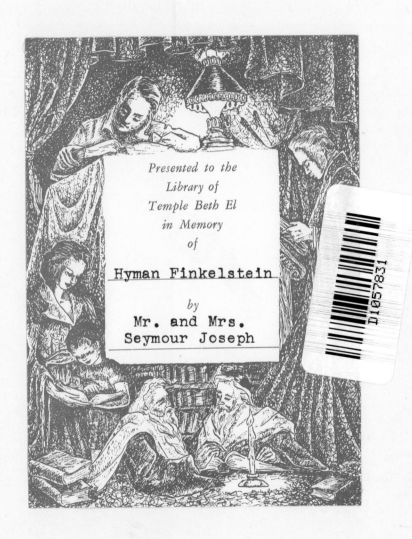

White Eagle,
Dark Skies

WHITE EAGLE, DARK SKIES

Jean Karsavina

Charles Scribner's Sons · New York

In memory of my father,

ADAM FATERSON,

who never understood why,
in success, he was still doomed
to defeat

❧ *Foreword* ❧

THE POLAND I have written about has only one parallel in the Western world—the Ireland of Sean O'Casey's biography. Today the parallel no longer exists. But in the time of WHITE EAGLE, DARK SKIES the unceasing struggle against foreign occupation was a fact of daily life. In this respect my own earliest childhood memories, dating back to the beginning of World War I, are no different than Adam Fabian's, a generation earlier.

The book is based on those memories, almost tribal in quality. It is also bolstered by careful research. To an even greater extent it is based on family legend, on tales told by all the adults who counted most in my childhood world. Although I have taken a great many liberties with the story line—inventing whole relationships out of bits and pieces and the merest hints of possibility, imagining what might or must have happened between characters seen through the prism of an admittedly romantic imagination—Adam Fabian is basically my father as a young man, my father long before my own time. Others in the book are patterned after relatives and family friends, and though in the writing they have inevitably parted company with strict reality and acquired lives and dimensions of their own, at heart they remain the men and women I knew.

Here and there I have even used real names. It hardly matters, for the people themselves are long since dead. So far as I know, the last traces of them disappeared when their children—my own generation—were starved and tortured and gassed and executed during the Nazi invasion of Poland. In between there was World War I. There was Poland reconstituted by the Treaty of Versailles. There were the Herculean efforts of people of good will to build a new life for the country, and there was corruption in high places. And the battle for human dignity went on.

During my research I tried to find traces of my remembered dead, and twice I succeeded: two of my cousins, university students, were among the young partisans who gave leadership to the anti-Nazi resistance. They died by firing squad, and their names are inscribed in the old Pawiak Prison, now a national shrine.

Thus the story had gone full circle. Symbolically, all that remains of Dziula and Jadzia are two songs they wrote together, songs which became a call to arms for the anti-Nazi resistance. I hope soon to write of them too, and of what shaped them into the women they became. For it was in the lives of boys and girls like these two that one finds the seeds of a singing tomorrow.

JEAN KARSAVINA

New York, October 24, 1973

❦ *Contents* ❧

White Eagle,
Dark Skies

❧ *Cast of Characters* ☙

THE FABIANS

Jacob
Bluma (*née* Grossglik)

their children

Adam
Viktor
Idka
Izidore
Rosie
Kazik

THE SEGALS

Karol
Balbina (Bluma's sister)

their children

Kuba
Jadwiga
Regina
Two younger boys

Leon Grossglik, *brother of Bluma and Balbina*

THE POZNERS

Maurice
Pani Konstancja

their children

Marek
Missy (Maya)

THE TWORSKAS

Pani Emilia

her daughters

Eugenia (Baroness Kronenberg)
Clara
Salome (*later* Salome Grossglik)

OTHERS

Olek Piotrowski ⎫
Henryk Meisels ⎬ *Adam Fabian's lifelong friends*
Juzek Meisels ⎭

Maryla Gorska, *Olek's sweetheart*
Wanda Borowska, *her roommate*
Jacek, *Olek's uncle*
Felix Gronowicz, *an exiled revolutionary*
Jan Rosol, *an Underground organizer*
Antek Rosol, *his son*

PART ONE
Spring 1890

❦ *One* ❧

A COLD WINTER TWILIGHT would always, for the rest of his life, remind Adam Fabian of March on the Vistula. He was still a good half-hour's walk from home, a flat in a run-down building on Nalewki Street in the heart of Warsaw's Jewish quarter, and he was tired and hungry. The wind blew raw from the river, which was at its broadest here and still frozen solid but beginning to rumble and crack in anticipation of the first thaws. The snow was high on the approaches to the Alexander Bridge—named after one of the hated Romanov Tsars—but it had taken on the weary look of winter's end, grayish-brown from months of carriage and sleigh traffic. Night was falling. The lamplighters with their long poles were beginning their evening's work, and the gas lanterns as they flickered on seemed to beckon to the boy like so many will-o'-the-wisps.

High on the Citadel defense tower a trumpeter blared out the hour, as generations of other trumpeters had done before him. Five o'clock. Adam could not see the man from so far away, but he knew exactly how he looked, ramrod straight in military regalia, moving clockwise around the balustrade, pausing to blow his horn northward, then east, then south and west. It occurred to Adam how cold the touch of the mouthpiece must be against his lips. But the sound came out clear and pure, and you could set your watch by it, as Adam now did. Five o'clock and all is well. Then silence. The man by now must have vanished inside, doubtless to thaw out so that at six he might repeat his performance as a giant human cuckoo clock.

What a strange use of human energy, Adam reflected. What a waste—yet something that for once one could not blame on the Tsars. The tradition went back much further than the last partition, the final dismemberment of Poland, and Russian rule—back to the days when the seat of the old Polish kings had been moved from ancient Krakow to the more modern, westernized Warsaw.

The new capital had been made beautiful by architects brought in from France and Italy, its palaces fashionably baroque or neo-Greek, its great formal gardens an echo of Paris, its broad boulevards carefully laid out and lined with acacia and linden trees. But the city lying in the vast open plain had been vulnerable from the start. Thus it became the first trumpeter's duty to search the horizon hourly for advancing enemy armies.

A useless precaution, as it turned out. The worst enemies had been within the gates—in the mansions of the magnates, inside the royal palace itself. And now the great palace in Sigismund Square served the Russian governor-general, while half the mansions housed one department or another of Muscovy's vast government machine. And flying over the city in place of Poland's white eagle was the double-headed black eagle of Russia. And Russian soldiers made up the permanent garrison. You saw them at the entrance of every official building, warning off the populace with bayonets. The *Moskals** did not trust a conquered people.

Adam knew all this in his bones and blood and angry passions, as did all Poles. But right now, at the end of a cold winter afternoon, all he could think of was getting home. It had been a long day for him. It was always a long day, beginning before sunup, with his mother shaking him awake. Quickly, then, he would dress in the dark, careful not to rouse his younger brothers, with whom he shared a room, and tiptoe into the kitchen. There, while the rest of the household was only beginning to stir, he could have a whole precious hour in which to finish the homework he hadn't had time for the previous day.

At seven o'clock his mother set some rolls and scalding tea

* Pejorative popular word for "Russian"—i.e., Muscovites.

before him and he gulped it all down, his eyes still on his books, while she stuffed more rolls into his book bag. By then it was time to start on his tramp across town to the government *gymnasium,* there to meet a younger boy whom he tutored in Latin until the school bell called them both to classes. During the midday recess he gave another lesson, in Greek grammar. And after school he went on to a third boy's house. This time, working not for pay alone but in exchange for a solid main meal, he spent two long hours coaching a rebellious ten-year-old in arithmetic, history, and Russian. The child was a dolt, he resisted learning in spite of constant threats and frequent parental beatings, and Adam sometimes wondered why it should matter so much to the mother and father that their offspring remain in school when a trade apprenticeship would have been more to the point. But that was really not his business, and he knew he would keep the thankless job until something better came along. A free meal was a free meal, and every kopek he earned or helped conserve was needed at home. At fifteen, he considered himself the second breadwinner in his family.

The heavy silver pocket watch he had just checked against the trumpet call was proof to him that his parents felt the same way. It had been his grandfather's, and only yesterday, his birthday, they had made him a gift of it. "You need a reliable timepiece more than I do," his father had said. "Will my customers stop buying from me if I'm five minutes early or late? Will I sell one *sheitl* less?" Jacob Fabian was a dealer in hair goods, and, since in a poor Jewish neighborhood like theirs the women still shaved their heads and donned wigs when they married, he was assured of at least half a living. "No, it isn't the lack of a watch that will put me out of business, but Father Time himself. Time, moving forward in a great civilizing leap, putting an end to what I consider," he went on to philosophize, "a barbarous medieval custom. Wigs! Bah! So, my son, use the watch in good health."

And Adam had understood how much the gift really implied. It was his parents' way of letting him know they relied on him, considered him adult, hard-working, and responsible, yet at the same time were not taking his contribution for granted. They appreciated what he did, were even proud of him. At the same time it was a constant source of worry and grief to the elder Fabians that their son, who was such a good student, should have so little leisure.

"Now if only I were a better businessman, I could make you a gift of hours of reading . . . ," and the regret in Jacob's voice almost made up for all the books that remained out of reach— Newton and Spinoza, Thomas Aquinas and Leibniz and William Shakespeare—all the riches, the father never tired of telling his son, that waited on the shelves of the world's libraries. "Still," he would conclude, consoling mainly himself, "there will be your university days. By then the younger boys will be doing their share. But until they're old enough, well, you see how it is, don't you? We just don't have a choice."

His mother only said, using the affectionate diminutive of his name, "You're such a good boy, Adash, such a good son." Then, reaching up to stroke the black springy bush of his hair, "Like Papa told you, use the watch in good health. You've surely earned it." Had it been up to her, Bluma Fabian's gift to her first-born would have been not so much time for reading but for being a boy—for skating on the frozen Vistula, playing ball in the yard. Only it was as her husband had put it—they didn't have a choice.

Generation after generation, everyone grew up too soon in Nalewki Street. It was work and more work from dark until dark merely to keep one step ahead of desperation, while one's eyes wore out for the stinting on candles and lamp oil. Jacob liked to tell the children how once their mother's eyes had been large and darkly luminous and her hair a glory. Now the hair was wispy and prematurely streaked with gray and the eyes were faded as flowers fade in rooms without sunlight. Her small, slight body sagged with neglect and childbearing, her hands had coarsened, the skin cracked, the fingers scarred with years of sewing and mending and scrubbing.

Yet she neglected only herself, never others. Six children living, twins stillborn, a baby daughter lost during last summer's dysentery epidemic and still bitterly mourned—Bluma found time for each of them, giving freely of her love. Unlike the neighbors, she seldom raised her voice and only raised her hand to them if they tried her beyond the limits of human endurance. And when that happened, afterwards she would cry. The traditional cat-o'-nine-tails hanging on a peg in the Fabians' kitchen was allowed to gather dust. Jacob shared his wife's aversion to corporal punishment. "If I can't reach my children with words," he would say, "then I've failed as a father." In this respect the neighbors and relatives thought the Fabians a bit odd.

Outwardly, theirs was the most ordinary of households. A maid of all work shared her mistress' labors, and between them the two women managed to keep up an atmosphere of shabby gentility. Their backs might ache from the weight of slop pails carried down three flights to the courtyard, the clean water carried up, the piles of dirty wash scrubbed and boiled and wrung out and hung to dry in the steamy basement laundry, the great baskets of fresh clothes that between them they barely managed to drag up again. The mounds of potatoes they peeled might seem like Mount Ararat, and the ironing was without end. But the kitchen chores were never permitted to get out of hand. The two front rooms that Jacob used as showroom and office were kept neat and swept, all the beds were made up each morning, and it was a point of considerable pride with Bluma that the overstuffed sofa in the dining room—the Fabians did not boast a parlor—was not used for sleeping unless a guest stayed overnight.

The rest of the apartment consisted of bedrooms. One for the parents, one for the boys, one for the two girls. The maid slept in the hallway leading into the kitchen. The windows throughout the house, double-paned and sealed tight against winter, were never opened, except for tiny transoms, from October until well into April, so that the air was always slightly fetid yet none too warm at that. Coal came high and was used freely only on Fridays to heat water for everyone's weekly bath. Then a great fire was laid in the huge tile stove built catty-corner, as was the custom, in the center of the apartment so that each of its sides threw off heat into a different room. The tiles stayed hot throughout the evening and all through the night, and getting up on Saturday morning was a pleasure.

In the dining room, by the sofa, stood Bluma's one personal

treasure, her one great luxury, her one concession to the fact that she was smaller and less physically strong than other women—a footstool covered in grospoint of her grandmother's workmanship. Bluma was so tiny that, when now and then she took time to sit down, her feet did not quite reach the floor. Then she would say, as though apologizing for an incomprehensible weakness, "Bring me my footstool, somebody, please. . . ." The tone of apology both amused and exasperated her husband. "Little she may be," he once remarked to his sons, "and soft-hearted, and quick with the tears. But in her own way your mother is a giant!" Sometimes it seemed to him that if the home ran smoothly, if the family held together and his own heart was whole, it was because his wife willed it so.

"How did I ever manage without you?" he liked to ask, kissing her in front of the children, or even a guest, until she blushed to the roots of her graying hair. And the neighbor women commented enviously, "Your man spoils you. You don't know how it is with most marriages!"

But she did know, and she wanted her children to know she knew.

"If God gave each of us only what we deserved, I'd never have merited your father!" she would tell them.

She had been twenty-four at the time of her engagement, an old maid by every standard of the world she lived in. The oldest child, she'd been forced to leave school at the age of eight, on the death of her own mother in childbirth, in order to care for the new baby, Leon, and a little sister, Balbina. After a decent interval her father remarried, and she eagerly brought up the subject of returning to classes. But the new stepmother put her foot down. Illiterate, and pregnant right away, she saw no reason for coddling her stepdaughter. And anyway a girl's place was in the kitchen, not the schoolroom. So the years passed. There never was a time for youth in Bluma's life, nor for courting. Nor had she a dowry to help attract eligible young men.

Then one day the local matchmaker came running to her father. He had such news! A fine young man, substantial, nearing thirty and with a business of his own, needed a wife. "And mind you, he doesn't even *care to meet* any pretty sixteen-year-olds! Says he'd rather have someone older, but gentle, sensible, quiet. So right away I think of your Bluma. There's just one thing, I tell him, she doesn't have two groshen to her name. And he says, 'If I like her she doesn't have to have money!' No dowry! No dowry, he says—now what do you think of that! For your Bluma, the match is heaven-sent!"

She went to her husband meekly, resigned to exchange one tyranny for another, but also with a secret surge of hope. She had read about love. Now, unbelievably, she found it. The humiliating arranged marriage turned into a love match, for the simple reason that it was in the nature of both partners to give of themselves rather than ask what the other was giving.

And yet at the last minute the wedding almost did not take place. Jacob, up to his neck in hairpieces and rats and false curls, took one look at his future bride's great chestnut braids, so long they reached her ankles when she let them hang free, and announced that on no account was she to shave her head when they married. Bluma's stepmother promptly made a scene, demanding that the engagement be terminated then and there. But her father was willing to listen to reason. After all, it wasn't as though the girl had a suitor for every day of the week! The wedding came off as planned, for all that tongues clicked and clacked for days. Bluma herself walked away from the marriage canopy expecting God's thunder to strike her down.

But nothing of the sort happened. And the next morning, as she combed out the heavy braids, her clear shining eyes met her husband's and she blessed him. A new world opened up to her, and she no longer feared retribution. After all, she told herself, it wasn't of her own volition that she'd defied rabbinical law. Had she done so, it would have been sinful. But in keeping her own hair she had only obeyed her husband's wishes as any good wife must do, and therefore she hadn't sinned.

With the years, Bluma continued to ease the rigid, age-musty religiosity that bound so many of her Jewish neighbors. True, she still lit candles on Friday night, still followed the dietary laws and fasted on Yom Kippur, the Day of Atonement, and unlike other "godless" husbands, hers never interfered. He even gave his consent for Adam, and after him Viktor and Izidore, the next two boys, to be sent to *cheder*, the Hebrew school. "What can it hurt?" was his answer to other men with atheistic views who criticized him for it. "Let them make up their own minds. Then, if they do reject the mumbo-jumbo, at least they'll know what they are rejecting. In the meantime they can learn something about their own people, and that, I believe, is good. . . ."

In time Bluma began to suspect that outside the home neither her husband nor her sons adhered to the rules she herself lived by. But this no longer worried her deeply. Only when there was illness in the family, or a death, did she grow fearful once more. When that happened, she would keep a candle burning in her room all day and all night. For the rest, she merely prayed silently, entering into a kind of private covenant with Heaven, asking forgiveness for her beloved infidels. Still later, even this began to seem disloyal, and it was no longer forgiveness she asked but only that nothing evil should befall her man and her household. She did not see how even a jealous God could be vindictive enough to visit His wrath on her Jacob. But, of course, one never knew, and it was as well to be on the safe side.

Jacob's private covenant—for always he remained careful of his wife's feelings—was with his oldest son. With Adam, he felt free to discuss his views, but only when they were alone. "God is for women and for the masses that live in darkness," he would say. "It's all superstition, that's what it is! But someday, believe me, someday when everyone has a chance at education and there's real enlightenment in the world . . . ," and he would wave his hand, leaving the sentence to hang in midair, some inborn sense of drama telling him it was more effective to let his son fill in his own interpretation.

These past two years, on Yom Kippur, he left Bluma safely praying in the women's gallery of the synagogue and took Adam on long walks into a Christian neighborhood where no one knew them. There, in a workers' lunchroom, they feasted on sausage and goat cheese and fresh bread. "But not a word of this to your mother," he cautioned, giving his son a delicious sense of conspiratorial intimacy. "I believe with Karl Marx—you know who he is, don't you?—that religion is the opium of the people. But with life so hard, why take the opium away? It's the same with us as with the Catholics. They too can't bear their lot, so they fill the churches. . . ."

The most frequent of all these father-son discourses took place on Saturday, at the far end of the inner courtyard of their house, where there was a row of privies. Jacob Fabian was an inveterate smoker, and rather than distress his wife needlessly by breaking the Sabbath law right in front of her, like many another Jewish husband he used the stinking cubicles for indulging his craving for tobacco. He and Adam made a game of going downstairs together, and once or twice Jacob even offered his son a cigarette. But Adam never did develop a taste for smoking, perhaps because for him it was not, as with other boys, a forbidden pleasure. In fact, the smell of cigarette smoke became associated in his mind with the stench of open privy pits. What he did hugely enjoy, however, was the man-to-man solidarity of those stolen moments with his father.

Sometimes one of the neighbors would join them in conversation and the talk turned to politics. Only this past week Adam had heard the medical student who boarded with the Liebmans on the landing below their own say with a kind of controlled fury, "Religion and the Russians . . . we and the Catholics are chained together in the same double yoke. Yet how many of us are ready to admit it's *double* slavery? Tsarist slavery—yes. We're born and we die dreaming that someday we'll throw the *Moskals* out, that we'll again become an independent, sovereign people. We sing *Poland Is Not Yet Lost* whenever we're sure there isn't a gendarme around or an informer to railroad us to jail. Yet even if we get our independence back, how free will we be if we don't stop bowing down to superstition?"

Adam's father explained afterwards that the Liebmans' boarder was a radical political activist, one of those who maintained it was not enough for the secret underground movement to set its sights on national liberation alone. To them, ridding the country of the Russian invader seemed only half the battle. The other half was social liberation. In that distant future when Poland was Polish again, they wanted it reconstituted as a true republic, with the power of the great magnates and great wealth strictly curtailed in favor of the common people.

"That's the viewpoint of the Social-Democrats," Jacob had said. "They lump the Church and the magnates together, saying that the hierarchy is nothing but these same magnates in clerical dress, using the name of God to keep the poor and the ignorant under their thumb. And unless the people are forewarned they'll gain nothing by any upheaval except to exchange one set of masters for another. It's an argument I can't fault. On the other hand, you know the way I feel about religion for those whom it happens to suit. It's not all black-and-white. Nothing ever is!"

Now, as he walked down the long Marszalkowska thoroughfare with its storefronts and milling crowds, Adam thought about that conversation, and wondered. He was disposed to agree with his father rather than with the medical student. Let those who could find consolation in prayer have their religion—why not? Besides, he happened to have a sneaking fondness for the centuries-old structures that were Warsaw's great churches. The domed, ancient Romanesque ones, the tall Gothic ones with their spires and arches and their magnificent stone carvings and stained-glass windows covered with the dust of ages—how could these be a threat to his intelligence? Only when he passed the huge Russian Orthodox cathedral did his anger boil up. But in this he was not alone—merely reflecting the feelings of the whole city.

The cathedral, so new its glaring whiteness blinded you, was the Tsarist government's latest insult to the people of Warsaw. Graceless, arrogant, and much too large to fill any religious need the city's Russian colony might have for a house of worship, it had been deliberately designed as an eyesore. Its five fat gold-leaf cupolas—the five sanctified onions, a wit had called them, and the name stuck—gave it a kind of overfed new-rich look, and it squatted like a giant brooding hen in the middle of the old parade ground that once had been laid out so carefully to show off the beauty of the classical palaces surrounding it. Now it was said that if you looked out of any window on the square, you risked having your eye put out by a gilt onion top.

Just thinking about it made Adam furious, helping him forget his tiredness and his empty stomach. He spat to relieve his patriotic feelings, then remembered something a boy at school had recently told him. It seemed that superstitious Russians—and this apparently included just about all of them—crossed themselves whenever they walked by a church; but whenever they passed a *pop,* or Russian Orthodox priest, they spat. *Not* to spit would, they believed, bring them bad luck. The thought enchanted Adam, comforted him, making him feel infinitely superior to "those Asiatics," the invaders who'd been there as far back as the oldest inhabitant's memory reached, but against whom the struggle never ceased and never would cease. Or so he let himself dream.

The dream of freedom was always there close to the surface, like a racial memory, a legend to be cherished and handed down in sacred trust to new generations, and someday he too would pass it on to his children, to sustain them as they in turn picked up the burden of the common cause. So it had been for a hundred years now, since the last of the three partitions. So it had been when Napoleon marched east, and the Polish legions under General Dombrowski marched with him, ready to die for him, thinking him a savior.

Poland is not yet lost, they sang, their standards with the white eagles flying. *Not while our hearts keep beating!*

But the song was all that remained of them after 1812. It was all that remained of the abortive uprising of 1831. And finally, in 1863, the very time, ironically, when he was liberating the serfs, Tsar Alexander II dealt Russian Poland the most vicious blow of all.

The Congress Kingdom, as it was still called in those days, revolted one last time. Within the year, in retribution, its last vestiges of self-government were taken from it. Even the history books were rewritten, and the Polish language itself was forbidden in official usage and in schools.

Then while all Europe gasped in horror over the brutal mass arrests, the executions, the deportations to Siberia, while Victor Hugo and Garibaldi and Kossuth added their voices to the thousands protesting the cruelties, the very name of Poland was expunged from all records. And the Russian viceroy was no longer called the governor-general of the vassal Polish Kingdom, but governor of the "Provinces of the Vistula."

And still the Poles dared to continue dreaming. And one day, Adam told himself, one day, who knows, if not his own children then maybe his children's children would live to see the dream become reality. And when that happened, the white eagle would fly proud and joyous once more where the odious, black double-headed predator now threatened. And men would speak their minds in the hearing of others without fear of arrest. And a boy could sing the national anthem at the top of his lungs if he pleased.

Poland is not yet lost. . . . Defiantly he whistled the first few bars, thinking back to the day his mother had first taught it to him, after gravely cautioning him that he must never, under any circumstances, be caught singing it in public. What a heavy responsibility to put on a child, he reflected, from the vantage point of his fifteen years—and yet one that all the children he had ever known shared.

Poland is not yet lost. . . . He had better stop whistling, or the next man he passed might trail him and denounce him and it might lead to the arrest of his whole family—faceless informers paid to accuse so many persons a day, a week, were an ever-present danger. "Stop pretending to be so brave!" he admonished himself. But the feeling of defiance persisted and he continued whistling, shrilly but tunelessly now, ending with a sharp blast through the teeth that nearly made the policeman on the next corner jump out of his skin.

"Warsaw hooligan!" Adam heard the Russian mutter.

Again he felt cheered, having contributed to the discomfort of the enemy. Miraculously his tiredness vanished and even the book bag slung across his narrow shoulders no longer seemed so heavy. He heard his stomach growling and his thoughts shifted from the dream at the rainbow's end to the pot simmering on the stove in his mother's kitchen.

❧ *Two* ❧

WHEN FINALLY he reached Nalewki Street he noticed unaccustomed activity in the yard. But hungry as he was he paid little attention. Sara Liebman from the third landing, who generally could be heard quarreling with her husband or yelling at her children, was downstairs, surrounded by neighbors. She was quiet and seemed strangely subdued. Maybe someone's ill, Adam thought, maybe there's been a death. But he only mumbled a greeting and started up the creaking wooden stairs.

The thought of hot soup sustained him on the long climb. He let himself in. But at home, too, everything was unnaturally quiet. His father was in the dining room instead of in his shop, as would have been usual at this hour. He sat with his elbows on the table, neither reading nor smoking but only staring into space. His mother, too, just sat unmoving, which was even more unusual. Her eyes were red and puffy. The younger children, Rosie and five-year-old Kazik, huddled on the sofa, seemingly frightened into model behavior. When the door opened they cringed, as though instead of their brother they expected the devil himself with his pitchfork.

All five pairs of eyes now turned to stare at Adam, and he forgot about his empty stomach and tired, cold feet and the welcoming kitchen aromas. "Bad news, huh?" he finally choked out.

His father nodded. "They've just taken Liebman from the third. The gendarmes were around for an hour."

His mother wiped her eyes, only to have fresh tears roll down her cheeks.

The Liebmans had always known that renting out rooms was risky business and renting to university students riskiest of all. As the saying went, scratch a student and find a radical. Not that there was anything so very wrong with radicals—weren't they forever fighting the battles of the underdog?—but if you happened to have one living under your roof, and he was picked up by the secret police, right away you were in for trouble. Still and all, money did not grow on trees, and how could you let an empty room go begging?

So they took chances. For years they'd taken chances. And now they'd taken one chance too many. One of their boarders turned out to be a provocateur.

"Not the medical student—that one was the salt of the earth," Jacob said, and Adam noticed how already his father spoke of the youth in the past tense. He was finding the news hard to swallow. He kept remembering the conversation in the privies only this past Saturday, and he wanted to shout that what his father was telling him couldn't possibly be true.

"No, not the medical student, the other one, the philosopher who said he was from Vilno," Jacob went on. "Who would have believed all this time he was nothing but a stoolpigeon! Imagine, a Jew informing on other Jews!"

"A *Litvak,**" Bluma put in. "What can you expect?"

"Now don't go condemning two million people all in a lump," her husband admonished mildly. "There must be *some* Litvaks with some good in them. Just the same, you're right in a way. With a Litvak, Liebman should have been doubly careful." Russian Jews were not trusted by Polish Jews, unfortunately with good reason.

Adam was only half listening. He was thinking of yet another forbidden song learned in childhood, *Smoke of the Ruins*. A hymn of mourning, it tore at your heart and kept you ever aware of the country's unrelenting struggle. The words he had been taught never to sing in public, now painfully relevant, echoed in his mind.

* The word "Litvak," technically denoting anyone from Lithuania and originally applied to Lithuanian Jews, eventually came to refer, among both Christians and Polish Jews, to Russian Jews in general.

God of our fathers, where is Thy mercy?
What is this anguish we call our fate?
Half of us Cains killing our brothers,
Killing each other, living in hate. . . .

Ah, but our crimes are not of our making
Though we be guilty, guilty oh Lord,
Blame not the tool of the forces of darkness,
Strike down the hand, and not the blind sword!

The song, dating back to the first of the three partitions, when the Congress Kingdom had been seized by Russia, Galicia by the Austro-Hungarian Empire, and the Northwest by Germany, had begun as a cry of protest against conscription into three enemy armies; and how many times had it happened that men from the same area, the same village, the same family even, had been forced into facing one another on the battlefield! Now it seemed to the boy the same thing applied to the Jews inside the Russian lands, who for a crust of bread, because they were starving, turned traitor to one another. But weren't they, too, only blind tools and the real culprits the viciously cunning, powerful men in high places?

Adam did not remember, although his parents did, a time when relations between Gentile and Jew in Poland hadn't been so strained. Since early medieval times the native Jewish population had sunk its roots deep in this land, it had a share in the country's history. But during the past decade everything had changed. Right after the assassination of Tsar Alexander II, with a wave of government-inspired anti-Semitic terror sweeping the country, a full-scale pogrom had broken out in Warsaw during Holy Week.

He had been just seven then, his brother Viktor five, Idka a baby and Izidore not yet born. What he remembered most vividly was that he hadn't been allowed out of doors for a week. But he also remembered the wailing of the women and the men's helpless query, repeated over and over, "How can such things be?"

The violence had been only the opening salvo in a wave of persecutions under the guise of a holy crusade. Alexander III and his evil genius, Count Pobiedonostzev, once his tutor and now Proc-

...... of the Holy Synod and the power behind the throne, set ...... id Mother Russia of the *"Zhid"* vermin." The Empire's ...... problem, as the Count put it, was to be solved neatly by liqu...ation: one-third conversion to Christianity, one-third starvation, one-third emigration. On May 3, 1882, new laws were promulgated to accomplish this goal.

Ironically, May Third was also the date of Poland's outlawed national holiday, Constitution Day, commemorating the last brave, stubborn stand of a handful of revered patriots in the *Sejm,* led by Kosciusko and Rejtan and Pulaski, who immediately following the first partition succeeded in forcing King Stanislas-August and his magnates to institute a series of democratic reforms, while at the same time defying the encroachments of the invaders. The reforms came too late to save the country. But May Third remained forever after a day of ferment and political protest.

Year after year, long before dawn, unseen hands managed to hoist the red-and-white flag in public places through the city, so that when the sun rose the national colors were already flying high. And floating on the Vistula where they'd been tossed from bridges in the night were red-and-white garlands of spring flowers. Later on there would be marching and singing in the streets, and student demonstrations. But in the end, like a black curtain falling, there were always the cossacks. Cossacks erupting at a gallop from side streets, their whips, the *naghaikas,* raining blows on backs and heads and upraised arms, their horses trampling those who fell. And then would come the arrests.

On that May morning in 1882 there had been gloating in the official press. Pobiedonostzev and his Black Hundred followers had achieved a signal victory: Virtually all Jews were being suddenly, summarily expelled from the main cities and here and there from whole regions of Great Russia, where until then the more privileged—those wealthy enough to own land or a business, those with an education or special skills whom the country needed—had been allowed to reside and to work. The new edict was so drastic, so brutal, so totally without recourse, as to make the original Laws of the Pale, which had "merely" restricted the mass of poor Jews in Great Russia proper to the ghettos of certain Eastern towns and to the *shtetl,* seem mild by comparison. Naturally enough, there was panic. Thousands, as during the Spanish Inquisition, converted. The few who could afford it resorted to bribes. But thousands upon thousands of unfortunates grabbed up their children, their feather beds and their pots and pans and a new exodus began. They headed for whatever seemed to them the new Promised Land—Germany or Britain or France, the Americas, Palestine, even the British colonies in Africa.

Yet, for all too many of the exiles, flight toward survival ended where their strength gave out—on Poland's soil. Here they dropped exhausted, and here they stayed. Unwelcome, swelling the country's Jewish population to three times its former size, resented by their own coreligionists, whose already meager livelihood they threatened, they became *luftmenschen,* creatures living on air: the despised Litvaks.

Unable to find work, they wandered from town to town. Soon the native Jews were blaming them for the fresh, violent anti-Semitism that ground them all down. To make matters worse, the Litvaks felt no allegiance to their unwilling hosts. What was Poland to them that they should care about its fate?

The secret police were quick to take advantage of this division between their victims. Soon the Litvaks were notorious as a breed of informers. Unaware that they were making common cause with the true enemy, they warmed themselves at the feeble fire of spitefulness.

"Yet you can't really blame them too much," Adam's parents had once tried to explain on a quiet evening when there'd been time for talk. "When a man's children cry for bread, his loyalty must go deep indeed for him not to weaken. And these people are after all strangers among us." His mother had been the one to put it most vividly. "It's the whole difference between being a stepchild in your own country and a foundling. For the stepchild keeps hoping to be loved like an own child by the stepmother and he'll keep trying to win her over. But the foundling groveling for scraps will turn on anyone."

So she had spoken when nothing threatened them. But now

that *Pan* Liebman was in jail she looked at things differently. "No Polish Jew in his right mind takes a Litvak into his home or talks to him about things that matter," she insisted.

And Jacob did not gainsay her, adding with quiet fury, "No wonder that—that *philosopher* never seemed to work for a living! And all those books he owned—Marx, Engels, Adam Smith, Dostoyevsky, Voltaire! Always showing them to you, always trying to draw you out, to get your opinion on everything!"

A chill went through Adam. Only the other day the "philosopher" had cornered him and his father on the stairs, whispering he had something to show them. His latest acquisition, he boasted. A gem. A copy of *Memoirs of a Revolutionary* by the exiled anarchist Prince Kropotkin.

The text was in French, printed in Paris and obviously smuggled in, and Adam, for all that his French was too shaky for easy reading, had been intrigued; so it had come as a distinct shock to him to hear his father say quickly, without so much as a glance at the book, "Please, spare us this nonsense—who needs it!" Now he understood. Speaking through his father's lips had been the caution bred into the bone and marrow of every Warsaw citizen. He also understood that the longer you lived, the deeper the caution, until it became second nature, a kind of animal instinct. But poor old Liebman's instinct hadn't been sound enough.

"The son-of-a-bitch," his father, who never swore, said distinctly. And his mother, more startled than shocked, whispered, "Jacob, please!" indicating the children. But his father was too bitterly angry even to apologize.

"That son-of-a-bitch deliberately trapped Liebman and the medical student! He was always starting the arguments, always talking revolution and armed uprising! He made it all sound so *possible* they stopped using their heads. And finally they started speaking freely in his presence."

"Yes, and look where it landed them," Bluma wailed, grieving as though for her own. "Tonight they'll be sleeping in Pawiak prison. And in the end it'll be Siberia. And *Pani* Liebman left alone with all those children to raise! How many more times must it happen, how many more times to how many more of us? No one is safe anymore, no one, I tell you. . . ."

You'd think, Adam told himself, a person could get used to living with fear, with uncertainty, in a constant state of alert. But you never did, no more than you got used to the pain of a wound that was torn open over and over. You just vowed that when the time came you would join the great surging movement that someday must put an end to the outrages.

After a while the front door opened and first Viktor, then Idka and Izidore, came home. Each in turn was told about the calamity that had befallen the neighbors on the floor below. And because they were still so young, Bluma again sounded the warning she no longer felt she must pound into Adam and never permitted herself to direct at her husband, no matter how much she might tremble for his safety.

"Now do you see," she admonished with all the eloquence that terror inspired, "why it's so important to guard your tongue! Always, always—in the street, at school. Because you never can tell who's listening! Because with the *Moskals* around, even the walls have ears!"

The youngsters nodded gravely, and even their father felt impelled to add for good measure, "Never forget—no blabbing. For all our sakes, keep your mouths shut." It was a conversation that in one form or another was being repeated in a million homes.

❧ *Three* ❧

AND THAT, so far as the neighborhood knew, was the end of Liebman and the medical student. The Pawiak had no oubliettes like those of the Bastille, but otherwise it was in the same tradition. Built early in the century, it consisted of a series of dark, damp dungeons guarded by high, thick walls and gates of solid iron, over which might well have been engraved the legend *Lasciate ogni speranza.*

And indeed those who entered might well abandon all hope, especially if they were political prisoners rather than common criminals. Once accused, they were seldom found innocent unless money and influence were available for bribing their way to freedom. Those who had access to neither—and this included not just fiery leaders but an endless procession of faceless men and women—were *a priori* doomed. Routinely they were left to languish in their cells for a year or two, just waiting for a hearing. Then, if the charges against them were all but unfounded, their punishment might be deportation to some distant town in northern Russia, there to survive as best they could among strangers whose language they did not even speak. If they were lucky, the verdict might even be merely exile abroad.

Those not so lucky—and often this was a matter of pure chance—were transferred by convoy to Moscow, to the infamous Lubianka or the Butyrki prison, there to await trial. And when at last they were hauled up before a tribunal, it did not take much to draw five years in a Siberian penal colony—with the time already spent in jail never taken into account. Yet even this was not the worst that could happen. A shadow of guilt, and the sentence might readily be ten years at hard labor in the Ural mines.

Pani Liebman wept, less perhaps for her man, since there had never been much love between them, than for being deprived of a provider, ineffectual though he had been. She began to refer to her children as "my poor orphans," and the neighbors echoed the phrase.

"And isn't that just about what they really are?" Bluma Fabian commented sadly. "God alone knows when, if ever, they'll have a father again! I hear people die like flies in that hell-hole, what with the slops they're fed and the filthy water giving them typhus or at the very least dysentery, and the lice and bedbugs and fleas! So just remember, all of you," she would conclude for the benefit of any of her own brood who might be listening, "just you remember to keep your traps shut when you're out where people can hear you! Because you never know who's a spy!"

The warning became her *leitmotif*. And yet not even she, the timid, the fearful one, thought of urging them never to do what might lead to trouble. She only asked that they be careful. For she knew well enough that sooner or later one or another of her children would be drawn into the unending battle. This was how it had been for generations. All she could hope for was that they would not get caught.

The arrests made a deep impression on Adam. It was not the first time such an event had touched him closely; one was constantly hearing about friends or at least acquaintances being picked up. But at least those were people actively engaged in underground activity. Some were avowed Socialists, Social-Revolutionaries or Social-Democrats, or else active in the Jewish Bund. They might be factory hands planning a work stoppage or students banding together to read and distribute forbidden literature. Or perhaps their crime was that they'd journeyed into the villages, there secretly to teach peasant children to read and write Polish. Or they had belonged to that amorphous but never-idle mass of patriots who simply kept the ferment of national rebellion alive.

It was all proscribed activity. The list of offenses was without end. Defiance was everywhere, handed down like a precious heirloom in every family. It was nurtured, tenderly yet with a burning passion, until it became a kind of tropism that kept all their faces turned always toward the sun of an independence that someday, somehow must surely come.

Arrest for patriotic resistance Adam could understand. But *Pan* Liebman! Liebman had done nothing, nothing at all. He was, in fact, one of those who hardly cared one way or the other, a frightened little man feeding exclusively on his own troubles, a human worm, a cipher. But the Russians, like the ancient Romans before them, needed so-and-so-many ciphers to throw regularly to the lions.

There seemed to be a wave of arrests throughout the city that night, and the following morning Adam's *Gymnasium* was alive with whispers. Like himself, the other boys well understood the need for caution. The teachers were either Russians or in the Russians' pockets. Just as importantly, one had to be careful of classmates who were the sons of Russian army officers, government clerks, postal employees, and of those whose fathers, though Poles, were in government service. Government salaries were notoriously low, and unless a man had private means at his disposal he was not always above eking out a meager income with spying, selling tidbits of information to the secret police.

In addition, the Russians always took unholy pleasure in lording it over ordinary Polish citizens, never failing to squeeze every last drop of satisfaction out of a cheaply gained sense of superiority over the "natives." And, of course, it was a case of like fathers, like sons. Some natural bullies delighted in openly baiting their Polish classmates, while others more subtle tried to win their confidence. They were the truly dangerous ones.

Cautiously, all morning long, the whispering reached out. You listened, you responded to a seemingly casual remark with an equally casual one of your own, and suddenly there would be a spark, a moment of recognition. And then the talk would begin in earnest, gradually more open, more frank as each sought reassurance in an exchange of experience, a sharing more easily achieved with coevals than with adults.

At noon in the school yard where they all ate their lunch, Adam found himself standing next to a tall youth with a broad peasant face, whom he'd always wanted to get to know better. "Know what this reminds me of?" the boy, Olek Piotrowski, said, around a mouthful of bread and cheese. He was addressing not just Adam but half a dozen others around them. "We're like a bunch of hound dogs brought together for a hunt—I've seen it many a time on the estate where my uncle is gamekeeper. They're all from different kennels, they smell strange to each other, so they sniff and growl, growl and sniff, till something tells them they've found a friend. Then all of a sudden the tails start wagging. Well, that's us!" The remark brought laughter, and tensions eased.

Ordinarily most of the brighter upper-classmen spent their midday recess as Adam did, coaching younger or duller boys, for the need for money was universal. No family, whether Jewish or Gentile, sent its children to a public Russian school if it could possibly afford a private one. This in itself created a basic solidarity among the boys, and class-conscious, realistic, surprisingly adult attitudes predominated.

Thus on the day after the arrests the recess quickly took on a curious character. The boys who gathered in the cobblestoned yard pretended to study as usual, the younger ones standing around with their Latin and geometry books open. Small groups had formed, and to make everything appear normal sounds of cramming could be heard. But in fact very little boning-up was going on. No one's mind was on lessons.

"*Gallia est omnis divisa in partes tres* . . . . Say, did you hear what went on yesterday on the waterfront?"

"No, but I can tell you all about the raid in Mokotow. . . ."

"*Arma virumque cano.* I sing of arms and the man. Just you wait—some day we'll make *them* sing a different song. . . ."

Pythagoras' pants? Who cared about Pythagoras' pants, or anyone else's for that matter, when the violet uniforms of the police swarmed everywhere?

"It was awful, I tell you, awful. They came in the middle of the night. The apartment next door. Right on our landing."

"With us it was the neighbors downstairs. The *struzh*—the concièrge—denounced them. . . ."

"In our house it was a boarder on the third," said Adam. "A real first-class rat."

"Did they find anything? Pamphlets? Books? Addresses?"

In some homes they did, in others not. Nearly everyone had a story to tell, and that noon it didn't matter whether a boy was a dunce or belonged to the intellectual elite so long as he was no Russian and could be trusted.

After a time Olek Piotrowski confided that a favorite uncle—"not the gamekeeper, my uncle Jacek—we're a big family"—had been caught red-handed, printing an illegal newspaper. The whole group stared in awe as though it were Olek himself who'd done something heroic, and he tried to look modest. "But fellows, that's only half the story. Because guess what—my uncle Jacek got away! He's strong as an ox, used to be a blacksmith. And growing up on the waterfront and all, he knows how to fight with his feet same as the other river rats!"

"Got away? You're not making this up, Piotrowski?"

"As God is my witness! He just kicked right and left, and by the time the guards picked themselves up he'd vanished—whoosh!—and go look for the wind in the fields, as the saying goes!"

It was a victory in which they all could share, and it lifted their spirits to the skies. Now they pressed around Olek, bombarding him with questions.

"Do you know where he went? Is he safe? And anyway, how come you know so much?"

Olek just laughed. "The 'violets' themselves told us, that's how. Dumb, they are. Two in the morning, they come knocking on our door looking for him. As if Jacek would be fool enough to hide right where they can lay their hands on him! Idiots! But then," he finished with fine contempt, "that's *Moskal* mentality for you."

"And . . . your uncle?"

Olek shrugged in a carefully offhand manner. "Oh, we probably won't hear from him for a while. But I'll bet good money he's safe. Maybe he's crossed the border into Germany. Or maybe the comrades are hiding him till the time is right for him to surface again. Then when we're least expecting it there'll be a knock on the door and there he'll be, looking like he'd never been away. And my mother will kiss him and cry a little. It isn't the first time, it won't be the last. He's got nine lives, that one, like a cat."

Recess was coming to an end. The last of the bread and sausage and cheese, the apples and the chocolate were gone. And still they were reluctant to separate. Adam said, speaking, he was sure, for others beside himself, "I wish there was something we could do. Right now. Without waiting till we're older."

"You mean that, Fabian?" Olek took him up quickly, eagerly.

"Who doesn't?" someone else put in.

Olek looked around, slowly sizing up his audience. He seemed to be weighing something in his mind; then he reached a decision. "You know something?" His voice dropped to barely above a whisper. "We could start one of those secret study circles. We could meet on Sundays, at each other's houses. . . ."

"What would we study?"

"Well, there's a lot to choose from. Polish history for one—I mean the *true* history, not the way the Russians teach it. And literature—there's so much censored stuff . . ."

"And political economy, maybe?" an older boy, Henryk Meisels, suggested. "I'd like to know about the Utopian Socialists and the trade union movement in Germany and England and the world ferment all this started." Henryk, the school's acknowledged big intellect, was the only one whose curiosity extended that far.

"Political economy too, why not?" Olek conceded grudgingly.

The others were even less enthusiastic. Economic theory seemed vague to them and dry, while other subjects touched a live chord in their hearts and made them feel kin to the great patriots, the martyrs whose names were like the names of household gods.

"I propose a class in Polish history to start," Adam said formally, just as the school bell sounded.

There was a murmur of approval.

"Everyone agreed?" Olek questioned. "Good." Quickly, then, he began issuing directions, organizing everything like the old hand at conspiracy he already seemed to be. "Now listen carefully, all of you. We'll have to break up into two groups, no more than six each. That's for safety." He made a few quick notes. "I'll ask my father to help us get the right books. We'll need a little money, not much, and anyway that can wait. And we have to have places to meet. Of course the best thing would be to rotate. That avoids attracting attention."

As they walked toward the school entrance and afternoon classes, they were already arranging details. Adam, Olek, Henryk and Henryk's younger brother Juzek would make up the core of one group, their first meeting would be at the Meisels' apartment on Wilcza Street. The Meisels' father was a dealer in furs, which meant there was always a good deal of coming and going at their house. No one would pay the slightest attention to a few extra visitors.

"Maybe people will think business is extra good—they'll take you for errand boys," Henryk laughed. "Just remember *not* to wear the *Gymnasium* uniform." They dispersed feeling life had a bright side after all.

"What I don't understand," Olek said later as he, Adam, and the two Meisels boys started walking home together after school, "is why you fellows are getting into this so deep. After all, you're Jews, the three of you—it isn't really your fight."

"What do you mean, not our fight?" Adam instantly challenged him with ominous quiet. "Whose fight d'you think it is? Maybe you've got a monopoly on it?"

"Now don't get mad, I'm not trying to bait you," Olek countered, not in the least disturbed. "I just want to understand, is all."

"What's to understand?"

"Well, for one thing," Olek said tentatively, rubbing the side of his nose in a characteristic gesture, "strictly speaking you aren't *really* Poles. So you could have it a lot easier if you wanted . . ."

Adam didn't let him finish. "To become informers, is that what you're trying to suggest?" He was doing his best to keep his voice controlled, but a tingling had started at the back of his neck. My hackles are rising, he thought. Literally. I'm like those hunting dogs he was talking about. "Just what do you take us for, Piotrowski?"

"I already said don't get mad. I'm only asking because I want to understand. We can't be friends unless we understand each other, and we can hardly be in the same study circle unless we are friends—comrades in the truest sense. Because we've got to trust one another in every way. So go ahead and explain it to me, Fabian. If you can."

Adam hated to fight. He was not a coward. Wiry and tough, he had long ago learned to take care of himself in street fights. But physical violence was repugnant to him. His palms still sweating, he forced himself to calm down, relieved to be back once more in the realm of ideas, not fists.

Answering Olek's question was not easy. What makes a Jew a Jew? It was something he himself had asked many times, something others were forever asking. A dozen answers, all complicated, did not add up to the whole answer. He made a valiant effort.

"Let's take it from the other end. You're a Catholic, aren't you, Olek?" This was a safe assumption, since with the rarest exceptions all native Poles were Catholics. "But just being a Catholic doesn't make you a Pole—I mean, there are French Catholics and Italian and Spanish ones, Catholics all over the world. Well, as I see it, being a Jew is like that too—a man still has to have a nationality. I think it's a question of where you're born."

"That's not the way our rabbi puts it," argued Juzek. "Or my mother either. With them, being a Jew is a religion and a nationality both."

"And a profession, don't forget," his older brother put in *sotto voce*. But only Adam heard him.

"That's just what I was trying to say," Olek now spoke directly to Juzek. "I wasn't able to put my finger on it, but that's exactly it. Don't your prayers all have to do with the promised land? Isn't every Jew supposed to dream of a homeland in Palestine?"

"Only on paper," Adam said, "and in the synagogue on holy days. Take me, for instance. If I did go to Palestine, what would I do there? It's a desert, it's full of Arabs, and I don't even know the language. Sure I've gone to Hebrew school, but what you learn there is the classical language, like classical Greek. And sure they say 'Next year in Jerusalem' in some of the toasts on the high holidays. But in Jerusalem I'd just be a foreigner."

"You know, I never thought of it that way," Juzek commented.

"Well, think about it now," Adam answered, "and never mind your mother and the rabbi." He was instantly sorry—it was a tactless remark. "I'm talking too much," he went on, trying to cover up. "Suppose you fellows tell Olek why you're joining."

"Well, for one thing, it's the decent thing to do," Henryk offered, sounding a trifle remote. "I mean, all the people one admires are on one side, opposing the Russians, and that makes the rest seem like turncoats. But it's really more than that," he added, with a kind of honest emotion he seldom allowed himself. "Much, much more. You're born in a country so it's your own. Like family. Can there be a better reason?"

"Yes, I see," Olek admitted, still grudgingly.

For a while they walked on in silence, four abreast, in step like young soldiers, their dark-green military-cut uniforms flapping in the wind, their flat student caps jauntily aslant and their book bags making humps across their shoulders. To the casual eye they offered a superficial appearance of regimented sameness, which their build and their faces belied: Adam slight, black-haired, gray-eyed, with the prominent nose and strongly cut features that proclaimed his Semitic ancestry; Henryk and Juzek tall and slender, olive-skinned, with finely etched classic features, looking less like Jews than young hidalgos. And finally there was Olek, not yet grown to full stature but already powerful, square-shouldered, his sandy hair and high Slav cheekbones and round, cropped head so typically peasant he might have sat for Matejko's paintings of village youth.

"Well," Adam asked after a while, "are you beginning to understand us, Piotrowski? My family were patriots fighting beside

Kosciuszko. My great-grandfather served in the Dombrowski Legions in Italy and my grandfather knew Mickiewicz—they corresponded after Mickiewicz went into exile. My other great-grandfather was thrown in jail for wearing the *konfederatka* * after Napoleon's defeat. And my mother tells about a pogrom of Catholics when she was a girl, when the Jews on Nalewki Street hid your people from the cossacks."

"Come to think of it," Henryk added with pride, *"our* grandfather was chief rabbi of Warsaw at the time. Dov Berish Meisels. You must have heard the name, Adam. Only my mother," he smiled sardonically, "prefers not to be reminded. Because, to her, her father-in-law was just the kind that likes to borrow trouble. Let sleeping dogs lie, she always says."

They reached the corner of Wilcza Street and the two brothers said goodbye and turned toward home. Adam and Olek walked on together.

"You know, Fabian, it's all beginning to make sense," Olek finally admitted. "I learned a lot today. I really did."

"That goes for both of us. You make me sort out my own ideas."

"Good. I've heard so much idiot talk on the subject all my life, so much senseless arguing pro and con. You know, of course, that when Christians are alone they talk differently. Even the ones that *say* they're without prejudice"—he grinned sheepishly—"like me. My Uncle Jacek once tried to explain to me about anti-Semitism, about the ruling class making scapegoats of Jews—the divide-and-rule principle. Only it all sounded like so much theory to me then. Now with you it's been different—you know, man to man."

"Then I'm glad we had it out," Adam said. "Let's shake on it." They walked on without further words, companionably at ease with each other.

* The *konfederatka* was the traditional square cap with sharp corners, frequently embellished with peacock feathers, worn by the Polish nobles as well as the Legionnaires and their generals, and also part of the national dress. Hence it became a symbol, and was therefore forbidden by Russian authorities.

❦ *Four* ❧

Pani Emilia Tworska was very jealous of the fact that she was a lady born and bred, and she let no one forget it. True, she was a lady whose husband's early demise had left her with only a pittance on which to raise and educate her three daughters, but she was determined not to let such a handicap declass her. This was more or less what she told her husband's solicitor when that gentleman came to suggest she had best sell her more valuable furnishings, cut expenses to the bone, and move into humbler quarters in some less fashionable section of town.

"What! And leave Count Berg Street where I came to live as a bride! I wouldn't think of it. After all, to give up gracious living would be like giving up one's birthright! Moreover, it would mean abdicating my girls' right to *their* birthright, and that would be far worse!"

The solicitor argued, then washed his hands of her after making all sorts of dire predictions concerning her future.

Within the year she had proved him wrong. True, she did for a time cut corners, but only to the extent of dismissing the servants, with the exception of one docile, browbeaten girl from the municipal orphanage, on whom she systematically piled all the heavy work. The marketing and the cooking she now did herself. She also moved her daughters with all their belongings into her own bedroom and a small adjoining boudoir. This left a whole wing of the apartment empty and free for renting. She refurbished it, then let word get around that her home, only a stone's throw away from fashionable Nowy Swiat, was open to a few select boarders, well-born young gentlemen from the provinces whose families sent them to the capital to be educated.

Having boys board with a private family rather than in school dormitories was an accepted practice of the time, good homes were hard to find, and even the fact that *Pani* Emilia was Jewish had little effect on the success of her scheme. Not a few of the landed gentry seemingly took the attitude that a place to board was like an inn—one only stopped there temporarily, after all— and inns throughout the country were traditionally run by Jews. Thus, from then on *Pani* Tworska's household, except for vacations and holidays, was generally teeming with well-mannered, well-scrubbed youths who came back year after year until finally they grew up and left for the Sorbonne or Cambridge or Oxford. But not even their departure created a vacuum, for younger brothers and cousins and friends arrived next fall to fill the empty places.

All in all it was a pleasant arrangement. Soon *Pani* Tworska's purse was again comfortably full. There were also other advantages. For one thing, she had no need to worry about appearances, as she might have if her boarders had been grown men. Still more important, her daughters were now in daily contact with the scions of some of the country's best families. The girls, especially the youngest one, Salome, were growing up into beauties, yet their mother was sufficiently realistic to realize it was not going to be easy to arrange advantageous marriages for them without dowries to smooth the way. Well then, they would have to depend on the magic of love. In which case getting to know so many sons of the wealthy could do no harm. She became fond of quoting the old adage about how it was just as easy to fall in love with a rich man as with a beggar.

The fact that her boarders were Gentiles, aristocrats, from a social stratum that did not countenance misalliances, did trouble her, but not for long. Just let the right man come on the scene, *Pani* Tworska spun her dream, and the rest would take care of itself. After all, when the powerful and the wealthy fell in love, barriers that to ordinary mortals might seem insurmountable could simply be swept away.

In the meantime she was at least able to send her daughters to a desirable private school, not the *gymnasium*. The *pension* she chose was one where the emphasis was less on scholarship than on polish. Eugenia, Clara, and Salome learned to speak French with what passed for a Parisian accent, they learned all the fashionable dance steps and the fine art of reading aloud, they took singing lessons and piano lessons, did fine embroidery, and were at ease in a drawing room.

Yet by some strange quirk the sisters, or at least the two older ones, were not seduced by their mother's romantic plans for them. Eugenia especially, at an age when most girls have their heads stuffed full of dreams and fancies, was already showing a sensible, practical side to her nature. She was calmly aware that one day it might be up to her to shoulder the family responsibilities. She also knew there were two ways for her to accomplish this—by making a good marriage or earning a good living. A natural sense of independence and dignity made her lean toward the second course.

Clara, more pliant and much less determined, might have been content to allow her mother to arrange her life for her, except that Eugenia was there to influence her. Consequently she, too, was not deluded. True, there were enough yearning young men always underfoot for her to realize that dowry or no dowry, sooner or later she would find a husband. But a brilliant match might not exactly be in the cards, and so she, too, like her more forceful sister, learned to face the fact that an education in what their mother called the ladylike graces might not be enough. In spite of *Pani* Tworska's protests both girls taught themselves to mend and to sew, to run a household and supervise its kitchen, nor were they helpless when confronted with account books.

Only Salome, the youngest, by her own choice, but also with the encouragement of the rest of the family, developed into a hothouse flower. Where Eugenia was exceptionally tall for a woman, and handsome rather than beautiful, where Clara was softly pretty with a freshness that someday would fade and turn to fat, Salome was delicate perfection. Slight, built like a Tanagra figurine, her skin the color of pale new ivory, her hair blue-black and her heavily lashed eyes the shade of cornflowers, she bore a striking resemblance to the Empress Eugénie, the last queen of France. She had the power to startle and to enchant.

That she must have everything life could offer a lovely woman became for her doting family an incontrovertible dictum. They took it so much for granted that in time the girl herself began to expect no less. Had she had the capacity for it, she might have developed a true sense of destiny, except that her horizons were comfortably limited. She burned with no special ambition. The fire in her eyes was an accident of nature, the high smooth forehead and beautifully modeled, sensitive features masked a mind that was quite ordinary, and she accepted her world as the best of possible worlds so long as she could be its very center and her garden was cultivated for her.

In short, she was like a pedigreed Persian kitten that everyone is happy to pet and spoil and admire and of whom nothing is required in return except that it look pretty and respond with an occasional purr. In a sense it was really a tribute to her innate sweetness of character that she did not grow up insufferably self-willed and self-centered.

When Salome was sixteen and Clara already a year out of school, Eugenia scandalized the family by announcing that she had found work that suited her and she was going to leave home.

She was by then twenty-three, she had already turned down a couple of offers of marriage that had flattered but not tempted her, and for the sake of giving her sisters a chance at something better she was ready to resign herself to spinsterhood. But she had no desire to be a spinster in her mother's house.

The position she was being offered came her way purely by chance, through the mother of an old school friend, and for anyone else so young to take it on would have been unthinkable. It was the kind of employment considered suitable for widows or genteel unmarried ladies of a certain age, women who after managing large households for husband, father, or brother were suddenly left alone and destitute, and rather than accept the grudging charity of relatives found a refuge of sorts below stairs in the homes of rich strangers. In this case the stranger was the recently widowed Baron Kronenberg, whose mansion, the size of a national museum, stood well back from the street on the corner of the Square of the Three Crosses, where Aleje Ujazdowskie began.

The Baron, an international banker, prided himself on his antecedents. Late in the thirteenth century his ancestors had migrated to Poland from the Adriatic seacoast to escape persecution, and he cherished a parchment with the signature of Casimir the Great, dated 1334, in which, along with other privileges, the king granted them liberty of domicile anywhere in the land. Like his father before him, he was a regally unconscious snob. Since his business dealings were largely with the French branch of the House of Rothschild, he was a frequent visitor in their Paris *hôtel* and their châteaux in France's wine country. But he had reservations about them. Weren't they after all just a few generations removed from being new-rich?

By the same token he maintained few ties with the Polish-Jewish aristocracy, and being hard to please he married late. When he did, he marked the occasion by presenting his bride with a diamond pendant said to have been part of the famous Queen's Necklace that in the end had cost Marie Antoinette her head.

And now his wife was dead and the child born of this union between two people too old and too highly bred for happy, easy parenthood was being raised by a succession of starchy governesses. The great mansion had taken on the look and mood of a mausoleum, from which the Baron stayed away as much as his affairs permitted. Unquestionably he needed a gentlewoman to take charge.

Curiously, it occurred to no one, not even *Pani* Tworska who otherwise duly lamented the economic necessity for her daughter's move, to warn Eugenia that there might be impropriety, not to say a certain danger, in staying, unchaperoned, under the roof of a man who was now a bachelor, a man of the world used to having his own way, a man old enough to be her father but with a sophistication her father had never possessed. Eugenia was Eugenia. Therefore she would be safe.

And indeed she was. Within six months the Baron's staff adored her, the house ran on oiled wheels, the *fraulein* had been replaced by a considerably less rigid *mademoiselle*, and Eugenia herself had established her right to oversee the nursery and on occasion even spoil the child.

The Baron's three-year-old son Lucio was badly in need of spoiling. He was a stolid, none-too-bright, frightened little boy curiously devoid of natural charm and thus from babyhood robbed of a child's most precious asset. Timid to begin with, he had been made painfully shy as a result of the *fraulein's* determination to toilet-train him, house-train him, and otherwise turn him into the perfect little gentleman his father would surely expect her to turn out.

Eugenia's heart went out to the youngster. She could not bear to see anything so young and small be so browbeaten. She began to spend much of her free time with him on the pretext that *mademoiselle* needed the rest. She played with him, often taking him herself to the Lazienki Park, encouraging him to play with other children while she sat on a bench among the governesses and nannies and an occasional young mother unwilling to trust her young to hired help.

Long before Victorian Europe had heard about progressive methods of education, Eugenia did the right thing by instinct. She seldom scolded, nor did she demand perfection. Lucio blossomed. His somewhat limited intelligence seemed less limited because he was no longer intimidated. He learned to smile, stopped wetting his bed, and began to get over the stutter that earlier had made him the butt of other children's jokes.

One day about a year after Eugenia had become part of his household Baron Kronenberg, arriving home ahead of schedule after a lengthy absence in Western Europe, walked in on his son and his housekeeper unannounced. As he came upon them he felt as though suddenly he were standing in a patch of sunshine after living a long time in the dark. For a moment he stood quietly watching the small boy and the tall, stately young woman playing together on the floor. She was being a lion, moving about on all fours, roaring at Lucio who was convulsed with laughter, shaking her bangs at him, her hair in her eyes, tendrils of it escaping the combs that ordinarily held it up so neatly. The Baron savored especially the incongruity of catching his dignified housekeeper with her skirts hiked up to expose a shapely calf.

Until then she had been a cog in a mechanism. Now for the first time he saw her as a woman, young, fresh, vital. He saw the marvelous long lines of her body and a pair of provocatively well-turned ankles. More than that—he saw her as a human being.

He coughed to make his presence known, and instantly the scene froze into a still life. Then, recovering, Eugenia scrambled to her feet. He noticed with approval that she was neither embarrassed nor flustered. The child, sensing that this time his father's coming was somehow not a threat, ran to him in a spontaneous outburst of glee. Baron Ludwig picked up his son, swung him high, then kissed him. He felt tears stinging his eyes.

That week and the next, he dined at home at least every other night. Finally, after considerable reflection and some discreet inquiries, he sent word to Eugenia that he would like to have her join him for dinner. She came in wearing her good gray dress with a touch of real lace at the high neck and wrists, her hair freshly brushed and once more shining, and she sat relaxed and calm at his table as though all her life she had belonged in baronial halls. Again the Baron noticed she showed no signs of self-consciousness. He knew that any other girl in her position would have been so preoccupied with why she was there that she would have been either struck dumb or else coy and overeager. Eugenia merely accorded him the deference due any man twice her age, and left the conversational gambits entirely up to him.

In the drawing room over coffee he proposed. He was crisply businesslike, unemotional, apologizing for not going through the accepted formalities of first approaching her mother through an intermediary. "I admit I wanted to sound you out first. But of course if you feel strongly about it, I shall be as correct as you like."

He then went on to explain that he needed a wife and his son needed a mother, that recently he had come to understand Eugenia was already, of her own accord, being a mother to the boy in spirit and so she might as well become one legally, and that he felt the arrangement would be advantageous to everyone concerned.

Finally he added that he hoped the difference in their ages would not frighten her off, taking care to make it plain he did not intend the marriage to be a business arrangement pure and simple.

"I respect you a great deal, my child, and could easily become extremely fond of you," was the way he put it. "That is, if you'll have me. Tomorrow I suggest you take the day off, go home, and discuss matters with your family." It did not occur to him that his housekeeper might turn him down.

It hardly occurred to Eugenia herself.

She weighed what the Kronenberg money could do for her mother and younger sisters. She thought of Lucio, and how much more she would now be able to do for him. Yet her ultimate decision was not based on sacrificial considerations. Eugenia was no martyr. From the very first she had appreciated her employer. People said of him that he was cold, but she had the perception to sense the hidden warmth behind his massive reserve. She sensed it in the delight he took in his collection of Flemish paintings, in the way he would sit absorbed in a string quartet on the rare occasions when he gave musicales in the barn-like ballroom. Most particularly she saw it in his awkward attempts to play with his son. As for the age difference, this did not seem at all unreasonable in an era when a young girl was considered fortunate to marry an established man with graying hair.

At least, Eugenia thought irreverently, the gray hair is thick—but not his waistline!

Aloud she said, after only a moment's consideration, "Thank you, Baron. Of course I'll talk to my mother at once. But I can tell you right now that she *will* expect a more formal proposal!"

"Am I to understand, then, that you yourself are not against it?"

She smiled—and she was one of those women whom a smile makes beautiful. "No, I am not against it."

"In that case we will consider everything settled in principle," he said, reaching for her hand and kissing it. "Thank you, my child, you have made me very happy." He rose, indicating the evening was over. Then, offering her his arm in an old-fashioned courtly gesture, he led her up the stairs to the second floor, where her room and his private suite were at opposite ends of the long hall. "Thank you again. Sleep well. I shall see you at breakfast."

It was a good marriage. As the years went by the Baron became so doting he sometimes embarrassed his wife. How could anyone so generous and so kind, she thought, be so humbly grateful for a little happiness? For the rest of their life together she never really appreciated how much she herself was giving him by merely being herself. She watched over his interests almost as tenderly as she watched over Lucio, and when the Baron's generosity threatened to go beyond the bounds of reason she stopped him. "No, Ludwig, it's too much. You overwhelm me. Thank you, but no." Eventually he learned to believe there was no need to bribe her in order for her to be fond of him.

His largesse was soon spilling over to include her family, and he would have taken care of them completely had Eugenia permitted it. But again she put her foot down.

"I don't believe it's in their own best interests," she would say in her thoughtful, quiet way. "Much as I love my sisters I know they are inclined to be vain and rather flighty. Oh, I know it's part of their charm, but," and here the Victorian moralist in her came through, "who knows what lies ahead for them—what kind of men they'll marry. Let's not spoil them too much, just in case they have to stand on their own two feet some day. Later on, when they're settled and my mother is alone, if you want to provide for her I won't say a word!"

"At least let me hire a couple of competent servants for her. And start taking Clara and Salome to your own dressmaker whenever you like. There's no need to stint." He was thoughtful a moment. "By the way, I don't know how much of this you'll want to discuss with the girls themselves, but do assure your mother that I mean to give each of them a dowry."

Clara got married that year, not a brilliant match but a satisfactory one—her husband was a young lawyer-accountant who represented some of the Baron's interests abroad. They moved to

London and Pani Emilia and Salome were left alone, each at last enjoying the privacy of a room of her own.

Gradually other changes took place in the apartment. The maid of all work was replaced by a cook and two chambermaids, one of whom, Julia, had been trained to wait on table properly and knew how to answer the door and announce callers. The living-room furniture was redone and new draperies hung. As a final touch, a magnificent Bechstein was delivered one morning to replace their old piano. Unfortunately the mellow-voiced instrument did nothing to improve Salome's playing, but as Eugenia remarked to her mother, Baron Ludwig was not, after all, a magician.

That summer, with the current crop of boy boarders dispersed through the provinces, the house began to echo with loneliness for its two occupants.

"This is the time of year when I miss your father most," *Pani* Emilia confided one evening to her youngest daughter. "It does seem so strange not to have a single man around. Not right at all. Why, at night it hardly seems safe," she added plaintively.

Salome, nearing twenty, barely remembered her father but she too felt restless in a house without men. For herself she was not concerned, since she was just leaving for a month's visit with the Kronenbergs in their summer villa. But she was uneasy about her mother. *Pani* Tworska, who never enjoyed the country, had stubbornly refused to close the house and come along.

"Maybe we could afford a footman," Salome suggested.

"What you really mean is, maybe we could ask the baron! Salunia dear, whatever are you thinking! That's not nice—that's, well—making demands."

"Is it? Yes, I suppose you're right. Well, I hadn't thought." The girl shrugged, and let it ride. "In that case, Mama, maybe you should look for a boarder for the summer months. Just until school reopens. You know, some older man, well recommended. It couldn't hurt. And it would give us a little extra income into the bargain."

Pani Tworska thought this a capital idea. "Now why didn't I think of it myself? Yes, I think I shall do just that."

The following morning she swung into action. And on the very day Salome left for the country, friends recommended the ideal person. He was Leon Grossglik, a man in his early thirties who despite his comparative youth held an extremely responsible—and well-paid—position at the *Gmina,* the community association of Warsaw Jews. The friends thought it proper to warn *Pani* Emilia that Grossglik's antecedents were lowly, not to say plebeian—his family came from the Nalewki district, where his brother-in-law, one Jacob Fabian, dealt in wigs and false hair. But he had another brother-in-law who was a doctor, and he himself was a university man, he had studied law, had good manners, and seemed a gentleman in every sense of the word.

Pani Emilia thought it would do no harm to look the young man over. After all she could always say no to him, and anyway it need not be a permanent arrangement—in the fall she could tell him all her rooms were spoken for. So an interview was set up, and that same evening Leon, the baby brother Bluma Fabian had mothered at an age when other little girls still play with dolls, was ringing *Pani* Tworska's doorbell.

❧ *Five* ❧

THE VERY WORD *gmina* was a misnomer in relation to the Jewish *Gmina* of the City of Warsaw. For *gmina* implies that its members are lowly—the common folk. But this *Gmina*, though technically a self-help organization, existed on charity. It maintained itself almost exclusively out of the donations of the wealthy and the self-exalted, to whom the teeming North Warsaw slums were an embarrassment.

The Jewish bankers and industrialists who comprised the board of directors were apt to blame the phenomenon of anti-Semitism on the Jewish masses themselves, who with their long flapping black coats, their side-curls and *yarmulkas*, and their use of the despised Yiddish jargon created, as it were, the symbolic obstacle in the way of assimilation. At least, by taking care of the poorest poor, the upper crust—whose charity was more modestly backed by contributions from the middle stratum and the genuinely pious—hoped discreetly to eradicate this blot on their pride, for weren't Jews traditionally known to take care of their own?

Like so many other philanthropic organizations, the *Gmina* was riddled with snobbery, with palace politics, with jockeying for positions of prestige. But this appetite for self-aggrandizement did not extend to the paid staff, composed mostly of dedicated men, men of conscience and integrity and strong social conviction.

Even among his selfless colleagues Leon Grossglik stood out, and not for his ability alone. He worked early and late, frequently dipping into his own pocket to ease someone's misery rather than get entangled in red tape. Indifferent to the small luxuries, he never owned more than two suits of clothing at a time, at least one of them shiny and threadbare. His sister was forever reminding him that his shirt collar needed turning. Promotions came regularly, but they brought little change in his personal habits, so that for years he continued to live in the same furnished hole of a room, a few blocks away from the Fabians' flat, into which he had first moved as a student. He always had something more urgent to do with his money than spend it on himself. And when he wasn't giving it away he was buying books.

Bluma Fabian was inordinately proud of her brother, but she worried about his welfare. "That Leon! Someday he'll walk in here barefoot because he met a beggar in the rain who needed shoes!" It never occurred to her that he was the way he was largely because, long ago, she herself had inoculated him with her own romantic idealism.

From his birth she had loved him fiercely, protectively, and for many things. He had cost her her childhood, this squalling infant who'd also cost their mother's life. But instead of resenting him as the worst of her chores she saw him as a consolation and a joy. Her sister Balbina, five years her junior, eluded her. Already too old to be babied, Balbina was nevertheless still baby enough to adjust, to accept, even to win over the benighted stepmother whom the distracted father had brought into the household as soon as the period of mourning for his first wife was decently over. This made Bluma feel doubly cheated. In her loneliness she turned to the little fellow, making him all hers. She allowed no one else to do for him. Later, when he was old enough, it was she who helped him with his ABCs, she who encouraged him to get good marks at school. In the cold, newly harsh atmosphere of their father's house she tried to build for just the two of them a secret, separate world where harshness had no place and where the wellsprings of everything were affection and kindness.

In time the brother-son grew into a responsive, studious, sensitive youth. He understood his sister better than she understood herself and even tried to serve as a link between her and the new family where, like Balbina, he too had found a place. When Bluma would have none of it, he made her exile in the kitchen more bearable by studying beside her while she peeled potatoes, swept out ashes, and scoured blackened pots.

He also began to bring her books to read and study. And if in time Bluma taught herself to quote Polish poets by heart and knew her country's history, if she learned enough French and German to read them fluently, it was all so that Leon need not be ashamed of her. At first there had been the need to keep one step ahead of the little brother still asking questions. Later on, it became important to her to earn his admiration and talk his language. Still later she discovered the pleasures of learning for its own sake, and then to her love for him was added deep gratitude. "If it weren't for him," she told Jacob one day, "I'd have been"—with a nod toward her stepmother—"like her."

It was in a sense inevitable that Leon, not merely a product of Bluma's training but very much a child of his time, should want to dedicate his life to the welfare of others. From boyhood on, medicine had attracted him. But there hadn't been enough money for him to follow this inclination. Next he thought of law, seeing himself as the mouthpiece and champion of the ill-used and ill-fed. He enrolled in law school. But again lack of funds threatened to defeat him.

Ironically, it was the nagging stepmother's early insistence that whatever other education he got, he must above all attend Hebrew school—for he could then coach his half-brothers in all he learned, thus saving the family the price of three more *cheder* enrollments—that in the end was instrumental in determining his profession. His knowledge of Hebrew, coupled with what legal training he already had, resulted in an offer from the *Gmina*. It was a way to earn a livelihood with dignity and self-respect—harrowing work, to be sure, but to a man of Leon's temperament highly rewarding. The term social worker had not yet come into use, but essentially that was what he became.

After the third or fourth promotion, colleagues began to urge him to allow himself a few creature comforts.

"Stop thinking you're Jesus. You're not going to feed the multitudes with five or even fifty loaves of bread!"

"Does it really profit the poor if you spend two hours a day chasing streetcars? Contrariwise, they might profit if you got more sleep. At least, move closer to your work!"

He himself was beginning to feel the need for a change. So that when the executive secretary of the *Gmina* announced he would be retiring soon, and at the next directors' meeting strongly urged that Grossglik, for all his youth, be appointed as his successor, Leon decided that maybe it really was time for him to move. No one doubted that the important new post would be his in a matter of months. He started looking around for more suitable quarters, preferably a place where he could take his meals. Someone suggested the widow Tworska, who had a spacious bedroom-and-study suite to rent in her once elegant apartment in a non-Jewish residential section only a short distance from the *Gmina* offices. Leon called on *Pani* Emilia, they discussed terms, and within the half-hour everything was settled. He moved in by the end of the week.

Pani Emilia was well satisfied with her new boarder. Plebeian though his origins might be, he seemed cultivated in every sense of the word, well-spoken, well-read. "One of nature's gentlemen," she described him when next she wrote to her married daughters. "And his conversation at the dinner table is certainly a welcome change from schoolboy chatter!" She also approved of the fact that he was punctual at meals, while the chambermaid reported him neat in his personal habits. "Best of all, he never even quibbled over my rates, which I'll admit I had set rather high on the assumption he would want to bargain like everyone else!"

Had Leon been twenty or even fifteen years older, she might have been tempted to think of him in terms of a husband for herself. But in view of his age she began to weigh other possibilities. *Pan* Grossglik was young but not too young, he was serious, stable, financially secure even if not in any sense a moneyed man, and he had the respect of the best people among Warsaw's Jewry. He also had considerable personal charm. If not a husband, he might make her a most satisfactory son-in-law.

Pani Emilia laid her plans carefully. Within days after Leon was installed in his new quarters the maids were taking down and polishing all the good family silver. The Sèvres china service was unpacked and put into constant use. By the time Salome came home from her month in the country, meals at *Pani* Tworska's had become daily works of culinary art served in an atmosphere of engaging intimacy. It was still a whole month to the opening of school—time enough for anything to happen.

Salome was one of those fortunate females born with all the instincts of her sex in wonderful working order, and nothing had ever happened to change this. Around her, women were beginning to question the justice of a world where men had all the say, they were beginning to demand such outlandish rights as equality before the law and in education, the right to earn a living and manage their own money and even choose their own husbands. Salome felt no need for self-assertion. If she gave such matters any thought at all, it was to shrug them off as "borrowing trouble."

Eugenia's insistence on going to work she had always mildly deplored, even if in the end it had led to a spectacularly happy ending. Her own future, in her mind's eye, revolved around her becoming the center of some yet-faceless man's lifelong devotion, a devotion engendered by her beauty and charm, of which she had long been aware. This feminine power she meant to wield not only over her husband but over a large circle of friends, a magic circle disturbed only by an occasional ripple of trouble when some "other man" would fall desperately in love with her. But she of course would remain faithful—though she wasn't exactly sure what being faithful really entailed—and everyone would agree how lucky her husband was. In short, her concepts of marriage were still confined to the drawing room and the tea table, or possibly a rococo boudoir at the door of which a husband always knocked. And to having her hand kissed rather than her lips. This was how life appeared in the novels of Marcel Prévost and Octave Feuillet, and this was what a girl of her background expected.

Leon Grossglik had over the years come in contact with a great many women of fashion, charity-ball patronesses and the like, and being a personable bachelor hadn't been allowed to remain wholly naive about man-woman relations. On the other hand his only intimate knowledge of family life came from observing his two sisters' households. Thus the unreal world Salome's mother was creating had no relation to anything in his previous experience. He was delightfully bewildered. For the first time in his life he was actually in daily contact with a future great beauty, a kind of budding femme fatale, who was at the same time truly an innocent. Soon Salome began to seem perfect in his eyes. He was finding her innocence enchanting, her passivity feminine and disarming, and he made no attempt to equate what he felt in an often wildly beating heart with what he knew in his sensible bones.

By the time school reopened and *Pani* Emilia's regular boarders once more overran the premises, the romance was on a safe, decorous course. For Salome, an unquestioned order of things had been established—she was being courted with both ardor and patience, and with a devotion deep enough to contain any unseemly, disturbing outbursts of passion. As for Leon, he now believed nothing could ever give him greater joy than to be allowed to pamper and cherish this lovely creature for the rest of his days on earth.

All his habits changed. For years he had brought paper work home, spending his evenings at his desk. Now he found himself spending them holding skeins of silk yarn for Salome to wind into balls for her embroidery. Or standing beside her at the piano while she tripped through the easier Chopin waltzes, humming the melodies in her clear, casually inaccurate little soprano. Leon, as it happened, had a fine natural ear. But the warm flower scent of Salome's hair which he inhaled each time he bent to turn a page of the music made him quite deaf to the wrong notes, the slurred bravura passages, the fact that the Bechstein needed tuning or that his beloved's voice, which nature seemed to have keyed permanently a trifle sharp, often made the performance sound as though it came from a human hurdy-gurdy.

When the Philharmonic season opened he ventured to invite both ladies to a concert. From this he progressed to a performance of Moniuszko's *Halka,* followed by *Aida.* When the first snow fell, the old woman selling flowers on the corner of Nowy Swiat across from the Copernicus Monument already knew him for a steady customer and always had a special smile for him. "I've saved my prettiest violets for your young lady." Or mimosa, or roses, depending on what she happened to have that day.

In midwinter the old *Gmina* secretary officially announced he would be retiring by spring, and Leon finally felt free to speak to *Pani* Emilia about his matrimonial intentions. She heard him out, went through the motions of dabbing her eyes with a hand-kerchief, as was expected of a mother about to relinquish her last chick, and admitted she was not surprised. Later she called her daughter into her bedroom for an intimate little chat. After informing her that *Pan* Grossglik was about to ask her hand in marriage, she asked Salome how she herself felt about it.

What Salome really felt was that twenty years old was no longer dewy-young and that a bird in the hand was a bird in the hand. But she cast down her eyes, managed a blush, and gave the answer protocol demanded. "I will do whatever you think best, Mama," she said with a show of meekness.

Well satisfied, and again following protocol, the mother countered, "My darling, I do want you to follow your own heart!"

They were like two characters in a highly stylized play, both enjoying the orderly flow of the dialogue while knowing perfectly well just what the outcome would be. And now that their scene had been acted out, all that remained for them was to sit back and wait for Leon's proposal.

But the proposal did not come.

The wave of arrests in which *Pan* Liebman had been caught was taking a long time to subside, and suddenly Leon, for all that his commitment to Salome was now total and irrevocable, began to be tortured by self-doubts. It was not his love he questioned but his right to the luxury of personal happiness. For wasn't it a kind of sinful indulgence to allow oneself the joys of home, family, all the creature comforts, so long as the Motherland remained in chains and millions of her children starved?

Incredible as this may sound to modern ears, he was not at all unique in his impulse toward these extremes of self-sacrifice. Rather, his scruples reflected the viewpoint of many of Poland's young liberals at the turn of the century. Within a few more years these doubts would crystallize in Stefan Zheromski's novel *The Homeless People,* its quixotic protagonist, Tomasz Judym, becoming the symbol of the nation's conscience. The book's climactic scene, when in an agony of self-abnegation the impassioned young doctor-turned-social-activist breaks with the upper-class woman he loves, would be quoted everywhere:

> *Oh, don't you see, I can allow myself nothing—nothing and no one—of my own! No, neither mother nor father, brother nor sister nor wife, so long as conditions in our land are what they are . . .*

Poor Leon struggled with his dilemma in silence, unable and unwilling to burden Salome with it and sensing, though vaguely, that to try sharing it with her would not help. In any case the decision must be his and no one else's. He vacillated endlessly. One moment he was sure that his only choice was renunciation. Next he felt equally convinced he would be as nothing, and his work nothing, unless he could have Salome by his side as his wife. He became taciturn, restless, ate little, slept hardly at all, and puzzled the household with his dark moods.

After a week of this private Gethsemane he woke one morning and knew that he could no longer go on this way. Ordinarily closemouthed about his personal affairs, he determined to talk things over with his sister Bluma. Bluma and Jacob might not be the most practical people when it came to ordering their own lives, but he trusted their instincts where others were concerned.

This much of the decision made, he felt better. It was Sunday. He began to plan his day. He had a report to write: a fire in the largely Jewish Praga district across the river had wiped out a row of wooden tenements along with the local synagogue, and funds were desperately needed for the burnt-out families. In the afternoon he must make some quietly determined calls on affluent *Gmina* patrons whose contributions had fallen off. But toward evening he might manage to get over to the Fabians' early enough for a private talk with his sister before she became absorbed in the hubbub of the supper hour.

He dressed hurriedly, had his early morning coffee, took a

long walk, came home with the newspapers, took second breakfast with the ladies, and before getting back to his desk to struggle with the report regretfully explained that an unavoidable family commitment would make it necessary for him to forgo the
pleasure of spending the rest of the day in their company.

On that same morning the Fabians, who for days had been
watching the Liebman children beg food from the neighbors,
sent down a peck of potatoes to the "widow" along with a sack
of coal. Then they talked the situation over and concluded that in
the face of such stark need even poor people like themselves
might try pulling a few strings. After all, with Bluma's brother
such an important man at the *Gmina,* what harm could there be in
turning to him for help? Surely if anything could be done, the
Gmina was the organization to do it and Leon the man to see to it
that the wheels were set in motion. If nothing else, perhaps the
Gmina could ease the lot of the two arrested men by sending a donation directly to the Pawiak authorities. Or perhaps it could
allot a few kopeks a day out of some special charity fund for milk
and bread for the little Liebmans.

"It isn't as if, God forbid, we were asking for ourselves,"
Bluma was quick to justify her decision in her own eyes, "though
I hate to add to Leon's burdens. He works so hard, always so
pressed, always running. . . ."

"And doing what brings him most satisfaction," her husband
was as quick to remind her.

"Yes, but just the same he's killing himself, doing only for
others!"

"Is it any wonder? Look who brought him up! Seems to run in
the family," he couldn't resist teasing her.

"Please, Jacob, don't make a joke of something that's not
funny!"

"Who's joking? It's God's own truth." Then, relenting, "All
right, I'll keep quiet. And as you say, it isn't as if we were asking
for ourselves."

"Heaven be blessed for that," she answered fervently, "I
hope we never have to. It's all settled, then? I'll send right over
and ask him to supper tonight. It'll be a pleasure," she smiled,

"to have an excuse to invite him. Now that he lives clear across town we hardly ever see him. If I didn't know him so well I'd start thinking he's getting too grand to visit us like he used to. But not him. Not my Leon!"

Adam came into the room just then to tell them he was going out, he and some fellows from school were going to study together. It was a neat way of accounting for his time while remaining carefully vague about the study circle, and when his mother asked him to stop off at Count Berg Street with a message for his uncle, to her surprise, he looked annoyed.

"It's going to make me late, can't you send one of the others?"

In the end they compromised. He would do the errand on his way home.

❧ *Six* ☙

T<small>HE FIRST MEETING</small> of the study circle turned out to be an
unsettling experience for Adam. He and Olek Piotrowski arrived
together, after arranging to meet on the nearest street corner. But
though it helped to have each other for moral support, they both
felt uncomfortable in the Meisels' home.

Even the building where the Meisels lived was unlike any
Adam was used to. A vast, ornate structure of the kind that had
become fashionable in mid-century, it stood on Wilcza Street, in
the heart of what was known as the gold-plated ghetto. It had a
great *porte cochère* and a landscaped inner courtyard with a fountain and mews to one side. The apartment itself was only one
flight up and at the front of the house, not in back where rents
were cheaper. From the street one saw its balconies and tall
jalousied windows. The stairway leading to it was marble with a
curving banister and red plush carpeting. The entrance doors
were massive oak. The boys read and reread the engraving on the
polished brass nameplate before ringing the doorbell: Y<small>ANKEL</small>
M<small>EISELS</small>, D<small>EALER IN</small> F<small>INE</small> F<small>URS</small>.

"Some class," Olek whispered as a parlormaid was letting
them into the entrance hall.

Here, too, everything was ornate. High carved ceilings, chandeliers, and what seemed to Adam acres of polished parquet
floors covered with rich carpets. He had a glimpse of huge rooms
furnished in gilt and damask, with dark velvet draperies at doors
and windows, and walls crowded with paintings of cows grazing

and nymphs in diaphanous garments cavorting, all against similar bucolic landscapes and in similar heavy gilt frames. "What did we get ourselves into?" Olek whispered, nudging Adam and winking. They asked for Henryk and Juzek.

The maid, though she eyed their shabby clothes with the obvious, ill-concealed distaste of the servant identifying with the employer class, nevertheless admitted that "the young masters" were expecting them. "Straight down the hall, last door on the right. Guess there's no need to announce youse."

A door slammed and Juzek came running, followed more slowly by Henryk. "Hello. Just the two of you? Where are the others?"

"Seems like they got cold feet," Olek said, adding contemptuously, "One fellow claims his father won't let him come. The idiot, why'd he have to ask permission in the first place? The other didn't explain, but I guess it's more of the same. Which makes us kind of exclusive for the time being."

It seemed to them Juzek looked relieved. "Maybe it's just as well. The folks aren't exactly overjoyed about the whole idea." He seemed embarrassed, as if regretting his fine impassioned words of the other day about being as much a Pole as a Jew.

Henryk, too, though he managed to maintain the aloof, slightly superior attitude of one who was only a few months away from matriculating at the university, gave the impression he wasn't quite sure how he had got himself tangled in such a strange and daring venture. He tried to be offhand. "The mater is really the one who's been raising holy hell—says she can't see why we had to get mixed up in something that was bound to be illegal. But then," he shrugged, "you know how women are."

Olek was beginning to bristle. "Look, you want us to go, we'll go. Just say so. Don't beat around the bush."

Juzek turned red but he stood his ground. "Naah. You're here, you might as well stay. Besides, we don't have to do everything *she* wants. What the hell. Only let's not stand around, let's go inside, we'll be more private."

He led the way past the huge parlors where, oddly out of place, Adam noticed several elaborate armoires with mirrored doors that caught the light.

"The showrooms," Juzek explained. And suddenly Adam stopped feeling awed. The Meisels might be very grand, but when all was said and done this was just another tradesman's house, and therefore not essentially different from his own home.

In actual fact Yankel Meisels catered exclusively to Warsaw's carriage trade and was extremely proud of this, as though to satisfy the whims of the titled and the very rich was the highest kind of responsibility, the highest honor one could aspire to. He liked to stress that he did not sell to "just anybody." No one came off the street, and only the city's finest furrier-tailors sent their clientele to him, often coming along themselves to help assist customers in their choice of pelts.

If not accompanied by her tailor, a lady generally arrived with her husband, a brother, or perhaps another lady, in which case there would be a footman or at least a lady's maid in attendance. Often the client would be a man, a dandy not content to let his furrier pick out the mink or sable skins for the lining of a new greatcoat. Yankel Meisels greeted them all like honored guests. He would then seat them ceremoniously in the green damask armchairs facing the mirrors, then call for a helper to bring out bundle after bundle of matched pelts from the unlocked cupboards. "There are skins *and skins,*" he was fond of saying. "Here we handle only the kind a prince would be proud to own."

If the customer were making a first visit, the proceedings were rather formal. But since many came back year after year, it was not unusual for Yankel to conclude a transaction with a health drunk in old French cognac, even older Polish mead, or fine Spanish sherry. The ladies might be asked if they preferred tea. And if they did, Yankel would pull the bell cord and his wife would bustle in, followed by a servant with the tea service on a silver tray.

The tea ceremony was a cherished ritual with Sara Meisels, her entrée, or so she felt, into the rarefied atmosphere of the world where it was given to her husband to rub elbows with the privileged, the great. As soon as she ascertained that an expected customer would be a woman, she got busy setting out her translucent Dresden cups, her gleaming sugar bowl and creamer and tea strainer, the monogrammed sugar tongs and spoons and lace-edged napkins. She sliced the lemon. She filled the sugar bowl. Then she sat back and waited. She knew exactly when to ring for the boiling kettle, when to make the infusion so that it would be neither too strong nor too weak. Fortunately not many ladies refused tea, not even in a Jew shopkeeper's establishment; and *Pani* Meisels' proudest boast was that she had lost count of the cups of tea with and without lemon she'd served to Poland's nobility—and them supposed to be such anti-Semites and snobs, too!

She liked her life, and the last thing in the world she wanted was to risk having it endangered. Yet if her sons persisted in this new habit of bringing riffraff home from school, that was just what was bound to happen. "You mark my words, Yankel. Nothing good can come of it. A little *sans-culotte* from Nalewki and an ox of a *goy* one step removed from the plough. I don't like it, I don't like it one bit. And all this meddling in politics before they're dry behind the ears! Better the boys should start thinking about making real contacts, the kind that'll stand them in good stead when we're dead and gone. . . ."

"Contacts, at the *gymnasium?* Mama, be reasonable! and they're not meddling in politics—all they're after is a little honest learning. Is that bad? Grandfather Meisels would be proud of them. Besides, boys should get to know all kinds, otherwise how'll they ever pick and choose their friends in later life?"

Mention of Grandfather Meisels always upset Sara. His name might be an honored one among the country's Jewry—who hadn't heard of Dov Berish Meisels, chief rabbi of Warsaw?—but what people really remembered about him was not his scholarship, not his position, but the fact that twice in his long life he had played prominent roles in the resistance.

First, as a youth, he'd been an officer in the "Beardlings," the Jewish regiment that fought in the uprising of '31. Three decades later he dared join the Archbishop of Warsaw in officiating at a mass public funeral of victims of the blood bath of '63. It was a display of interfaith solidarity such as had never taken place before or since, and Yankel still cherished a yellowed photo of the two holy men standing together during the ceremony, together blessing the crowds.

All very fine and noble, Sara Meisels reflected, taking great care not to let her husband suspect her thoughts, but she could have done without an ancestor like Reb Dov Berish. For even the dead have a way of getting one in trouble. However, it was the living who were her main concern. "Take it from me, Yankel," she now warned. "Better put your foot down. Or else we'll live to rue the day."

She was wishing she herself had taken a firm stand regarding the study group the moment her sons had first mentioned it. But perhaps something could still be done. "Take it from me," she said again, as she fussed about the showrooms that Sunday helping Yankel shake out and rehang bundles of precious furs. "Even your business stands to suffer," she ran a small, plump, ring-laden hand lovingly over some sables, "if you're not firm with your sons."

Yankel sighed. As tall and spare as his wife was round, with something of his grandfather's fire in him but none of the courage and fervor, he often wished he'd arranged his life differently. But to do so he would have needed a different wife, a spirited woman to encourage him. Now maybe his sons would surprise him. For himself, he knew he didn't really have it in him to take risks. And there was Sara—Sara who wanted everything nice and safe.

Take the matter of a wig, for instance. Though he had never cared one way or another, she still insisted on wearing one. "It looks better to the world," she would say to him, "to the Jews and the *goyim* both. It's what they expect." If a woman went wigless, she reasoned, right away she was tagged emancipated, a freethinker—so why look for trouble? Better let people approve of one, it was best for business.

Of course when they traveled abroad, that was a different matter. *Pani* Meisels thought nothing of taking off her *sheitl* in her compartment on the European Express as the train sped toward the German border. Just the way her husband took off his long gabardine coat. He changed into a conservative "European" suit of clothes, she combed out her curls, kept short but not too short, into a fashionable pompadour over which she pinned a perfectly matched coil of human hair, and the metamorphosis was complete. When in Rome, she argued. Besides, it really was expected of you—everybody did it. And if friends from Warsaw should catch you in Karlsbad or Marienbad wearing your natural hair, why, there was no need to fear gossip for they would be doing the same. The pot had better take care not to call the kettle black! But here at home there were other rules. . . .

"I think the sables are all in order now," Yankel said wearily. "Let's check the broadtail."

"Please, don't go changing the subject," his wife answered sharply. "About the boys. I meant what I said. I don't want them associating with riffraff."

"Yes, I know. You've said it all before."

"All right. So you know. What are you going to do about it?"

Since no customers were expected yet and all the doors were standing open, the voices of the older Meisels reached the hallway with unfortunate clarity.

Henryk and Juzek exchanged exasperated looks, then suddenly, in the hope of drowning out their parents' voices, began talking fast and loud, and both at once.

"Sure glad you two fellows could make it, anyway. . . ."

"It's too bad about the others, but we'll manage without them."

"I say to hell with them."

The adult voices dropped. But they could still be heard.

"You should have listened to me in the first place, Yankel," *Pani* Meisels was now being plaintive. "We should have sent them to private school right from the start. It isn't as if we couldn't afford it, and it's never too early to start making connections with a better class of people. . . ."

"Shh, Sara, they'll hear you. . . ." A door closed firmly, too late.

Juzek's face was red as a beet. "Snobs," he muttered. *"Her,* especially. Who does she think she is, a lady of the nobility?"

"Don't you know what's biting her?" Henryk said, speaking directly to his brother. "This is the day the man from the *Gmina* is due—the one who comes every year to collect a big fat contribution. She likes to impress him. Everything has to be just so." He smiled with one side of his mouth, his young face sardonic and unexpectedly bitter. "Too bad we aren't a couple of years younger—then she could put us into Little Lord Fauntleroy suits. . . ."

"I still think we'd better leave," Olek offered stiffly.

"Don't be an ass!" Henryk said. "Besides, it's really a matter of principle now."

And Juzek, wishing the earth would swallow him, insisted, "We'll do as we please and to hell with it. Only . . . well . . . I'm just sorry you had to be exposed to all this . . . shit. . . ."

The Meisels boys' quarters, in contrast to the rest of the apartment, were simple and uncluttered. Each had his own room, his own desk. What luxury, thought Adam, used as he was to reading and studying in the midst of family confusion, to be able to close a door and shut out the world!

There were books everywhere, some of them—those in expensive leather bindings, those in special sets—even arranged in bookcases with glass doors. On the walls hung reproductions of Michelangelo and Da Vinci. Best of all, in Henryk's room there was a Blütner upright.

"You play?" Adam asked enviously.

"We've both taken lessons. Neither of us is much good at it, but we do a lot of stuff for four hands. And sometimes a friend of mine brings his violin. Beethoven comes out badly and Bach abominably." Henryk laughed and shrugged. "You care for music?"

"I don't get much chance to hear any," Adam said. "But we do have a neighbor who . . . In the summer, with her windows open, it makes good listening."

"Ever been to a symphony concert?"

"Once. I saved up and went standing room. I'd go more often, it's just that I don't have the heart to spend all that money on myself. The family needs what I earn." As soon as he said that, he wished he hadn't spoken. It sounded like a plea for sympathy.

But Henryk Meisels, from the vantage point of his eighteenth year, was struck by the ingenuousness of the younger boy's words.

Here is someone, flashed through his keen, cool, sophisticated brain, who hasn't yet learned not to speak his mind. And he found himself wanting to make a gesture that would bring pleasure to his guest. At the same time he saw a chance to do something to annoy his parents, for whom at the moment he was feeling little affection and a great deal of contempt.

"Tell you what, Fabian. The family have season tickets—my mother thinks going to concerts is socially correct. But the fact is good music bores her—she's always torn between going and being seen, and staying home, so quite often I get to take a friend. The next time there's a ticket going begging, suppose I let you know."

"Oh, would you? Would you really?"

"It would be a pleasure," Henryk said with the lordly generosity of the affluent patron of the arts. "And a pleasure to sit next to someone who really listens instead of snoring in my ear. . . ."

All in all, the afternoon was not especially productive. None of them knew enough Polish history to make the discussion rewarding, and they hardly knew where and how to start. Even the help Olek had hoped for from his father turned out to be limited— most of the books on his list were unavailable except through underground sources. And contact with those sources had been broken because of the disappearance of Olek's uncle.

"Guess we'll just have to wait till a member of Uncle Jacek's cell turns up. Which is bound to happen sooner or later, because that's the way the group operates. When one member goes into hiding or gets arrested, someone else takes over his assignments. Trouble is, it takes so much time. . . ."

"You sound like it's an old story to you."

"In a way it is. It's happened before. And I've gotten books before. But even with Jacek around it's never easy. First I have to tell him what I need. Then he has to pass the list on to the literature agent at his Socialist circle. Then the agent tracks down the titles. Then . . . But maybe I shouldn't talk about the details." The unspoken inference was that the less was known about procedures, the safer for everyone concerned.

"So what'll we do in the meantime? Forget our meetings?"

"What, and make my mother happy?" Henryk objected. "Look, I've a better idea. How about switching to literature for the time being? We could all read the first act of *Dziady*—everyone knows Mickiewicz crammed it full of hidden meanings, that's why the work is so important. Let's have a discussion on that next time."

"Good enough," Olek seconded him. "Everybody agreed? Only let's not meet here. Come to my house. It's crowded, it's noisy, but you'll be made welcome."

Henryk smiled his crooked smile. "And the mater needn't know where her darlings go on a Sunday afternoon." Adam and Olek picked up their caps and overcoats.

In the hallway they were just in time to collide with the elder Meisels, who had rushed to the door because the bell was ringing. Sara's prayer that the *Gmina* man might be late, that by some miracle all contact between him and "those ragtag street Arabs" might be avoided, had not been heard in heaven. At the exact moment when the maid opened the front door, her sons escorted their guests into the foyer. "Mama, Papa," Henryk took wicked pleasure in rubbing it in, "we haven't had the chance to introduce . . ."

Caught between the desire to pretend the boys did not exist and an equally strong wish to appear the gracious lady in the newcomers' eyes, *Pani* Meisels was briefly rendered speechless. Yet there was nothing for it but to make the best of a bad situation. Looking daggers at her sons, she extended the tips of her fingers to the two shabby boys. "So nice that you were able to come," she murmured. Perhaps, she tried to console herself, the *Gmina* man would choose to interpret the little byplay as a gesture of generosity, of sweet charity toward the underprivileged, something for which the Meisels deserved special credit.

Instead, the *Gmina* man did something wholly unexpected.

Without so much as divesting himself of his hat and fur-lined coat he went directly to one of the boys. "Why, Adash!" Using a pet name, too! "I never expected to find *you* here!" His gloved hand resting on the boy's shoulder, he turned toward his hosts. "My very favorite nephew! What a coincidence!"

Adam laughed. "Double coincidence, Uncle Leon! As a matter

of fact you just saved me a trip across town. Mama wants you over for supper." He searched his pockets for the note Bluma had written. "Here you are. Now I don't have to drop it off."

Well, who'd have thought it, *Pani* Meisels reflected, sighing in inaudible relief. This attractive, polished, *civilized* man and the shabby *Yidlach*—relatives. Ah well, stranger things than that happened. Now she was all smiles. "Indeed, *Pan* Grossglik, your nephew is one of our boys' closest friends." She hoped God would forgive her the white lie, forgive her for having doubted His boundless kindness even for a minute. In token of this she caught her husband's eye and by a system of communication known only to those who have been married for many years conveyed to him that the donation they would make to the *Gmina* this year would be considerably larger than usual.

Leon Grossglik in the meantime gave her a polite, absent-minded nod and continued to address himself to Adam. "I was planning to drop by your house anyway, as soon as I leave here. Suppose you wait for me. It shouldn't take long."

"Yes, do wait by all means," *Pani* Meisels urged. The invitation pointedly did not include Olek.

Suddenly Adam found he was in a great hurry to be out of there. He wanted to breathe air that was not laden with camphor, perfume and hypocrisy. Henryk's and Juzek's mother sickened him, and he was ashamed and sorry and embarrassed for his two friends, so embarrassed he could hardly look them in the face.

"I'm sorry, Uncle Leon," he said, knowing perfectly well he was being rude, that it was to the lady of the house he should have addressed himself, "but I've a lot of homework to do. I really must leave now, I can't wait."

"Have it your own way then," Leon gave in cheerfully. "And tell your mother I'll be there as soon as I can. Tell her I'm just as anxious to talk to her as she is to talk to me."

"Fine, I'll tell her," Adam promised. Then, remembering his manners, he bowed in the direction of *Pani* Meisels and clicked his heels. "Come on, Olek, let's go." Briefly, his eyes met Henryk's and just as quickly he looked away. Then, careful not to slam the heavy doors, he and Olek made their escape.

As they clattered down the broad staircase, he was trying to decide how he really felt about Henryk Meisels. Standing behind his parents, Henryk had taken in every nuance of the little drama that played itself out in the ornate foyer. And it had seemed to Adam that he was trying to control a smile with an undercurrent of malice that was disconcerting.

"Now why do you suppose Henryk takes such pleasure in feeling superior to his own folks?" he asked Olek. "Did you see how he actually gloated over the way his mother was placed in a false position? As though it pleased him. If it were me I'd have wanted to drop through the floor."

But Olek said he wasn't wasting his time in such speculations. "Anyway, who can ever tell what goes on in the bourgeois mind?"

Adam looked baffled. "What the devil are you talking about?"

"Just that the convolutions of the middle-class mentality are a total mystery to the ordinary working stiff."

His manner—the elaborate patience of an adult explaining something to an obtuse child—goaded Adam into snapping, "You're just saying the same thing in two different ways and explain nothing. The fact is, Piotrowski, I don't really understand *either* them *or* you."

Olek shrugged. "Sorry. I know I get carried away." And Adam wasn't sure, but thought it was meant as an apology.

They reached the corner where their ways separated and for a moment stood undecided, half hostile, measuring one another like a pair of young tomcats not quite certain whether to fight or merely growl and back away. "You know," Adam finally offered, "you don't make things any clearer when you start in with all those high-sounding phrases. At least not to me."

"Well, maybe when there's time we can talk about it some more. Or try to."

"Yes, maybe."

They shook hands, signifying a truce.

"So long. See you tomorrow in school."

❧ Seven ❧

ADAM WAS ALREADY deep in the next day's trigonometry when Leon's familiar ring, one long and two short, announced his arrival. Bluma, just starting to set the table, hurried into the hallway to greet her brother. But Kazik and Rosie were there before her, squabbling over who would take Uncle's hat and coat and walking stick, swarming over him, demanding attention.

"I have to talk to you alone," Leon whispered over the children's bobbing heads. And Bluma knew without being told that he was in one of his states, those moods of excitement, anger, depression and despair he had been subject to ever since going to work for the *Gmina*. Well, small wonder, she thought, a man would have to have a heart of stone not to let all that human misery get him down once in a while! And here she was going to add to his load of troubles, knowing at the same time that add to them she must.

"And I have to talk to you," she said, standing on tiptoe to kiss him. "I hope it was worth while, visiting those people where Adash ran into you. I hope they were generous. Because I'm going to have to ask a favor of you. Not for myself, of course," she added hastily.

He shrugged, as if to say, "It's all in a day's work," but otherwise made no comment, and now it struck her that today he was possessed by other, private demons. Her own request would have to wait.

"Come into the bedroom with me," she said, taking his arm. "We'll close the door. Idka, darling," she turned to the older of her little girls, "be a good child and finish setting the table while I talk to Uncle. Let Rosie help you. And keep an eye on Kazik. I won't be long."

Once they were alone, she gave her brother her complete attention. "So now tell me what's wrong. Is it your work? Your health?"

"No." But he said nothing else, just started pacing back and forth across the cramped little room, his face such a study in misery that she grew alarmed in earnest. "Have you lost your job? You haven't, God forbid, got a girl in trouble? Whatever it is, Leon, you can tell me. Only for heaven's sake get it over with!"

He ran his hands through his thick, already mussed hair till it stood on end. "It's none of these things. In fact, I don't even know how to put it into words because on the face of it it sounds so simple. Just . . . I've fallen in love. With the most beautiful, the most wonderful girl in all the world. I want to ask her to marry me."

Relieved, she repressed a natural desire to laugh. "And is that bad?" But he continued to look so woebegone that again she became uneasy. "What's wrong, then? Doesn't she love you? She'd have to be crazy! She isn't—I don't even want to say it—a Catholic?"

"No, oh no! And she'd make me an ideal wife. You've met her. She's *Pani* Tworska's youngest daughter, Salome. She's not only lovely to look at but gentle, modest, cultivated, beautifully brought up. In a word, perfection itself. They tell me several young men have already lost their heads over her. But she wasn't interested."

"Are you afraid she won't have you?"

He shook his head. "I've already talked to the mother and I've reason to believe . . . to hope . . . that she'll say yes. And I can afford marriage now, I can afford a family. I'm due for a big promotion, my future is secure."

"Then why in God's name don't you just propose?" she asked, puzzled yet a trifle impatient.

Leon sighed as though his heart were breaking. "Before I answer that, suppose you tell me what's on *your* mind?"

"Now? You want to hear about it now, right in the middle . . . ?"

"Please," he said, "don't argue. I have my reasons."

She shrugged and sighed, as if to say, "Who'll ever understand a man?" But if that was the way he wanted it, she might as well make the best of it and plead the Liebmans' cause.

"It's our neighbors from the third," she began. "The husband got pulled in during the last trouble. They came to arrest a boarder, and took him for good measure. And now the wife and the children are starving. So Jacob and I got to thinking, maybe through the *Gmina* you could do something. Help with a little food, a little coal. Maybe ease things for poor Liebman himself in the Pawiak."

"I figured it was something like that," Leon said. "I'll do what I can. The food and coal I know I can promise you. The rest may not be so easy. You know yourself the Russians don't care if a man is guilty or not, just so long as they keep their jails filled with politicals. But if the *Gmina* intervenes formally, through channels, at least the guards will let him have the packages his wife sends. I'll see about it all tomorrow."

"Thank you, darling. I'll tell *Pani* Liebman. She'll bless you."

"I'm only doing what I can," he said. "And now shall I tell you why I made you talk about it? Because, just as I expected, it helped me prove my point. With so much suffering, so much injustice around us, do I—does any man—have the moral right to turn his back on society and think only about his own happiness—drown in it, as the song tells it?"

She nodded and began to hum the words he meant, a stanza from the *Warszawianka*, the song that not many years later was to become famous the world over as *Whirlwinds of Danger*:

> *Today, when our land lies hungry and bleeding*
> *Shame on the man who wallows in pleasure,*
> *Shame on the one who turns from his brothers*
> *Silent and meek for fear of the gallows . . .*

Tears stood in Leon's eyes. "I knew you'd understand," he said with sudden humility. "Now do you see just what I'm up against? What shall I do, Bluma? Tell me what to do!"

For a moment she saw him as the child she had raised and mothered, who had run to her whenever he'd been hurt, expecting her to kiss the hurt and make it well. But how do you tell a grown man that the kind of soul-searching he is insisting on really belongs to adolescence? What do you say to him? And even if I found the right words, she thought, would he listen, or even hear me?

"Are you a monk," she finally asked, "that you think you must wear a hair shirt? Do you honestly believe your getting married or not getting married is going to change anything?"

"Now you talk as if everything were all cut and dried! But there is such a thing as principle."

"I'm not denying that. But believe me, my dear, permitting yourself some happiness—*indulging* yourself, as you put it— isn't going to interfere with your work. You'll still be the same Leon Grossglik, you'll go right on turning yourself inside out to make the world a better place. And maybe, who knows, maybe you'll even do it better because you're happy, with someone to share your life, make a home for you, see you're taken care of. Ah, Leon," she pleaded, "it's no good trying to carry the weight of the whole world on your shoulders! It's too heavy for any one man. You're only liable to trip and go down with a crash."

In spite of himself he smiled at her way of putting things, and she breathed easier and pressed her advantage.

"Believe me, there's enough sorrow around without your adding to it by making yourself miserable for nothing. Now let me advise you," she used an old phrase that had been a private joke between them in their grim childhood, "like your very own sister. Go to your girl. Tonight. Bring her a big bunch of flowers and ask her. But first let's have supper. Before the food gets cold."

With her hand on the doorknob she paused, searching for a way to encourage him without sounding mawkish. "You'll do a better job of proposing with a good meal under your belt," she finally said. "That much I promise you."

Leon laughed, and she knew she had found the right words.

After they had eaten, Bluma and Jacob accompanied Leon down to *Pani* Liebman's. The "widow" wept, cursed out the authorities, thanked her good neighbors, thanked them again, swore she would never say another unkind word to them or about them, let alone spreading gossip behind their backs, and ended up, to Leon's intense embarrassment, by kissing his hand. Then she insisted on giving him a precise account of what she intended to do to help herself and feed her brood.

"Charity bread is bitter bread, we won't be eating it for long, of that you may be sure!" She explained how, much as she was reluctant to go back to such a risky business, she planned to start taking in roomers again as soon as the dust settled. "After all, with three empty beds! Only this time, you can bet your last shirt on it, I'll not be renting to intellectuals! And I'll give all of them, no matter who they are, a wide berth. No passing the time of day, no getting friendly, nothing. Just a civil good morning and good evening and please, I'd like my rent money on time. And if I catch any of my kids trying to socialize, I'll beat them."

They finally broke away from her, returning upstairs for a fresh round of tea, just the three of them this time, for the older boys were studying and the little ones were getting ready for bed. Bluma would have liked to share with Jacob the news of Leon's forthcoming engagement. But Leon had sworn her to secrecy.

"Wait till it's all settled. Wait till she says yes."

Like a fond mother, she'd answered, "If she says no she should have her head examined!" Nevertheless she did as he asked, intending, of course, to tell her husband all about it as soon as they were alone—something Leon himself suspected.

But he didn't really mind, for a great feeling of elation, of lightness, now came over him. It was as though his sister had taken his putative sins onto her own shoulders. He wondered if that was how Catholics felt as they came out of the confessional. Afterwards he walked home through the dark streets like a schoolboy drunk on his first wine. He found a florist's shop along the way that was still open, and following Bluma's advice to the letter armed himself with a huge bouquet of mimosa and two bunches of Parma violets, one for his landlady and one for her daughter. Then he continued in long, impatient strides toward Nowy Swiat and Count Berg Street.

It was still fairly early when he let himself in with his own key. As usual on Sunday night, the house was quiet, the Tworskas' young boarders all busy with next day's Latin and algebra and Greek and the two ladies alone in the living room.

Salome was at the piano, her mother bending over an embroidery frame. Since breakfast they had had plenty of time to discuss Leon, whose behavior was seriously baffling them, and the mother had already given her daughter the standard advice women everywhere give young girls in similar circumstances: Give him some competition, that shouldn't be hard! Let him see you flirting with someone else, worry him a little. Let him imagine he's in danger of losing you!"

Salome herself thought this might not be a bad idea. But now suddenly here he was laden with flowers, smiling, eager, indeed a wholly different man from the morose bear who had stormed out of the house in the morning. She had been determined to punish him, but her determination quickly melted.

"Oh, Mama, look!" she cried, burying her face in the violets. "*Pan* Grossglik has brought spring into the house!" She fluttered her long, thick lashes and raised her eyes to him. "Is this a peace offering for having deserted us for the whole day?"

"Call it that if you will. . . . But it's also something else. . . . Something more . . . much more . . ." He was blushing and stumbling over his words like a schoolboy. *Pani* Emilia, skilled in interpreting such signs, picked up the mimosa and murmuring something about going to find the right vase for it quickly left the room so the two young people could be alone.

There was a moment of uneasy silence while vaguely Leon wondered just what he must do next. Get down on his knees like a knight in a medieval tale? In one way he felt this would be no less than Salome's due. On the other hand the idea made him feel thoroughly foolish. He thought better of it.

She had carefully seated herself in one corner of a delicate little sofa just wide enough for two. Now she patted the seat next to herself. He sat down quickly, took her hand and raised it to his lips. "Miss Salome," he began a trifle shakily, then, using the diminutive of her name, "Miss Salunia, Salunia darling . . . darling . . ."

She smiled and waited, and went on smiling.

"My darling, you know of course that I—you *must* know how much I love you!"

"Yes," she whispered, and the ice was broken, and it was all he could do not to grab her in his arms and smother her with kisses. But he knew he didn't have the right, quite yet. With a tremendous effort he disciplined himself.

"Perhaps your mother has already told you . . . I . . . I have her permission . . . But her permission means nothing unless you yourself give your consent. Because in the end it's you who must decide. . . ." His voice cracked like an adolescent's. "Darling, would you consider sharing my life, letting me love and cherish you to the end of our days together?"

For once Salome forgot all of her mother's training. She forgot to be coy. "I was beginning to think you'd never ask!" And like a little girl who wants to thank an adult for a big, very special present, she threw her arms around his neck and kissed him— on the cheek.

Bemused and delighted with her, he thought, How pure she is! Pure and childlike and untouched, and she's going to be all mine! His throat hurt. His eyes were stinging. Desire shot through him and he began to tremble.

Late that evening, after telling *Pani* Emilia their news and receiving her blessing, they sat pressed close together, hands interlaced, discussing their future. The house was quiet and the scent of the flowers Leon had brought hung sweet in the air. They seemed to him a token of eternal spring.

"You realize of course I shall never be rich," he warned his future wife. "I'll never have much more to offer than—well, just flowers. Oh, there will be the big promotion soon, and later the usual salary increases, and in the end a comfortable pension. But nothing grand. Nothing like the kind of life your sister Eugenia has. Not even what you were accustomed to as a child. Are you sure you can be satisfied with that? You deserve so much more! And of course you could have more with some other man. You could have the whole world at your feet! So think it through very carefully, my dearest. And should you decide this isn't for you after all, I'll understand."

She said she had already thought about it. She said she would be proud to share what she called his Spartan existence. She said, "I would rather marry for love and be poor than make a rich marriage of convenience." And in her own way she was being sincere, for in her own way she did love him. But her way was also to scheme, without the slightest sense of guilt, how to make their existence considerably less Spartan. For surely, with Eugenia so rich, there would always be enough to go around, and more. Surely ways could be found—tactful ways, maybe at times even invisible—to get Leon to accept a share of those riches.

And then it was *Pani* Emilia's turn to make turns.

"I don't really know what you children are worrying about! None of us need be poor! And there's really no reason why you should be spending money on another home when you can just as easily stay here with me. At least until you start raising your own family, that is. And even then we needn't be crowded—I can merely stop boarding so many boys. Oh, we'll be very happy together! And that way my little girl needn't be lonely all day while her husband works, and there won't be any sudden difficult changes for her, she needn't bother her pretty head with any nasty housekeeping. . . ."

It was like being engulfed by a strong if kindly centrifugal force named woman. For a moment Leon felt he was drowning. Then he told himself groggily it was probably all for the best. All for the best that decisions about the routine of daily living were being firmly taken out of his hands. He should be happy with any arrangement that made his bride happy—he really had no right to demand of her that she subject herself to unnecessary rigors, though just what those rigors might be he wasn't quite sure.

Hadn't he just said himself that maybe, in agreeing to marry him, Salome was giving up too much? Well, this way she could still live graciously. It would all work out. It would work out just so long as there was no question of their becoming Baron Kronenberg's retainers, of living on his bounty the way Clara and her husband were doing.

Finally, he remembered what Bluma had said about his doing better work once he was happily married. With no household problems to plague him, his own time would be well spent on

Gmina business. He would be really free, and able to continue giving of his own income wherever it was most sorely needed, and all without forcing his young wife to deprive herself. And later on, as she grew older, her ideas about many things would change. This domestic arrangement wouldn't be forever.

He went to sleep that night exhausted but blissful.

✎ *Eight* ✎

Even if privately the Fabians had a few qualms about Leon's choice of a bride, they were careful not to let him suspect it. But alone with each other they did not pretend. "Such rarefied circles your brother travels in now!" Jacob commented later the following evening, after Leon had rushed over to make his somewhat awed announcement that he was now formally engaged. "Baron Kronenberg's sister-in-law, no less! My, my!"

Bluma sighed, for her husband's words uncomfortably echoed her own unspoken fears. The Tworska girl was not just young and known to be frivolous, she was an acknowledged beauty, a fledgling social butterfly. Probably spoiled rotten. What kind of wife, what kind of helpmeet was this for a dedicated man?

But staunch believer that she was in giving everyone the benefit of every doubt, and possibly also to console herself, she instantly came to Salome's defense. "Leon tells me they've discussed everything, that he's warned her there'd be no living on anybody's bounty. That she'll be allowed to accept personal gifts, but nothing else."

"And?"

"He claims she's satisfied. Seems she's assured him she expected to defer to her husband in all such decisions—those are her very words—the way a good wife should. What more can anybody expect?"

"Ah, you," he said, "you always see good in everyone."

"Why go out of your way to look for the bad? Besides, you

never really know, a good marriage will sometimes change even the flightiest. . . . Oh, dear, here I go sounding as if I had something against her already. . . ."

She sat down next to her husband on the edge of their big bed, took his hand, and pressed it against her cheek. "Maybe I'm just jealous. Already I sound like a mother-in-law! Jacob, if that's the way I am about my brother, what'll I do when it's our own sons' turn to get married? Promise me you won't let me turn into some kind of shrew!"

He held her close and laughed at her. "You a shrew! *That* I would have to see!" More soberly he added, "Besides, in a way Leon is half your son."

"You think that's what's eating me? Yes, I suppose you're right. Which brings me to the next point. Leon must have a proper engagement party. And it'll be up to us to give it to him. After all, whom else has he got? We'll have to invite all the relatives so the two families can meet each other."

Jacob agreed, and, relieved to have something concrete to turn her mind to, she immediately set about making plans.

"I've already told Leon he must get over to Balbina's house right away, give her and Karol the news in person—it's only right. Then we'll have to agree on a date. But I'd better not wait for that, I'd better get busy at once or I'll never have the house ready! So much to be done! We haven't used the good table linen since I don't know when, it's probably all yellow by now and needing a good boiling and bleaching and ironing. And the curtains have to be taken down and washed, and the windows too, and there'll be the children's best clothes to check and your cutaway to air—it's a good thing you're not one of those men who runs to fat with the years! And all the baking to do, and supper to plan. . ." Already she was feeling better.

To Bluma's intense relief neither one of the future bride's sisters could come to the party. Baron Kronenberg was just leaving on an extended business trip, and since he seldom traveled without his wife these days Eugenia, too, would be away. Clara, who was pregnant and not too well and therefore afraid to travel, remained in enforced exile abroad, though she hoped to be able to come to Warsaw for the wedding. Bluma was touched and flattered by their warm notes of regret and loved the armfuls of flowers Eugenia sent, but she thanked her lucky stars that she did not have to entertain such exalted company.

She had taken great pains to arrange things so that the future bride and her mother might be the last to arrive, and miraculously, in a city proverbial for its lack of punctuality, everyone else came early. The Segals—Balbina and her husband and their four children—and the Grossglik stepbrothers with their families, and even the old stepmother, no longer the fearsome witch of Bluma's childhood but a wizened, stooped old crone creaking with arthritis.

When at last Leon ushered in *Pani* Tworska and her daughter everyone beamed at them, and the old stepmother hobbled up and kissed each in turn, wiping rheumy eyes and telling them in her strongly accented Yiddish-Polish how she had been a mother to the whole tribe, giving up her whole youth, in fact her whole life, not just to her own but to another woman's children. "They were little and they needed me and how could I help but love them like my own flesh and blood?" By now she believed every word she said and no one disabused her. What would be the use? Besides, it was exactly as Bluma put it when she made up her mind to invite her: High time to let bygones be bygones.

Only when Leon introduced Salome to his sister Balbina was there a moment's chill. Balbina Segal had not, as she later explained to her husband, expected the girl to be quite so la-di-da. "He couldn't settle for someone plain like the rest of us? Oh no! He's got to rub elbows with the aristocracy! Soon, mark my words, none of us are going to be good enough for him!" It was not in Salome's nature to look for slights—she expected the whole world to love her and generally it did—but even she couldn't miss the lack of friendliness.

In all the ways that counted, Balbina was different from her brother and sister, calculating where they were generous to a fault, and with a special, instinctive ability to turn everything to her own advantage. Only three years older than Leon and unable to remember her own mother, she learned early to wangle her way into her stepmother's good graces while at the same time extracting various small advantages from being an "orphan." Neither as intelligent nor as sensitive as the other two, she tended toward the conventional and grew up uncomplicated and generally well satisfied with herself.

By way of reward her stepmother, so indifferent to Bluma's welfare, had seen to it that in time she got a husband who was a professional man. Doctor Karol Segal might be only a neighborhood practitioner whose patients paid fifty kopeks a visit and sometimes never paid at all, but he was a doctor nevertheless. Balbina could be proud of being *Pani Doktorowa,* and she made Karol an average-good wife. She kept the office accounts, nagged her husband into collecting fees that were due him, determined early to send all her children to private schools, and secretly—for there was no use in "spoiling" a man with praise—congratulated herself on having done fairly well.

For Leon's party she had laced her corsets tight, gotten into her good black silk dress with the Venice point lace, added the dog collar of seed pearls that had been her mother's and should rightfully have gone to Bluma, and insisted on Karol's wearing the tailcoat he hadn't had on since their wedding. He hated such fuss, but since he hated arguments with his wife even more he went along with what she wanted.

The two boys—Kuba, who was eight and just Izidore Fabian's age, and little four-year-old Edek—wore suits with velvet collars and were warned that they could play with Aunt Bluma's boys all they liked, but if they spilled anything or tore their clothes they could expect a whipping once they got home. The girls—seven-year-old Jadwiga and Regina, who was five, only six weeks older than her cousin Kazik—needed no such warnings. Their starched white dresses, blue-sashed and worn over starched and ruffled petticoats, made them feel so important they moved like mechanical dolls, good as gold and perfectly safe.

"It's all for Leon's sake," Balbina had told her husband as they finished dressing, "and someday it's going to stand him in good stead. Let his new in-laws know that he, too, has a few relatives who are of some account. Because just between you and me I don't trust our Bluma to arrange much of an affair. You know her and her easygoing ways—her food is never much, and the table

she sets has no style, and her children are always into everything!"

Karol, who thought the world of his wife's sister, merely
grunted. More than once he had wondered what it would be
like to have a wife who made a man feel like a king in his home,
and for no reason except that she wanted it so. Ah, well, he
tried to shrug the idea off, not everyone could be lucky like Jacob
Fabian. And what was the use of complaining? Life did not go by
exceptions, only by the rule.

As the evening wore on it became a truly joyous occasion. Even
the younger children somehow sensed its special mood, so that
there were no squabbles, no crying, no broken plates, or spilled
milk. A separate table had been set up for them in the room next
to the dining room, and there they amused themselves in relative
freedom, with the women taking turns keeping an eye on them.
In addition, Bluma, who would have been surprised to hear she
was following a radical trend of progressive child-rearing, had
come upon the idea of telling her older daughter that she was
being put officially in charge of the little ones. Idka, of course,
responded with the deepest pride to such a delegation of responsibility and was absorbed in her new duties, never so much as
suspecting that one purpose of this ploy on her mother's part was
to avoid having her at the main supper table.

Of the younger Fabians, only Adam and Viktor were seated
with the grown members of the party. They were even served
wine like everyone else, and as the toasts went round they began
to feel progressively solemn. This was especially true of Adam,
who was coming more and more under the spell of his future
aunt. His eyes riveted on her, he forgot all about the good food
heaped on his plate and at one point, when glasses were raised in
a health to the engaged couple, his brother had to nudge him.

He was thinking that he had never seen pure beauty in the
flesh before. So far, women to him had meant his mother and the
various aunts, they had meant the female population of the courtyard, and others like *Pani* Meisels about whom he sometimes
wondered whether, if you stuck a pin into them, they would
deflate. Girls were mostly the sisters of classmates, shy or bold or

indifferent depending on whether they were younger or older than himself, with dark school uniforms taking the place of bodies. There were also drab factory workers streaming down the streets while he was on his way to school. Sometimes, too, they were the sluts on street corners. They used words and gestures meant to be inviting, to which in spite of what his mind told him he felt a disturbing response, but not because of their looks.

There was also a world of women seen at a distance along Marszalkowska Street, Aleje Ujazdowskie or the Lazienki and Saxon and Krasinski parks. He had observed them walking in and out of elegant shops or stepping into their carriages—women in furs and plumed or flowered hats, their gloved hands buried in muffs in winter or holding lacy parasols in summer. They belonged to the world of fashion and never seemed real to him at all.

And now just such a person was seated at his parents' table, hatless, her marvelous blue-black hair piled high on her head, her sapphire eyes sparkling, her neck like a white swan's (Adam's romantic vocabulary stemmed quite naturally from the poets he had read), her little ungloved hands slender and smooth, with long fingers and long, unbroken nails.

A woman like that coming into his own family? He tried to envision her as Uncle Leon's "better half," as the saying went. Having breakfast with him each morning and in the evening gracing his supper table, maybe mending his socks or sewing buttons on his shirts, planning his meals and the marketing with the maid, and—Adam's imagination shied away, then came back to the ultimate—sharing his bed.

There was a sudden trembling in him and he felt the heat of the room like a blast against his face.

Would there be children? Would *she* bear children like everybody else, her willowy body slowly distending and her movements growing awkward? And later on would she nurse them as his mother nursed child after child, giving of her breast to the greedy mouth and clutching baby fingers, not caring that the sucking hurt, that the breasts grew heavy and started to sag and the blue swollen veins stood out?

He had never given much thought to childbearing and endless baby-tending. It was all part of the routine of family living. Now suddenly, in terms of Uncle Leon and this ravishing creature, it all became unthinkable. Not gross exactly, but something his mind could not encompass. Beauty like this woman's must remain unflawed, it must not be permitted to reduce itself to the level of ordinary human functions. It must be guarded and preserved, cherished and worshipped. Now if it belonged to him. . .

The collation was over and now the younger children were allowed in. Immediately the little girls gravitated to the beautiful newcomer. Shy at first and intensely curious, they surrounded Salome, fascinated by the swish of her dove-gray taffeta gown, the diamonds sparkling in her ears and the watch that hung from a gold and pearl fleur-de-lys brooch pinned to her bodice.

"Pretty, pretty," they kept saying, touching everything.

Salome, anxious to show herself in a flattering light to her fiancé and his kin, encouraged them. She even slipped off a diamond and pearl ring she was wearing—not Leon's gift, he could never have afforded anything half so fine, but a family heirloom her mother said it was proper for her to have, now that she was engaged—and let them play with it.

With this their shyness vanished, and first Regina, then Rosie, climbed into her lap and even Jadwiga, just enough older to be more reserved, pressed against her.

Suddenly Balbina sounded the second harsh note of the day.

"Jadzia, Ginia, stop making pests of yourselves. Get off the lady's lap this minute—you'll ruin her dress! Your fingers are all sticky, and your shoes. . . You'll get dirt on that good silk!" If Bluma didn't know enough to discipline her brood, *somebody* should!

Quickly and graciously Salome defended the youngsters. "Oh, please, *Pani* Segal, please don't scold them! Really, I don't mind a bit! Even if my dress does get a smudge on it, why, it's only a dress, it can be cleaned."

Balbina sniffed, bringing Adam out of his reverie.

All his life Adam had accepted young children in the family as small unavoidable nuisances, the source of noise and confusion, of unwanted responsibility and interrupted reading and lost sleep, little thieves who stole your occasional hour of quiet. Yet they could no more be helped than sun or rain, and finally, just when you had almost given up, each in turn began to grow up, becoming a person in his own right. Then, when you weren't engaged in an endless tug-of-war with them, a *modus vivendi,* even a kind of friendship became possible. But very small children were for the women. Or were they? He had often caught a certain look in his father's eyes when the little ones were around, a special kind of tenderness, something he still was able to sense only dimly.

Now, watching Salome with the starched little girls, seeing the softened smile and listening to the lilt, even the changed pitch of her voice, he began to ask himself what it was that eluded him. "It's there all right. Even Aunt Balbina feels it sometimes—I know, because I've caught her watching them at play. . . ." And he remembered a puppy they'd had briefly some years before. At first, when Izidore found him and dragged him home, Bluma had raised her voice in stern protest, calling the little creature filthy, declaring she wouldn't stand for the extra bother and the mess. Yet within a day or two she was as loving toward it as the rest of them, and when in the heat of summer it died of distemper she was disconsolate.

Protective love. The word came into his head as if of its own accord, but actually it was a phrase he had read somewhere and stored away until he had need for it. Protective love. Now he was beginning to understand. This was what he read in Salome's face right now, and in Uncle Leon's face when he looked at his bride-to-be, and sometimes in his father's face and at other times in his mother's. It was there all around him, making him feel safe.

Again his thoughts turned, as they had been doing all evening, to his uncle's beautiful future wife. Would he ever feel really at home with her, get to know her, be able to approach her in the easy, casual way of a mere relative? Would there ever be a time when he felt free to come and go at her house the way Leon came and went here—Leon who always said that Bluma's was his second home? And would Salome welcome him, accepting him casually, easily, simply because he was her husband's nephew and because the bond of family encompassed them all, always elastic enough to bind the newcomer rather than break and exclude?

He had never yet felt any real need to seek others out, always on the run from early morning until bedtime. Even his friendships at school had until recently been too casual to matter one way or the other. But now everything seemed to be changing, and all at once. At school there was Olek, the Meisels—especially Henryk—and the study circle. He had a sudden sense of new foundations being built, of new currents that would make a difference, that would change him. It was a sense of mounting suspense, as if new, important questions were about to arise at every turn, crowding in on him, demanding his attention. But what these questions might be puzzled him, and it was all very vague still, hardly definable.

He returned to watching Salome.

The table had been cleared of everything save the big copper kettle and teapot and glasses. The men sat around discussing the latest Black Hundred outrages. The old step-grandmother was cackling something to which *Pani* Tworska listened politely. Salome herself had charmed the little girls into a circle around her—she was telling them a story.

"And then the little princess came to the door, and there stood the prince bowing ever so politely. . . ."

"And then what did she say? And what did he say?" Adam heard his cousin Regina ask in her piping voice. In spite of her mother's sharp *don'ts* she was securely ensconced in her future aunt's gray silken lap, the toes of her small square black shoes turned in, the long white stockings wrinkling over short little legs that hadn't yet lost their baby fat. "Tell us what they *said!*"

Startled, Adam saw suddenly that in her own way the little girl too was uncommonly beautiful. Her face turned up confidently toward her new friend, her glossy black curls dancing, her skin with only a shadow of color in the cheeks transparent and very fair, like Salome herself she seemed a creature out of another world. He had never before bothered really to look at her, but now it struck him that she was a changeling in her own family. Where Jadwiga was square-built and solid like her mother, Regina was a fairy child, an elf. Neither Segal nor Grossglik, she might have been Salome's own daughter, so much alike were they in coloring, in delicacy and grace.

The picture they made with their two heads close together reminded him of a Fragonard he had once admired at the museum—or was it a Greuze? It was hard for him to believe that loveliness such as this should be here within his own home, so close he could put out his hand and touch it. Not only that, but it was in a way a permanent part of his life. Finally it also came to him that the woman his uncle was marrying could be no more than five or six years older than himself, and for some reason this was a most unsettling thought.

He had no way of guessing that he was on the verge of a dozen other new discoveries, nor that of all of them this would be the one that eventually would have the greatest and most lasting effect. He didn't understand what was going on inside him, and would only begin to understand little by little. He had reached that moment in adolescence when secret doors seem ready to start opening, and he felt restless and anxious to begin exploring whatever lay beyond. The greatest restlessness, he finally realized, was in his loins. It was a sensation he recognized and at first would have preferred to deny, for until now it had always been connected with the street-corner sluts and with words written in chalk on the walls of *Gymnasium* privies and whispered lunch-hour talk that he was embarrassed to join yet even more embarrassed to stay away from.

He thought he ought to be ashamed of himself but instead felt only elation, a kind of sensual joy that so far he had only approached when savoring the sound of music or of the written word. That living beauty could so rouse him was a fresh miracle. The restlessness in his loins continued, but now he welcomed it even though in its intensity it was beyond bearing. He closed his eyes and gave himself up wholly to sensation.

PART TWO
Winter–Spring 1898

❧ *One* ॐ

OUTWARDLY a centuries-old city does not change much over the years except as it is scarred by man-made upheavals. So the Warsaw of Adam's boyhood remained unchanged into his university days. Here and there a wall cracked, a building was declared unfit for human habitation. But the trumpeter atop the Citadel tower continued to herald sunup and sundown. In the Old Town market square pigeons still congregated around the water well and Fukier's wine shop did a thriving business in gold-flecked Danzig vodka, and mead dating back to the days of the kings, while a stone's throw away the great Cathedral of St. John kept its doors always open to those who felt in need of consolation and prayer.

Along the fashionable boulevards—the Aleje Ujazdowskie and the Jerozolimskie—an occasional modern apartment house went up, taking shape slowly as hod-carriers, bent double under their loads of brick, climbed in unending procession to unprecedented heights—six stories, seven even—until people said it was like building the pyramids again or, worse yet, the Tower of Babel. But for the future tenants there would be no climbing. Gilt-cage elevators were being installed, and here and there electric lighting and private telephones. Only the façades of the tall new structures didn't look new, designed by clever architects to blend with the eighteenth-century mansions that gave this part of the city its character.

Adam Fabian had occasion to frequent the Aleje regularly now, albeit as a backstairs visitor. His days of tutoring for thirty kopeks and a plate of cabbage soup were at long last over. Slowly he had established a schedule of decently paid private lessons at well-to-do homes until finally, at twenty-three and more than halfway through the university, he was even able to turn down a new pupil now and then. And if it was the servants' entrance he must use as he came and went, if his shiny suit and threadbare overcoat evoked the unconcealed contempt of footmen and parlormaids, he scarcely paid attention. He would merely remember with mild amusement how his old friend Olek Piotrowski explained such attitudes. "All these lackeys of imperialism," Olek had once erupted in a fine frenzy of oratory and mixed metaphors, "are more royalist than the king and more Catholic than the Pope and their only gauge of a man's worth is the size of the tip he leaves, so just tell 'em to kiss your . . . elbow."

With no tips of any size to hand out, Adam could hardly expect to be popular among the hired help. But the money he gave his mother at the end of each month made a great difference at home, and for the time being that was all that mattered.

The constant wear-and-tear of making ends meet had aged Bluma Fabian so much during the past few years that even a son noticed. She was now completely gray, the once-luxuriant hair thinning visibly, the once-luminous eyes colorless, as if bleached by too much exposure to the painful glare of daily living. Only her high domed forehead remained serene, retaining its look of polished ivory in an otherwise lined and sagging face. And when he thought about it at all, Adam was able to find strange comfort in the mere fact of its smoothness, as if this symbolized his mother's essential strength in spite of the many small weaknesses he had learned to recognize as he changed from boy to man.

His father, too, was showing signs of deep weariness. True, he was making a living of sorts—he would always make a living so long as Jews continued to get married and the new brides hid their hair under matron's wigs. But he never did learn to stand up to a haggling customer, and word had long ago spread throughout the Nalewki district that anyone could beat Fabian down on price. And if that weren't bad enough, he was constitutionally incapable of refusing credit to any young girl who, money or no money, had to have her *sheitl* ready when she came away from the wedding canopy. Nor did he have the heart to hound young husbands for payment later on, especially if he knew that a baby was on the way.

So with every year Jacob's shoulders grew rounder and the lenses of his steel-rimmed spectacles thicker, and his smoker's cough plagued him more and more until his wife would beg him with tears in her eyes to give up the habit. But he only shrugged and said please, let him be, leave him at least this little bit of pleasure and relaxation. And quickly she would pat his hand and promise to stop nagging. "Especially since it won't do any good anyway. Just the same," she would add, "can you blame me if I want what's best for you?"

Often, watching these two, Adam wished he could take the full burden of family off their shoulders. He did what he could, and now at last the end was in sight. Viktor and Izidore were earning their own way through school and even brought home a few rubles now and then. Kazik, the baby, Bluma's spoiled and petted darling, was attending the *gymnasium*. Fourteen years old, tall and strikingly handsome—too handsome, his mother sometimes worried, for his own good—Kazik was the only one among the Fabian boys indifferent to serious learning. Instead, he talked about making a pile. He laughed at his brothers for being content, as he put it, merely to grub; and recently, instead of looking for tutoring chores like the rest had done, Kazik had apprenticed himself to a goldsmith and was even considering leaving school and going to work full time. To Adam he seemed a stranger, but stranger or not, at least he, too, would soon be on his own.

That left only his sisters to provide for—but provide for them he must. Because, for girls, what other acceptable future was there save marriage, and how were Idka and Rosie to find husbands if they remained dowerless? Idka especially, who in spite of the great shining braids inherited from her mother was painfully plain, a square-built, heavily freckled carrot-top to be exact, would have to have something more than her good heart to offer if the marriage broker were to busy himself in her behalf. But even vivacious little Rosie, for all her sparkle, would fare no better if beauty were to be her only bait for catching a bridegroom.

"Maybe they'll be lucky," Bluma sometimes said when the girls were out of earshot. "Maybe somewhere there are two more men like their father. . . ." But Adam knew without having to have it spelled out for him what his mother really meant: If the girls weren't to end up old maids, it would be up to him.

In the meantime he was doing rather well, and he had his beautiful aunt by marriage to thank for it. From the earliest days as a member of the family, Salome Grossglik had cast herself in the role of Lady Bountiful to her husband's oldest nephew. Her original reasoning, which to do her justice she had long since forgotten, had stemmed only partially from a sincere desire to help. Looming as large had been a wish to show Leon, with an eye to their own future, what valuable connections she could tap in Warsaw's Jewish *haut monde*. And finally there had been Adam himself, unformed still, gauche, dazzled, silently admiring. Flattered at first, then touched, she had set out to mold him, civilize him, guide him.

From her mother she had a practical streak. Planning her campaign carefully, she began by suggesting to a few of *Pani* Tworska's young boarders, who continued to occupy one wing of the vast Count Berg Street apartment, that they might be glad of Adam's help at examination time. Later she mentioned his name to the Kronenbergs as a possible tutor for Lucio. Poor slow-witted Lucio, anxious above all else to please his adored stepmother, was making Herculean efforts to learn, but to little avail. He barely managed to hang on at the second-rate if exclusive academy where he was enrolled, and his parents despaired of him.

Adam Fabian or some other tutor, did it really matter? "We'll try it for a few months, then we'll see," Eugenia told her sister without much hope. And then, miraculously, the impossible began to happen. Between her own encouragement and the new tutor's patient prodding, Lucio was keeping abreast of his class. At the end of the year he was promoted.

Overjoyed, the Baron took time to thank Adam personally, raised his wages, and started recommending him to friends. Salome's biggest coup came when her protégé was hired to teach the twin children of the textile magnate Maurice Pozner, Marek and Maya. "Imagine, dear heart," she bubbled as she relayed the news to her husband. "Imagine what this can lead to! Not now, but later on when our Adash has his degree and there's his career to consider! In the meantime," she stopped dramatically, as though afraid Leon might fail to appreciate all that she had accomplished, "here he is, barely out of the *Gymnasium*, and already the money for the rest of his education is as good as in the bank!"

The Pozner fortune derived from the textile mills of Lodz. But in common with other factory owners the family preferred to avoid that dreary, sooty provincial town and maintained a residence in the capital. Here Marek and Maya, or Missy as she had been nicknamed by some long-ago English nanny, had grown up. Here they studied, with private tutors as was common among the well-to-do, following the official school curriculum and taking formal examinations every spring.

The difference in age between Adam and his new charges had at first been enough to establish a relationship of discipline and respect. But now, at seventeen, the twins were no longer children and the lines were becoming obliterated. The end of their schooling in sight, Marek was beginning to look forward to going to England to round out his education. Missy, on the other hand, much to her own disgust, would be launched socially, and eventually a suitable marriage arranged for her.

Brother and sister both had a great deal of natural intelligence; but while Marek was indolent, interested only in dogs and horses and more recently in women, Missy was a voracious reader and her sharp intellectual curiosity made it a pleasure to teach her. What a pity, Adam sometimes reflected, that all her gifts must eventually go to waste. Yet her parents categorically refused even to consider the possibility of allowing her, too, to go abroad for further study. Her father, who adored her, merely lamented the cruel trick of fate that had endowed his girl-child with all the qualities he would have wanted in a son.

What good was a steel-trap mind to a woman, Maurice Pozner frequently complained to anyone he could buttonhole, including

Adam. With Missy's looks and money, did she need brains too? She'd be lucky if those brains didn't scare all the worthwhile suitors off and if a husband could be found for her who one day could be trusted with managing the family holdings. Because that would be the only way to keep Marek from letting both his own and his sister's patrimony—the whole cotton empire so painstakingly built up by their father—slip through his fingers!

Missy knew exactly what her parents had in mind for her and resented it bitterly. Seeing a friend in Adam rather than a teacher now that she was more woman than child, she often managed to turn their classroom discussions into conversations about her future.

"I'm Papa's old-age insurance," she once said in a moment of cynical self-abasement. "I'm supposed to marry whomever he picks for me. Because of course fathers know best! Oh, you should see him at parties, sizing up the men! He doesn't miss a one. And he's not what you'd call subtle! It's humiliating, it's degrading, it's. . ." She broke off, seemingly giving her full attention to curling the end of her long, thick chestnut braid around her index finger. "Know what I've been wondering lately, *Pan* Adam?" She gave him a slow speculative look from under lowered lashes. "If maybe Papa has you, too, earmarked for a candidate. . ."

She let that sink in, then raised her eyes to his face—oddly slanted almond eyes which, people sometimes told her, gave her an inscrutable, Oriental appearance. She was doing her best to look bold, provocative, sly. "Well, after all, why not? You're a worthy young man—poor but honest, as the saying goes. I could do worse, you could do worse. I'm rich, and you're no furtune hunter. And at least we know each other, we even like each other. Best of all," she started to laugh shrilly, "we'd make such *intelligent* babies!"

He was shocked, as of course she had meant him to be.

"Missy, you mustn't talk like that!"

"No? Why not? Who's to stop me? You? Hah! Try telling Papa, and he'd only fire you for daring to discuss such things with me!" She laughed again, gloating to see him helpless.

"Well, it's just an idea, you understand. You or some other suitable male, what's the difference?"

On other occasions she talked about running away. "I'll go to Paris and never come back! I'll set myself up in grand style and I'll have a salon where famous men will flock to talk brilliantly by the hour, I'll be another Madame Récamier and they'll all vie for my favors. . ." For a moment she sounded like any other schoolgirl indulging in daydreams, then abruptly grew shrill again. "No, wait, I've an even better idea. I'll marry a Count—a blueblood with a huge dilapidated estate that needs restoring. That shouldn't be difficult now that we're such good Catholics!" For reasons of pure expediency the Pozners had recently converted, which made contact with the aristocracy possible at least in theory. "Papa can afford an impoverished count for me. He can afford a count but what he really wants is an accountant," she finished acidly. "Well, why don't you laugh, *Pan* Adam? I really think I'm being very witty!"

He didn't know whether to console her or shake her. Yet his impatience did not last, for he sensed in her a deep unhappiness, a misery that deserved respect, because already a wasted future was casting its shadow on her for the sole reason that she was a woman. Would it help her find herself, he wondered, give her direction and purpose and that sense of human dignity she now only dimly sensed she needed, if she were directed toward the underground student movement? With the right kind of influence, and time on her side, she might easily turn into another Nora Helmer, slam out of her doll's house and become a rather remarkable human being. Certainly she would be a happier one. He must ask Olek if he shouldn't talk to her about the Floating University, that illegal self-help network of study circles that was the alma mater of so many of their mutual friends. Even if Missy wasn't old enough to join, even if she had to wait a year or two, the mere knowledge that it existed and was within reach might give her a new perspective.

There had never been a time, it seemed to Adam, when he hadn't known about that particular secret organization. But until recently his concept of it had been vague—like the heartbeat, he'd taken it for granted without giving it further thought.

Then Olek Piotrowski had been expelled from Warsaw University for organizing a demonstration. He'd quickly made contact with a group, and instantly, for such was his way, managed to make the whole operation come intensely alive for Adam as well, mainly by drawing him into his new circle of friends.

Hardly anyone remembered exactly how the concept of a secret institution of learning had taken shape, or when. It must have been sometime between the first uprising after the partition, that is, after 1831, when Nicholas I ordered the universities of Warsaw and Vilno closed, and 1869 when Alexander II had them reopened as wholly russified schools. By then the Tsar was enraged and embittered because his brief early phase of would-be enlightened liberalism had gone unappreciated. (Was it his fault if the serfs he had emancipated were improvident enough to continue starving? And how dare his Polish subjects continue to seek self-government, autonomy, independence even, after all his assurances to them—always delivered in French, to be sure, for no Tsar of all the Russias would deign learn even a few words of the Polish "dialect"—that he had their own best interests at heart?) And the Tsar turned from a benevolent despot into an absolute one.

Whereupon the authorities, in their effort to stamp out the very traces of Polishness from the lands henceforth to be known only as The Vistula Territories, expunged the name itself of Poland, of the Congress Kingdom, from official documents. And the use of Polish was forbidden in the higher schools. Moreover, since all educational institutions throughout the Empire were considered hotbeds of radicalism, revolution, and godlessness, secret police agents and provocateurs began to infiltrate the lecture rooms.

Eventually Alexander II was assassinated for his pains. But even though the assassin was a native Russian and the killing a thousand miles away, the new Tsar, Alexander III, used his father's death as a pretext for further crackdowns. Adam himself could vaguely remember the edict that forbade the use of Polish even in elementary schools. He also remembered how the Jewish quotas, already stringent, were further tightened. And, of course, for women there were no quotas of any kind—they were simply denied all rights to an education beyond the *gymnasium* level.

The Floating University was the phoenix risen out of the ashes of the holocaust. It functioned exactly as its name implied: it floated. Groups met in private homes, behind darkened store fronts, in laboratories, in libraries shut down for the night. Its faculty consisted of dedicated teachers, scientists, historians, economists, philosophers, literary figures. Textbooks were in the main smuggled from abroad. There were no diplomas, and the only tuition fee apart from donations for more books was the students' pledge to become in their turn educators, extending the network of rebellion to factory and farm.

Because of the danger of attracting police attention, classes were seldom larger than eight or ten. Discovery meant arrest for teachers and students alike. Every applicant must be vouched for. Yet in spite of the risks the work went on, and it was astonishing how many of those who gathered in the secret little enclaves eventually found their way to the great seats of learning in the West—like the physicist Maria Curie-Sklodowska, just beginning to make a name for herself in France.

Abroad, the young émigrés inevitably gravitated into the orbit of Poland's exiled intellectual elite, many of whom were leaders of both the purely nationalist and the social revolutionary movement. It was also largely the university centers of Western Europe that served as a meeting ground where Poles and their Russian counterparts learned to make common cause, thus helping feed and swell the surging torrent that one day was to sweep away the Romanovs.

"If you're looking for an example of the dialectic of change, I can't think of a better one than our own situation," Olek Piotrowski told Adam one day in an effort to explain basic principles to him. Entranced by his own concept, he enlarged on it. "One thing leads to the next, they mesh, and a beautiful pattern emerges—the more the bastards persecute us, the faster they help dig their own graves!"

This seemed to Adam the perfect moment to bring up the subject of Missy. "Then how about an extra gravedigger?" he asked between sips of strong black coffee. "There's this pupil of mine, a girl, rich, bright, completely at sixes and sevens. She needs something to fasten on to, something bigger than herself. I think she has possibilities. Exposed to the right influences she might even, who knows, turn into another Morozova." His reference was to the Moscow sugar heiress reputed to be a heavy contributor to the Russian Social-Democrats. "She has good instincts that otherwise will go to waste. And from your point of view, helping her would be—what's that phrase you're so fond of?—oh, yes, an act of enlightened self-interest."

Olek listened attentively, but as soon as he heard Missy's last name he shook his head. "The Pozner girl? Too risky. From everything you've ever told me she sounds like a spoiled brat. Self-centered, undisciplined, immature. It would all be only a game to her—how would we know we could trust her if the going got rough?"

"How can you know with anyone?" Adam countered with some heat. "You take risks constantly. I tell you she has good instincts."

"If she does," Olek said calmly, "they'll keep. So let's just wait till she's dry behind the ears." And as Adam was about to protest once more, "Don't forget we aren't playing for marbles exactly. Not that we ever did, not even in the old days of the *gymnasium* study circle. And it's a far cry from that to what my new friends are doing. The Black Hundred would love to get its hands on us!"

The Black Hundred, whose more formal name was the League of the Russian People, was the secret organization most beloved of the Tsar and his dignitaries, and the scourge of the whole Empire. Made up of the worst reactionary elements among the native Great-Russians, and with a generous sprinkling of hooligans and ex-convicts, it dedicated itself to spreading terror among political activists and plain liberals alike. For money and pleasure both, its members spied on patriotic and labor groups, Pole-baited, Jew-baited, incited pogroms, acted as provocateurs and informers, and otherwise made themselves invaluable to the secret police. Olek Piotrowski had good reason to be wary of them.

Grown into a great oak of a man with a zest for living as huge as his commitment to the social cause was now complete, Olek had become a full-time, professional revolutionary. By day he worked in the underground print shop run by his Uncle Jacek, the one who had vanished eight years earlier but had long since surfaced again. By night, when he wasn't studying, he wrote leaflets to feed Jacek's presses or met secretly with groups of factory workers, teaching them to read and write Polish, which was forbidden, and also preaching organization—organization which, he never tired of explaining, was their only hope of easing their subhuman working conditions. In between, he also taught classes in history and somehow found time to court his girl, who fortunately shared all his convictions and interests.

"Try to see it our way," Olek told Adam with studied patience. "Just because we do dangerous work doesn't mean we *welcome* danger. To put it another way, just because I risk my neck ten times a day doesn't mean I don't value it. Quite the contrary. I intend to keep alive and well and a thorn in His Majesty's side for years and years. So let's simply keep an eye on your little Pozner heiress for the time being. Later on, if you still think she's worth worrying about, you can reopen the subject."

Regretfully, Adam had to admit that Olek with his greater experience was probably right. And in a sense he was rather relieved to let the matter drop. For purely personal reasons he was beginning to think he should never have allowed himself to be drawn into Missy Pozner's problems. He was still, after all, merely the poor tutor using the servants' entrance, and one ill-advised word from his capricious pupil might cost him his job—a chance which, considering his obligations, he could hardly afford to take. He was not yet his own man, and this was something he must not allow himself to forget.

❧ *Two* ❧

In LATER LIFE, when neither he nor the century were young, Adam often thought back to his university days and wondered how he and so many others he knew had endured them. Even under the best of circumstances the minimal curriculum stretched five grueling years. But the large majority of students, forced to eke out a living, took six or seven or eight. Some— those who were deep in secret political work, for instance—took longer still, while others turned into university bums, "eternal students" as they were called, becoming demoralized and incapable of facing examiners so that they never did get degrees of any kind.

He would remember their chronically undernourished bodies and the monkish lives they were forced to lead while in theory celebrating free love as the only admissible relationship between men and women who valued their dignity. There were few early marriages among them. Very few started families before earning a doctorate, and if they did it was generally by accident.

And where, he would speculate, where under the circumstances had they got their dedication to pure learning, that simple-hearted passion that seemed to him to vanish on university campuses around the time of the First World War? He decided it must have stemmed from an innocence of mind lost when the fourth dimension ceased to be an intellectual's fancy bracketed with the search for the philosopher's stone. Once the true structure of matter had been glimpsed by Einstein and the Curies, once modern science challenged Newton's laws as the bedrock of physical knowledge and the world became at once both more finite and less definable, younger generations, pursuing their complex specialized goals, were never again to experience that total wonder of discovery that marks the beginning of a new scientific era.

Then again he would ask himself how much of the lean and hungry time of his youth he was seeing through a haze of middle-aged nostalgia. He forced himself to remember the steady grind of teaching and learning, learning and teaching, and the daily trek across town from Nalewki to the university to the Kronenbergs' to the Pozners' and back again, none of it really different from his early *gymnasium* routine except that he no longer needed to stint coppers from the autobus.

Actually, there was another difference, and an important one.

When Salome Grossglik had started him out on the routine of tutoring her mother's boarders, she had also opened her house to him, telling him he must feel free to come and go and stay to meals, just as once Leon had made himself at home at his parents' place. "Your dear mother did so much for him, and now here's our chance to do something for you. Not that one keeps score, of course! But after all, to Uncle Leon you're like a son, and as for me, well"—she paused for effect, well aware of the absurdity of what she was about to say and the effect it would have on him—"I can't exactly pretend I feel like a second mother to you, not" with a little lilting laugh, "at my age! And *stepmother* would hardly be appropriate. But oh, you must know what I'm trying to say!"

He wasn't sure and didn't know how to tell her so, but it hardly seemed to matter. "The whole point is," Salome continued, "that we're anxious to make life easier for you, save you a certain amount of wear and tear." But to Leon she confided that it was all part of a larger plan to start exposing his nephew to certain refining influences that later on, when he was ready to face what she called the great world, would serve him in good stead. "For he needs polishing, our precious diamond-in-the-rough! And your dear sister isn't exactly the one to—not that I'm criticizing, you understand, far from it, I do respect and admire her!—but there are certain things she simply hasn't the, shall we say the *wherewithal,* to accomplish?"

Leon, whom marriage to this exquisite creature had left permanently bemused, said of course she must do as she thought best. As for the still-unformed Adam, he didn't need to be asked twice. Thus began a lifelong relationship which, for better or worse, was to have a profound influence on everything that mattered to him from that time on.

Not Adam alone, but most of the young-men-of-good-family who year after year still arrived from the provinces to board at the Grossgliks', fell under the same spell. That they, too, should adore Salome while remaining properly respectful was a considerable tribute to the skill with which she handled them, since these boys, young as they were, were by and large far more worldly than Adam. On country estates sexual innocence was rare, and the sons of the landed gentry learned early to seek and find casual gratification with married women. But in regard to their beautiful landlady—*Pani* Tworska having long since handed the reins of the business over to her daughter—they were, to a man, punctiliously correct. In another age they might have yearned to tilt lances and kill dragons in her honor, or at least throw cloaks down in the mud to spare her dainty shoes. Failing such possibilities, they contented themselves with becoming her errand boys.

In time Adam's own feelings for his uncle's wife passed from mute worship to comfortable affection and trust, occasionally tinged with exasperation. The boys, on the other hand, always at the same impressionable age level though their faces kept changing, continued as her willing and romantic slaves. She thrived on this, for the admiration of males of any age was meat and drink to her.

Besides, devotion such as theirs could occasionally be put to very special and practical use. In a country where the whole corrupt government apparatus, not to mention the civil service network and the schools, was run on a system of bribes and pull, influence-peddling and protection, it was good to know that among the men in high places there were by now dozens who cherished fond, even tender memories of her, and that they could always be appealed to for help on the strength of old relationships. Whenever anyone Salome cared about needed her, she always seemed to know what to do. "That's something Count X can help with—I'll speak to him tomorrow. . . . No, I don't need an appointment, he'll receive me any time. Why, he used to carry my books when I was a schoolgirl! . . . The younger Prince Y? Of course I have entrée to him! Years ago he was so in love with me he actually proposed! But then *his* mother came to town to see *my* mother, and naturally I gave her my word that nothing would come of it because of the religious difference. The family's never forgotten it! They'll still do anything in the world for me. . . ."

None of this was as much of an exaggeration as it sounded. And Salome did manage to get things done that even the most influential among Warsaw's Jewry, like her august brother-in-law and various *Gmina* directors, were powerless to accomplish. She could be relied on to discover who among the Tsar's high command was most receptive to bribes, and what the size of each bribe should be, depending on whether one needed a passport in a hurry or a prison key. And since she never asked favors on her own behalf, but only to help others, she hadn't the slightest hesitation about sweeping up marble stairways straight into the sanctums of the mighty.

"After all," she became fond of saying in the tone of one delivering a profundity, "in this ugly society it isn't what one is but whom one knows that counts, and I simply don't see why I shouldn't act on it! Besides," she would add with a touch of coyness, "we all know there are times when a woman, even a mere nobody like me, can accomplish what no man could so much as attempt!" Her husband began to believe she could move mountains.

"You're the most remarkable woman I've ever known," he never tired of telling her.

He said it again on their seventh wedding anniversary, arriving home with great armfuls of roses and a small jeweler's box in his pocket. "The most remarkable, the sweetest, the purest, and, I needn't say, the most beautiful. Perhaps that's why others besides myself find you irresistible when you ask a favor!" He kissed her hands, then slowly walked her over toward a mirror so that as he talked, he addressed her reflection. "On second thought I'll amend that. You're not just beautiful—you're loving and unselfish. And oh, what a rare, inspiring combination that is!"

She sensed he was leading up to something and stood there calmly expectant, leaning back against him, smiling, holding the roses. She saw him dig for the velvet box and hold it out to her. She put the flowers down, snapped open the lid, and gave a sharp little exclamation of delight. Resting against the blue velvet was a gold filigree lavallière studded with tiny pearls and diamond chips, modest but exquisitely wrought.

"Oh, it's lovely!" she cried, and he saw her eyes take on the glow of splendid sapphires.

"Not half so lovely as you, my darling," he said gallantly. He took the necklace from her and fastened it in place, kissing the nape of her neck. Then, still to her reflection, "Has anyone told you you're even more beautiful than when we were first married? Your waist as tiny, your skin as flawless, but your face—it's more perfect somehow, more finely molded, the way a young girl's face hasn't had time to be. . . ."

She turned in his arms and stood on tiptoe to rub her cheek against his. "What a delightful compliment for an old hag who's pushing thirty!"

He laughed as she had meant him to, and kissed her hair. "Ah, my love, to me you're still—you always will be—my child bride!" He spoke with that odd mixture of courtliness and formality he retained when approaching his wife, handling her as though she were a doll, and breakable. "Sometimes I even still think of you as my betrothed. And sometimes it seems as though you could happily remain an engaged girl all your life." It was not the first time she had heard him say this, only now she thought she detected the oddest expression on his face, half-wistful and half-ironic. But it vanished so quickly she decided she must have imagined it.

That was how Adam found them as he let himself in with his own key a moment later. Informed about the occasion and made to admire the necklace, he reflected how unlike his own home everything here was. When, if ever, had he known his father to bring a gift to his mother—a real gift, that is, not something she desperately needed? And although one part of his mind whispered that such grace notes, while pleasant, didn't really matter, still the whole life style of his relatives' existence was something he regarded with a touch of envy. And this troubled him, for in some obscure way it seemed to be clouding his judgment precisely at a moment when he needed clarity.

He had come that day on impulse, anxious to talk over with them something that overnight, unexpectedly, had become a matter of vital importance. A decision he had been half-heartedly avoiding, involving his whole future, could suddenly be put off no longer. He had in his pocket a notice from the university stating he had successfully completed the last of his required courses and was now expected to specialize. Translated into practical terms, this meant that the end of his student days was finally in sight. It also meant he would have to settle on a career, and considering his true predilections he did not trust himself to make the decision alone.

He couldn't, he realized, have come at a more inopportune moment. Urged to stay to dinner, he pleaded pressure of work and was quickly off again, feeling restless and lonely and left out, and wondering what to do next. Should he go home and talk things out with his father? Or perhaps look up Olek, who at this time of day could always be found at the flat his girl, Maryla Gorska, shared with a fellow student?

He decided against both alternatives. He was, he told himself with a kind of inverted anger, a man grown, presumably capable of reviewing the situation and drawing his own conclusions, knowing his own mind. "Know thyself," he heard himself mutter aloud so that a passer-by started at him. That's the first step, know thyself. And like a cat stalking his own shadow he set out for a brisk walk.

Choosing a specialty was distasteful to Adam mainly because the possibilities open to him were so at odds with his inclinations. Reason dictated something safe and practical, like law.

Law was what Leon and Salome had long been urging on him, for it would mean a good living rather quickly attained. But his enthusiasm for it was nil.

His real love, he had learned long ago, was mathematics. The youngster who at one time used to work extra algebra and trigonometry problems for the sheer pleasure of it had grown into an avid reader of theoretical texts by the world's masters of the exact sciences. Physics fascinated him, astronomy made his head spin, and his intellectual ancestors, he sometimes felt, were Archimedes and Kepler, Copernicus and Newton. But it was the beautifully inevitable symmetry of numbers that set his imagination aflame. Numbers in the proper configuration, he liked to argue, held the secret of the universe. "God," he told Olek in the course of one of their interminable discussions, "is he who can put the world into an equation. And don't ask where I read this because it's my own definition. I just made it up."

Unfortunately pure scientists, while they no longer risked the stake or the rack, could still quietly starve before they achieved anything of distinction—unless they were willing to put their knowledge to mundane, uninspired use. Of course, a scientist could always teach. But that, for a Pole, meant accepting a curriculum of often outrageous distortions, which in addition he must convey to Polish students in the hated Russian language. It meant knuckling down under the constant surveillance of Russian bureaucrats, licking the boots of Tsarist inspectors. Finally, for a Jew who wanted advancement, it also meant conversion. And this, in spite of his total indifference to religion, was repugnant to Adam.

Briefly he had considered medicine, but here again was the problem of additional long years of study without income, something to which he felt he hadn't the right to commit himself. True, with a minimum of work he could always become a neighborhood practitioner like his aunt Balbina Segal's husband. But this prospect, too, filled him with acute distaste. Only a day earlier he had gone to see Uncle Karol, and the interview began and ended on a note of bleak discouragement: he was left with a feeling that Karol treating the ills of the human body was like a deaf man trying to tune a Stradivarius.

"I'm not without a conscience," the pudgy, balding little doctor had said, out of the depth of some private despair. "I'm not indifferent to suffering, just woefully ignorant. Most doctors are. The years pass us by, we stop reading, stop trying to enlarge our vistas. We don't even attempt to keep up with the advances our profession is making. True, most patients don't ask for more than I'm able to give." He looked around his shabby office, empty on the Sabbath, and his voice hardened as though he were passing judgment on himself. "Just so long as I take their pulse, make them say 'ah' and prescribe cuppings and leeches, they're satisfied. And God forbid don't let me send them or their children to the city hospital to die! But if death does come, the poor wretches don't blame the doctor—they only cry out to Heaven against the injustice, or blame themselves for not having prayed harder. . . ."

Adam was beginning to feel uncomfortable, like a man inadvertently eavesdropping on a confession. But then Karol shrugged and smiled wryly. "Fortunately, by the law of averages, fewer people die than get well! Just the same, half the time I feel like a *felczer,* a barber-surgeon, a buffoon Figaro. So there's your answer. Stay away from my kind of butcher work, Adash, or you'll end up like me, your thinking mechanism atrophied and your skin turned to elephant hide. Now how about joining the family for a cup of tea?"

Thus, no matter how often he reconsidered, it always came back to law. Walking along the windswept Vistula embankment, he could hear Salome's soft urging, repeated time and again. "Think of the opportunities! We could be so proud of you!" Once she had added, "Women do so love being proud of their men!" And the subtle use of the possessive just about melted him.

Until recently he'd had no very clear concept of what becoming a lawyer might mean. Uncle Leon, for instance, had never actually practiced. On the other hand there were world-famous court cases where lawyers played a pivotal role. Freshest in his mind was the Dreyfus affair, which had rocked France and the world and was not yet over by any means—in fact, Emile Zola's noble cry of protest, *J'accuse,* was only a few months off the presses. And in the past there had been trials like those of the Decembrists. And less spectacular but no less in need of champions were the political prisoners crowding every jail.

None of this, of course, was what his beautiful aunt had in mind for him.

"I'm afraid you aren't thinking in very practical terms, dear heart," she liked to point out, patting his cheek with her cool hand. "Oh, I do realize you're much too much an idealist to consider such crass aspects as honorariums, but no one has ever made a living defending 'politicals'! On the contrary, it's always a sacrifice, so that first you must become established. And people like the Baron and *Pan* Pozner need lawyers for all sorts of things. In fact, just handling wills and estates and giving advice on business matters can make a man a tidy fortune. You wouldn't really object to a fortune, would you, dear heart? Why, I'm looking forward to the day when I can boast about my successful nephew, the legal expert *Pan* Fabian. . . ." Almost she persuaded him.

Olek Piotrowski had his own opinion about his friend's projected career in law. "Don't let the unsavory aspects bother you —what else can you expect when you're dealing with corrupt authorities?! We have to fight fire with fire, don't we? Just think in terms of how you can help the movement. You've a good head on your shoulders. Now if only you'd make up your mind which way it's really turned. . ."

Adam sighed. Just thinking about Olek's uncompromising insistence made him uncomfortable. For the hundredth time he had pleaded family obligations, and remembered how unimpressed that had left Olek: "You're not the only one with responsibilities, you know." He remembered his own quickly flaring anger. "Don't preach at me!" And then as quickly a flash of clear-sightedness. "But basically you're right. Tell me, Olek, aren't you ever plagued by doubts?" Yet even as he asked, he knew the answer to his question. "No, you're not. You're a monolith. You know exactly where you're going. You've always known. Sometimes I suspect you were born knowing."

Olek had only shrugged. "I just don't have your petit-bourgeois illusions, is all. It's the difference in our backgrounds,

I suppose. I'm a worker—you know the dirty word—a proletarian. And you're essentially middle class. By definition."

"Definitions be damned. I see more similarities between us than differences. For one thing, we're both poor as church mice."

"Granted. But people like me *expect* to stay poor, and what's more, they know why. They know they're being exploited, and that they have to fight tooth and nail for everything they'll ever have. They don't rely on the kindness of an employer's heart—they organize. Knowledge like that is in the blood. It's been pounded into us, generation after generation, and it's something a man doesn't lose sight of even if he doesn't always understand it with his head."

By then Olek was launched on another of his favorite topics. "What I mean is, don't expect every factory hand to spout off about the class struggle, but in his bones he knows that the lion doesn't lie down with the lamb! While the petit bourgeois spends his life killing himself, never really making ends meet yet always deluding himself that if only he can learn to make each copper do the work of two, his children will finally have a place in the sun. And in the end he dies defeated, a poor little would-be *rentier,* but without ever admitting how miserably he's miscalculated. . . ."

Adam said, "You've just described my father."

"And you, too, Adash, unless you wake up. . . ."

Adam had felt anger stirring again. "What would you have me do? Take a factory job for the good of my soul?"

"Don't be an ass. It's not that simple—not a one-to-one correlation. And by the way, you're even worse off than I am—you happen to be a Jew."

"What's that got to do with the price of cheese?"

"Maybe more than you know. Seriously, Adash, I wish you'd find time to attend just a few of our workingmen's circle meetings. Or even just drop in more often at Maryla's house. You know you're always welcome."

He was not far from that house now, he realized, having turned west from the river to cross the Old Town market square on the way home. He was tempted to turn off into the narrow alley where Maryla and her friend Wanda Borowska shared a cramped two-room attic. Olek was doubtless there, and even if he was not, the girls would make him welcome. He felt badly in need of more talk. Yet perversely he decided not to indulge himself. Then he understood why. What he really needed in order to get to know his own mind was to figure out more clearly not so much what he ought to do, or was expected to do, or felt he must do, but what he might do had he a free choice.

The evening shadows had lengthened and there was a chill in the air, and he realized he was hungry, having forgotten to eat all day. He didn't care. Because suddenly this hour alone with himself was important. He had to think. All his life, a true child of his time, he had always unquestioningly followed the patterns of his class and his social milieu, so that like a horse in harness he had moved in a straight line along the road of prescribed duty. Now it occurred to him to wonder about that far-off time when all obligations had been discharged and he was free to live for himself. What then?

Slowly the mirage of a promised land flashed before his eyes and it bore a strange resemblance to a picture postcard Henryk Meisels had recently sent him from Paris. He saw the main building of the Sorbonne, the broad steps leading to its main entrance. Across them, Henryk had penned in his precise, elegant handwriting, "To some, this is the fount of true knowledge."

Since Abelard's day philosophers and scientists had streamed toward the ancient seat of learning from all over Europe, and now Adam saw his own face turning west regardless of how long, slow, or even tortuous the road might be. Perhaps the day would eventually come when he would have the right to take it. It was a new thought, and it filled him with mounting excitement.

For the first time he was able to see that by doing exactly as Salome advised he could in the long run not only hasten that day but also make things considerably easier in the meantime. If he did take up law, if he worked diligently and began earning well, he could start saving, not just for his sisters' dowries and the family's needs but for himself. And when finally he had a nest egg large enough, he could leave for several years' study abroad. Even thirty-five wasn't too old to become a science student, was it?

God is he who can put the world into an equation. . . . Numbers in their proper configuration hold the secret of the universe. . . .

He had no idea where the search might lead, but at least he knew now where to begin.

He knew all this in a brief flash of insight illumined by a glory that by morning would be dimmed, and he would hardly remember it afterwards, overwhelmed once more by daily routine. But even this one glimpse would suffice to sustain him. His step quickened, he hurried home, went to bed early, and slept like a log.

The following week he began to read law.

❧ *Three* ❧

THE HOUSE on Count Berg Street continued to draw Adam like a magnet. He told himself it was really only a convenience, a home away from home, a place where he always felt welcome and could drop in any time—for half an hour's conversation, a catnap between lessons if he happened to be reeling with fatigue, or a hot midday meal when he wasn't in the mood for dry bread and sausage purchased from a street vendor. But the truth of the matter was, what attracted him was the atmosphere Salome created. He frankly relished the elegance, the gracious ambiance. And while he did not consciously envy his uncle, he did consider him the luckiest of men, sometimes even wondering whether someday he, too, might not stumble into a similar charmed life.

Yet at other times, generally after an evening spent with Olek and Olek's friends, he would ask himself whether there wasn't such a thing as paying too high a price for such blandishments. And the answers always made him uneasy. Here he was, a member of a persecuted race as well as a vanquished nation, raised in a virtual ghetto, awake to social injustice, immersed in the tradition of freedom, and as good a patriot as the next man— yet when Olek taxed him with being a petit-bourgeois at heart he knew with a sinking feeling that there was some justice to the charge. Otherwise why become so entranced with the mere outward trappings of fine living? Where was his sense of values? A more dedicated man would have remained indifferent. Like Olek. Olek, he thought, could live in a cave if need be without noticing or caring.

Adam thought of the times he had observed his friend at street meetings, at demonstrations. Olek never seemed to mind the stench of poverty but mingled easily with the rag-tag crowd, striking up conversations with those elbowing him as though secure in the conviction that all men were his brothers. But Adam shrank from the odor of stale sweat, nor could he help turning away from the pockmarked, those with foul breath and decaying teeth. But though he disliked himself for it, he felt powerless to change.

As he tried to sort out his thoughts it occurred to him that even in his choice of friends he sometimes allowed himself to be influenced by externals. Nor was this Salome's influence alone: he recalled the start of his friendship with the Meisels brothers, especially Henryk the fledgling sybarite, who at first had so awed him with his carefully cultivated tastes, his pose of connoisseur of fine wines and painting and music and a calm insistence on having only the best. Today Henryk's tastes were no longer a pose— he had become as single-minded in his pursuit of the good life as Olek was in his dedication to a cause. All well and good. But what of himself, just where did he fit in? And what was the synthesis he needed of dream and reality, of inner spiritual satisfaction and practical achievement? He knew he was not another Henryk, whom he could never match in ambition. But neither was he another Olek. *Who are you, then? Where are you heading? Quo vadis?* He continued to walk the streets nights, searching for answers, or sit for hours in a café that stayed open late, nursing a cup of black coffee grown cold and waving away a discouraged waiter.

Bluma grew used to his not turning up at the family supper table and was grateful that he at least came home every night to sleep rather than stay out God-knows-where. But she worried about his superhuman schedule and his not getting enough rest, and accepted the money he gave her every month with pity in her eyes. Yet she was careful not to embarrass him with effusive thanks. Only Jacob knew what a source of grief it was to her that her first-born, forced to shoulder an adult's cares almost since childhood, was now being cheated of the lightheartedness of youth as well.

"Someday it's all going to change, wait and see, I can feel it in my bones," she vowed, her husband her only witness. "It's bound to. Our Adash was never made for a petty life."

He was the only one of her children about whom she had such a conviction. The others she merely loved without illusion, but Adam seemed to her to carry within himself the seeds of destiny. "Whether that's good or bad I'm not ready to say. Just it wouldn't surprise me if we lived to see him enormously successful, and wealthy. Or better still, famous."

Lying side by side in their big double bed, both of them too tired for sleep, Bluma and Jacob often held long conversations for which there never was time during the day. "Oh, he'll go far, that one . . . but at what cost to himself! Because he's the kind that's bound to travel the hard road. It's his nature. I sometimes wish he were a little more selfish, like other people."

And Jacob would find himself wondering how, after all the years of marriage to her, he could still be startled by his wife's insights.

Jacob and Bluma were not the only ones to worry about Adam. In an attic atop a wooden building on Zapiecek, a crooked alley in the heart of Old Town, three Floating University students discussed him with affectionate despair.

"What are we going to do with him?" Olek Piotrowski moaned, pacing the creaking floor until it seemed the small space that served its occupants as living room, study, dining room, and kitchen must explode with his caged energy. "Because it's clear we've got to do something! We can't abandon him at life's crossroads—not and let that aunt of his put a ring through his nose! Because once she does that"—as usual when he became excited he launched into rhetoric purple with mixed metaphors—"once she does that, it's the end! She'll have him gliding down the primrose path toward the fleshpots of capitalism and. . ." He stopped, at a loss for a sufficiently grim image. "We'd better draw him into some sort of meaningful work now, at once. There's not a day to be lost!"

His sweetheart and future wife, Maryla Gorska, let him rant on for as long as she could bear it, knowing he was just letting off steam. A tall, handsome young woman with ash-blonde hair, brown eyes, and dark brows meeting over the bridge of a fine straight nose, she possessed a strength that her delicately classic features belied. Fearless, determined, and in every way a match for her man, Maryla shared all of Olek's passionate beliefs and was ready to work side by side with him regardless of consequences—ready to follow him to Siberia if need be.

She understood the man he had become, understood his elemental capacity for love and hate, fury and joy, and that he was incapable of doing anything by halves. And she wouldn't have wanted him different, but at the same time she also knew there were times when he needed to be firmly muzzled.

"You're not making a street-corner speech, my dear love," she now said tartly, "so let's have a little less oratory." But a quizzical smile softened the impact of her words. "Though in substance I couldn't agree with you more. The only question is, what do you have in mind? Exactly what do you propose?"

"That's just the trouble," he sighed, intent on the subject at hand and not the least ruffled by her criticism, "I only wish I knew. Easy enough to say, let's draw him in—but doing what? Frankly, my mind is blank. How about you?"

She shook her head and he resumed his pacing, turning at length to the third occupant of the room, Maryla's roommate and childhood friend, Wanda Borowska. "What about you, my dear? Any ideas? Here you've been letting us do all the talking and not a peep out of you!"

Addressed directly, Wanda raised her eyes from the pile of old gloves and stockings she had been mending. "As a matter of fact I've been sort of wondering. . ." Her face as she spoke was intense with concentration and her warm, slightly husky contralto came hesitantly, as though she were still thinking through what she wanted to say. "I don't really know your friend Adam very well but I've been observing him. And it seems to me if we really want to reach him, it'll have to be on his own terms." She paused, then added a trifle diffidently, "I think I'm on the trail of an idea. But you'll have to let me figure it out."

Wanda Borowska was the quiet one in the group. She had always been the quiet one. At school, at children's parties in the small provincial town where her family of impoverished landed gentry still cut a swath, they called her "mouse" or else, because of her darkly vivid coloring, "the gypsy." Her earliest act of open rebellion, which had astonished even more than it had shocked, had been to take up with a classmate from the lower strata, the daughter of Gorski the stationmaster, notorious for hitting the bottle and gambling at cards.

Forbidden to associate with Maryla, she had in spite of threats and punishments remained quietly defiant. The friendship flourished, inevitably developing along iconoclastic lines. In time the two girls, both of them disowned by their people as freethinkers and "emancipated women," made their way to the capital. Here they found poorly paying jobs in a *pension,* a young ladies' seminary where the only qualifications needed for teaching were a secondary-school diploma and good manners. Here, too, they soon made contact with the illegal student movement. They enrolled in a pre-medical group and were saving every kopek they could against the day when they had enough to go abroad to an accredited university that admitted women.

Then Maryla met Olek, became serious about him. And in no time, as is the way of women in love, she was trying to matchmake so that her friend, too, could know happiness. So far nothing had come of it; Wanda was still so uneasy with city people, so innately reserved and stiff and shy, that despite her darkly lovely face and slender, graceful figure the students who nightly filled the flat in Zapiecek thought of her as only a good comrade, nothing more. And if occasionally one of them did single her out she gave him no encouragement—she simply didn't know how, and would have considered it below her dignity to try.

But recently, after watching her closely whenever Adam Fabian was around, Maryla had begun to suspect a strong attraction, which Wanda would sooner bite her tongue out than admit. Her woman's intuition alerted, she now thought she saw a chance to help matters along. "I've always said," she murmured, assuming a look of bland innocence, "that you have a way of seeing things the rest of us miss. A way of understanding difficult people."

She had said nothing of the kind, but Wanda let that pass.

"Well, it seems we're always being told that the best way to recruit into the movement is through whatever interests each person most. Then let's ask ourselves what really absorbs Adam. Not politics, certainly, but science. So why not ask him to give a course—no, on second thought maybe start with a lecture or two. . . . I can think of a dozen subjects that would suit both him and us. Like Copernicus and the Church. Or Roentgen and X-ray. Or the Curies—polonium and radium are still so new they're just words out of the newspapers, and Maria Curie-Sklodowska one of us until not so very long ago! Or he might want to talk about Lobachevsky and Reimann—how many of us know anything about non-Euclidean geometry?"

As she spoke, she kindled to her own excitement. "Let him pick his own topics, start researching, lead a few discussions; before you know it he'll be in our work up to the hilt!"

"Hey," Olek cried, "why didn't I think of this myself!" In two strides he was across the room, catching her in a great bear hug. "Wandusia," he said, using the affectionate diminutive, "you're a genius! If I weren't already in love I could fall in love with you with no trouble at all!"

The attic rooms were ideally situated to serve as a center of underground activity. Zapiecek, or Chimney Corners, was an extension of Bakers' Row, the street that in earlier centuries had supplied the city with bread. Today the only picturesque thing about the alley was its name. Antiquarians and wealthy purists were forever talking about restoring the entire area to its seventeenth-century beauty, when the house fronts facing Old Town Square had been painted in designs of Byzantine splendor and the stained-glass windows of St. John's shone like jewels. But now everything was shabby, flea-ridden, infested with vermin. The great virtue of the dark narrow alleys, however, was that rents were cheap, and they were so crowded with a migrant population of beggars, pickpockets and drunks that eager young radicals passed unnoticed and were thus relatively safe from the prying eyes of housewardens and police informers.

Wanda and Maryla kept open house for the small group of men and women who, drawn into Olek's orbit, met there to study, dream, and conspire. And if in winter the rooms were frequently so cold both hosts and guests were forced to keep their outdoor clothing on, the reason was not always that coal was dear. The tile stove made such an excellent cache for illegal literature that building a fire was simply out of the question.

The people who wandered in at all hours of the day and night were rebels and revolutionaries of every color and stripe. They ranged from simple nationalists, who merely wanted to see the Constitution restored along with a modicum of token autonomy, to Nihilists, Polish Socialist Party members, Jewish Bund members, and finally the Social Democrats working closely with such famous exiles as Rosa Luxemburg, Leon Tyszka and Julian Marchlewski, who edited the banned *Workers' Cause* from abroad, and also with the Russian party headed by Vladimir Lenin. They disagreed constantly and violently, their voices rising in heated debate until long past midnight. But a common cause—the cause of independence and freedom—nonetheless united them, and to that extent overshadowed all other considerations.

Now that Olek felt he knew what to do about Adam, he began to make it a point to invite him over at least once a week. He was shrewd enough not to rush matters, hoping to draw his old friend in bit by bit, so that when finally the question of lectures did come up Adam would find it difficult to refuse. So the rest of the winter passed. Spring was in the air, and still they were marking time. The only difference was that as the cold receded and with it the indoor clamminess, Adam began to find Zapiecek more and more to his liking.

In the beginning, still completely under the spell of Salome's studied charm, he had been shocked and somewhat repelled by the young women in the group. Some of them wore their hair short. A few smoked. They uniformly scorned frills of dress and the small social graces, the coquetry and show of helplessness that supposedly made the female irresistible to the human male.

For the first time Adam was in contact with girls who not only asked but *expected* to be treated as equals, who refused to accept the often degrading role society assigned to them in marriage and were willing to do battle for the single standard. Adam watched couples forming liaisons without benefit of clergy, not because their morals were casual but as a matter of principle—because omitting the marriage ceremony, making a public avowal of free love, meant to them a defiance of the status quo.

Alternating with political discussion he heard frequent talk about social issues. From there it was only a short step to literature with a social content. Between gulps of scalding tea someone would mention Ibsen, Strindberg, the early Hauptmann, a recently translated collection of unperformed plays by the Irishman George Bernard Shaw.

The *leitmotif* was always the same—freedom, dignity, human rights for all men, all women.

A girl would say, "It's you men who're hardest for me to understand! Why should any living creature with a good mind of his own deliberately pick a mate unable even to think of herself?"

"Well," came the answer, "it's taken the powers that be centuries to train us to think that way. Now nine men out of ten will quote you the Bible to prove that's how the world was ordained ever since creation!"

"So here's something else we have the Church to thank for!"

"The Church *and* the government—one is the arm of the other, don't forget."

Adam would only listen, seldom joining in the conversation. He would think of Salome and wonder.

Olek, on the other hand, always had a great deal to say. "In the village where my grandfather lives, half the men beat their wives when they're drunk Saturday night. And they'll tell you the women like it that way—makes them know to whom they belong. But would the women really stand for it if they were economically independent? The hell they would!" He paused to take a large bite of black peasant bread and sausage. "I say the characters in *A Doll's House* are no different. More polished, yes. More civilized. But basically it's the same social forces at work—that's what dictates the relationship."

His eyes sought out Maryla and his broad, high-cheeked face broke into a gargoyle smile. "Me, I'd rather have a woman I can call comrade. I don't need a pet anymore than she needs a master." His large square hand covered his lover's in a brief, husbandly gesture of comfortable intimacy. Adam, watching them,

saw Maryla's fair skin turn pink with pleasure and embarrassment. He found himself thinking: Why, for an emancipated
woman she's quite deliciously feminine! and was startled by what
still seemed to him a contradiction.

His train of thought was interrupted by Wanda, asking if he
wouldn't like another glass of tea. "You've been as silent all evening as you've been abstemious. Tell me, what's *your* opinion on
the woman question?" At a loss how to answer, he remained
silent, but she kept after him. "What? No opinion? No opinion
at all? Then maybe you're too hungry to think—you haven't
touched the food. Eat something, *Pan* Adam." Suddenly for no
good reason she reminded him of his mother, though the two
were in no way alike. She seemed to him to have Bluma's concern
for anyone within her ken. She'll make a marvelous doctor, he
thought, if she ever manages to become one.

"Well, can't I fix you something?" Wanda continued to urge.
"Bread and cheese? Hunter's sausage? Then maybe you'll have
the energy to join our discussion!"

Adam laughed. "How can I resist such a nobly motivated
offer? Or such wonderful-smelling sausage? That's one thing you
won't find in a kosher household—good sausage!" For the first
time in their acquaintance he was really looking at this girl, and
liking what he saw. "But seriously, Miss Wanda, if I've been
silent it's because I've nothing, really, to contribute, and I hate
to talk just for the sake of making a noise."

Her eyes, since she was tall for a woman and he of only medium height, were on a level with his. She looked straight into
them. "I can't imagine how anything you say wouldn't be worth
hearing!"

She was forcing herself to flirt with him, doing her awkward
best to draw him out, and because he didn't answer at once she
became suddenly convinced she had failed miserably. It made her
feel cheap, as though she had openly made advances to a man and
been rebuffed. Her pride wounded, she made some lame, abrupt
excuse and left him.

Afterwards, when all their guests had gone and she and Maryla
were putting the place to rights, she unexpectedly exploded.

"That Adam Fabian! He isn't even human! I've been trying and trying to make him notice me, and look what happens!" She started to put the tea things away on a shelf in a curtained corner and dropped a glass. On her knees to clean up the mess, she wailed, "What do I do that's wrong? Am I being too forward? Or what?"

Maryla, who had never heard her talk so openly, looked at her with concern. "I don't think the trouble is you at all. Not at all. Olek tells me that Adam simply has never. . ." Whatever she had started to say, she now thought better of it. "You aren't falling in love with him, are you, poor darling?"

Wanda, still on her knees, looked up with an expression of pure misery. "Is it that apparent? I didn't want anyone to guess, not even you." She picked herself up, taking exaggerated care not to scatter the pieces of broken glass. "Promise you won't tell anyone, not even Olek! Because if he knew, if anyone knew, I think I'd die!" She seemed on the verge of tears. "Maryla, Marysh, what am I going to do? I just don't seem to be made like other women—I don't ever know the right things to say, the right way to act. . . ."

Maryla said loyally, "There's nothing at all wrong with you, and if Adam Fabian doesn't notice you he's an even bigger ass than I thought! Or maybe he just needs more time."

But in her own mind she decided she had better take a hand in pushing matters along. As soon as she could, she must talk to Olek again about their plans for Adam. It was high time.

❧ *Four* ❧

AND THEN unexpectedly events themselves took over.

The "violets," the people of Warsaw said, referring to the Tsarist police in their purple-blue uniforms, came up in profusion that spring, blooming early and late. Eighteen-ninety-eight was a season of unrest not only in Poland but throughout the Empire. In spite of rigid censorship, stories circulated about strikes in distant cities, occasionally successful, like the one in St. Petersburg that forced the government to make a few concessions to labor, including shortening the working day from fourteen to eleven-and-a-half hours.

All this had an effect on Poland's industrial towns far more complex than most political leaders were yet able to grasp. On the one hand the business boom of the decade, now already past its peak, had brought on a certain amount of labor organization and with it a strongly emerging labor consciousness. On the other, fresh calamity was hitting from the east: Great Russia, in its attempt to catch up with the rest of the "civilized" world in industrial development while at the same time giving employment to its own restless labor force, had recently ringed itself with walls of protective tariffs against manufactured imports from abroad, and this extended to goods it had previously bought in its own more advanced conquered territories.

For Poland this meant that, for the benefit of the Empire, it was to be reduced to the status of a backward colonial possession.

Its iron and steel plants, its textile centers, its leather and shoe industry and lumber and sugar plants were threatened. Warsaw and Lodz were particularly badly hit.

The factory owners, seeing the handwriting on the wall, resorted to direct bribes to ensure special treatment. They sent petitions to His Majesty and prepared for special pleading. They issued additional stock in their firms and offered it cheap to Russian investment bankers: the surest guarantee, it seemed, against the ruinous discrimination. And in the meantime, while waiting for one or another of these measures to bring results, they cut production. If not whole plants, sections of plants shut down. There were mass firings. In the textile industry, more and more men were being replaced by women at the looms, not just because womanpower was cheaper than manpower, it was also more docile. Within months average wages fell by thirty per cent.

With hunger and unemployment a specter over the land and fear already beginning to paralyze the working masses, a series of sporadic protests against the wage cuts nevertheless broke out in Lodz. This led to a lockout at Scheibler's. The local military garrison was called out to deal with what the government-controlled press called "anticipated rioting." And Governor-General Gurko issued the laconic orders for which he was to be remembered ever after. "Shoot. Don't grudge them bullets."

The words and the shots echoed around the country. And fear and apathy gave way to anger. The political climate grew more heated. In Poland's ever-seething if disorganized underground the first rumblings could be heard of the storm that must inevitably, a few years hence, explode into revolution.

Within the resistance movement itself there was no cohesion. Independence meant too many things to too many factions. The royalists talked seriously of restoration of the monarchy, while the far Left dreamed of socialism. In between, a vast gray mass was ready to settle for moderation, meaning accommodation to a vague form of pseudo-autonomy. Meanwhile the romantics, the tilters at windmills, talked bravely of armed uprising. Unmindful of past defeats, they argued that freedom could only be gained through open war; that once a national army rose up against the

Romanovs, the rest of Europe—no, not Europe alone but the whole world—would offer its support. They refused to remember 1831 and 1863.

It was at about this time that the Social Democratic Party, decimated because arrests had been heaviest among them, received unexpected reinforcement. A youth named Felix Dzierzhynski arrived in Warsaw from his family's country seat near Vilno. Already, at twenty-two, a veteran of Tsarist jails and recently escaped from Siberia, he surfaced in the working-class suburb of Praga at the home of a former cell-mate, Maciej Rosol.

He came bringing greetings from the Russian Social Democrats, who, in a plea to their Polish counterparts, were calling, begging, for unity. Only by joining forces against the common oppressor, they wrote, could the long-suffering peoples of the Empire, native Russians hand in hand with those in the outlying provinces who were subjugated aliens, hope to topple the whole vast rotten structure of Tsarism. And when that day came, the annexed lands would automatically gain independence, since no new, democratically constituted Russian government could ever betray the revolution by keeping others enslaved.

"But remember, neither we alone nor you alone are strong enough to win out," the message warned in conclusion. "Fraternal unity amongst all working people is essential for victory."

As both Dzierzhynski and Rosol understood from the start, such a message would hardly sit well with the masses of Polish labor, who in their hatred and distrust of all Russians, working people and intellectuals included, were no different from other sections of the population. Emotions were bound to get in the way of sober common sense. Nevertheless here was something to build on.

The two men put their heads together. They were an odd pair, Dzierzhynski, the youthful aristocrat with elegance bred into his slender bones, and Rosol, the grizzly, craggy bricklayer whose father had been born a serf. Each cherished the other's special abilities, complementing them with his own. Unreservedly Felix put his keen, trained analytical mind and organizing talents at the service of Maciej's broader experience in mass work.

It so happened that Maciej belonged to a numerous, dedicated, indefatigable family of underground activists—the legendary tribe of Rosols, brothers, sons, nephews, and their connections by marriage, who among them seemed able to reach into every conceivable branch of the labor movement. Now Maciej rounded up the family group and with them formed the nucleus first of a citywide, then a national, organizing committee. The task they set themselves was to shape the inchoate longing for freedom and a decent life into a conscious conviction that all this was indeed possible, but that it couldn't come about unless the workers and the peasants made it happen—they had to have a program, they had to formulate demands for basic human rights.

Suddenly there seemed to be Rosols everywhere. Perhaps fifty in all, they became a yeast of ferment throughout the country. Maciej himself worked not just with bricklayers but with the whole building trade—masons and roofers and the lowly hod-carriers. Jan, a master bootmaker, took on the starved-out leather and shoe industry. Walenty started a special committee to reach out into the foundries and forges, the steel mills and mines. Bartosz made himself responsible for railroads. A cousin on the distaff side, Marcin Kaspszak, a typesetter, joined forces with Olek Piotrowski's Uncle Jacek in the illegal print shop. And so it went.

Rosol being the Polish word for soup stock, word began to get around that the good soup was now bubbling away on the stove and would soon be ready. "The good soup's a-simmering" became a slogan, a password. *What can be better for empty bellies than good hearty soup? Hurrah for the soup pot!*

It was slow, uphill work but here and there one saw the first signs of progress. Strikes and demonstrations became more frequent until they formed a pattern. And more and more often stacks of "tissue paper"—illegal handbills and even shop newspapers which got their name from the thin paper they were printed on—could be found in factories when the gates opened for the day.

The "violets" redoubled their activity. Men, and women too, were trailed in the streets and arrested on the flimsiest of pretexts. Student groups especially became a target for harassment, since to the government the very existence of young Polish intellectuals spelled trouble. In April and early May, doubly a time of defiance since both labor's May Day holiday and the Polish national holiday, May Third, were forbidden—there was a fresh wave of house searches and arrests. Some of the Floating University's leading teachers were caught in the dragnet.

But the classes did not fall apart. Forced to meet without discussion leaders, the students, buoyed by patriotic and political fervor, quickly re-formed into self-study groups. Yet though morale remained high, sooner or later the situation was bound to deteriorate unless a continuing, systematic program was provided, and this the more experienced organizers understood very well. New teachers had to be found, a new curriculum quickly arranged to carry the classes through the summer months.

It was at this point that Olek Piotrowski abruptly decided he had had enough of trying to handle Adam Fabian with kid gloves. To hell with carefully worked-out gambits and the niceties of a subtle approach! Since obviously Adam would make an excellent replacement teacher, he, Olek, must persuade him to become one, putting the proposition to him as directly as he knew how. "You've always been a dabbler in science," he would say, "Now is your chance to make use of your avocation. Just choose your subject and teach it to your heart's content. You'll be helping the movement—and maybe even doing yourself a favor!" Olek reflected with some irony that essentially his appeal differed little from what Wanda Borowska had originally suggested. Except for the timing. This in turn prompted him to jot down among some notes for a future lecture of his own: "In re talk on Plekhanov's *Role of the Individual in History* (just smuggled in, very new): if A.F. does abandon his ivory tower to lead a class, what a perfect example from life of how individual choice is determined by historical necessity!"

But Adam, although he listened attentively and sympathetically to everything Olek had to say, at first only shook his head. "I'm honored. More than that, I'm touched that you trust me so much. But first of all, where in the name of heaven would I find the time to prepare such a course, and secondly, do you really think a man in my position has the moral right to take the risk? Where would my family be if anything happened? Maybe at some later time, if my situation changes. Right now I can't help feeling"—he cast about for words that would sound convincing —"I can't help feeling it would be, on my part, a kind of self-indulgence. . . ."

Only then did Olek realize how much he had been counting on a different answer. He didn't trouble to mask his disappointment. "So you're still singing the same old tune!" he barked out harshly. "Well, then, I'll answer your question with another question. Does anyone, anyone at all who understands what's at stake today, have the moral right *not* to take risks? Oh, I don't mean foolhardy risks, like taking in that rich little pupil of yours into a group!" He let that sink in. "But helping maintain an organization that's the lifeblood of our youth movement—yes, I think any risk is warranted!"

In order to be able to talk freely they had arranged to meet in a public yet very private spot, the fountain of the Lazienki Park. Here in the cool spring twilight it was possible to sit on the stone parapet without attracting undue attention. Their backs safely to the water, and with a good view of the approaches, which at the moment were deserted, they were safe from the long ears of informers. Yet both men, no matter how heated their argument, automatically kept their voices low.

"There are times," Olek continued accusingly, "when I simply don't understand you at all. It seems the longer I know you, the less I know you. Are you really so indifferent to the common good?" Adam, troubled, tried to think of an answer but the other man plowed on, "We've been friends for so many years. . . . Remember what brought us together? It was at a time like this, when they were arresting people right and left—my Uncle Jacek, that man in your building. . . . And we formed a study group. It was a good beginning . . . what happened to you? Why are you so afraid of getting involved with the rest of us?"

"You know what happened. I don't have to keep explaining," Adam flared. But in the face of the direct challenge, he found himself squirming. He remembered how Olek always answered his carefully structured excuses: *You're not the only one among us with responsibilities!* The implication seemed to be that he was using his family obligations as a smoke screen for something else—a kind of inner need to avoid all feeling, to continue functioning like an automaton. Could it be that the implication was true?

Determinedly, he rejected the suspicion. "You know all there is to know about me," he said defensively. "There isn't any more. As for involvement, I don't even know what you're driving at. What kind of involvement? With the movement? With a woman? I always come back to the same fundamental answer: Where in the world would I find time?"

"I didn't ask whether you had a mistress," Olek said with heavy-handed irony. "Just if you ever take down that fence you've put up around yourself. Just if you ever permit yourself to care about anything at all?"

Adam knew he ought to resent this. But his anger had by now evaporated and he felt helpless, with a sudden tremendous urge to speak out openly.

"To tell you the truth I sometimes wonder myself. . . . In a general sense of course I care. As much, I suppose—no, that's an exaggeration, not as much, but almost—as the rest of you. It's just that I'm always so swamped. I'm always running. I've been running so long I sometimes think if I allowed myself to stop I'd lose my bearings. Maybe once I have my degree things will be different."

"You're fooling yourself," Olek said. "Teach yourself to stop thinking, and first thing you know you'll have learned not to feel either. The head can kill the heart, you know. Oh, very easily."

"I'll have to take that chance, then."

"Won't you reconsider?" Olek tried urging. "It would only be one evening a week."

"Look," Adam said, resentful all over again. "Just let me outline my typical day. I get five hours' sleep a night. I do my studying before anyone else stirs in the house. I'm out in the street by seven, and when I'm not in a lecture or the library, I'm tutoring. I eat on the run. Worse, I think on the run. . . ."

"I've said it a dozen times and I'll say it once more," Olek answered, unimpressed. "You keep outlining the typical day of the typical poor university student."

"Not typical. There are things I haven't mentioned. My father isn't well. I don't know how much longer he'll be able to work. My sisters will soon be needing dowries. Already my mother worries herself sick that they'll end up old maids. You know how it is—no dowries, no husbands."

"All the more reason," Olek deliberately needled him, "why you should want to help change our lousy social system."

"You know, Piotrowski, sometimes you give me a pain. I've been trying, in all honesty, to explain something. And you. . ."

"*Mea culpa, mea culpa,*" Olek intoned like a sinner in the confessional, and because he was feeling slightly guilty Adam got the impression he was being deliberately provoked. "But come to think of it, if you're so poor and driven and you have all those contacts with the Rothschilds of Poland, has it ever occurred to you that if you play your cards right you might find your answer right there? How about that poor little very rich girl whose cause you once pleaded so eloquently? Huh? The heiress and the tutor—I must say the situation has possibilities. Remember your Balzac?"

"I do, and you can kiss my ass."

Olek's laugh echoed hugely among the park's old trees. "Well, at least you speak the vernacular. That's a comfort. It tells me you're human." And suddenly relenting, "Don't mind me, Adash, I only wanted to hear in your own words where you stand. Because there's been gossip and, well, I was beginning to think. . . But never mind. At any rate I'm glad to know money doesn't tempt you. Because it can be tempting, make no mistake. All things considered, I'm not even sure I would have blamed you."

It had grown dark. A night guard passing on his late rounds eyed them curiously, and they stood up and began walking toward an exit gate. Olek said, "Coming back to my original request, Adash, don't give me a categorical no. Not just because we need you, but for your own sake. So that maybe you can start questioning the accepted social values. So that you'll stop running, doing what's best for everyone but you, waiting to become established, respected, safe, and then suddenly remembering your starved-out self and marrying late in life, marrying something young and nubile and empty-headed and producing children that will be like grandchildren to you. . . ."

"You don't have to make me sound so pathetic," Adam bristled.

"Who said you were?"

Adam let that go. "The answer is still no. And no, I don't want to start worrying about the common good! And if this shocks your proletarian mind. . . ."

"Adash, Adash, I'm not setting myself up as judge," Olek said with a compassion rare for him. But seeing his friend so stirred and so hostile, he understood that here was a man driven by forces quite out of control, a man in danger of being buried alive because he lacked the elementary life urge to defend himself.

"All I ask is that you think about what I've been saying. I want you to consider that it's possible for a man to be a good son, a responsible member of society and a good provider, and still allow himself to do something for the good of his own soul. . . . And maybe in the process learn to call other men brothers. . . ."

The conversation died. They walked side by side in the darkness, their footsteps on the gravel echoing like the marching feet of a whole column of men.

"Will you at least think about what I said?" Olek asked one last time as they reached the street.

"I'll think about it—but don't get your hopes up," Adam said too quickly. Then, "A few lectures this summer, I think you said? That's all?"

"That's the immediate need."

"Well," said Adam. He had started to make his refusal absolute. Instead, to his own surprise he heard himself saying, "Well, if you can wait another month, until year's-end examinations are over, maybe I can squeeze it in after all."

"You mean that, Fabian?"

"Yes, I mean it."

"Why you old son, you!" Olek's huge hand descended like a bear's on Adam's shoulder. "That's great, that's capital! Come over to Zapiecek a week from tonight. Others will be there and we can make plans." They shook hands and started walking in opposite directions when Olek suddenly remembered something, turned, and called out, "I forgot to tell you—Wanda Borowska sent you greetings!"

But Adam was walking fast and did not hear him.

❦ *Five* ❧

As SPRING advanced that year the prospect of another long, dull vacation in Milanowek, the family estate halfway between Warsaw and Lodz, began to fill Missy and Marek Pozner with pure boredom. For a time they did their best to tease their parents into taking a villa for the season on the French Riviera, as the Kronenbergs were in the habit of doing. But to Maurice Pozner it was unthinkable to absent himself from his business for more than a week or two, especially in a time of crisis, and his wife refused to budge without him. At Milanowek he could at least join the family on weekends and be looked after properly. Villas on the Riviera, *Pani* Konstancja told her sullen children, would have to wait until they were married and had households of their own.

This triggered another of Missy's cycles of daydreams, in which marriage always became synonymous with freedom.

"You, of course, are too young," she taunted her twin brother, "but I'm a girl and girls can get married any time. For all you know, next year I'll be inviting you to visit me on the Côte d'Azur."

"You?" Marek snorted. "Who'd marry *you* in such a hurry?"

"I'm not ready to answer that," said Missy, looking appropriately haughty. "Just don't be surprised if it happens, is all. Of course, I'm not promising anything definite. . . ."

Alone in her room later on, she spent a restless hour turning over in her mind all the possible ways of making good her threat.

Whom did she really know who would make an acceptable bridegroom? She thought of all the dancing fools her brother was forever dragging home to dinner or out to the country for hunting and riding and tennis. She thought of the brothers of various friends of her own, and they seemed no more appealing. Children, all of them—callow, gauche, often still pimply. If her father's money was to assure her a husband, at least let it be a man, not a boy. And so, unbidden, her thoughts again turned to Adam Fabian.

Ever since her conversation with him some months earlier she had watched her tutor daily, and the fact that he continued to be calmly unaware of her as a woman only whetted her appetite. Her imagination began to run riot. Anyone so unimpressed by the advances of a rich heiress must indeed have his mind fixed on higher things, which argued a noble nature. She liked that. The only question was how to reach him. And suddenly she felt she had the answer—through his interest in science. Obviously he and she had this much in common: they were both deprived, he through poverty and she because her parents wouldn't see reason, of the joys of the quest for pure knowledge. Well, then, rather than try to seduce him with promises of wealth for its own sake she would let him understand that she could help him spend the rest of his life as a gentleman scholar. Thus, if she played her cards right, her ends would not remain unattainable after all. Her father, delighted and relieved and certainly surprised at her choice of such a stable, serious, and brilliant man—one with a spiritual outlook and none of the earmarks of a fortune-hunter—would of course settle a huge sum on her and an equally huge sum on her husband, and there would be no further dreary country summers, and she could do as she liked forever after.

This much decided to her own satisfaction, Missy cast about for someone to whom she could turn for help with her scheme. After days of mulling it over, she finally settled on Eugenia Kronenberg, not only because the Baroness was one of the few friends of her mother's whom she liked, but because she remembered there was some connection between Adam and the Kronenberg family, which in itself might be useful.

Eugenia Kronenberg and Konstancja Pozner had at one time cherished the hope that Missy and Lucio, once he was a bit older, might make a fine match, not just for their own sakes but because it would be a marriage between the Kronenberg banking network and Pozner textiles. But slowly it had begun to dawn on the Baroness that her stepson's interests might not center on women. And she couldn't rid herself of a feeling of guilt, as though in some obscure way she herself was responsible for Lucio's inadequacy. The guilty feeling gradually extended to encompass Missy, so that she tried to make up to her for this supposed failure by showing her special affection, encouraging her confidences.

Sworn to secrecy, Eugenia now let Missy unburden herself, then promised to do what she could. Which is to say she discussed everything first with Salome, who was unreservedly ecstatic, then with her husband. And when the Baron pointed out that he could think of more improbable alliances, that he saw nothing outlandish in the idea, that, in fact, it might serve the interests of everyone concerned, Maurice Pozner included, Eugenia—again in the strictest confidence—broached the subject to Missy's mother.

Whatever Eugenia might have feared, *Pani* Konstancja did not turn a deaf ear to her daughter's yearnings nor did she throw up her hands in horror. On the contrary, she sat back and listened carefully. Husband-hunting for one's children, she was thinking, was after all an art that required shrewdness and imagination. One had to look for potential candidates in the oddest places. They were like plants for one's conservatory—some had to be nurtured patiently, others forced, still others cultivated from wild stock, and it was these in the end that often produced the most extraordinary flowers and fruit.

As she talked, it seemed to Eugenia that she could hear her friend's mind like an abacus clicking off the plus and minus aspects of what she was proposing.

"My husband thinks," she then said, embroidering a little and aware that Konstancja Pozner would consider whatever the Baron thought worth reckoning with, "that Adam Fabian would be a kind of investment in the future—not just for Missy but for the business as well. Like a surrogate son to *Pan* Pozner, only bound to him by ties of gratitude and loyalty—something that, I don't have to tell you, one doesn't always find in one's own children." The reference to Marek was tactfully oblique but unmistakable. "As for our dear Missy, she'd have a fine, trustworthy husband, someone sufficiently mature to keep her firmly in hand yet not so much older as to be . . . well . . . a second father. . . ." Embarrassment made it impossible to be more explicit, but there was little doubt in *Pani* Konstancja's mind that the Baroness was thinking of her own husband's venerable age. And Missy's mother reflected rather smugly on certain obvious differences between Eugenia's aristocratic Baron and her own plain Pozner. She was lucky—she had no complaints. If God was good, her daughter wouldn't have any either.

"To sum it all up," Eugenia brought her back to the business in hand, "Missy seems to have quite lost her heart to Adam Fabian."

"Missy," said Missy's mother, "doesn't yet know she has a heart. Besides," she added piously, not wishing to appear overeager, "we all know that real love comes after marriage. However, what you've just confided to me bears thinking about. Though, of course, we're going to have to be very careful, very discreet. That Missy! If she got so much as an inkling of a suspicion that her father and I approve, she'd lose interest. You see, I know my own children, that I do! Anyway, leave everything to me—and don't be surprised if nothing happens for quite a while."

In the end it was agreed that *Pani* Eugenia would make Missy a promise of a soirée or garden party at which Adam too would be a guest, so that the young people might for once meet more or less on an equal social footing. But this would take time, and meanwhile the school year would be winding up and Adam's examinations would absorb him and then suddenly it would be summer—and nothing much else would happen until fall.

"And by then," *Pani* Konstancja smiled, a plan of her own beginning to form in her head, "Missy may decide she has other fish to fry. And if not, well, then my husband will take over. He'll know just what to do—and without tipping his hand to that little minx, you may be sure!"

Carefully choosing a time when Pozner was in an expansive mood, which meant after a good meal during which there had been no arguments with the children, *Pani* Konstancja sat her husband down for a sensible, down-to-earth talk about their daughter.

Knowing they would have the evening to themselves—Missy had announced she had a new French novel to finish and Marek was off for an evening of theater—she waited until Maurice was comfortably settled in his favorite chair in the small living room where they liked to sit if no company was expected, and made sure his bottle of port and his cigar box were at his elbow. Then she poured herself a cup of steaming after-dinner coffee, topped it generously with whipped cream, sipped appreciatively, and said by way of opening up the discussion, "I don't know if you've noticed, Papa, but our little girl isn't a little girl any longer. She's a young lady. It's time we were treating her like one."

Just as she had anticipated, his first reaction was to shrug this off. "Missy a young lady? Bah. She's a child."

"She's seventeen. At seventeen I was already starting to plan my wedding, remember? Of course it took three long years because you were so set on making a pile of money first. But at least I was spoken for. It's easy for a girl to wait once she's spoken for. She knows exactly what will be, so she's less apt to get restless. Otherwise. . ."

"Mama, you trying to tell me our Missy needs a husband? That's nonsense! She's too young!"

"You didn't think I was too young."

"That was different," he argued with conviction. "Times were different. You were different. Brought up different."

"True," she said. "It was a different world altogether, and not such a sweet one." She'd been born and raised in a *shtetl*, a small, crowded, rigidly authoritarian Jewish townlet, whose ruling autocrat had been the conservative rabbi and the rabbi's brother— her father—the richest man. "I used to think the orphans in the convent school down the road had more freedom than Papa let me have. But once he got everything settled with you, I didn't mind so much. The end was in sight, I knew it was worth waiting for, so I didn't have to worry any more."

Maurice knew his Konstancja—he remembered when her name had been Hanke, and he still called her that sometimes when they were alone. He was beginning to see where the conversation was heading. "Ach, Hanke, Hanke, why don't you just tell me what's on your mind? You worried about our daughter? What's she been up to?"

"Nothing—so far," his wife said, glad to have the preliminaries over with so easily. "But she will be, if we're not careful. What I mean is, you know what she's like. Like her father. For two groshen she'll take matters into her own hands. So naturally I worry."

Maurice picked a cigar, bit off the end, lighted up. "I give those brats everything, and they're not satisfied! What does she want?"

"A life of her own," her mother said. "A man. At her age it's natural. And all *I* want is, she shouldn't do something foolish. Because I see signs." And she began a detailed account of everything Eugenia had said to her and what she had said to Eugenia, and how they'd come to the conclusion that a girl as independent-minded as their Missy might best be kept in line by being allowed the illusion—only the illusion, mind you—of having things her own way for a while.

"*Pani* Eugenia says Missy's lost her heart to young Fabian— those are her very words, lost her heart to him. And you know, Papa, maybe that's not so bad? After all, it's the Baron who recommended him, he's sort of related, from a respected family. Which is more important to us than a son-in-law with money. Provided, that is, our Missy really wants him. And that," she added, "only time will tell. And in the meantime we've got to see she doesn't do anything wild just to spite us, which I wouldn't put it past her." Then she offered her clincher. "Even the Baron thinks we could do a lot worse."

"Hmp," said Maurice. But he was listening with both ears. Because on the rare occasions when his wife spoke at such length, long experience had taught him she really had something to say—and doubtless was leaving even more unsaid. The chances were good that she already had a whole complex plan of action ready, one she was anxious to share with him as soon as he chose to draw her out.

It was a game they had played often over the years to their mutual satisfaction. He understood that the next move was up to him, and prepared to make it. Relaxed now that the first shock of her disclosure about his adored daughter had worn off, he puffed on his Corona-Corona and slowly sipped his port. He didn't offer his wife any, though there were two glasses on the tray. She seldom drank—she preferred her coffee.

"So," he asked, following the rules. "What do you want I should do, Mama?" Away from the children and the servants, it was a pleasure to lapse into the vernacular.

"You know best," she said. "You're a good judge of men."

"Hmp. Still, I won't deny I've had my eye on that boy for some time. And no, I haven't forgotten my friend Kronenberg has a personal interest in him. Not that I need a Kronenberg to tell me what's what," he added hastily, "but a good connection is a good connection and never hurt anyone."

She knew better than to argue the point and went back to her own main theme. "From what Eugenia tells me, Adam Fabian has always been the way he is—a good son, devoted, loyal, dutiful."

"Priceless qualities," her husband agreed.

"His parents don't know how lucky they are! Or maybe they do." *Pani* Konstancja, too, now spoke in the heavily accented sing-song of the far-away *shtetl,* the voice of her Hanke days. "That kind would never spend his wife's money on other women, he'd never break her heart. Still," and now she began to play devil's advocate, "there's also another side to the question. Such a serious young man, so intense. Even if Missy thinks she wants him, can he make her happy? I wonder."

"Happiness," Maurice reminded her, "no one can guarantee." He was thinking that she was talking out of both sides of her mouth, but then she sometimes arrived at her conclusions by devious ways. "So again I ask you, what do you suggest?"

"We-e-ll . . ." her sing-song became for all the world like her uncle the rabbi's, "on the one hand she's got her heart set on him. On the other hand next year her tastes may change. So I say let's give a little and take a little. First throw them together, but God forbid she should guess we planned it that way. Then take her away for the summer and see what happens. In other words, make haste slowly."

She picked up her coffee cup, sipped, and put it down again with distaste. "Cold as ice. I'll ring for some fresh."

They waited while the footman came in, retreated with the tray and reappeared, the interruption giving them both time to sort out their thoughts. Not a bad idea, Maurice was thinking. Find Missy a husband old enough to have some authority, yet young enough to be trained and molded into a business successor. For a long time, ever since he'd been forced to face the fact that his own son was a wastrel in the making, this had been the old man's cherished hope. It only remained to be seen how someone of Adam Fabian's temperament would take to being a business-man. Still and all, the man had not yet been born who couldn't be taught and shaped, provided he had the brains and the will to carry through—and the right inducement was there.

If we throw them together often enough, Konstancja thought, it'll probably all blow over of its own accord. But if it doesn't, I wouldn't really object, if he's what she wants. Only he's got to be in love with her, really in love. And why shouldn't he be, I'd like to know? She's pretty, she's clever. And like they say, it's just as easy to fall in love with a rich girl as a poor one!

Aloud she said, "Just don't you let that Fabian boy suspect you're leading him by the nose! Just you be careful, Papa. Gam-ble on what a man is at heart, I always say."

"All right, all right. So now I see you're ready to tell me what you want I should do. Offer him a good job in cotton, maybe?"

"Not even that," she said. "At least not yet. First start paying some attention to him, make him think you're interested in him, himself. Ask him what he wants to do when he has his diploma. Get him to talk. Eugenia tells me he's starting to study law. Well, then, tell him law's a great profession and you'd like to help him get started. Tell him you'll maybe be able to use a good lawyer when he's ready. Tell him. . . But why ask me?" she interrupted herself. "When the time comes you'll know exactly how to handle him."

He nodded and beamed. "Ach, Mama, what a head you have on you! No wonder I never even look at another woman! Not even," patting her fat rump, "after twenty years! So all right, it's settled then? All settled? Let's drink on it!" He poured a fresh glass of port for himself and a few drops for her. "Here's to our daughter's future, whatever it may be!" The ruby wine sparkled against the crystal as they clinked glasses. "If that boy is what she really wants he's as good as hooked already. And he'll never suspect a thing, not a thing, I promise you."

He sat back, congratulating himself on the wonderful helpmate he married, preparing to enjoy a slow, patient campaign. After all, there was plenty of time, and he was not Maurice Pozner for nothing.

❧ *Six* ❧

LATE on a hot lazy afternoon that felt like the middle of summer Adam Fabian sauntered aimlessly down the broad white steps of the main university building, his shoulders aching and his head full of cobwebs. He had just finished his final written examination of the year and was hoping to run into someone with whom he might hold the usual postmortem. Other students were milling about, talking in small groups, but they all seemed to be from other departments. Too tired to do anything else, he decided to wait and see who else might emerge from the building.

Leaning against the balustrade, his eyes half closed, he let his thoughts drift, disorganized, from thing to another. He was remembering the promise he had made to Olek Piotrowski about teaching some classes this summer. It was a promise he felt honor bound to keep, although reluctantly. Now there would be no putting it off, and tonight, tomorrow at the latest, he must get over to Zapiecek to talk over plans.

From there his mind jumped to the party at the Kronenbergs' to which, much to his surprise, he had been invited the previous week. Missy Pozner had been among the guests, looking delightful in something frothy and blue instead of the schoolgirl brown he was used to seeing her in. She teased him into trying to waltz with her, and when he stepped all over her feet she said, "Anyone can see you're not a lady's man. That's why you would make such a good husband. But I already told you that once, remember? Don't let me repeat myself!" And although she laughed, and he with her, he sensed she was only half joking and felt she was somehow demeaning herself, and wished she wouldn't, but without knowing how to tell her so.

Afterwards, sitting next to her at supper, he had begun wondering, not so much about Missy as about women in general, and finally about his own future, about marriage. He had never before given the subject much thought except to suppose that like everyone else he would eventually marry. But try as he would, he could not form any picture of the woman who someday was going to fill his life. Would she resemble his mother, devoted and selfless, patient and uncritical and a little sad? Or was it going to be someone strong and brave like Olek's Maryla? Both of them, he knew, were admirable, each in her own way, as indeed Missy, too, might grow up to be in spite of her money. But his senses did not quicken at the thought of sharing the future with someone like any of them.

And then, as his eyes had traveled the length of the glittering table where he felt rather out of place, he caught Salome Grossglik's eyes and she smiled at him. At the same time he could see Leon smiling at her. And there was such a look of love and adoration and pride in his uncle's face that his breath caught. And much as it surprised him, he had the answer to his own riddle. His wife, that feminine presence which would someday be part of the very texture of his existence, was going to resemble his aunt. For it wasn't intellect or loftiness of purpose that really captivated him, but beauty and soft charm and grace. "Good Lord," he thought, "Salome's just a birdbrain—I must be losing my wits!" But the concept refused to go away. "Ah, well," he consoled himself, "it's perfectly possible for a woman to be all these things and clever as well!" And anyway it was going to be years before he was able to consider marriage, so why worry? He had turned back to Missy, asking about her plans for the summer now that vacation was only a week or so away, and let her complain to her heart's content about the dullness of Milanowek.

The sun felt good on his face and after a while he felt refreshed as after a long nap. He roused himself and continued on his way. Then he heard running steps behind him and felt himself being jostled. Turning to protest, he recognized a youth he knew only vaguely, Zenon somebody-or-other, one of the Zapiecek crowd. Unaccountably, Zenon was pumping his hand, as though rejoicing at having found a long-lost friend.

"Adash! What luck to run into you like this! And here I thought I'd have to go jackassing all the way across town to your house! I have a message for you from my sister. She's having a party this Sunday and she says you must, absolutely and without fail, be there." He put an overfriendly arm around Adam's shoulder. "She says she'll never talk to you again if you don't come! So what shall I tell her?"

Since they were little more than nodding acquaintances and Adam had never even heard of Zenon having a sister, he understood at once that the message had another meaning. He had the presence of mind to fall in with acting out the charade. "Tell your sister I shall be delighted. In the meantime, how about going somewhere for coffee? I've been writing steadily for three hours and my brain is numb."

"Coffee by all means," the other man agreed.

Arm in arm they ran down the remaining steps and turned toward a main thoroughfare. It was not until they had rounded the corner and walked a block or two that Zenon pressed a fold of paper into Adam's hand. "Read it when you're alone," he whispered, the tone of false cordiality falling away. "You'll find out all you have to know. Phew! I'm glad I found you so easily. About the coffee—maybe some other time. I've about ten other people to contact before evening."

They shook hands, Zenon hailed a passing hack and was gone, and Adam sauntered down the avenue, pausing to look into shop windows, buying a paper, even stopping for a beer. Not until after turning a half-dozen corners did he finally unfold the note.

It was in Olek's handwriting but without salutation or signature. *"What a spring! Even in our little attic the violets are in full bloom. The scent is overpowering. Besides, it's a pity to stay indoors. Meet me in Lazienki instead. Eight o'clock at the fountain, and be on time."*

Adam's hands were shaking. He could feel a prickling under

his skin and sweat beginning to drench him. At the same time all tiredness fell away and his mind cleared, beginning to function calmly and efficiently.

He had never before had to deal with a coded message, yet was experiencing not the slightest trouble deciphering it. The violets, of course, were the police. They must have overrun the Zapiecek apartment, and God only knew what they found; and Olek was assuming the place would remain under surveillance for some time to come. Therefore as many of its habitués as possible were being warned to stay away. Finally, since Olek was doing the writing he was not in jail, but obviously he needed help. Otherwise he would not be exposing both of them by requesting a meeting.

It was the kind of situation they had all envisaged so often, the kind everyone was always discussing, warning themselves that one must be ready for such contingencies at all times, yet never quite believing it was going to happen. But it had happened, and now that he was part of it Adam found he had no wish to avoid involvement. On the contrary, he felt rather proud that of a dozen trusted friends Olek should have chosen to turn to him.

But it wasn't Olek he found waiting for him at the appointed place and time. It was Wanda Borowska. Her clothes looked as though she had slept in them, her eyes were red-rimmed, and several times as she recounted the details of what had happened the previous evening her voice shook and grew hoarse with repressed tears.

"They got Maryla. She's at the Pawiak. Olek is sick with worry. Fortunately there's not much they can pin on her—it was right after a distribution of literature and there wasn't a pamphlet, not a handbill in the house. But they did come across some old letters—from a cousin of hers who died last year of typhus in Tula, in exile. He'd been arrested several times and they were very close, the letters sounded that way, so that makes her suspect. We can't think who could have denounced us. . . ."

They were sitting on the edge of the fountain, breathing the warm scented air and watching the swans slowly circling the artificial pond. Wanda had had the foresight to bring stale bread to feed to the birds, and in the dusk of the June evening they might have been any pair of lovers keeping a tryst under the acacias in bloom.

"We'll have to organize help," Wanda whispered urgently. "And we'll have to raise money. The comrades will give what they can, once we spread the word. We've already started. Zenon and a few others are running all over Warsaw. They're warning everyone to keep away from our place. Olek said to tell you to do everything you can. . . ."

"It's strange," he said, voicing the thoughts he had had earlier. "No matter how well you know about these things, you're never really ready."

She nodded. "It's . . . it's like death. Someone is mortally ill, your head tells you it's hopeless, but you're still not prepared for the actual blow." It seemed to help them both to talk in abstractions. It gave them time to come to grips with reality and with themselves.

What surprised Adam most was that he was feeling very little fear—only a shattering sense of devastation. He was remembering scenes out of his boyhood, the arrest of harmless little *Pan* Liebman from the floor below, *Pan* Liebman who had never come back from prison. He was remembering how the man's wife came to be known as the "widow" Liebman while they were still trying to get her husband released.

"It was dreadful," Wanda was whispering, not daring to raise her voice. "Dreadful. I can't begin to tell you—the humiliation. They searched everything, emptied every drawer, every box, then threw everything in the middle of the floor. 'We're looking for incriminating evidence, girlies, and just wait till we find it!' They tore pages out of books, ripped up notebooks. One of them kept examining papers upside down—he couldn't even read. Then they ripped up seams of dresses—destroying, destroying for the sheer pleasure of it, making coarse jokes about how they'd get down to searching our persons next." She shuddered. "Somehow, they didn't. But that isn't important. It's done. What's important is Maryla. I'm afraid for her. You know how it is." And she quoted the tag line of a recent political joke that told of a man fleeing the country because a new Tsarist edict was out on the compulsory gelding of camels: "I'm not taking any chances! They pick you up, they do it to you, then go prove you're not a camel. . . ." She was trying to laugh, and instead broke into harsh, terrible sobs.

Without thinking, in a completely spontaneous gesture, Adam put his arms around her. "Wanda, Wandusia, don't cry, please don't cry." And when she didn't stop, "Crying isn't going to help. You've got to get hold of yourself. Wandusia, Wandeczka, Wandziula," the diminutives of her name came to him naturally, sounding like caresses. "Please, darling. We can't afford to attract attention. . . ."

But she had reached the end of her tether, the events of the past twenty-four hours overwhelming her, her reserve, her control shattered. She quieted, but went on making great gulping sounds and a violent trembling took hold of her and her teeth chattered. Adam pulled her head down to his shoulder and held her close. After a while her sobs subsided to a barely audible keening. Then she buried her face against him and gradually even the keening was stilled. But the trembling went on. She tried to say something, but her teeth chattered as during an attack of malaria, and no words came.

"Hush," Adam kept on whispering gently, "you hush now," still holding her, rocking her as he had seen his mother rock the little ones when they were hurt, waiting for the pain to subside before asking questions. "Hush, little one, hush, hush. . . ."

Then he felt her body sag as she huddled against him, seeking the comfort of a stronger, calmer presence. Her arms went around his neck, her forehead pressed against his cheek, until finally she relaxed as a child does when at last its crying is stilled. And still he held her, his hands stroking the dark damp mass of her hair, the thin taut shoulders.

He had never before realized how slight she was, all nerves and sinews and frail, slender bones. The new woman? The emancipated woman? She was nothing of the sort. She was just woman, and she was leaning on him.

"Wandusia, Wandziula, Dziula . . . Hush, dear heart . . . Hush, don't cry any more. . . ." She sat up straighter, tendrils of her hair brushing his face. And in his eyes she became beautiful, and his face flamed and he was kissing her, the matted hair, the hot forehead, the weary eyelids.

Suddenly he felt the thin body tense in a different way, coming alive, responding. "Adam, Adash, oh Adash . . . ," she whispered. And then she was kissing him back, not for comfort this time but in passion.

On the lake the swans had grown quiet. The late strollers paid little attention to the young couple with their arms around each other, a boy and girl with, doubtless, no other place to go to do their courting. Even the uniformed guards bypassed them. A city in spring is full of lovers, and who would want to disturb them except perhaps the street urchins?

At last they drew apart. Wanda settled back against him once more with a contented sigh. "I never thought it would happen. . . ."

"Nor I," he said, misunderstanding completely. "Imagine, all those months, seeing you constantly yet never seeing you at all. I must have been blind. . . an idiot. . . ."

He sat tracing the curve of her cheekbone, letting his fingers learn its pure and lovely line. He kept shaking his head in disbelief, as if still unable to comprehend what was happening to him. He was twenty-three years old, and for the first time he had just kissed a woman in passion, in love. He was totally overwhelmed by what until that day had been unknown quantities in his makeup—profound emotion and equally profound physical need, direct, all-consuming, exactly what he had always guarded against and sternly denied himself.

He remembered one of his last conversations with Olek, remembered his own insistence that he must continue to live by a blueprint, a human abacus by his own description, since circumstances allowed him nothing else. He remembered Olek's answers and how right they had been. But now everything was changed, and his whole being was chaotically awhirl. Only this was no time for chaos.

As if echoing his last thought, Wanda said, "We're letting ourselves forget the others. . . ."

She was making desultory attempts to tidy her hair. She leaned over and in the spray from the fountain dampened a handkerchief and bathed her face. In a voice that tried, unsuccessfully, to sound matter-of-fact she added, "There's so much to be done. And so little time. . . ."

Adam stopped her fussing by taking her hands in his and kissing them. They were rough and red from constant work in some secret biological laboratory, not soft and white like Salome's. She must have been working earlier that very day, for there was a faint odor of formaldehyde still clinging to her fingers.

"This was the night I was going to talk to Olek about giving a course," he mused aloud. "I'd promised, yet I didn't feel at all sure I'd do it. And now it isn't even a question of choice. Now I'll simply be doing what I have to do." He smiled speculatively. "Olek has been sweating bullets trying to pull me in—and here everything is falling right in place!"

"I know," she said, with her characteristic honesty. "I know all about it."

"You do? You mean he told you?"

"Not . . . quite," she said, looking embarrassed and guilty. "You see, Adash, I . . . ." She stumbled over her own words, stopped, then with an effort started over. "Adash, I'd better tell you the whole truth right away. Because from now on that's the way it has to be between us. No secrets, ever. We have to be completely honest and frank with each other."

He looked completely bewildered. "Darling, I don't understand. . . ."

"How could you? Let me begin at the beginning. This plan to get you to give lectures—it was my idea. Olek and Maryla and I were so anxious to draw you into our work, and none of us could figure out how to do it. So then it occurred to me . . . and I said . . . ." She stopped again, then finished with something like her old exasperation over the aloofness of Adam Fabian, "Well, nothing else seemed to reach you, so I said maybe we should try to trick you!"

She was afraid he might be angry with her, but he only smiled. "I wonder what would have happened if you yourself had simply asked me."

"Oh, you'd have said no to me even faster than to Olek."

He laughed out loud. "Maybe you're right at that." He pulled her to him again and again held her tight. "But no more. I can't imagine ever saying no to you again."

The disciplined part of her mind couldn't help whispering that there were better reasons for a man to join in the work of the underground than for love. But she had the instinctive wisdom not to say so. She was standing tall and straight beside him now, her inner strength restored, and briefly there seemed to be no trace left in her of the soft clinging she had permitted herself in her moment of weakness, so that he almost felt intimidated. Words from one of the forbidden songs flashed through his mind:

> *Lend us your courage, sisters in struggle,*
> *That we, your brothers, too may be brave. . .*

But he reached for her hand, felt its strong answering pressure and was reassured. He began to cope with his own momentary paralysis. "Will it be possible to reach Olek right away?" he wanted to know. "Because I think there may be a way to help Maryla." A plan was forming in his mind that might or might not work but was certainly worth trying. He would go to Salome. "You know I have relatives with all kinds of connections, even in government. . . ."

She said fervently, "Then may they know the right doors to knock on!" Now they were both intent only on what had to be done. "But it's too late to catch Olek tonight. We'll have to wait till morning. In the meantime we'd better get out of here before someone gets too curious." Their arms around each other, they walked into the street.

Suddenly it occurred to Adam that he was now responsible for this woman who, by asking nothing of him, had bound him to her. "Have you a place to stay tonight? I just realized you can't go back to your own rooms." She admitted she hadn't even thought that far, but only knew she must stay away from Zapiecek and look elsewhere for a night's lodging. "In that case," he announced, "you're coming home with me. Don't argue, it's all settled. My mother will take care of you."

❦ *Seven* ❧

ON THE LONG omnibus ride from Lazienki to his own neighborhood they sat pressed close together, fingers intertwined, silent a good deal of the time. Every once in a while Adam glanced at Wanda, then shook his head like a man trying to shake sleep out of his eyes.

Everything tonight was assuming a dream quality. He had gone out to meet an old friend in trouble, and instead had found love. And now he was taking his love home to his people, he who had never so much as dated a girl in his life. And all this was happening while they were still half-strangers, because in these hurricane days there was no time for the slow voyage of exploration that by rights should belong to all lovers. And yet, he thought, in a way even time itself was on their side, for wasn't it the headlong pace at which things were happening that had jolted him out of his isolation?

Wanda's eyes were closed. He pressed her hand again and felt the instant response, but she neither opened her eyes nor did she speak, as though too emotionally drained to make the effort. Too much had happened to her since the night before and she was letting herself drift. The rhythmic swaying of the horse-drawn bus, the rattle of wheels on wood-block pavement, the clatter of hooves, and the flicker of street lamps all merged into a phantasmagoric lullaby that soothed and rocked her, bringing a measure of quiet. Soon she must force herself to be fully alert once more, clearheaded and practical, for there were plans to be made. But for a little while longer let her remain as she was. Like a child that has stayed up long past its bedtime, she refused to be reached.

"Tomorrow," she heard Adam say, as if from a great distance, "you and Olek and I will go to see my Aunt Salome. If anyone in Warsaw can help Maryla, she can. I know this is hard to believe, but then, she's an unbelievable woman. Let me tell you about her." But her murmured answer was so vague he realized she was incapable of listening.

By the time they reached the Krasinski Gardens she roused a little. She looked up and caught him studying her as though he could not quite believe what he saw. The smoke-gray almond-shaped eyes were filled with wonder and with questions. "Wanda," he whispered, "my Wanda. . ."

"Yes?"

"Nothing. Just . . . Wanda. I love saying your name. It fits my lips."

She smiled, coming suddenly and fully awake, sitting up straighter but still leaning against him. "Adam. Adam, the first man."

Hungry for the touch of each other, they could barely refrain from kissing. But even their intertwined fingers were attracting smiles from the other riders, and Wanda, suddenly painfully self-conscious, tried to snatch her hand away. But he was holding it fast and she did not try very hard.

"I keep thinking of all those times I would start flirting with you and you never even noticed! I used to get so furious. And really the whole trouble all the time was me. I'm not very smart about that sort of thing, I'm afraid. Other girls know just what to say, what to do. But not me. They know dozens of little tricks. . . ."

"Don't ever learn tricks, darling. Don't ever change."

He was remembering the Kronenberg party and how he had pictured his ideal woman, and had a great desire to laugh. He couldn't conceive of Wanda indulging in the thousand little artifices that so charmed him in Salome. With her there would never be any pretense or coyness, no *doubles entendres* to keep him unsure about her true feelings. Love could never be a game to a sister-in-struggle. With her hand securely in his he was experiencing not just male desire but a new inner sense of worthiness and of strength. Tomorrow he would take his place in the ranks of the patriots—and it was all her doing. She had lent him courage and now he, too, felt brave. And he had a great urge to tell her about it, tell her he had just found the missing axis around which his life must revolve, found it where he had least thought to search, and if he recognized it instantly as right and even inevitable that was because it had existed all along, only he'd been too obtuse to see it.

He wanted to tell her all this and much more, but the words seemed grandiloquent and empty. So he just said, "Now that I know I love you everything has become simple. Won't Olek be surprised, though! You know, Olek has always been after me to stop running long enough to find out if I can feel, like other humans."

"I used to wonder myself," she confessed, and they laughed companionably, their heads so close together that each could feel, without touching, the heat of the other's skin.

"Well, now you know." From the more reserved, slightly archaic *you,* common in peasant speech and affected by university students in order to avoid the cumbersome third-person form of address that makes Polish one of the most formal of languages, they had switched quite naturally to the very personal *thou,* reserved for family and intimates. "As you said, between us there must never be any secrets. But you'll have to help me, Wandusia, because it's very hard for me to talk openly, and I don't know how to ask questions. So you'll just have to assume I want to know everything about you, and tell me things."

She was finding his stumbling admissions immensely touching, especially since during all the months he'd been a regular visitor at Zapiecek, during all the nights of talk and discussion, she had never heard him make a personal statement. "You know," she said, "I remember one night particularly. I was terribly angry and upset after you left, and I said to Maryla, 'I bet when that one gets home, he doesn't go to bed like other people—he crawls inside the pages of a book!' "

"Was I really that bad?"

"That bad and worse." And how different, she thought, from Olek with his huge appetites, whose love for Maryla was mixed with the earthy realism of the Vistula waterfront. Olek, she guessed, had probably sampled every experience life had to offer. While Adam—her Adam now, she reminded herself tremulously—hadn't even bitten into the apple yet.

She raised their interlocked hands to brush his against her cheek, not caring who stared at them. And finally she began to talk. By the time they reached their stop Adam knew that in the small town where she was born, her mother still went out one afternoon a week wearing a plumed hat and tippet and much-mended cotton gloves, to leave calling cards at the "best" homes. Only she went on foot because it had been years since she'd had the use of a carriage, and there was never any returning of calling cards.

He also knew that her father just barely kept his head above water by selling off land he'd inherited—heaven forbid he should soil his hands with work!—and that like himself she was the oldest of six children. Like his own, her early youth had been one long relentless round of hard work, mainly lessons given outside the home. Later there'd been summer governess jobs in fine villas where she was treated like one of the servants. But the humiliations could be taken in stride because in the fall she came home with money in her pocket, some of which went to her mother and some for her own schooling.

Her determination to become a doctor dated back to a night when a younger brother died of croup because the local physician had been too busy attending a ball given by the military governor of the province to drive clear across town for a sick child. "I battled the family, battled the priest who threatened me with hell and brimstone if I persisted in what they called 'my unnatural, unwomanly desire.' I was threatened with excommunication and I said I'd risk it if I had to. They prayed over me and burned candles in church, and told me I needn't expect any help— which, of course, they couldn't have given me anyway. I said nothing could change my mind. Then for a while I was really scared—waiting for God to strike me dead. When He didn't, no matter how much I blasphemed, well, I decided He couldn't have much power. That's when I stopped going to church."

Mention of a priest made Adam uncomfortable. A close relationship with a Catholic, even a non-practicing Catholic, was something he had never yet countenanced. "You know I'm a Jew, don't you?" he asked abruptly.

"Of course." She was about to shrug off the subject when a new thought occurred to her, and a wicked little smile made her wan face light up like a skinny urchin's. "And won't *that* scandalize my people when they find out!"

Adam was wondering, a little uneasily, how his own mother would react when he introduced to her a girl whose name was Wanda Borowska. But he said nothing, afraid that if Wanda got so much as a hint of the fact that he anticipated trouble, she might not want to go home with him.

He need not have worried. Bluma took one look at the tense drawn face, the feverish eyes of the girl her son brought into her house and thought only that here was someone in need of a hot meal and a bed. Besides, she was a friend of Adam's—that alone made her welcome. Who she was and what she was scarcely mattered. Explanations could wait.

It was not until later, after she had warmed up a potful of thick barley soup, cut thick slabs of bread and, pushing aside the piled-up books that Viktor and Izidore were studying by the light of the big overhanging lamp, had set two places at one end of the dining table, not until they had eaten and she'd poured tea for everyone and called Jacob to join them and was herself able to sit down with her guest—not until then did she take a second look at the newcomer, and noticed her son looking at her. Then she knew at once that this was no casual acquaintance. And although she had long been telling herself the time for something like this was overdue, the knowledge came as a shock. Adam, her first-born, was in love. Adam would soon belong to someone else entirely. . . .

She glanced at her husband to see whether he, too, had

guessed. But Jacob was too absorbed in what the young people were saying. "Another wave of arrests. . . . The girl I share rooms with, Maryla . . . arrested on such ridiculous evidence. . . ."

Not Jacob alone, but Viktor and Izidore and Idka were hanging on every word of the conversation. Izidore's eyes especially were alight with an excitement his mother had never seen, and she caught him exchanging a secret glance with Idka, the sister so close in age to him they might almost be twins. It was a conspiratorial glance, and it seemed to say, "Imagine, this is going on right under our own roof!" And Bluma sickened with fear, for until today these two had seemed to her little more than children; yet here they were, intensely alive to the politics of resistance, startlingly aware, informed. She tried to pretend she was just imagining things but knew she was lying to herself. And anyway, what did she—what did any parent for that matter—know of the thoughts of children growing into adults?

The sense of impending danger grew sharper the longer she listened. It was there all around her, in the eager eyes, the busy tongues, the young, brave, daring talk at her table. She sighed. She'd heard it all so many times, from her own generation and from those who were already old and tired when her generation was young.

"The Pawiak . . . maybe the Citadel. . . . Tomorrow we'll know, tomorrow we'll see what can be done. But the work can't stop, the work must go on. . . ."

She forced herself to pay close attention, less to the talk itself than to what her intuitive ear might catch of clues to the relationship between Adam and the girl. And as she listened she grew more and more uneasy. Yet it was not the girl's religion that troubled her as Adam had feared, nor yet the fact that Wanda was obviously one of the "new women." Rather Bluma was remembering how she and Jacob, lying awake half one sleepless night, had talked about their son. And she saw how already her predictions were being fulfilled. Whichever way he chooses in life, Adam is bound to travel the hard road, she'd said. And this girl, this Wanda Borowska, was exactly like him. Two peas in a pod. She would never shield him, as most women tend to shield their men, or keep him safe, doing the safe things. Not she. She would travel the hard road with him.

Someone, Bluma could no longer remember who, had once said, "In our country you can't be a self-respecting family and not have at least one member in and out of jail." And it was true. And now it had caught up with them, the day of decision, the day of danger, the day when she must begin to live with an ever-present ache of fear for her children's safety. Today, without warning, it was beginning with Adam. Tomorrow it would be one of the others.

Wanda's voice, controlled yet passionate, seemed to her an echo of her own thoughts. The girl was telling them how it had been in the garrison town where she grew up. "The only difference between the city and the provinces is that out there everything is simpler because you can see it in black and white. You know the enemy face to face, you pretty well know who's the potential informer. Sometimes when I go back for a visit I get the feeling I'm walking into a scene from Gogol's *Inspector General*. Except of course that he was satirizing Russian officials for the Russians themselves, while in our case the corruption is also foreign corruption, and twice as savage."

It was said so knowledgeably—as though this young girl had already lived through a lifetime of the eternal warfare—that Bluma's heart contracted and she no longer saw Wanda as an outsider. But mostly she was thinking of Adam, not her son Adam but Adam the whole man, the man who had just brought his first sweetheart home to his family for shelter and who must do whatever he had to do, just as Wanda was doing, just as later on, inevitably, the other children would. And she understood, painfully but with a kind of new clarity, that no matter how much she trembled for them she hadn't the right ever to try to dissuade them or let her own timidity influence them. The best she could do for them was to cherish them and if possible smooth their way.

"It's getting terribly late," she finally said, speaking in her everyday voice, as though her only concern were household schedules and everyone's comfort, "and tomorrow there's going to be a great deal to do. Let's all go to bed now. Adash, help me set up the extra cot in the girls' room. Come, *Pani* Wanda," she turned to her guest, "I'll show you where you can wash up. By the time you're done the bed will be made. In the morning everything will look better."

❧ *Eight* ❧

ADAM WOKE the next morning to the aroma of fresh coffee, and was astonished to see his brothers' beds empty and the sun already high. He threw back the covers, stretched, then lay for a moment longer savoring a wonderful sense of well-being. He couldn't remember when he had slept so deeply. He felt refreshed, strong, ready for anything.

The events of the previous night came back to him in a rush, and it struck him all over again that Wanda was here under his own roof and that in a few moments he would see her at the breakfast table. Once again, as on the previous evening, he shook his head to clear it of an impossible dream. Then he heard her voice from beyond the closed door and knew that nothing was impossible any more.

Within minutes he was in the dining room.

"I overslept. Someone should have doused me with cold water."

"Whatever for?" his mother said, as though such late company breakfasts were an everyday occurrence. "There's plenty of time, and you've got a long hard day ahead of you."

Wanda only smiled and said good morning. She, too, looked fresh and rested and glowing, and he wished he could go straight to her, take her in his arms and kiss her, on this their first morning together. But that would have to wait. He sat down in the chair next to hers, which had been left vacant for him, and when no one was looking reached for her hand under the tablecloth.

Over coffee and rolls he listened to the conversation his entrance had interrupted. His brothers and the older of his sisters were trying to prepare Wanda for the phenomenon that was their Aunt Salome, and he was startled, as his mother had been the night before, though on another plane, by their sharp adult awareness, their whole clear-eyed approach.

"Uncle Leon likes to call her his child bride, then says he'll probably never stop being amazed how anyone so fragile and pure can do what she can." That was Viktor. Izidore added, "He claims she can move mountains—and sometimes she can. I think it's because it's never even dawned on her that there are some doors on which one doesn't go knocking! In fact, we think she doesn't even knock—she just marches in."

Idka said—and this surprised Adam most of all since generally she was such a quiet person—"We'll be talking to her, wondering if it's at all possible to approach this bureau chief, that government department head or minister, and she'll say, 'But my dears, it's really perfectly simple, he was one of my mother's old boys. . . .'" Idka interrupted herself to explain about the Tworska-Grossglik ménage with its frequently illustrious young boarders. "She'll say, 'He was so in love with me he threatened to kill himself, but I helped him see how silly that would be and now there's nothing, but nothing he won't do for me just so long as I ask him personally, as a very special favor. . . .'" She even managed to mimic Salome's high, fluted voice to perfection, and everyone laughed, even Jacob and Bluma, who probably shouldn't be countenancing such disrespect.

It was Izidore who had the final say. "You'll probably find it hard to believe she's real, but take it from me, she can be very useful. She steps down from her carriage, sweeps past all the flunkeys straight into some sanctum sanctorum, and boom, she's got what she was after. The movement," he added, sounding like an old hand at conspiracy, which this time somehow didn't even surprise Adam, "can use more friends like that."

He pushed back his chair, slung his book bag across his thin shoulders and said he'd better be going. "Last week of school," he commented cheerfully, "then we'll have the summer free for more important matters. Right, Miss Wanda?" He winked at their guest. "Goodbye, good luck, and maybe next time we meet, it'll be on the barricades."

"Izzy!" his mother and father instantly protested. "Watch what you say! Don't you ever talk like that outside!"

The boy gave them a pitying glance. "D'you think I was born yesterday?" The hall door slammed and they heard him running down the stairs, whistling off-key.

Viktor left shortly afterwards, and finally Jacob excused himself to go into his shop. Bluma urged a second cup of coffee on Wanda, and Idka brought more rolls. There was dark buckwheat honey in the comb, which they cut with a knife like runny candy. "Try some, Miss Wanda. You too, Adash. It's delicious, the woman who brings our milk brought it this morning. Her husband raises bees." They munched as they started planning their day.

Adam made sure Wanda memorized Salome's address and arranged to meet her there late in the day. In the meantime she must contact Olek and find out whether he had been able to learn more of what was going on. If he thought it at all wise, she would bring him along to the Grossgliks'. As for Adam, he would drop in during the morning and warn Salome to expect them. He also would try to find Zenon. And, of course, he must keep to his tutoring schedule as if nothing had happened.

He fought down the temptation to cancel all his appointments, stay with Wanda through the day, never for a moment letting her out of his sight. But that could well be a disservice to all of them. It was a rule of the underground never to do in pairs what two could do separately. For one thing, a single person attracted less attention than a couple—one face was easier forgotten than two. For another, if you worked separately you covered twice as much ground. And finally, Wanda would be seeing contacts it was best for him to know nothing about.

They didn't even leave the apartment together. In the early morning the courtyard was always teeming with activity, the men going to their jobs, the women busy with household chores, sweeping stoops, hanging out wash, beating the dust out of carpets. The *struzh,* the eternal concièrge, was at the water pump keeping a weather eye on all comers. It was impossible for a stranger to pass unnoticed at this hour. But later on he would go about his errands, and then Wanda would throw a shawl of Bluma's over her hair and shoulders, and the two of them, armed with straw marketing baskets, would slip off together. To a housewarden all women with marketing baskets looked pretty much alike.

Shortly after noon, Adam rang the bell of the Pozner mansion.

"Miss Maya and Master Marek are in the schoolroom," said the footman who took his battered cap. Wooden-faced and straight out of a Strauss operetta, he had absorbed all the snobbery of the servants of the rich. He was willing to forgive his employers their Jewishness, not because they had converted, which, of course, fooled no one, but because they were millionaires. But this shabby Jew-boy with the reserve of a count made his hackles rise. And Fabian didn't even use the back stairs any more, and neither the master nor the mistress seemed to care! It was enough to make a man want to give notice!

Unaware of the resentment he was stirring up, Adam went to join his charges. The door of the schoolroom stood open. Marek, one leg over the arm of a chair, was sketching a naked woman riding a circus horse—a crude attempt, but unmistakable. Missy as usual had her nose in a book. Glancing over, Adam saw it was a copy of *Salammbô* and his eyebrows shot up: precisely what Missy had hoped for. "Well, teacher," she said, deliberately provocative, "aren't you going to tell me this is nothing for a young lady to be reading?"

Ever since they had been supper partners at the Kronenbergs', she had alternated between flirting with him and doing her best to play the haughty lady, not certain which approach might be the more effective. At the same time she really wanted to have him admire her. Occasionally she even tried to convince herself that she was badly hurt by his coldheartedness, his indifference. Then a streak of honesty would force her to admit she was play-acting, that mainly she was annoyed at not getting her own way—which undermined her performance.

When she saw he wasn't going to make an issue of her choice of reading matter she tried another tactic. "As you see," she smiled archly, "I'm improving my French. Flaubert is a marvelous stylist, don't you think?"

From across the room her brother guffawed. "If you're going to read smutty French novels, then read them—don't apologize!"

Whatever Adam might have said to either of them was cut short by the reappearance of the footman. The Master wished to see *Pan* Fabian in the library without delay.

He saw Missy smile a malicious little half-smile as though she knew something about the summons which no one else did, and he felt suddenly uneasy. Was something wrong? Surely not his work or there wouldn't have been all those periodic raises. Was he perhaps too lenient with his charges? Or did their parents have other plans for them after the summer? Oh God, he thought, don't let the lessons stop now, not now when we still need the money so badly! Sweating uncomfortably, he excused himself and walked out of the room.

In the library Maurice Pozner greeted him from behind his massive mahogany desk. "Good morning, my boy. Or I should say, good day. Did the children tell you you're staying to dinner? No? Just like them! Always forgetting, thinking about nothing but their own concerns! Anyway, I hope you can join us," he finished, jovial but perfectly aware that to someone like his children's tutor an invitation to his table was in the nature of a royal command. "I hope this isn't disrupting any of your other plans."

If he were firing me, there would be no dinner invitation, thought Adam. He breathed easier and said he was free until well into the afternoon. Pozner nodded. "Good, good. In that case sit down, sit down." He leaned back in his chair, playing with the heavy gold watch chain stretching across the expanse of his London-tailored vest. "There are some matters I wish to discuss with you."

As he talked, Adam studied him. A large, paunchy man—his son took after him in heaviness of body—the great financier-industrialist had a strongly modeled face, a prominent nose that barely escaped being bulbous, heavy eyebrows, and a walrus mustache. His head was clean-shaven, as was the fashion among the older men of the day, giving it the look of a large cannonball. But otherwise there was nothing military about him. His expression was deceptively benign. His bearing—strangely in contrast to his wife's, Adam always thought—was that of a *grand seigneur*.

The young tutor sat gingerly on the edge of the chair his employer had indicated, waiting for the conversation to start. Common sense told him there was nothing to be afraid of. Or had Missy's father perhaps become aware of Missy's silly attempts to flirt with him? It was the only other thing he could think of.

His eyes stared unseeing at the flower garlands on the magnificent Aubusson rug covering the library floor. "Cigar?" he heard Pozner ask. "You don't smoke? Very sensible. Very. Someday you must tell me how you escaped. Curse of my life. Schnapps? Don't tell me you don't drink either?"

The "schnapps" was seven-star Martell, which Adam tasted that day for the first time and which later he was to adopt for his own. *Pan* Pozner raised his glass in a quick toast. *"Prosit, prosit, my boy."* He sipped the golden-brown liquor. Adam sipped his. No, this certainly did not seem like the prelude to trouble.

After a moment Maurice cleared his throat. "I presume," he began, "you've been wondering why I sent for you. Well, I'll not beat around the bush. I've been observing you, I like what I see, I have confidence in you. So now suppose you tell me what you plan to do with yourself once you have a degree?"

It wasn't in the least what Adam expected, and it took him by surprise. He found himself thinking wryly that any accurate answer would have to wait until he and Wanda had a chance to talk about the future. Then he said something vague about hoping to find employment in a good law firm in need of a diplomate clerk, and let it go at that.

Pozner nodded. "Hm. Yes. Just as I thought." Then he lowered his voice. "Obviously, you haven't heard any of the rumors."

"Rumors?" Adam repeated, totally at a loss. "What rumors?"

Pozner said, elaborately casual. "Of course this may be just gossip, but there's been talk that a new edict is imminent. I have it from an acquaintance in St. Petersburg, a man rather highly placed, that restrictions are to be placed on the right of Jews to practice law. Law school quotas are to be made more stringent—though, of course, that needn't worry you, since you've already been accepted. However," he improvised, deliberately making the future sound as ominous as possible, "no one really seems to know whether or not the regulations are to be retroactive. So you see, there's really no telling what'll happen to men like you, who're still in school."

For a moment Adam just sat there immobilized, staring. "What you're really saying is there's a chance I might never be able to—" He broke off, then exploded, "The swine! The lousy bastards!" And his anger had little to do with any impending threat to his own future, since from the very first a career in law had been only a lukewarm choice of livelihood. It was that the whole idea was monstrous, a denial of the last vestiges of freedom of choice, of personal dignity for his people. Besides, if this year the government forbade Jews the practice of law, next year it might be medicine or engineering or architecture. Or clerking in food stores, for that matter. "The filthy bastards!" he said again.

Well pleased, Pozner suppressed a smile. "Quite so, my boy." He was trying to gauge the young tutor's reaction and draw the proper conclusions. *This is the day,* he thought, *when I can make him feel indebted to me for life. Even if it's all a false alarm, even if he should never need my help, he won't forget I offered it.* And he congratulated himself on having so skillfully manipulated the information to suit his own purposes.

Actually, he had had to stretch the truth a little—a little, but not much. The edict was indeed in the offing and would soon be made public, as vicious a piece of legislation as ever came out of St. Petersburg. But Pozner's informant had said nothing about retroactivity—only that a cut-off date would be announced for accepting Jews into law school. For the rest, the purpose of the measure was clear. It would become the latest building block in the infamous Black Hundred master plan devised by Pobiedo-nostzev and the Holy Synod for "liquidating" Russia's Jewish problem once and for all. One-third starvation, one-third emi-gration, one-third assimilation—the new law would fit this basic formula with double-edged precision. Not only would it succeed in depriving future generations of Jews of lawyers of their own faith; it would also hold out to the educated elite an additional inducement to convert.

Pozner waited until the silence in the room became appropriately oppressive. Then, assuming that the news he'd just dispensed had had the desired effect on Adam, he took his strategy one step further. "I can see," he said, sounding sympathetic, "that you hadn't an inkling. But that's the way life is." He puffed on his cigar. "Call it one of the more refined cruelties His Imperial Majesty subjects us to. How very satisfying it must be not to let one's victims be forewarned! What a delicious joke, to let young people like yourself work hard, build up their hopes, then find everything tumbling around their ears like a house of cards!"

"Yes," Adam nodded. "Yes." He was thinking that however reluctant a choice the law had been for him, if there was any chance of all this resulting in a body blow to his future earning capacity he had better reconsider, in practical terms. "What would you advise me to do, *Pan* Pozner?" he finally asked. "Wouldn't it be a waste of time under the circumstances to continue working for a diploma?"

"Now that you ask," Maurice refilled their glasses, gazing into his as into a crystal ball, "I wouldn't say so. And for a number of reasons. First, there's always the chance—slim, I'll grant you, but a chance nevertheless—that the rumor is only a rumor after all. Secondly the timetable hasn't been set yet, so maybe you're in the clear. And finally," doling out a carefully weighed initial crumb of solace, "a resourceful young man with a diploma and, I hope, a brilliant school record is always able to manipulate. So now, my young friend," here his voiced dropped to warmly confidential, "I'll come to the real point, the real reason I called you in here. I wanted you to know that should the need arise, I can always find room for you in my business. For one thing, I've enough legal work to keep a man busy full time. And if worse comes to worst, there are other alternatives. For instance," he paused dramatically, "how would you like to go into the cotton business?"

"Me?" Adam said. "In business? What do I know about cotton?"

"Nothing," Maurice laughed. "And that's the least of it, for I can teach you. On the other hand you've other qualities that an employer values. You're honest, hardworking, conscientious. A bit impractical, perhaps, an idealist—but that will pass. If my own son were in the least bit like you, believe me, you wouldn't be sitting here now, drinking my cognac. Or if I could be sure my daughter would marry someone I'd want for a junior partner. Trouble is, I can't afford to wait and find out. So better I should train my own man."

Adam's hand shook so visibly he was obliged to put his glass down. At that he miscalculated, nearly snapping the stem as it hit the marble top of the chairside table. Martell sloshed on the priceless rug. A sunbeam danced through the half-drawn draperies. Somewhere in another part of the house a silver bell tinkled, announcing dinner.

Adam rose to his feet but Pozner was in no hurry.

"They'll wait for us. As I was saying, I just wanted you to be forewarned. I know your circumstances, that you have heavy responsibilities and can't afford to be long without work. And obviously you can't plan to be a tutor all your life!" He chuckled at his own joke. "Of course, as I said, this may all come to nothing. But in the event things do go wrong, my offer holds good. They say of cotton that all around the world it's king. Egyptian cotton and American cotton and cotton brought via the Caucasus from all over the Near East. As you know, I supply half the textile mills of Poland. I have the city of Lodz in my pocket. Frankly, my boy, I never did quite picture you as a lawyer—you lack the devious temperament. But put yourself in my hands, and I'll make you rich. How does that strike you, eh, Fabian? Getting to be a rich man, a *really* rich man?"

Inwardly Adam was not so bedazzled as Maurice had hoped, for the whole proposition seemed unreal to him. But he had the presence of mind not to say so. "To tell the truth," he hedged, "right now nothing strikes me hard—I'm not even thinking clearly. You'll have to forgive me, *Pan* Pozner, my mind is in a whirl. The last twenty-four hours have been a strange time for me . . . strange and . . . unsettling. So much so that I'm not doing justice to what you said. . . ."

Pozner chose to interpret this as the reaction of a young man overwhelmed by his own good fortune. He became more benign than ever. "Relax, relax, my boy, you don't have to give me an answer this minute! Certainly not while we're both hungry! Business, like armies, marches on its stomach. So now shall we go downstairs? Food will restore you."

As they entered the dining room, he caught his wife's eye and signaled to her with a wink and a nod that everything had gone off in fine order. Leave it to Pozner, the gesture seemed to say, to invest shrewdly not just in cotton and securities, but in human beings.

❦ *Nine* ❧

ADAM FINALLY managed to get away from the Pozner mansion, still in plenty of time to keep his appointment at the Grossgliks'. As he walked the short distance from Aleje Ujazdowskie he was feeling slightly lightheaded. *I've just been asked to become a rich man,* he kept telling himself as though the proposition concerned someone else. *Ridiculous!* He could hardly wait to tell Wanda about it and hear her laugh.

At first he hadn't been able to understand why his interview with Pozner, significant as it was in so many ways, had made so little impact on him. Now he knew it was because all during it, with all his being, he'd been straining toward Wanda. And even the news about the impending anti-Jewish edict, shocking though it was, had struck him mainly as part of the overall outrage they were exposed to. The monster that threatened to deny him a livelihood was the same monster whose tentacles had caught up Maryla. His own potential predicament, since nothing could really be done about it for some time to come, was, under the circumstances, secondary.

As for his employer's offer, he was simply unable to consider it seriously. "How would I like to be a rich man? Well, how would I like to grow a second head?" The single-minded pursuit of wealth, he thought, was something he would never understand.

It had rained briefly during the dinner hour, one of those summer downpours over almost as soon as it starts, and all up and down the avenue there was a fresh fall of acacia blooms and the yellow-green blossoms of lindens. After the early heat the air was washed clean, spring-fresh and fragrant. As he passed block after block of fine apartment houses it occurred to him that should he accept Pozner's offer and become successful, he would eventually be able to move his family out of the Nalewki flat, perhaps even free his father of the hair-goods business. And there would be money for Wanda to study till she became a first-rate doctor. This was what she wanted most in life and this was what he might make possible. He would send her to the best university in Europe. . . . But no, if she became his wife how could she leave him for years on end?

It was at this point that the fantasy lost its meaning. He could hear Wanda's laughter and Olek's more sober response. "Never trust a rich man bearing gifts," Olek would warn. "The old man must want to buy you. Why? God knows what's in a rich man's head! But if you ask me, it smells of a bad bargain. Don't be naive, Adash, old friend. . . ."

So on a conscious level at least, he dismissed Maurice Pozner as thoroughly as he himself had been dismissed, and the rest of the way to his uncle's house his thoughts were all on Wanda. By the time he rounded the corner of Count Berg Street his heart was racing, and not from the exertion of walking.

He was the first to arrive at the Grossgliks'. The maid Julia— *Miss* Julia, now that she was no longer young and had been promoted to housekeeper—met him at the door and said Madam was in the drawing room and to go right in. As always when he walked into her presence he was struck afresh by Salome's beauty, as though her cameo-like face couldn't possibly be quite so perfect as he remembered it. Perhaps because her marriage had never been blessed with children she seemed never to change, neither aging nor putting on flesh like other women, her expression ever serene, her lips set in the permanent half-smile which was good for discouraging wrinkles.

At the moment she was sitting very straight, as girls of her day had been trained to sit, her dark head on its long slender neck inclined over an embroidery frame. She was absorbed in selecting just the right shade of gossamer ribbon for the elaborate rococo flower motif she was working on. She tried first one combination of colors, then another. The light from the bay window made a hazy aura behind her, and she looked like a woman Botticelli might have painted had he worked with Palestinian models rather than North Italians.

Adam had the fleeting impression that she was aware of his presence well before acknowledging it. When it suited her, she raised her head and bestowed on her nephew the full radiance of her smile.

"I'm so glad you came early, there'll be time for a chat. Izidore warned us this morning you've invited some friends to tea. How absolutely delightful of you."

It was one of her special talents to be able to give the most commonplace statements a gracious little twist, somehow conveying the impression that in the doing of a favor she was the one being favored. Even now, when under the circumstances the pretense was just a bit silly, she couldn't resist working her charm on Adam exactly as she did on her husband every day of their lives.

He bent over her hand, then said rather gruffly, "The friends who're coming aren't exactly company. They're in deep trouble and I was hoping you could help." Quickly he went on to outline what had happened. "Olek Piotrowski's fiancée—you've heard me speak of Olek, he's my oldest friend—was arrested night before last, her place raided. We think she's locked up in the Pawiak."

He added that as of the previous night there had been no word of the prisoner. But Olek and the girl who shared her flat, whom for some reason the gendarmes hadn't even bothered, would be here soon with, perhaps, some fresh news.

"This other girl's name is Wanda, Wanda Borowska, and last night, just to be safe, I took her home with me. I wasn't going to let her stay the night alone in that empty house. Though I must say she herself has been wonderfully brave. So clear-headed and calm. . . ."

His voice took on a tone that wasn't lost on Salome. "A special friend of yours?" she asked, all innocence.

Adam let that pass. "About Maryla," he said. "We don't even

know what the charge is or what can be done. But as my mother told Wanda this morning, if anyone will be able to help, that person will surely be you."

"Your mother flatters me." Automatically, Salome began the usual graceful disclaimer. But the stark look on Adam's face conveyed such a sense of urgency that her drawing-room manner dropped from her like a superfluous garment. "Darling, of course. You know you can depend on me. I shan't leave a stone unturned, I promise you."

Miss Julia came to the door asking whether to serve tea now or later, and as if by prearrangement they cut their conversation short. Miss Julia might be an old, trusted, devoted retainer, but the less known by the fewer people, the better. "We'll wait until our other guests arrive," Salome decided quickly.

The little French gilt clock in the Louis XVI curio cabinet chimed the hour, and Adam, more and more restless, began pacing the floor wishing Wanda and Olek would hurry.

"Don't worry so, dear heart," Salome soothed. "They'll get here." And to distract him she began to talk about the man she thought would be the right person to see. "That nice young man who used to board with us before I ever married your uncle. One of Mama's favorites . . . what was his name? Only dear me, he's not such a young man any more! Why, he's older than I am! Maryan . . . Maryan. . . You'd know in a minute if I could only be more explicit. . . . He's the Governor-General's right hand now. . . . Maryan . . . oh, yes, Count Maryan Walewski. Descended from *that* Countess Walewska. . ." Her voice dropped discreetly. "You know, the one Napoleon fancied. . . ."

Adam rather wished she would get to the point, but Salome was in no hurry. "Well, so now we've got him placed. And I daresay you don't approve—naturally idealists like you think of men who collaborate with the Russians as traitors. But I always feel that if one needs a favor, the best thing to do is go to those with the best connections, regardless. And those," she added, "who you know will be willing to put themselves out for your sake. Like my friend Maryan. He was so in love with me, poor boy, he actually tried to persuade me to elope—though I had better sense than that, thank heaven! And later he was forced into a miserable marriage of convenience. Naturally he's kept only the warmest, most beautiful memories of our romance. So now if I ask for a favor, he listens."

Adam pulled out his old watch, which after all the years was still doing yeoman service. "At this point," he said dryly, "I'd accept favors from the devil himself."

She nodded approval. "I'm glad you're being realistic."

He didn't answer, just walked over to the bay window to watch the street, and his restlessness was so apparent she wished she could do something to comfort him.

The doorbell rang at last and Adam in his relief rushed into the foyer ahead even of Miss Julia. "Wanda, you're here. . . . I was getting worried. And Olek. . ." He drew them inside and quickly closed the drawing room doors.

Forever afterwards, even after he learned to see Salome from the vantage point of mature experience, he remained grateful to her for the way on this one occasion she very simply shed her role of charming hostess, cutting through the amenities and the small talk which ordinarily she considered mandatory. Even the presence of another, younger woman, and one so obviously important to Adam, made no difference.

"First of all, my dears, you must tell me the whole story right from the beginning," she began without preamble. "Leave nothing out. Sometimes it's the little details that really make the difference—little details that can make a story so appealing. . . ."

Olek nodded, and Adam saw to his amazement that these two understood each other perfectly. "Adam already told you about the search," Olek said, "but let's go over everything again exactly as it happened. Maryla and Wanda were having a study group at their house—they both belong to the Floating University as I think you know—and they had tea and food on the table to make it look like a social occasion. Ordinarily that doesn't fool the gendarmes, they pull everyone in; but they didn't bother the others—not even Wanda. So the study group can't be what the search was about."

He was sitting stiff and uncomfortable on the edge of a small gilt chair that looked as though at any moment it might collapse under him. His big, raw wrists stuck out inches beyond the cuffs of his ill-fitting jacket, his boots made smudges on the rug, and in his nervousness he kept twisting the cap Miss Julia hadn't had the chance to take from him. Had he held a horseshoe in those powerful hands, he would be bending it double. Now if only those hands could have closed around the neck of some gendarme!

"We've managed to find out where she is. In 'Serbia.' " Serbia was the name of the women's wing of the Pawiak, originally a military hospital during the Turkish-Serbian-Russian War. "Tonight's her third night there, and she doesn't even have a toothbrush or a piece of soap. They wouldn't let me send in a package—I'm not a relative, you see. And I didn't have the ten rubles to bribe the guard." He swallowed hard, mauling his cap as though it were the prison guard's own person.

Salome asked if they had any information on what Maryla was being accused of. It was Wanda's turn to explain, since she alone among those in the room had been present at the time of the arrest. "They said they were taking her in on suspicion. That it was part of a roundup of some sort in preparation for the Grand Duke Paul's visit next week. The authorities are anxious to forestall student demonstrations, so they're looking for *potential* troublemakers. Or so they said. But all they found was some old family letters." Suddenly her face crumpled and she looked as though she were about to cry. "I told her and *told* her," she wailed, "that she should burn them . . . that she was being dangerously sentimental. . ."

"Hush, Wandusia," Adam whispered, patting her hand.

Olek said in a hoarse voice, "They were from a cousin she loved dearly. He died in exile. He was my friend too—in fact, it was through him that we met."

"Well," Salome asked reasonably, bringing them back to the business in hand, "were the letters significant? Incriminatory in any way?"

Olek and Wanda, both of whom had read them, agreed they were not. "Mostly family talk. But his name was on them, and that was enough."

"And you're sure," Salome continued probing, "you'd swear on a stack of Bibles that they found nothing else?"

"Not unless they planted something themselves. You see"—
Olek pushed back his chair, crossed the room quickly, and unexpectedly threw open the foyer door. Satisfied that no one was listening on the other side, he relaxed a little. "You see, we all
knew there were demonstrations planned for next week, but not
by our organization. That's all anarchist stuff and leads nowhere.
A lot of heads broken and nothing accomplished. And so to answer
your question, yes, I can swear on *two* stacks of Bibles. But go tell
that to a deputy of the Tsar, and he a Russian Orthodox bastard,
begging your pardon. . . ."

"My friends," Salome said in a voice like shattering crystal,
"that is precisely what I propose to do—tell it to a deputy of
the Tsar! And now stop worrying, my children. Tomorrow morning, for today it's already late, I intend to drop in on Count
Walewski unannounced. . . ."

When she added that within twenty-four hours she expected to
have Maryla safely home, they stared at her as though she had
taken leave of her senses.

"How can you be so sure?"

Olek asked bluntly, "But aren't you jeopardizing your own
safety? Aren't you in the least afraid?"

Salome actually giggled. "Afraid of Maryan? Oh, my dear,
don't be silly! He'll be flattered beyond words!" Then, serious
again, "Just the same, if I were you I'd start making arrangements to take your girl out of the city. As they say, the Warsaw
climate probably won't be healthy for her, nor for any of you, for
a while. At least not until the Grand Duke has concluded his
visit. And now, my dears, shall we all have tea?"

❦ *Ten* ❧

NONE OF THEM ever knew what black magic Salome worked on her once-susceptible count, but the following evening, just as the prisoners lined up for their supper of thin soup and moldy bread, the Pawiak gates clanged open for Maryla. Knotted into a kerchief she carried a toothbrush, a comb, and a piece of soap. Her purse, with whatever money had been in it, was gone. So was her enamel lapel watch and the tiny gold buttons she'd worn in her ears since childhood. But these were small matters. She was free.

Olek was waiting for her on the nearest corner. When he saw her come out he ran to meet her, arms open wide. Tall as she was, he swept her up off the ground.

"I've just found out how much I love you," he said in a rare outburst of unashamed emotion. "You're my good right arm and all of my heart."

"But what happened?" she questioned, still not quite believing her incredible good luck. "How did you manage? You're sure they didn't let me out just so I can lead them to . . . the others?"

"Nothing of the sort. We find," he grinned broadly, "that we've connections in high places."

"Stop making fun of me."

"I'm not. It's the truth."

"Olek, talk sense!"

"Well, it *is* the truth. You've Adam Fabian to thank. Just as we were beginning to think we'd never get you out, up he comes with this relative, this beautiful piece of fluff who knows just about everyone from the Governor-General down and doesn't know enough to be scared to ask favors. She'd flirt with the devil himself if she met him face to face—and get the best of him!"

Maryla laughed for the first time. "It hardly sounds real."

He nodded. "I know. But you'll see for yourself. I'm taking you over to her house right now."

She started to protest. "Olek, I can't go like this! I'm filthy. I probably have lice. I must get back to my place and strip and bathe and wash my hair. . . ."

He said she would be doing all that at the Grossgliks'. "It's all arranged. You're not to go near Zapiecek. And that's orders."

"What do you mean?"

He began to explain what they'd been advised to do. Both she and Wanda were to move bag and baggage out of their attic, and the sooner the better. "Wanda has already brought a box of your things to this *Pani* Grossglik's, then she and Adam will take care of everything else."

Maryla, who could not remember having cried since she was a baby, suddenly felt her eyes beginning to sting. "Lend me your handkerchief, mine was stolen." She blew her nose hard. "Bless them," she said, all choked up. "Adam Fabian of all people! Imagine! Who'd have suspected it!"

They celebrated that night, the four of them, with a trip down the Vistula on a sand barge belonging to one of Olek's innumerable relatives. They brought a picnic supper in hampers—steamed crayfish and dilled cucumbers in sour cream, fresh crusty bread, cheese and apples, vodka and wine. Olek's cousin piloted the craft, an occasional thrust of his long pole keeping them on course as they drifted slowly downstream through the broad, shallow reaches of the gray river. Warsaw winked from one bank, Praga from the other. After a while they began to sing.

They began with *The Song of the Vistula Bargemen*, familiar from childhood, inoffensive in content, safe:

> *Gliding down the river, down our native waters,*
> *God be with us, brothers, till we're safe in Danzig. . .*

But once past city limits, other songs took its place. First the drinking songs, *Gaudeamus Igitur* and *Savor the Golden Hours.* Then *The Song of the Philarets:*

> *Shed your worry, shed your sorrow,*
> *Let's not fret about tomorrow.* . .

But if you knew your history you knew that the Philarets had been a fraternity of doomed heroes and banished poets—men like Mickiewicz and Czeczot and Zan—banded together in the early days of the resistance. And then for your ears the brave, gay words acquired a deeper significance.

Still farther out, the commercial wharves left behind and the river banks unpeopled now and greenly wooded, they at last felt free to raise their voices in forbidden fighting songs. They sang *Poland Is Not Yet Lost.* They sang *The Smoke of Ruins* and *Whirlwinds of Danger.* They sang *The Red Banner.*

> *Lend us your courage, sisters in struggle,*
> *That we, your brothers, too, may be brave.* . .

And Adam's arm tightened around Wanda's shoulders and Olek held Maryla close. And the songs of joy and heartbreak and the songs of patriot and partisan and the songs of labor merged into one great paean of protest as the music rose and swelled and floated out on the warm summer wind.

How they had all come to know the words, from whom they had learned, none could have really said. Only that it was in their blood, part of them, part of their heritage and strength, of what gave them courage and created the unbreakable bond between each of them and the land.

At the Grossgliks', Maryla had said very little about her experience with the police. Now at last she was ready to talk. She spoke of the brutish, stupid, snarling guards and of the grapevine that went into operation the moment a newly arrested "political" arrived in jail.

"I've learned a very important lesson from all this," she also told them. "It's about fear. You all know how, most of the time, no matter how brave we think we are we're really scared of getting caught. Well, once a person really does get arrested, something happens: you stop being afraid. In fact, you become very calm. I suppose it's the anger that sustains you—it's hate for the system that keeps you from falling apart. That, and what you feel for the other prisoners. You actually begin to see that you're not alone facing the guards, you're aware you have a responsibility to your cellmates, that you have to sustain each other. So you help each other remember this isn't the end of the world. And pretty soon you realize it really isn't, not by a long shot!"

They listened, a little awed by her, and very still. Olek, standing behind her now, pressed the length of her body against his. Adam and Wanda drew even closer together. The bargeman continued to pole and steer by turns, but his attention was not on what he did.

"It's the anger that you feel most keenly," Maryla went on, "because you really begin to see how much those bullies *enjoy* pushing us around. They even pretend they don't understand a word of what you say. Prisoners are supposed to speak only in Russian, and never mind whether they know the language or not." She took a sip of wine, savored it, took another. "There were women in there who've waited a year, two years, without a trial. Some never have visitors any more—they're the ones who lose hope. And suddenly more than wanting your own freedom you want to help them—help them believe that outside there are still thousands who haven't given up the good fight. . . ."

Olek whispered, his voice rough and shaking, "My own brave wonderful girl. . . ."

Maryla shrugged. "Let me tell you, I didn't always *feel* very brave! I shook in my boots." Then, in a deliberately cheerful voice, "So now let's drink to a better world. And isn't it time one of you fellows spelled our bargeman? Olek, your cousin's arms must be falling off. . . ."

Coming back much later, as they rowed hard against the current, they held a strategy session. The city was swarming with Russian soldiers in gala uniform. In addition, for every uniformed man there were several members of the secret police. Without such protection a Grand Duke's life wasn't worth a broken kopek if he ventured onto subjugated territory, or so Lloyd's of London had informed the Tsar known hopefully to his Polish subjects as Nicholas the Second and Last. Every precaution was being taken against demonstrators. This was true of Russia proper, doubly true of other provinces, and triply true of Poland, especially the capital.

"For myself, I'd feel better if Maryla never even went back to town tonight. But since that can't be managed, she's going home with me. And tomorrow we'll think of something. It's almost vacation time—who'll notice if she drops out of the study circle a little early?"

"We could both go to my family for July and August," Wanda suggested, but without enthusiasm. "They've never approved of us but they're not informers either."

She was voted down. In a town as small as theirs, they would be too conspicuous. Besides, Maryla's drunken father might decide to make trouble.

"The safest place I know is my grandfather's farm beyond Lowicz," Olek finally said. "And I think you'd best come with us, Wandusia. The sooner both of you quit the city, the better."

From the stern, Olek's cousin contributed the information that he knew a reliable drayman who wouldn't even charge them for the trip provided they bought the oats to feed his nag. If his cart were piled high with hay, who'd search for books and papers underneath? "For the rest, just wear peasant skirts and shawls, and no one will give you a second glance."

"The way no one looks at a woman going to market with a basket," Wanda laughed, recalling how she'd left Adam's house the morning before, with his mother. "Sure there's room for me at the farmstead, Olek?"

"One more, one less—in the country who's counting! Besides, you don't really think we'd let you stay in Zapiecek alone?"

"It's just. . . ," she answered, looking at Adam while she spoke to Olek, "I hadn't thought of leaving right now." Her heart was in her eyes.

Adam sighed. "You know how welcome you'd be at my mother's house. But it just wouldn't be wise."

"I do know, Adash. I understand." They all did. An overnight guest was one thing, but to have Wanda stay at the Nalewki address on a more or less permanent basis would simply mean inviting more trouble. Government regulations demanded that any lodger—any visitor, in fact, who stayed twenty-four hours—must hand over his passport to the *struzh* for registration at the local police precinct. And while a five-ruble note slipped into the man's hand might result in a convenient oversight, it was always risky, especially in the case of a young, attractive woman, and one so obviously non-Jewish, in a Jewish district. "I'll do it Olek's way," Wanda finally agreed.

There remained the problem of packing up whatever the girls wanted to take with them from the Zapiecek attic. And again it was Olek who decided how this should be done.

"Adam and I could easily take care of everything. But two men going up to a place rented by two women wouldn't be too smart either. Suppose you, Wanda, and you, Adam, get it done between you. If you enter the building with your arms around each other, you'll be like the woman with the marketing basket. A pair of lovers are by definition invisible. . . ."

So it was arranged that they pack in the night. Then, at daybreak, the drayman would load up his cart and drive in the direction of Zhelazna Brama, the Iron Gate, at the city line. "And while he's paying his toll he'll see two peasant girls anxious to get back to their village after selling their produce at market. He'll offer them a lift in exchange for a pound of butter. . . ."

Everything was timed with careful precision. Adam and Wanda reached Zapiecek after dark, yet early enough so that there was no need to ring for the *struzh* to unlock the house gate. For the rest, there was no need for pretense or play-acting. If anyone did notice them as they started their steep climb to the attic, he only saw a pair of lovers with their arms tight about each other, their cheeks touching, their eyes eager.

Adam could feel his heart hammer against his ribs, but not from exertion. "My darling," he kept murmuring against Wanda's warm hair, "my dearest darling. . ." And the words were a litany, they were blessing and prayer. When finally they reached the top he took her key and turned it in the rusty lock, and for the first time they were alone together with a door between them and the rest of the world.

The attic rooms were as the police had left them: every drawer open, the curtain torn off the corner shelves that had served as cupboard, the beds ripped apart, pillows and feather quilts slashed. From an overturned glass tea had dribbled onto the green baize table cover, staining it dark brown. Books and papers littered every conceivable surface.

"Welcome to my happy home, Adash," Wanda said bitterly. "Pretty, isn't it?" Trembling, she turned to him, and without a word he took her in his arms.

They clung and kissed. In this room that had been violated and now seemed an enemy wilderness, they each felt a terrible need for the comfort of the other's body. Yet they were both so new to love they felt strange with one another, shy and self-conscious. "I . . . I had best get down to work," Wanda stammered, slipping out of Adam's arms, and started to pull the hatpins out of her hat. Then out of habit she went to hang it on its accustomed peg among the debris in the corner. "It shouldn't take long. We want to be out of here before they lock up at midnight."

Not knowing how to be of use, he sat on a vandalized cot while she went methodically about her tasks, checking drawers and shelves. She took down and folded the few clothes she and Maryla owned. Adam, watching her, was experiencing a piercing sense of intimacy. With every movement she was uncovering something of her everyday life, of those hours in every human being's daily routine that should and must remain private.

When she started to strip the bed on the opposite wall, suddenly he felt like a husband watching his wife dismantle their home, watching her strip the nest so that it might be put together again, safe and warm, in another spot. "Isn't there something I could be doing for you?"

"Not really."

When she was done with the other bed she came over to where he sat. He started to get up but she motioned him to sit still.

"Never mind, we'll leave this until last." There were still books to sort, there were letters and papers.

For a while they worked side by side in silence, cramming everything into cardboard boxes which Adam carefully secured with twine, until finally there was nothing left to pack save only the bed on which he had been sitting. The spread had been so badly ripped it was not worth saving. The gaping featherbeds and pillows Wanda secured as best she could with safety pins. "My sheets were ready for laundering anyway," she tried to joke.

It came to him then that this was the bed where for over a year she had slept alone night after night, dreaming dreams he knew nothing about. A rumpled nightgown lay there as if to prove it, and the thin white stuff seemed to him warm with the imprint of her body. He stood staring down at it, and felt his own body burning, felt the blood rushing to his face.

"My darling," he said again as though this were the only word in his vocabulary. And again pulled her to him, then slowly sank down with her onto the creaking springs.

As an extra precaution they had been working by the light of a single candle, of which only a stub remained. Outside it had grown completely dark. A lone lantern illuminating the courtyard gave the illusion of moonlight. On the steps of the house opposite, someone sat playing *Sorrento* on a harmonica.

"Someday," Adam whispered, "we shall be in a house of our own, and there will be no fear. Someday. . ."

"Don't even make such promises," she whispered back, "the waiting might be too long! We've wasted too much time already. . . . All those months when I . . . when we might have. . . And who knows if there'll even be a tomorrow for us. . . ."

"Are you afraid, my love?"

"Only that we may be separated. Suppose they arrest me and you're left alone. . . ."

"Don't say it! Don't even think it! Think only about the here and now. . . ." His fingers twisted into her hair, his mouth covered hers. Then his hands began to travel downward, tracing her face, her neck, touching her thinly covered breasts.

She kissed him back, the newness of their love no longer a barrier. Fumbling and awkward, he found the buttons on her blouse. She did not try to stop him. But there were so many little buttons and he had never undressed a woman before. He was lost. "Darling, help me. . ."

She did. There was about her no false modesty, no coyness. The blouse fell away, then the corset-cover and the petticoats. The long lines of her body finally lay revealed, the dark skin with the woman fragrance offered itself for kissing.

Adam tore at his own clothes. Free of them, he came back to her. He buried his face in the hollow of her throat and for a long moment breathed her in without moving. Then his lips started tracing the swell of a small taut breast to the hard nipple, flew down the soft flanks and over the hard young belly and down the thighs.

She responded to his every touch, arching her back, guiding him.

"How beautiful you are," he whispered in awe. "Nothing in the whole world is so beautiful as your body. . . ."

"Adam," she whispered back, saying his name over and over. "Adash. My dearest. My love. . ."

After a while they slept, woke, made love again and again drifted off. The candle flickered and finally died. The harmonica player gave up and went home. From the distance came the clatter of hooves and wheels rumbling over cobblestones.

They continued to lie there, absorbed in one another, Wanda's hair spilling warm and soft over Adam's naked shoulder. Until finally it was she who said, "We mustn't stay any longer. It isn't safe."

He stirred, sighing. "If only I could say to my people tonight, 'This is your new daughter.' But I can't, not yet, not the way things are. You understand that, don't you, dearest?"

"Of course I understand. Don't worry so!" Then a new thought struck her. "But won't your people hate it when you marry a . . . *goyka?*"

"*Shikse,*" he corrected, laughing and glad of something to laugh at. "You might as well start learning the right words, my *shikse* bride! But to answer your question—no, I think they already know and have accepted you. Because that's the way they are, both of them."

Wanda and Maryla left Warsaw the following morning without further incident. But the city continued restive. There were more searches, more arrests in the middle of the night. Then a peaceful demonstration in Theater Square turned into a bloody massacre. Mounted cossacks charged the parading crowds from side streets, trampling them down, *naghaikas* raining blows on the heads of men, women, and children alike. Skulls were broken. Several of the young leaders were arrested and sentenced to hang.

Olek Piotrowski was suspect not only because of his connection with Maryla but in his own right. Adam, for all they knew, might be suspect also. "Come away with me," Olek began to urge him. "A little country air is the best thing in the world for you right now."

"You mean I should drop everything and just go? How about my teaching schedule? I don't see how I can drop it so soon. . . ."

"Look," Olek interrupted with unconcealed impatience. "Suppose the 'violets' get you? What'll happen to your schedule then?"

Adam did not answer at once. The sudden need to make all these unaccustomed decisions was unsettling. For the first time he was becoming aware how completely and irrevocably his life was being rechanneled.

Only a week ago, until that evening in Lazienki Park, he'd been a free agent. He had actually had a choice: to be or not to be part of the movement. Then he'd discovered a Wanda he had not known, and everything changed. He, Adam Fabian, the eternal onlooker, had become a participant in something so vast it was all-engulfing, yet so personal he did not feel engulfed.

He knew by now that it was not love alone he had discovered. Was it Shakespeare who once wrote, *No man is an island?* No, it was some other English poet whose name he had once known briefly. *I've been an island all my life,* he thought in wonderment, *and now I'm part of a great land mass.* . . . . And he knew there was no going back.

"Olek, suppose I leave the city now. Pozner will fire me."

"So? You'll find other work. If need be you'll ask your beauteous aunt and she will help you."

"My people need what I bring in every week."

"If you're thrown in jail you'll bring in nothing. Anyway, if you ask me, it's too late to worry about things like that."

"You have an answer to everything—as usual," Adam said.

But the truth was he wanted to be convinced. Already he was missing Wanda more than he had imagined possible. And that other new feeling, the sense of belonging, was adding an astonishing dimension to his whole existence. "I don't recognize myself any more," he said, musing aloud. Then he made his decision. "All right, Olek. I'll go with you any time you say."

Silent tears coursed down Bluma's pale, lined face as she packed a rucksack for her son the following morning. From the moment he had come home with Wanda that first night she had been afraid for him, and now already she thought of him as a fugitive. And her heart ached both for him and that girl of his. But she was careful not to betray her fears. By the time the rucksack was ready for him to slip over his shoulders she was outwardly composed once more, her eyes not even red.

"Just take care of yourself. Don't take chances you don't have to take," was all she said. "God be with you."

She handed him a paper bundle with bread in it, cold leftover meat, apples, a slab of chocolate. "There's enough here to last you and Olek a couple of meals." At least, she thought, they could avoid stopping at roadside inns until they had put some distance between themselves and the city. It wasn't much to do for them, but it was all she could think of doing.

Before leaving, Adam solemnly shook hands with his father, who then embraced him. They kissed three times, right cheek, left cheek, and right once more, as was the custom. "Well, it won't be long before we see you home again," Jacob said, hoping this was the truth. He looked so drawn and thin that briefly his son wondered whether he shouldn't reshuffle his plans and stay home after all. But Jacob, as if reading his thoughts, said, "You're not to worry about us. Do what you must."

"I will," Adam answered, and the moment passed.

He kissed his mother, said goodbye to Izidore and Idka who, curious and excited, were there to see him leave, and was off to meet Olek. Walking away from Nalewki, he might have been just any student on the way to join friends for a day's outing beyond city limits. The anonymity gave him an added sense of security, and this led to the observation, which rather amused him, that already he felt like an old hand at conspiracy, he who only a week earlier had still fought off being drawn into political struggle.

He also reflected that in this new world he had just discovered he was finding not love alone, but comradeship. He was even beginning to understand what Olek had so often told him about putting one's faith in people: even those from whom one expected nothing were sometimes full of surprises. He had just had proof of this with Maurice Pozner. The day before, on the shortest of notice, he had gone over to see Pozner in order to explain that quite unexpectedly, for urgent reasons of health, he must go to the country. And the old industrialist, after taking a long, hard look at his children's tutor over the tops of his gold-rimmed spectacles, had nodded, then winked, and said yes, of course, a man's health could be most unpredictable these days and for Adam not to worry. "Come what may, you can have your job back in the fall." He also pressed a hundred rubles on him, by Adam's standards a staggering sum. "Take it, take it, Fabian, no need to be stiff-necked. Call it a bonus for having achieved the impossible—my son Marek was actually seen reading a book the other day! Besides, you're going to need money while you're away." He hadn't been able to resist adding, "And while you're gone, think again about what we discussed that other time. I might add that your leaving now makes no difference for the future. Under the circumstances you may decide mine isn't a bad offer—not a bad solution at all. But one way or the other, good luck."

Just as the girls had done, so Adam and Olek left by way of the Zhelazna Brama toll gate, where human traffic was heavy and guards tended to be lax. As they skirted the marketplace, a secondhand clothes peddler wearing a *yarmulka* and a *kapota,* the long Jewish coat, looked after them with scorn. "What's the matter," he yelled at Adam in angry Yiddish jargon, "there aren't enough Jewish boys around that you suck up to a *goy?"*

Adam shrugged and walked a little faster, a sickness in him mixing with pity for the old man. "It's still the Dark Ages for them," he said, translating the heckler's words for Olek. This was not the first time he'd heard such taunts, but today he was freshly aware of everything they implied, and newly vulnerable. "In Yiddish," he said, "we have an expression, 'It's hard to be a Jew.' Well, I'm beginning to think it's just as hard to be a human being. . . ."

"In Polish," Olek answered, "we say, 'It's hard to live when you're not used to it.' Same difference. But then who ever claimed life was easy? Come on, old friend, don't let it get you down. The sun is shining. It'll be a fine day for walking."

A hundred yards beyond the gate a heavyset peasant woman sat beside a homemade stand, dispensing lukewarm lemonade. "Two groshen a glass, young men! Only two groshen! Treat yourselves!" And she reached for her measure, ready to dip and pour. But when she saw they weren't stopping she shook a gnarled, malevolent finger after Olek, calling out viciously, "You should be ashamed, a fine upstanding Polish lad taking up with a Yid!"

"As I was saying," Olek commented. "Same difference!"

They walked on in silence. The city ended abruptly, as though the vanished walls that in medieval times had ringed and protected it were still there to contain it, keep it from spilling over onto the countryside. Soon the green meadowland came into view, and the checkerboard fields of ripening wheat and oats and barley, the stands of birch and of pines, the fruit orchards, and as far as the eye could see, sandy ribbons of rutted road sparsely outlined with poplars winding in and out across the cultivated plain.

The afternoon sun grew hot on their backs. Each time a coach or hay wagon passed they choked on clouds of dust. Soon their boots were gray and their eyebrows and mustaches hoary like those of young actors impersonating old men. A slight breeze rose over the wheat fields until they looked like shallow water rippling on a bright day. On a far slope they could see a herd of cattle grazing. Dogs barked lazily.

They came to a well, drank, ate some of Bluma's food, rested briefly, and were off again. Toward sundown they came to a nameless village, the rutted road suddenly calling itself a street. The houses, some whitewashed, others colored a chalky blue, were still deserted, but soon the children would be bringing the herds in for milking and the grown folks returning from work in the fields. Most of the houses had thatched roofs and a pot of geraniums blooming in a window. The dooryards were diminutive, crowded, each with its plot of verbena and wild thyme and nasturtiums, a sunflower or two nodding above them just beginning to turn to seed. It was a picture out of an idyll—provided you did not look too closely, provided you chose to remain blind to the poverty and the ignorance.

But Adam was thinking of none of these things, only of a line of poetry he had long ago committed to memory:

> *Hushed, our peaceful Polish village,*
> *Stilled, our joyous Polish farmland. . .*

And it was his country he saw, and love of country was an ache inside him, making his throat hurt and his eyes burn. And he thought of everything the people must endure, and he with the rest, because there was no other way. And his love choked him, and the flat fields seemed all of a sudden terribly his own, and Poland was the mother, his mother too, but a mother who like the vicious old woman at the lemonade stand cruelly rejected him. And just as a child, unwanted, continues to offer his love hoping to win the mother over, so he knew he would go on loving this cruel, tragic country which despite his centuries-old roots in her soil so often told him he should feel himself an alien.

And then he saw the mother country with wiser eyes—saw her for what she was, beaten down, brutalized, dragging on her knees but fighting to stand proud once more some day. But the *naghaika* kept her down, the knout and the bayonet would not let her rise, and the wounds were never allowed to heal. Torn open again and again, they festered, gangrenous, and it was the degradation that made Poland what she was, an ugly, rejecting stepmother. And because he understood all this he could forgive the hurts she dealt him. More deeply than ever before in his whole life he understood the meaning of the forbidden song that was a kind of national prayer. Walking down the empty road, hardly raising his voice above a whisper, tentatively he began to sing:

> *The smoke of fires, the stench of killings*
> *Carry our voices up toward the sky,*
> *Hear us, oh Father, pity our anguish,*
> *Help us, oh help us before we die. . . .*
>
> *As for our crimes, they're not of our making*
> *Though we be guilty, guilty, oh Lord,*
> *Blame not the tool of the forces of Satan,*
> *Punish the hand and not the blind sword!*

They had been walking silently for what seemed to him hours, and now suddenly he felt the need of talk.

"How much longer, Olek? How much longer can the slavery go on? Will we ever see liberation, do you think?"

Olek, who had been matching his giant stride to Adam's shorter step, turned and frowned. "Why ask me—I'm no prophet! But this much I promise you. The day will come. It must. If not for us, then in our children's time. Someday there's going to be freedom, and not just in Poland but everywhere. And now for heaven's sake will you stop glooming! If you must sing, sing something we can swing to, not that dirge!"

"Was I singing?" Adam said, looking surprised. "I didn't realize."

Olek stood looking at him tolerantly. "Adash, Adash, get hold of yourself! We're on vacation, you idiot! We're out of the damned city, and free, and on our way to be with our women. Besides," he added, "it's time you started learning that in our kind of business you've got to take each day as it comes. It's no good borrowing trouble."

The air started to fill with evening sounds, lowing of cows, dogs barking, voices calling to each other. In the distance church bells rang for vespers. But it was the time of year when darkness doesn't fall until late, and although they were beginning to feel weary they decided not to stop but to cover as much distance as possible while there was still daylight.

They walked on. "By tomorrow," Olek decided, "I'll feel safe trying to hitch a ride in a hay wagon."

"Suits me," Adam agreed. "Because to tell you the truth all I want right now is to be where my girl is!" Suddenly he grinned. "Well, come on, I'm getting my second wind. You wanted something to swing to, how about this?" And he launched into their old favorite, *The Song of the Philarets:*

> *Shed your worries, shed your sorrow,*
> *Let's not fret about tomorrow,*
> *Pop the corks and grab your forks*
> *And let us all be gay!*

They fell in step, two young, vigorous men marching toward the future, singing at the top of their lungs:

> *Now it's time to lift our glasses,*
> *Drink the health of our fair lasses,*
> *Molly, Polly, Yula, Dziula,*
> *Let each toast his own!*
> *Drink to Yula, and drink to Dziula. . .*

Dziula, thought Adam, joyfully and with longing, *My Dziula. Wandziula. Wanda.*

PART THREE
Summer—Fall 1898

❧ *One* ❧

ADAM AND OLEK reached the village of Karelice before the end
of the week. Traveling mainly on foot, sleeping under haystacks
in the open fields, buying no provisions until their own had been
completely exhausted, they managed to arouse no suspicion.
And now suddenly the city seemed a thousand miles away, and
not even a line of telegraph poles to remind them of urban civilization. The cadence of peasant speech around them was archaic,
Biblical. It transported them into another time, into a world of
peace.

This last was an illusion, of course. Each hamlet had its own
troubles, particularly where even four decades following the abo-
lition of serfdom the landowners still acted as though they owned
the peasants body and soul, extracting personal tribute and taxes
in medieval fashion. In addition, the countryside was as much at
war with the authorities as were the cities. Yet paradoxically it
was this very state of war that served as the traveler's best guarantee of personal safety. Local garrisons showed little interest in casual summer guests. They had headaches enough as it was, what
with collecting crown revenues, and seeing to it that they themselves were fed and their mounts kept in oats, and that each year's
quota of conscripts was duly herded to army recruiting points in
sufficiently good condition for pressing into service. Because with
those damn Polaks you had to look sharp every minute—nothing
they wouldn't do to get out of serving the Tsar!

For years Olek had been telling Adam how in their unending

battle of wits with the Russians their one great precious advantage was the unbelievable stupidity of the official mind. During their days on the road Adam had seen enough to understand that Olek was right. The countryside crackled with hate. And yet the two sides hating one another so fiercely might easily have been brothers. The soldiers, ordinary conscripts, were for the most part themselves peasants, the villages where they were stationed differing little from their own except in crops and size of farmholds. But they were peasants from Great Russia or the Ukraine or western Siberia or the Caucasus; they spoke other languages, worshipped in the Russian Orthodox, not the Roman Catholic, Church; and they'd had it dinned into them that the Poles were blasphemers against that church, hence also against its head, the Little Father, Tsar by the grace of God of the Holy Russian Empire. So that to them the local inhabitants were infidels, subjugated enemies whom they could bedevil at will for the pure sport of it. The village men had long ago learned to leave the tavern in twos and threes, especially of a Saturday night. And no straying barnyard fowl or suckling pig was safe in the road. And no girl or woman was safe in the fields alone.

"Be all that as it may," Adam argued as they neared their destination, "how can you be so sure they really will ignore us once we get to your people's farm? You're known. We won't be casual travelers any more. . . ."

But Olek was unperturbed. "Hell, that's a chance we've got to take. Besides, I doubt the Warsaw police have bothered to send out an alarm—we're not all that important. And anyway, what's the sense of worrying? You know my motto—*sufficient unto the day*. . . . Do you have wind enough left for a song to keep us going?"

The sun was setting when at last they reached the village. Karelice was much like all the other hamlets they had passed through: a single long street, a tavern with a shed serving as a kind of store, a smithy. The whitewashed houses stood separated by small gardens, each one neatly fenced off. In the dooryards were cramped, painstakingly cultivated flowerbeds full of midsummer color—pinks and nasturtiums and heliotrope and mignonette, and standing tall and regal, great sunflowers in bloom. In the windows, between starched curtains, pots of geraniums alternated with begonias, the kind even the Polish winter does not easily discourage. Hens with their chicks pecked about in the dirt.

Hushed, our peaceful Polish village,
Stilled, our joyous Polish farmland. . .

In the distance they could hear lowing and a tinkling of bells. A dog barked. Another answered. A fife shrilled.

"The herds will be coming in for milking any time now," Olek said. "The men are about done in the fields, too."

He turned off at the last gate, at the compound that was the Zaremba farmhold, where his grandfather's place dominated the other buildings as a rooster does his hens. Bogumil Zaremba did not believe in keeping his tribe living together, all under the same roof. He had been generous with his sons and daughters as they married. But there was never any doubt as to who was chieftain. In the summer, when work in the fields was heaviest, half a dozen families sat down to meals together in the "big house," the women taking turns with the cooking. As Olek pushed open the door and motioned for Adam to follow him inside, tantalizing aromas assailed their hungry noses. Great caldrons of steaming potatoes and bubbling cabbage soup hummed on two enormous wood stoves. A bent crone and a vigorous young woman in her early thirties were busy stirring and tasting.

"Granny, Aunt Kasia, we're here!" Olek called.

The old woman dropped her spoon, her leathery face lighting up. "Well, heaven help us, you got here at last! And up to your old tricks, too, sneaking in on cat's feet! Nearly scared the wits out of me, you did! But then I don't hear so well as I used to. Don't see so well either. Can't be helped. Main thing is, you're here, and all in one piece. Welcome, sonny. You too, mister." She turned to Adam, wiping her hands on her apron, bowing low from the waist, not subservient but following old custom. "A guest in the house means God's in the house," she quoted. "We're honored to have you." Then, politeness satisfied, she spoke once more to her grandson. "We been waiting and waiting . . . specially those two girls, heheheh! You'd think they expected the second coming!" She laughed, youthful and ribald, exposing great gaps between yellowed teeth. "Every night they're down to the crossing, watching the road!"

"And where might they be now?" Olek asked, doing his best not to sound anxious.

"In the barn, helping my Bossie calve," said the younger woman, who had not yet spoken. Her voice was low-pitched and there was a heaviness of spirit about her. Kasia was recently widowed, left with three children to raise and only her father to depend on. She generally did her best not to spread sadness about her, but there were times, like now in the face of Olek's ill-concealed eagerness to find Maryla, when it was an uphill struggle.

She made an effort to lighten her tone. "Those friends of yours have sure been a godsend to us! The doctoring that's been going on since they got here, you've no idea! First it was just our young 'uns—a boil, a sty, a bellyache, what have you. Next thing you know, they started in on the cattle. Better'n any vet, I tell you! Talk about earning their keep. . ."

"Kasia, for shame!" her mother interrupted. "It's our guests you're talking about—whoever heard of guests having to earn their keep!"

But the young widow stood her ground. "That's not how I meant it and well you know it, Ma. I'd have lost Bossie if it hadn't been for them two, so what's the harm in saying I'm grateful! That fool cow of mine," she went on to explain to the newcomers, "swelled up on too much grass, and she about to drop her calf any minute. So we told your doctor ladies what to do and they did it and old Bossie's as good as new. Now they're both with her, midwifing, you might say. . ."

That's Wanda and Maryla she's talking about, Adam thought, not yet quite able to take it in. And then he was just thinking, *our women . . . my woman . . . mine. . .* and it was all he could do not to run out shouting Wanda's name for everyone to hear.

Olek sensed this and was quick to warn him. "When there's birthing in the barn, you stay out of the way. We're more careful of animals here than of people, they're our bread and butter. That," he added wryly, "is life close to the soil. You'll have to grin and bear it, and so will I."

Soon the room began to fill, as one after another the clan gathered after the day's chores. Adam shook the hands of a dozen men and youths with Olek's face, Olek's high, broad cheekbones and massive shoulders, and each powerful handclasp reaffirmed their general welcome, their acceptance of him, and a kind of pride. Pride in Olek which now washed over him too simply because he was Olek's friend. "Up to your old tricks, eh, you and your comrade? And your women. All cut from the same cloth . . . we might have known. . ." Implicit praise that in his own case, Adam felt, was undeserved.

Finally there was a stomping outside and Bogumil Zaremba himself, Olek's maternal grandfather, came in. He stopped in the doorway, dwarfing the room and those in it, and if one had been looking for the archetype of a Polish peasant patriarch to paint, here was the ideal subject. His white handlebar mustache stained with pipe smoke swept down well below the jawbone, the white mane on his head was as thick as on his wedding day, his shaggy brows met over eyes that could still spot a hawk before even the barnyard creatures sensed danger circling overhead. A benevolent despot, he held the family together because he held control of their acres. "So long as we work the land undivided," he was fond of saying, "none of us will ever know want. But let me parcel it out and each of you separately will starve. Like some others in these parts I'd rather not name." And it never occurred to his sons, or the husbands of his daughters, for that matter, to argue the point.

Of all his children only Olek's mother had defied him. Her dream of becoming a teacher took her to the city where she soon married for love, married a factory hand and so was lost to country life forever. And her father had never quite forgiven her, yet his delight in her was greater than in any of the others. "Smart as a whip she always was, my Amelia. Walked off with all the prizes in school. Always with her nose in a book. Too good for the rest of us, guess she decided she was. . . ." But woe be it to anyone who dared agree with him when he was running her down. "Since when is an education a bad thing, you lunkheads?" he'd thunder. "If the rest of you had done half what she did, you'd be a lot more use to your old father now. . . ."

His greeting to his grandson was typical. "Still running to us when you're in trouble, eh? That's what comes of being a university man, a student, a political, and with politicals for friends. . . . But there's no gainsaying it, your kind of trouble is honorable—those who risk their necks for the rest of us are the best. And that makes you, Bogumil Zaremba's seed, part of the country's best. Which is as it should be." Now he embraced his grandson, who stood almost as tall as he, then shook hands with Adam, nearly crushing his fingers as he did so.

"My house is honored." Bowing from the waist as his wife had done, he repeated the ancient saying, "A guest in the house means God in the house." Then, changing his tone and his mood, "Hey, wife! Hey, Kasia, Zoshka, Magda! Break out a keg of mead, we must toast our guests the old Polish way!"

Afterwards the men all sat at the long table and the women served them before touching a morsel of food themselves. Adam hardly tasted what was piled on his plate for watching the door. It was Wanda he wanted, not meat and potatoes. But someone said Bossie wasn't done calving yet and the "doctor ladies" would get here when they got here. No point holding up supper.

When they came in at last, halfway through the meal, it took a conscious effort on his part not to push his chair back and rush to Wanda and take her in his arms, which Olek had managed to warn him would be a great breach of decorum. To make matters worse, their places were at opposite ends of the table, with Wanda and Maryla among the unmarried girls, so that there was no chance for even a private word of greeting, a touch of hands, much less a kiss.

He could only watch hungrily, and it seemed to him that in the short space of her stay here she had been renewed, the drawn lines of her face smoothed out, and the borrowed peasant clothes she wore—borrowed, he guessed, for protective coloration —were quite startlingly becoming. Her skin had taken on the tones of darkly sun-ripened peaches. "How beautiful is my love with shoes. . ." *How beautiful with peasant blouse and coral at her throat. . .* The ache of wanting her was almost beyond bearing.

It was not until much later that they were free at last to be alone together. Supper over, the custom of the house was for everyone to remain in the communal room. After the tables had been cleared each member of the family settled down in his accustomed place with an accustomed chore, the men mending harnesses or honing knives and scythes, the women mending, carding wool, spinning, the children polishing copper and brass.

Meanwhile old Bogumil, having lit his pipe and surveyed his "seed" to his satisfaction, reached for his worn copy of Mikolaj Rej's *Zwierciadlo* (*The Mirror*), that classic of Renaissance wisdom so dear to the Polish heart. It was his favorite book for reading aloud. "Better than the Bible, may God forgive me," he often remarked to his wife, "for it'll pour Polishness into the very marrow of the children's bones. Religion they'll get willy-nilly from the priest. But this, ah, this . . . let them once absorb what Rej has to say, and no matter what, no matter where or when, they'll always know who they are." And so every evening, while the others worked or tinkered, he read to them for an hour. This was how it had been for as long as any of them remembered, taking the place of what in other households might have been evening prayers.

The old man read well, savoring the flow and the rhythm of the majestic prose, and it was plain to see where Olek's mother had got her love of the written word. But not even she, the quick, the perceptive, the educated one, had ever guessed that her father's reading ability was, in fact, cruelly limited, that he would have stumbled like a schoolboy over any new, unfamiliar text, that the phrases rolling so grandly off his tongue sounded as they did only because with the years they had practically been committed to memory.

Adam and Olek among the men, Maryla and Wanda among the women, had no choice but to sit politely listening with the others in deference to their host. At last, however, the reading came to an end. Bogumil closed the book, a signal that the others might now rise. Benches scraped, the children said goodnight and were packed off to bed, the adults put their work away.

Bedtime came early on the farm. There were a few stifled yawns, then one by one couples murmured goodnight and God be with you. Then, armed with candles, they were off, each to his own cottage.

Adam and Olek were informed they would be sleeping in the hayloft along with several of the younger boys. Wanda and Maryla shared a room in Kasia's house, the only one without a man and thus the least crowded. Fortunately it was situated beyond the courtyard and barns, and there was no moon but plenty of trees, and soon the dark swallowed whoever walked in that direction.

Kasia herself passed them, a sad knowing look on her face. "Goodnight. Sweet dreams." Olek and Maryla went by and vanished into the shadows. And now at last they were alone, eager hands reaching out, eager bodies free to press and cling.

"Darling, my darling, I've missed you so . . . I've worried. . ."

"I know. But now we're together. And you're safe. That's all that matters—you're safe."

"At least for now," she said, and suddenly laughed. "There are so many Zaremba relatives and connections in the village, the local garrison can't possibly keep track."

He kissed her. "Look at the stars. Have you ever seen such a sky?"

They stayed together until the first rooster crowed. And then it was another day, to be followed by a long succession of days uneventful yet crowded, smooth-flowing, days when the body labored in the broiling sun while the mind drowsed sweetly, when muscles ached then hardened, and nerves unwound, and one could almost believe in a future of unclouded happiness.

A week went by, and another and another, without so much as a newspaper to intrude. It was a time like a waking dream, a time of magic unflawed and unreal, for even the cares around them were not really their own.

❧ *Two* ❧

On Sundays, every last inhabitant of the village including even the halt and the lame piled into carts and hay wagons for their weekly trip to the nearest church, the ancient Lowicz Cathedral not many miles away. Shedding their drab field-work clothes, they donned traditional regional garb—brilliantly striped homespun skirts and aprons for the women, embroidered bodices laced tight over fine white linen blouses, and flowered kerchiefs, and beads of coral and of amber tied with ribbon streamers, and store-bought shoes on their feet; the men wearing trousers of the same homespun, wide and stuffed into high polished boots, and felt jerkins over shirts of linen almost as fine as their women's, and hats with peacock feathers.

Again, as on the previous Sunday, Kasia and her mother dug into carved and painted dower chests for clothing that would fit their women guests. In the meantime Bogumil Zaremba took his grandson aside to discuss a worrisome point of protocol. "What do you think we should do about our Jew-boy friend? To leave him behind would make him a sitting duck for trouble. But to take him with us into God's house . . . well, I just don't know. . . ."

"Something tells me," Olek replied dryly, "that God will not be insulted. Or do you think he's got nothing better to worry about?"

"Hold your tongue, you blaspheming pup!" the grandfather

thundered. Then he winked slyly. "Let's say that between the two of you you'll help me follow the *padre's* Latin."

So Adam was decked out in borrowed finery, making an altogether unconvincing peasant with his thin scholar's shoulders and feet too narrow for the heavy boots. "People will think we're harboring a pair of gypsies," their hosts said when they saw him and Wanda together. "First thing you know the neighbors will be locking barns and stables as we pass!"

There was general laughter, and Kasia's youngest, flaxenhaired six-year-old Kasienka, who had taken to following Wanda like a puppy, instantly begged, "If you're going to be gypsies, will you steal me like the gypsies do and take me along? Please please please, *Pani* Wanda!" She kept it up until finally her mother explained that this was all make-believe—yes, indeed, grown-ups too sometimes played make-believe—and there was to be no more talk about it, and above all neither Kasienka nor the other children were ever, under any circumstances, to mention their visitors' masquerade around the village. "Not unless you all want a taste of the strap on your bare backsides," she added for good measure while Kasienka's eyes grew round with fear. For the life of her she couldn't understand what she had said that was bad. And she pressed against Wanda's skirts for reassurance, and Wanda would have liked to comfort her, but what was there to say?

"Tell you what," she finally suggested, stroking Kasienka's cornsilk hair, hoping to reassure her without at the same time undoing whatever good the threats might have done, "suppose we take you with us for just a little while? Suppose you ride with *Pan* Adam and me as far as the church and back. In the hay wagon. Would you like that?"

The small blonde head nodded vigorously and Wanda smiled, looking more like a gypsy than ever with her black hair in long braids and the red flowered kerchief tied loosely over them and the row on row of dark-red coral circling her slender neck. She seemed to Adam truly a changeling among the stocky, round-faced women of the region. "A changeling." Echoes of old wives' tales overheard in boyhood came back to him, tales of stolen children picked up when he and his brothers made Sunday visits to Aunt Balbina Segal's rented summer cottage near Otwotsk.

The cottage had been a primitive affair rented from a farmer, within a stone's throw of the barnyard and the potato patch, and it bore very little resemblance to the elegant villas of Otwotsk itself, the resort town less than a mile away. But to the Fabian children it had spelled luxury quite beyond reach, and exploring the farm, playing with peasant youngsters, helping them look for eggs had all added excitement.

One Sunday morning Adam and Viktor and Izidore had arrived to find the whole village agog because a caravan of gypsies had come in the night and pitched their tents in a fallow field. The little Segal cousins were as breathless about it as everyone else, wanting to have their fortunes told and watch horses being shod. But like the local youngsters they had strict orders to stay close to home and go nowhere without an adult in charge. And if a gypsy woman approached, Aunt Balbina like the rest of the mothers would yank her offspring into the house and slam the door.

"If you're not careful the gypsies will steal you!" she'd warned, believing the myth as implicitly as little Kasienka did.

"Indeed they will," the Segals' peasant landlady solemnly backed her up. "For it's a fact they'll steal anything that isn't nailed down. Turn your back for five minutes and everything's gone—chickens, featherbeds, horses, children. . . . And you know what they do to children? You'd never believe it, but they stain the skin dark till their own mother wouldn't know them. Do it with hot butternut oil, they do. First they boil the nuts with the skins on, a regular witches' brew. Then they let it stand overnight and boil it again. And then a third time, till it's good and thick. Rub a baby's skin with glup like that and it'll turn for life. No amount of scrubbing will take it off. . . ."

Exactly why the gypsies should have wanted to steal children when they had so many of their own no one ever stopped to consider. The peasants said the gypsies sent them out begging, trained them for pickpockets. "Do their dirty work for them, and who cares if the poor tykes get caught and sent to jail! So you be careful, *Pani* Segal," the peasant woman admonished, "and don't you let your young 'uns out of your sight! The little girls particularly. You people may be Jews and all, but you've always been good tenants and I'd hate to see anything like *that* happen to you. . . ."

Adam remembered his cousins repeating it all to him like so much gospel. He also remembered Regina, the younger girl, who even then was beginning to be vain about her delicate good looks, adding airily, "Of course, it would take an *awful* lot of butternuts to make *my* skin dark enough. . . . I'd probably be much too expensive to steal! And my hair is all curls, they can't do much about that. Anyone just looking at me would know right away I was a changeling. . . ."

"Are you a changeling, my love?" he suddenly whispered to Wanda. And she, who could not possibly guess what he meant, smiled, playing up to him. "Why yes, of course, didn't you know?"

In church he sat among the other men, less tempted than they to doze through the services, for the unaccustomed pageantry, sumptuous and so different from the synagogue, fascinated him. The chanting, the flickering candles, the incense, the glorious symmetry of the vast Gothic structure itself, the sunlight slanting obliquely through the jewel-toned, stained-glass windows, all stirred him to profound hedonistic pleasure. The priest's deep voice lulled him into a curious state of oneness with the worshippers that had nothing to do with religious faith, and before giving himself up to pure sensation he thought, surprisingly, of his old friend Henryk Meisels, Henryk the esthete, who once had tried to tell him about his own vicarious experience with cathedrals and Catholicism. But at the time none of it had had any meaning for him.

Henryk, toying with becoming a convert, not for practical reasons but as a sensation seeker, was an anachronism of sorts, Adam thought, just as the Lowicz Cathedral was an anachronism, rising illogically, inexplicably on the flat Mazowsze plain. Here it had stood for hundreds of years in the midst of wheat fields and orchards, resisting invasion and wars and plunder, a monument to one of the great feudal houses of the realm. Who exactly had ordered it built, and on what occasion, he had no idea. Olek would probably know. Of such details is one's sense of history made.

Carefully, not wishing to offend his hosts by merely gaping around during the solemn prayers, he let his eyes travel from face to sun-browned face while keeping his own head politely down. Once his glance met Olek's, and in his friend's expression he read impatience mingled with distaste. Almost he could hear Olek's thoughts. *Sheep,* was what his friend was probably thinking. *Poor benighted sheep willingly bleating and begging to be allowed to lay their necks down on the slaughtering-block. Don't they know the church is the instrument of the rich against the poor?* That was all Olek did see in the sumptuous ritual. "Religion is the opium of the people. Marx said it all when he said that, I tell you."

And again as on a thousand occasions since their boyhood Adam found himself marveling at the monolithic quality of his friend's makeup—marveling at the single-mindedness, the untroubled forward line of Olek's thinking, the lack of any inner need to complicate his concepts by speculating on the various shadings between the black and the white. It must be comfortable to know exactly where one stands, what one wants and where one is going, he thought with a touch of envy. Just the same, he himself could never so cavalierly dismiss the hundreds of human beings bent in prayer, even though the Being whose praises they sang did not exist for him. A latent streak of mysticism made him wish he could delve into viewpoints not his own, made him want to try to lose himself in the beliefs of others at least long enough to experience what they were experiencing. Looking around, he could see here and there faces bathed in tears. And while it made no sense to him really, he was deeply moved.

The priest's sonorous Latin, of which most of the congregation understood not a word, had woven its spell. And now the services were drawing to a close. *Pax . . . pax . . . pax vobiscum. . . .* The smell of incense intensified, filling the church. Far across on the other side of the aisle Adam caught a glimpse of Wanda, to whom church services were as much part of childhood as had been her mother's lullabies. And he saw at once that she was as much at home here as were the women among whom she sat, although she was as far away from prayer as he himself, or Maryla or Olek. And he understood what it was, really, that lent her protective coloration: not her borrowed Lowicz finery but her being at one with her surroundings—for if her responses were easy and automatic, it was because a lifetime of habit had gone into shaping them.

Suddenly he felt a great surge of loneliness and a sharp need for physical contact with her, as if just by touching her hand he might be able to break out of the isolation of his alien self. And then the last benediction was over. And the crowd surged out of the semidarkness, spilling into the hot sunshine, exploding into color and noise.

As soon as they reached the churchyard the women all stopped to unlace their shoes and pull their stockings off. Laughing in sheer relief, wiggling cramped toes in the blessedly cool grass, they tied the laces together and threw the shoes over their shoulders. Unlike the men who always wore boots for field work, the women went barefoot six days in the week and would have done the same on the seventh had the choice been theirs. Custom, of course, decreed otherwise. But now they could be themselves again. Thus with a single gesture they dispelled the mood of solemnity as though it had never been.

On the way home in the hay cart someone suggested a boletus hunt later in the day.

"A hunt?" Adam recoiled, instantly alarmed. "Not me! I can't abide the thought!" He was startled and rather annoyed at the shrieks of laughter that greeted his protest. Even Wanda, usually so reserved, laughed till tears came into her eyes while quiet, shy little Kasienka went into spasms of giggles. And the old nag pulling the cart, hearing the commotion, obligingly gave a start and quickened her pace to a brisk trot.

"He won't hunt boletus because he hates the sight of guns! Oh no, that's too much! You wouldn't use a gun on one if it came up and bit you? Wouldn't even defend yourself? It's against your principles maybe?"

"What's the matter with all of you?" Adam kept asking indignantly. "What's so funny? What did I say? . . . ."

"The b-b-boletus . . . ," Kasienka finally managed between giggles. "Oh, *Pan* Adam, don't you know *anything?* The boletus isn't an animal, it's a mushroom! And we call it a *hunt* because they're hard to find under the trees. . . ."

Mushroom picking, he soon found out, was the sport of children and courting couples. The place to search for them was deep in the woods where the ground was moist and cool and the carpet of last year's pine needles thickest. Under the giant firs no underbrush grew and walking was easy. By unspoken agreement the couples separated, each pair wandering off in a different direction, each with a single basket to fill.

Soon even the echo of other voices died away. Adam and Wanda found themselves completely alone with only the birds and red squirrels for company.

"What would happen," Adam said after a while, "if we were to go back with an empty basket?"

"They'd say we were unlucky."

"Would you care?"

"Would you?" She laughed, this time not at him but with him. Overhead a tomtit chattered.

Without a word he took the basket from her and hooked it over a low-hanging oak limb where later he hoped they would not forget it. He held out his arms and she came to him quickly, meeting his kiss halfway. They stood for a moment pressed close together, mouth to mouth, each feeling the pounding of the other's heart. Then hurriedly he began to undress her, his fingers trembling as he searched for buttons and hooks in her voluminous borrowed clothes. The heavy strands of her coral beads fell to the ground together with the ribbons that tied them. The laced bodice went next, and then the blouse and bright skirt. Her many petticoats spread over the thick fragrant carpet of pine needles made them a fine bed, the branches overhead their canopy.

They had made love many times these past weeks in Karelice, but always stealthily, in darkness. Now in the green shade latticed with sunshine they felt joyously unrestrained. Tall as she was, he lifted her easily, as if it had been for this alone that the strength of his new-found muscles had developed while he labored in the fields.

She threw her arms around his neck and held on tight, and he knelt, still holding her, and lowered her to the ground. "I love you so," he whispered, although there was no need for whispering here in the woods. Still kneeling, he unbuttoned her shoes, pulled them off, unhooked her stockings and pulled those off, too, then kissed her arched, slender feet while her fingers began to caress him. *How beautiful is my love without her shoes.*

Out of a kind of leftover shyness she had kept her shift on, but he slipped the straps off her shoulders and pulled it down until she lay naked before him, her skin soft and golden against the white linen. Only then did he think to get rid of his own clothes. Afterwards, stretched out alongside her, he lay for long minutes motionless, raised on one elbow, lay looking at her without yet touching her, deliberately holding himself back, drinking in the lines of her body as if to memorize them.

"Every time we're together it's like a miracle." He was still whispering.

"Do you think other people can feel like this?"

"No. No one in the world. Only you and me."

She smiled and murmured something he couldn't quite hear and turned toward him, the hard points of her breasts thrusting against him, and the woman smell of her assaulted his senses and the need for her overwhelmed him and there was no more holding back, only the swelling hunger and the surge toward pleasure. And then at last his body covered hers. And the wind sang its own song in the branches overhead.

✵ *Three* ✺

For the first time in his life Adam was discovering leisure. Not time stolen from work or frittered away, but time that truly belonged to him so that it could be savored in all its sweetness without the bitter admixture of guilt. He could not remember this ever happening to him before. Since earliest boyhood he had hardly known what it meant to play after school without having his ears boxed for it afterwards—and knowing it was necessity that forced his parents to such severity had made it no easier.

In Karelice too, six-year-olds like Kasienka and her little cousins all had their share of chores—carding and spinning, and carrying slops, and watching over cows and sheep and babies only a little younger than themselves—but the work was somehow always naturally interlarded with play. As he minded the flocks, a small boy was free to whittle in the shade of a great tree, to cut himself a reed pipe out of a length of willow and try his skill with it. The boletus hunt became a game even if its purpose was utilitarian. How different from the grim awareness of duty he had grown up with! He could still clearly remember the first five groshen he'd earned, the first silver coin, the first gold piece, none of it his to spend because family needs always came first. By the same token his time too had been a commodity he'd never felt free to dispose of. It belonged to those who depended on it.

Now for a little while everything was different. He had no need to hurry, no need to push relentlessly from one task to the next, his feet pounding the pavements and his mind drugged with fatigue. He woke up mornings with a luxurious sense of well-being and filled his lungs with the fragrant air of the hayloft. He would continue to lie there, unhurried, making lazy note of the cracks in the thatch roof through which the early sun was already shining, and stretch, and doze again, and finally be ready for the new day.

"One thing more, and I'd think I was already in heaven," he once told Wanda. "If only I could have you lying beside me when I go to sleep, find you there when I open my eyes. . ." For it was becoming increasingly hard, especially after that afternoon in the woods, to make love catch-as-catch-can, then separate for the night.

Yet neither they nor Maryla and Olek had much choice in the matter. In deference to the strict mores of the patriarchal household, outward conventions had to be observed. The village accepted both couples as betrothed. But it also expected brides to be virgins, with blood on the sheets to show for it on the morning after the wedding.

Morality was rigid in other matters, too. The oldest inhabitants could still remember how faithless wives had been dealt with in the old days: stripped naked, tied hand and foot and with honey smeared over their sinful bodies, they would be carted out into the woods, there to be dumped on giant ant heaps. Later, their clean white bones would be buried in unhallowed ground. And for the sin of fornication unmarried girls were punished by being driven through the village atop a cartload of manure. Should word ever get out that Bogumil Zaremba's grandson and his Warsaw friends lived loosely, "like students," the old man would never again be able to hold his head up.

"Why didn't we think to tell them we were already married!" Olek started to grumble. "Then everything would be simple."

"Simple now and twice as complicated later," Maryla tried to argue. "Just think—something still can go wrong. I may have to hide longer than we anticipate. Or the police may decide to go after you, too. How would it be if your people found out from the authorities we'd been lying! Think of the added pain, the humiliation. . ."

"I see what you mean," Olek admitted grudgingly, "but it's still a big nuisance. And time's a-wasting. . ."

Another week, and his patience was completely at an end. "Enough! Enough of this sneaking and hiding like children! Besides, we'll be getting married sooner or later, so why not get it over with?"

In this quiet corner of the world the old arguments against sanctioned marriage had gradually lost their validity for him. The climate of the university had failed to carry over to this spot where all values seemed different, where, as the song had it, a girl's dowry was a pot of clabber and four cheeses, a man's four cheeses and a rick of hay. "Marry me, Maryla. Now. At once. And to hell with the way we used to talk. . . . ."

It was not a romantic proposal, but Maryla heard in it all the things her lover left unsaid and she nodded and kissed him hard on the lips. That night at supper they announced their decision. Old Bogumil broke out another crock of mead from the spring house, and toasts were drunk and *vivats* shouted and everyone embraced the future bride. On the following Sunday the banns were published, and the Zaremba household began to prepare for the wedding.

For Adam and Wanda the situation was becoming more and more painful each day. "When will it be our turn? What will become of us?" they kept asking themselves and each other. Wanda by now had learned a good deal about her sweetheart's background and, of course, she had met his family. She knew he was tied to them by bonds of loyalty and affection all but incomprehensible to her in terms of her own parents. Sometimes she even wondered—and would instantly hate herself for her lack of heart—whether his selflessness didn't go beyond what was expected of the best of sons. But she would have been the last person in the world to point this out to him.

The troubles he had left behind in Nalewki Street, which earlier he had allowed his new-found happiness to submerge, now surfaced suddenly, at the first hint of impending decision setting up a kind of mute pleading. And feeling torn, feeling cornered, he became like a man unable to stop probing his own wound even though all he succeeded in doing was to make the pain worse.

"I'd give my good right arm to be able to say, 'Let's make it a double wedding,' " he kept telling her. "You know that. But my hands are tied. You do understand, don't you, dearest? What right do I have to a life of my own so long as things at home are the way they are?"

She was tempted to cry out that he had every right, the right, old as history, of each man to start a hearth and a home of his own. Besides, she might have added, marriage to her would not mean turning his back on his people's needs. For she was not like most women, she expected to go on working, she wouldn't even consider it a sacrifice to forget her chosen studies for the time being and find employment of the kind available to her sex. And they could crowd in with the rest of the Fabians if need be, with only a corner to themselves, and still manage.

But to tell him all this would have been, to her, tantamount to begging. And this her pride would not permit. Just as his pride as a man would have made it impossible, she realized, for him to accept such an offer had she made it. So they got nowhere, and their discussion ended up as all the others had done, in desperate love-making.

To make matters worse a letter came from Bluma the very next day, to be followed by another and another, and the news was deeply disquieting. His father was not at all well, she wrote in her meticulous, microscopic hand. "You know how he hates to admit to feeling ill. But he tires so easily these days, and he keeps coughing, especially at night, and his voice is always hoarse, his throat a little sore. I've begged him to smoke less but he just shrugs me off. Says it's one of the few pleasures left to him. And maybe he's right. I haven't the heart. . ."

Conquering her natural distaste, Bluma left the sanctuary of her kitchen to deal with the customers out front, so that Jacob might have a chance to rest more. She wrote that Idka and Rosie, too, had been pressed into service. "But it isn't right, especially not in our business. You know how it is with the choosing of wigs—the talk that goes on, the coarse jokes not fit for the ears of young girls. . . . It hurts me that your sisters have to hear such things, but what else can I do?"

Unspoken, but plain between the lines was his mother's warning that soon he might have to help even more than in the past. Exactly how serious was his father's illness? Would he soon be incapacitated? Was he dying? If so, who would be the family mainstay if not himself?

He shared the letters with Wanda, and it was hard to believe that only a few weeks earlier his mood had been one of pure joy. "I can't turn my back on them now. I want to belong to you, but I don't even belong to myself! Wanda, my own love, my darling, what are we going to do? I want to call you wife before the whole world, but how long must we wait? Maybe," he was finally driven into goading her one day, "you should forget about me, find someone else. . ."

"Just like that?" she demanded. "What do you take me for?"

They had been walking hand in hand through the pine woods and had stopped at a brook in a clearing. In an effort to hide her misery, Wanda knelt and began to splash water on her face. Instantly he was beside her. "Darling, don't turn away from me! Even if you're angry don't turn away!"

She had no wish to punish him, only to persuade him. "When I was in trouble, did you turn away?" she said, caressing his cheek. "No, you made my trouble yours even before we knew how much we loved each other. That's how we really found out, remember?" And her arms reached out, and she began to rock him, soothing him with her voice and her touch. "Don't make it more difficult for me than it already is," she pleaded.

Still, with all the wedding preparations under way, it was hard to be comforted. He tried not to think of the menacing tomorrows and cursed his fate. The days was still golden, still outwardly an idyll. The wheat was ripening, full and heavy on tall stalks, the apples and pears took on color, and there was talk of a bumper crop. And to judge by the newspapers, the unrest that earlier had had such a grip on the country seemed to be receding. Everyone breathed easier. Adam alone could not lay his burden aside, until Wanda, sensing how he was torn, urged him to go home, if only for a day or so, and see for himself whether things were as bad as he imagined. But the temptation to let sleeping dogs lie, to prolong the uneasy truce with his own conscience, was too strong. "If I go I may not get away a second time." He stayed where he was. And compromised by continuing to reproach himself.

In the meantime the Zaremba household was buzzing with activity. Since Olek was the eldest grandson, the family would have found it unthinkable to let the marriage be celebrated in anything less than traditional style. After much discussion and coaxing, and Olek acting like an irritated hedgehog, Maryla told him it was decided to delay the ceremony just long enough to coincide with the year's harvest festival, *dozhynki*. That way, with the heaviest field work out of the way and the grain threshed and stored, there would be time for days of feasting and drinking, for music and dancing, and for making all guests properly welcome.

At first Olek resented the hubbub and to-do as going counter to his deepest convictions. "The most private act of a man's life, and they have to make a circus of it!"

But Maryla who, now that their relationship was out in the open, was enjoying the fuss her future relatives made over her, did her best to calm him down; and even Adam, despite his own aversion to public display, tried to make him see reason. "Your people are old, and proud, and this has great meaning for them. Take it with good grace."

"As if I had any other choice!"

"All the more reason to be amiable."

Olek shrugged, then laughed, helpless and rueful. "They've even invited all the Warsaw relatives. Not just my mother and father but aunts and uncles and cousins. I'll never hear the end of it, especially from Uncle Jacek!" The illegal printer had already sent word he was coming, although in theory he was as dead-set against legalized marriage as was his nephew.

"I only hope," Maryla said gravely, "that we won't attract too much attention and alert the police!" But they all assured her a peasant wedding was a far cry from a student demonstration. The authorities seldom closely watched what they considered "good-natured" peasant activity, especially at harvest time when the whole countryside was celebrating anyway.

And now the women in the family finally took over. Grandmother Zaremba, her daughters and her daughters-in-law all dug into the carved and painted presses where linens and homespuns, embroidered cloths and extra featherbeds were kept. Nothing would do but for Maryla to have a proper hope chest. They engulfed her, decked her out in the very best they had to offer, outfitting her from the skin out. She was no longer *Pani Doktor,* the doctor lady with the formidable education and city ways, but one of their own, and a bride besides.

So they brought her white shifts and petticoats with beading, long-sleeved, high-necked nightdresses edged in tatting, snowy blouses with riotous embroidery, and kerchiefs, and strings of bright beads, and earrings intricately carved out of cherry pits. They piled up length upon length of the brilliant, highly prized, striped Lowicz homespuns that could be used not just for skirts and capes but also for rugs and wall hangings. For her future home there were linen sheets and pillowslips and tablecloths with fine drawnwork, and it was all fruit of their own looms, the work of hands tirelessly busy on long winter evenings. How many hours of Bogumil's reading aloud, Maryla wondered, overwhelmed by so much generosity, did the piled-up gifts represent?

"With the kind of life we'll be leading, when will we ever use all this?" she remarked privately to Olek. But she dared not refuse any of the gifts for fear of hurt feelings. "I did try, just once, to explain to your grandmother and to Kasia about our work in the underground. They just smiled and looked wise. Your grandmother looked positively smug. 'Wait till the children start coming, you'll be wanting a snug nest then.' Your Aunt Kasia was just as bad. 'Think I'd let you marry my own sister's son with only the shirt on your back? Now stand still and let me pin this bodice so it fits properly when you walk to the altar. . . .' " She began laughing. "What could I do but give in?"

If Maryla's dowry was to be put together out of whatever was at hand, her wedding dress at least must be made to her measure. So now the evening hour of family reading was given over entirely to fine needlework. Meanwhile the uncles examined the pots and pans, the knives and spoons the young couple were being given to start their own kitchen. Word went out for the itinerant tinker to come around in time for the copper utensils to be relined and mended.

Suddenly, to Olek's surprise and somewhat to his annoyance, the sensible young woman he thought he knew so well seemed to become just one of the womenfolk. What's more, surrounded by his giggling, squealing, chattering cousins, she acted as though she belonged with them. Unlike him, she was completely at home in the close-knit tribal group. She who had never known what family ties really meant, who had grown up ashamed of her own father, and humiliated, now learned that to belong to one Zaremba was to belong to them all.

For the unmarried girls, a wedding always had a very special significance. A few of them were already spoken for, a few just beginning to court, still others on the lookout for steady, likely lads to pair up with. And what better auspices for putting ideas into the young men's heads than the days of wedding festivities, what with the fiddlers giving everyone itching feet, the dancing making for proximity, and the wine, the mead, the vodka flowing freely, setting off a string of ribald jokes to help bashful swains over their shyness while pushing the less bashful ones off the psychological fence.

"I envy you . . . how I envy you!" Wanda admitted to Maryla late one night in the room they still shared in Kasia's house. She managed a smile. "Funny I should be saying that, isn't it?" She was thinking what a long way they had come since the days they'd both so vehemently denounced marriage as a degrading institution to which the only possible answer was a free, voluntary union between a man and a woman! "What wouldn't I give to be in your place. . . ."

Maryla frowned, looking searchingly at her old friend. "I've been so engrossed in my own affairs I forgot that you and Adam . . . I mean, things aren't going right for you, are they?"

Wanda flushed. "I wasn't complaining," she mumbled. But the look on her face was one of hopelessness, and as she sat listless on the edge of her narrow cot, head bent and hands tightly interlocked, Maryla saw with a pang how thin she had grown since the beginning of summer.

"Are things that bad?"

"Bad?" Wanda echoed, and laughed, but without mirth. "On the contrary, they're good, they're wonderful. He loves me as much as I love him and a couple of months ago I wouldn't have dared hope that could happen! So in a sense what more could I ask?" She unbuttoned her blouse, shrugged out of it, then automatically began pulling the bone hairpins out of her hair. "But oh, Maryla, he's so defenseless! Something's going to happen to separate us unless we, too, manage to get married! I know it . . . I feel it. . . ."

Maryla would have liked to reassure her, to ply her with all the comforting platitudes one generally offers people in trouble and in pain in order to help them over their worst moments. *Take each day as it comes. . . . Don't borrow trouble. . . . Look on the bright side of things. . . .* She couldn't bring herself to say any of them.

"Do you really believe," she finally managed, "that the legal sanction of a wedding ring would protect you or him or any of us against . . . well, you know, what the song calls the whirlwinds of danger? Jail will still be jail. Exile, Siberia, it's all still in the cards. Even the gallows. They can separate us, pick us off one by one. . . . The trick is not to let ourselves be immobilized by danger, by threats. Not to lose the courage to find personal happiness in spite of everything, and live out our lives. Otherwise one might just as well throw a rope over a crooked tree limb and stick one's neck in the noose . . ."

"I know all that," Wanda agreed tonelessly, "and none of it is what bothers me. As long as we're talking you might as well know. It's Adam's family. He's convinced they come first, that he has no right to think of himself, of us. And how can I argue the point when his father is mortally ill? Maryla, Maryla, what am I going to do?"

"Oh my poor lamb," Maryla sighed, hugging her. She was ashamed for having suspected her friend even fleetingly of envy or lack of courage.

❧ *Four* ❧

ON THE LAST Sunday in August, with only a week to go to the wedding, little Kasienka refused to get up with the others and get ready for church. Not even threats of a good sound whipping had any effect, and big Kasia was beginning to wonder which herb tea to dose her with when Wanda and Maryla, still only half dressed, heard the scolding and crying and came out of their room to find out what the trouble was.

The child's face was flushed, the flaxen hair damp with perspiration, the cornflower eyes lackluster under their film of tears. Her throat, she moaned, was so sore she couldn't swallow. Maryla bent down and felt her forehead. It was burning hot. Her pulse was racing.

"This child needs a doctor," she told the now alarmed mother. "Is there one we can send for right away?"

Kasia sighed. The only doctor within hailing distance, she said, lived halfway between Karelice and the Lowicz Cathedral but he rarely troubled with home calls to peasant households. He would quite likely be at church, however, in the company of the big local landowner *Pan* Zbigniew Korsza, for the two were in the habit of spending their Sunday afternoons together playing whist. "Maybe," Kasia offered dubiously, "I could bundle the kid up and take her along on a chance he'd consent to look at her then and there. . . ."

The two friends exchanged glances. Both had by now come to the same conclusion—whatever the diagnosis, this was no casual summer complaint. There might be danger in moving the child, worse danger in exposing others to her illness.

"Do you have a thermometer in the house?" Wanda finally asked.

"And how would we come by a contraption like that?" her hostess wanted to know. Then her face cleared. "I just remembered. The *felczer*, the barber-surgeon, he's got one. Used it last year when my man fell ill." She considered a moment. "If we're lucky, if he's not still so drunk from last night that there's no rousing him, he'll lend it to us. I'll send one of the boys. His house is right down the street."

The barber-surgeon was known to spend more time at the tavern than tending to the cuppings, bleedings, and similar chores that had made his profession an honorable one since the Middle Ages. He had, in fact, long ago abdicated to the local midwife, who knew as much and more about doctoring than he did, tending the sick regularly between birthings. On a Sunday morning he was always especially hard to wake. If one did try, it was with the added precaution of using the polite time-worn fiction that he was being disturbed while getting ready to attend holy services.

Knowing all this and observing protocol, Kasia coached her small son to be sure to repeat exactly what he was told: that the *Pan Felczer* was to excuse his neighbor for presuming on his good nature, that she, Kasia, well realized he was busy and had no time for the likes of her, only this was an emergency. Oh, nothing that required his presence, he needn't worry, he could go about his business with a clear conscience. But first would he be pleased to lend them a piece of his valuable equipment, namely his thermometer, of which the young ladies from Warsaw would take the very best of care until it could be returned later in the day. Translated, all this meant he was free to sleep off his drunk and no one would hold it against him.

The thermometer registered 104° and there were nasty yellowish spots on the child's enlarged, inflamed tonsils. Her pulse continued to beat wildly. The two friends decided that one of them had best stay with her while the other went to Lowicz in hopes of catching up with the doctor and convincing him how badly he was needed. "You go, Maryla," Wanda urged. "You belong there with Olek anyway, today of all days. Then later you can spell me and maybe Adam and I can take a walk." She also managed to persuade the now weeping Kasia there was very little to be gained by her, too, staying in the sick-room. The distracted peasant woman finally agreed.

"I'll say special prayers for her, and you, too. Burn an extra candle to Our Lady."

Doctor Dobrzynski did not arrive at church until the very last minute, so that Maryla was unable to approach him until after services were over. Then, escorted by Olek, she went up to him as he was crossing the church courtyard toward Squire Zbigniew Korsza's waiting carriage.

She introduced herself and explained her errand, but he listened with only half an ear, noting in the meantime that the liveried coachman perched on his high seat already held reins in hand and that Korsza's magnificent dappled grays shivered restlessly, ready to shy from the boisterous peasant crowd.

He had been looking forward to a fine midday meal at the manor, to superior wines and a chance of fleecing his host at cards as usual, for he was the shrewder player of the two. And did this wench who wore regional clothes like carnival dress really expect him to give up his Sunday pleasure for the sake of some village brat, merely because she asked in city accents? "Bring the child around tomorrow," he began. "It will be time enough, I dare say."

But Maryla was not to be brushed aside. "We think it's diphtheria, sir," she said politely but urgently. "My friend and I have done what we could to make the patient comfortable, but I'm afraid our best isn't good enough. And if this were to start an epidemic. . ."

She let the sentence trail off, but by now she had his full attention. "So," he said acidly, his pince-nez quivering and his voice heavy with sarcasm. "So. It seems you've already made a diagnosis. But if you and your, er, friend, whoever that may be, are so competent, why am I needed at all?"

Maryla flushed but stood her ground. "I didn't mean to presume, sir," she answered with what she hoped was the proper degree of deference. "It's just that last year we, my friend and I, spent some time working in a children's clinic." Carefully she omitted mention of the kind of clinic it was. "We had the opportunity to observe the disease in all its stages. I mean, all the symptoms seem to indicate. . ."

From crimson Dobrzynski's face turned purple. "Hear hear! *The symptoms seem to indicate.* . . . So now we have women doctors, eh?" He turned to Korsza. "What's going on among your peasants, my friend? Are the newfangled notions from the city seeping in even here, subverting the good people?"

Pompous old goat, Maryla thought, feeling rage beginning to mount. Now she understood, too late, that she should never have mentioned her clinic experience. Heaven alone knew what kind of hornet's nest this might stir up in the future. She glanced sideways at Olek and was aware of the suppressed violence of his own reaction. Her hand caught and pressed his, as if willing him to control himself at all costs. For at this moment nothing was so important as getting adequate medical help for Kasienka, and neither her pride nor his must be allowed to get in the way.

Then, unexpectedly, they were finding an ally in Squire Korsza. The craggy landowner was studying Olek, and his look of slight puzzlement changed to one of recognition. "Why, I know you, boy! You're old Zaremba's grandson, from the university!" He laughed, a deep, benevolent, expansive sound. "You've gone a long way, haven't you, since you used to steal my green apples! A long way indeed!" Then he whispered something to the doctor, who instantly lost some of his truculence. Old Zaremba, went the gist of what Korsza was saying, wasn't "just anybody" but one of the wealthier villagers, and to be reckoned with in local matters. His family must not be ignored without good and sufficient reason.

Doctor Dobrzynski had no wish to antagonize the biggest landowner in the district even if it should cost him his Sunday plans. "Very well," he said, sighing audibly. "Duty is duty. The Hippocratic oath and all that." He turned to the young people with a great show of magnanimity. "You may expect me sometime later on in the day."

By the time he reached the cottage Kasienka was delirious. He did what was necessary, swabbing her throat and prescribing for her; was reminded that medicines were unobtainable this far away from a city; considered, seemingly waging battle with himself; then, making up his mind, rummaged through his satchel and came up with what was needed. "By a fortunate coincidence I happen to have just the right drugs. . . ." He appeared anxious to erase the unfortunate impression he'd made earlier, for if Squire Korsza felt these people were worth bothering with it might be to his advantage to play along. Besides, secretly he was relieved that the two city bluestockings, as he had labeled Maryla and Wanda, had had the presence of mind to do what they had. Without their quick action, their isolating the child, already a real epidemic might have been in the making. And wouldn't *that* have spoiled the rest of the summer for him! Best of all, that handsome Brunhilde in the peasant getup and this other one, the skinny feminist with the black look, could be counted on to relieve him of other trips to the village. So, treating them as he might two novice Sisters of Mercy on a hospital charity ward, he left them a pile of instructions, medicines, alcohol, another thermometer, and, of course, orders to keep in touch along with directions for reaching him at his villa in case of emergency. Then he drove off, well satisfied. Diphtheria was, after all, not necessarily fatal.

Kasienka did not die, but two other small pine coffins were taken to the cemetery in a matter of days, votive candles and prayers notwithstanding. A sadness fell on Karelice and not even the gold of the bumper grain crop lifted the people's spirits. The harvest festival that had promised to be so joyous would now be a hushed affair, for who had the heart to dance the nights away when there was mourning to the left and to the right in neighbors' houses?

The wedding itself would be quiet, too, quietly solemnized.

"Perhaps we should put it off a couple of weeks," Grandfather Zaremba wondered out loud. "There's still time to tell the priest and send word to the folks in the city. Well, children," he turned to the bride and groom. "It's for you to decide."

The grandmother agreed with him. "Gloom on the wedding day is ill luck," she warned.

But Olek and Maryla had begun to feel uneasy, as if time were suddenly running out for them. "We should be getting back. There's work to be done," they both insisted. "We've stayed away long enough as it is."

In the end it was decided to have only the church ceremony and a family gathering afterwards—though even a family gathering meant dozens of guests in the compound. Well, Olek thought wryly, at least he and Maryla would be spared the public circus, the jokes at the expense of newlyweds. It was an ill wind that blew no good!

The wedding day arrived, and with it Olek's parents, a married sister, and then Uncle Jacek, Olek's hero since childhood, the one who was always in and out of jail. Adam had not been sure what manner of man to expect—no doubt someone larger than life—and was startled to find himself shaking hands with an ordinary Warsaw workingman. Jacek Piotrowski was a half a head shorter than Olek and Olek's father but like them was broad-shouldered and powerfully built, with graying hair, a broad nose that once had been broken, and a grip that bespoke his early training as a stone-cutter. "Well, did I think he'd appear wearing a halo or a martyr's crown?" Adam chided himself ironically, and had to admit this was precisely what his imagination had been conjuring up. So much for boyhood dreams.

Olek's mother had not seen her family in more years than she cared to count on her fingers, for when was there ever time for visiting? As happens so often in such circumstances, she was shocked to find how very old the old people had grown, how even her own generation had weathered, like timber left out in the rain.

With her new daughter-in-law she was unexpectedly shy, much more so than her village kinfolk, who by now had accepted both "doctor ladies" without reservations. This was especially true since Kasienka's illness. They suspected, and rightly, that it was less Dr. Dobrzynski's ministrations than the round-the-clock nursing the girls had given her that had saved the child's life. But Olek's mother saw Maryla mainly as a lady, educated, upper-class. And while she and her husband had long ceased to be surprised at their son's choice of friends, that he should choose such a wife was difficult to countenance.

It remained for Uncle Jacek to cut through nonessentials and welcome the bride in the name of his generation. "We're proud to have you in the family, *Pani* Maryla—or should I really say, *Comrade* Maryla?" And his eyes twinkled while his voice boomed. "As you can gather, I've heard all about you. Our Olek is a lucky man to've found you. For courage and principle are rare at any time and a priceless dowry with which to begin a marriage." And right then and there, dusty as he was from the road, nothing would do but that he must link arms with her and drink a *bruderschaft* toast, so that they might start calling each other by their given names and say *ty,* thou, to one another instead of using the cumbersome *pan* and *pani* form of address.

Soon it was time to start for church, with the bridal pair heading the caravan in a hired hack and the others in assorted carts and hay wagons, with half the village turning out after all. Try as they all might, the atmosphere of mourning couldn't entirely subdue their high spirits. The Zaremba women had decked Maryla out in their regional best, they had woven a garland of cornflowers and poppies for her hair and pinned it like a diadem over her bridal veil, and she was looking softly radiant and surprised even herself by feeling every inch a bride.

Olek, who hadn't let her out of his sight since the women had done with her, could hardly take his eyes off her. "Would you believe it," he admitted to Adam, sheepishly, at the last moment, "I feel positively awed. It has nothing to do with the claptrap, the mumbo jumbo—it's just something inside me. Can you understand that?"

Adam nodded. He did understand, and only too well. It seemed to him that for days now there had been a dull pain where his heart ought to be, and the pain quickened every time he looked at Wanda or permitted himself to dwell on his friends' bursting happiness. Not that it was a happiness he begrudged them, but it made him all the more aware of his own dilemma and Wanda's obvious distress.

"Why couldn't it be us?" The question tortured him, and in turn he tortured her with it. "Why not us too? Why, why, why?"

But she could only look at him and shake her head. For how does a woman tell a man that the fault is really his, that he himself is causing the misery by remaining stubbornly blind? How does she say, "Take a chance, then, marry me, we'll muddle through!" She wanted to, she tried, but pride stood in the way and kept her from choking the words out.

He saw only that he was hurting her, that nothing was to be gained by more talk unless he could bring himself to make a move. He was like a swimmer trying to dive, knowing exactly what he must do yet standing immobilized at the water's edge, incapable of taking the plunge. *Come on, it's easy, just hold your breath and let yourself go.* He remembered his brother Viktor throwing the words out like a challenge during some half-forgotten outing. But he hadn't jumped and finally had turned away shamefaced. Something of the same paralysis gripped him now. Why couldn't he take the risk? Would the family really be that much worse off if he and Wanda were to marry? Must it mean shrugging off all responsibility? Surely with his diploma in sight and Pozner's offer of a job, they could manage. Besides, he knew that for Wanda it would be a matter of principle to keep on earning her own way, so that between them they would be able to go on helping his parents even if for a time it might mean moving in with them. Why then was he so afraid? Was it because he must seem to be a model son at all costs? Because everything he did must be done not less than perfectly?

They had planned from the start that Wanda would stand up for Maryla. But Adam, as a Jew, could not be best man, and that honor had gone to Uncle Jacek. Now, as the ceremony progressed, he felt devastatingly alien and alone in the great church, wedged in among the Zaremba men in a pew reserved for the wedding party. All around, the crowd was absorbed in the pageantry of ritual. The sun slanting through the stained glass windows hurt his smarting eyes. And suddenly it was no longer the marriage service he was hearing but words spoken by Jacek a few hours earlier. *Courage and principle are a priceless dowry with which to begin a marriage.* Wanda had courage, the kind generally expected of men, not of women, and he found himself wishing desperately, with a kind of envy, that his were a match for it.

The bride and groom were exchanging rings. They were kissing and being blessed. Women wept, as women always seem to at weddings. Organ music swelled and faded. There was a shuffling of feet, and then the general exodus began.

As soon as she was able, Wanda made her way through the crowd to join him. She, too, was decked out in the peacock finery the occasion called for, the peasant dress and flowered kerchief and beads and ribbon streamers adding to the gypsy look that so enchanted him. But he saw that her cheeks had none of their accustomed color and her eyes were darkly circled.

He knew she had gone many nights without sleep during her vigil by Kasienka's bedside, yet her pallor seemed to him more than plain weariness. "Are you all right, my dearest?" he whispered anxiously, taking her unresponsive hand.

"Never better. Just feeling the heat a little," she whispered back. "For heaven's sake don't worry about me! I'm never sick!" Did he imagine it, or was there an edge of irony to her voice?

There were times, and this was one of them, when she intimidated him, as if austerely withdrawing behind a curtain of private thoughts and feelings where he was not welcome to follow. It left him bewildered, and he was about to ask whether he had done anything to offend her, when he felt her sway against him. "You're not all right! You look ill! Please, darling, let me take you out of here. . . ."

But already she was regaining control. "It's nothing. Nothing, I tell you. Just help me outside so no one will notice. After all," she forced a laugh, "fainting's for brides, not for bridesmaids! Come. I should hate to do anything to spoil the festivities."

On the way back to the village they hardly spoke, grateful for the hubbub around them that made their own silence pass unnoticed. And later on he felt more and more like the proverbial ghost at the wedding feast. Wanda, seemingly recovered, joined in the dancing. He watched from the sidelines as she whirled by, bright skirts and ribbons flying, and he marveled at her sudden effortless change of mood. It never occurred to him that she might be acting out a part in order to prove a point to him. *See, I'm well and gay and quite able to take care of myself, me, myself, alone, without help from you. . . .* The curtain she had so imperceptibly lowered between them refused to lift.

Night fell. Long tables were set up on the grass to accommodate the overflow of guests. As musicians and dancers drooped, hoping for their second wind, suckling pigs were lifted from the pits where they had been roasting. Great mounds of potatoes and black bread and steaming kasha were brought on. Wine flowed freely, vodka was plentiful, men cracked smutty jokes, slapping each other on the back and guffawing loudly while the married women joined in and young girls giggled. Round after round of toasts were drunk and so far no one seemed the worse for it.

By and by Bogumil Zaremba went down in person to the spring house for some of the special mead he'd been hoarding since his own wedding day. And when it had been rolled uphill and the bung pulled, he announced that now there was only one more keg left, and this he was saving against the day—with a broad wink at the bride—when his first great-grandson was christened. And, he added, while the mead might grow mellower for the waiting, he himself wasn't likely to, so they had best not try his patience too long. The speech was greeted with more laughter and the toasts began again.

It was already well after dark when with a great clatter of hooves Squire Korsza's familiar carriage and pair pulled up at the Zaremba gate. There was momentary respectful silence as the coachman climbed off his high seat and went around to open the door. But the carriage turned out to be empty—the man merely reached in and produced an enormous basket of fancy fruit, oranges and peaches and God alone knew what else, that could only have come from the landowner's hothouses.

A gift for the bride and groom, the coachman announced importantly, and a note for them, too, to which he had strict orders to bring back an answer. And this in itself might have seemed queer, had people still been sober enough to notice. For whoever heard of a wedding gift that called for a thank-you by return messenger, like a telegram?

It was Jacek, in his role of best man, who now came forward to relieve the coachman of his awkward package. But the other said no, he'd been told to deliver it into the hands of the newlyweds and no one else. "The way I figure it, Master meant to make damn sure they got a taste of all them goodies 'fore the guests could get at 'em!" He chuckled, shedding some of the dignity of his job, then dug into an inside pocket. "Here's the note, though. Master said to carry it safe and separate. Well, it's safe enough now. Who'd want to sink his teeth into a piece of paper!"

Jacek glanced at the envelope, and his eyebrows shot up. For it was addressed, not to the bride and groom at all, but to the bride and her maid of honor. He wondered how the coachman had failed to notice and decided it could only be because he couldn't read. *Was this perhaps why Korsza had chosen him to make the delivery?*

His trained conspirator's mind now fully alerted, he called to one of the women to bring the new guest food and drink and see that the horses were watered. "Rest yourself, friend," he elaborated, "for I may be a while." He was playing for time. "You know how it is with newlyweds. . . . Ten to one they're holed up in one of the barns!" He was rewarded with a poke in the ribs and a guffaw. Fine, he thought, now *that's* taken care of.

On his way into the house he caught sight of Adam and signaled him to follow. "Something's up," he whispered urgently. "Help me round up Olek and the girls. And old Bogumil." In the doorway he turned and shouted, "Hey, fiddlers, basses, give us another tune! Do your resting tomorrow!" Immediately couples began to pair off for another mazurka. And that, too, was as it should be, for the more merrymaking, the more noise, the better.

In a small room away from the crowd of celebrants Jacek and Adam were joined by the grandfather, then Olek. "The girls will be here as soon as they can get away," Olek said, "but we'd better not wait." Jacek broke the seal on Korsza's note and they crowded together, reading over his shoulder.

There was neither salutation nor a signature, and at first glance it made very little sense:

> "*Jus primae nocti* being an ancient, time-honored custom," Korsza had written, "I shall be expecting you girls on my doorstep at midnight. And escorted by your young men, just for good measure. Since I prefer to keep my household in the dark about my private life, don't ring or knock but use the French doors on the terrace. They lead directly into the library, where I'll be waiting. My wife is used to my keeping odd hours and the servants sleep in the back, so it'll be quite safe. Above all don't disappoint me. *For my friend D. has been telling all and sundry about you smart young ladies and what you can do, so naturally I'd like to get my licks in before his other cronies.* If I can manage that, I promise the whole thing will be well worth your while."

On the face of it, it sounded like a smutty proposition from a horny old roué, and one who had taken leave of his senses to boot. Lords of the manor hadn't exercised their prerogative to deflower virgin peasant brides since a century before the serfs were freed. Was Squire Korsza out of his mind and living in another time? Was this his notion of a joke, crude and in poor taste? Neither conjecture squared with his reputation.

"*Jus primae nocti* be damned," old Bogumil muttered. "You young squirts know more Latin than I do, but if it means what I think it means. . ."

"It does, but if you ask me it doesn't add up," his grandson answered. "You've known Korsza a lifetime, Grampa. Would you say he's crazy? Or an old rip?"

"Far from it."

"And here's another thing," said Adam, puzzled. "*Jus primae nocti* never did extend to bridesmaids. Not even in *Figaro*." Then, realizing how little meaning such a reference would have for the old peasant, he went on quickly to his next point. "And what's all this about expecting us to bring him our women ourselves? As if any man in his right mind would do such a thing of his own free will. . . ."

"Precisely," Jacek agreed. "Unless, of course—" And he began rereading the note as if searching for the missing parts of a puzzle.

Wanda came in, and a moment later Maryla, and Olek held out the note to them. "As you can see," he told his bride, attempting a lightness of tone he didn't feel, "already I'm acting like a husband, opening your mail!" Then, serious again, "Can either of you make head or tail of this? It has the rest of us stumped."

They studied the curious document in silence, while from beyond the thin walls came laughter and the screech of fiddles tuning up between dances. Presently Adam noticed that Wanda, whose face had at first flamed with shock and anger, turned quite pale. "It seems to me," she began slowly, feeling her way, "that all the rigmarole at the beginning is so much flimflam, a red herring. The whole gist of the message is in the last couple of sentences. Listen." She glanced at the note for confirmation, "listen to what he's saying. *My friend D.*—and that's got to be Dr. Dobrzynski, we don't know anyone else he knows—had his nose badly out of joint that time Squire Korsza made him come for Kasienka. Remember how nasty he got, how sarcastic?" She began quoting, mimicking Dobrzynski to perfection: " '*Oh, so now we have lady doctors. . . .*' We ruined his Sunday for him and maybe made him lose face, so he's got even. How? By *telling all and sundry about us.* Telling whom? The authorities, of course— who else would be interested? In other words, Dobrzynski has denounced us."

"Good God! Then the letter's a warning!"

"And an offer of help. Korsza says he hopes to *get his licks in before D's other cronies.*"

"I was beginning to figure it that way," Jacek said, "and now it's all falling into place. You're to go to his house in the dead of night when his household is safely asleep. Above all, you're not to disappoint him. Which probably means he hopes to see all four of you miles away from here by morning."

Bogumil Zaremba swore under his breath. Then, unable to contain himself, exploded loudly, "Goddam that little bastard, may he roast in hell! What's our country coming to that even a man's wedding night isn't sacred any more. . . ."

Outside, the music started up again and there was the stamping of feet. Men were swinging their partners, couples whirled round and round, and those on the sidelines clapped in rhythm. The party had turned into a true Lowicz wedding after all. And this was just as well, for no one heard what was going on here in this room, no one cared or paid the least attention.

A moment more, and there was a knock on the door. Squire Korsza's coachman wanted to know how much longer he would have to wait for his answer. Olek found a blank sheet of paper, wrote the one sentence, "We'll be there," folded, sealed, and addressed it, and took it out. Then he came back for Maryla, so that together they might return to their guests. "Above all," Jacek warned them, "keep acting as if nothing had happened. Let the party spirit wear itself out. After the men start rolling under the tables it'll be safe for you to leave."

Maryla smiled bitterly. "I always knew it was too good to last. Come, Olek."

Wanda, her hand in Adam's, said nothing.

The grandfather was still cursing. "God damn it to hell, what a way for the children to spend their wedding night! God damn Dobrzynski! God damn the *Moskals*."

"At least this time we're seeing the *Moskals* outfoxed," Jacek consoled him.

The fiddlers went on fiddling and the accordionist filled the air with his sharp wailing. The mazurka ended, and Olek claimed his bride for the final oberek.

❧ *Five* ❧

THE LAST GUESTS were still lingering when Wanda left the main house and made her way through the wet grass to Kasia's. Out of habit she looked in on the sleeping Kasienka, still isolated from the rest of the family in a hastily improvised sickroom, and couldn't resist an edge of self-pity creeping into the tenderness she had developed for the child. *My first patient,* she reflected, *and you'll never know what you're costing me!* Yet she knew that had she the same choice a second time, she would not do anything differently.

In the room where she and Maryla had roosted all summer she methodically stripped herself of the peacock plumage of her bridesmaid's attire, folding each article carefully, stacking everything neatly on the cot where she wouldn't be spending another night. Then she changed into her own dark, plain city clothes, undid her long braids, brushed them out, pinned her hair up in conventional fashion, and set about packing her things.

This was quickly done, for there were no choices to make, no sorting out of any kind. *Omnia mea mecum porto* flashed through her mind. The phrase seemed cruelly apt. Yet it was not the meagerness of her possessions that hurt, but the realization that like a wanderer with only a bundle over her shoulder she was adrift and had no place to go, and between herself and Adam nothing was settled.

For the first time she understood how much her living with Maryla had come to mean to her. What had it mattered that her parents had neither room nor a welcome for her so long as the Zapiecek flat had been home and an anchor? Well, that, too, was gone, and nothing—she forced herself to face and to admit it—nothing promised to take its place.

Earlier in the day, before there had yet been any inkling of the fresh trouble, she'd said something of the sort to Maryla. They had been dressing for church, and Maryla, seemingly intent on lacing the bodice of her wedding dress, had listened, then in her practical, matter-of-fact way urged her to share her misgivings with Adam. "Maybe all he needs is to be told how you feel. Just say you dread the thought of having to live alone. Bring it out in the open. Why not? You've nothing to lose and everything to gain."

But Wanda could no more bring herself to do this than she could admit—to Adam, or Maryla, or even to herself—that a new and worse fear was beginning to gnaw at her. For the past week she hadn't been feeling her usual robust self and resolutely put it down to overexertion and excitement. Everyone knew that excitement and overexertion did sometimes make a woman miss her period. *But they didn't cause sore nipples or swollen breasts. . . .*

Even when she had almost fainted in church she had stubbornly refused to face what might really be wrong. "It'll all blow over. . . I'm being a hysterical female. . . ." And as always in moments of crisis a perverse kind of pride sustained her, making her incapable of asking for help. She also had a deep need to prove that her emancipation as a woman was something she could achieve alone, with no succor from any direction. At the same time—and this was feminine pride of a different kind entirely—she yearned for her lover to anticipate her terrible need, to outguess her, lay siege to her reserve, and conquer it, conquer the obstacles she herself was putting in his way because she must have additional proof that she was cherished.

Her conscious reasoning told her none of this. She knew only that time was running out and she no longer had weeks or even days in which to figure what to say to Adam in order to convince him, and she began to feel trapped and her head started spinning and she dropped down on the hard stripped mattress and briefly indulged in the luxury of unashamed crying, spinning the childish fantasy that if only he might come upon her and see her thus, heartbroken and bewildered, he would take over and start making the decisions and set her world to rights. *Oh Adam, Adam, help me!* Then, as abruptly as it had started, the weeping stopped, and she just sat there motionless, eyes closed and forehead pressed against the cold iron bedpost.

"What's the matter, Wandziula, aren't you feeling well?"

She hadn't heard Maryla come in and was nettled at being caught out in this moment of weakness. "I'm fine. Why? Why does everyone keep asking me how I feel?"

If only you could see yourself! Maryla thought, but let it pass. Instead she said, "Since you're all packed and ready, maybe you'll give me a hand with this veil. I'm so afraid to tear the lace." Deliberately, she turned. With her back to Wanda it was easier to ask questions. "Have you had a chance to talk to Adam yet?"

"At the rate things have been going? How could I?" Wanda sounded weary beyond caring. "Besides, now that we're on the run again what does it matter? Nothing will ever be the same."

"No, but you still have to make plans for the future. Both of you. Together or separately. And maybe together would be better."

She didn't answer but turned abruptly, trying to read in Maryla's face whether possibly her friend had guessed the whole truth about her. If so, there was bound to be further probing, and the best way to ward that off was by direct attack. "What am I supposed to do," she said nastily, "get down on my knees and beg him to make an honest woman of me? Like . . . like Olek did for you?"

Maryla saw that it was Wanda's misery speaking and would not be provoked. "Sarcasm does not become you," was all she said. Without further comment she, too, began changing into her city clothes. Wanda sat watching her, and within moments began to feel ashamed of herself, aware that part of her bitterness had been jealousy pure and simple.

All the fight went out of her. "Don't you see," she finally said, "much as I love Adam I've no illusions about him. He's not like the rest of us—he doesn't seem to feel the need to go after what he wants. Or maybe he's just convinced he has *no right* to want anything for himself. Other people have always come first in his life. That being so, he won't even face the wanting—it's easier that way. After all," she went on with an objectivity Maryla was finding thoroughly disconcerting, "if a man doesn't know where he wants to go, he can't be lost, can he?"

"And so you won't lift a finger to help him find himself?"

"Now who's being sarcastic?"

"I just think," Maryla said quietly, "that maybe you're underrating him."

"Do you, my dear? I wonder if Olek would agree. Has it been deep conviction that made Adam join in the struggle? Remember how we used to plot and scheme to draw him in, and how nothing really worked till it became a personal thing with him? It was only when he and I fell in love, and he knew I was threatened, that. . . Then he had no more doubts. Oh, he stood by me," she admitted, still with that same merciless detached clarity, "but make no mistake about it, he's with us out of personal loyalty. Loyalty to me, to Olek, to you. His heart's in the right place and he'd give each one of us the shirt off his back. But the understanding, the need to do, aren't there."

Maryla still wasn't convinced. "And you don't think him capable of changing, growing?"

"We're all capable of growing," Wanda said rather loftily, "but not at anyone else's pace. Certainly not if we're pushed, or appealed to. Or because someone begs us in the name of love—love crying out for help, for a little pity. . . ."

"So there you have it in a nutshell," Maryla said, making a final attempt to shock her friend out of her self-destructive mood. "As I see it, you're so afraid of admitting you might need help you won't even try the simplest move. . . . I suppose if it came to moving mountains you'd try doing that alone, too!" She snapped the lock on her suitcase with all the finality of slamming a door. "There, I've had my say. But it's your life. I've no right to force advice on you."

Because all day long there had been so much coming and going through the village, no one was likely to pay attention to one more cart jogging along the road late at night. Nevertheless they decided it would be safest for them to leave as part of the caval-cade of Warsaw relatives bound for the railway station. At the crossroads they would simply turn off and double back toward Squire Korsza's villa. The driver, one of Olek's numerous cousins and thoroughly trustworthy, would let them off at the edge of the Korsza apple orchard, through which it was an easy walk to the manor house.

It was a quiet leave-taking, with few words spoken and em-braces that were quick and hard, for who could tell whether the old people would live to see the grandchildren again? Grand-mother Zaremba wiped her eyes with the corner of her apron as she stood in the doorway waving to them. And even her husband was seen to give his nose a mighty blow as he chewed fiercely on his walrus mustache.

Through it all Adam sat in hurting, frozen silence. He and Wanda hadn't exchanged two sentences in private since the cur-tain of her withdrawal had first descended, leaving him helpless, making communication impossible between them just when they most desperately needed to talk. Had he been able to hear her mute appeal he might have found the words to convince her that now of all times she shouldn't be holding herself back from him, shouldn't be so forbidding and stern. Had she known how will-ing he was to listen she might have pleaded that this was just her way and begged him to bear with her and try, oh please try, to make a first move of some kind. But neither knew how to break the impasse and so the moment was lost, and the estrangement, the resentment, grew and rankled.

Years later, when his character had been set in a definite mold and the streak of youthful mysticism that for a while, under Olek's influence, he had ignored, began to reassert itself heavily laden with overtones of fatalism, Adam would think of this night as the first of a series of crucial turning points in his life—moments of prevision when, in a flash of something akin to sec-ond sight and clearer by far than mere premonition, he would an-ticipate what must surely come later. At times the insight would take the form of a prophetic dream. At times it would be a wak-ing certainty so strong that when the events themselves finally did take shape nothing came as a surprise. All this only served to increase his fatalism, for on such occasions his destiny seemed to unfold as if preordained, like well-rehearsed lines in a play finally being enacted on the living stage.

That all this was merely part and parcel of his own character—stemming from that basic sense of unworthiness which sometimes causes a human being so to doubt himself he will make no direct demands on life but will rather let events buffet him—this he never learned to suspect. And if ever such a suspicion did come nibbling around the edges of his mind, he firmly shut it out. *What must be, must be.* Whatever happened, he told himself stoutly, at least he had the comfort of knowing he would always act honorably, out of a sense of responsibility. For Adam, like so many men eternally in harness, equated the discharge of responsibility with moral strength, never dreaming it might merely be propitiation of the gods. Eventually by this tortuous path he would reach a stage where he would find it increasingly difficult to make decisions of any kind and finally all but impossible to keep from making ones he knew in his bones were wrong for him. But that wouldn't happen until much later, when he was older, and successful, and unable to countenance success.

On this particular fall Sunday at the turn of the century his inability to take action simply brought on the feeling that doom was hanging over his head, and Wanda's coolness in church had done nothing to ease his depression. The arrival of Korsza's messenger at the wedding feast served to reinforce his sense of foreboding, so that when Jacek called him away from the guests he was tempted to say yes, of course, how else could the day have ended except in calamity? And in a sense he even felt relieved that the thread on which the sword of Damocles had been hanging over his head all day at last had snapped. Yet still it did not occur to him that he might, in fact must, take his fate into his own hands if he was to save his soul.

As they jostled along the dry and rutted road, he tried to see into the future. But the pictures his mind conjured up only confused and distressed him. He saw Wanda arrested, sentenced to jail, to Siberia, denied forever the privilege of continuing with her life's work. But where was he while this was happening? Why wasn't he beside her, accepting voluntary exile rather than separation? It seemed inconceivable that he did not join her, yet try as he might, the waking dream showed him staying behind.

What seemed to keep him from following was that he couldn't shut out an insistent voice whispering accusingly that his life was not his own to dispose of. At first he thought it was his mother talking, but as words and sentences emerged he knew them for Salome's familiar flute-like tones. *A young couple can afford to wait, dear heart . . . Why not consider yourselves engaged, wait a couple of years . . . ? You have your whole life ahead of you, but to abandon your people when they need you, when you're just beginning to be a real help, isn't that selfish? Wouldn't it be best to remain free and unencumbered a little while longer?* Against these arguments, hoarse and hollow yet surprisingly firm, his father seemed to counter: *A man must do what's best for him, he must not do violence to himself!* But his father's voice was gradually drowned out by the sweetly reasonable terrible insistence of the other, until finally the rattle of turning wheels obliterated all other sound.

He was no further along with his thinking when they reached the apple orchard. As he and Wanda started toward the villa through the dew-wet grass he reached out, drew her to him, kissed her hard. "I love you," he whispered. "No matter what happens I'll always love you. Never forget that."

She was no longer forbidding but soft and yielding in his arms. "I know. Because that's the way I love you."

Yet both knew that this was no longer enough.

Zbigniew Korsza was as good as his word, waiting and watching for them, letting them in before they'd had time even to knock. "Welcome. I see you had no trouble figuring out what I meant!" He led them into the library where a fire crackled merrily against the chill of the fall night. The room was decorated with mounted boars' heads and antlers, the bookshelves holding at least as many trophies of the hunt as books. On a leather-covered desk stood decanters and crystal glasses on a silver tray.

He gave them brandy to warm themselves, apologizing for not having anything more elaborate to offer. But, he explained, he wanted no trace of unexpected midnight visitors. Not even his wife need suspect. "The cardinal rule of this business is never to talk to others about what you can accomplish alone." With that one sentence he let them know how much he had guessed about them and also where he stood. "By the time the household stirs in the morning you'll be gone, and no one the wiser. It's the safest way." Then he broke off, habits of a lifetime asserting themselves. "But what am I thinking, starting to talk business before even making you comfortable! Forgive me, ladies!" Effortlessly, he slid into the role of courtly host. "Country living makes a boor of a man. I'm being insufferably rude!"

"You're being wonderfully kind and generous."

"Stuff and nonsense! Should I stand by and let the Black Hundred pick you off like starlings on a fence?" He gestured toward an elaborately framed portrait of Kosciusko hung prominently in a place of honor. "Why, old Tadeusz's ghost would come to haunt me, should I allow anything like that to happen! Did you know he was a friend of the family? He and my grandfather fought together, and before that they hunted bison together in Bialowierza. He's the only patron saint I need or want, and how could I sleep soundly nights, were I to disappoint him!"

He raised his glass so that the light caught the amber liquor and made it sparkle. *"Prosit,* friends! *Poland is not yet lost!* And do you know why? It's because generation after generation young people like you carry on the good fight! You pick up where we oldsters have to leave off. . . ." He insisted on clinking glasses with each of them in turn. Then he cursed his oncoming gout that was forcing him to the sidelines of struggle, and finally cursed out the doctor.

"Damn skunk, damn craven little turncoat! So anxious to get on the good side of the *Moskals* that. . . When I think of all the money he's won from me at whist! And all the good food he's had at my table—he should have choked on it. Well, never again. . . . But enough of that. The real question is, what do we do with you? Have you made any plans yet?"

Olek said they had thought of hiding out with friends in the city until things quieted down, but Korsza shook his head. "Not good enough. They'd only smoke you out. That louse Dobrzynski, forgive a rough country man his language, ladies—that louse, I've good reason to suspect, has really extended himself.

He was determined to cook your goose—or is it geese?—so we must get you far away from Warsaw."

They asked if he had any counter-suggestions.

"As a matter of fact I do. Wouldn't a trip abroad be in order? Presuming, that is, you're all free to travel. Is there anything particular to hold you here?"

Listening to him, Adam felt a first unreasoning surge of hope. Had it come, then, the miraculous categorical imperative he had been waiting for? *We'll go, just go, and worry afterwards. . . .* Practical considerations seemed suddenly to fade away, so much so that when Olek pointed out the obvious—that traveling cost money—his immediate reaction was annoyance, impatience.

But the squire seemed to have an answer to that, too. "It's not an insuperable obstacle," he answered calmly, rising and crossing the room. With a key he wore on his watch chain he unlocked the glass doors of a bookcase filled with gold-tooled, leather-bound volumes which Adam assumed were treasured first editions. Reaching in behind some massive tomes, he pulled out a soft string purse. From this he extracted a dozen gold pieces. "A cache entrusted to me for just such contingencies," he grinned. "So you see, that clears the first hurdle."

Before they had recovered from the shock of this he moved on to a large map hanging behind his desk, and like a general accustomed to mounting campaigns began to explain exactly what he had in mind for them. "Now here is how we get you out of the country. First, using the less traveled roads and changing horses at inns where we know the people, we get you safely to Lodz." And they understood that his deliberate, repeated use of the "we" was intended to make it perfectly clear that he was indeed part of the vast network of an underground that reached out everywhere, into workers' compounds, and middle-class homes, and manor houses like his own. "Once there, you simply contact friends who'll know what to do. From Lodz it's only a skip and a jump to Kalisz, to the German border. After that you'll be on your own. Unless," he added, turning directly to the two girls and smiling, "you ladies should feel inclined to make your destination Zurich. Because at the moment we have good friends there, too, friends who could help you find your bearings. Zurich," he added, "as

I'm sure I don't need to tell you, has an excellent medical school, one of the best in Europe. One which happens to admit women."

"Zurich!" Maryla and Wanda repeated in unison. If either had been given to flowery speech she would have said this was like the promise of a dream come true. Finally Wanda, speaking for them both, answered soberly, "We've always said . . . if we had a choice of all the medical schools in Europe, Zurich is where we'd go. A degree from there means so much!"

Korsza nodded approvingly, looking rather paternal. "I figured that's how you'd look at it. Someday, let's hope, the country will welcome you back, two fine full-fledged doctors, in which case, hah-hah! that swine Dobrzynski has really done you a favor! And wouldn't he be livid if he knew! Hah!" He laughed hugely, relishing the joke, then in a quick change of mood became serious and businesslike once more. "It's settled, then? Zurich as your final destination? Good. Now let's get down to details."

❧ *Six* ❧

It TOOK A WHILE for the situation to begin to seem real to them. For it is one thing to have absorbed as an elementary fact of life that in order to be effective in the underground one must become adept at dodging informers and the police, and quite another to find this law of survival applied, in a seemingly wild fanciful game of cops and robbers, to one's own self.

They had run away once before, yet their flight had meant no more than a trip to Olek's native village, and thus was easy to take in stride. But to sit here in this baronial room, under the watchful eyes of the great Kosciusko himself, and hear the grandson of Kosciusko's friend jingle gold coins and plot a course for them as though they were characters out of a novel by Dumas père—this was more than their minds could yet encompass.

Even Olek, the most seasoned activist among them, was visibly shaken. Escape in the night, uprooting oneself, going abroad to live, learning to draw nourishment from foreign soil might all be part of the warp and woof of anti-Tsarist resistance, but he had always thought of such derring-do as reserved for the important figures in the movement. The leaders, the organizers of working-class groupings, the radical philosophers and men of letters from all parts of the Empire were forever being spirited across the border to escape jail, hard labor, sometimes torture and death. But these were the giants of thought and of action, men and women who belonged to history before they could belong to themselves. They were the ones inescapably touched with greatness. To live turbulently, rootless yet never without roots so long as they felt at one with the masses of people around them—such was their lot, accepted proudly and consciously as part of the price of being professional revolutionaries. How could four undistinguished university students equate themselves with such as these?

As he sat digesting Squire Korsza's proposals, Olek reflected on the never-ending traffic in precious human cargo smuggled in and out of the country by an underground that led to stations in England, France, Germany, Switzerland, distant America—all the places people liked to call the civilized world. England, where Marx and Engels had found a haven, where Robert Owen had gathered disciples, where the concept of personal freedom was said to have originated and the dignity of man first codified in the Magna Carta and a man's home was called his castle and to enter it the police had to have a search warrant. France, after her three revolutions, giving shelter to Prince Kropotkin and that other permanent expatriate whose writings Olek himself had recently been finding so useful, Grigori Plekhanov. And in Berlin Rosa Luxemburg was active these days, in close touch with her native land, managing trips home regularly, surfacing like a diver in troubled waters whenever she was needed. Olek had met her, he had heard her speak during some of those carefully engineered appearances of hers at illegal gatherings, heard her tell of the strong, class-conscious trade union movement of Germany and entreat her compatriots to quit squabbling among themselves and organize, organize, organize. . . .

Not long ago Rosa had begun to make frequent reference to a small group of Russian exiles with headquarters of sorts in Switzerland. She spoke with particular enthusiasm about one of their leaders, the red-bearded young veteran of Tsarist jails and Siberia, Vladimir Ilich Lenin, with whom sometimes she worked closely and sometimes violently disagreed. Olek had read a little of Lenin, was intrigued by what he knew of his scathing polemics against lukewarm liberal reformers and his position on equality for the subjugated peoples of the Empire. He remembered someone mentioning that Lenin was starting a secret newspaper as a means of unifying all the widely scattered revolutionary groups both at home and abroad. The paper would be called *Iskra,* The Spark, and on the masthead would be a line from a Pushkin poem dedicated to the Decembrists: *The spark shall kindle the flame.* It would be smuggled in, to start fires wherever people read it—even under the Tsar's very nose.

The underground with its channels into other parts of the world was in a sense the life stream that kept alive the movement for independence and freedom and sweeping social change. It also kept alive—literally, not figuratively alive—the leading cadres, the brightest minds. And what Olek kept coming back to, his mind boggling, was the absurdity, the presumption, of somehow finding himself and his bride and their friends suddenly bracketed with those illustrious others. It was like casting callow apprentice actors in roles created for a Bernhardt, a Rejane. And all without so much as time for rehearsal, time to say yes or no or will you accept the part or can you handle it? Just the lights dimming and the curtain going up.

And yet of the four Olek was the least perturbed. He had known for so long that this was where his life must inevitably lead that slowly the night's events began to seem to him merely a matter of advancing the timetable a bit: the inevitable had come a trifle sooner than expected. He certainly didn't relish finding himself, on his wedding night, caught up in what the song called "the whirlwinds of danger." Yet already future possibilities began to occur to him. Something he'd read fairly recently in the illegal magazine *Scientific Review,* something to do with the role of the individual in history, kept nudging at him. And then it came to him. Of course! It was that essay by Plekhanov himself, which in the spring he had tried to apply to Adam Fabian. History, Plekhanov insisted, determined its great men. And then he thought of another famous saying—who the devil was it ascribed to, anyway?—about some men being born great, some achieving greatness, and still others having greatness thrust upon them.

Now you're indulging in illusions of grandeur, he told himself wryly. *Maryla has to make a run for safety and you're running with her and that doesn't make you one bit more heroic than you were yesterday. All you'll be doing is taking a train past the checkpoint—and shaking in your boots till you're past the frontier guards.* But part of his mind whispered, *All very true but the train is being pulled by the locomotive of history and it's an express train at that.* And the fact that they would be surfacing in Zurich of all places, and who their new friends turned out to be, might determine the whole future course of their lives. And nothing would ever again be humdrum. Horizons would open up before them they had never even dared contemplate. In spite of himself, Olek's strongest emotion was a profound sense of excitement.

Adam's strongest, and all-engulfing, emotion was uneasiness with an admixture of shame. Since he'd had no chance to explain his presence here, Squire Korsza was simply assuming he was in trouble along with the others. It made him feel like an impostor. Perhaps he should warn the old gentleman that he was accepting his help and hospitality under false pretenses? At the same time the temptation was overwhelming to say nothing, just let events take over and drift in the silence of acquiescence, letting the tide sweep him wherever Wanda went—toward hardships but toward happiness, too.

In the meantime the squire continued to make plans.

"Do any of you have any connections of your own in Lodz? Because you may have to scatter while you're hiding out. The trick will be to fix you up with passports that look thoroughly authentic, and what with four of them, this may take a while. Once your papers are ready you'll be sneaked on to the European Express, which leaves late in the evening and gets to the border in the small hours, when customs officials are asleep on their feet. It'll be safe enough. It's the time in between that can be risky."

"The Pozners, the family where I've been tutoring," said Adam tentatively, "have a residence in Lodz on account of their textile business. And their summer villa is very close, in Milanowek. They're well disposed toward me."

But Olek felt Maurice Pozner was too much of an unknown quantity, and this was no time to find out where he really stood. "What about your Aunt Salome, Adash? She helped us once, and she seems to know everybody everywhere. If only we could get in touch with her, and fast! *Psiakrew!*" he swore, running his fingers through his hair. "The problem isn't a lack of contacts, it's how to reach them in a hurry!" Then, since Korsza was looking puzzled, he elaborated, "You see, sir, my friend here has this aunt, a perfectly unbelievable woman. Knows everyone, pulls all kinds of strings; it's like a game to her. Last month she even got my wife out of the Pawiak overnight—which is how we came to spend the summer with my people in the first place. If anyone can think of someone in Lodz," he concluded, "it would be Salome Grossglik."

As he talked a curious change came over old Zbigniew Korsza. His face broke into a beatific grin, he drew himself up, the tips of his mustache rose to stand at attention. "Salome Grossglik? *Pani* Leon Grossglik? I can hardly believe it! The most beautiful, the most charming woman my wife ever had cause to be jealous of. . . ."

"You know my Aunt Salome?" Adam asked incredulously. "But how? From where?"

"My oldest son," the old man said, still grinning broadly, "was one of her mother's boarders some years ago. She was Salome Tworska then, and already irresistible. He was wildly in love with her, and so if the truth be known was I. Of course it was all hopeless. For me because I'd reached the age of discretion. And for the boy—well, because he simply had to marry money." Tactfully, the squire skirted around the fact that under no circumstances could a scion of the Korsza clan have been permitted to join in wedlock with the Semitic beauty. "We had quite a time of it, convincing our Tadek—he's named after Kosciusko, of course—that neither of them would get very far in the world if he persisted in his determination to lay his heart and life at her feet. My duty as a father became especially painful considering," his smile became a mixture of nostalgia and self-indulgent amusement, "considering how much I sympathized with the boy. But all that's water under the bridge." He raised his glass, toasting the past. "What a small world we do live in! So you think, young man," addressing himself directly to Adam, "that *Pani* Salome could be helpful?"

"She'll do anything for anyone she's fond of, sir."

"In that case *Pan* Leon Grossglik is a lucky man," mused Korsza, wandering away from the main subject. "Not that my son didn't marry well, too. His esteemed father-in-law is Count Roman Lubienski. Unfortunately, my daughter-in-law Caroline is one of the *ugly* Lubienski women, not the least like some of her famous ancestresses. Small close-set eyes, a nose like a snout. . . . Of course, lack of beauty isn't necessarily a disadvantage in a bride. Sometimes quite the contrary. The dowry's apt to be larger, and the wife stays faithful. Still, I'm glad to say none of my grandchildren favor her. . . . "

Olek, impatient with the digressions, tried to direct the talk to better purpose. "And is your son in Warsaw now? Because if he is, that might simplify matters a good deal."

The ploy worked. Korsza hit his forehead with the palm of his hand. "Of course! Old fool that I am, why didn't I think of it myself? At dawn I send a messenger with a sealed letter to my son. I tell him to contact *Pani* Salome at once, warn her that her nephew and his friends are thinking about a little vacation trip abroad. You, young man," again he addressed Adam, "write a note to your aunt, which I shall enclose. If I know my son, that's all that's needed. We can rely on the two of them to do the rest."

For the second time they all felt like people in a book, still unable to accept the unbelievable masquerade. Too much had been happening too fast, and now they were beginning to feel numb, content for the moment to let someone else do the thinking and the manipulating.

Abruptly, their host stood up, indicating there would be no more discussion tonight. "You must compose your letter at once, *Pan* Adam, and I will do the same. Just keep in mind that even with a trusted servant carrying the message, the less committed to paper the better. Is *Pani* Salome good at reading between the lines?"

Adam, who had let his mind wander, did not answer at once. He was thinking how for years he had lived on the edges of conspiracy, but always vicariously. To Wanda, Maryla, and Olek conspiracy had long been daily reality, and to Aunt Salome a titillating if risky parlor game. There had been echoes and shadows of it everywhere around him. And now he was irrevocably part of it. And it seemed to him that from Olek to Maryla to Wanda to himself a strong chain had been forged, a chain of clasped hands, and if he tried to let go the whirlwinds of danger would surely engulf them. The time for decisions was past. He leaned over to Wanda sitting quietly beside him and touched her arm. "You see," he whispered, "I couldn't leave you now if I wanted!" But she didn't smile, didn't look pleased or happy, and he felt strangely disconcerted.

He became aware of Squire Korsza repeating his question, a touch of impatience in his voice. "Well, young man, what do you think? How much can we really expect of your aunt?"

Rousing himself, choosing his words carefully, he did his best to be precise. "It's hard for me to say what her connections may be in Lodz. I do know her sister's husband, Baron Kronenberg, has a *pied-à-terre* there—he travels back and forth a good deal and when he does, he likes his comfort. But the Baron and his wife are in Nice, and my aunt may not feel free to give their house-keeper in Lodz orders. Though on second thought she's not one to be stumped by protocol. . . ."

"From what I remember of the lady this will all be grist to her mill," Korsza said, rubbing his hands as if everything were falling in place to his satisfaction. "Between your aunt and my son and . . . a few others, I'd say you're in good hands. And now for the letters, and then you really must get some rest, for you'll have to be on the road by daybreak. Forgive me," he went on, "if I don't put you up in the guest wing, but as I've already pointed out, the fewer people see you, the better. So it'll have to be the barn for you, and new-mown hay. But you'll not mind that. Ah me, when I was your age. . ."

Adam held his love in his arms for what was left of the night, in turn adoring and overwhelming her with a hunger born of des-peration. Whatever had been wrong between them in the past few weeks was for the moment swept aside as each gave the other the sustenance that only passion mingled with deep tenderness can give. But dawn came, inevitably and too soon, and in the light of morning the language of loving bodies would no longer be enough. "Have you forgiven me for the way I've been shilly-shallying?" Adam suddenly asked, between kisses. She kissed him back but said nothing.

Slowly, a sound at a time, they listened to the countryside coming awake. An owl hooted. Then sharp and sweet came the pre-dawn trill of the nightingale. A cock crowed, a dog barked. The occasional chirp of a bird became the twitter of hundreds. A gate creaked, a cow mooed. There was the clatter of milk pails and a woman calling the barnyard fowls, "Tsip-tsip-tsip, my biddies. . . ."

Beyond a thin partition Olek snored evenly.

"That one never wears himself out worrying," Wanda said abruptly, and Adam could not tell whether the resentment in her voice was directed against the sleeper or himself. "Nerves of iron."

"He's been that way ever since we were boys," he answered. "No doubts, no hesitations. I've often envied him." In an effort to know what she was thinking he raised himself to look at her, but though the light was strong now it wasn't much help. Her expression remained closed.

With his free hand he began slowly to trace the long lovely line of her body from shoulder to hip—it was always easier to talk, he had learned, when he was touching her. "Maybe you should have found someone like him," he goaded her. "Someone strong and clearheaded."

It was his way of begging her to tell him she was accepting him as he was, that she could do without the uncomplicated power of a monolith. And she understood very well, but her uncompromising awkward honesty made it impossible for her to say the easy, soothing words. Her very silence became an accusation.

"I suppose you think me a coward," he went on painfully, his need for self-abasement like the need of a man in the confessional seeking absolution. "You can't have much respect for me."

"Don't," she tried to stop him. "Please. We all have the right to be afraid."

"You too? You seem so calm."

"Do I? Feel my heart." She pulled his head down and held it against her warm flesh and as he buried his face between her breasts he felt the pounding. "You see, that's how calm I am." She went on holding him and he smelled the unaccustomed sweat. "And now, before I lose my courage, let me say something I've been trying to tell you ever since all this started. . . ."

Beyond the partition the snoring had stopped and new sounds reached them—yawns and whispered words and then a rhythmic rustle of hay.

"They're awake," she said. "Soon we'll all be up, and then it will be too late. All day long we'll be with people and the Lord only knows when we'll have ourselves to ourselves again. I've got to say this to you now, Adam. Adam, listen to me. . . ."

She pressed close, not wanting him to see her face, to read the pain in it and guess the effort the words were costing her, the words she knew she must say. All night long she had debated with herself, weighing one thing against another: Maryla's unbidden advice against her own stiff pride, fear of sacrificing principle and independence against love and need and hardy common sense.

"Adash, you must listen carefully and then think about what I tell you. First, I want you to know that *I know* I've been making it hard for you ever since Olek and Maryla decided to marry. Part of me wanted so badly to have everything neat and settled for us, too, that I haven't been fair to you. Because we aren't them and they aren't us and this isn't really your battle. I pulled you in. Simply because I'm caught up in this mess doesn't mean you can't back away. I won't hold it against you if you do. I never want you to feel that I've trapped you. This is *my* politics and its *my* life—" *Yes, and maybe my baby too,* she longed to add, and bit back the impulse because to say it would have been a cry for help, negating everything else. "What I mean is, I really do understand that for you nothing has really changed and if you still feel your family comes first, why, you must do what you think is right. You must go back and just let me muddle through alone as best I can and. . . . Oh, I'm saying it badly, but the point is I wouldn't want you to stay with me just out of that sense of obligation of yours. . . ."

Whatever he had expected, he was completely unprepared for this outburst. And he knew that in a way he ought to feel relieved, that this was indeed the absolution he'd craved, that if she was willing to forgive him ahead of time, then he was free to follow his conscience and later, when he was ready, come back to her. She was offering him the gift of time. Yet he was no more able to accept the gift than she was not to hold it out. He began to feel a cleansing anger. "You can't think very much of me to say all this! Do you think I'd abandon you now?"

"Don't twist what I'm saying."

"I'm not. And maybe I deserve all of it. Maybe you've every right to doubt me. Because in a way I've been playing games, like a schoolboy. Even when I made love to you I've been like a schoolboy without a thought for tomorrow. But all that has got to change."

Now that she had humiliated and hurt him she could afford to be magnanimous. She found herself coming to his defense, just as earlier Maryla had defended him to her. "You've been completely loyal."

"Yes, like a schoolboy in love."

"Oh Adam, be reasonable! It isn't your fault the way things are for you. The rest of us are answerable each for himself alone. But you have others depending on you so for you it really is different. Believe me, dearest, I'm not demanding that you choose between them and me."

She was fighting with the last of her strength. A trembling was taking hold of her body and she braced herself to keep her teeth from chattering. *Now. If he tells me now that nothing matters except for us to stay together, that wherever I go he must go, I'll not have the strength to stop him.* But just as surely as she longed for this, so she put one final obstacle in her own way, hoping against hope that this, too, he would know how to push aside.

Like yesterday in church, she became austere and distant even while her flesh still radiated the warm afterglow of love. She freed herself of his arms, sat up, her own arms crossed over her breasts and hugging her naked body. Adam felt the chill instantly. "What you're trying to tell me is that you're strong enough not to need me, that whether I go with you or stay behind can't make too much difference because either way you'll manage just fine!"

"No, Adash, no!" But then she realized she was on the point of giving herself away. Pretending a calm she was far from feeling, she said evenly, "Still, you may be right." The need for self-immolation driving her on, she added, carefully choosing words that would wound him, "At least don't make any chivalrous decisions on impulse. After all, at the rate we'll be traveling it's going to take us a good two days to reach Lodz, after which there's bound to be more waiting. So please, I beg you, take that much more time to think over what I just said. That isn't too much to ask."

She was shutting him out again. The old separateness was closing in, and he could think of no greater cruelty than her seeming indifference. "You sound as if you don't really care what I decide." She shrugged, and one last time he appealed to her. "Don't you want me—just simply want me, Wanda?"

You'll never know how much! she thought. But what she said was, "Oh, Adam, you insist on misinterpreting everything I say. I only want you to think of what's best for you, not me, so that afterwards you can never say you're sorry." And still wrapped in her austerity she stood up and began to go through the motions of tidying herself and dressing.

Downstairs the great double doors of the barn creaked open. They heard Zbigniew Korsza's heavy footsteps, then his bluff voice calling to them to come down. Wanda hastily finished buttoning her blouse and hooking her skirt. Then she ran a comb through her hair, crammed the last of her things into her satchel, and without looking at Adam or attempting to touch him moved toward where a ladder stood against the haymow. Olek and Maryla, looking sleepy and rumpled, crawled out of their cubbyhole and followed her. Adam, silent and hurt, came last.

Their host had brought them a breakfast of milk still warm from the cows, and bread and cheese, and apples. "Sleep well?" he asked, but didn't wait for answers. "My valet is ready to leave and I thought I'd check. Any last-minute messages? Any changes? Have any of you anything to add to what we decided last night?"

No one did, until suddenly Wanda seemed to make up her

mind. She took a long breath, and looked from one face to the next, and when her eyes met Adam's she quickly averted hers and he thought he heard her murmur words that sounded curiously like, "Forgive me, love," but he couldn't be sure. For now she was speaking in a high, thin, brittle voice. "As a matter of fact, *Pan* Zbigniew, there *is* something. Could . . . could whoever you're sending delay a few more minutes? Because, you see, I've just thought of a much better solution. . . ."

She waited until she had all their attention and went on, "The change is really very simple. We didn't go into details last night, but Adam Fabian is not suspect like the rest of us. And since this is so, since the police aren't interested in him, wouldn't it really be more satisfactory, rather than sending a servant with a written message, if he were the one to go into town? I mean, that way nothing would be committed to paper, which certainly means one danger less. Also, there'd be no chance of any misunderstanding, therefore fewer delays. He'd just explain everything to your son and to *Pani* Salome, and the three of them together can set the wheels in motion, and once everything has been taken care of, someone—not necessarily he at all, it could be someone else entirely—can catch up with us in Lodz and tell us what to do next, and no slip-ups. Best of all, Adam *won't* have to run with us. He can stay behind if he chooses. Now I ask you, all of you, isn't this the most practical plan?"

A trifle startled, but knowing of no good reason to argue the point, Korsza nodded. "Seems reasonable. Practical enough."

"Practical enough if that's what you want," muttered Olek as he and Maryla exchanged puzzled glances.

Practical as buying a loaf of bread, thought Adam bitterly. Outside a hen cackled, mocking him.

Korsza said, "Well, if you're all agreed, I'll just tell my man not to saddle but get the carriage ready instead. For if you're really safe traveling openly, *Pan* Adam, you'll make much better time by taking the train. And if you hurry you may even catch the Warsaw express at the Lowicz station. That was good thinking, Miss Wanda. Excellent."

Olek added, "Now all we have to do is agree on where and

when to meet in Lodz. You or whosoever you send must be able to find us." He named a small park he knew, and they arranged several alternate times. "Well, do your damnedest for us, Adash."

Adam, standing motionless, did not even answer. He felt as though the ground had been cut from under him, unfairly and without warning. And there was nothing he could do to change things. Wanda, for some obscure reason that completely eluded him, had seen to that.

❧ Seven ❧

SQUIRE KORSZA'S dappled grays were swift and the Warsaw express miraculously on time, and the trip that had taken days while he and Olek were making it stealthily and on foot was over for Adam in a matter of hours. Heartsick and still bewildered though he was by what he could only explain as a cruel, senseless whim on Wanda's part, and weary for lack of sleep, he nevertheless forced himself into immediate action, going directly from the railroad station to call on the younger Korsza. Here the combination of the message he carried and mention of Salome's name seemed to work its own magic. Pan Tadeusz, a younger, handsomer edition of his father, reached for the telephone, broke appointments, rearranged his whole day, and by noon the two men were climbing the stairs to the Grossgliks' apartment.

Midday was an unheard-of hour for visitors, especially male ones, and the mistress of the house was feeling rather casually put together. She had only just returned from marketing, a chore she invariably insisted on sharing with Miss Julia. "Mama always taught me that servants *will* take advantage no matter how long they've been with you," she was fond of explaining, virtuously, to a skeptical Leon. And when he continued to look unconvinced would add, "I'm sure even our Julia has her little weaknesses. I'm not saying I've got to watch her like a hawk, but let's not put temptation in her way either. . . ."

Instead of coming out to her guests in rustling silk she appeared in her severely tailored morning suit, gray with only a touch of white at neck and wrists and no ornaments save a gold lapel watch hanging from a pearl-encrusted fleur-de-lys. Her hair was slightly flyaway, for there hadn't been time to primp after taking off her hat.

"Oh dear me, I must look a fright," she apologized at once, perfectly aware that her old admirer was finding her appearance charming. "The duties of a housewife, you know . . . ," and did not fail to note the light in Tadeusz Korsza's eyes as he bent to kiss her hand. However advantageous a marriage he might have made, she was thinking, his eye for beauty, and more especially the beauty of his first love, had not dimmed.

Satisfied with the effect she had produced she rang for Miss Julia, telling the men they were just in time for second breakfast. "Tea or chocolate? Chocolate, I think, it's so much more nourishing." There was no attempt to say anything of consequence until the tray with the chocolate service, the country butter, the wild strawberry preserves and buckwheat honey in their twin Sèvres jam pots had been brought in and the housekeeper had retreated and they could hear the pat-pat of her slippers down the corridor.

"Now then," Salome began, her long white hands busy pouring the steaming thick liquid, the profile she turned to Korsza itself like fine Sèvres—the face of an alabaster-skinned shepherdess masquerading in somber city dress. "Aside from the fact that I'm always delighted to see you, Tadek my dear—how many years has it been? You must admit you've neglected me shamefully!—what's the occasion for this call?" She gave him her dazzling smile. "Politics, of course, you don't have to tell me! Isn't it always politics! And to have you and my nephew turn up together . . . what a surprise, I might even say what a shock! But oh, don't let me chatter on like this. Gentlemen, I'm all attention."

During the weeks away Adam had forgotten the quicksilver charm of this contradictory woman, forgotten the hothouse ambience of his uncle's house. Daily contact with simple folk who belonged to the earth, intimacy with Wanda who never so much as gave a thought to any effect she might be producing, had already changed his values. But right now he was angry with Wanda as well as hurt and needed to deny whatever she stood for, deny her in any manner that presented itself. So that, perversely, he was again finding Salome's airs and graces appealing. He told himself he was as enchanted with her as on that long-ago day when Leon had first brought her, his future bride, to Bluma's to meet the relatives.

"Now then," Salome's lilting voice brought him back to the present, "tell me who's in trouble this time and what I must do?" In a few sentences Adam brought her up to date on what had happened in Karelice. She listened attentively enough. Nevertheless, he became gradually aware that he was viewing her more critically than in the past. The old enchantment no longer held him spellbound and slowly irritation was taking its place.

For the first time he saw her from the vantage point of his ripening maturity—a woman playing to the hilt a role she hugely enjoyed, playing it skillfully, deriving as much satisfaction from it as a professional puppeteer in charge of an intricate production. And preparing to pull strings better than any puppeteer.

In this questioning mood he also found himself wondering about Tadeusz Korsza. He had no clues at all to him as a person beyond what the Squire had said, but the son's instant response to the father's message, just as the father's matter-of-fact assumption that the son would know exactly what to do, and with a minimum of fuss, argued membership in some well-organized secret group. But if this were indeed the case, Tadeusz Korsza seemed to Adam to have to be two people—one the underground activist, the other a successful man of the world cynically enduring a loveless marriage as the price of a brilliant career. Otherwise how reconcile the two? Was his secret work, perhaps, a kind of respite from reality, just as this brief, unexpected contact with the woman he had once loved represented a lost dream?

But why am I sitting in judgment? What would I myself have done in his place, Adam suddenly asked himself, experiencing one of those rare flashes of almost prophetic clarity that even the most honest self-searcher hastens to blank out lest it reveal a side of his nature he would rather not see. Which way would I go if my own dream were suddenly destroyed? It was a hypothetical question, since even angry as he was with Wanda he could no longer imagine a future separate from hers. Yet suppose, a part of his mind persisted, just suppose for the sake of argument that I let her slip away from me? Wouldn't I then be tempted to jump in the extreme opposite direction, if only to deny the pain of the loss? How easy to become another Tadek Korsza then!

While all these thoughts kept flashing through his mind, part of him was taking an intelligent, active part in the conversation, so that he, too, was like two people, participant and observer, actor and audience at once. It was a strangely unsettling experience, this duality in a moment of crisis which should have held him to the exclusion of all else since it affected him to the core of his being. And because it did not, a doubt arose in his mind that was to return to plague him again and again in the years to come. If he had the capacity so to remove himself from himself in this difficult hour, surveying his own situation with such clear-eyed detachment, then just how strongly was he capable of feeling anything, he wondered. How deep and genuine were his emotions? And wasn't this very detachment proof of some sort of lack within? He could find no answer and felt curiously unworthy.

In the meantime Salome was recapitulating the facts the two men had given her. "You say your friends will be in Lodz tomorrow, Adash, and that you've arranged to meet Olek in the little park on Ewangielicka? By sheer coincidence that's practically around the corner from the Kronenbergs' place. Which gives me an idea. It so happens that my step-nephew Lucio—you remember all the excitement when my sister Eugenia married Lucio's father, don't you, Tadek?—well, Lucio is about to join his parents for a few weeks on the Côte d'Azur, and I've been invited to go along. I was going to say no, it seemed too cruel to abandon my poor husband for all these weeks, but now I think I'll change my mind. Because this may turn out to be the most useful of excursions. My poor darling will just have to fend for himself. After all, first things first, I always say."

Her plan was to have the fugitives travel as part of the Kronenberg entourage until they were safely past the border. What could be more natural than for the young Baron to be going abroad accompanied by a tutor, while his aunt took along not only her own personal maid but her sister's as well? "So now all we have to worry about is getting the documents ready in short order. Three passports to forge . . . but I'm sure you'll take care of all that for us in record time, won't you, Tadek dear? As you see," and again she turned the radiance of her smile full upon her old sweetheart, "I think of you as a man who can perform miracles!"

Tadeusz Korsza started to say something when Adam broke in sharply, "There's just one thing you forgot, Aunt, and that's a cover role for me. There are four of us to think about."

Salome looked startled, her astonishment perfectly genuine. "But surely, Adash, you aren't thinking of leaving the country too! Why exile yourself when you're not being hunted?"

"Because it's what I want," he answered rather too sharply. "Because there's no other way for me. Because I must."

Having once said so, he now fully believed this was the only possible truth. Wanda, he decided, all his anger gone, Wanda acting instinctively had done exactly right: she had forced his hand without meaning to. "But I never had any intention other than to go," he assured himself. "How could I possibly stay behind?"

"It's that girl, isn't it . . . ," Salome started to say, looking, he thought, not at all pleased. "But surely. . ." However, it wasn't a point one could argue in front of a near-stranger. So she smiled, as if determined to take her defeat with good grace. "We can talk about it again later, dear heart. In the meantime," she managed an airy little laugh, "one passport more or less, what can it matter, especially if it's a legitimate one! N'est-ce pas, Tadek? As for your role, Adash, you can be the Baron's secretary going to join him or else Lucio's valet, whichever suits you."

Tadeusz Korsza now became extremely businesslike, reminding them that while the validation of a legal passport for foreign travel was accomplished in minutes if one slipped a five-ruble note to the right clerk, forging three others might take a good couple of days. So the problem now was to find a hiding place in Lodz where the fugitives would be safe until everything was settled. The Kronenberg apartment did not seem to him a prudent choice. "For one thing, too many people arriving at once might cause a stir. For another, there's the *struzh,* the concièrge, to consider—always an unknown quantity." Indeed, the *struzh* never ceased to be a key figure when it came to hiding political suspects in private homes. He might be a friend, or amenable to bribery. Then again he might be an informer. "I'd feel better if we could find something more trustworthy."

It was then Adam remembered Olek's uncle Jacek with his connections wherever working-class organizations existed. Surely in the country's largest textile center Jacek would know someone they could turn to. Careful not to mention names, he said he could probably track down an address or two before the day was over. By next morning, when they met again to report to each other, he was sure to have the information. Afterwards, he added, thinking with satisfaction that Wanda wouldn't find him so easy to be rid of after all, as soon as Korsza had definite word on the passports he would at a moment's notice be ready to start for Lodz, making contact with Olek and the girls and serving as liaison between them and Salome. She, for her part, would not leave Warsaw until she had all their documents in hand. They would rendezvous at the Kronenbergs'.

Thus everything seemed to fall in place, except that Salome still looked troubled. "Since you are determined to leave the country, dear heart," she murmured, seizing this one last chance to influence him by indirection, "shouldn't you at least stop home to say goodbye?"

Inwardly Adam cringed, for a confrontation with his parents was exactly what he wished to avoid. He could so clearly see the scene of his unexpected arrival, the hubbub and the excitement, his mother's glad cries and his father's quiet pleasure, the talk, the questions asked and those left carefully unasked, and finally the moment when he must tell them he was only there in passing. "I'm going abroad. No telling when I'll be back." And Bluma, unlike Salome, wouldn't try to dissuade him, though she too would know his going had to do with Wanda. She would say nothing but her face would be the face of Niobe. And he would wish he could tear himself in half. No, he was not anxious to go home.

Fortunately, Tadeusz Korsza came to his rescue. "I frankly

think the less attention *Pan* Adam draws to himself, the better. So far as his parents or anyone else knows, he's still in Karelice. Let's keep it that way—it may be for a shorter time than we think." And Adam breathed easier.

The following noon, his head crammed with addresses Jacek had made him memorize—"If you can't make contact with one person, you will with another!"—Adam set out for Lodz in the company of a somewhat astonished but docile Lucio. Lucio, whose adoration for his beautiful aunt was surpassed only by his love for his stepmother, was beside himself with happiness at the thought that very soon he would be vacationing in the company of both of them at once. Now grown into a large, flaccid youth with the capacity for devotion of a Saint Bernard and a similar eagerness to please, Lucio had nodded compliance when Salome explained that he was to travel to Lodz with "Cousin" Adam while she took care of some last-minute business and packed, and in the meantime it would help her a lot if he and Adam interviewed some people Mama had hired by mail. If they did that, rather than wait until she herself was ready to leave, they could all start on their holiday trip that much sooner. She then went on to admonish Lucio to be a good boy—she still talked to him as if he were a six-year-old—and not give "Cousin" Adam any trouble.

The early years before Eugenia had come into his own and his father's life—the years of uncaring nursemaids and governesses—had left Lucio so permanently scarred that even now he was inordinately grateful for every scrap of kindness. For Adam he felt an affection based on the, to him, astonishing fact that in all the years of their tutor-pupil relationship the older boy had never once cuffed him around or screamed at him or called him a lunkhead for his slowness to learn. Besides, he was lonely in the great house in Warsaw. He went with Adam willingly, full of talk about Nice and Saint-Jean-de-Luz and bursting with importance because the new people Aunt Salome said were being hired had in a sense become his responsibility.

Until the last moment before the train left Adam expected another argument with Salome about his leaving the country. But she seemed to have made her peace with his resolve and, like

Lucio, talked only of the hot white sands and the blue waters of the Mediterranean, the shops and the casino and the interesting people one was likely to meet, and he could not rid himself of the impression that for all her generous efforts in behalf of himself and his friends, his charming relative was glad enough of this excuse to kill two birds with one stone, or if one put it another way, have her cake and eat it. For now no one could accuse her of selfishness if she chose to travel abroad while her hard-working husband stayed behind with his nose to the grindstone. And should Leon himself, for that matter, show signs of displeasure because she was accepting more of her wealthy sister's largesse than he considered proper, couldn't she point out virtuously that she was crossing the border in order to help victims of Tsarist tyranny escape to safety?

It had been arranged with Tadeusz Korsza that, barring the unforeseen, she would start for Lodz exactly forty-eight hours after Adam and Lucio's departure. In the meantime Adam would not only contact his friends, but would also buy reservations for the whole party on the midnight express to Berlin. "Just remember, dear heart," Salome admonished him one last time as they all stood together on the station platform, "first-class tickets all around." She stood on tiptoe to kiss him and murmur in his ear, "You've plenty to pay for everything, yes? It's all Eugenia's money, of course, but when I explain to her why I spent so much I just know she won't say a word. On the contrary, she'll be proud to've been able to help." She turned to Lucio and kissed him, too. "Well, have a good trip and I'll see you soon. Come, Tadek, the train is starting. Let's get away before we're black with soot . . ."

In Lodz that afternoon it did not take much to convince Lucio that what he really needed after the slow, dirty train ride was a bath and a nap before supper. Thus Adam, free of his charge until evening, was able to leave the Kronenberg flat in plenty of time to keep his appointment with Olek in the park off Ewangielicka Street.

They had separated less than two days earlier, yet it seemed to Adam a lifetime had gone by. The village idyll was a thing of the past, vivid in the way of fragile, cherished memories. So many things had got in the way—Warsaw and Salome's drawing room and Tadeusz Korsza and the slow-witted Lucio, but most of all the visit he had avoided making to his parents' house and the long, looming shadow of the gendarmerie.

He was so completely over his anger at Wanda, so sure she, too, must by now have forgiven him whatever it was had mysteriously troubled her, that all he wanted was to hold her again. "I was hoping," he said, disappointed to find Olek waiting alone, "that the girls would be with you. Where did you leave them?"

Olek explained they were at the public baths. "The poor people's hotel," he quipped. "But since Jacek has been so generous with addresses we might as well go pick them up right away. Come on, it isn't far to walk."

As they started down a gravel path, they brought one another up to date on what had happened. "Things have really worked out surprisingly well—better than I'd dared hope," Olek commented after hearing Adam out. And after a while, "Well Adash, how do you feel now you've received your conspirator's baptism of fire?"

"Like hell, if you must know," Adam answered, thinking of his unresolved problems.

The other man started to laugh. "What? Not even the least bit heroic?"

"Stop it, Olek. I'm not in the mood for this kind of talk."

"No? What kind of talk do you want?"

"None, really."

Olek stopped laughing, studying him in concern and puzzlement. "Well, that makes two of you." He plowed in with his customary directness, "Have you and Wanda had a fight? Certainly sounded like it when she offered your services to *Pan* Korsza without so much as a by-your-leave! Was she trying to get rid of you? What's got into her, anyway?"

"I was hoping you might know," Adam said, no longer pretending indifference.

But Olek was no help to him. "All I can tell you is she's been about as cozy to have around as a hedgehog. Ever try to domesticate a hedgehog, Adash? Only thing less satisfactory by way of a pet is a skunk. I remember once, when I was a kid, dragging one home and. . ."

"Shut up, Olek, will you? I'm not even in the mood to listen."

"Oh, all right," the other took the rebuff good-naturedly. "I was just trying to cheer you up." His face grew sober. "Adash, this is no time for the two of you *not* to be pulling together. Want to try telling me what you think has gone wrong?"

"I only wish I knew," Adam answered despondently. "I'm not sure she knows either. Just that we've been at sixes and sevens ever since the Sunday before your wedding. I somehow haven't been able to get through to her. I've tried—it wasn't any use. She seemed to be holding something against me, something she wouldn't explain. Then, before we had time to get back on an even keel, this thing with Dobrzynski came up and we were on the run. And there was no more time for straightening anything out. For a while, that night in Korsza's barn, I thought it was going to be all right. But in the morning she deliberately picked a quarrel. And then, well, you know the rest. . ."

"Women . . . ," Olek muttered helplessly, "holy Jesus, women!" and added a trifle vaguely, "Maybe she wasn't feeling well, is all . . . you know those female upsets. . . . In fact, Maryla hinted something of the sort." Suddenly he struck his forehead with a huge open hand. "She . . . she couldn't be pregnant, could she? It sometimes happens no matter how much you take care. . ."

Adam looked horrified. "Pregnant? Good God, Olek! But surely she'd have told me!"

"Maybe yes, maybe no—who's to know how a woman's mind works?" Olek let his arm fall heavily on Adam's shoulder. "Well, you'll be able to ask her yourself soon enough. Still, for both your sakes I hope it isn't that. Because a baby *now* would be one hell of a complication." He broke off, embarrassed. "What I mean is, well, Jesus Christ, there ought to be a time and place for everything. . . ."

Adam hardly seemed to have heard him. "If that's what it is," he said, pursuing his own thoughts, "there can be no more ifs or buts. She's just going to have to agree to marry me at once. Only you and Maryla will probably have to help me. You know her, you know how she is. . . . She might even try to hide the truth from me. Under the circumstances she'd feel that—how did she put it the other night?—that it was, well, applying unfair pressure. And she'd get distant again, she'd get unapproachable, and I couldn't do a thing with her. . . ."

"I don't envy you, my friend," Olek said, and muttered one last time, "Women . . . women. . ."

❧ *Eight* ❧

Now that the suspicion was planted, he was in a frenzy to act on it. He would have to convince Wanda to marry him at once, as soon as they came to some sort of haven. There could be no waiting to find out whether or not Olek's guess was correct. In fact, the one thing he must shield her from, he realized, was any lingering fear on her part that his decision might after all be predicated on the possibility of a pregnancy. Whatever else happened, he must guard against so cruel a blow to her pride.

I wonder how an expatriate makes a living abroad, he found himself thinking. How *did* a man support a wife and child in a strange land? *Wife and child.* The words startled him and he rolled them on his tongue, liking the sound. Well, how did other exiles manage in Europe's liberal university centers? Besides, he and Wanda were after all no novices at penny-pinching. They would survive. And when finally it was safe for them to come home both would be armed with imposing foreign degrees. And their child would be bilingual from the cradle.

Now that it was all clearly worked out in his own mind he found it hard to believe he had ever wavered. He thought about how he would break the news to his parents. They would be stunned, but would never hold it against him. When he wrote them after he and Wanda were settled, he would explain the speed with which everything had been done—the sudden flight, and why he had not stopped to say goodbye, and the rushed marriage—as part of the same overall urgency. And they need never know—especially since Salome would bear him out—that part of what he wrote was a white lie. Why, after all, strain his parents' tolerance by demanding that they condone a premarital relationship and the possible birth of an embarrassingly premature grandchild? Why shock and hurt his mother unnecessarily? Besides, it was an extra precaution against exposing Wanda to gossip and future slights. Let it merely be known that they got married sooner than planned in order to simplify their arrangements abroad. . . .

On the religious score he felt sure of acceptance, for here it was his father whose opinions prevailed, and Jacob was ahead of his time in such matters. The family had never been against mixed marriages in principle. Whenever the question came up for discussion, and it was always coming up, Adam heard his father take the position that it was more important for a man to find himself a good, staunch, understanding wife than one who kept a kosher house. As for his mother, she might shed some token tears, she might pray hard to a very personal God not to hold it against her son that he had married a *shikse,* but she would do it less out of deep religious conviction than as a kind of insurance against the future.

There still remained the problem of continued help to his people. Well, he asked himself, suppose the situation had been reversed and he the one hounded by the police, he and not Wanda forced to leave the country—what would the family have done then? They would simply have had to manage without him, and it would have been the turn of the two next-oldest boys, Viktor and Izidore, to help out more. His brothers, he reflected, were no longer children. They could pitch in. And adjust. And survive.

Astonished at feeling no particular guilt once the first pangs of it were out of the way, Adam found himself at last questioning some of the rules of conduct which until that day he had accepted as eternal verities, much as his mother in her youth had accepted religious dogma. *The eldest son shall take over, he shall be as a second father to the clan.* . . . But had this ever really been demanded of him or had he merely set up his own impossible code, finding a source of enormous gratification in his ability to shoulder a disproportionate burden, proudly and alone?

He was too lacking in experience, too unaware of the complexities of human reasoning, to question his own motives. It never occurred to him that generosity could be a fault and the illusion of being indispensable a form of arrogance. But at least he no longer felt driven or deeply troubled. No one need go hungry because he was leaving. And even if, with his father's health failing, the day must eventually come when it would really be up to himself to provide for his mother and the younger children, that time was still a long way off. Besides, he and Wanda would surely be home again by then and in a better position financially.

Having thus reexamined the situation to his own satisfaction, he felt suddenly lighthearted, and with good reason. He had just won his first skirmish in a war of attrition that would rage, devastating him, for the rest of his life. It was a war in which the defeats would, alas, outnumber the victories, in which he would do battle against the never-ceasing temptation to make sweeping gestures of generosity at exorbitant cost not just to himself but to those who were nearest and dearest to him. But so far he had no premonition of any of this.

By the time he and Olek reached the public baths, the two women were waiting in the doorway. Their hair still damp from the steam room, they both wore a fresh, scrubbed, rested look. But next to Maryla's robust vitality Wanda, grown thinner than Adam had realized, seemed strangely frail. The tension in her face was unmistakable, the skin taut over her cheekbones as though after long illness. He could see the worry lines between her brows and around her mouth. Her eyes were lackluster and her natural high color, usually so striking in so dark a skin, now gave the appearance of the dry flush of fever.

"Are you all right?" he asked as soon as they had a moment alone together. "You're not looking at all well, darling."

"Oh, I'm fine. You're just imagining things." She still sounded remote although she took his arm, managing a smile which he realized was wholly perfunctory. "Just tired from the trip. Traveling in a coach-and-four may sound romantic but it's not exactly restful. How far is this place you're taking us to?" Determined not to get into any heart-to-heart conversations, she pulled him along the narrow sidewalk, trying to catch up with Maryla and Olek, who had outdistanced them.

But he was equally determined not to be put off. "You aren't telling the whole truth, are you?" It was an accusation rather than a question, and this time he didn't even care if he provoked her to further anger, so anxious was he to bring things out into the open, then set them to rights once and for all.

A block ahead they could see Olek and Maryla stopping a passer-by to inquire for directions. They were headed for Industrial Town—by sheer coincidence the first address Olek's uncle had given them was in the Pozner compound on Cegielniana— and already the streets were progressively dirtier and shabbier. Strangers to the city, they did not know how soon they would be reaching their destination where unknown friends were waiting.

These were their last moments of privacy, with no time left for leading up to what should really be discussed slowly and tactfully, no time for reestablishing the kind of rapport that can make intensely personal talk not only possible but fruitful and deeply satisfying—certainly no time for avoiding issues.

"Look," he began awkwardly, working his way around a shyness that was rendering him tongue-tied, "Look, Wanda, you've got to be frank with me. I have to know. What I mean is, Olek said something today that . . . that made me think. . ." He stopped and tried again, "Please, darling, don't hedge. Is it true what he seems to think . . . that we're going to have a baby?"

She stopped short, sucking her breath in sharply as though hit in the solar plexus. "Olek said that! He had no right. . . ."

"Well," he interrupted, "Is it true?"

"I wish he'd kept his mouth shut!" she exploded, then stared at him as if trying to read his thoughts while sorting out her own.

"Is it true or isn't it?" he asked again, gravely.

Still she did not speak, and when at last she did, her voice came with difficulty. "I don't even know myself yet. It's just

. . . just I haven't felt too well this past week. Maybe it's only a false alarm. With all the trouble and the excitement and the sickness in the village, that's not impossible. I was going to wait and see, but this morning I fainted, and was sick to my stomach afterwards, and Maryla saw me and I guess she jumped to conclusions. Anyway, one way or another it's too soon to tell. And oh, Olek had no right to worry you!"

"On the contrary, he had every right. Because I *should* be the first to know. And," he accused, "you weren't going to tell me."

"No, I wasn't." Her look became one of defiance. "Of course not. You've had enough trouble on my account."

"My God, Wanda," he cried, "don't you realize your trouble is my trouble? Don't you know I love you?" When she refused to answer he chose to find her silence insulting. "Don't you trust me at all? No, obviously you don't. You must think I'm ready to turn my back on you!"

They were standing on a curb, arguing back and forth, waiting for a break in traffic. Suddenly Adam dashed across, pulling her with him so abruptly that she stumbled. Then, as always when he was agitated, he began to walk in long strides, a man pursued by furies. She practically had to run to keep up with him and was having trouble catching her breath. "I just finished telling you I wasn't sure! It may be something else entirely. . . ."

"But that's no longer the point," he fairly shouted at her. For by now the issue, at least for himself, had ceased to be whether or not she was pregnant. "The real point is that you had no right, do you hear me, *no right* to shut me out as if I were a stranger! I don't see what you were trying to do. I don't even begin to understand you. . . ."

Then the picture flashed vivid into his mind of their abortive attempt at closeness during the night in *Pan* Zbigniew's barn, of their estrangement despite the physical lovemaking, and the way Wanda had so suddenly and wholly without warning maneuvered afterwards to send him away. Had she acted in resentment against his hesitation to commit himself? Had she perhaps tried to forestall disappointment, rejection, by hitting out before herself being hit? Worst of all, was she still unable to forgive him for not having spoken out earlier, before Olek's wedding? Suddenly he knew with absolute certainty that he had stumbled onto the truth. And because this made him feel guilty again, and ashamed, and anxious for justification, he let his guilt take on the form of fresh suspicion and anger.

"One would think you were trying to get rid of me! I'm good enough to be your lover but not good enough for a husband!" He cast about for the most wounding accusation he could make. "Is it because I'm a Jew?"

The attack was so unfair she gasped as though he had slapped her. "Adash, how could you?"

He was instantly sorry, but still he blustered, "Well, is it? Answer me!"

She wanted to plead, as she'd wanted to so many times in the past week or two, "Don't you see, I'm only trying to do what's best for you, even if it means breaking us up. If I'm wrong tell me so and make me believe it! Tell me I'm being a fool and that nothing matters to you but me and you won't let anyone or anything come between us! Once I believe this I can stop fighting you!" But all she really said was, cool and dignified, "You can think what you like. Draw your own conclusions. I won't even try to defend myself."

They had been walking and halting, halting and walking, with Olek and Maryla getting farther and farther ahead until finally, coming to another intersection, they realized they'd lost sight of them and weren't even sure where they were going. It was a small thing but it brought them up short. They stood staring at one another in horror for the way they'd permitted their tempers to flare.

Adam was the first to capitulate. "Darling, I must be out of my mind to treat you like this. Forgive me. It's just that I've been beside myself with worry. . . ."

It was not enough but it was a beginning of reconciliation, and she accepted it, at least to the extent of listening quietly while he floundered on. She made no move to help but neither did she hinder as he tried to extricate himself from the morass he had wandered into.

"All I'm trying to say is, will you marry me no matter what? Let me stay with you no matter what? It's what I want more than anything in the world. . . ."

"You're sure?" she asked one last time, no longer hostile.

"So very sure!" And now the enormity of the chance that he might lose her became more than he could countenance. And the barriers were swept away, and he heard himself rushing on with all the persuasiveness he could muster, "Darling, listen to me! We have all of tomorrow to make plans. Nothing can go wrong now, I promise you! Twenty-four hours more, and we'll be out of the country. Then, as soon as we get to where we're going, we'll take care of the legal arrangements. Oh dearest, the important thing is to settle this *before* you're sure about the baby. That way, you can never again think that I only . . . that maybe I just. . . ."

"Don't say it." She stopped him with her hand over his mouth, and he kissed the palm, rough and hard from her work in the fields, and then kissed the fingers. "Trust me, Wanda, just trust me. Dearest love, will you trust me and let me be your husband?"

Great happy tears were rolling down her cheeks. A boy darting into the chaotic traffic stared back at them and whistled, nearly paying for his curiosity with his life. It was a strange proposal, on a strange street corner in a strange and ugly city, but neither Adam nor Wanda was aware of the fact. The world had all at once become simple and, briefly, beautiful. Adam tucked Wanda's hand securely under his arm and then peered up at the street signs, trying to figure out in which direction to go.

Then he noticed a flower vendor at the curb, selling limp roses and fresh forget-me-nots and mignonette in small bunches. He reached into his pocket for loose change and the woman, quick to spot a customer, began chanting, "Flowers! Buy my lovely flowers! Flowers, sir, for your lady!"

He picked two bunches of forget-me-nots and paid for them without bargaining, much to the woman's astonishment. "Don't you think a bride should carry flowers?" he said, offering them to Wanda.

The old woman overheard and broke out into a snaggle-tooth

smile. "A bride, did you say, sir? Tsk, tsk. . . . May the good Lord bless you! May he give you long life and happiness, and big healthy children!"

Wanda swallowed hard, then said, finding her voice at last, "Thank you, mother. You're the first to wish us luck."

She breathed deep of the damp fresh fragrance of the flowers, and for a moment herself felt like a parched plant to which water has been restored after a long drought. The fear that for days had been knotting her entrails relaxed its stranglehold. Miraculously the nausea receded. When she looked up again Adam saw that the dry look of fever had gone and a glow taken its place, smoothing out the tiredness in her face.

They found their way once more without much trouble, catching up with Maryla and Olek after an unexpected turn into a side street. The others were waiting at the gate of a vast compound where, encompassed by the same tall fence, Pozner's palatial residence sat with its back turned on his huge smoking mill. In between was a cobblestoned yard the size of a city square, and on either side, forming a quadrangle, stretched two long rows of workers' barracks, and in the farthest corner, the stables. A gate-keeper directed them toward "one of them family shacks over yonder," otherwise showing no interest in them whatever.

Wanda, deliberately hanging back, signaled Maryla to fall in step with her while the men went ahead and out of earshot. "He's just asked me to marry him!" she burst out. "Maryla, Marysh," she went on, using the affectionate diminutive of her friend's name, "you were so right and I so wrong! Would you believe it, he actually forced the issue! He wants us to be married *before* I can be sure about the baby—so I can never throw it up to him that we *had* to get married! As if I would! Oh, Marysh, Marysh, pinch me, tell me I'm not dreaming. . . ."

The factory was going full blast, smokestacks belching, steam vents hissing, the whole compound reverberating with the hum and whir of machines so that everything they said to each other seemed set, as to mechanical background music, to rhythmic sound. In the center of the yard, moving to the same rhythm, a laborer stripped to the waist was working a water pump. Arm working like a piston, he was pumping to fill huge reservoir drums atop the roof of the mansion so that its residents might have running water for their plumbing system. Several ragged, barefoot children stood in line beside him with pails as large as themselves, patiently waiting their turn at the pump. As the visitors advanced deeper into the yard an unbelievable stench assailed their nostrils: a large cesspool behind a row of outhouses was being emptied, for the city of Lodz was without sewers.

But not even this picture of Poland's Manchester at its worst could dampen Wanda's spirits. "I'm so happy, happy, happy," she chanted like a refrain. "Now at last I can allow myself to feel again. . . ."

They were nearing the door of the shack their men had already entered, their moment of confidences drawing to a close. "You know something, Wanziula," Maryla said. "Far be it from me to start preaching the bourgeois virtues and all, but some social institutions do have their good points, don't you think?"

Wanda smiled, and her voice was soft as she answered, "I think I know what you're trying to tell me, Marysh. Let's put it this way. When the sun shines day after day, it really does become possible to work in the communal fields—and still cultivate one's own garden." And she thought she must share this new discovery with Adam.

❧ *Nine* ❧

As she waited for Tadeusz Korsza to procure the forged documents—her own and Adam's having indeed been validated with lightning speed, as the liberal greasing of palms always made possible—Salome Grossglik fussed happily in preparation for her journey abroad. Two trunks and half a dozen valises, hatboxes and portmanteaux stood open in her bedroom. The large bed, the chaise-longue, the boudoir chairs were piled high with froth and gossamer. Laces and ribbons spilled from half-closed drawers. Tissue paper made mounds of meringue on the rug, while in the midst of the confusion Miss Julia scurried in and out, carrying with her the warm smell of freshly ironed linens.

"Don't bring much," Eugenia had written on first extending her invitation. "Should you need anything, there's a little dressmaker here, a veritable genius, who can fix you up. Afterwards we'll be stopping in Paris, and Ludwig says I can order new things for you as well as for myself." But not even a little French genius could whip up a dress in a day, and in the meantime she couldn't very well disgrace the Kronenbergs by appearing at the Biarritz casino in rags, could she? Even though by now she had thoroughly convinced both Leon and herself that her trip was purely a mission of mercy, Salome did not for a moment lose sight of these delicious trivia.

Helping her pack, along with the housekeeper, was her favorite niece by marriage, Regina Segal, who was spending the day with her and whom she hadn't seen since late spring. During the summer months Regina seemed to have undergone one of those startling metamorphoses that sometimes, overnight and without warning, transform a child into a young girl in bloom. Not that she had grown in height; like Salome, she would remain slight and small-boned. It was the lines of her body that had changed, her breasts beginning to swell, her hips rounding out, her calves and ankles elegantly shapely in defiance of the thick, black schoolgirl stockings.

Delighted with what she saw, Salome decided that even full of her own affairs as she was, she must take a few moments for a talk with her niece that really shouldn't be put off. "A year or two more," she began, regarding Regina with a mixture of satisfaction and exasperation, "and you'll have a lovely figure. You can even be beautiful if you try. But my, oh my, what was your mother thinking, letting you get sunburnt like a common peasant! Look at you—nose peeling and all those freckles! Ugh! You must start using my cucumber lotion and the rose-and-almond cream—I'll give you some of both. And for heavens' sake no more soap on your face! Wash only with sweet cream, or use a bit of butter, then finish with more cucumber lotion so you'll smell sweet. *But no more soap!*" she repeated emphatically, as though drilling the girl in the ten commandments.

"I don't think Mama will like that," Regina answered a trifle timidly. "She always makes us scrub."

"Like it or not, we can't have you developing a skin like leather! I'll talk to her." In mock despair Salome put her arm around her niece's shoulders and drew her toward the large, well-lighted mirror of her dressing table. There she bent her own graceful head closer, so that they stood reflected cheek to cheek. The contrast, she felt, would bring the lesson home more eloquently than any words.

People always said they looked like mother and daughter, but now Regina saw the difference as well. And she was mortified. For it was true that with her coloring the sunburn was singularly unbecoming. Indeed, the whole striking alabaster-and-ebony effect of flawless white skin and blue-black hair, which she already knew was her greatest claim to beauty, seemed to have vanished. And small wonder. During vacation her days had been crowded with the usual summer diversion—berrying, mushroom hunts, boating and croquet and occasional lawn tennis with her brother and sister and their numerous friends, and she hadn't given a thought to her looks. But had the game been worth the candle?

Her older sister, who claimed to care nothing for the feminine graces, might think so, but she, Regina, had in the course of this past summer read her first forbidden romantic novels and she was beginning to wonder. Partly as a result of Salome's long tutelage but also because such was her nature and the time was ripe, she had recently become aware of her brother's friends as future men. Young as she was, just turned fourteen, several of them had already looked at her with interest and there had been excitement in it. Jadwiga might say what she liked, but the real fun might not be in winning on the tennis court. And in that other game other things counted for more. A poem of Ronsard's which she'd had to learn by heart in French class hummed in her cool little brain. *Mignonne, allons voir si la rose | Qui ce matin avait éclose.* . . . And how did that song go that Aunt Salome was always singing? *Jeunes fillettes, profitez du temps.* . . . Well, she would gather rosebuds and she would profit, starting with any advice her aunt—her second mother, as they were both fond of saying, chose to offer.

Facing her beautiful mentor in the mirror, so that their cheeks touched, she thought of sharing some of her observations. But all she actually said was, "Can I undo the damage, Auntie, do you think, if I do exactly as you tell me?"

Salome smiled, thoroughly pleased. "I should think so. But do stay out of the sun from now on, and if you must expose yourself, wear a big hat or carry a parasol. And remember about the sweet cream and the cucumber lotion. I'll keep you supplied. Twenty years from now you'll thank me. A girl can't start too early taking care of her skin!"

Miss Julia interrupted them, coming in with another armload of lacy underthings that needed ribbons run through the beading, and immediately Regina offered to do the job. "I love to handle your things, Auntie, they're so pretty!"

Salome hugged her again, delighted that the girl derived the same sensuous pleasure out of small luxuries as she herself did.

And she thought this was exactly the kind of relationship she would have enjoyed with a daughter of her own—provided, of course, daughters could be acquired without the pain and travail of giving birth, or nursing them and seeing them safely through babyhood. Or without the risk of sacrificing one's figure. . . .

"Would you like to know what I've been thinking, dear heart? I wasn't going to say anything until I was back from my trip, but this seems as good a time as any. . . . Your mother has her hands so very full, while I have no one. . . ." She let the words trail off and began again. "How would it be if I suggested to her that you come to stay with us for a while when school reopens? It would mean less of a walk to classes for you, and we could pretend you're the little girl I've never been blessed with. . . ." In that moment Salome sincerely believed she had yearned for children ever since her marriage, and that she had been truly denied.

Regina's eyes lighted up. "Oh Auntie, what fun! But do you think Mama and Papa would agree?"

"We'll see what we can do," Salome promised in a tone that said, *Consider it done.* "Of course, you can only come if we can trust you to be every inch a lady. For in the fall my house will be full of boys, and you'll have to learn how to carry yourself in their company." And what better way to start a young girl off on her career as a woman, she added wordlessly, than in such a milieu? In the course of the next few winters dozens of the country's future eligible bachelors would be spending their most impressionable years right here under her roof. Let Regina get used to taking such company for granted. Training in the stalking of desirable husband material, like training in the care of the complexion, could not begin too early. She made a mental note to have long talk with her sister-in-law Balbina at the very first opportunity.

Thinking about all this, she began to see herself as part diplomat serving the best interests of her large family and part master juggler accomplishing the most dazzling feats of legerdemain. Adding to Leon's prestige at the *Gmina* through the Kronenberg connection, for instance. Shaping Regina's life. Shaping Adam's. And, of course, there was more to come.

Her mind back on Adam, she began to worry about him all

over again. Perhaps something could still be done to keep him from going abroad with that girl—and what did he see in that flat-chested bluestocking of his anyway? If he went off with her now he would surely come back married—and what a waste! She must make one last effort when she caught up with him in Lodz. Maybe if she stressed his father's failing health, he could be swayed. . . .

Leon, when she spoke to him about it that night, the last they were to spend together in many weeks, looked dubious. He had just heartily endorsed her suggestion to have little Regina come to stay, thinking it would be rather like giving his wife a great living doll to play with; but on the score of his nephew he had reservations. "Wouldn't you call that meddling, dearest?" He still always called her dearest, and whether it was because he'd never got over the miracle of her sharing his bed and board, or out of habit, he did not stop to analyze. "What right does anyone have to interfere between two people so obviously in love?"

"Ah, but there's love and *love*," she crooned, and in order to muster her arguments she bent her head over the embroidery hoop in her lap, glad that she had decided to pick it up rather than busying herself with last-minute mending. For Leon loved to watch her absorbed in this delicate and rapidly vanishing art, and she often found it a weapon far more useful than any direct approach when she wanted to have her own way. "There is also this thing they call infatuation. True love, as who should know better than you and I, dear heart, is a tender plant that needs long cultivation. But a wild summer romance withers in autumn like leaves blowing on the wind." She knotted a fresh length of silk floss, biting off the loose ends with her white, even teeth. "I should think if this girl truly loved him, she would be willing to wait until he can claim her with his conscience clear. But if we let him run off with her, to live among strangers. . ."

She paused to pick her words, and in the meantime held her breath so that a hot flush simulating embarrassment suffused her neck and face. "What kind of marriage will it be, with such *messy* beginnings!" She looked up to meet her husband's eyes, then dropped her own with appropriate modesty. "After all, my love, the days of her betrothal are a time every *real* woman wants to be able to cherish among her most beautiful memories." She permitted herself a little catch in her voice.

How pure she is, her husband reflected for the thousandth time—forever virginal, still somehow untouched by the grosser passions so that each time he wanted her he must woo and win her, his eternal bride. A woman never to be taken for granted. He felt his need for her, unblunted, sharp as on his wedding night. Yet somewhere in the back of his mind a vague sense of exasperation pulsed undefined. How comfortable it might be to live with someone more like his sister Bluma, someone who allowed a man the luxury of emotional house slippers. . . .

He pushed away the disloyal thought. "Not all women are like you, my dearest," he finally said, with a touch of asperity that was wholly lost on her. "As I've told you so often, *you* could have remained an engaged girl all your life." As always she chose to take this as a tribute, storing the remark away to be quoted again and again in years to come. She gave him a misty smile, and Leon got up, went over to where she sat and took the embroidery out of her gently resistant fingers. "Come, you've worked long enough. What's left of the evening belongs to your husband." She did not gainsay him, and the subject of Adam and "that girl" was momentarily put aside.

But the seed of doubt had been planted. A few nights later, feeling at loose ends without his wife and reluctant to face a solitary meal served by an oversolicitous Miss Julia, Leon decided upon leaving his office to detour to Nalewki Street and take pot luck at Bluma's, as he'd done so often during his long-ago bachelor days. He found his sister just setting the table for supper. He thought she was looking unusually harrowed, eyes suspiciously red-rimmed.

"Something wrong?" he queried, after kissing first her hand, then her soft flabby cheek.

She hastily sent young Rosie, who was helping, to the kitchen on some improvised errand. "It's Jacob. I'm so worried about him. He—" She gestured toward the front rooms which her husband still used as his shop, and lowered her voice. "He coughs constantly now. It's got so bad he hardly gets any sleep. And he's hoarse all the time. And still he won't see a doctor. Talk to him, Leon. Maybe to you he'll pay attention."

In the three or four weeks since he had last seen his brother-in-law, Leon found him shockingly changed. Jacob had lost a great deal of weight. His clothes hung on him. His skin looked greenish-gray. Several times during supper he seemed to swallow the wrong way, choking on his food. But he was still a chain smoker, and when Leon suggested a throat specialist he stubbornly refused to consider it. He hated doctors.

"Butchers, all of them! Suppose they put a name on what ails me and try curing me—their cures are often worse than the disease! Look what they did to old Kaiser Frederick. Cut out his gullet, gave him a silver tube for a throat, and what happens? Six months, and he's dead of cancer. If *that's* what's wrong with me, I don't even want to know about it. At least let me die in peace. . . ."

In the end, Leon gave up the fruitless argument. But as he walked home, his last conversation with Salome came back to him in vivid detail and he began to think his wife had been right, that Adam's place really was here, that they should never have helped him leave so long as things were the way they were, and he himself was in no immediate trouble with the authorities.

Would he have come to the same conclusion had Salome not spoken as she had? Would he have interfered had Adam and Wanda already been man and wife? He did not stop to consider, then or later. But the following morning on his way to work he stopped off at a telegraph office. He sent an urgent message to his wife, hoping it would overtake the travelers before they went their several ways.

The telegram caught up with them in Berlin.

Salome's trip to Lodz and her meeting with the young exiles had been uneventful, the forged documents adequate, the railway tickets in order. The use of the Kronenberg name secured for them the kind of preferential treatment conductors and station-masters always extended to persons of note. In the early dawn of the following morning, as the train started westward from the frontier checkpoint, all danger was over. They were on foreign soil.

They reached their Berlin hotel in a state of nervous exhilaration, crowding into the suite which the Baron had reserved for his sister-in-law and young son. Feverishly they thanked Salome and congratulated each other. Nothing more threatened them. Certainly they did not feel threatened by the thin blue envelope waiting propped up against a huge vase of yellow roses in the bay window.

Salome herself had no premonition of trouble. She had been expecting some welcoming word from Leon, so that she reached for the envelope eagerly, tore it open, and began to read. Then her expression changed. She turned away. No one noticed. They were far too excited still, and all of them talking at once about what arrangements must be made next and whom they must contact, and whether there would be time for a celebration before they entrained for Switzerland.

She waited until the bellhops had done with carrying in the luggage and until the young people were trooping out to their cheaper rooms on another floor. Then gently she put her hand on Adam's arm. "Stay a moment. This concerns you, too." Only when they were alone did she show him Leon's laconic message:

FEAR ADAM'S PRESENCE URGENTLY NEEDED HOME STOP
FATHER MORE GRAVELY ILL THAN REALIZED STOP BREAK
NEWS GENTLY BUT IMPRESS ON HIM MUST COME HOME
STOP ALL MY LOVE

It was a long time before either of them spoke. Then Salome threw her arms around him and kissed him. "I know how hard it is for you, believe me." Her regret was all the more genuine because the blow that had been dealt him was not, she felt, her doing after all but seemed God's own intervention. "You'll have to go back, dear heart, I see no other way. To tell you the truth, Uncle Leon and I were afraid of something like this. But when you first came home last week we weren't sure, and besides, there was the question of your personal safety. But that's never really been an issue, has it? Would Uncle be sending for you if he thought there was any risk? So. Your friends are safe, everything that could be done for them has been done. Now it's time to give thought to your parents."

Still Adam did not speak. So this was where it was ending. The days of doubt, the fighting with himself, the scruples, the decisions arrived at so slowly, so painfully—it had all been for nothing. And now the brief reaching out for happiness was over, the flight toward the sun ended, the wings of wax melting as he plummeted into a sea of inevitable lifetime patterns, to drown in acceptance. And had he really believed only yesterday that he could escape? And then he knew, in another of those moments of cruel clarity, that the telegram was not actually an unexpected blow. Rather, it was a *coup de grâce* he had always known must come, with only the direction whence it hit not entirely predictable.

Finally he roused himself to give some semblance of an answer. "Yes, yes, of course, I see, I see it all now. . . ." He picked up the thin blue paper, scanning it as if in hopes that the words had changed. IMPRESS ON HIM MUST COME HOME. . . ." He passed his hand over his eyes and turned to Salome without really seeing her. "If you'll excuse me, Aunt, I've got to . . . that is . . . I must. . . ." He stopped trying to explain and walked out into the hall like a man who cannot hold his vodka.

Upstairs, the door between their two adjoining rooms stood ajar. Maryla, hearing him come in, called out that Wanda was down the hall taking a bath. When he did not answer she came to see if he had heard. Adam's look of utter dejection, his eyes devoid of all expression, frightened her. "Good heavens, Adash, what's happened to you?"

"Not to me," he corrected. "It's my father. He's dying. I've got to go back." He spoke in a strange, hollow, lifeless voice. "I suppose in my bones I've always known it would end like this." He showed her the telegram.

"Oh, dear God!" she exclaimed, handing the paper back to him. "Oh, the poor man. . ."

But she had learned in a hard school and women like Salome

Grossglik were anathema to her. After the first shock passed, her instinctive distrust reasserted itself. "Are you sure things are exactly what they seem, Adash? Is the situation really different from what it was the last time you heard from your mother?"

He failed completely to grasp the intent of her words. "I don't understand. What are you trying to tell me?"

"Just—that this aunt of yours isn't exactly enthusiastic about any of us, Wanda in particular. That's been plain to me as the nose on my face. Maybe I'm meddling, Adash, but how come your immediate family hasn't said anything to you directly? I mean, if it's really a life-and-death emergency, wouldn't your mother have written . . . ?"

He said, "Leon is my mother's brother. They're very close. If he's taken it upon himself to step in, it can only mean one thing. I'm needed. I must go."

"And Wanda? Don't you think Wanda needs you, too? Isn't your first obligation to her now? Or maybe just because you haven't put a wedding ring on her finger, you think you can. . ."

"Maryla! That's enough!" Olek bellowed from the next room. He came to stand in the doorway. "You're butting into something that doesn't concern you!"

"Oh, doesn't it?" she shot back, sweeping both her husband and Adam with a look of scorn and anger at their unbelievable male stupidity. "I smell a rat, I tell you! It's a trick to break them up. And am I expected to sit back and watch my best friend sacrificed . . . and just at a time when . . . when she. . ."

"Enough, I said!" Olek shouted. He had never before used such a tone with her, and for a moment both were startled into shamed silence. But it was already too late. The door from the corridor opened and Wanda walked in.

"What's going on?" she asked, alarmed. "Why is everybody mad?" She closed the door and, leaning against it, scanned their faces. "I could hear you all the way down the hall. What's wrong?"

"Nothing much," Maryla blurted with heavy sarcasm. "Just that your man is about to leave you and trot obediently home because they've pulled the leash on him. And I've been trying to make him see that now he has other obligations. . . ."

Wanda blanched. She turned directly to Adam. *"You* tell me," she demanded. "In your own words."

Instead of answering he handed her the crumpled piece of paper. "So you see," he pleaded while she read, "I've got to go."

She raised her head and said with a kind of deadly calm, "And you want to be released from your promise, is that it?"

"No, darling! No! What a horrible thing to say! Only. . ." He swallowed. "Only we'll have to put things off for a while. Nothing is changed between us, nothing will change! Except. . ."

In the meantime, almost by main force, Olek half dragged, half pushed Maryla toward their own room, closing the door firmly behind them. Neither Wanda nor Adam paid attention. Wanda, her face still deathly white, was rereading the telegram exactly as he had done, as though to give it some degree of reality.

She hadn't moved, still leaning against the door for support, her dressing gown drawn tightly around her, a damp bath towel over her arm, a soap dish gripped tightly in one hand and the telegram in the other. "Tell me again from the beginning," she finally said. "I've got to hear you say it."

He said bleakly, "That's all there is. I know Leon. He's not an alarmist. He wouldn't be sending a message like this unless . . . unless my father were. . ."

He began pacing the floor, stumbling against a chair in the narrow space between the untouched double bed and the window. "God, how I wish now you were pregnant for sure. Because then I couldn't leave you no matter what. . . ."

Still she offered not a word of help.

"You heard Maryla," he floundered on. "She thinks if I go back it means I don't really love you! Not love you? Christ!"

She thought, *His father is dying but inside my body his child is quickening. And if he doesn't know it, it's because he doesn't want to know—he just wants me to tell him what to do. And I won't, damn him!* Her face did not soften, nor did she hold out her arms to him, either in appeal or for comfort. "And you, Adam? What do you think?"

"Does it *have* to be either you or them? I'm not trying to abandon you! Why am I being forced to choose?"

"I must know what you really want, Adam."

"I want you. I love you. I can't see a life without you. You know that. But if I ignore this telegram and then the worst happens, I'll never forgive myself. And I'd be no good to myself or to you. Dearest, you've always been strong. . . . You could manage alone for just a little while longer. But they . . . my people . . . especially my mother. . ." And he added in a suppliant's voice, "Darling, I know I said this before and now I'm begging you. . . Trust me, trust me for only a little while longer. . . ."

She shut her eyes tight, her face contorted as if in great physical pain. She crossed her arms over her chest, and the soap dish clattered to the floor, skidding into a corner where it came to rest against an open suitcase. Neither of them heard, nor moved to retrieve it. She continued to stand in the same position, hugging herself, swaying like a mourner. Briefly she was tempted, sorely tempted, to tell him the whole truth, to use the one sure weapon at her command. Knowing all she need say was, "But I am sure, I've been sure for days," she remained silent. She couldn't bring herself to do it. A grim, perverse sort of pride forced the silence on her. She would not beg for what he was unable to give freely. She would not whimper.

Afterwards Maryla would call her a fool and maybe she would be right. But being herself, she could not do otherwise. "You've always been strong," he had appealed to her. She wanted to be strong. To stand alone. And when the baby came she would raise it alone if she had to, feed it, cherish it, be both mother and father to it if need be. *But she would not be mother to a grown man.*

"If you go now, you'll not come back to me, Adam."

"I will! I give you my sacred word. . . ."

She shook her head. "Not the way things are. For one thing, where would you find the money a second time? Face it, Adash. You'll get caught up in that other life and nothing will ever be the same. Not you. Not me. Time will make us into two different people. There's no such thing as turning the clock back. They say not even the slowest-flowing river is the same two moments in a row. . . ."

"You mean you refuse to wait for me?"

"I merely refuse to delude myself. We'll be lost to each other. So why raise false hopes?"

"No!"

She sighed. "Have it your own way. I hope with all my heart that you're right and I'm wrong. And now would you please leave me so that I can dress and repack? I understand a train for Zurich leaves in a couple of hours. If we hurry we can make it. I'm sure Maryla and Olek won't mind."

He caught both her hands in his, kissing them, not daring to touch her more intimately, still fighting the inevitable. "Dearest, don't act as though you hated me already!"

"Please," she whispered, nearing the end of her endurance. "Please don't make it harder for us than it already is. . . ."

She forced herself to pull her hands away, to start in on some small, meaningless chore she could pretend to become absorbed in. Then, because he hadn't moved, more sharply, "Adam, please, I asked you to leave." She waited, bending down in the meantime to pick up the piece of soap she had dropped. When she had it, she used the damp hotel towel to rub furiously at the bits of grime it had accumulated, as though cleaning it off were the most important thing in the world.

Only when she heard the door close behind him did her face crumple. She threw herself across the bed and began to sob hopelessly, giving herself over to unbearable pain, overwhelmed by a sense of total loss.

Later, on the railroad platform, she managed once again to appear calm, composed, serene. *What a cold creature she is,* thought Salome, watching her without seeming to do so. *Unwomanly, that's what. What a narrow escape for our Adash! Ah, well, there we have it—the proverbial ill wind. Of course, he doesn't know it yet, but some day he'll thank me for this. . . .*

The train for Zurich was filling up. The Piotrowskis were already settled in their compartment, and although Wanda told herself she would have preferred to avoid any last-minute talk, she and Adam were left standing alone together.

"Write me the moment you get there," he kept begging. "The moment you have an address, send it to me. Promise me, Wanda. Wanda, do you hear?"

"Yes, I hear."

"And we'll be together again before you know it. I swear it. And if . . . if you *are* pregnant, and need me, write at once. Or better still, wire me, and I'll move heaven and earth to come to you. . . ."

"Yes, maybe. . . ."

"And above all, always remember I love you."

The first warning bell sounded, and then the second and the third. Olek and Maryla called to her and she scrambled up the steps just as the stationmaster bellowed a Prussian command to board. The train began to roll. Adam started to walk, then run alongside the open window of the Piotrowskis' compartment. "Always remember I love you. . . ." But the locomotive hooted, drowning out his words.

Around him, others who had come to see friends and relatives off stood waving handkerchiefs. He felt a tug on his sleeve. Salome stood beside him, giving him her most tender smile. "Well, they're gone. Come, dear heart, no sense standing here any longer. We've another hour to wait for your train home, longer for the Transcontinental for Lucio and me. I'd say what we all need now is a cup of good, hot, strong tea. I've already sent Lucio ahead to the station buffet to order for us. Well, what do you say?" He let himself be led away like a sleepwalker.

Now that it was done, her heart did truly ache for him and she was doing her genuine best to console him. "I know, my pet, how hard it is for you. But the day will come when you'll be glad you did the right thing. You'll be glad to have a clear conscience. Believe me, in the end it will all turn out for the best. . . ."

When he failed to respond, when she was unable to draw even the palest semblance of a smile from him, she tried another gambit, and yet another. Finally with a helpless little shrug, as if to say, "Well, heaven knows I've done my best," she stopped talking.

PART FOUR
Winter 1899—Spring 1901

❧ *One* ❧

HIS DISLIKE of doctors did not help Jacob Fabian. First they took away his tobacco, then they made him cut out salt and pepper and spices until it seemed that even the smallest pleasures of life were denied him. And when none of it did any good they made a slit in his throat and inserted a length of silver tubing.

"Only it's going to help me like cupping helps a dead man," he remarked wryly shortly before the operation, when he still had his natural voice. "Exactly like the old Kaiser." It was a subject he kept harping on, since unfortunately the much-publicized, useless operation in which the Prussian ruler had been given a "silver throat" a decade earlier had made an indelible impression on him, doubtless because Frederick, too, had been a heavy smoker. Now he had very little faith in his own future. But he tried to be resigned. "Well, so be it, if it'll make the rest of you feel you've done everything for me that could be done. . . ."

He saw his wife and children wince, but was no longer able to control the hurtful gallows humor that eased his spirit. "A silver throat should, by rights, give me a silver voice. But will I sing like a nightingale? On the contrary, I'll croak like a frog. There's probably a moral in it somewhere. If any of you find it, make the most of it. . . ."

Afterwards, for a long time he could only make his wants known by writing on a tablet. Yet once home from the hospital, he continued to work, hating the enforced idleness, refusing to lie in bed, to let himself be coddled into total helplessness by

Bluma, who would gladly have waited on him hand and foot. "Just let me live as normally as I can for as long as I can," he grumbled. And when her answer was to dissolve in tears, he patted her hand in awkward tenderness. "Tell you what—let's make a pact, you and I. I'll stop the jokes if you promise to stop crying. That way we'll both be happier."

Between him and Adam there had always been a kind of inarticulate affection, a latent friendship, for all that in the past they had lived like strangers under one roof. Perhaps, for Jacob, it had been mainly a matter of waiting until his eldest was a man grown, and now was the time. They found to their mutual pleasure that they enjoyed exchanging ideas, that they had an all-encompassing curiosity in common.

"Desperately as I miss you," Adam wrote Wanda a few weeks after coming home, "in one way I'm glad I came back. No, glad is hardly the word, for I've abandoned you and that's torture to my soul. But dearest, if only you knew how much I was needed! Nothing will help my father now, but he's going to take a long time to die. In the meantime I seem able to offer him a special kind of comfort. . . ."

It was ironic that the discovery of each other should have come so late for father and son, at a time when that least appreciated, that most taken for granted of all sound instruments, the human voice, was failing Jacob as a means of communication. Adam, by nature a man of few words, now had to learn to talk for two. He solved the problem to some extent by reading aloud for hours on end. "Anything and everything I can lay my hands on," he told Wanda in the same letter. "Spinoza and Adam Smith, Lomonosov, Voltaire, the new Zheromski novel that the booksellers have been forbidden to carry, a history of the French Revolution, Dickens and Darwin. . ."

Jacob would listen, his writing tablet and pencil at the ready, and when he wanted to interrupt, the pencil would start tapping. Between the hoarse, whispered comment and the written one he managed to make himself clear. Slowly his speech began to improve. It would never again be normal but at least he wasn't mute.

Often Adam forgot that he was there to help distract a sick

man. The ideas themselves would take over, and he talked to his father as once he had talked in the garret on Zapiecek Street. After a while he even started reading from the illegal leaflets which again were making their way into the house, this time smuggled in by his brother Izidore and his sister Idka inside their schoolbooks. Adam knew better than to question them about their source of supply. But secretly he was pleased. So was their father, judging by the gleam in his eyes.

"I will not live to see it, but your generation may, and your children for certain," the dying man would lie there spinning a cherished dream. "There's change in the wind. A day will come when not only Moscow, but Berlin and Vienna, too, will be forced to disgorge what they've swallowed but never digested. Then we'll again be united, independent, a sovereign nation. No longer will brother battle against brother. . . ."

His caring so deeply startled Adam. "How little I've known my own father!" he would conclude. Then vividly his mind conjured up those long-ago Saturday morning excursions to the back-yard privies, the smoking and the talk and his own swelling pride in being initiated into the weekly ritual of rebellion that implied the beginnings of a masculine camaraderie between father and son. And he remembered *Pan* Liebman and the medical student, and the politics that were never long absent from the conversation. He thought of Jacob unfailingly anxious to spare his wife's feelings, and how in contrast to most of his neighbors he was always encouraging her to think of herself as his equal. Even his deception of her had been gentle and loving. "What she doesn't know won't hurt her." As if it were yesterday he could see his father light his first cigarette, then puff on it greedily the way an alcoholic swigs liquor straight from the bottle after being too long deprived.

Now, watching him bite on the stem of a cold and empty pipe, his son found the memory both painful and poignant. "I never even suspected how far ahead of his time he always was," Adam's next letter to Wanda confided. "But now I find he's been most of the things you taught me a man should be! I find myself wishing I'd learned to appreciate him sooner. Why must there always be this chasm between parents and children?"

Why, why? The letters followed one another, three and four to one of hers, passionate outpourings of a kind he had never found possible before. Alone at his desk in the small hours, enveloped in the quiet of a sleeping house and with only the glow of a student lamp for company, he was able at last to let himself go. "I love you, you and you alone . . . you're flesh of my flesh and heart of my heart. . . ." And when his own words seemed pale, he again turned to the *Song of Songs*. "Thy love is better than wine. . . . Oh when shall I lie again all night between the breasts of my beloved. . . ."

Wanda never made any comment about his lyrical outbursts. Her answers were becoming more and more stilted, brief, the underlying hurt only barely discernible now and then. Often he wondered if she would be less unforgiving now if he'd learned to speak out more freely earlier. Sometimes he asked himself if he would ever know—if there was going to be a second chance.

Worst of all, no matter how often and how urgently he begged her to tell him about her physical condition, she made no further mention of it. "Please, I implore you," he wrote, "give me a simple yes or no. After that time in Berlin, what happened? Was it a false alarm after all? You've never said one way or the other. . . ."

She answered airily that the Swiss climate was doing her a world of good and please to stop worrying—didn't he have enough on his mind as it was? Her tone was deliberately patronizing, on the verge of insult, as though he were a child that needed to be put in his place. And yet he had the nagging impression that, masked by the cold, arrogant words, was a cry for help.

And then her letters stopped altogether. Adam waited a month, and another, and another. Finally, in desperation, he wrote to Olek, demanding to be told the truth, whatever the truth was.

❧ *Two* ❧

At DUSK on an afternoon in early April, Olek Piotrowski left the omnibus at a stop in Aussersil, Zurich's working-class district, and slowly made his way through a maze of steep, narrow alleys lined with gingerbread cottages, moving in the direction of the small shabby *pension* he, Maryla, and Wanda now called home. Originally directed to it by the landowner Korsza, they had been living there ever since first arriving in Switzerland. And the place did indeed have the feel of home—a corner of the motherland tucked away on alien soil—for it was peopled almost exclusively by exiles, and run by the widow of an old revolutionary who herself could never go home again.

Behind him as he walked was the embankment of the cool blue Limmat. Far off in the distance rose rolling hills beyond which wooded mountain slopes wore year-round bonnets of snow as white as the clouds into which they poked their heads on overcast days. But Olek had no eyes just then for the picturesqueness of the Linth Valley or its spectacular environs. He was bone-weary, for his day began at dawn and his work was back-breaking. Employment for a foreigner, especially one with only a sketchy knowledge of the local German, was not easily come by, so that when a chance presented itself to join a street-paving crew he had jumped at it, considering himself lucky. At least pay scales here were better than in Poland, and besides, unlike most of the other expatriates, he could stand up under hard physical labor. He was thus able to support himself and the two women who depended on him without being forced to turn for help to the hard-pressed Exiles' Assistance Fund, a fact of which he was justifiably proud.

After three or four more turns along the winding streets he reached the boardinghouse, let himself in, and began the climb to the cramped bed-sitting room he and Maryla called their apartment. He remembered that this was a late lecture day for his wife and Wanda at the University and that he would have the luxury of an hour to himself. Time to wash up and relax, or perhaps start jotting down notes for the report he was due to make the following evening at a meeting of their political group. He decided to forget about resting and concentrate on the report. He could relax another time.

When he reached his own door he found a rolled-up twist of newsprint wedged in behind the handle. He recognized the paper's format and the type. This was the latest issue of *Iskra,* The Spark, the new illegal publication of the Russian Social-Democrats, edited and largely written by Vladimir Lenin. Scribbled across the masthead legend, *The spark will kindle a flame,* was the notation: "Thought you'd appreciate a quick look at this. But I must have it back tonight without fail, and no nonsense. F.G."

The initials were those of their neighbor across the hall, Felix Gronowicz. An exile of a somewhat earlier vintage, Felix had at first been merely a useful acquaintance, showing them around the strange city where he had endless connections and knew his way around. But very soon, partly because he shared their political views and partly because, like Olek, he was Warsaw-born and bred, a kinship developed between them that was warm and close. Since, as chance would have it, Felix was also a fellow medical student at the university and even Wanda's laboratory partner, he gradually became a fixture in their lives. With no personal ties of his own, he often shared their meals and their evenings, and being something of a clown could keep them entertained for hours on end with yarns of the Vistula waterfront told in the inimitable idiom of the river rat.

Arrival of the paper changed Olek's plans. Barely taking time to shrug out of his work clothes, he settled down to read. The lead article at once caught his attention. It had to do with the principles of underground organization and stressed the need for total discipline as the only way to avoid the pitfalls of anarchy while at the same time lessening the danger of falling into traps.

He became completely absorbed. But it was hard going. His Russian was far from fluent, his head spun with fatigue, and the small, smudged print, the paper purposely tissue-thin for easier smuggling into the Empire from wherever it happened to be printed abroad, were hard on eyes even less tired than his. He was beginning to nod in spite of himself when there was a knock on the door. "Hey, Piotrowski, you about done with my little 'Spark'?" Without waiting for an invitation Felix stuck his head in. "I promised it to a fellow down the street. Such a to-do every time an issue arrives, you'd really think we're starting fires!" He chuckled. "Makes me feel rather like Prometheus!"

Olek's head came up with a start. "What? Oh. Have a heart, this isn't something you read on the run like a penny-dreadful! This takes digesting!"

Instead of answering, Gronowicz pushed the door open all the way and came inside. He was an immensely tall man, taller even than Olek, and so thin he seemed all length and no width. Long arms, long legs, long, narrow hands and feet, a long, skinny neck stretching above the confines of a celluloid collar, and balanced on it precariously, like a ripe fruit on a thin stem that might snap any minute, a long, dark head with bushy beard and hair. All this, plus the fact that even with his glasses he was hopelessly myopic and had formed a habit of peering closely and curiously at the world around him, and finally the years of bad posture due to his great height, combined to give him the semblance of a some-what startled bird of prey. Until he smiled. Then he didn't look the least bit like a predator.

"Good stuff, this *Iskra*, huh? Solid. On second thought why don't I let you keep it another hour? I really should be getting back to the lab anyway. Wanda's been glued to the microscope since morning. We've got this fantastic experiment going. Live bits of tissue taken from a carcinoma patient, and the cells have gone wild! No wonder she can't tear herself away!"

In spite of drowsiness Olek warmed to the other man's enthu-siasm. A good egg, this Gronowicz. "Whatever would we do without him?" the three of them often asked one another. Felix the Fixer, they'd nicknamed him, and even called him that to his face, to his good-natured amusement.

"Well, I'll leave you to your reading, then," Felix said. But he made no move to go; obviously he had something else on his mind. "You know, Olek," he finally began, and hesitated, "I'm getting awfully worried about that girl of ours. Drives herself too hard. On her feet too much. Dedication to science is all well and good but there are limits. Especially in her condition." He was referring to Wanda's pregnancy, now in an advanced stage.

Olek suspected something more than dedication to science was driving Wanda, but that was none of Felix's affair. He made no comment. But Felix persisted. "Talk to her, can't you? Or ask your wife to."

"Wouldn't do much good," Olek growled. "We've both tried. But here's a stopgap proposal. Why don't you both quit work early and then you can eat with us. There's always an extra potato. And now go, go, go and let me read in peace. Or else you won't get your paper back tonight," he threatened. But once Felix had left he found he couldn't keep his eyes open.

When he woke, it was because Maryla was shaking him, saying supper would be on the table in five minutes. "Felix and Wanda are bringing up the stuff from the kitchen right now." The kitchen, on the floor below, was something of a communal affair even though technically this was a *pension* with a regular dining room. But the landlady's sympathy with her tenants was such that she simply looked the other way when they cooked their own meals in order to save a few sous. The Piotrowski ménage had long ago given up all pretense of doing anything else.

"Felix says you invited him to take pot luck with us," Maryla was commenting dryly, "so just remember to fill up on bread. It's fresh from the bakery and there's plenty for a change." She began clearing the clutter of books and papers from their only table so they could eat on it.

"Any mail?" Olek questioned, watching her arrange the ill-assorted crockery. He stretched and yawned. "That was a good nap. Good evening, wife!" He drew her to him and kissed her soundly. She kissed him back, then reached into her pocket.

"This came after you left for work." She handed him an envelope with a Warsaw postmark and no return address. "Makes me homesick just to look at it! Adam's handwriting, isn't it? How come it's you he's writing to?"

Olek tore open the envelope, feeling uneasy. He scanned the single sheet of paper covered with minute script, reread it, and without comment handed it to her. She read quickly, and she, too, seemed uneasy, at a loss for comment.

"Wish I knew what to say to him," Olek finally grumbled. "Wish that fine friend of yours weren't so stubborn and so bitter."

Maryla sighed. "Sometimes I think she's cutting off her nose to spite her face. I used to think Adam was the villain of the piece—I blamed the whole fiasco on him. Now I'm no longer sure. That Wanda! The walls are so thin—do you think I can't hear her cry in the middle of the night? So why doesn't she write and tell him the truth? Will a crown roll off her head if she admits she's human like the rest of us? But no. She eats her heart out here, he eats his heart out there. . . . It's the old story of the irresistible force and the immovable object—but at least if they got on a collision course something might happen, something that would surprise her!" She slammed plates down on the table noisily. "The worst of it is, those two really do belong together! Honestly, *people* . . . what a mess!"

In spite of the urgency and the concern they both felt, he couldn't help laughing. "Well, well, I never thought I'd hear this from you, my girl! What a difference from the tune you used to sing! Could it be," he added slyly, slapping her on the rump, "that just being married to me has made the difference?" Then, serious again, "I've felt right along that a man has the right to know what's what in a situation like this. After all, it's his baby, too. I've even been tempted to meddle, though she's dead set against it."

"Perhaps you really should write and tell him," Maryla began. "Perhaps. . ." But Felix's voice in the corridor interrupted whatever else she meant to say.

"Gangway! Hot soup coming!" Clowning as usual, Felix made a grand entrance with the steaming tureen. "Make way for the cook!" Wanda followed, carrying a tray laden with thick-sliced bread, cheese, a mound of potatoes. She moved awkwardly, her walk a kind of waddle, her belly huge. Her face had lost its usual high color, her features were bloated and thick.

All day long, in the laboratory, at lectures, the demons had been after her. As luck would have it, it had been she who picked up the morning mail. Adam's familiar handwriting had leaped out at her, and instantly she had felt resentful. "Oh no, not again! Why doesn't he just leave me alone!" Then she noticed the letter wasn't addressed to her after all, and her carefully worked-up anger vanished. Sick with disappointment, outraged, and at the same time strangely frightened, she had barely managed a shrug of indifference as she handed the envelope to Maryla. "This one's for your husband. And here I was about to open it!" A letter from Adam to Olek—what did it mean? Were they discussing her? If so, how dare they? Then other possibilities suggested themselves. Perhaps something dreadful had happened, something he didn't have the courage to tell her directly. Perhaps he was in trouble himself and asking his old friend to break the news to her. Perhaps. . . She broke a test tube, spilled the contents of another. To make matters worse, Felix the Fixer hovered over her, clucking. "Don't you feel well, Wandeczka? Tell Uncle Felix. Your hands are shaking and you look like a ghost."

You're wrong, she wanted to cry out, *I am a ghost and I'm seeing ghosts.* She fended him off as best she could. "I'm fine. Just naturally clumsy."

But he refused to leave her alone. "You've worked long enough for a lady in your delicate condition. Come on, let's go home."

She became irritated out of all proportion, snapping at him, yet at the same time it felt good to be fussed over. Finally she gave in, but with bad grace. "Just this once I'll let you take care of me." *Only why does it have to be you? Why isn't it him? It should be the. . .* Startled, ashamed, she stopped. She had almost said *the man I love.* "But I don't love him any more. I hate him!" She did not realize she had spoken the words out loud until she saw Felix staring at her oddly. "Whom do you hate, little one?" she heard him ask softly.

It was late in the day and the laboratory was deserted. Not a soul in the building, just white rats in cages. A fine private place for a private talk—if that's what one wanted, which she did not. But again Felix would not be put off. "Whom do you hate so much? Why are you so unhappy?"

She tried the same airy little laugh she sometimes used with Maryla. "Me, unhappy? Me, hate anyone? Don't believe everything I say! Why, I love everybody. . . . I'm just brimming full of the milk of human kindness for the whole goddam human race. . . ." And to her horror she burst into a storm of weeping.

He let her cry herself out. Without a word he put one long arm about her and with his free hand pushed her head down against his bony chest. It was like being comforted by a skeleton. When at last she quieted down, he handed her his handkerchief and turned his back. "Now I understand a lot of things I only suspected before," he said gruffly. "He doesn't love you enough to marry you. It's an old story. Only believe me, it isn't the end of the world."

Instantly she felt compelled to fly to Adam's defense. "You don't understand a thing! It was never that simple . . . it was political, and we had to separate before. . . . What I mean is, I never let him know for sure about the baby. Besides," she finally admitted, knowing he would realize that to her this was the crux of the matter, "I wasn't going to have him feel he *had* to marry me. . . ."

"And that, too," Felix commented, "is an old, old story. People like us want to change the world, we live according to our conscience, and what happens? Babies happen, same as with anyone else. Babies, you see, are the great imponderable." Listening to him, she hardly knew whether to laugh or to cry again.

Now in his abrupt way he strode to the microscope they shared, peered at the slide under the lens as if it were far more important than anything they were saying to one another, made an adjustment, jotted down some findings, and put a cover over the apparatus. That done, he turned back to her. "Now what do you say we close up shop? Olek said if I dragged you home early I could eat with you."

Without waiting for an answer he took his student cap off its hook, then helped Wanda into her coat which no longer fitted her swollen body. "You know, Wandeczka," he finally said, offhand, in his most cheerful Felix-the-Fixer tone, "I've thought and thought about your predicament, and I think I finally know what you could do about it. You could marry me. I don't see why it shouldn't work."

"Marry you?" She stared at him stupidly, and he began to talk fast and thick as if determined not to let her answer yes or no.

"Why shouldn't it work? We're good friends. We have the same convictions and the same interests. You're alone. I'm alone. And I love kids. I wouldn't care that this one isn't mine, I'd make it mine, I promise you." As he talked, he took down his own coat, shrugged into it. A button popped off. "Besides," he said, holding it out to her triumphantly. "Here's proof that I need a woman to take care of me."

"Oh, Felix," Wanda finally managed, "Felix, this is crazy. . . ."

"Crazy? Why? I might even end up falling in love with you." His long, cadaverous face suddenly turned beet-red, and in that moment she understood the one thing he had left unsaid: He was already in love with her, but wasn't going to use this as an argument.

She felt infinitely touched and curiously humble. "Felix, my dear, you're too good for this sort of bargain."

"Who says? Let me decide that. Just think about the proposition, is all I ask. Don't give me an answer now. There's no rush. No rush about anything, in fact, except—" again he resorted to clowning, "that matter of supper. If we don't get out of here pretty soon the four of us will starve to death."

She went over to him and patted his bearded cheek. She had no intention of accepting his proposal, but her battered self-esteem was somehow less battered.

All that evening she waited for Olek to bring up the subject of Adam's letter without being prodded. When he failed to do so, she put it down to their having company. But eventually Felix left, and then it was almost bedtime, and still he hadn't volunteered any information. Finally, unable to stand it any longer, she swallowed her pride and questioned him point blank. "I know you heard from him. Doesn't he even send me his regards?"

Olek looked at her owlishly and scratched his head. "You're a funny one, Wanda. Can't make you out. Mad at me because I haven't said anything. But you know perfectly well if I'd tried to talk to you about him you'd just have told me you didn't want to hear." He rubbed the side of his nose. Maybe, he was thinking, all she really needs is for someone to shock her into thinking straight.

She flushed. "I'm sorry," she said with stiff dignity, "if I've been hard to live with." Her heart had begun to pump hard, making it difficult for her to breathe. And though she tried to tell herself it was only because she was so upset, she was by now doctor enough to know this was not the whole story. Something else was wrong. Otherwise why, with the baby's birth only weeks off, should she still be bothered with constant nausea? And why the unrelenting headaches, the palpitations, the dizzy spells? Why the painful swelling of her feet and ankles and the ugly blotches on her face?

She was doing her best to ignore her physical misery, steadying herself against the table. She heard Maryla say, "That's enough, both of you. Olek, you leave her alone. I'm going to put her to bed." She roused herself and stood straight again. "No. This is a conversation we've got to finish. Well, Olek, what have you to say in defense of your friend?"

He thought, it's the hurt in her talking, and when he answered his voice was measured and he chose his words carefully, speaking slowly, "As a matter of fact, my girl, you and only you are what he's thinking about. Begging me by everything that's holy to tell him the truth. He's no fool, he's known for a long time you've been hiding things from him. If you need him, he writes, just say the word and he'll pack a bag and come to you."

It was what she had longed to hear for so many months, only it had come too late. In her overwrought state she was not to be appeased. *"If I need him . . . ,"* she mimicked in a high, shrill voice, not her own voice at all. "He'd do me that favor, would he? That's noble, that's rich! But tell him from me—no thanks. Tell him I wouldn't dream of accepting such a sacrifice! Tell him to keep right on putting his family first!" She began to laugh.

Olek stared at her, shocked. "Wanda, what's come over you? I hardly know you any more. You sound so . . . heartless. . ."

"Heartless—me?" The laughter grew louder. "Just because I'm in no mood to accept his favors? Oh, you fool . . . you utter fool. . . ."

Olek saw that she was on the verge of hysteria and did not press her. Maryla came up to her and put her arm around her. "Hush, darling, hush. You'll make yourself sick."

Suddenly they saw her double over and clutch her abdomen. "Help me, help me . . . ," she moaned. Beads of sweat stood out on her forehead and upper lip. "It was like a knife in the back. . . ." Another spasm hit her. "The baby . . . I think it's coming. . . . But it can't, it's too soon! Maryla, help me! Olek, tell Felix! Felix is the only one who understands. . . ." The moaning turned into a sharp cry. "Felix! I want Felix . . . Felix, Felix. . . ."

It took the baby two nights and two days to fight its way into the world. And when at last they could be sure that both mother and child would live, when the midwife had left and the doctor come and gone, Olek took pen in hand and composed a stiff, formal letter to Adam in Warsaw. In it there was no word about the daughter he had fathered. Olek just wrote, "For your own sake as well as hers, leave Wanda alone, old friend. That's all I can tell you. Forget her and give her a chance to forget you. Believe me, Adash, it's the only way." He repeated the last phrase and underscored it heavily. *The only way.*

❦ *Three* ❧

JACOB'S ILLNESS seemed to draw together not just the immediate family, but all the relatives, until it seemed that the Fabian home was once more as Adam remembered it from childhood, the hearth around which the clan gathered. In practical terms it meant he was very seldom alone, and for this he was grateful, for such an almost tribal way of living left him little time to brood. He was being forced to shift his center of gravity, as it were, outside himself. Now in a very real sense he became head of the family, advising his mother, making the decisions with which his father must obviously no longer be burdened, shouldering more and more of the bills, always on hand when it became necessary to confer with the doctors or when Bluma, utterly drained with worry and the constant effort at self-control, needed a shoulder to cry on. Thus the classical roles of parent and child were being reversed, and reversed earlier than happens in most cases.

During that year Adam also became newly aware of his younger brothers and sisters and it was a startling discovery to him that they were not merely his siblings but individuals—and that he did not have equal affection for them all.

He found a friend in Viktor, the second eldest, also by now a student at the university. Viktor, determined to be a great engineer, talked with single-minded absorption about the modern approaches to designing bridges, but he also shared Adam's interest in pure science and was much the best chess player in the family. Occasionally one of the brothers would begin a game of chess with their father while the other watched, and all three would pore silently over the chess board for hours on end. It was exactly the kind of companionship Adam needed, the mental gymnastics, with no threat of emotional encroachment to cut through his spiritual solitude, offering him a kind of cool solace.

Izidore, seventeen and in his final year at the *Gymnasium,* was still a question mark. It made Adam proud that the boy's youthful political passions were carrying him far beyond where he himself had once cared to venture: Izzy had none of Adam's propensity for watching from the sidelines. And if the eldest brother, in his new role of *paterfamilias* so unceremoniously thrust upon him, was finding it hard to rest comfortably on nights when the younger, out without explanation on business which must remain mysterious, was late getting home, he tried to remember this was all part of the warp and woof of the times and could not be avoided. What did disturb him, however, was that Izidore's enthusiasms all seemed to stem from a grasshopper turn of mind. He was forever skimming the surface of things. In quick succession he could become enthralled with the study of Sanskrit, the seven stages of Yoga, the founding of an underground student newspaper, and peasant art as reflected in wood sculpture. Each time he was like an explorer touching new land. But the enthusiasms seldom lasted, and Adam suspected that the boy mainly relished the impression he was creating. He even wondered how much of his brother's life outside the home, including his outbursts of patriotic activity, was for show. Still, he reminded himself, Izidore was really too young to know what he wanted. One must reserve judgment.

Idka and Rosie, he was finding out to his surprise, were now budding young women, and soon it would be up to him to make their future secure. Idka, only a year older than Izzy, was Izzy's shadow. But where he sparkled, she was solid, plodding, thorough. What he started, she finished. Thus when it was a matter of organizing student demonstrations, Izidore might plan but it was Idka who worried about details. If he wrote the fiery manifestos, the calls to action, she saw to it that they got printed and eventually distributed. And when a history instructor at Izidore's *gymnasium* was thrown into prison, it was she who, without telling anyone, stole out of the house alone long after dark to dispose of the pamphlets her brother had been hiding, which would have linked him to the arrested man. He himself would not have thought of it. But she was like a mother hen, protecting him.

Unfortunately, all these sterling qualities were hidden behind so unpromising an exterior that Adam understood why his mother sometimes said, "Poor Idka'll need a really *good* man to appreciate her!" and worried constantly about her daughter's future. Stocky, with heavy breasts and a face astonishingly lacking in the freshness of youth, Idka was, to put it mildly, plain as a mud fence. Even her one claim to beauty, the great shining braids she had inherited from her mother, failed to make her proud, for they were carrot-red, a color considered downright ugly, and she had the freckled skin to go with them. Already she had resigned herself to the life of an old maid, talking about earning a teacher's certificate, then finding work in some girls' school, preferably one where room and board was offered in addition to a salary. As he listened to her making her plans, Adam quietly promised himself he would do everything in his power to save up a decent sum against the time when their mother was ready to start negotiations with a marriage broker. If there was a dowry, Idka just conceivably might find a husband. Not that he himself would have objected to a sister of his making her own way in the world; Wanda had taught him that much and more. It was the prejudgment which he found so maddeningly unfair, the cruel cutting-off of a young girl's hopes.

Rosie, of course, would never have Idka's problems. Pretty, vivacious, uncomplicated, pliable, gifted with a truly sunny disposition, Rosie would make her own happiness wherever she went. "That one," Bluma said of her, "will neither give nor make trouble." Dowry or no dowry, it was somehow taken for granted that Rosie would marry early and immediately start producing healthy babies for the man lucky enough to get her. Adam saw no reason to doubt the predictions.

He wished he could be equally easy in his mind about Kazik, the baby of the family and the only truly handsome one. A throwback to some tall, blond, blue-eyed ancestor, Kazik had a good deal of Rosie's charm and easy-going ways, but none of her sweetness. People said of him that being the youngest he was naturally spoiled, and that he would outgrow it once the outside world gave him a knock or two. But Adam thought he could already detect a steely kind of selfishness beneath the charm. In fact, although he was profoundly ashamed to admit it, he was beginning to realize he didn't much like this youngest brother. Was it possible, then, not to love someone who was flesh of the same flesh, blood of the same blood—and practically a child at that? Well, it would seem so. . . .

If none of this was the stuff to absorb a man on the threshold of his own life's work, at least it served to fill a terrible vacuum, and for the time being it would have to suffice. Adam almost welcomed the worries, the responsibilities, the constant demands on his time—welcomed the fact that between these, his tutoring chores, and his own studies, all the hours of all his days were so crowded as to make thinking all but superfluous. Thus the whole academic year went by, a year that forever afterwards remained vague in his memory, a year through which he moved like a sleepwalker. And then it was examination time again, and because he really did not care enough about anything he forgot to be nervous, and acquitted himself brilliantly as a result, and emerged in possession of his sheepskin. At twenty-four he finally had a degree in law.

It was at this point that he roused himself sufficiently to consider with acute distaste a decision about his future which he could no longer postpone. He could no longer mark time, tutoring Lucio Kronenberg and Marek and Missy Pozner. His diploma meant he must embark on a career of some sort. Uncle Leon and Aunt Salome, and through them the Kronenbergs whose contacts reached out in every direction, were offering letters of introduction that could be enormously helpful. Armed with these, he should have no trouble finding a clerkship in some established, respected law firm. It was an auspicious beginning—there was no reason why he should not look forward to eventual success.

There was no reason, yet there was every reason. For now that his years of slaving for it were behind him, he knew at last how much he hated to think of himself in the legal profession, hating everything the profession itself represented within the framework of Tsarist rule.

"How can I make a living at law and remain honest?" He finally posed the question to his father, not really expecting an answer but rather by way of thinking out loud. "I must have been an idiot not to ask myself that in the first place!"

Jacob had no ready answers. "Still, a degree is a degree and may turn out to be of some use to you regardless," he tried to console him in his raucous whisper.

"If only teaching paid a decent wage!" Adam said in quiet desperation. "There's self-respecting work for you! To mold young minds, and continue to learn while one does it. . . . Then eventually to go more deeply into the exact sciences. . . ." He sighed. "Oh for the world of pure science where there can be no corruption!" *Yes, and no human entanglements, either. . . .* "That's where I would really feel entirely at home."

"Perhaps," Jacob offered, slowly exploring the idea, "perhaps you owe it to yourself to consider just that. After all, as a family we're not really desperate—the others would help more if they were asked, I think. The whole responsibility should never have been dumped on just your shoulders. Believe me, Adash, your mother and I appreciate all you've done, the way you've taken over. Just the same, you've the right not to be smothered by us. Remember, there's great happiness in doing work one is fitted for. So try not to do violence to yourself, son."

It was, for him, a very long speech, and as always when he tried to say more than a few words Jacob was seized with a spasm of coughing, so that in the end the true sense of his warning was lost on Adam. For at the sound of his father's distress he was reminded how much sicker Jacob was than either he or anyone else was willing to admit, and he cursed himself for all kinds of a fool, wishing he had never brought up a subject that clearly caused the dying man worry, and did his level best to help him forget it.

Then suddenly a practical solution presented itself.

It was now exactly a year since Adam had first been summoned into the presence of Maurice Pozner for that conference about a possible job in his cotton empire. As the school year drew to a close, the old man decided the time was ripe for a second interview.

Only recently *Pani* Konstancja had reported that their daughter's infatuation with her tutor was not entirely a thing of the past. Missy was not exactly pining over Adam, but in between flirtations with her brother's friends she still occasionally sighed over the raggle-taggle youth who had proved to be so impervious to her feminine wiles. Here and there she'd heard talk about his "noble sorrows"—some story about the lost love of his life, a heroine of the underground movement whom he hadn't been able to follow into exile because of his father's illness—and this, to a girl of eighteen, made him seem so lofty and tragically romantic that at times she considered herself positively unworthy of even trying to make an impression on him. She also became convinced that no other man of her acquaintance could so much as hold a candle to him. Her whole attitude toward her tutor changed. She began to treat him with a curious kind of diffidence. What it actually amounted to as far as Adam was concerned was that he saw her as somehow gentled, and, putting it down to the beginnings of a very becoming maturity, began to feel easy with her.

Missy's parents, however, saw the matter differently. "It's time to make the next move, Pozner," *Pani* Konstancja said to her husband one night in the privacy of their bedroom. "I'm talking about your Fabian. Offer him a job now, don't wait till next fall. With Missy away all summer it'll look more natural, and neither he nor she will suspect a thing. It's always good to be prepared."

Sitting on the edge of the enormous double bed she had never considered exchanging, like so many of her friends as they reached middle age, for separate beds or, worse yet, the separate rooms they said were even more fashionable, she thoughtfully began undoing the long row of buttons down the front of her blouse. Her ample bosom, pushed upward by the thrust of her corsets, emerged as if ready to spill over, but miraculously did not. Konstancja was fat but not sloppy fat, and took pleasure and pride in keeping Maurice well aware of her opulent charms. "I'm not even sure Missy will care one way or the other by the time she's home again and the fall season starts. But when it comes to a thing like that one can never have too many irons in the fire. Anyway, he'll be earning his salt, and the Kronenbergs would be pleased, which can't hurt either, and you've always said you'd like to have him in the business. You've nothing to lose."

He had just dropped his trousers and was standing in his long underwear, grinning at her appreciatively. "You know, Mama, you should've been a prime minister, not my wife." He kicked the trousers out of his way, strode purposefully to her side and without warning plunged a hand deep between her breasts. "On the other hand, what would a prime minister want with these?" His hand slid deeper, feeling its way.

She slapped it away. "Later. Now I'm trying to talk to you, and I want you should listen." But she kissed him full on the mouth, and he laughed uproariously. "About your daughter . . . ," she began.

Thus it was that Adam found himself, a couple of days later, once more sipping seven-star Martell in Pozner's study while his employer asked, as if picking up a conversation interrupted yesterday rather than left hanging a year, "Well now, my boy, suppose you bring me up to date on what's been happening to you. From what I hear, you have your degree at long last. So what do you plan to do? Still intending to go into legal practice?"

He asked the questions as if by the way, then added offhandedly, "Of course, by now we both know how all those warnings I gave you last spring haven't amounted to a row of beans—the way the new edict will operate lets your graduating class in under the wire. Lucky, eh? Very lucky. Still, how long do you figure you'll have to spend clerking," he interjected with a fine show of innocence, "before you start earning a decent wage? Two years? Three? Rather a long haul, I'd say, when one considers how badly you need the money. Which really brings me to what I have to say, and I'll not beat about the bush. Have you had time to think seriously about the offer I made you a year ago?"

Adam admitted that he had. "But frankly, sir, I can't quite see it. What's my value to you? Why should you want me?"

"Not," Pozner chuckled, "for your legal experience, that I'll warrant. Fact is, it's your diploma itself that matters here. As I told you last year and I'll repeat now, I'm at an age where I need someone young to train as, well, a kind of personal representative, someone who'll do my leg work for me but with a good head on him, too, and honest. A man I can send with confidence—once he's learned his business, of course—to any part of the Empire where I might need an agent."

"But what has my diploma to do with it?" Adam asked, honestly puzzled. "Isn't it all a matter of experience rather than education?"

"I see," said Pozner, "that you're not aware of the fine points of the Laws of the Pale—most people aren't who haven't felt them where it hurts, on their own skin. Well, it so happens that when it comes to traveling through Great Russia, and staying in the big cities, the average Jew has problems—he's only given a transit permit. As for any protracted visits, that's a privilege reserved for men like me, who pay taxes in the highest category, or men with domestic university degrees—domestic only, mind you, not foreign—in other words, men like you. I could also, of course," he went on, "look for someone to fill the bill who simply isn't a Jew. But just between you and me it sticks in my craw to hire *goyim* unless I have to. So you see." Carefully, he blew a large smoke ring which he then followed by another, smaller and faster one that floated through the first. "This is not exactly an altruistic offer. To put it another way, we can be valuable to each other."

He downed the rest of his cognac and let Adam consider while refilling both glasses. "Well now, my young friend, here is what I propose. Come to work for me right away. I'll pay you well from the start simply because I'm convinced I can get more out of an employee who isn't always full of money worries. I'll start training you. At the end of a year, if my hunch is correct—and I flatter myself I'm seldom wrong about such things—all that fine legal training of yours may be rusty, but you'll be worth everything I invest in you and more. Plus even a bonus and a raise."

Adam shook himself and passed his hand over his eyes. "I still say I don't know the first thing about cotton. Or about business—any business—for that matter."

"And haven't I just finished telling you," Pozner snapped, impatient now, "that I'll see to it you learn? When I'm through with you, there isn't much about cotton that you won't know." Deliberately, he began to concentrate on more smoke rings, a whole series of them, each smaller and faster than the preceding one. "It's like I said, I've a nose for such things. One of these days you'll be worth your weight in gold to me."

Abruptly changing the subject, he began talking about his textile factories that consumed the cotton from the East, about the growers and brokers in the Caucasus, in Persia, all through Asia Minor who cheated him, cheated all Europeans for that matter, right and left, even about the big banks in Moscow and Petersburg through which he did business. "None of them have a conscience. Granted, they can't afford one—but does that mean I must put up with what they try to ram down my throat? Now do you see why I need my own man, a man I can trust, since I'm getting too old to travel all the time. . . ."

Adam sat silently twirling the stem of his glass, watching the sun break light into dozens of prisms against the deeply cut crystal. And Maurice Pozner grew lyrical about the complexities of cotton. Raw cotton, cotton on the stalk, cotton in the boll, long-staple, short-staple, baled and shipped and processed. Then abruptly he became matter-of-fact once more. "What I propose is that you agree to work for me for five years. At the end of that time you'll probably want to go into business for yourself, and why not? The factories of Lodz are a big, big field, a good man would be a fool not to want to try his wings. Only born flunkeys remain employees. When the time comes I may even want to stake you. Or make some other arrangement, like give you a share in the business. We'll cross that bridge when. Well, what do you say, boy? Are we agreed?"

They had discussed no terms, he had named no salary, yet he seemed to consider the matter closed. He raised his glass. "Well, *prosit*. Believe me, you'll never regret it."

"But," Adam interjected, "but. . ."

Pozner held up a large square hand that peremptorily silenced all opposition. "If we're agreed in principle, everything else is detail. I already said I intend to pay you well from the start—the less you worry the faster you'll learn—you'll be valuable to me that much sooner. So? Do you want more time to think it over? Very well, give me your answer tomorrow."

He rose, indicating the interview was over. The truth was, he was anxious to report on his progress to *Pani* Konstancja.

Adam promised to stop in the following afternoon, which was also to be the last of his tutoring sessions with Marek and Missy. But when he came home, it was to find that his father had taken a sharp unexpected turn for the worse and had been rushed to the hospital. That evening he went into a coma out of which he emerged for only short periods from then on. In a matter of days he was dead.

Bluma managed, by sheer willpower, to hold herself together through those final days by her husband's bedside and through the funeral. Then she went into a depression so severe that Karol Segal, in his role of family physician, expressed fears for her sanity. Already numbed by double grief and double loss, Adam now found himself functioning like an automaton. As soon as he was able to start thinking clearly, he knew he must bury his own misery under a semblance of total outward calm and begin doing whatever needed to be done. For he was now truly head of the family, its only head.

One of his first actions after the services for the dead were over was to send word to *Pan* Pozner that he would be ready to start work as soon as certain urgent family matters had been attended to. This taken care of, for the first time in days he took time to undress and get into bed, actually to sleep between sheets. But his sleep was disturbed by recurrent dreams in which he sat by his father's bedside, holding the conversation there had never been time for in real life.

And "Don't go into business," his father kept urging him in his old, normal, good voice of long ago. "Choose work you are fitted for. That's where happiness lies."

Finally, at daybreak, his head heavy and his heart pounding, he jumped up, pulled on his clothes, and went to stand on the narrow balcony outside his window. The city was only beginning to waken, the sky still gray with a faint tinge of rose. The footfall of an occasional passerby, the rattle of a milk cart on the cobblestones, were all that disturbed the silence.

Well, what am I fitted for? he asked himself in desperation. *And how can I take time to find out when there are all those mouths waiting to be fed?*

And then he knew with a terrible and painful clarity that his real choice had been made long ago, in a hotel room in Berlin. Which course he took now—whether it would be law or the cotton business or something else entirely—did not really matter.

❧ *Four* ❧

A WEEK PASSED, and another and another. Bluma continued to sit motionless in her chair by the window, without a word for anyone, the tears streaming ceaselessly down her cheeks, her great gray eyes no longer luminous but bleached colorless by salty grief, her gray hair wispy, a monotone study in lifelessness. Her daughters dressed her every morning and undressed her at night, her sons came to lead her to the family table at mealtimes. She allowed herself to be handled, docile as a sick child but with no will of her own.

For years she had been the heart of the household, the pivot they had taken for granted, on which everything revolved. Now suddenly she was no longer that, no longer the mother incarnate but only a woman mortally stricken. When spoken to, she answered in monosyllables. When asked a direct question she said, "I suppose so. I just don't know. Whatever you say." And the answer was always the same whether it was a question of shutting off the rooms Jacob had used for business or shutting the window against driving rain. Even the youngest and least sensitive of them, Kazik, accepted the fact that for a while at least he wouldn't have her to cater to him, and tiptoed around as if afraid of rousing her from a deep sleep.

When at the end of a month she showed no signs of improvement, Uncle Karol gave up trying to treat her with strong herb infusions and valerian drops and brought in a specialist for consultation. The specialist diagnosed acute melancholia and advised sending her to a sanatorium for an indefinite period.

"Your mother," he explained, turning to Adam and Viktor, who participated in the family council, "is in that critical period of a woman's life . . . the change, surely you've heard of it . . . when the nerves are highly unstable. A severe emotional shock— in this case your father's death—can trigger a total emotional collapse. From what you tell me she and your father were devoted to each other, and now she's paying a terrible price—she's feeling her loss a great deal more deeply than most wives. It's as though she had nothing left to live for. She's withdrawn into a world where no one can follow her. Left alone, she might try to do herself harm, or simply *will herself* to die—which does happen. That's why she must be put in a safe place, a place where she can be watched. Eventually she may snap back. . . ."

They said they understood, but they did not understand. Besides, it seemed to them indecent to hear her discussed like this, indecent to be told she was a woman like other women, with emotions and needs and an inner life that had nothing to do with them—that, indeed, their parents had been two sexual human beings first, and mother and father secondarily.

But there was no time to dwell on such matters. Arrangements had to be made, money found to take care of the heavy, protracted medical expenses. In addition, there was now the fresh problem of running the household without adult feminine supervision. Aunt Salome and Aunt Balbina immediately offered to take in the three younger Fabians, but at this point the practical, dependable Idka protested. "What's all this fuss?" she demanded to know. "Why break the family up, make things even worse? Rosie and I are no longer children. We'll run the house. We'll manage. Especially if we can keep the maid-of-all-work. Then we can do the marketing and get the meals and take care of Kazik and keep everyone's clothes mended and your socks darned—and not even drop out of school. Don't you think so, Rosie? It shouldn't be too hard."

The younger girl agreed instantly. "Of course! Besides, it isn't as though this was going to be forever—only till Mama gets better. Adash," she turned to her eldest brother to coax prettily, "do you really think we can—I mean—keep the maid?"

Already, Adam thought, they were taking him for granted as

the mainstay. And he was grateful for their offer, grateful and relieved and touched. At the same time he saw that once again an old pattern was repeating itself. His sisters, like himself, were being robbed of their years of adolescence, that should have been carefree. And who could tell how soon Bluma would really be home? Maybe in a matter of months. Maybe next year. Maybe never.

"Yes," he said quickly, without even stopping to consider how he would manage it. "We'll keep the maid and pay her somehow. And by the way, with so much happening I haven't even had time to tell you, but I'm taking a position with a regular salary. Not in a law office—something that will pay better right from the start. I'll be working for Maurice Pozner. In his business." It was said so casually that no one, not even Viktor who knew him best, guessed how much the decision had cost him. "I'll start work as soon as we have Mama settled. So you see, we aren't going to be all that badly off."

As she sat watching her daughters pack a suitcase for her, Bluma did not so much as give a sign of awareness.

"You'll be taking a lovely trip to the country, Mama," Rosie told her. "We're taking you to Otwock. Imagine, you'll wake up every morning to see trees right outside your window. And hear birds singing! Won't that be lovely!"

"I suppose so. Yes. If you say so."

Rosie bit her lip, trying hard not to cry. "Oh, you're going to love it there, Mama, you'll see!"

But Bluma only continued to sit staring into a void, hugging herself as though the world had grown unbearably cold and she had no way of warming her lonely flesh. And the tears continued to flow until her daughter dried them, as a mother dries the tears of a hurt child.

The sanatorium was only about a mile away from the suburban railroad station, with trains running frequently, especially on Sunday, which was visiting day. The soil of the region was sandy, with pine woods growing thick except where they had been chopped down to make way for sketchy civilization. By some freak of nature the area seemed like a pocket version of those spas in the Black Forest or the foothills of the Alps to which all Europe traditionally traveled "for its health." The air sparkled, the wind was fragrant with resin, and even in winter there was none of the penetrating dampness that made the Warsaw climate so harsh. Children's health centers and convalescent homes studded the countryside, retired gentlewomen made a good living running year-round boarding houses for the elderly. In time, the doctors pointed out, when she began to improve, Bluma might be able to take walks without taxing her strength and even meet new people, possibly even make a few friends among women of her own age. In the meantime she would be only a stone's throw away from her family.

But although not a single visiting day went by without one or another of her children coming to see her, Bluma remained indifferent to them all. She would greet them with a coldly vacant stare as if asking why they persisted in troubling her with their presence. In the end the doctors themselves decided it would be best to discontinue the visits for the time being. "You'll have to wait until she herself asks for you. In the meantime, just keep in touch with us." Thus the visits dwindled to one a month, Adam and Viktor making them alternately for the purpose of discussing their mother's case with the medical staff.

In time the household in Nalewki Street settled down to a fairly smooth routine, and Adam, now that he was on salary, was enjoying the unprecedented experience of having money in his pocket. True to his word, his employer had been openhanded in the manner of a *grand seigneur,* so that not only was there enough to meet current expenses, including the household help his sisters had so wistfully asked for, but he could afford an occasional gesture of generosity as well. That fall there were new school uniforms for the girls, and for Kazik new shoes, and meat on the table two or three times a week, and even, though rarely, gallery seats to a play or a concert.

He worked conscientiously and hard, yet by comparison with his student days he had a modicum of leisure. It seemed practically a luxury not to be constantly running from one tutoring job to the next, regardless of weather; his desk in the Pozner office seemed a veritable oasis of peace. He was even getting enough sleep and began to look rested. His employer was pleased with the way he was learning cotton and taking hold. All in all he should have been deriving satisfaction out of the new situation. But satisfaction eluded him, for in his own way he had grown as uncaring as his mother. He felt empty, hollowed out.

He no longer heard from Wanda, nor even from Olek for that matter. After Olek's strangely ambiguous response to his own impassioned appeal, he had tried writing Wanda one last time. But she had ignored the letter, and when several endless months of waiting passed he was finally forced to admit the inevitable: she had gone out of his life.

For the rest, he had no real friends in the city and avoided contact with those who might have become his friends, since they were all part of the circle that once had gathered in the Zapiecek flat. The Meisels brothers, so far as he knew, were in Western Europe, Henryk having gone to the Sorbonne and Juzek to Düsseldorf. The only one from his past he still saw occasionally was Missy Pozner. It was inevitable that they should continue to run into one another, since her father's offices, as was the general custom, were right in the Pozner mansion, occupying one whole wing of the house.

Once in a while he ate lunch with the family, and sometimes *Pani* Konstancja invited him to some large, impersonal gathering. Adam knew, and did not care, that the invitations were merely for the purpose of making sure there would be more young men than girls at the parties. The gatherings were a big bore to him, although Salome Grossglik and even the Baroness Kronenberg, both of whom he generally glimpsed among the guests, had more than once hinted broadly that if a youth were smart and ambitious, he could easily draw plenty of advantages from rubbing elbows with the right people.

This was the period when he first formed the habit of turning to solitary esthetic experience to fill a human void. He started reading voraciously again, as he hadn't done since his teens, and could lose himself for whole evenings in Dante or Balzac. The *Divine Comedy* and the *Human Comedy* created for him worlds where he was free to live vicariously, without pain, absorbing a great deal of theoretical knowledge about the human condition while risking, and learning, nothing.

New theories of mathematics also fascinated him all over again, for it seemed to him they were pointing out ways to bring order out of the chaos he felt surrounded him. One day, browsing in a secondhand book stall, he came upon a dog-eared copy of Camille Flammarion's *Astronomie Populaire* in the original edition. He brought it home in triumph and spent weeks absorbing its contents. For some reason he kept being reminded of his own aphorism, coined during a long-ago discussion with Olek Piotrowski, and could not resist writing it out on the flyleaf: "God is he who can put the world into an equation." It gave him a sense of achievement for a good twenty-four hours.

He began to frequent museums, then contemporary art galleries, teaching himself to see painting, especially Impressionism, which was new to him, with his own eyes rather than relying on established critics for permission to admire or turn down. Next, in a rare moment of self-indulgence he bought a mellow-voiced old violin and began taking lessons. But the ability to draw pure sounds out of the instrument required more time and dedication than he was willing to give, and his occasional, hard-to-repeat successes only served to exasperate his now sensitized ear. Quickly he realized he would never become an even passably good amateur musician, and after a few months he simply slammed shut the lid of the velvet-lined case, which from then on was left to gather dust in a corner. But the money he saved on lessons he used for a series of tickets to the Warsaw Philharmonic. There he would lose himself for a few hours now and then in the sheer joy of listening to great music masterfully played.

One night during intermission between Mozart's Haffner Symphony and Beethoven's Seventh, he heard his name called and turned to face a slender, elegantly tailored dandy behind whose lovingly tended beard and silken mustache he recognized the sardonic smile of the older of the Meisels brothers.

"Henryk!"

"Adam! I thought it had to be you! That wild head of hair. . ."

They shook hands, then impulsively embraced. "It's good to see you. I had no idea you were back in Warsaw!"

"Back a month. Well, I see you're still addicted to solitary concert-going! Which I admit is better than sitting next to the wrong person, having to listen to a lot of insipid comments. . . ."

"And you're still the perfectionist," Adam retorted, "still the esthete." He did not go into the fact that his own solitude was not a matter of choice. "By the way, did you know you were the one who actually introduced me to concert-going? For which I owe you a sizable debt of gratitude."

Henryk looked pleased. "In that case I'll exact payment. Have coffee with me after the performance, and we'll bring each other up-to-date on everything that's been happening to us."

The cafe Henryk chose was not one Adam normally frequented. The decor was luxurious, the napery sparkling white, the coffee and pastry superb. Among the after-theater crowd one recognized well-known faces—critics, literary figures, popular actresses and titled personages.

Henryk, clearly an habitué judging from the headwaiter's reception, waited until they were seated and their orders taken. "Now then, where do we start? Cigarette?" He pulled out a thin gold monogrammed case which he extended to Adam. "Turkish tobacco. Excellent. You still don't smoke? An ascetic all the way?"

Coming from anyone else the remark might have annoyed Adam, but the relationship of long ago was reasserting itself and he was willing to grant Henryk special privileges. Besides, he was feeling mellow. "Is that really how you remember me?"

Henryk threw back his head in a slightly theatrical gesture and laughed out loud. "Oh, definitely. I used to observe you from the vantage point of my three years' seniority, you and that proletarian friend of yours who started the study circle, what was his name?"

"Olek. Olek Piotrowski."

"Yes. I tried hard to feel superior to the two of you because you seemed to have something I only vaguely sensed existed, a sense of direction maybe, a sense of commitment. And it made me uneasy so I resented it. I was full of cheap cynicism then, full of borrowed quotations about how every man has his price. And all the time I knew none of it applied to you. So I patronized you because I envied you."

"How young I must have seemed! How young we all were!"

Henryk gave him a searching look. "Don't tell me it was just youth, and that you, too, have learned to compromise."

Adam shrugged. "What else was I to do?" he said flatly. "My father died last summer and my mother had a breakdown. She's in an institution. Keeping the family together is mainly my responsibility. Compromise! Why, I'm full of the prose of life!" As briefly as he could he sketched in the story of the past few years, including his arrangements with Maurice Pozner.

Whatever he had expected, Henryk's reaction startled him.

"So I was right after all. You haven't changed, not really. Still willing to immolate yourself. Well, when all is said and done none of us change much. Take me. With my princely tastes and my snobbishness I, too, have gone into business. But for different reasons. I'm still the hedonist, still living for pleasure, and so, for me, the road from my father's fur parlor has led by a logically circuitous route into international banking. Nothing grubby, you understand! I'm determined to make a fortune and propose to enjoy every skirmish along the way. Whereas you, you're equally determined to feel you've stepped into a squirrel cage. You may turn out as successful as I hope to be, but you'll manage to make it torture for yourself every inch of the way."

He signaled the waiter, who presently brought them fresh, steaming, fragrant brew. "And Olek? What happened to Olek?"

"He and Maryla had to leave the country." Adam forced himself to sound offhand. "There was a lot of trouble. I was with them at the time. . . ."

"Yes," Henryk nodded, his handsome face sober. "And that, too, is in character. I remember hearing something about it at the time. . . . Funny thing," he added speculatively, "but in the days I knew you best I would have sworn that was the direction you, too, were heading in. Politics, or at least the national independence movement. Socialism maybe. Your head was so high in the clouds. How did you escape getting embroiled more deeply?"

"I told you I had no other choice. My father. . . ."

Henryk nodded, but he was looking skeptical. "As I remember, there was a girl, a student at the Floating University. What was her name?"

"Wanda Borowska." For the first time in over a year Adam spoke her name aloud in the presence of another person. He hoped his voice had not given him away. "She had to go with them. They're all in Switzerland now. Olek writes both girls are working toward medical degrees."

"Borowska? A woman doctor, still an interne? Well for heaven's sake! I think I ran into her only a month ago, in Zurich." Adam tensed, said nothing, and waited. "It was at the house of some Polish friends. Tall, thin, terribly intense. No wonder the name was familiar. . . ."

"Wanda? You saw Wanda?" Adam was finding it hard to breathe. "What a fantastic coincidence. . . ."

"Not really." Henryk either failed to notice or chose to ignore the effect of his remarks. "You've no idea how it is in the big cities. All the expatriates exist in tight little colonies, homesick, hungry for fresh news from home, and anyone they're reasonably sure is not an enemy is welcomed as a friend. Come to think of it, I'm only surprised that in the whole week I was there I didn't also run into the Piotrowskis. Well, to get back to your Wanda, she's working part time in a small private maternity clinic. And I don't know if you know this or not, but she has a child to support. There's also a husband, another medical student, from what I was able to gather another starving revolutionary. . . ."

Adam sat staring into his empty coffee cup. Now everything was falling into place. His head buzzing, he thought back to Wanda's growing evasiveness, his questions always left carefully unanswered, and eventually the silence. He was beginning to understand the veiled implications in Olek's last letter.

But why hadn't she at least let him know the truth, cruel as that was? And then his brain began to work again. He remembered the seesaw of his own emotions—love versus duty, duty versus love—and finally the pressure Salome had so skillfully brought to bear. Small wonder Wanda had fallen back on her stiff-necked pride.

And afterwards? He tried to imagine her alone, terribly and hopelessly deserted, her misery all the more glaring because it stood out in bitter contrast to the happiness of the only two people she had for friends, with whom she was forced into inescapable daily intimacy. Worse, she was forced to lean on them, without a whimper in his, Adam's, direction. Wanda the uncompromising feminist stonily living up to what she felt was right. And he cursed himself for a spineless fool.

There were many ways, he suddenly saw, in which a man can sell his soul.

❧ *Five* ❧

H E WALKED THE STREETS half the night, knowing there could be no sleep for him, in his mind writing and rewriting a long, bitter, angry letter to Olek. "In the name of common decency, why didn't you at least warn me she was really pregnant—I would have come! Or was it already too late? Had she just turned around and found someone else right away? You might have told me that much. And that I had a daughter. . ."

He suspected, of course, it had never been that simple, but the fury building up in him as he accused his old friend of betraying their friendship was easier to bear than self-blame and fury at himself. He had thrown away the one thing in life he had wanted—and for what? His sacrifice hadn't helped his father stay alive nor his mother hold on to her sanity. Besides, there never had been, there could not be any such thing as a system of checks and balances between the generations. A bewildered small boy can say to his widowed mother, "Don't cry any more, Mama, you're not alone, you have me, *I'm* not going to leave you!" and the mother will hug the child to her and even feel comforted. Not so in the case of the grown man. Bluma had known this. In her simplicity she had not been deluded. It was he who had deluded himself.

He turned toward home at last as the church bells through the city were chiming three. He let himself in quietly, then realized the light in the dining room was still burning. Idka and Izidore sat huddled at the table, their heads together, whispering, arguing, busily jotting words down on a sheet of paper.

When they became aware of him they quickly covered the paper with an open book.

"What are you doing up so late?" Adam growled, sounding rougher than he had intended. "Izidore, there's school tomorrow—haven't you any sense!"

The boy growled, "For heaven's sake, we're old enough to take care of ourselves!" But a surge of enthusiasm carried him over his annoyance. "Have you forgotten what time of year this is? A week from today is May Day, and two days after, Constitution Day. But since both come in midweek, all the demonstrations are set for this coming Sunday . . . a dozen of them at different points in the city. You probably don't know it, but this is the tenth anniversary of the first May Day ever observed *anywhere* within the Empire, and we Poles started it. So the PPS (Polish Socialist Party) and the SDKP (Social-Democrats of the Kingdom of Poland) and the Jewish Bund are all calling street meetings. But we students have decided to stick to the old patriotic tradition. We'll have a wreath ceremony in honor of May Third and Kosciuszko. And that's what Idka and I were busy with—working out a placard and some leaflets."

His thin, good-looking face was aglow and his eyes—Bluma's eyes of a long-ago time—radiated excitement. A phrase from an old legend flashed through Adam's mind. Dragon's teeth. Kill a dragon and scatter his bones to the winds, and a new generation of heroes will spring up from the dragon's teeth. This was right, this was as it should be. And even though only a little while ago he could have sworn he was done with such concerns, it pleased him to know his brother and sister were not.

"We're going to float garlands of carnations and roses on the Vistula," Izidore was saying. "We'll drop them down from Alexander Bridge, deck out the river in the national colors for the holiday. . . ."

"Yes, and get yourselves into a peck of trouble!" Adam grumbled. But it wasn't in him to try to dissuade them.

The floating of red-and-white garlands on the river had a long history. It infuriated the police, for invariably the crowds materialized suddenly—always in different spots and at different times—and vanished as suddenly, not dispersing gradually like ordinary demonstators who could then be conveniently shot at, but melting away like ghosts. This year's choice of Alexander Bridge, thought Adam, contained its own irony. For the vast structure, directly visible from the old royal palace, now the residence of the Governor-General, was named for the foreign tyrant who presided over the First Partition, who annulled the Constitution of 1791 that was to have been the country's salvation—annulled it almost as soon as it had been enacted—Alexander I of Russia.

Today, after a hundred years and more, Constitution Day remained sacred to patriots. May Third was still a time of rededication to the cause of independence. Adam had never been able to go along with Olek's position that the call for independence without social change was an empty slogan, and utopian and suicidal besides. He tended to side with those who said, "Forget May Third, and it's the final capitulation." Now he himself had almost forgotten. But Izidore and Idka remembered, bless them. It jolted him out of his self-absorption.

He searched for a way to express his gratitude. "Let's see what you've done. Maybe I, too, can help."

One arm on the back of each of their chairs, he bent over their shoulders to read. The lettering on the double sheet of paper began simply enough:

POLAND IS NOT YET LOST. . . . IT SHALL RISE AGAIN!

"We were wondering what to say next: 'Out of the ashes like a Phoenix' or 'Out of the waves like Venus'—you know, Venus on account of the ceremony on the water. . . ."

He thought both suggestions a bit self-consciously literate but hesitated to say so lest he hurt their feelings. "I think I'd keep it plain if I were you. Why not just, *Poland is not yet lost / So long as we still live?* You'd be quoting the first two lines of the national anthem. Everybody knows the rest, they'd pick it up and you'd have the whole crowd singing."

"Of course!" they cried in unison. "Why didn't we think of it ourselves. Adash, you're a genius!"

He squirmed. "Genius is a pretty strong word. Don't forget I, too, have had some practice—long before you two were dry behind the ears."

Idka said in her diffident way, "If you must know, we kind of thought you'd forgotten. Look, you wouldn't like to come to a meeting with us, huh? You'd run into old friends, I shouldn't wonder."

At that he recoiled as though she had touched a raw wound. "I've had my share of *jugendkrankheit,* the youth fever. And," he couldn't resist adding for good measure, "one of these days so will you."

As his own guard went up, so did Izidore's. "Don't you make a joke of what we're doing, big brother. People lots older than you are in the movement, working night and day."

"Sure, sure. But as I said, I've had my share. No more. Besides, I've other things to worry about now. Like Mama. And seeing the bills get paid." As soon as the words were out he regretted them, for implied was a rebuke they did not deserve. And so, although all he wanted all of a sudden was to get away and be by himself again, he searched for something else to say so as not to leave them on a harsh note. "Well, anyway, good luck," he managed lamely. "And try to stay out of trouble."

A few nights later he saw Henryk again and in the hope of gleaning additional details about Wanda again questioned him. But Henryk had already told him what little he knew. Now he just raised an eyebrow. "Still agonizing, eh, Adash? I believe what you need is a handsome young filly to take you to bed with her. Which shouldn't be much of a problem. Warsaw is full of delightful women married to pompous old bores with nothing to offer save money. A liaison with someone their own age, and no entanglements—what could be better? Say the word and I'll see what I can do!"

The idea seemed to Adam singularly unattractive. "I appreciate your concern, but no thanks. Besides, I haven't got time."

"There is always time for *l'amour*," Henryk chuckled, adding, "The French have a proverb: *Il faut un clou pour chasser un autre*— to drive out a nail one needs another. A romp in bed would do you worlds of good."

"Thanks again, but no."

"As you will."

Obsessed with the need to know more about Wanda's new life, Adam tried to hunt up various old acquaintances from the Zapiecek days. But most of those he had met there had either moved away or else were in hiding or jail or Siberia, while others, like Wanda herself and the Piotrowskis, had emigrated. Still others had cut all ties with the movement. He found out nothing. Finally, in desperation, he went to call on Olek's uncle, the illegal printer Jacek.

Jacek Piotrowski greeted him like an old friend and plied him with vodka, but had no information to give him beyond what he already knew. Yes, Olek had indeed mentioned that his wife's friend was married now and had a child. And yes, she was still studying, and doing work at a free clinic besides. As was Maryla. "Maybe by the time they're full-fledged doctors things will change enough so they can come home and set up practice. Legally, I mean. It's not impossible."

He was talking, it seemed to Adam, to make conversation—as if to fill a void while making up his mind whether or not to say anything more. Then, after refilling their glasses and downing another drink at one gulp, "I don't mind admitting my wife and I were pretty disappointed in that girl. Married so soon after you two . . . what I mean is, you seemed so right for each other . . . as my wife put it, everything seemed like nature really intended it, and then, bam! Out of sight, out of mind. Well, some women are just so anxious to have a *missus* in front of their name, they'll get it by hook or crook. It's the system," he added. "Only I wouldn't have thought it of Wanda. Not with her understanding of the social forces at play. But then again, who's to know? People do strange things, especially uprooted like she was, on foreign soil, alone in exile. . . ."

He thanked Jacek for his hospitality and was about to leave

when his host laid a detaining hand on his arm. "Wait. Since you're here anyway, I'd like to put a question to you. How is it we never see you at any of our gatherings any more? When my nephew and those girls were here. . . . You know, there's a lot more to life than love. . . ."

Adam mumbled something about a changed family situation and how he could no longer afford to take personal risks, but Jacek did not sound convinced. "You think the rest of us have it any easier? That's all beside the point—our work must go on. Besides, frankly, I'm also thinking of you yourself. That girl, she hurt you bad. You're crying inside. Your soul—if you'll forgive me using such a word—needs sustenance. And nothing feeds the soul like the common cause. When you link arms with strangers and they call you brother, something feels whole," he tapped his chest, "in here."

Still Adam could only shake his head. The common cause, to him, meant Wanda; he wanted no further part of it. Not from Izidore. Not from Jacek. All he really did want was to be left alone to lick his wounds and somehow learn to live with what had happened.

But Jacek would not let go. "Forgive me if I sound like a padre in a pulpit, only the comrades all say the same thing: when life starts to get you down, go out and find yourself a tough assignment. It won't keep your feet warm on a cold night, but it sure helps."

Yes, thought Adam, provided political convictions are part of the warp and woof of your makeup. But his own had always been tangential, not to say vicarious. Wanda had seen through him. Maybe that had been the real trouble between them. Hadn't she practically hinted as much?

Absorbed in his own thoughts, he stopped listening to whatever Jacek was saying, when suddenly a phrase came through. "Sunday . . . May Day." He pricked up his ears. "In addition to the usual demonstrations there's to be a protest meeting in solidarity with the weavers of Lodz, who are on strike. Considering who your employer is, you ought to know all about that!" And indeed he did know. At the Pozners' this spring hardly a day went by without talk about strikes and lockouts and the insolent demands of the textile workers. "We're having a last-minute strategy meeting here tomorrow evening. There's talk of a one-day work stoppage throughout the country. Personally I'm against it, not in principle but because there hasn't been time to organize it, and without solid organization it can only turn into slaughter. But the youngers, the students, are hotheads. Which reminds me. There's an Izidore Fabian I've been seeing a lot of. Relative of yours?"

"My brother," Adam said, surprised at the quickening pride he felt at this, but added, "If he gets in trouble it'll just about finish off my mother. . . ."

"In that case," Jacek said slyly, "come to the meeting and maybe you can make him listen to reason."

"Perhaps I will," Adam began, almost persuaded. Then he remembered that on Sunday he had an appointment with the doctors at the sanatorium and he must be up at dawn. It was a relief to be able to tell Jacek so.

On Sunday morning he woke with the sparrows, dressed hastily, bolted down a breakfast of stale rolls and warmed-over tea, and set out in the direction of the railway station. Along the whole length of Marszalkowska Street he noticed an uncommon amount of activity. Ordinarily only a few devout old women would have been out at this hour, on their way to early mass. Today men and even young girls were hurrying along in small groups, purposeful and preoccupied. They were not dressed for church.

He arrived in Otwock much too early for his appointment and decided to walk the mile and more from the station. The morning was fresh, a light mist that later the sun would burn off hung over the meadows, high overhead a skylark was pouring out his full-throated music, and in the distance church bells called the faithful to matins, while wispy curls of smoke rose lazily from chimneys above thatched roofs.

Here there was not an echo of city turmoil and rebellion, here the day was one of quiet and rest. *Hushed our peaceful Polish village / Hushed our joyous Polish farmland.* . . . But as the lines of poetry flashed into his mind they instantly destroyed all semblance of peacefulness. For they kept calling up memories of another morning when it hadn't been safe to remain in the city.

"Good God, will everything always remind me of *her?*"

The interview with the doctors was surprisingly encouraging. When at last he was allowed to go to her, Bluma smiled at him for the first time in months. "Adash. My son," he heard her murmur as he bent to kiss her. "All morning I've been waiting." She patted his face, stroked his hair, then made a place for him beside her on the visitors' bench. "Here, sit here close to me and tell me all about everything at home. . . ."

It was as though the same sun that burned off the fog in the fields had warmed and cleared her mind. Doubtless the improvement had been gradual, but to Adam, who hadn't been close enough to observe the cumulative changes, it seemed dramatically sudden.

"Mama, it's so good to see you looking so well!" Later, remembering, he would say that it had indeed been like having someone come back from the dead. "We all miss you so, the house isn't the same without you. And now it won't be long until you can come back to us."

Again she smiled. "Home. . . ," she repeated. Then suddenly she was all worry. "Oh my, I've made so much trouble for you children! The household must be at sixes and sevens! My poor lambs . . . who cooks for you? Are you getting enough to eat?"

She sounded so much like her old self that he began to laugh. It was good to laugh. "Now, Mama, you're not to agitate yourself! The girls have taken hold beautifully, everything's under control and we've not had a bit of trouble. We're all well fed and our socks are mended and no buttons missing! That isn't at all why we want you home. . . ."

She was by now thinking clearly enough to be able to appreciate the incongruity of her questions and to laugh with him. But her anxiety had not lifted entirely, and quite suddenly she started crying. "My children miss me and want me home with them. . . ." She said it a couple of times, as though the news were a source of infinite wonder. "They want me for myself, not for my cooking or mending. . . ." Then suddenly she became impatient with her own display of emotion. "I don't know what's been the matter with me," she said in her old normal, everyday voice. "I cry so easily nowadays. . . . You must forgive me, Adash, it's just that for a time . . . for a long time . . . I felt so useless, so entirely useless and alone. . . . It's a terrible thing," she finished, as if trying to explain something that her son couldn't possibly understand, "to feel you aren't needed. I hope it never happens to you."

By the time he left her he was no longer haunted by a sense of meaningless, quixotic sacrifice. His mother was coming home sane—and to some extent at least this had been his doing.

Back in the city, still buoyed by his visit, he decided rather than going straight home to share his good news with the Grossgliks. At the crossing of Nowy Swiat, where the statue of Copernicus stood, he paused, intending to buy a bunch of spring flowers for Salome. Only then did he become aware of an unnatural quiet around him. The plaza dominated by the statue was strewn with red and white carnations. But the flower vendors themselves, of whom there were generally three or four in the area, were not at their accustomed corners. Sunday strollers were conspicuous by their absence, no fashionable carriages rolled by, and only the pigeons strutting and pecking among the debris cooed unperturbed.

Although it was still an hour to sunset, he noticed that at the Kronenberg mansion, which he could see in the distance, all the shades were already drawn.

Then he heard the echo of hoofbeats and from a side street a platoon of mounted cossacks emerged. He could not distinguish their faces, but their swords were drawn and their dreaded whips, the *naghaikas,* stuck out of the tops of their boots, leather thongs hanging loose, ready for action.

They rode like conquerors, caps jauntily cocked and handlebar mustaches bristling, and the infrequent passersby scurried out of their way, hugging the sides of buildings, prepared to dart into the nearest doorway at the first sign of trouble. One of these jostled Adam, then, with a hasty "Excuse me, sir," quickened his pace to a trot.

Adam tried to detain him. "Wait. Tell me what's been going on. I've been out of town, I only just got back. . . ." But the man only shook his head, raised his eyes to heaven, and began to walk faster. One could almost smell the animal fear on him.

At the Grossgliks', a tearful, voluble Miss Julia responded to his ring. "Bless you, *Pan* Adam, you're here at last! Such a day it's been! A shame, a crying shame! Has the good Lord gone blind, may I be forgiven for blaspheming, that he doesn't avenge our wrongs? But here I go beating my gums when clearly you know it all yourself by now—else you wouldn't have come in such a hurry!"

Bewildered, he finally managed to stop the flow of words. "I know nothing. I just got off the train. What's been happening? Where is everybody?"

For an answer Miss Julia burst into a torrent of noisy tears. Then his young cousin Regina came running. She, too, looked as though she had been crying. "Oh Adash, you're finally here! We've been waiting and waiting. . . . Uncle tried to telephone the sanatorium but he couldn't get through. . . . It was so awful, so awful. . . ."

"*What* was awful?" he kept asking. "Has something happened to Uncle Leon, to Aunt Salome? Please, won't one of you tell me. . . ."

But Regina only threw herself into his arms, wound her own tight around his neck, and began to sob. "No, it's not them, they're safe. . . . It's . . . it's. . . oh, I can't bear to say it. . . ."

Thoroughly alarmed though he was by now, he realized he must first of all try to calm her rising hysteria, and the effort it-self steadied him. "Now, now, Ginia, my dear, don't cry, please don't cry," he murmured ineffectually. "Crying won't help. Here, take my handkerchief. Dry your tears like a good girl."

She dabbed her eyes and relaxed against him. The dark mass of her hair lay warm against his cheek and he was assailed by the fragrance—half clean-child smell, half woman—of her young body. He was shocked that he could be so physically aware of her when clearly his mind should have been on some unknown emergency. "Now then," he tried once more, "suppose you begin at the beginning and tell me everything."

This only brought on fresh sobs, through which he was able to make out separate words. "Wreath ceremony . . . demonstration broken up . . . the cossacks. . . ."

Izidore flashed through his mind. And he no longer felt protective or charmed by her, but only wanted to shake her. "Regina, for pity's sake get hold of yourself and start talking sense!"

She was saved the effort. A key turned in the front lock and the Grossgliks trooped in together with all the young Fabians—Idka and Rosie, Viktor and Kazik. Four pairs of stricken eyes met Adam's questioning ones. Then Salome spoke, all the lilt gone out of her voice, "You might as well know right off. Izidore has been arrested."

Bit by bit they gave him the details. There had been demonstrations all over the city from morning on, mostly labor parades and meetings to mark May Day. The Socialist Party, the PPS, had gathered in the Aleje Jerozolimskie, while the Social-Democrats and the Jewish Bund held a joint rally in the Ujazdowskie. The security police with their well-oiled spy system had been ready for them—there had been violence all day long, blood and broken heads. In the "panhandle" in front of the Café Sans-Souci a pitched battle erupted, leaving three hundred dead—many of them, thank Heaven, neither Poles nor Jews but men in violet-blue.

And while all this was keeping the gendarmes and the soldiers hopping, a different kind of demonstration was getting under way—the one the students had planned to honor Constitution Day. On schedule, when the churches opened their doors after midday services and the worshippers began pouring into the streets, whispers spread like wildfire through the crowds of the faithful. *Don't go home. . . . Go to the river. . . . This is May Third, help us celebrate. . . . Show you're a good Pole, a patriot. . . .*

Hundreds, and then thousands, trooped to the embankment.

Some, forewarned, still carried the lighted tapers that ordinarily they would have left at the altar of the Virgin Mother. Others carried fresh flowers. It had looked like a church procession, solemn, innocent.

They began to sing. First the ancient, slow chant with which in centuries past Polish armies had marched into battle:

> *Mother of God, holy Maiden,*
> *Blessed art Thou amongst women. . .*

And because it was a religious anthem the police patrolling the streets let them pass unmolested as far as Sigismund Square. There, within sight of Alexander Bridge, they were joined by the delegation of workers from the struck factories of Lodz that Jacek had mentioned to Adam. Around the delegates had been an honor guard of university students, and mingling with the students, boys and girls of school age whose assignment had been to obtain red and white flowers in profusion and weave them into garlands for the wreath ceremony.

Up until that moment there had been no signs of placards or banners. But now suddenly as they converged on the bridge, to be joined by a similar outpouring from the Praga side, a forest of signs interspersed with red and white banners blossomed overhead. As in years past, the white eagle was flying on his field of amaranth, flying high in defiance of the hated double-headed black eagle. And the crowd broke into a single *Vivat!* that made the earth shake, and again they began to sing—not religious hymns this time but *Whirlwinds of Danger,* the *Warszawianka,* the *Red Banner,* and finally, triumphantly, *Poland Is Not Yet Lost.* Thousands of young, exultant voices rose in unison, and the bargemen on the Vistula echoed them.

But the glory of the forbidden songs as they reached the old royal palace sent the Governor-General into a rage. It was said that he personally gave the order for the cossack attack. Hardly had the first garlands gone spinning down on the water than horsemen emerged at a gallop from side streets on both banks of the river. Swords whirling as they rode, shouting savage, unintelligible words, spurring their mounts, they charged directly into the crowd, slashing to the right and to the left with sword and *naghaika,* trampling men, women, and children, cutting off retreat.

There was no time to sound a warning. Those already on the bridge were trapped. Some, to escape the savage lash, jumped blindly, many to their death. Others stumbled and fell and were trampled beneath the hooves of the rearing horses. Those left alive were arrested. Izidore had not only been among them—he had been caught with a garland of roses in his hands.

"I should have been there with him," Adam heard Idka say dully in a choked voice, and from the way she looked he realized she must have tried. "I should have stayed close. But we got separated. Maybe," she whispered, shuddering, "maybe I could have saved him if. . . ."

"Hush, there's nothing you could have done." Uncle Leon was doing his best to console her.

"Then I should have been arrested with him."

"Darling, be sensible! What good would that have done?"

"I don't know, I don't know!" She began to rock and moan as though in physical pain. "I only know I can hardly stand it. . . ."

Adam, who so far hadn't been able to utter a sound, went over to her and put his arm around her. "Idziunia," he used the all-but-forgotten pet name of her childhood. "You've got to get hold of yourself. If only for Izzy's sake, you've got to be brave."

She gave a long, shuddering sigh. "Yes, Adash, yes, I know." Then she said something wholly unexpected. "You know, I'm glad you and he had that chance to talk like . . . like friends . . . the other night." She sounded so like an old woman his heart broke for her.

And now he looked at her, really looked this time, and saw what the day had done to her. Her face, plain at best, was mottled and puffed, and there was a deep purple bruise under one eye. Her blouse was ripped across one shoulder, the hem of her skirt torn, the great braids that ordinarily gleamed like copper were mussed from the jostling she must have had. And suddenly Adam saw his sister not as she now was but as the woman she would one day become, blessed with less than her rightful share of the feminine graces and ready to take on more than her rightful share of trouble. And he felt a rush of unaccustomed tenderness for this girl whom until a week ago he had more or less ignored. He would have liked to tell her so, to say something that would show his concern. But the habit of not putting things into words was too strong. Besides, it would only have embarrassed both of them.

In the meantime there was the immediate problem of Izidore's arrest and what could be done for him.

"The jails are full," Leon was winding up the long account, "at least three thousand prisoners herded together like cattle—at the Pawiak, the Citadel, the St. Alexis dungeon. The leaders, the activists, the suspect, the youngsters whose only crime was to have been there . . . no differentiation being made, they say. All of them lumped together as 'politicals'—and where do we go from there?"

It was a question to which he expected no answer. But his words, like a familiar cue, seemed to electrify his wife. She pulled herself up very straight, as if donning invisible armor. A faint smile played on her delicate lips. "Why, I do think, dear heart, the first thing will be for me to see someone important in government. A key man—and I think I know just the one. Count Dembinski—that used to be Leshek Dembinski, remember, one of Mama's boys when you were first courting me—a little young in those days, of course, but simply mad about me. Always swore there was nothing he wouldn't do if only I asked. . . ."

"That was rather a long time ago, don't you think, love?" Leon put in wearily.

"Well, yes," she shrugged in dainty impatience, "and, of course, it's true that he's become awfully important. But it won't hurt to try. And it isn't as if I were asking something for myself! No, no, I shan't hesitate one bit to go to him. In fact, I've already sent word that he must absolutely, absolutely and without fail, receive me in the morning. . . ."

But Leon Grossglik was right and his wife overconfident. For all that he had been "her" Leshek once, the Count was no Tadeusz Korsza. He saw no reason for taking risks just as a favor to a woman at whose feet he'd worshipped as a romantic young fool.

"I'm desolate, simply desolate, my dear darling *Pani* Salome," he moaned the next day. "But you must understand . . . my hands are tied. Oh, I'll do what I can—a discreet word here, a few rubles there, but don't count on it." He lifted a well-groomed eyebrow. "After all, these are no routine arrests. The governor-general has given strict orders . . . prisoners are to be treated with the utmost severity. He's determined to use this as an object lesson—if I interfered, it would mean my political neck. . . ." He had the grace to squirm under Salome's reproachful blue gaze. "I can, however, promise you this much. Once the smoke clears, we can talk about it again. It may be possible to separate your nephew's case from the more serious ones. If only," he added unctuously, "if only his name weren't Izidore Fabian and his address the heart of the ghetto! You do understand my position, don't you, dear lady? Please tell me you understand!"

His distress sounded so genuine, he had by now so completely convinced himself that he meant every word of his vague promises, that she could even feel sorry for him. "I understand more than you think," she finally said, with a dignity that was chilling. She rose, then, remembering her manners, gave him her hand to kiss. "I understand that it's one thing for a young boy to dream of laying the world at the feet of a lady he thinks he adores, and quite another for a career politician to endanger himself for the sake of. . . ." She had been about to say, for a little Jew-boy from Nalewki Street, but reconsidered. "Well, goodbye, Count Lehon. I won't trouble you again." She no longer addressed him as Leshek. "Wouldn't it be interesting if someday we were to meet again, in happier circumstances—in a free Poland, for instance?"

And she swept out of his office with her back very straight, her head very high, quite as though she hadn't just suffered a crushing defeat and a shattering humiliation.

❧ *Six* ❧

No ONE KNEW how soon the prisoners would be allowed visitors, but the rumor spread that if one walked by the Pawiak's north wall there was a chance of glimpsing their faces through a row of third-story windows. So the people kept converging in a steady stream on the vast fortress-like building they generally would have avoided like the plague. They came from all four corners of the city, from the farthest suburbs, from Praga, from Saska Kempa on the waterfront. They walked slowly, stopping every few paces at what they hoped was a safe distance, their heads upraised, their eyes scanning the small, deeply set barred apertures that stared back like so many malevolent little eyes.

The rumor turned out to be without foundation. The prison windows were set too high for even a tall man to be able to look out onto the street. But the hope persisted. "Maybe they climb on each other's shoulders," Idka Fabian speculated. She was taking her beloved brother's arrest hard, harder even than her father's death and her mother's illness. "I've got to see for myself. If I could only just wave at him. . . ."

She was so miserable that against their better judgment Adam and Viktor decided to humor her. On a day as gray as the mood of the populace the three of them joined the unending procession of slowly shuffling men, women, and children on Pawia Street, a procession, this time, without banners or slogans or even rhythm. The people all knew that the slightest outcry, the barest hint of a demonstration, would only make things worse for those on the inside.

They reached the corner of Wiezienna, Prison Street, turned, turned again into Dzielna to skirt the Pawiak's long southern wall until they reached the women's block, turned back, and retraced their steps. Over and over, over and over. And gradually, as he trudged back and forth, his arm linked through his sister's, Adam began to feel a deep primitive hatred, a personal fury against this stone monster with sightless eyes that fed on human beings. It swallowed them. Ten years ago it had swallowed poor, harmless little *Pan* Liebman. Summer before last it had tried to swallow Maryla. Now it had swallowed his brother.

The memory of how he had come here with Olek brought back with it the sharp sense of loss that still was never far from the surface, but this time, strangely, it also brought him a sense of closeness with Izidore. It brought new concern, making him feel more alive than he'd felt in many months and for this reason he welcomed it. He wished there were some way of telling Izzy. Failing that, he pressed Idka's arm, then with his free hand patted her hand. "You mustn't lose courage, people live through worse than this," he said gently, thinking that someday he must tell her about dragon's teeth, "and still they come back to fight the *Moskals.*" She nodded, her lips trembling, and clung to him.

They rounded the corner again and the prison's main entrance came into view. The iron gates had sentry boxes on either side. In front of each a soldier stood at attention, holding a bayonet. The soldiers on duty were Kalmyks, yellow-skinned, slant-eyed, short with powerful shoulders and the bowlegs typical of their tribe—some said because they grew up riding wild horses. They looked savage, they had been trained to kill, they spoke no language save their own, so that even the Russian officers had to address them through subalterns acting as interpreters. This, of course, was all part of the Tsarate's plan: use one subject nation against another. Build up the hatreds lest the people discover common ground and unite in revolt.

Someone not far from the Fabians thought he saw a face at a window and waved and called out a name. It was an illusion. But instantly out of the *porte cochère* four more soldiers emerged. These four were cossacks, the inevitable *naghaikas* stuck into the tops of their ill-smelling, tar-smeared boots, their heads shaved hairless beneath their flat caps, beardless but with long curling mustaches nearly meeting beneath their chins.

"Hey you, Polaks," yelled the one who wore a sergeant's stripes, "what d'you think you're doing, sniffing around here like a pack of bird dogs?" His voice had the drawling sing-song of the Don plains and the words came out like a string of insults. "Get gone, clear out, you hear? Anyone still around five minutes from now gets his guts ripped open!" And lest there be any mistake as to his meaning he lowered his bayonet, then jerked it upward. "Like this. And I don't aim to tell you twice."

The crowd began to melt away. Still not satisfied, the sergeant turned to the first man he could collar at random, which happened to be Viktor. "You! What's your name? Let's see your papers." Viktor had no choice but to reach into his pocket. The cossack scanned the registration form. "A Yid, too. I might've known!" He turned to one of his men. "What'd you say, Vasia, shall we run them in? Too much trouble?" He spat. "Then just write down the name and address and we'll make a report."

That same night, somewhere between the hours of two and four when the house was at its quietest, heavy boots sounded on the stairs leading to the Fabian flat. The doorbell rang, shrill and persistent.

"Telegram."

It was the standard announcement that fooled no one. Adam and Viktor rushed into the hallway hastily pulling trousers on over their nightshirts.

"House search," a Russian voice barked through the crack in the door. "Take off the chain. Police."

Adam's first thought was that at least, following Izidore's arrest, they had cleared out all suspect pamphlets and books. He began to breathe easier. Let them look! It gave him real satisfaction to see the searchers huffing and puffing as they pushed heavy furniture away from walls, peered behind massive wardrobes and underneath Bluma's sideboard. Nothing. The cupboard with china. Still nothing. Then one of them muttered, "Hey, let's look in the tile stove. My old woman says, you want to hide something and hide it good, put it in the stove." He strode purposefully toward the big central tile stove that warmed the whole house in winter and hadn't been used since spring weather set in. Adam held his breath. They had forgotten to check the stove.

The kneeling searcher clicked open the iron door, plunged his arm in, and gave a grunt of satisfaction. "Well now, what did I tell you? Ve-ry interesting." He pulled out a neatly tied package of literature. A few books without bindings, a newspaper printed on onionskin, a sheaf of undistributed May Third leaflets. Adam could read the words of the call he had helped Izidore write.

"So. Here we are. Now what d'you have to say about that, you Polak Yids, you?"

Adam and Viktor exchanged glances, their helplessness momentarily paralyzing them. Then out of another time Adam heard Olek's voice patiently coaching him. "If they catch you, always try to brazen it out. Lie in your teeth. You've nothing to lose. If they don't believe you, you're no worse off, they've got you anyway. But sometimes—and more often than you'd think—you can get away with it. Because chances are you can think circles around them. Because you're one hell of a lot smarter. Never forget that."

Putting on a show of surprised innocence and careful to address only the leader, he said in Russian, "Why, officer, we're just as surprised as you . . . hadn't the slightest idea anything *like that* was in there! Please consider. With the Warsaw climate what it is, only an idiot would make the stove unusable! Why, just this evening there was a chill in the air, and my sisters were going to build a fire. Only reason they didn't—we're out of coal. What I mean is, only an idiot would think of stuffing the stove with . . . so it must have been that idiot brother of ours who's already 'sitting'! Crazy!" He turned to Viktor, doing his best to sound indignant and injured. "That crazy kid wouldn't care if he got all of us in trouble with his idiot pranks!"

No one had coached Viktor, any more than he himself had been coached, but it was exactly as Olek had said—a quick, bright mind is always at an advantage in a battle of wits with dullards. Viktor gave no outward sign, but he picked up the line Adam had thrown him. "Of course, that must be the answer, officer. Do we look stupid to you? Is it likely we'd be leaving such poison around if we knew about it, and risk freezing our asses off into the bargain?"

The man in violet-blue looked unsure. "Well, I don't know. . . ." He riffled through the small pile of publications. Fortunately none was so recent as to give the brothers the outright lie. "Maybe yes, maybe no. How'll I know you're telling the truth?"

It was working. The quick lie was working. As far as Izidore was concerned, putting additional blame on him would make no difference—the charge of possessing a few illegal pamphlets more or less would alter neither his present situation nor the punishment which was already preordained, depending on the general line of the eventual mass trials. Evidence scarcely ever mattered, it was probably not even sifted. What was important now was to save the skins of those who were still at liberty.

"Answer when you're spoken to. Can you prove you're telling the truth?"

"Not meaning any disrespect, sir, that should be perfectly obvious to you. Did we try to stop you when you started the search? I mean, did we try to distract you? Nothing of the kind! Did we act guilty in any way? No again. You were watching us—well, weren't we as surprised as you when you came on all this . . . this rubbish?" Viktor was laying it on thick, and Adam could only admire him.

"Hm. Yes. Well. Perhaps." The uniforms needed more time to figure that one out. "We'll let that go for the moment. Who else is in the house with you?"

"Just our two sisters, your honor. Another brother—he's just a boy, a child really. The hired girl—she sleeps in the kitchen."

"Get them all in here. We'll question them all. Afterwards we'll see. . . ."

Brazen it out and you can outsmart them. Never forget that, Olek's voice seemed to continue to urge. Adam took over now, saying with a considerable show of meekness, "Yes, officer, of course, right away. But please, girls and children get frightened so easily. . . . Won't you let us go in by ourselves to wake them? It won't take but a minute. . . ." And the searchers, glad of this chance to sit down and have a smoke, agreed.

Brazen it out. Quickly, as he shook his sisters awake, Adam whispered to them an explanation of what was going on, and what they must and must not say. As quickly, as she rubbed the sleep out of her eyes Idka began to object. "It seems like selling Izzy out! It might hurt him!"

"It can't hurt him. He's already in jail. Don't argue, there isn't time." Then Adam had an inspiration. "Look, nothing worse can happen to him than has already happened, but if you're stubborn the rest of us will get hurt, and that'll kill Mama. Do you want to kill Mama just to have your own way?"

A heavy fist pounded on the door of the girls' bedroom. "Hey, you in there, what's taking you so long? We haven't got all night! Keep up the monkeyshines and we'll put all of you in for questioning!"

"You see how it is," brother whispered to sister. Then in a louder voice, "Right away, officer. They're dressed now. We'll be right out."

All the fight seemed to go out of Idka. "For Mama's sake I'll do what you want. But it doesn't seem right." And so their skins were saved, at least for the time being.

For a long time inside the Pawiak prison morale remained high. By sheer luck and mostly for reasons of bureaucratic inertia the "politicals" were left together, unsegregated, dozens of men and boys herded into enormous communal cells in one wing, dozens of women and girls in another. There had been so many arrests, people had been dragged in so indiscriminately, that everyone was convinced some sort of sifting must soon, inevitably, begin. Surely, they told themselves, any day now half of them would be allowed to go home. At the same time no one wanted freedom at the expense of his comrades in misfortune. The spirit of solidarity was strong among them—all for one and one for all. This was particularly true of the youthful, the ardent, the ones like Izidore.

The older men, hardbitten professional revolutionaries who

had spent a lifetime in the underground, were not so sanguine. Neither, for that matter, was the youth who slept in the cot next to Izidore's. This was Antek Rosol, son of Jan Rosol, nephew and grandson of two Maciejs, all of them of the legendary Rosol clan. Yet even he was not really downhearted: there was a reason, he painstakingly explained to his new friend Izidore Fabian, why police repression should be so brutal this year. It wasn't just Warsaw or Lodz, nor even just Poland, that the Tsarate was fighting. Unrest was everywhere, in the heart of old Mother Russia and among all the conquered nations on the periphery of the vast Empire, in the Ukraine and Lithuania, in Byelorussia and Finland and the Transcaucasian lands and even Asia. Change was in the air, blown in on winds of progress from the West, and the Tsarate could no longer have everything its own way.

This was how Antek and some of the men who were his father's fellow conspirators analyzed the situation as they waited for fresh developments. In the meantime, conditions were not yet too outrageous. After the first few weeks parcels from the outside were permitted, and even reached those for whom they were intended, after the guards had taken their cut in food and cigarettes. And the old hands at "sitting" busied themselves with organizing study and discussion groups. As a result, time did not drag so unconscionably and even the least politically aware did not become completely disheartened.

But as the weeks dragged by, as the heat of summer began seeping into the damp, fetid cells, breeding lice and ticks in the straw of their pallets and making sleep a misery, as food spoiled and the first cases of dysentery and typhoid and typhus broke out, the endless waiting began to take its toll.

Now and then a guard came in and called out a name, and a prisoner answered and was told to come along, and that was the last that would be seen of him. But the grapevine, that inexplicable yet uncannily accurate news service in prisons the world over, would report the outcome sooner or later. In nine cases out of ten the man who was singled out was someone well-to-do, someone from a well-connected family, in which case he was simply given his freedom. Occasionally, if he happened to be a professional revolutionary or a labor leader, he vanished. When that happened he was quietly mourned, even though in later years his name might turn up in connection with some prison far north in Great Russia or in a hard-labor camp in Siberia.

Gradually a pattern began to emerge that even to the uninitiated became self-evident. There was to be punishment for the best among them but freedom for those with enough money or connections to buy their way out. Many years later, while working on an ambitious, carefully documented autobiography, Izidore Fabian did his best to reconstruct from memory the lists of those who were summarily sentenced and those who were "sprung." He then tried to follow up their individual careers. He was not surprised to discover that those sentenced, if they survived, remained by and large faithful to their beliefs. But those who went free chose, almost to a man, and woman too, to forget all about any patriotic or revolutionary fervor they may once have burned with. A few even preferred to remember nothing at all.

The heat continued, and slowly the miasma of apathy was becoming felt. The discussion groups lagged. Then a provocateur was discovered among the students. Before the cell leaders could stop their younger comrades, he was badly beaten. Briefly morale soared, the outbreak of violence serving as a kind of shot in the arm. But once the now-useless stool pigeon was removed— whether to be freed as a reward for services rendered or punished for stupidity, the grapevine never did manage to learn—the authorities retaliated by putting all political prisoners on bread and water for a week.

The bread was moldy and the water unfit to drink. Dysentery and typhoid assumed epidemic proportions. Cases of typhus were promptly isolated by being dragged off to solitary, where more than half as promptly died. When there had been enough deaths, the prison doctors finally stopped the punishment. For a while only boiled water was issued for drinking. By then it was assumed morale had been broken once and for all.

"I am beginning to understand what it means to give one's all for the Motherland," Izidore said wryly the next time he was finally allowed a visitor. The visitor was Adam, because Idka, the one he really wanted most to see, was home in bed with a bad throat. But even Adam was a welcome sight these days for his younger brother. "Let me explain," the boy grinned. "I'm now consciously prepared for every sacrifice, including a two-week siege of the runs. What more can my country ask? And if you think that's a joke. . ."

Adam studied him, his own feelings a mixture of impatience, affection, and very real admiration. Izidore was maturing. Steel was beginning to show under the flighty exterior, along with humor at his own expense. At the same time it was clear that Izzy had no real inkling yet of what might be in store for him, no awareness of the enormity of the punishment in relation to his offense, no understanding of having been caught in an unbreakable net. Part of him was still frighteningly young, he still seemed to be playing a game, still somewhere at the core of his mind convinced that when the game ended he could go home to a good supper and sleep in a soft, clean bed. It was maddening and it was also wonderfully heartening.

"Do you have any special messages for anyone?" Adam asked at one point in the conversation. "For Mama, for Idka? We've good news about Mama, they're sending her home. But I'd better warn you—we probably won't let her come to visit you, at least not for a while. In fact. . ." He looked abashed. "The truth is we haven't even told her about your trouble. The doctors said we shouldn't, that we'd have to make up a story about where you've vanished to. Knowing might be too much for her, the state she's in. Luckily, because she's still a little vague about things, so far she hasn't asked; but of course once she's home. . ."

Izidore's first reaction was to be indignant. "What makes you so sure she couldn't take it? Just maybe she'd be proud of me."

"Izzy, that's not the point," Adam did his best to soothe him. "Of course she'd be proud. We all are. But she'd also worry. And that might put her right back where she started."

"Yes, I suppose you're right." The boy's thin shoulders sagged. "Makes me feel kind of abandoned, though. But if it has to be, it has to be." He made a final effort at bravado. "If I could survive two weeks of the runs I'll survive this, too." It was a feeble joke, but it made him feel better.

The autumn rains came, then sleet and snow. The Warsaw winter, always hard, was a punishing time for the "politicals." Not a day went by without some of them showing the symptoms of grave illness. Pneumonia, pleurisy, tuberculosis were taking the place of typhoid and dysentery. No date had so far been set for a trial or even hearings.

In time Salome Grossglik recovered from the humiliation of her encounter with Count Dembinski and redoubled her efforts in her nephew's behalf. She even had Dembinski and his wife to tea. She had Tadeusz Korsza to tea. She ruined the hems of her best gray afternoon taffeta and her violet broadcloth suit—"the new one banded in velvet, but, of course, the binding can easily be replaced!"—sweeping in and out of the inner sanctums of the powerful and the near-powerful.

Everywhere it was the same story. The men who as boys had worshipped at her feet, grown momentarily nostalgic over the romantic past, still treated her with consummate gallantry—but that was all. "Dear, darling *Pani* Salome, who could ever willingly deny you anything? If any woman can make miracles happen, that woman is surely you. But these are parlous times. The behavior of the masses has so enraged the Tsar. . . ." The voice would drop and the speaker would glance uneasily to the right and left, and especially behind him. "The truth is, everyone is shaking in his boots, from the Governor-General down. Bribe-taking isn't what it used to be—one hardly knows whom to approach any more. Perhaps during the holiday season. . . . Now, unfortunately, all we can do is hope. . . ." And somehow the interview was over and there was nothing to show for it save a trail of Salome's special scent, a subtle mixture of iris and amber.

Without telling either his wife or his sister-in-law for fear of raising false hopes, Baron Kronenberg made a few discreet inquiries on his own, hinting that he was willing to pay handsomely for oiling the wheels of official corruption. But not even this yielded results. Word had come down from St. Petersburg that the Polish rabble must be taught a lesson they would not soon forget. There must be no favoritism, no leniency. Similar "lessons" were being taught the whole length and breadth of the land. Wherever there was protest, the reprisals were savage.

But in spite of punishment the protests kept spreading. In Siberia, miners dared refuse to go down into the pits for their twelve-hour shift unless their pay was raised by ten kopeks a day and their wages paid out regularly once a month. A supervisor promised to meet their demands but welshed once the men had gone back to work. He was set upon and roughed up. The next day the local authorities decreed floggings—eight-five lashes to a man on the bare buttocks, to be administered in the public square. In a cold of 20° below zero they lined up in long queues to await punishment, and each as his turn came was ordered to drop his pants and lie on a narrow wood bench. And when the pain started, the sweat on their genitals froze to the wood, to the amusement of the gendarmes who went to work on them.

In the Tula factories it was the women workers who went on strike. They demonstrated, carrying their children in their arms. They were met by a charge of mounted cossacks, beaten with knouts and rifle butts, and trampled.

On the Trans-Siberian railroad and on the Moscow-Petersburg line, labor was herded from local villages with knout and bayonet and the use of hunting dogs. Forced to dig in the deep mud, it was no unusual thing for men dropping with fatigue to drown. For those who survived no pay was forthcoming. There were mass defections from the labor gang, and again dogs were used to hunt down the runaways. It was great sport for the hunters.

What all this had to do with Warsaw *gymnasium* students joining with other students in the traditional wreath-floating ceremony was not entirely clear. Among all those other threats to the monarchy, this threat was so mild. But the case was not one for logic.

Eventually, however, the Baron was able to accomplish one thing with his "oiling"—while remaining locked up in his communal cell, Izidore was at last allowed to receive gifts of books, all the books he wanted, provided they passed the censor. And so began for him a period which all the rest of his life he recalled with a grim kind of pleasure and pride. In the eyes of those who knew him he had become something of a hero. Being one of the young and untried prisoners, he had also become something of a pet in his cell. Now, with time on his hands, and all that reading, he was getting a reputation for learning. He couldn't resist the temptation to show off, and offered to teach a class.

Then came the incident that ended his boyhood once and for all.

It was almost spring again. The air of the cells was warmer but not yet fetid. Death had thinned out the prisoners' ranks, and those who survived felt like blood brothers. The previous day had been Sunday, and visitors' day. Adam had been particularly generous with books, and all evening until darkness stopped them Izidore and Antek Rosol had taken turns reading aloud, with many comments, while a group of their cellmates crowded around them.

In the morning they were wakened even earlier than usual and ordered to get dressed and be quick about it. The usual slops that went by the name of breakfast were not served up. Instead, they were all herded out into the prison yard where a strange dark shape loomed in a corner still left in shadow by a reluctant sun.

Instantly, though conversation was forbidden, the whispers started. "We're being deported . . . Siberia . . . and not even a trial. . . ."

Then the dark, angular shape in the corner was rolled out. It seemed massive, and was shrouded in black cloth. As two guards pushed it toward the center of the yard, its wheels ground over the cobblestones and the sound was like the sound of a hundred horses' hooves echoing in the prisoners' ears.

"We're not being deported. That's a cannon. We're to be executed here and now . . . ," someone decided.

"Naaah, that's no cannon. Must be one of those new Western rapid-fire guns that kill fifty men at a clip," Antek Rosol guessed. "Pretty fancy for mere politicals like us."

Izidore had read about summary executions. They were not rare. Dostoyevsky, too, had faced a firing squad without so much as a day's warning. Of course, in his case it had turned out to be just a sham, a form of deliberate torture, a Tsarist joke. As he stood facing what he thought was death, a reprieve was already in the hands of the prison's military commander. The point of the joke had been to prolong the comedy until the very last minute. "But there will be no reprieve for Polish patriots. . . ."

Izidore and Antek stood very straight, very proud, and, to their own astonishment, not especially afraid. They were expecting the worst. But at least soon the waiting would be over. Now two soldiers in uniform joined the prison guards, and following them a man in civilian clothes, who went to stand behind the infernal draped object. There was a whispered consultation among them, and a good deal of laughter.

"The bastards," Antek said to Izidore under his breath. "Killing Poles must be very, very funny."

Before Izidore could think of an answer, an order rang out like a gunshot. "Atten-shun!" They obeyed. "Line up in straight lines! No talking! No moving!"

They stood still and waited. They continued to stand and wait, denied even the comfort of their usual breakfast of stale bread and watery tea, until the sun was high and hot on their faces.

"Atten-shun!" came another order.

Those who were beginning to droop pulled themselves up.

There was another consultation with the man in civilian clothes, who then took a position directly behind the shrouded machine. "Clearly the executioner," Antek whispered. And Izidore thought, *If I'm going to die, at least let it be with dignity.* He had a moment of fear, but it passed. *Patriots are not afraid,* he reminded himself. And he made up his mind that when the shots rang out he would fall shouting, "Long live Poland!" Those would be his last words.

"Atten-shun!" the order rang out a third time, itself like a bullet. They stood ramrod straight. "None of you bastards blink an eyelash! Ready! One . . . two . . . three. . ."

They haven't even bound our eyes, thought Izidore, shutting his own in spite of himself. He held his breath, the cry, "Long live Poland!" ready to burst from his lips.

There was a tiny puff of an explosion, then a click. Nothing happened. Nothing seemed to have hit him. Was death so painless, then? Cautiously he opened one eye, then both.

Not only he but all his comrades had remained standing. The

black cloth was off the dark mass, which stood revealed neither as a small cannon nor a machine gun but as a large professional box camera on wheels. The man in civilian clothes was no executioner, he was the cameraman. Calmly, he was taking out one glass plate and putting in another, while the guards roared with laughter, slapping their knees, slapping each other on the back, wondering out loud how many prisoners had wet their pants.

Izidore's knees buckled, and if Antek and the man to the other side of him hadn't caught him he would have fallen.

❧ *Seven* ❧

DURING the last week of April 1901 the industrial cities of Russian Poland, or the Congress Kingdom as people still called it, began to resemble a vast armed camp. In preparation for May Day new army contingents started arriving to reinforce local garrisons and the gendarmerie. The streets filled with uniforms, causing the timid to predict a bloodbath that would make the previous year's violence pale by comparison.

But though the towns bristled with bayonets, the May Day demonstrations turned out larger than they'd ever been. Twenty thousand marched in Warsaw alone instead of an expected ten, while in Lodz, where a dozen large factories had been shut down by strikes, the whole working population seemed to pour into the streets. Dressed in their Sunday best, unmindful of the hunger that stalked them, they paraded up and down the main thoroughfare singing all the forbidden songs. And although there were a certain number of arrests and beatings, though a carefully engineered pogrom in the Jewish district of Baluty did provide an excuse for a brief cossack stampede, by and large the day was a victory for the anti-Tsarist forces.

When presently work did resume in the struck textile plants, the weavers, men and women alike, had had their hourly pay raised by a few kopeks. At least one overseer had been fired. And the mercantile dynasts weren't resting easy in their beds. More and more often, not just here in the Congress Kingdom but all through the Empire, a word was being repeated that deviled

them. The word was *proletariat,* and various people used it with
varied emphases. In the language of the theoreticians of the Left it
kept its classical meaning: the class that labored for wages, for
hire, owning neither property nor capital but only its ability to
produce. But the daily press deliberately corrupted the sense of
the unaccustomed term until in the minds of the middle class it
came to have a nasty sound equated with words like rabble,
hooligan, vulgarian, mob. It was as though the wealthy and powerful hoped that if only one expressed sufficient aristocratic contempt for them, the masses would remember their place, slink
back where they belonged, and give no further trouble.

But the proletariat stubbornly refused to let itself be cast in the
role assigned to it. There were fresh outbreaks in Tomaszow,
Zhyrardow, Zgierz. Then came news of unrest in the countryside, and the frightened industrialists, bankers, and great
landowners petitioned the Tsar, affirming their loyalty and begging for protection against possible armed insurgence.

The underground press responded with bitter denunciations of
the self-serving, classless stand of the bourgeoisie in its battle
with labor. And from somewhere in hiding—wherever he edited
the banned newspaper *Sprawa Robotnicza,* The Workers' Cause—
Julian Marchlewski sent out his memorable broadside calling for
the overthrow of the Tsarate. "Alone, the despised wage slave,
the workingman," the paper thundered, "dares to *demand* his
rights while others cringe, licking the Tsar's boots and begging.
Alone the workingman dares threaten while others crawl!"

And it was true. With so little to lose, the workers were no
longer humble.

In his daily contact with the Pozners, Adam was finding himself uneasy that spring. His loyalties were painfully divided. On
the one hand he was what his very nature dictated, hardworking,
conscientious, a model employee. On the other hand he kept
thinking of his brother Izidore sweating out the months at the
Pawiak, and knew that his own carefully cultivated aloofness
could no longer be counted on to serve.

As far as the business went he was learning fast, availing himself of every opportunity for advancement that Maurice Pozner

offered. He often brought work home nights, and after a hasty supper would excuse himself and retreat to his room, one of the two that once had served as his father's shop and office, there to sit until long past midnight poring over financial statements, brokers' and agents' reports, sales-and-profits sheets. More importantly, he would study samples of raw cotton by the hour, examining them under a magnifying glass, rolling them between thumb and forefinger, pulling and pressing until the very feel of the springy fiber telegraphed to his brain everything he needed to know before giving an order to buy. He was making excellent progress, and the Old Man made no secret of his plans to start delegating serious responsibility to him soon.

But there was also the reverse side of the coin.

For all his benevolence, all his avowed sympathy with the previous year's demonstrations, in regard to his own mills Pozner seemed no different than the Silbersteins, the Scheiblers, the Thonet brothers, the Kindlers of Pabianice, and scores of other owners. Catholics or Protestants or Jews, Poles or foreigners from the West, in fighting their mill hands they united in a single phalanx.

Long ago Maurice had suggested that Adam take his midday meal with the family, and now from his lowly place at the foot of the long table he daily heard conversations which made the excellent food difficult to swallow. Never before had he heard labor policy discussed privately among employers. Frequently their approach horrified him.

The worst offender of all was handsome, thirty-five-year-old Miecio Silberstein, champion polo player, tennis player, art collector, man-about-town, and elusive, exclusive, inveterate bachelor. A frequent guest, vaguely related to both the Pozners and the Kronenbergs, and darling of the whole clan, Miecio had his own formula for dealing with factory workers. "I simply refuse to deal with them. It's the only way. Lock them out, starve them out, treat them like the dirt they are, and when their kids start dropping like flies they'll come around. And *beg* to work for any wages you care to offer."

Others among Maurice's guests, though less coldly direct, could see nothing wrong, when business was bad, with adding an

hour's unpaid overtime to the legal eleven-and-a-half-hour working day. Or with employing children to do men's work at half-
rates. "They should be grateful we put bread into their mouths!"
Still others openly advocated making every possible use of the
Tsarist police, informers, provocateurs, and even the military.
"Why not? Everyone knows the Governor-General has orders
from St. Petersburg!"

Adam did not consider himself naive—ever since the old
study circle days he had known that the rich traditionally formed
a solid front in defense of their wealth. But he had never before
heard it admitted so bluntly. What he found hardest to stomach
was that native Poles—Polish Jews at that, even though assimi-
lated, even though converted—should casually advocate turning
to the Tsar for armed backing against their own people.

One day after a particularly bitter discussion at table, Missy
cornered him. "I never see you any more," she complained half
flirtatiously. "I do wish you'd come and talk to me once in a
while like you used to. I mean, about things that matter." She
lowered her voice. "I'm not a schoolgirl any longer, I've a right to
be treated like a person, a person with a brain. But if I ask Papa
what's going on he only laughs and says, don't bother your pretty
little head. It's insulting. Just because I'm a girl doesn't mean I
have to be an idiot. Which I'm not. Please help me, Adam." It
was the first time she had called him by his given name, bridging
the distance, sweeping away the old differences between scholar
and pupil. "You can trust me, you know," she added in an un-
dertone.

Remembering his discussions with Olek about her, Adam was
not surprised at the outburst. What did surprise him was the
change in her. He had hardly seen her since the tutoring had
stopped, for she and Marek had been away abroad a good deal.
And now here she was, poised, her features honed to a new maturity, and if not exactly beautiful in a classical sense, certainly extremely attractive. A fresh hair style and a chic frock—by
Worth, but how was Adam to know?—accentuated a slightly
oriental, exotic quality he had never noticed before.

But mainly he was touched by her stubborn insistence on continuing to think for herself. "I wish I knew what to tell you," he

answered honestly enough. "But I'm no longer in touch with my old friends, they've all been exiled. I only know what I read in the press, same as you and everyone else."

"No," she countered. "It's not the same, for you know how to read between the lines. Which is a lot more than I do. On the other hand you're not hateful like these . . . these. . ." At a loss for the right word she borrowed one straight out of Balzac or Flaubert, "These rich *tradesmen.* . ."

"Missy, Missy darling!" *Pani* Konstancja's peremptory summons came loudly across the room. "Missy, I need you to help pour the coffee. . . ."

"You see," the girl whispered with all of her old impertinence, "Mama fears her little golden bird may escape its golden cage." She started to walk away, then threw over her shoulder, "But I'm not giving up. I'll find ways to talk to you, see if I don't!"

By now Izidore's detention had become a kind of inescapable fact of life to his family. The monthly visits continued, the parcels of food and books were a scheduled budget item over which only Bluma's doctors bills were given precedence. Even for Idka the sense of shock passed, as it passes when one must learn to live with the knowledge of incurable illness.

For a while the problem of how to break the news of the jailing to their mother had continued to trouble the young Fabians, but once the date of Bluma's discharge from the sanatorium was actually set, the doctors, with whom Adam and Leon discussed the whole matter frankly, had taken a stand diametrically opposed to their own. "No, don't lie to her. Try that and she'd only sense it, and that may be worse. But if you tell her the truth, who knows, it just may help jolt her out of the past, turn her face toward the future. Another link to reality, as it were. Only be sure to stress that your brother's situation isn't hopeless, and above all keep telling her how much he's looking forward to seeing her."

The doctors turned out to be right. Bluma cried one whole day over Izidore's plight but almost immediately her sorrow turned into ordinary, practical worry. Did he have enough warm underwear? Could they afford to buy him apples? And what about bananas? He always did love bananas, though, of course, they were terribly expensive and scarcer than hen's teeth. But maybe if she economized on something else. . . . From worry over Izidore she then switched to worry over what a drain all this was on her eldest son. In short, from inconsolable widow she changed back into protective mother.

Slowly the old warmth crept back into her relationship with all her children. She was still distressingly docile, but she was beginning to take a normal interest in her household. She sewed and she mended, on occasion supervised the kitchen, and finally one Friday morning dressed early for the street, announcing she was going down to the fish market for some live carp. "High time you were having some of my good gefüllte fish on the Sabbath eve." She then spent the rest of the day chopping and stuffing and fussing, and supper that night was served on a white tablecloth, and she herself lit the candles. If she'd served them peacock's tongues, her children could not have been more delighted.

That day was a turning point. She became capable once more of spontaneous affection, the light pat on the shoulder, the quick kiss, the smoothing back of unruly hair. With her daughters, there would be the gently critical appraisal of a bow carelessly tied, a braid unevenly plaited. "And just look at that shirtwaist! What's the matter, can't we afford more starch? Next time I'd better do it myself." With Kazik, long past the stage of even wanting to be babied, she was like an old cat with her last litter of one. Tucking him in at night, slipping a slab of chocolate into his school bag along with his midday snack of bread and cheese.

Now that everything seemed to be going so well for the Fabians, Salome Grossglik began to think it was high time to start concerning herself once more with Adam's future. So far, she had accomplished everything she had set out to do regarding him. Wanda Borowska was out of his life. He had a good job. The family was on an even keel. He had earned the right to a little happiness.

By this, of course, she meant marriage, one that would be both solid and advantageous. But how to go about it she wasn't sure. Normally one would begin by arranging a young man's social life. The trouble was, as she complained to her husband, Adam was getting to be such a big bear of a recluse that, try as she would, she could not reach him.

She gave herself one more chance. Cornering her nephew in his own room one Sunday while she and Leon were visiting, she started in her usual roundabout way, "Your mother is getting along splendidly, dear heart, and no one knows better than Uncle and I how much of this is your doing. If you hadn't sacrificed so generously for the family. . . ." Grave blue eyes open wide, she raised them to the ceiling as though somewhere right above it a recording angel were waiting to take notes. "Don't ever think we aren't aware just how much you did sacrifice! It ought to be a great consolation to you to know you've given your mother something to get well for."

"Please, I'd rather not talk about it."

"Well, in that case let's talk about you. Your mother tells me you've turned hermit. All you do is work. You never play, never go out among people. At your age, that just isn't *normal!* We'll have to do something about it!"

Adam felt a slow wave of heat travel from his stomach to his neck. "I like things the way they are. As for going out more, I just happen to have a low tolerance for human company."

She patted his cheek. "A phase, my pet, I promise you. It will pass." But his expression became so closed that she did not press him. Instead, she decided to enlist the help of his mother, who also worried over him.

"So moody, my poor Adam, so moody," Bluma responded to mention of her son's name, then quickly added, fearful lest they think she was criticizing, "Sometimes I have to remind myself he's not mad at us, it's just the way he is. He can no more help himself than I can help my migraine headaches. Such a good boy, such a good son and brother, but there's this unhappiness inside him. His heart is always heavy. . . ."

"I suppose it's still *that girl,*" Salome whispered. She had closed Adam's door to make sure he couldn't overhear, but it paid to be careful. "My dear, for such an obvious malady there's an obvious remedy. What our Adash needs at his age is a wife. We must think about getting him suitably settled."

"If it would make him happy . . . ," his mother began. "Yes, but where does one start? He never so much as looks at a girl!"

"All the more reason, then, to take matters into our own hands. Why, the right young lady would make a new man of him, don't you agree, Leon darling?"

She smiled coquettishly at her husband and managed to achieve the blush of which she was still capable on occasion, the blush she hoped still had the power to reduce Leon to mush. "Well do I remember the days of our courtship. . . ." Then her tone changed from dreamy to businesslike. "I'll get my mind going on the problem, and in the meantime, since these things don't happen overnight, let's hope your daughters get settled. Surely with the dowries Adam is planning for them, and a little help from the marriage broker, there ought to be no trouble there."

As always when the discussion turned to her girls, Bluma sighed heavily. She had never ceased dreaming of something better for them than arranged matches. And yet wasn't that exactly how her own had finally come about? And could any woman find greater happiness than she had found with her Jacob?

"About Adash," she finally said. "I suppose I've been selfish. Somehow I've let his welfare always be put last." She was silent a moment. "Well, how would we go about doing what you propose? You'll have to help me, coach me. . . ."

"Just leave everything to me," Salome purred, completely in her element now. "Let me do all the planning. We might start with . . . let's see . . . a Sunday afternoon tea party at our house. No, on second thought better make it an evening affair, a musicale. Yes, that's it. Oh, Bluma, Leon, what fun! I always say there's no greater pleasure for a woman," she wound up, "than to help her near and dear ones with their life problems!"

Her husband made no comment. He was wondering if he could count the times he'd heard her use those same words.

Doing something for Adam would compensate her for her failure to do something for Izidore. Eagerly Salome rolled up her metaphysical sleeves and went to work. The very next morning, instead of going to market with Miss Julia as usual, she paid a visit to her sister Eugenia. This, she felt, was the best way to begin. For the Baroness knew everyone who mattered in Warsaw's Polish-Jewish social world. She could be counted on to know exactly who had marriageable daughters and which of these might be out of bounds for Adam Fabian because their fathers needed them for effectuating financial mergers, and which were attainable.

Eugenia was more than willing to be helpful. "As you know, my dear, there are plenty of girls whose families are looking for new, healthy blood," she remarked. "Shall we start making lists?"

They settled down happily to jotting down names. Salome was adamant about ruling out a couple of heiresses so ugly it was common gossip their parents would marry them off to anyone willing to take them off their hands. "I'll not have our Adash saddled with a wife he can't bear to face across the breakfast table!" Only in deference to Eugenia herself did she make an exception of Lucio's twin cousins on his dead mother's side, the Silberstein sisters, who bore him an unfortunate family resemblance. "After all, other young men at the party will have marriage on their minds!"

Slowly, the list grew. When Missy Pozner's name came up, both women agreed she could no longer be considered a prospect, which was really too bad since she, for one, did not have to marry money. "They know each other too well. Besides, if there'd been any kind of spark there it would have flared up by now. No," Salome concluded. "I'm afraid it's one of those cases where the folk saying applies: 'From this flour there'll be no bread.'"

"Let's invite her all the same," Eugenia suggested. "She and Adam have gone through so many stages in their long acquaintance, you never can tell. And it won't hurt to let her family see him for once not as an employee but as a young man with social connections of his own."

"How wise you are, big sister," Salome murmured admiringly. Now why hadn't she herself thought this out? Of course, the soiree must be used not merely to launch Adam on the marriage market but also to let it be known that he had powerful friends in the world of commerce and finance. The Kronenberg sponsorship might even, who knows, produce a useful change in his relationship with Pozner. As for him and Missy, perhaps if they were thrown together afresh, on neutral ground. . .

"It's settled then. We invite Missy? Her brother? Marek's personable, and we do need our quota of personable young men. Who else? Adam's friend Henryk Meisels. Your own Lucio. Then, let's see. . . ." And they went on sifting, discarding, reconsidering; and when it came to the men, they were especially careful not to eclipse Adam himself.

"It's beginning to sound absolutely delightful," Salome said at last, rising and pulling on her gloves. "But I've been thinking—there's another bird we could be killing with the same stone. It may be time to do something for that darling little Regina Segal. I've given up on her sister, but Ginia's already past fifteen and the most charming, disarming, poised fifteen-year-old—because like you and me she's always been used to having a lot of boys around. In fact, her mother tells me Ginia is quite the belle of the ball. But so far she's only been meeting her brother's friends, and everyone knows that isn't always the best source of husband material. These can be dangerous games. I won't rest till I see her start moving in other circles. . . ."

"If you don't think she's too young," Eugenia said.

"Not really. And I'll have her come with Kuba—after all what's more natural than to invite my own niece and nephew to my party? And here's an idea, they're both excellent pianists. We can have them provide part of the entertainment. Something for four hands. Or we'll start with Regina playing a few Chopin waltzes solo. It'll all seem so very natural!'

Eugenia laughed. "When the country starts planning its next uprising, little sister, you should be a member of the general staff."

Salome relished the compliment but chose to be deprecating. "If only everything were that simple! Well, I must leave you now or my whole household will be at sixes and sevens!"

And so the date was set, the invitations were sent out, the apartment on Count Berg Street was scoured and burnished. The rugs and draperies were taken down to the courtyard for dust cleaning, professional waxers hired to do their ritual dance of polishing the parquet floors, the piano tuner and the florist alerted. Eugenia promised to lend Salome her own butler and a couple of footmen, and Miss Julia started losing sleep weeks in advance, agonizing over which cakes should be baked at home and which ordered from the caterer.

Now that the wheels had been set in motion, Salome could think and talk of little else. For the time being she forced herself to forget her other nephew who was being devoured by lice in Pawiak prison. The echoes of the weavers' strikes, the ferment following May Day and May Third, touched her as little as they touched the *jeunesse dorée* who were going to be her guests. As for Adam himself, she kept him carefully in the dark about the purpose of her party, not even letting him suspect that he was the guest of honor.

He knew only that he was invited, and he was none too pleased. The prospect of an evening in the company of persons most of whom he barely knew and didn't particularly like was not an appealing one. He detested chitchat, and at any large gathering invariably felt like a fish out of water. He began considering not going at all.

"Oh, but you can't refuse Aunt Salome," his mother pleaded anxiously. "You can't disappoint her. You know how much things like that mean to her!" Because it seemed to matter so much to Bluma, he finally promised to go through with it.

So he let himself be persuaded, managed, pushed around; after all, it would be for only one evening. And maybe, came the consoling thought, he would enjoy the music. And with Henryk Meisels invited, there was sure to be some good conversation. So he agreed to do whatever was asked of him, even promising to let himself be measured for a new suit, and made his excuses, and as was his habit vanished into his room for the rest of the evening. There he sat down to work out a chess problem that the night before had thoroughly eluded him.

It eluded him again tonight. A sixth sense was giving him

warning that something out of the ordinary threatened the insulation he still did his best to maintain around himself. How long had it been since he'd attended a social gathering of any sort? Two years, or thereabouts. And that had been in another world entirely, a world he had schooled himself never to think about. It suddenly struck him that this would be the first party he had ever attended without Wanda. He dreaded it.

What was that other thing Henryk Meisels was so fond of telling him? "Time you were meeting other women. Let one of them take you to bed one of these days. Shall I arrange it?" Henryk also liked to remind him that the past was dead. "It's dead, now bury it. Let the sap of manhood flow!"

But regardless of all this cheap wisdom there wasn't so much as a stirring in his loins any more. He wondered if there ever would be again.

❧ *Eight* ❧

O<small>N THE MORNING</small> of the day of the party, a Sunday, a small boy, tough and self-assured and speaking the lingo of the waterfront, climbed the stairs to the Fabian apartment asking for Adam. Having first made sure he was speaking to him and no one else, he dug into his pocket and produced a crumpled, smudged, but carefully sealed envelope.

"For you. From a friend. I'm supposed to wait for an answer."

The message, unsigned, was unmistakably in Olek's handwriting. Adam felt the blood rush to his head and realized his hands were trembling as he read. "The kid who brings you this is my cousin. You can trust him. He'll lead you to me if you care to come. But you must come now, at once. And if that's impossible, tell him where I can find you late tonight."

He read the note a second time, and only then became aware of the child's young-old eyes watching him intently. "Well, mister, you going to give me an answer or not?"

Adam pulled out his pocket watch. It was still early. "It says here I can go back with you. Wait for me. I shan't be five minutes." Leaving the boy in the hallway, he went inside to tell his mother he was going out and wasn't sure when he'd be back.

Bluma looked up from her eternal pile of mending. "You've not forgotten about tonight, have you, dear?"

As if any of this mattered, when somewhere in the city his old friend was expecting him! But he bit back a sharp answer. "Don't worry about me, Mama, I shan't get lost."

The little street Arab, after volunteering only the information that his name was Franek, accepted Adam's offer to pay his omnibus fare, but only on condition that Adam take a seat inside while he himself remained standing on the back platform. "If we sat together we'd only attract attention," he explained with the aplomb of an old conspirator. "A tramp like me and a gent like you! Back where I live it won't matter so much—no one will watch us, they see all kinds."

They traversed Warsaw and the bridge into Praga. Here the streets became progressively narrower and shabbier. Almost at the end of the line Franek signaled it was time to get off. He led the way through dirty, tortuous alleys and finally stopped in the doorway of a tenement that made Adam's own apartment house look like a palace. "In here. Other end of the yard, back building, fourth floor, left-hand door. And don't bother ringing, the bell don't work. Just knock."

He started to walk away. Adam detained him, and after fishing in his pocket handed him a five-kopek piece.

"What's that for?"

"Buy yourself some rock candy."

"Mister, didn't your Ma ever teach you not to take candy from strangers?" He spat neatly and accurately through his teeth, deliberately just missing the tip of Adam's shoe. "I don't run nobody's errands for pay. Olek and me, we work together, see? For the cause."

"No offense meant," Adam apologized gravely.

"Yeah. So now you know how it is. *We work together.* We're comrades. Well, like I said, fourth floor, left-hand door. And tell Olek for me, if he can't spot me through the window, not to work up a sweat. I'll catch up with him the minute you're gone."

Whistling, with an elaborate show of unconcern, he sauntered down the street. It was as though he hoped to make himself invisible the better to watch over his big cousin's safety.

Adam took the steps two at a time. His heart was pounding hard enough to burst his rib cage, but not from the exertion. Though he hadn't consciously admitted it, he was still hoping for a miracle—that beyond the door on the fourth floor not Olek, but Wanda would be waiting. His throat was dry and his palms wet. He knocked. A querulous voice inquired about his business. He identified himself and at last heard the bolt being pushed back and a chain clanking. Then the old crone who let him in shuffled away, and in the dim light of the hallway another figure, massive, broad-shouldered, familiar, detached itself from the shadows.

"Olek!"

"Adash! Son of a gun, you made it!"

"You didn't think I'd stay away?"

"These days one takes nothing for granted."

They embraced, kissing three times in the traditional manner, then holding each other off at arms' length to stare, still unbelieving, each trying to assess the changes time had wrought in the other.

And each saw that the other was looking shockingly older, all youthful exuberance gone. It was damage done not so much by time as by the times. Adam wondered whether Olek had known hunger in exile to make him so gaunt; Olek, whether the look of comparative affluence combined with a certain lackluster expression meant Adam had capitulated completely to the demands of the system.

Olek was the first to break the silence. "For a while there, I was afraid Franek might not reach you. When one is so pressed for time, waiting comes hard. I must be out of the city by daybreak, catch the train for. . ." He broke off. "But don't let's stand here. Come on in, come inside where we can talk."

Adam was still finding it difficult to talk. He merely pressed the other man's rough, powerful hand, and it was as though his other, good self were waking from a sleep induced by an evil drug. A few more minutes, and the world would right itself.

They went into a room furnished sketchily with a table, some straight chairs, a narrow cot, and in a corner a tile stove like the one on Nalewki Street, also obviously used for purposes other than to heat the house: its iron door, pushed carelessly closed, gaped to reveal a stack of "tissue paper" a foot high. On the table lay another stack, along with a candle and a stick of sealing wax.

"Just like old times," Adam finally grinned.

"Business as usual." Olek grinned back, indicating the paraphernalia with a sweep of his hand. "As you may have guessed, that's why I'm here."

"Alone?"

"Maryla and a—a friend from Zurich—are in Lodz. Never mind the details. We have to be like the wind in the fields these days, blowing here, blowing there before the storm breaks. And there's going to be a storm—of that you may be sure. And what a storm! It's blowing up from the east. Contrary to what our parlor socialists from the PPS may try to tell us, when Polish independence is finally won it won't be because a bunch of knights in armor decide to declare war on Russia. It'll come as part of Empire-wide revolution, the Polish masses and the Russian masses and all the other subjugated nationalities, led by the proletariat. . . ."

They might have been resuming a conversation interrupted the previous night. And yet Adam had the distinct feeling that his old friend was talking so furiously in order to avoid having to get around to other, more personal subjects.

"I don't know how much you know about what's going on among the exiles abroad," Olek was saying. "But the Social-Democrats—that's Lenin for the Russians, and for us Rosa Luxemburg and her group—are raising the Polish question as an international slogan. Polish labor and Polish independence both are very much on the agenda. Ergo, it has become obvious that our own delegates had better find ways to attend the next SD congress, which will be held in London, or maybe Brussels, soon. Prior to that there's to be an internal organizing congress on Polish soil. I don't need to explain that that's going to take a lot of doing—a lot of people will have to be able to travel fairly freely back and forth across the border, which means arranging for false papers, places for them to stay, a foolproof system of communicating with one another, and, of course, money. That's one reason we're here. The other is that at long last we're starting a newspaper of our own. In other words, nothing has changed, it's just got hotter, if you know what I mean."

"I know only too well." Slowly, painfully, the self-hypnotic excitement that had gripped Adam for the past hour was ebbing.

Wanda was not here, he had never really believed he would find her here, but at least now he could talk about her, speak her name.

"Later. Tell me about all that later. Olek, listen. That last letter I wrote you and the way you answered it. . ."

Olek Piotrowski sighed heavily, like a man on a witness stand who can no longer avoid answering his interrogator. "All right. I suppose we might as well stop beating around the bush. I always did mean to write you again, at more length, but after all what more was there to say? No, that's not true. There was a lot to say, only none of it would have done you any good."

"So she's married now. I know, someone else told me. Does she love him?" Just to voice the question was to twist the knife in his own festering wound. "More than she ever loved me? No, don't even bother answering that, it's so silly! A fat lot she must have cared about me to be able to console herself so soon. . . ."

"Adash, stop talking drivel." Olek spoke sharply, more sharply than he had intended, but this turn in the conversation was more than he'd been prepared for. It embarrassed him, and for Adam's sake as well as his own he wanted it over with. "She did love you, with all her heart. But her pride was mortally wounded—that infernal pride of hers. We tried, Maryla and I, to persuade her to let us write you about the baby long before it was born. We were even thinking of doing it against her wishes. But then she went into labor prematurely. She nearly died. And you weren't there, and Felix was, and he wanted her. Wanted her knowing everything about her—even that she didn't love him at the time. Wanted her and that poor little mite of hers, and nothing that's happened since has made any difference. He adores them both. And she needs him. They need each other. . . ."

Adam was reminded of his mother's words that first time she had spoken to him rationally at the sanatorium. *It's a terrible thing not to be needed. . . .* He suddenly had a painfully vivid picture of Wanda big with child, alone in her room after saying goodnight to her good friends who were a couple. Alone and prideful he saw her, a woman born to give of herself but where was the taker?

"God, if only I had known the whole truth! Somehow I would have found a way to come to her. . . ."

"Would you, Adash? Would you really? Be honest with your-self. You were so torn. Just think of the words of the marriage ceremony: *forsaking all others.* Would you have been ready to for-sake your people, your sick father? So perhaps it is all for the best."

The painful truth of this made him snarl, "Don't give me cheap consolation!"

Olek let that pass. "It wasn't your fault if your hands were tied because of the way things were. And babies don't wait. And soci-ety can be hard on a woman who dares flout the conventions. Just be glad Wanda has someone to share her burden."

"Burden?" Adam was quick to fasten on to what sounded like an offensive phrase, relieved to be able to channel his anger. "Since when is a child such a burden?"

Olek's face expressed surprise, then softened with compassion. "Sorry, I thought you knew." He sighed. "All right, I had better give it to you in detail. The child's a cretin. So you see, Wanda needed all the help she could get."

"My child—a cretin?" Adam repeated, unbelieving. This was something Henryk Meisels had not included in his account. Per-haps he hadn't even known. Or hadn't cared to mention.

He became aware that Olek was still talking, gently, ra-tionally. "It's one of these things that happen, no one knows why. Seems there's a lot of cretinism in Switzerland—some say it's the climate, some the soil—they're only just beginning to study it."

He wasn't listening. He sat rigid, his face gone gray. Olek went over to a cupboard, brought out a bottle of vodka and filled two glasses. "Here, have a snort. We both need it." He downed his own drink at a gulp. "Yes, Adash, life isn't pretty. How does the saying go? Like a baby's shirt, it's short and full of shit."

The burning liquor seemed to bring Adam out of his trance-like state. "A cretin. Not even a normal child," he repeated. Then savagely, "God damn it, what kind of monster was I to let her go through all this alone! I should have been there with her, giving her strength, loving her. But no, I had to be the dutiful son, the son everyone admired. . . ."

Now he surrendered to self-abasement, self-torture, wallowing in them like a man who hopes to rid himself of all responsibility for his sins by reciting them before a priest. He could see only the dark side of what he had done. "My father wasn't asking for sacrifice. In fact, he warned me. To the very last he kept saying a man had a right to his own life. . . ."

"Adash," Olek finally broke in. "Listen to me. Stop tearing yourself apart. It's over. You've got to accept that it's over." After having for so long held Adam's defection against him, he understood now that whatever this man had done or left undone was far more hurtful to himself than to the woman he had hurt. His punishment would have endless ramifications, for it would go on and on, and someone should try to ease it. "Look, don't even think of the baby as yours. It's theirs. Say it. *Their* child, *their* little girl. Don't ever again think of her as having to do with you."

"Olek, what's her name?"

"Felicja, Felka—*after her father.*" He poured two more drinks, as if to anesthetize his friend against the blows he was dealing. "And Felix is wonderful with her. He doesn't seem to mind that she's not like other children. Even more than her mother, he keeps looking for every least sign of improvement he fancies he sees. A scientist . . . maybe he should know better, but in this he seems to be a father first and foremost. So infinitely loving and patient with her. . . ."

"Do me a favor," Adam interrupted the flow of well-meant words. "Shut up. Just shut up." He was shaking and his voice came with difficulty.

"I just felt you ought to know, is all," Olek finished firmly. "Surgery may hurt like hell, but still it's better than gangrene."

And deliberately changing the subject, he launched into further discussion of his own work and the political situation. Adam listened, but only heard every fifth word.

"I can't even pretend to care about any of it," he finally said. "Not right now. Maybe someday, maybe the next time the wind blows you back, I'll feel different. But today. . ." He shook his head in wordless helplessness. "Today nothing makes sense, nothing matters. Forgive me, but I think I'd better go."

They embraced one last time.

"Stay out of jail, Olek."

"And you, don't turn your back on the world—come back among the living."

"I don't know that I ever will."

"Sooner or later one always does. Scar tissue gets pretty tough. Well, *servus,* goodbye, old friend."

"Servus."

The chain on the entrance door clanked again like the chain of a prison. Adam walked down the stairs slowly, like an old man who doesn't trust himself.

He remembered with a start that he was two months past his twenty-sixth birthday. He felt like a hundred.

℀ *Nine* ℈

WHAT IN THE WORLD can be keeping Adash?" Salome wondered aloud for the third time, and only her husband was able to
catch the faint annoyance edging her bright company voice. "I've
never known him to be inconsiderate! Nearly an hour late, and to
his own party!" Leon wondered whether to remind her how carefully she'd concealed from Adam the fact that it *was* his party. He
decided against it. His wife's spurts of irritation seldom lasted,
and this one would vanish the instant Adam came through the
door.

"I do wonder what's keeping him," she said one last time, but
already somewhat vaguely, her role of hostess too absorbing for
her to allow herself to be distracted from it. "Leon, my love, keep
an eye on the door. Be sure to take the boy in tow the second he
gets here. In the meantime, be an angel and check that the men
are being properly looked after. After all, Eugenia's people don't
really know their way around, and Miss Julia's nose is a wee bit
out of joint, and I shudder to think of the explosions in the
pantry if she should take it into her head not to cooperate!" She
raised her eyes to heaven. "So be my own sweet darling and do
what you can." And she swept off to her next chore, lovelier than
ever, Leon thought, in her new dove-gray satin and the pearls
borrowed from Eugenia for the occasion. He wished he could afford to circle her throat with her own pearls. But that could never
be, and the best he could do for her at the moment was to see to
the comfort of their male guests just as at the tea table his sister-
in-law was seeing to the ladies.

Salome, in the meantime, felt free to devote herself to the younger people. It was, after all, of the greatest importance that they be encouraged to mix as much as possible. The shy ones especially must not be left to hide in corners, talking only to old acquaintances. If Adam must be late, she thought, then at least let her use the time prior to his arrival to good account. Let the stage be perfectly set, everything ready for his entrance. And like an expert choreographer making shrewd use of his corps de ballet, she passed from group to group, changing the composition of one, the mood and tenor of another.

Out of the corner of her eye she had noticed Lucio Kronenberg standing silent with one arm on the back of his stepmother's chair, as if determined for safety's sake not to be separated from her for a single moment. Salome beckoned him over. "Lucio, dearest, Mama's going to be frightfully busy for a while, and I know you want to be helpful to her, so here's what I wish you would do." She spoke gently, as one does to a timid five-year-old. "Just take a cup of tea and a plate of cookies over to my niece Regina, you know her, you've met her here lots of times. This is her first grown-up party, she hardly knows anyone, and it would be so sweet of you to help her feel at ease!" Without giving him a chance to demur she added, "You'll enjoy talking to her, I know you will, for she's most knowledgeable about poetry, about music. . ."

To Regina she whispered to please help entertain Lucio because the poor boy was so very awkward and needed to be encouraged. "Now do as you're told," she added with just the right touch of severity when the girl made a little moue of distaste. "A *lady* has to learn to be gracious to all her guests, not just the ones she likes. Go on, march. And don't you dare be choosy. Not in *my* house, miss!"

Her eyes traveled around the drawing room and the study beyond, where the older people were playing cards, then scanned the brightly lit foyer and entrance hall. Still no sign of Adam. But Regina and Lucio were actually talking together in the embrasure leading to the balcony. She could see that Regina was being dutifully pleasant and that Lucio was coming out of himself a little. A good beginning. The girl could do a lot worse. Of course, she wouldn't be sixteen until summer and it was still too soon for serious matchmaking. But Lucio, for all his dependence on his stepmother, was of age, technically a grown man. Never undervalue the enslaving effect on a grown man of a very young, truly virginal, nubile woman. Once enslaved, and safely married, he would to his dying day see his wife as the child bride he'd initiated into the mysteries of conjugal love. He would think of her as totally his, and in return would be totally hers. Like her own Leon.

Clearly the time was coming for her to have another serious talk with Regina's mother.

Having disposed of one responsibility, she went on to the next. She hunted down Regina's brother Kuba and led him over to the alcove where the two Silberstein girls, Bela and Emmy, had converged on a rather supercilious Henryk Meisels. "My dears, I'd like you to meet my nephew. He and his sister are going to play for us later on." Since the time when she and Eugenia had drawn up their invitation list, she had been told on good authority that Silberstein *père,* the handsome Miecio's eldest brother, was giving away a factory with each of his wall-eyed daughters. She wondered whether either Henryk or Kuba knew this.

Henryk had risen at her approach and she thought fleetingly, her expert eye taking note of the cut of his Prince Edward jacket, approving his manners and the ease with which he handled himself, "Now here is a young man who knows exactly what he wants and is going to get it. A pity he's not in the family—I should have enjoyed helping launch him, too. . . ." Then, as he bowed over her hand, his eyes managed to convey a message of such bold intensity that she could not mistake its meaning. She flushed and became unsure. Henryk might be a prince among men, but keep the young girls out of his reach! When he did marry, as eventually his kind always did, unless he met his match his wife would very soon be in for some difficult times. So much for handsome, ambitious men.

"Adam tells me," she said presently, "that you've been living abroad. What brings you back to Warsaw, may I ask?"

"Why, the beautiful women, of course!" The naked provocation in Henryk's glance belied the silk of his voice. "No city in the world has women as beautiful as ours. Let's just say I came back to feast my eyes."

One of the Silberstein girls—Salome found it hard to remember which was which—giggled. "Ooooh, you talk like a poet, *Pan* Henryk!" She appealed to her sister. "Doesn't he talk just like a poet, Emmy? And such a flatterer!" There was a brief, embarrassed silence while Henryk and Kuba exchanged pointedly pained glances. "Oh, my," floundered Bela, "Did I say something wrong? I'm always saying something wrong. . . ."

Marek Pozner had come alone a little while earlier and had by now managed to insinuate himself between Lucio and Regina. But his father sent his regrets, and Missy and *Pani* Konstancja were among the late arrivals. Mother and daughter were hardly speaking to each other, for there had been quite a scene between the girl and her parents during the afternoon, starting at the luncheon table and eventually developing into a battle royal.

At table Missy had flatly announced that she would not go along with her parents' plans for her; she was not going to become the social butterfly they expected her to be. Now that her formal schooling was over and that she'd also had a taste of Paris during the past season, what she was demanding was not more money for clothes—which they would have been delighted to give her—but a chance to study at one of the Western universities that admitted women. "And why not, if you please?" she wanted to know. They were sending her brother, who didn't even care about going. Then why keep her back?

Because she was a girl, that was why, her father said. Girls didn't need a university education. What for? Was she going to start earning her own living? "Or maybe you're about to cut your hair and take up smoking cigarettes and become a feminist?" Of course, he admitted, if a woman were so hopelessly plain she couldn't hope to marry at all, that might make a difference. If she were a hunchback, say, or had a cleft palate and a harelip. But she, Missy Pozner! Out of the question!

Missy said, "That's the silliest bunch of reasons I ever heard! I want to study so I can learn things, that's why. The world is so full of things I don't know. . . ."

For once Marek sided with her. If his sister wanted to become a bluestocking, that was her business. But their father's only answer was to pound the table and shout that if his children didn't stop being impertinent he'd cut their allowances. Marek subsided. But Missy remained defiant. She spat out that being left without money would suit her fine for then she'd have a really good reason to start earning her own way. And to do that she'd be needing a higher education, all the education she could get, and to finance it she would sell all the jewelry they'd ever given her for when she was married. At that her father became apoplectic, and they were shouting at each other, and he ended up ordering her to her room like a naughty child.

Vaguely, as she flounced up the stairs, Missy heard her mother plead with him that a girl her age couldn't be handled by means of threats and punishment. She hardly bothered to listen. She slammed her door so hard the mirrors in the hall swayed on their hooks. Then she locked herself in, pulled out the forbidden novel of the moment, which happened to be Balzac's *Memories de deux jeunes mariées,* and escaped into the heroine's fortuitous escape.

Every few pages she would stop reading and begin to daydream. She reviewed all the old avenues of escape she had ever considered, and how once she, too, had schemed to find freedom by marrying her tutor. Only unlike the tutor in Balzac's novel, Adam Fabian was no impoverished foreign nobleman, and besides, fond as they were of each other, she was beginning to understand that whatever romantic interest in him she might once have had, had been generated mainly by perversity.

She revived various other fantasies: How she would get even with her parents by marrying a titled roué, a chic wastrel who would enthusiastically help her squander the family fortune, or else a Catholic, a real honest-to-God one and not merely a "paper *goy*"—her own private term of derision for anyone who, like her own people, had converted for practical reasons. If she married a real Catholic it would just about kill Papa, and serve him right. She might even start giving lavishly to the Church. . . . Thus

Missy embellished her dreams of revenge. But very soon the game began to pall, especially since deep down she knew perfectly well that she had no intention of cutting off her nose merely to spite her pretty face.

In the end, out of sheer boredom, she consented—but only after her mother had sworn that Papa was staying home—to dress for the party. She pulled out one of the Worth gowns *Pani* Konstancja deplored as too plain—ice green brocade with an off-the-shoulder décolletage and a real wasp waist, and rang for her maid to dress her hair in the new flat Cleo de Merode style everyone said was so glamorous. The maid also laced her corsets tight enough for the wasp waist to fit properly, which was a great nuisance, but worth it.

When she was ready, the young woman staring back from her mirror looked tall and lithe, the skin of her neck and arms a matte amber against the green silk, her high, young breasts filling out the artfully close-fitting bodice, the tiny waist accentuating the roundness of her hips, and even her long legs somehow, thanks to the couturier's art, clearly suggested under the folds of sweeping skirt drawn smooth in front and flowing into a short train in the back.

"My, but you look lovely, Miss," the maid pronounced approvingly. "Almost sinful lovely, I'd say."

"Do I really?" Missy, who was holding up one long gold-and-pearl earring and one small diamond stud and trying to decide which to wear, suddenly made up her mind. "In that case I'll wear the long ones. That ought to make me look really wicked!" She was hoping for trouble tonight.

Trouble, she soon regretfully decided, was not likely to materialize at the Grossgliks' party. But her mood was such that she felt completely detached from the roomful of people most of whom she knew almost too well, and this made her quite maliciously perceptive. Left briefly to herself after her mother had gravitated to the card game in the library, she stood alone in the archway between the two rooms, surveying and categorizing the guests and making uncharitable mental notes.

There across the long drawing room were the Silberstein twins, overdressed as usual in formal ball gowns with long trains and an abundance of flounces, bows, and silk flowers for decoration. The gowns were identical except that one was pink and the other blue, the last word in high fashion and both equally unbecoming. The sisters seemed to be working feverishly to keep the two young men they had cornered from getting away, and for once Missy pitied them instead of feeling superior. Their look of desperate animation was something she had by now grown able to recognize. Indeed, far more attractive girls than Bela and Emmy wore it at parties. It was the eager "for sale" look which was one reason for her own rebellion, and it made her feel ashamed of her own sex.

Next she took stock of the available bachelors, and distaste rose up in her like a hot wave of nausea. A few of them she did not know, or knew only slightly, but for the most part, what a revolting lot! Her own foolish brother, Lucio Kronenberg, a dozen others like them. And coming toward her right now—coming *at* her, as it were—was that insufferable bore she'd been dodging everywhere this past month, Adolf Scheibler.

Adolf had a ferret face and the bearing of a prince royal, his arrogance made somehow worse by the fact that, having been educated abroad, he now affected a faintly foreign accent, as if determined to remind one of his Prussian ancestry. She had loathed him on sight but he would not be discouraged. For the Scheiblers, who had large factories both in Lodz and in Pabianice, were now branching out into banking, and a merger with the house of Pozner would make everybody happy. *Everybody but me!* thought Missy dismally, *but what do I matter? If I weren't Maurice Pozner's only daughter I could have a face like Cleo de Merode herself and he wouldn't give me a second look!* Determined to be as rude to Adolf as she knew how, she deliberately turned her back on him—and found herself facing Adam, who at last had arrived.

If Missy's mood was one of gloom, Adam's was blackness itself. For the past few hours he had been in a state of disembodied unreality, and only his mother's distressed pleas that he couldn't, he really and truly couldn't affront the Grossgliks by staying away altogether had finally persuaded him to take himself in hand. His meeting with Olek had left him not merely bewildered but stupefied. He was like a man coming out of the anesthetic after serious surgery, before the anesthetic has begun to wear off. That this was also the beginning of healing, he had no way of knowing.

In her state of heightened awareness Missy saw at once that he was no more ready to enjoy himself than she was. This suited her perfectly: he could be made to serve as her refuge. She gave him a mirthless, knowing smile. "Quite a circus, don't you find it so? Whatever would the old ladies do for entertainment if they didn't have us to—to put on the auction block?"

Adam, his mind still a million miles away, looked vague. "Auction block? Whatever are you talking about?"

"Oh, you're hopeless! Don't tell me you really don't know!" She continued smiling. "Why, this is the marriage market in operation." And she began to chant in rapid sing-song like an auctioneer: "What am I bid for one poor but dishonest young man, ready, willing and able to marry daughter of a counting house? . . . Going for a song: rich troublesome virgin . . . first acceptable candidate for junior partner gets her . . . ! Come to think of it, you're an acceptable candidate for a junior partner, Adam. Or didn't you even know?"

"Missy, stop talking like a character out of a novel."

She laughed aloud, and the sound was not pleasant. "You don't believe me, do you? Well, for your information I've heard Mama and Papa and the Silbersteins discuss these things dozens of times. I'd hear my name, so naturally I'd listen at the keyhole. Oh, don't look so shocked—how else do you think a *jeune fille bien elevée* learns things? I've heard your name mentioned, too, don't think I haven't. There's nothing Mama and Papa would like better than to see me safely settled with a hardworking, responsible husband—so naturally you were considered. I think maybe they've given up on us, though, so just be glad you've made yourself invaluable to Papa in other ways. But I'm not the only heiress in this assemblage, not by a long shot."

He was looking incredulous. "I still think you're just talking to hear yourself talk." And yet, suppose she was right. He glanced about the room. Most of the faces were unfamiliar to him and he saw that there were more girls here than men. He also remembered the great fuss Salome had made over a new suit for him, and his mother's frantic anxiety of an hour ago. Was she, too, then, in on some kind of conspiracy? It was an idea he shied away from, and in his present frame of mind the whole thing was too much for him to cope with.

"If what you say is true, Missy, I'm leaving. Now. At once."

"What, and abandon me to the wolves?" Her laughter died, the malice of her smile vanished, and she put a detaining hand on his arm. "Please, please stay. You're my friend and I trust you, Adam. You can't possibly know how much I need a friend right now. Papa and I have been perfectly beastly to each other and nothing's right. . . ."

Even when she had been his pupil and so full of posturing it had often been hard to take her seriously, Adam had suspected she was really quite unhappy at home. Now he sensed in Missy's whole attitude a desperation that was not to be shrugged off. Concern over her won out, it began to act as an antidote to his own misery. "All right, I'll stay and watch over you." She brightened a little and he went on, doing his best to console her, "Believe me, Missy, every thinking person has these moments of being out of sorts with the world, even, I suspect, a young woman born with a golden spoon in her mouth."

"You think that's all it is—a kind of *Weltschmerz* or something? I wish it *were* that simple! But my father . . . he makes me hate just to be a woman! You don't really know how it is. . . ."

But he did know. This had been Wanda's battle, and recently he had begun to suspect it was also his sister Idka's, though not so intense. "If you're really serious," he said against his better judgment, "there are better ways of dealing with it than fighting with your parents."

"Then tell me how. Sometimes I think my only chance of escape is through marriage. To a good friend like you, who'd leave me alone and whom I would leave alone." She made another attempt at flippancy. "Remember how once I said you could do worse than marry me? Maybe you should offer to do just that. Believe me, it would be a kindness. And come to think of it, I wouldn't make you such a bad wife."

"Missy, dear, please be serious."

"I'm—almost serious." For the first time in the years he had known her he saw her eyes filming over with tears even though her face remained controlled. "When I was younger, for a while I was crazy about you. But this is something else—let's call it a business proposition. We like each other, we respect each other, so why not? Marrying me would make you rich, while all I'd be asking is to be free. I really wouldn't be a lot of trouble."

He was more and more uncomfortable. "Missy, you shouldn't joke about things like this. You don't know what you're saying. A girl your age—you should be thinking of falling in love. Believe me, you'll feel different tomorrow. . . ."

"In other words, you wouldn't marry me no matter what?" In a final flare-up of frustration and malice she added, "Not even if I threatened to get Papa to fire you for it?" He blinked, and instantly ashamed she said quickly, "Don't listen to me, I just said that to be mean. Papa really does need you in his business and he's much too hardheaded-practical to sack someone he needs just because I make a scene. Besides," she laughed, her good humor miraculously restored by her outburst, "I suspect he's much too fond of you to want to saddle you with me for a wife! We'll forget we ever had this conversation, and I'll start . . . no, I'll continue to look elsewhere."

He was desperately sorry for her. Poor Missy, poor little rich girl suffering from the increasing malaise of the woman of her generation. Judging by her performance of a moment ago she could easily, unless she found an outlet for her intelligence and energy, turn vicious like one of those highly bred but poorly trained guard dogs. He thought back to all the talks they'd had in the past, remembered trying to persuade Olek that perhaps the Pozner girl's salvation would be to bring her into some sort of underground work. He also remembered Olek's hesitation and now understood it. No matter how badly the movement needed patrons, needed money, it could not afford to expose itself to well-wishers who were ruled by mood and whims.

He was still thinking about all this when he saw Salome come to the center of the drawing room. She clapped for silence. "My dear friends, you've been invited to a musicale, and now we shall indeed have some music." She gestured for Regina to come forward and announced that her niece Miss Segal would give them some Chopin. "The *Minute Waltz* and the *Butterfly Étude* for a starter." The audience clapped politely. Kuba disengaged himself from the Silberstein girls and came over to the piano to turn pages for his sister. Later on they were going to play duets.

Adam hastily found seats for Missy and himself, then observed Henryk Meisels fidgeting to make himself comfortable on a delicate gilt salon chair scaled for people of another century. He kept crossing and recrossing his long legs while his fingers began a restless drumming and his handsome face settled into an expression of bland boredom. Emmy and Bela sat on either side of him.

Regina acknowledged the applause with a bow and a smile that had just the correct suggestion of shyness. She hadn't learned the music by heart and played with that prim correctness that bespeaks the amateur of any age. But her youth, her grace, her unspoiled beauty were exerting their own special effect. At the end of the first number the applause, especially among the men, was enthusiastic and spontaneous.

"She'll never make a musician, but give her a year or two and all males for miles around will be eating out of her hand," Missy remarked dryly, under cover of all the hubbub. "You should have seen my brother when he was talking to her—he was positively drooling, though usually he likes his women a bit riper. As for that Henryk What's-his-name, oh-oh-oh!" Actually she was embroidering a bit, mainly because it annoyed her that Henryk, with whom she had flirted outrageously at a party the previous week, should show interest in someone else. "Did you see how blasé he looked when she started playing? Well, look at him now!"

To his own surprise Adam reacted with something close to anger. "Really, Missy, you exaggerate every little thing. My cousin Regina is hardly more than a child and neither Marek nor Henryk could be seriously interested in her."

"You think not?" Missy's eyebrows quirked upward. "Well, that simply tells me something about you, too." For here, she realized, was jealousy—that pure, all-inclusive, primitive male reaction, even though not yet consciously directed—and her own female instincts caused her to recognize it even though she was not experienced enough to pin the proper tag on it. "Be that as it may," she added, cryptically, she hoped, "it's beginning to look as though the evening might turn out interesting after all."

And if Adam was stupid enough, she added to herself, he could interpret this as a reference to the musical program.

❧ *Ten* ❧

ALTHOUGH when she came out to play she managed to convey an impression of charming diffidence, beneath the shy exterior Regina Segal was amazingly calm. Whatever misgivings she might have initially harbored were already half dispelled by the attention she had been receiving, and not merely from Lucio, who to her was an old shoe, but from other, attractive, and more worldly men. Marek Pozner with his talk about a string of polo ponies—and a suggestion she might enjoy watching him play sometime—had intrigued her. And she had found Henryk Meisels' subtle compliments more heady than wine. She was not drunk on them, at least not yet, but she was savoring a delightful foretaste of feminine power which more than countered her uncertainty about her ability to hold an audience.

Young as she was, she took tremendous pride in whatever she did and was determined to make people admire her. All day long she had kept firmly in mind her piano teacher's words, intended to bolster her self-assurance. "Don't worry about your audience—most of them know a lot less about music than you do." And although, just as Missy had been quick to observe, she was not, and never would be, musician enough to be at one with her instrument, she struck no wrong chords and missed none of the grace notes and her tempi were all correct. At a time when musicales were very much the vogue, so that people were exposed to a good deal of really dreadful playing, Regina's performance came to her listeners as a pleasant surprise. When she finished there was a murmur of approbation followed by applause sufficiently spontaneous to make her believe it was for her artistry.

Adam Fabian's initial reaction to the performance had been much like Missy's. He resented having their conversation interrupted, resented being part of a captive audience—resented, in fact, everything about the occasion. But as the minutes passed he forgot to listen critically. His head began to fill with other sounds, echoes of other voices, and imperceptibly the girl at the piano, the child he had known all his life who was a child no longer, fused in his mind's eye with a memory out of the past, a memory that lay buried under everything else that had happened since, to mold him into what he now was.

Looking at the delicate profile he was reminded of the time Leon had first brought his future bride to Bluma and Jacob's to meet the relatives. He remembered himself as he'd been then, a boy in his mid-teens entranced for the first time by a woman's beauty. He turned from Regina to Salome, still lovely but so familiar now that nothing about her was mysterious or exciting any longer, then back to the familiar-unfamiliar figure who, if not Salome's daughter in the flesh, was surely her daughter in spirit. And exactly as once he'd sat at his parents' table sensing the sap of his manhood flow for the first time, so once again he gave himself up to pure sensation. The sensation was woman-hunger. He hadn't experienced it in so long that only a few hours ago he had been ready to swear he would never experience it again. It was as though he had been dead and had just come back to life.

When Regina stood up to make her bow after several encores, she was immediately surrounded, everyone promptly forgetting that there was to be a second part to the concert. Salome herself was too experienced a hostess to try to discipline her guests and only hoped Regina's brother would forgive the unceremonious way he was being scratched off the program. But when she started apologizing, Kuba, to her intense relief, only laughed. "Happily I don't share my little sister's penchant for showing off. Besides, no one seems to feel any further need for formal entertainment, myself least of all." And indeed no one had remained seated. Chairs scraped and already were being miraculously whisked back into their accustomed formal groupings, fresh tea was being carried in along with new mounds of little cakes, and a dozen conversations started at once.

Regina now seemed easily the most popular girl in the room, outshining even Missy, the matrimonial catch of the season.

" 'Twas ever thus," Salome whispered to her sister, surveying her handiwork and finding it good. "The freshest bud is the one to which the bees will swarm." Henceforth, she felt, her niece would have more invitations than she would be permitted to accept. Her social future seemed assured.

Salome wished she could have said as much for Adam, but unfortunately her nephew was making very little effort to be sociable. She saw with a certain amount of concern that he, too, had gravitated toward his young cousin, which was one sure way of getting him nowhere, especially inasmuch as others in the group—Henryk and Marek and Kuba—were old familiars and Missy the only other girl.

Considering the whole basic purpose of the party, she decided she must get him away from that charmed circle where obviously he was too much at ease, and get him tactfully into circulation. She surveyed the various knots of people talking together, noting carefully who was where and making a battle plan. Then she went into action. Signaling for Eugenia to spell her at the tea table once more, she started threading her way across the room toward the animated group around the piano and was just in time to hear Henryk Meisels invite Regina and Kuba, Adam and Missy and Marek to be his guests at the Philharmonic a fortnight hence. "Ysaye, the greatest violinist of them all, will be the soloist. I have a box. Afterwards we can all go on to supper at that new place that's just opened," and he named Warsaw's most fashionable *boîte* of the moment.

This was Salome's cue to interrupt. "It sounds delightful, but my dear *Pan* Henryk, whatever can you be thinking? I don't know what may be considered proper in the West these days, but here at home our young ladies don't accept invitations without their parents' permission! And what about a chaperone?"

But Henryk was ready for her. "Why, you're just one jump

ahead of me," he answered smoothly, "for I was on the point of coming to speak to you. Won't you and your husband do me the honor of being my guests as well?"

Disarmed, she forgot she had been meaning to break them up and even tried not to remember that Leon hated restaurants and late suppers and would have to be coaxed and cozened. But of course it would be a perfectly simple matter to handle Leon: all she need say was that they must do this for the young people's sake. "In that case, *Pan* Henryk, I don't see why we can't arrange it. In fact, I shall myself speak to *Pani* Pozner and my sister-in-law."

Inwardly Regina heaved a sigh of relief. Wheedling permission out of her parents might have proved troublesome. How much simpler to have Salome take care of everything! As her aunt linked her arm in Adam's, preparing to lead him away, Regina whispered to him, "Now if I can just tell Mama *you'll* be along, she won't even give Kuba orders to watch me like a hawk!" For good measure she fluttered her long lashes and smiled up at him archly. "Let's say you will be my bodyguard. Or better still, my knight errant. That's it! Will you be my knight errant, Cousin Adam?" Afterwards she could not imagine what made her say such a silly thing, what made her flirt with her serious, earnest, terribly grown-up cousin, especially when there were so many more interesting fish in the sea—except that he had never before paid her the slightest attention, so perhaps it was for the fun of finding out if she could make him do what she wanted.

Obviously she could. Because as soon as he was decently able, he broke away and came back to her. And later in the evening he promised, awkwardly, she thought, and with rather absurd formality, to call for her—no, for her and Kuba both—on the night of the concert. "I'll promise your mother to take very good care of you," he added gravely.

Just as gravely Regina thanked him. But she was fighting down an irresistible urge to giggle. One of Aunt Salome's long string of *caveats,* delivered on some other occasion, flashed through her mind. "There's nothing wrong with flirting—what pretty girl doesn't?—but you must also realize it's unkind, sometimes even downright cruel, to try and deliberately turn a man's head just for the pleasure of knowing that you can. Especially when you also know nothing can come of it! Men have feelings, too, after all. . . ." Apparently men not only had feelings but wore their hearts on their sleeves, she reflected. And now it seemed she could make them lose their composure just by crooking her little finger. She repressed the giggle as unsuited to her newly discovered sense of power.

After that night Adam was unable to get his little cousin out of his mind. Another man, more worldly, more knowledgeable, might have been instantly alerted by such an unbidden surge of feeling. Henryk, for instance, had he suspected the turmoil his old friend was going through, might have warned, "Take care, you may be mistaking the juice of your loins for your heart's blood!" But Adam was sharing his thoughts with no one, Henryk least of all, and was, moreover, totally without protective armor against an emotional reawakening.

As so often during his times of stress or crisis, his sleep was crowded with recurring dreams. Again and again he was following a woman whose head was turned away so that he could never catch a glimpse of her face. She was tall and quick, and as she moved on she laughed softly, and beckoned to him, and he followed. Then the laughter would change, grow harsh, derisive, and the figure stiffened and although he still followed he knew she had no welcome for him, for this was Wanda leaving him forever without so much as a backward glance, moving surefooted on toward high perilous ground which she seemed able to climb effortlessly while his own feet stumbled so that he was being left farther and farther behind. And he would wake, not rested but stiff and aching as after tremendous, unrewarding effort. And it would still be dark in his room and he would feel a desperate need for more sleep but feared to close his eyes lest the fruitless chase begin again.

But he drifted off in spite of himself, and now the sun warmed the high ground and birds soared and swift mountain streams leaped down the craggy slopes and around him was the kind of beauty only folklore and fairy tale promise. But as in any good folk tale, nothing was ever quite within reach. First he must cross a torrent, and no bridge in sight, and he knew, as one does in dreams, that to ford it could be dangerous. Dare he take the risk? As if in answer a treetop bent down of its own accord, and he sensed that all he need do was reach up, and the branches would swing him across. But it took him too long to decide, and when he finally did he could no longer touch the branches. And again he heard harsh laughter, and woke up, and it was morning.

The two dreams, with infinite variations, kept succeeding each other until he felt like a superstitious old peasant convinced that in the darkness the patterns of his future were in some mysterious way being laid out. He was annoyed at himself but unable to shake the feeling. Later on in life he would think back to this period as a kind of dying and total rebirth, a resurrection in the best tradition of folk heroes who must let themselves be hacked to bits before they are sprinkled with magic water and restored to new vigor. And just as the folklore figures always come alive again strangely stronger, so did he feel changed. He was restless yet tremendously aware of self, as though the slate had been wiped clean and was now ready for fresh writing, as though all his senses had grown keener in preparation for some new experience he only dimly anticipated, yet knew must come soon.

There was no further word from Olek. But reports kept coming of mounting unrest in the provinces, Lodz especially, and Adam suspected that Olek and Maryla and whoever had come with them might still be fairly close by somewhere. There were also whispered hints of solidarity demonstrations in Warsaw. Then, toward the end of the week, Idka took him aside, and after making sure, by the rattling sound of pots, that their mother was in the kitchen, whispered she had something to discuss with him.

"It's about Izzy. I heard there's to be a . . . what they call a housecleaning at the Pawiak. To make room for new arrivals, on account of all the arrests. They say they're going to ship all last year's politicals to Moscow, to the Butyrki Prison. You know what that means?"

He did know. Butyrki was infamous. And if a man survived it, he was generally given five years in Siberia just for good measure. "Are you sure, Idka?" he questioned. "Who told you?"

She evaded his question. "You hang around the prison, you can't help hearing things. You get to know people and they talk to you. No, I'm not sure, you can never be sure what they'll do till they do it. But oh, Adash, I'm sick just thinking about it. That trip into Russia by convoy, by *kibitka*. . . . They die like flies on the way." She burst into silent weeping, the tears rolling unheeded down her puffy cheeks. "We may never see our Izzy alive again!"

Awkwardly, because gestures of affection were never easy between them, he put his arm around her heaving shoulders. "Shhh, crying won't help." He added anxiously, "Does Mama know?"

She shook her head. "I've been afraid to say anything, afraid of what it might do to her." She lowered her voice still more, even though no one was near. "But that's not all. There's talk about a prison break. I keep thinking I ought to be doing something, helping. . . ."

"A prison break at the Pawiak!" Knowing so much better than she what effort, what organization it took to carry off the least political maneuver, remembering the slaughter of the innocents that last year's demonstrations had turned into, he was instantly alarmed. "But, Idka, that's lunacy! Have you any idea what's involved? When has there ever been a successful break at the Pawiak, or the Citadel either? Yes, I know, once in a blue moon a single prisoner does escape. But that's always some steeled revolutionary with years of experience, someone who's facing a death sentence anyway or at least life at hard labor so he hasn't got much to lose. But a mass action like this. . ."

She had stopped crying. She answered uncertainly, "They've been saying it would stir the people up—that it would be worth risking because it's a sacrifice for the Motherland. . . ."

Now all his senses were mobilized by fear and he knew he must stop her before she could add her share to precipitating a disaster. "These are just words," he said coldly. "Words and more words. Yes, and your friends are like children playing grown-up games they know nothing about. Keep out of it, I tell you!"

She looked at him in innocent amazement, hurt, reproachful, but also, he thought, with contempt. "You didn't always feel this way. You used to understand when someone risked every-thing for the cause. And I . . . I used to think you were so brave and wonderful. . . ."

She had touched a live nerve and he reacted instantly, without thinking. "I used to be a snotnose, too," he barked, then said contritely, "I'm sorry, I didn't mean that the way it sounded. But, Idka, Idzia, listen to me! You know so little about un-derground work. And even less about the people you talk to on the line. Suppose it's a provocation—that's not impossible! Be-lieve me, if you want what's best for Izzy, don't get mixed up in harebrained schemes." On inspiration he added, "Look, I'll make a bargain with you. If there's an ounce of truth in the whole rumor I'll find out for you, I give you my word of honor." He was whistling in the dark, but surely there must be some way of checking—possibly through Olek's uncle. The more he thought about it the more convinced he became that he must again con-tact the old printer. "In the meantime, not a word to Mama," he added quickly as Bluma's steps were heard in the corridor from the kitchen. "Promise me."

Idka sighed like a child too worn out with crying to put up more resistance. "All right. I don't want just to make trouble, honestly I don't." Their mother, coming in to lay the table for supper, found them like this, apparently deep in an absorbing conversation, and she looked at them fondly, pleased that her children should have so much to say to one another.

🌿 *Eleven* 🌿

Later on it occurred to Adam there might be yet another reason why he should visit Olek's relative, and this without delay. Could Olek's mission, whatever it was, be in some way endangered by the impending action around the Pawiak? The more he thought about it the more convinced he became that this was no time to indulge in guessing and speculation. Olek must be warned. He set out for the Praga district where Jacek lived.

As always, the old printer made him welcome, but this time heard him out without comment and seemed strangely uncommunicative. For once he did not urge Adam to consider attending meetings or otherwise contribute his time and effort. Nor did he offer the usual glass of wine. "What you've told me is very enlightening, and I thank you. Be sure and tell that sister of yours to stay out of crowds, understand? Tell it to her in just these words: *for the time being stay out of crowds.* Also, tell her to spread the word." He gave no further explanation, as if anxious to see his guest gone.

He stood up. "One thing is sure," he volunteered. "We're sitting on a powder keg. Set a match to it too soon, and we'll all be blown to hell and gone."

Adam nodded. He, too, stood up, shook hands, said goodbye. As he started down the stairway he passed a couple of men on their way up. They looked vaguely familiar. But, scrupulously, he made no effort to remember where he might have seen them, or with whom.

He relayed Jacek's message to Idka verbatim and hoped its cryptic words would be persuasive. Apparently they were, since the rest of the week passed and the threatened prison break failed to materialize. Nor were the prisoners themselves moved, at least not for the time being. He knew then that his suspicion had been correct: the rumor had been a plant, a provocation, and he had somehow played a part in helping expose it. For a day or two he felt good about it.

Then he put the whole episode out of his mind, for unexpectedly his own life took a fresh turn. Maurice Pozner sent word he wanted to see him on a matter of considerable urgency. And there they were again, facing each other in the old man's study after the midday meal, Maurice relaxing with his glass of port and his cigar, Adam, as in the past, still feeling absurdly like the schoolboy tutor working for a few coppers a day and a square meal.

But this time he sensed something unaccustomed in the air.

"I've sent for you," Maurice began once Adam had as usual declined a Corona-Corona but accepted the port, "because it's time for a change. I've been training and training you until there's nothing left for you to learn sitting here in Warsaw on your skinny behind. So now I have other plans for you." He blew a series of his beautifully precise smoke rings. "But first let me ask, how are things for you at home? Mother recovered, I hear? Emergency over? Good. I hope that means your presence here is no longer urgently required. That you're free to travel. How much notice will you need if I decide to send you away?"

Startled, but thinking in terms of the Pozner mills in Lodz or Piotrkow or Zgierz, Adam said he could be ready in the time it took to attend to his laundry and pack a portmanteau. "And," he smiled, "get my mother used to the idea of my leaving. She still clings a little, but she's a lot better. I'll just promise her to come home as often as I can."

More smoke rings. "I wouldn't make any such rash promises if I were you." Pozner sat back, eyed his protégé with considerable amusement, and dropped his bombshell. "Because where you're going, you won't be exactly within easy reach. My agent for the Caucasus is retiring—never was much good to me anyway. Took too many bribes from the Persian cotton merchants and it was costing me a pretty penny. With you I won't have such troubles. So. You'll be working out of my Erivan office."

"Erivan!" Adam repeated stupidly. "The Caucasus! You mean you're putting me in charge? But I never. . . ."

"I know, I know," the old man cut him off impatiently. "Don't start telling me it's too much responsibility. I'm aware of your lack of experience. But there's precious little you haven't learned about long-staple cotton. Also you're cautious, smart, and mainly you're a man of your word. With those Asiatics, believe me, that's what really counts. They've an ethic all their own, and they'd just as lief knife you as look at you if you rub them the wrong way. Most Europeans do. Treat 'em like dirt, an inferior race. They're getting tired of it. You'll do nothing of the kind, so you'll get along well. Let alone the fact that I myself can trust you, which is a relief." He paused, letting Adam absorb everything he'd said. "Needless to say I'll be giving you a fat raise in salary—to which I'm sure you won't object."

He didn't specify the exact sum, and Adam was wondering whether to ask, when Pozner began to laugh. "One of these days you'll probably get too big for your breeches. And if I'm still alive then, there won't be room in my firm for both you and me. But then, who knows, I might even help you set up your own business. Better," he concluded, "than having you compete on the inside."

Adam looked—and was—genuinely scandalized. *"Pan* Pozner! You know I'd never do anything disloyal! I owe you too much!"

Pozner laughed harder. "Yes, I know you're a fool in some ways, my boy. But business is business. I also know you've got, as they say, enough conscience to sink ten popes. And yet sometimes it's men like you, the dreamers, who make the fortunes. One way or another, you'll end up either a millionaire or a pauper—for you there can be no middle ground. And whatever happens it won't hurt you to have a friend like me. Though damned if I know," he added, "why I feel about you the way I do. For if ever we have labor trouble while you're around, ten to one you'll be siding with the workers. . . ."

It was the first time Pozner had ever directly broached the subject of his beliefs to him, and instantly Adam was on his guard. "What makes you say that?" he asked, neither admitting nor denying anything.

"Because I know human nature. Because I'm not stupid, or blind, and I can see farther than my nose."

Having no comment to make, Adam made none.

With his second glass of port Pozner became expansive. "It took me a little time to decide whether to groom you for Lodz or for the East," he admitted. "And then I said to myself, way off in Erivan my young friend Fabian can't do himself—or me—any harm. Cotton in the bale doesn't march. It doesn't sing songs that tug at the heart and inflame the imagination. It doesn't have a brother still rotting inside the Pawiak."

"You're very well informed, sir," Adam said quietly.

"Let's just say I wasn't born yesterday. And now to change the subject. Can you be ready to leave in a fortnight? Will that be time enough for you to wind up your affairs?"

It was more than enough, and he knew he ought to be feeling flattered, elated, even dazzled. Except that he had no desire to leave. But his employer left him no choice, having already in his lordly manner pushed everything around to suit himself.

He even had the details of Adam's departure figured down to the last detail. "If you need ready cash, have my bookkeeper give you a draft on my bank. Don't try to be frugal—you'll be going into a wilderness and you'll want to go well provided. I doubt there's a single decent tailor anywhere in the Caucasus, so take enough clothes to last you and keep you comfortable the year round. If you don't, you'll be freezing and roasting by turns and that wouldn't do the business much good—your work would suffer." He roared at his own joke, the heavy gold watch chain across his belly shaking and shimmering with his merriment. "It's all settled then? Here's luck, my boy! I'll telegraph my man in Erivan to expect his replacement three weeks from Monday."

They drank to it. And all the while Adam kept wondering why this promotion—this big feather in his cap—should leave him so cold. The Caucasus offered the escape he needed, an honorable escape from everything that had lacerated him these past couple of years. It was his chance to remove himself for the time being not just from the social life his relatives were urging on him but from the political scene with its painful associations. It could be a Nirvana where emotion would cease to matter. Yet he would have rejected it if he could. Why? Surely there was no happiness for him in Warsaw. Then why this sudden sense of desolation?

During the following week the house on Nalewki Street was turned upside down with hustle and bustle. Adam must have a warm winter coat, so his father's greatcoat with the beaver lining and the otter collar, the "good" coat Jacob had hardly ever worn, was taken out of mothballs and sent away for refurbishing. He must have a second suit and an extra pair of shoes and woolens and socks, gloves and a fur cap, and some blankets. Bluma and her daughters made round after round of shops and market stalls, to say nothing of the almost daily visits to the bootmaker and the tailor—everyone knew you must ride herd on tradesmen or nothing would be ready on time, and to risk sending luggage on by freight later, well, it was common knowledge how things got lost or stolen on the railroad!

There was also interminable washing and ironing, sewing and mending, and in the meantime the house was filled with relatives and friends and neighbors eager to help and share in the excitement. For it wasn't every day that one of their own, a shabby son of the ghetto, traveled to a land only once removed from Arabian Nights country, a fairytale wilderness where the exotic was an everyday occurrence.

Even the widow Liebman came trudging up the stairs with a gift for him. "Here, I've baked you some cookies for the road. With real butter. In a tin they'll stay fresh for weeks." She turned to the Grossgliks, who were over that evening. "Imagine *Pani* Fabian's Adam going all the way to Asia to live!"

"The Caucasus is hardly Asia," Leon corrected gently. "Not even Asia Minor."

"Minor, major, what's the difference? It's all heathen country . . . Huns, Tartars, Turks. . ."

Salome interrupted to speak of more practical matters. "I've been meaning to ask you, Adash, do you need extra luggage?

You can borrow from us. Especially," she sighed, "since again it's beginning to look as though my poor darling won't be able to accompany me when I go to Eugenia this summer. So take what you want. Come by any time. If I'm not home, ask Miss Julia. She has the keys to the storeroom."

Since in spite of his employer's largesse Adam was anxious to be frugal with money, it was an offer he appreciated. The very next day on his way from the office he detoured to Count Berg Street. No one was home, the housekeeper informed him, though through the closed doors of the drawing room the strains of Chopin reached him. "That's just Miss Regina, come to practice like she does every day. If you want, I expect you can go right in."

Quietly, though aware of mounting excitement, he pressed the door handle and opened the door. Regina was too absorbed in what she was doing to hear him. She had just started to decipher Chopin's technically complex last *Ballade,* Opus 52, which she had finally coaxed her teacher into assigning to her. She was savoring the sound of the Bechstein, still perfectly in tune after the party, for it was an instrument infinitely superior to the old upright in her parents' house and a joy to practice on. She was also pretending that it belonged to her, as did the elegant room with all its treasures. The fantasy spun itself out until she was making believe she was mistress of everything here, that the maid answering the doorbell was her servant and she needn't even turn her head until her guest was announced. She went on playing.

Adam took her absorption for true artistic concentration, and respected it. He paused in the doorway and stood listening, eyes half closed. When he opened them again, it was to add visual pleasure to the enchantment he was already experiencing.

How lovely she is, he thought, sitting there unselfconscious and unobserved, intent only on her music! Even lovelier with the late sunlight framing her than she had seemed the night of the party—and of how many women could one say as much? No artifice—just freshness and youth, purity of line, perfection of natural coloring.

Regina did indeed make a charming picture. She was wearing

her school uniform, dark brown, severely plain except for a bit of white ruching at throat and wrists, the obligatory black apron covering the front of her dress and standing out like dark wings at her shoulders. Her hat and book bag had been thrown carelessly on a chair and obviously she hadn't bothered to primp, for her hair was tumbled, a dark tendril escaping to curl over the nape of her long, graceful, very white neck. The coquetry of the other night was as if dormant, and she seemed to him to be working with that total gravity and concentration young children sometimes show when there are no adults to watch them.

He was still undecided whether to speak to her and disrupt her mood when she broke off in mid-phrase and wheeled around on the piano stool. "Cousin Adam! Oh, dear, you should have given me warning! Here I've been playing so wretchedly—I'm really very bad at sight reading and was making the most of being alone. . . ."

He wasn't sure if she was apologizing for all the wrong notes or because she'd been caught out while making a game of what should have been serious work. He assured her there was no need for excuses; after all, he was the intruder. "Besides, I thought you did rather well. You should hear *me* when I first read a new piece!"

"I didn't know you played."

"The violin. Or at least I try. But there's never enough time, and the violin is a jealous master. I'm afraid I shall never do it justice."

"I'm sure you're being modest—at any rate, why not let me judge for myself? Perhaps we could try duets sometime. We do a lot of that at home, you know. Kuba and I play four hands, and Sundays friends drop in, a classmate of Kuba's who plays the cello and another who's quite a violist. We have chamber music whenever we can. It's fun. Bring your violin and join us. Or if you want, just come and listen. . . ."

Already in his mind he was conjuring up the picture, the tone, the sound of the music-making. He could see Regina surrounded by her brother's friends, every one of them a male. And as on the night of the party, primitive jealousy gripped him. "Shall I come this Sunday, then?" he asked, not caring whether his playing would measure up or not. "It may be my last chance for a long time. You've heard I was going away?"

She nodded and said how sorry she was. "And just as you and I are finally getting to know each other better!" She smiled up at him. "It's all settled, then? We'll expect you?"

"I'll be there. In case an extra violin isn't needed, at least I can turn pages for you."

"You could turn pages for me right now, if you would." Her smile became grown-up, knowing, wise. "Sight reading goes so much better if one doesn't have to keep stopping all the time!"

"Now why didn't I think of that myself?" he exclaimed. And the music began again, halting and haunting by turns, interrupted only when Miss Julia came in to light the lamps and remind him about the luggage. Adam nodded, saying he would wait for *Pani* Grossglik after all. He had never been able to make up his mind which of the *Ballades* was his favorite. Now he decided it was the Fourth.

The very next morning the newspapers came out with great swaths of white cutting across their front pages. The blank columns left by last-minute censorship were mute testimony that something was happening about which the Tsarate had no intention of informing an already hostile populace. But Warsaw was well schooled in reading blank spaces—this was indeed a stillness ready to break into storm.

Now at last the occasional rumblings reaching Poland from the four corners of the land turned into a steady underground roll, echoing hunger and poverty and a thousand daily cruelties, injustices driving the masses to a desperation that transcended fear. *Maybe it's true, what they whisper in secret meetings—that we've nothing to lose but our chains!* Thus yet another new word crept into the vocabulary of the disinherited. Solidarity. *Workers of the Empire, unite! Proletarians of all tribes and all subject nations, don't let the Autocrat divide you! Rise up! Organize! Demand your rights!*

At industrial centers everywhere, in large factories and small shops, from the vast Putilov Works in St. Petersburg to the textile compounds of Piotrkow and Pabianice and Lodz, activists had long been saying these things. Smuggled newspapers printed so badly they were barely readable had long been preparing the ground. *Organize! Make your demands heard! Refuse to work more than ten hours a day for less than it takes to feed your children! And if the bosses won't listen, strike!"*

But among the workers of Poland there had long been an odd sort of confusion. Who was their real enemy, they asked themselves? Why, the Tsar. But the bosses were Poles like themselves, or at worst Germans, or Polish Jews. Then how could striking against them help a revolt against the Autocrat of all the Russias? What did the one have to do with the other? It just didn't make sense.

Patiently, as best they could, the more sophisticated leaders tried to explain the class struggle to men and women who were barely literate. "It's like this: the rich are on the side of the rich, and never mind nationality. Bosses and Tsar's men work hand in glove, with the cops and the cossack doing their bidding. And our brethren, the poor, work and starve and get stepped on. And no one will help us unless we help ourselves."

It had long been slow, uphill, ungrateful work. Then circumstances became the teacher. Wages were cut because business was bad, and cut again when a sudden rush of orders made overtime possible. Either way there was never bread enough for the children. In the marketplace a man was found trying to sell his youngest son, and when asked how he could do such a thing, he answered, "How could I *not* do it? At least he'll be fed, and with the money he fetches I can feed the others. . . ."

One day, goaded beyond endurance, the second shift at the Silberstein ribbon-and-elastics factory refused to start their machines. Men and women sat at their looms with arms folded, and no amount of threats, pleading, cajoling by the foremen moved them. Later, during their brief supper break, they called a meeting in the open quadrangle of the factory compound. A speaker mounted an improvised rostrum not far from the great ornamental entrance gates. "Brothers and sisters!" he shouted, "today is a historic date, and you the history-makers because you dare stand up for your rights here and now. And what you dare today, all the workers of Lodz will dare tomorrow. So glory be to you. . . ."

From the sentry booth beyond the gates a soldier emerged. He was well trained, a marksman. There was a single shot, scarcely louder than a pellet of hail against a windowpane. The speaker's voice was cut off in mid-sentence. For the briefest moment he stood swaying, disbelief written on his face. Then slowly he crumpled and fell backward into the crowd.

The soldier did not live to tell about his exploit. He was set upon and torn limb from limb. That day, many things which the patient, dedicated organizers had never managed to explain adequately became suddenly clear to the working people of Lodz. For it had been a *Russian* soldier doing the killing, a *Russian* on guard over the Polish, albeit Jewish, boss's property. At the first sign of trouble the Silbersteins had turned for help to the archenemy.

Overnight, not just the Silberstein mills but the whole city was crippled by strikes, and for the second day in a row the newspapers carried great, eloquent white spaces on their front pages. It was not a revolution, not yet. But it was a mass expression of solidarity without precedent. No one dared make predictions, but people saw in what was happening a beacon of hope—hope for whatever they wished to see. Thus one man predicted a powerful trade-union victory, another the Commonwealth reconstituted, and still another an independent Polish monarchy. Yet for the moment the ultimate goal became less important than the immediate action. For the first time in years freedom was in the air. "We'll soon have the great Autocrat running for cover," people congratulated one another. "He's probably already wetting his pants!"

Early on Friday Maurice Pozner sent for Adam once more. "What do you know about the Lodz riots, boy?"

Adam's face became carefully blank. "Nothing. Nothing everyone else doesn't know. What makes you think I do?" Privately he had already come to the conclusion that Olek's trip into the country must indeed have had some immediate connection with what was happening, but this was certainly not his employer's business.

"The Silbersteins are fools," Pozner said emphatically. He

hadn't, of course, expected any other answer from young Fabian than the one he had gotten. "Running to the Russians at the first sign of trouble—that's suicide! If they can ever live it down it'll be more than they deserve! It's like . . . like dragging the Pope into an argument between two rabbis! Fools, I say! Why couldn't they let it remain a *Polish* quarrel in a *Polish* city?" As he spoke, working himself up into a passion, he all but convinced himself that he was a patriot first and a capitalist second. "You don't do this kind of thing unless you're really pushed to the wall. As a last resort—perhaps. In desperation, when all other measures have failed and you're facing an angry mob *and* bankruptcy, maybe. But before even trying to negotiate, never. Not in this day and age. This way . . . ayayay! The worst of it is we'll all be paying for their idiocy!"

Adam made no comment, and suddenly it came to the old man that perhaps he had spoken too freely. His manner changed, became more distant. "But that's not why I called you in. Tell me, how good are your connections among the weavers of Lodz?"

Take care, this may be a trap. "Connections, sir? Why, I've none at all. Oh, I did know a couple of them once, quite briefly. But that was a while ago." He hesitated, then decided on an outright lie. "I wouldn't even remember their names."

"Could that have been when you left the country so precipitately?" By his employee's startled look Pozner knew he had hit right, and smiled slyly. "Come, come, don't look so surprised, I was well aware of your movements at the time. How? Because your beautiful aunt approached me, among others, for help. She, at least, had the good sense to know she could trust me."

Adam said, less respectfully than was his custom, "If you're already so well informed, then why question me?"

"Because," Pozner said, "I have a lot invested in you. Too much to risk losing it all to patriotic ardor. So I propose to make sure you're not sucked into any ructions; doubly sure the police don't take it into their heads to pick you up just on account of your brother and your old friends. And so, my boy, I'm advancing the date of your departure for the East. By one week. There's a train leaving Sunday night. Reservations have been made for you. Be sure you're on it."

He had spoken in a tone that left no room for argument, but now that orders had been issued he became more conciliatory. "In case your things aren't ready, go see the tradesmen at once and tell them you're paying double. Let them work through the night, hire extra help. I personally will underwrite all expenses. As for anything still on your desk that's left undone, either it will be taken care of without you or we'll forward it."

But it was not the state of his wardrobe or the papers on his desk that mattered to Adam. The following night, Saturday, was the Ysaye concert, and on Sunday he had planned to make music at the Segals'. He could still take in the concert, but that would be all. He cursed silently. Until that moment he hadn't known how much he had let himself look forward to the afternoon with Regina. "But," he ventured, "couldn't I have just one extra day?"

The old man shook his head, pursed his mouth, looked grim. "I just finished telling you. Everything has been arranged. So please plan accordingly."

For the first time in his adult years Adam tasted the full bitterness of being an underling. He was enraged. And helpless. Pozner was well aware of this but it suited him to ignore it. "And by the way," he added, conscious of, and enjoying, his power, "whatever else happens between now and Sunday—are you listening and paying attention to me, Adam?—whatever happens I want you to keep your appointment to hear Ysaye. Your last night in town I want you to be seen in public, in young Henryk Meisels' box, in the company of my son and my daughter. Believe me, my boy, this is for your own good. The more conspicuous your presence, the better. I understand you're all going on to supper later? Fine, fine, couldn't be better. I'll see that your departure is toasted in the best champagne—now does that tempt you?"

Adam said furiously, "I had every intention of keeping that appointment, sir. There's no need to bribe me." At least he would have that much to remember of this encounter.

❦ *Twelve* ❧

REASON TOLD HIM he should go straight home, inform his mother about the change of plans, and put himself at her disposal for last-minute errands. But he needed to sort out his thoughts first. As he left the Pozner mansion he deliberately started in the direction of the Lazienki Gardens, detouring whenever it suited his fancy.

He would only be gone a year, yet he felt he was taking leave of a city he would not be seeing again, the city of his youth. How many landmarks there were! The trumpeter atop the old tower still announced the hours exactly as he had done when Adam was a schoolboy living by the clock. (The horse-drawn omnibuses, though, were now in competition with electric trolleys.) Fukier's wine shop, unchanged in Old Town, and around the corner from it, off the Market Square, Zapiecek Street. Who now occupied the attic that once had been Maryla's and Wanda's, he wondered. Other students? Other patriots working toward the next uprising?

At the gate to Lazienki he hesitated briefly, then turned and made his way to the fountain. Since it was high noon the benches were full of children with their nannies and governesses. A band of small boys chased each other round and round along the fountain's narrow ledge, the ledge where long ago he and Wanda had sat pressed close together in the evening quiet. A woman yelled, "Get down from there, you rascals! You'll slip and fall in, and then you'll get it!" The children laughed. Adam thought of

Wanda and their first kiss and was startled that he could remember it without the familiar stab of pain.

He left the gardens by another gate and headed in the direction of Pawiak prison. Sunday would be visitors' day, and he'd hoped to go with Idka and say goodbye to Izidore. Now his sister would have to go alone. He must find time to have one final talk with her. He must impress on her that these were truly dangerous days and she should try to stay out of trouble. He hoped she would listen.

He passed a couple of newspaper kiosks and saw how still the people stood as they queued up waiting for the latest papers to be delivered. Warsaw, generally so gay, so brash, so full of talk even in bad times, seemed to have withdrawn into itself, as though husbanding its energies for whatever lay in store. To a casual stranger it presented a blank, bland, closed face. Adam stopped at a bistro for coffee, and although the place was crowded got quick service from an idle waiter who complained that business was lousy—folks were forgetting to order, all they wanted was to read the papers while their first and only cup of "black" got cold. . . .

Adam mumbled an answer but was careful not to let himself be drawn into conversation. Cafés and restaurants and newspaper kiosks were favorite haunts of informers, and only a fool would take chances. For all he knew the waiter himself might be a stool pigeon. He began to wonder if Pozner weren't right, if the city were indeed girding itself for a demonstration of solidarity with the Lodz strikers. If so, was he glad or sorry to have to miss it? He would never find out. *I used to think you were so wonderful,* Idka had reproached him. Maybe he ought to be ashamed of his lack of fervor. Then again, maybe someday he would feel it again.

He finished his coffee, paid his bill, walked out. The closer he came to the Pawiak, the more he was struck by the marked increase in the number of beggars, ragpickers, itinerant tinkers, and junk peddlers crowding the sidewalks. Even the perennial flower vendors at street corners seemed to have multiplied. Their language was oddly literate, their voices had none of the hoarseness that comes with hawking one's wares day after day, year after year, in all kinds of weather.

One of the beggars accosted him, asking for alms in a tone totally lacking in the beggar's whine. "Give to a better cause than my own, brother." Adam emptied his pockets of silver. The man eyed him up and down, nodded, and whispered, "Thank the Lord the people understand, they understand they've got to give. Yes, the good people of Warsaw understand everything very well. . . ."

When at last he got back to Nalewki Street, he found his mother and Idka in heated argument.

"Why can't you just be like Rosie?" Bluma demanded. Then she tried pleading. "I want you to give me your word that when you're doing errands that's *all* you do, and then come straight home. Stay away from meetings, stay away from the Pawiak, you hear me? If you don't, something terrible will happen to you, I know it, I feel it!"

She was making no impression on her daughter. "But, Mama," Idka kept saying, "what can happen to me if I don't talk to anyone? Honest, I just listen. Sometimes I hear something the movement ought to know, something that counts. If what I do turns out to be useful, won't you be proud of me, Mama?"

"Proud!" Bluma cried. "I already got one hero to worry about! Two of you in prison I couldn't bear!" She became aware of Adam standing in the doorway and appealed to him. *"You* talk to her, Adash! Maybe with you she'll listen to reason!"

He said he would talk to Idka later but first there were things he must discuss with her. "Come into my room, Mama."

She followed him and he cleared a chair for her. "What a time for you to be leaving!" she lamented. "What shall we do if there's more trouble, and the head of the family away?"

"Why, you'll just manage without me," he assured her, and meant it. For he saw that with so many cares piling up his mother was responding by being her old self, strong again under the surface weaknesses because her brood needed her. "Besides," he pointed out, "you won't be exactly without help, should you need it. There's Uncle Leon. And Viktor—you can rely on him." He made a mental note that whatever else he might or might not have time to accomplish, there were things he must talk over with his brother. "Viktor, by the way, may get a lot further with Idka than ever I could. You know how she and I sometimes rub each other the wrong way."

She said yes, she knew this, but just the same hoped that during the week left to him he would make another attempt to reach his sister. "Sometimes, I've noticed, you two get along so well. Try catching her when she's feeling real good. . . ."

He sighed and shook his head. "Trouble is, Mama, I seem to've run out of time. In fact, that's what I must talk to you about in the first place. Something's come up, *Pan* Pozner changed my schedule and only just told me. I'm leaving day after tomorrow, Sunday night."

He had half expected an emotional scene but his mother surprised him. Sweeping aside all other considerations, she was suddenly interested only in his well-being. "Oh dear, in that case let's not waste any more time! So much still to do!" She bustled to the door. "Idka, Rosie," she called urgently, "Where are you? I've got a list of errands for you a mile long and you'll have to hurry!"

When she had sent them on their way Adam finally got her to sit down again. "Mama, the packing will get done somehow— it's really the girls I want to talk about. In a couple of years they'll have husbands to worry about them, but in the meantime, while I'm gone, it's all going to be up to you." Lightly he kissed her cool, flaccid cheek. "Should the question of marriage for either of them come up, the final say-so will have to be yours. Even if you write and ask my opinion, how can I answer sensibly unless I know the men in question?"

She was looking troubled. "With poor Idka, you know, it isn't going to be simple."

"But at least there'll be no need to go to a marriage broker hat in hand. I promised long ago I'd provide decent dowries for them, and I'm doing it. Fifteen hundred apiece for now, maybe more later."

"So much?" Bluma's eyes widened in amazement. "I had no idea. . . . How have you managed?"

He shrugged. "Pozner pays me well, but he's also invested for me here and there. I've been lucky. And you, Mama," he added, "are a good manager. So there."

"Oh, you're my good boy," she said, looking at last as though she were about to cry. "If only your father could have lived to see this. But he knew. He always knew."

Adam reflected with some bitterness how easy it was to be considered generous for giving lavishly of what one valued very little.

He had always got along well with Viktor; ever since Jacob's illness the two had been in the habit of talking over family matters and had no difficulty in doing so now. But with his sister things did not go so smoothly. When he finally got Idka alone the next morning she was as full of sting as a stand of nettles. "What, you expect me to sit here doing nothing, with the whole country ready to rise up? With Izzy waiting for a verdict on exile? And people being arrested right and left! Adam, you simply can't mean that!"

"You're worrying Mama to death," he merely said.

"I can't help it!" And she flung a phrase at him he recognized for having heard it long ago from Olek. "If everyone always only did what was safe, we might as well resign ourselves to living on our knees."

It had the force of an insult as well as a reproach, and he lashed out in self-defense, "You talk about things you know nothing about!" He was shouting.

"And you, about things you know very well but are trying your damndest to forget."

Again he responded cruelly and at random. "Hah! Just how much d'you think it will help the cause of independence for one witless girl to run around the streets asking for trouble?"

For a moment she looked as though she were going to hit him. Then her face crumbled, her eyes and nose got red, and in his fury he felt like telling her she should never cry except in the privacy of some dark private hole, for crying made her even uglier than she was.

Then instantly he began to feel ashamed. After all it was

through no fault of her own that she hadn't been born pretty, any more than it was her fault that she was young and inexperienced. And besides, who was he to run her down? Also, in attacking her for the crime of immaturity how did he differ from the cynics who shrugged away all social and political dedication as something to be outgrown, like adolescent acne? If that were true, what sustained generation after generation of patriots in their heroic resistance? They did not all, as they aged, settle down to tankards of mead and a gouty retelling of exploits past, warmed by a winter fire and glad of the snug safety of bourgeois life spiced with romantic memories. For if they had, Russian Poland would not still be, after these hundred years, an armed camp.

He thought of the old landowner in Olek's native village, alerting them, giving shelter on a summer night to four shabby university students on the run. Zbigniew Korsza hadn't paused to count the risks. Nor could a casual sympathizer have done what he had done, just on the spur of the moment. Everything had swung into motion too smoothly for the machinery not to have been kept constantly oiled.

No, it was not the malaise of youth, *Jugendkrankheit,* that sparked the underground.

He thought of all the dedicated men and women who'd ever crossed his path. And he envied them—even envied poor, bedraggled Idka. And a truth he had long and stubbornly resisted seeing now hit him full in the face. He envied them because in spite of the blows life had dealt them they did not allow themselves to be immobilized.

They had the courage to live. Whereas he—only once had he ventured out of his shell, and that only because he had fed on the courage of a brave and gallant woman. Afterwards, rather than again risk the pain of disappointment and loss, he had barricaded himself behind a wall of fine talk about what he owed to this one and that one. Excuses, lies, all of it. For it was as Jacek had said: those in the movement, too, had families, had responsibilities, which didn't stop them. So it was—it always had been—a matter of choice.

The truth is I've been a coward, he thought, in a moment of self abasement and loathing. *I still am.* And he no longer felt superior to the girl who sat quietly watching him out of red, swollen, mournful eyes.

"Idka, I'm sorry," he said at last, hoping he could reach his sister and that she would be generous enough to forgive him. "Sorry I've been so nasty to you. Look, this may be the last chance we'll have to talk for a long time. So let's not fight any more. Let's just say I understand that you have to do what you have to do. Only for pity's sake take care. Try not to give Mama any heart attacks."

She blew her nose and nodded and managed a smile, and immediately they both felt better.

✌ *Thirteen* ☙

ADAM'S MOOD of self-abasement lasted into the evening. Following his conversation with Idka he was in a fever to escape, shake the very dust of his native city, lose himself among strangers so totally alien by language and culture that he could live among them isolated as an anchorite. It suddenly seemed to him that maybe, in the remote mountains of the Caucasus where there would be nothing to remind him of the rape of his native Poland, he might find a measure of peace of mind and a little clarity, an understanding of self and, through understanding, self-acceptance. Then perhaps the groping would end.

The hours dragged for him in the midst of the household hustle and bustle. A sense of unreality descended on him that he was unable to shake, not even as he took his seat in Henryk Meisels' box at the Philharmonic. It was as though not only he but all the others around him were mechanical dolls, so many automatons out of the *Coppélia* boutique going through their antics after hours. Henryk with his cultivated urbanity, Marek and Missy, his aunt and uncle elegantly turned out for the occasion were bowing and smiling to acquaintances in nearby boxes or eyeing the rest of the audience through opera glasses. They mouthed exactly the phrases expected of cultivated persons come together for an evening of cultivated entertainment, making all the appropriate comments on the people and the programming.

"The Beethoven Violin Concerto—a perfect choice for Ysaye!"

"And the unaccompanied Bach—that takes a past master!"

"But then," Salome stated decisively, "the Philharmonic always makes such *musicianly* choices!" Anxious to draw her niece and her other nephew into the conversation, she appealed to them for confirmation of her views. "Kuba, Regina, don't they make musicianly choices? You're the experts here among us—what do you say?"

Regina, who was sitting directly in front of Adam, turned, and his feeling of vagueness vanished as he lost himself in admiration of her profile. "I really don't know the Beethoven well enough to judge," she started to explain earnestly. "I've never heard it in concert, only in transcription for four hands. As for the Bach, a friend of Kuba's plays it, but he makes it sound pretty terrible!" This brought laughter, and she understood how young and naive she must have sounded for having spoken so impulsively. She colored, and Adam was delighted with her.

Inadvertently Missy came to her rescue by shrugging off the whole subject of music and music programs. "Oh look, everybody," she giggled irreverently, "over there, in the Silbersteins' box! Emmy and Bela have Lucio Kronenberg in tow, sandwiched solidly between them. I wonder," she added waspishly, "if they intend to draw lots for him?"

Missy herself was flirting outrageously with Henryk, as though, having lost her interest in her former tutor, she was determined to find escape by other means. Watching them together, Adam decided they might not make a bad combination. Henryk, of course, was sufficiently an opportunist to let the advantages of an alliance with the house of Pozner seduce and influence him, and Missy probably suspected as much. But somehow, over and beyond any such consideration, Adam thought they might suit each other. Missy with her sharp independent mind might even be woman enough to keep Henryk interested long after the honeymoon was over.

The members of the orchestra came on stage, took their seats and began tuning their instruments. Salome, keeping her opera glasses trained on the stalls and her voice low, said, "I see Countess Potocka just came in. Over there, in the sixth row." She hoped that in the din she would not be heard except by those for whom her remarks were intended. "As usual she's escorted by one of those . . . those *nephews* of whom she is said to have an inexhaustible supply. . . ." The two young girls on either side of her immediately made a pretense of not understanding a word. The men smiled discreetly.

Then Henryk, in an amused tone, identified the "nephew" as the impoverished son of another great house. Leon, anxious to guide the conversation into more conventional channels, pointed out other illustrious personages: the austere Prince Sapieha, Prince Radziwill, and Prince Lubomirski, three of the country's great landed magnates. Henryk began to tick off other names, and who was whose guest. In the Sapieha box sat a notorious Russian general, and next to him a Pole who lived permanently in St. Petersburg and was well received at court. Adam remembered a report about the landed gentry petitioning the Tsar to keep the peasantry "in its place." Which of the men being identified had signed the appeal, he wondered.

The polite small talk that passes for conversation under most circumstances continued to flow around him. Salome and Missy were smiling constantly and flirting with their fans. Henryk and Marek compared the merits of fashionable restaurants. Kuba was looking bored. No one had mentioned the unrest in the streets or the rumors of fresh arrests.

Regina, who said very little, sat with her eyes riveted on the audience below, drinking in the glitter, the ladies' fashionable gowns and jewels and boas. Just as the musicians trooped in she turned to Adam and said with breathless excitement, "I keep looking at her, at this Countess Potocka, and all I can think of is, she must be the granddaughter of that other one, in the famous portrait—you know, Delphine, Chopin's patron and friend. Imagine being descended from someone who helped Chopin! Do you think her grandmother used to tell her stories about him?" And again Adam was delighted out of all proportion.

Immediately afterwards the lights dimmed, the conductor and the great soloist came on stage to thunderous applause, and the concert began. Adam forgot about the mechanical dolls surrounding him and lost himself in the music. Ysaye's tone was dark and velvety, the low notes almost like a cello's, wooing and casting a spell not just over the audience but over the other players. At one point Regina caught his eye and they shared a moment of poignant beauty. From then on he was lost. He found himself taking as much pleasure in watching her reactions as in savoring his own. It seemed marvelous to him that she should smile at precisely the passages that touched him most deeply, that when the music stopped she did not immediately join in the applause but sat quite still, as if pulling herself back to the here and now.

His bitterness receded, his mood of self-hate lifted. He remembered, incongruously perhaps, a line from the Stefan Zheromski novel that served as a kind of Bible to so many people of his generation: Even knowing that because of the life he leads he must give up the woman he loves, Zheromski's hero cannot find it in himself completely to condemn the lighthearted, upper-class girl who does not share his views. "She is like the lilies of the field," he tells himself, "that toil not, neither do they spin. But no one thinks to trample them underfoot, nevertheless!"

During intermission he did not join in the general conversation though he stayed close to Regina's side. She chatted gaily, and he heard the lilt of her voice rather than the words. Her light, delicate flower perfume transformed the hot air of their box; if he closed his eyes it was as though he were being transported into a field in bloom. *Consider the lilies of the field. . .*

The house was asleep when he got home and for this he was grateful. He had been afraid his mother might be waiting up for him for a final heart-to-heart talk, and right then he wanted to talk to no one. In the stillness, savoring and reliving the evening, he undressed quickly, blew out the lamp, and was asleep the instant his head hit the pillow.

Again his sleep was restless as dream followed dream.

First he was at the Pawiak, standing in line on visitors' day waiting for Izidore. But it was Olek, not his brother, who emerged flanked by two guards. "So," Olek said, "you've decided to join us at long last, and now they've got you, too. Your Wanda is in here somewhere, too, by the way. Only she isn't *your*

Wanda any more, is she? You've taken too long to make up your mind." And he laughed, but not unkindly, and turned away, and was gone. And as Adam stood rooted to the spot searching for something to call after his friend, he felt a tug on his sleeve. And it was his father, trying to pull him away. "That's not for you, son. Time to be honest with yourself. Admit it—to belong inside, a man must be made of sterner stuff."

He felt ashamed that his father should see through him so easily, but again could find no words to express what he felt. Jacob, however, like Olek, seemed not to be condemning or even judging.

"A man is what he is," he said, "and sometimes he forgives himself for it." He chuckled. "As you see, I've become quite a philosopher. Here beyond the grave we have plenty of time to think." Adam tried to answer but no sound came. "And speaking of self," Jacob Fabian went on, "let me repeat what I said just before I died. The business world is not for you. Don't let yourself be dazzled by promises of a splendid future. Even if it should materialize, there can be no happiness in it for you. Find work you are fitted for."

Adam found his voice at last. "That's easy to say—but what? What am I fitted for?"

But his father only smiled, murmuring, "That's for the living to find out." And like Olek, he vanished into the gloom of the prison.

Adam woke in a sweat, threw off his covers, turned and twisted in the dark, searching for nonexistent answers, until somewhere on a church steeple the bells chimed three. For a while he considered lighting his lamp and reading, but his eyes were full of sand. He sighed, closed them again, and again was sound alseep.

This time the dream began in full sunlight, with the familiar chase after a familiar distant figure, continuing over rocky ground until the sun set and the shadows lengthened. The figure vanished and suddenly it was night, clear and starry. But the mountains were gone and the heights he had climbed were stairs leading to a balcony, the balcony off Salome's drawing room. The French windows stood wide open and he breathed the perfume of acacias in bloom and overhead the sky was a deep midnight blue and the stars were beginning to dance. As he stared, they formed into unaccustomed patterns—giant letters, he realized.

That was when he became aware he was no longer alone. A white, delicate hand rested on his arm. "I didn't like to think of you all alone out here," Regina said.

He didn't answer directly. "Look, look what's happening! The stars have gone crazy!" he cried. "The whole sky is one great initial—R.F.—*République Française!*"

Regina laughed the high, clear, lovely laugh he was beginning to find familiar. "But that's not at all what the sky says, Adash. You're so wrong!"

"I am?"

"Of course you are. Don't you really know what R.F. stands for?" He shook his head and she laughed again, teasingly. "Why, for Regina Fabian, of course. How could you *not* know?" This time, when he woke, the sun was high and the room seemed full of the fragrance of lilies.

He gulped the breakfast his mother set before him and with the excuse that he still had packing and errands to do retreated to his own room. He stuffed the last remaining necessaries into his valises, locked them, rolled up and secured the large hold-all borrowed from Leon. When everything was done it was still only mid-morning. His train wasn't leaving until mid-afternoon, and if he hurried he would have time to do what during the long restless night he had realized he must do that day.

Since it was Sunday, his brother Viktor was home and Adam appealed to him for help. "I've got to go out . . . something important came up last night. . . . It may take a while, so do me a favor, will you? See that my luggage gets to the station safely. Mama will want to see me off—see that she gets there. Here's money for a hack and for platform tickets. I'm traveling second-class sleeper." He gave the number of his railway car and compartment. "You'll have no trouble finding me."

Viktor promised to take care of everything but was understandably curious. "What's come over you that you've got to run like a madman all of a sudden?"

"Never mind. Just something I can't leave undone." To his mother he said, "I wish I could spend the rest of the day with you, but this can't be helped. We can still have a nice visit at the station." As usual, she neither questioned him nor complained.

Out in the street Adam hailed a passing cab, promised the driver a good tip, and crossed the distance from Nalewki Street to Szczygla, where the Segals lived, in record time. He knew he was doing everything wrong: this was no hour of the day to go calling, not even on people one knew well, not even relatives. But time was running out and the Segals would have to forgive him. He only hoped Regina was at home.

Luck was with him. She and Kuba were at the piano, going over their four-hand transcription of the concerto Ysaye had played. Jadwiga was reading, Uncle Karol and a friend were playing chess. Since it was the maid's day off, Aunt Balbina herself came to the door. She wasn't a gracious woman, but was glad enough to see him. "Adash, how nice! You've taken the trouble to come and say goodbye."

He declined Uncle Karol's invitation to sit in on the chess, refused the glass of tea that was automatically thrust upon him. "I'd just like to . . . sit and listen to the music, if you don't mind. My head's still full of what we heard last night. Then there's something I must ask Regina." He improvised. "Something I forgot last night. . . ."

Since he was family, Balbina let it go at that and went back to her own concerns. Adam walked soundlessly into the living room. Regina and Kuba, barely aware of him, finished the concerto and began the Egmont Overture, she taking the treble and he the bass. Without a word Adam stationed himself behind them and started turning pages. When it was over Kuba thanked him. "The angels must have sent you. What luxury, not to be constantly losing one's place!"

Regina giggled. "The angels didn't send him—I invited him, the night of Aunt Salome's party. Maybe I didn't tell you."

Adam mumbled something inane. Now that he was here, he was wondering how he had ever found the courage to come at all, and how he was going to manage to speak to Regina alone.

Fortunately the chess game seemed to get really interesting

just then and the players called to them to come and watch. Kuba stood up, but Adam found some excuse to stay behind. Now at last he had Regina to himself. And she was smiling up at him, long lashes fluttering, lovelier even than in his dream.

"Would you like me to play something for you, Cousin Adam? For you and no one else?"

He thought in panic, *I should never have come, I'm an idiot, a first-class idiot, I won't be able to handle this!*

"Well," she asked again, this time with a shade of impatience, "what shall it be?"

"N-nothing. . ." Only then did he know he was being boorish. "That is," he hastened to apologize, "not right now. And I didn't mean that the way it sounded! I mean, I should love to have you play for me, but please, another time." He was fumbling like a schoolboy while she regarded him with arch surprise. "You see, I'm here because there's something I must say to you before I leave. . . ."

She had no idea what he was leading up to, but was aware, and clearly, that she had succeeded in destroying his equilibrium. This pleased her, more than making up for her annoyance at being asked not to play. "What is it you want to tell me, then?" she asked, her fine black brows curving into delicate question marks.

He stammered, "Well, first of all, you know I'm going away in a few hours. And that I'll be gone a year and more. The choice isn't mine, believe me. If I could, I'd be staying right here, close to you." She went on looking at him in that arch way of hers, offering none of the encouragement a more experienced woman might have given. He gulped, inwardly cursed his own gaucherie, and went on. "The fact is . . . Regina, ever since last night I haven't been able to get you out of my mind. . . . I even dreamed about you, a . . . a kind of prophetic dream. . . ."

Now she was intrigued. "A dream? About me? What kind of dream?"

"I'll tell you later. But first there's something else. . . . Last night I . . . I realized I've fallen in love with you. Does that shock you? No, don't answer, don't say anything, just hear me out. And please don't say I shouldn't speak to you like this, that I should go to your parents first! I would, but don't you see, there isn't time. . . ."

She sat perfectly still, neither helping nor hindering, giving him no clue to how she felt. But there was no stopping him now. "Next year," he pleaded, "next year when I'm back I'll do everything the proper way—go to your father, ask for your hand in marriage. If you'll have me, that is. Next year I'll have much more to offer you. Oh, maybe not so much as you deserve. I know you could find someone more worthy of you, someone who's handsome, and witty, and rich. But never a man who'd love and cherish you as I should cherish you. Regina, Regina, don't turn me down because it's all so sudden! Say there's a chance for me, that you'll think about it during all those months while I'm gone. . . ."

She said neither yes nor no, and, terrified of being turned down, he stopped talking. He thought she might laugh at him. But Regina did not laugh. This was her first proposal, and it had come from a grown man, not a boy. It had, moreover, come from someone who everybody said had brilliant prospects. Adam Fabian, she had heard it prophesied, was going to be successful and rich.

Of course, he was a cousin, and that might cause difficulties. And there was the age difference, although that didn't really bother her. Besides, she reminded herself, nothing need be dealt with, much less resolved, right now. Right now what mattered was that a man was declaring his love and asking only that she think about it. This, to her, seemed proof that his love was as pure and noble as his intentions were serious. She was immensely flattered. *He's treating me like a storybook princess,* flashed through her mind. And wasn't that exactly as Aunt Salome said every girl should expect to be treated—if she were lucky, that is.

"Do you have an answer for me," Adam finally dared ask, "or am I asking too much?"

She was feeling pleased with herself and very proud. "Oh, Adash, of course I shall think about all you've said!"

"Does that mean you'll let me talk to your parents next year?"

"Perhaps."

"My darling, do you think you could learn to love me?"

"Perhaps."

He bent toward her, and again her perfume, faint though it was, overwhelmed him. "Consider the lilies of the field," he murmured.

"What did you say?" She wasn't sure she had heard him.

"Just foolishness. Oh, Regina, Regina, how happy you've made me just not to say no!" He rose. "And now I must go or I shall miss my train. . ."

She gave him a long, speculative look, then unexpectedly stood on tiptoe, pulled his head down and kissed him on the lips. "That is to show you *how* I shall think of you," she whispered.

When he left, he was walking on air.

PART FIVE
Fall 1901–Fall 1903

⚜ *One* ⚜

THE NEW CENTURY, ushered in by labor unrest and waves of protest strikes, had by now turned into a time of misery unparalleled in scope. Throughout the Empire a general crisis had brought on unemployment, and in spite of the revolutionary ferment in the land, of fiery manifestos and calls for a reasonable working day and a living wage, the plight of the Tsar's subject peoples continued to worsen. Then, as if that in itself were not calamity enough, two summers in a row the crops failed, forcing the poorest peasants into the cities in search of bread, pushing wages down lower still, since for every man who dared refuse the pittance offered him three others waited, hat in hand.

But though there was hunger in the land there were also those who grew fat on it. In Lodz, where bankruptcy threatened small businesses, the true magnates of industry found a comfortable way to survive. With labor cheaper than it had been in years, it became a simple matter to turn their backs for the time being on the shrinking domestic market and start developing contacts abroad. One reason they were able to do this was because they could well afford to undercut their Western competitors: unlike them, they were not up against a working class that was literate, nurtured on the democratic traditions of liberty, equality, and the Rights of Man, and backed by trade unions into the bargain.

Maurice Pozner's export business flourished to such an extent that he began expanding his Lodz plant and even built additional, completely modern factories outside the city, one in Zhyrardow and one in Pabianice. Zhyrardow was to manufacture passementerie and fancy elastics, while Pabianice turned out machine-made laces in imitation of the traditional Belgian ones, exactly as Manchester was already doing. It was a tremendous undertaking and for a while absorbed the old man completely. In vain did *Pani* Konstancja complain that this constant shuttling back and forth between Warsaw and the Lodz compound on Cegielniana Street was not for a man his age, that they never had any peace and quiet any more, and besides, weren't they rich enough already?

"What more do you want?" she demanded to know, her small, pudgy, ring-laden hands indicating in one sweeping gesture the conservatory with its palms and fruited orange trees bright green against the new snow beyond the windows, the marble colonnade leading to the ballroom no one ever used since Lodz was hardly the place for big parties, the liveried footmen whose names she didn't even know. "Two palaces, a third in the country that we don't have time to enjoy! Enough, Pozner, enough! You're killing yourself!"

He petted her, patted her, felt her up, and promised to settle down eventually, maybe next year. "In the meantime be glad you have a man who doesn't feel his years!" With a wink and a leer he added, "Want me to show you how little I feel 'em? Just come upstairs with me!"

She knew he was trying to change the subject and pretended to be scandalized. "Now? In the middle of the day? With all the servants underfoot? Ach you, you're incorrigible!" But for the moment she let him win the battle. "All right, all right, I'm not saying another word!"

One reason Maurice Pozner was able to be so lighthearted about his plans for expansion was that his troubles with growers of top-grade cotton had at last been resolved to his complete satisfaction. Adam Fabian was turning out to be his find of the decade, and all that year and for a number of years to come the old textile wizard never ceased congratulating himself, both in private and among his cronies, on his choice of a new Near Eastern agent.

"Haven't I always said I can smell out a good man like a gambler smells out good horseflesh? You either have a nose for it or you don't!" Adam Fabian, he maintained, was an investment better than a gold mine. "How did I find him? How does a magnet find a nail? My children's tutor, a skinny Yid with shiny pants and dandruff on his collar and friends in the underground, and here he takes to business like a duck to water! The shipments he's been sending—you should just see! Pure silk, I tell you, a pleasure. Long staple, if you didn't know different you'd swear it was Egyptian. Don't ask me how that boy does it, all I know is he just always turns up where the crop is best. And the prices he gets it at! A *wunderkind,* I tell you!" And on and on, between sips of his favorite port, between contented puffs on his Corona-Coronas.

Secure in the knowledge that the yarns his looms were spinning and the stuffs woven from the yarns were a soft cloud on which he would ride out the catastrophe threatening Russia, Maurice Pozner could well afford to be generous with his praise. Nor was he niggardly with financial rewards. Six months after Adam's arrival in Erivan, after a particularly successful shipment, the old man gave him his first really substantial raise in salary as well as carte blanche in regard to closing advantageous deals as he saw fit. Adam would henceforth have a free hand to buy on the spot, even to the extent of making commitments to growers concerning future crops. "And there will be other raises, I promise you, and maybe a percentage arrangement soon," Pozner wrote him. "Keep up the good work, and I'll make a rich man of you, like I said."

The idea of himself as a rich man continued to seem unreal to Adam. He still could not think in such terms. At the university, among his old friends, there had been different goals. And even when he had finally gone his own way, money had been just a means to keep his family in food and shelter. But wealth, even comparative affluence, was a concept with which he was not yet comfortable.

The old Adam, he thought, Wanda's lover, would have been contemptuous of it, or at least indifferent. But the old Adam was dead, he had died a violent death at the hands of an unforgiving sweetheart and the wake had been held months and years afterwards, in a shabby Warsaw flat to which the street Arab Franek who was really Charon grown young had piloted him across tortuous streets in a boat drawn by four black horses clip-clopping over cobblestones, and Olek had poured the libation of oblivion and they had toasted the dead and the dying in cheap vodka. The vodka turned out to be an anesthetic and when it stopped burning his guts, the pain was gone. Or maybe it had been gone a long time without his ever having noticed, killed by unspoken demands for something he could not give, killed by perversity, by time and distance, by words and the lack of words.

And into this new emptiness had come Regina. Regina, who was lovely and untouched, half malleable child still, so that a man could shape her to his desire while enveloping her in his dreams. Affluence would become Regina. She at least would not be contemptuous of it.

In the six months since he had last seen her and fallen so unexpectedly in love again, dreams had become Adam's daily bread. While part of him labored mightily in the Pozner vineyards, dreams gave his heart vague and comfortable sustenance with no yardstick of reality to measure against. It was all the feeling he was capable of for the time being.

Thus not even the casual tone of Regina's irregular answers to his letters seriously disturbed his frame of mind. His enforced exile suited him and he felt no immediate need for a personal life. Everything good, he kept telling himself, was in the future. In the meantime most of his time was spent in travel, since cotton had to be bought where he could find it—at the Astrakhan fair on the Caspian Sea, in Batum on the Black, in Tiflis, in Samarkand, or farther afield in Tashkent and south toward the Persian border.

He who had always been a city dweller now went to inaccessible places by open cart, by caravan, on horseback or by donkey. The wild, high mountains, the cascading rivers and winding precipitous roads of the Caucasus gradually lost their terrors as he learned to trust guides and drivers. Mount Kazbek began to look like an old friend. And when one day he found himself in the shadow of Mount Ararat, he felt as though he had just walked backwards in history and stumbled into the pages of Genesis. Yet he never once crossed the boundaries of the Russian Empire.

But in a way all these experiences only served to increase his sense of remoteness. And so he got into the habit of working without letup, often neglecting to eat, sleeping only when exhaustion caught up with him, substituting routine for thought. His quarters were two sparsely furnished rooms that served him both as home and office. His needs had always been frugal. He saw no reason to change them. It would no more have occurred to him to alter his scale of living simply because he was on an expense account than to start doling out his energies because he was working without supervision. When Pozner sent expressions of appreciation, they seemed to him all but undeserved.

In the meantime, partly as a result of all the hard work but also because, unlike his predecessor, he never attempted to split commissions or hint at fat bribes, he was making an enviable reputation for himself. The native Georgians and Armenians, as well as merchants arriving from Asia Minor, many of whom were Persian or Turkish by birth, liked and trusted the young Pole. They had all been accustomed, in greater or lesser degree depending on whether they were Mohammedan or Catholic or Eastern Orthodox, to slights and sometimes even gross insults at the hands of Western Europeans but especially of the Great Russian masters—for to the Russians they were at best "the natives" and more often "those yellow mongrels." But Adam Fabian treated them with unfailing grave courtesy, and for this they rewarded him in a most practical manner: they gave him first choice on their crops.

The Persian planter *Hadji* Irza, an older man and Adam's first real friend in the Caucasus, put it to him this way: "One hears a great deal about Christian humility, but all we ever encounter is Christian arrogance. They treat us like dirt and we get back at them by cheating whenever we can. You understand, don't you, why it gives us such exquisite pleasure to cheat them blind? But money alone never quite salves crushed pride, and pride is important to us. Also, not being disciples of Christ, we are not trained to turn the other cheek. The hate smolders. We never stop dreaming of revenge."

Adam looked at the tall, handsome, graying Moslem whose best customer he had become, and knew from the man's intense black gaze what kind of revenge his people yearned for. Yes, he assured him, he understood about the ways of Tsarism. "We in Poland know the same slights, the same yoke."

"So that's why you are not like those other white dogs."

"That's partly why. Remember I am also a Jew."

"Ah, yes. That explains a great deal, does it not?"

And Adam reflected with wry amusement that for once in his life being a Jew in the Russian Empire had turned into an advantage.

There were others. Brought up to respect the kosher food habits and religious practices of those among whom he had grown up (shades of his father smoking secretly on Saturday mornings!), it was only natural for him to take the unfamiliar mores of the Near East in stride. When it came to ordering a meal in a restaurant, from the very start he had the intuitive sense to defer to native customs, content with whatever was set before him. Since as luck would have it he hardly ever drank, he never offended by calling for wine or spirits in the presence of Moslems. And if at sunset a man with whom he was doing business excused himself, unrolled a prayer rug, and, facing east, knelt to worship Allah, he neither showed surprise nor felt impelled to make wounding comments.

"So now you know why we're honest with you," *Hadji* Irza informed him, "why we don't try to mulct you like the others. Soon you will find more and more doors opening to you that to other Europeans remain forever closed."

The *Hadji* kept his word, and the contacts Adam made through him stood him in good stead for years to come. Now and then he was even invited to a local home, not as a trader but as a guest. And he was fascinated by what he saw and learned, but in an oddly impersonal way.

"It's as though I'd stumbled into Scheherazade's world," he wrote in one of his early letters to Regina. "The women here really do wear trousers, they're veiled even in their own houses, they glide about silent and mysterious. . . ." But, typically for this period in his life, the doe-eyed, voluptuous beauties, serving him sweetmeats and coffee like hot, strong honey, made no other impression on his male consciousness.

Hadji Irza kept a watchful eye on him, decided the youth was simply slow to take fire, and when, by way of testing him, he suggested a visit to Erivan's red-light district and was politely turned down, he became more than ever convinced he had guessed right. And this too was a point in Adam's favor. Soon word got around that here was one European in whose presence one's women were safe—final proof that he was a man of rare discretion, a man other men could honor.

His Armenian landlady was tempted to give a different interpretation of his behavior. After months of bringing him his breakfast tray in the morning only to find him already up and at his desk she became frankly disgusted with this foreigner who lived like a monk. "What's wrong with him?" she commented indignantly to her husband. "Not once, when I knock on his door, do I hear whispering and giggling like with the other roomers! Not once does he yell for me to put his tray down and he'll get it later! Call that a man? Young, not half bad-looking, and never a woman around! It's unnatural, that's what it is!"

The husband shrugged and gave what seemed the obvious answer. "Maybe it's boys he likes."

But she had never seen evidence of that either. Was it asses, perhaps, or sheep? Not likely! That was for the rugged men of the mountains, not for Europeans.

Fortunately for Adam's sense of personal dignity, he never suspected that he was the subject of such speculations. In the meantime, again through *Hadji* Irza, he was given his first major indispensable lesson in the fine protocol of local hospitality, an area where simple ignorance of local mores often cost the foreigner dearly.

After a field trip which they took together, the *Hadji* invited the younger man to stay overnight at his country estate, a sumptuous villa built according to modern French fashion but furnished—superbly—in traditional Persian style. From the moment he crossed the *Hadji's* threshold, Adam was transported. Within the first half-hour he had particularly admired a rare six-teenth-century miniature, a chased gold goblet encrusted with precious stones, and finally an ancient silk prayer rug.

To his intense embarrassment, all three treasures were presented to him as departure gifts when it was time to leave the following day. And when he protested that under no circumstances could he accept such lavish presents, his host merely smiled and ordered a servant to load them into the waiting carriage.

"You mustn't insult me with a refusal, *effendi.* Besides, these are mere trifles—it causes me no pain to part with them. On the contrary, the giving fills me with joy. Just be glad," and his smiled broadened, "be glad you did not look with similar lust upon my wife or my daughter or my favorite stallion or youngest concubine. For had you done so, I should have been honor bound to offer you those, too. Such is our custom. But once you were on the highroad, no longer a guest under my roof—once the law of hospitality no longer protected you—I should have had to send my servants to overtake you. And then . . . and then. . ."

"Then what?" Adam echoed, his skin starting to prickle.

"Then—this." The *Hadji* drew his index finger across his own throat in a gesture as eloquent as it was universal. "And don't think such things don't happen, my friend. Many's the greedy traveler who, after spending a night under a stranger's roof, has ridden off in the morning with just such treasures. Afterwards, he'd be found in some ditch, a dagger in his back."

No more was said about the gifts, then or later. But Adam took care never again to repeat his mistake.

The experience, however, had another, completely unexpected effect. The rug and the golden chalice and the miniature, which he unpacked with awed care and placed where he could look at them constantly, not only transformed his bare room but filled him with a kind of glow, like the stirring of first love. And so was planted the seed of his taste for Persian art, which with the years was to develop into a true collector's passion. And now for the first time he understood his old friend Henryk Meisels of the sybaritic tastes. *Why, I could very easily get used to enjoying luxury!*

The thought made him slightly incredulous; but this time, as he remembered his employer's promise of wealth to come, he no longer found it disturbing. What did disturb him was the recollection of another of Pozner's remarks. *Cotton doesn't sing songs that inflame the heart. Cotton doesn't have a brother rotting in the Pawiak.* . . . For he knew it was one thing to have shaken himself loose from whatever bound him to Wanda, and quite another to turn his back on those basic issues no decent Pole must allow himself to forget.

For days he felt guilty about ownership of his precious new acquisitions. Surely he had no right to them. Should he perhaps convert them into hard cash to send to his family? The money would more than cover the sums he was putting aside for his sisters' dowries, and the rest could be used for bribes to make life in jail less grim for Izidore.

But no matter how much he argued with himself, he could not bring himself to act on the idea. He spent several sleepless nights wrestling with his conscience, and finally salved it by telling himself that one did not sell off gifts so generously given, especially not in a small provincial town where they would be immediately traceable, resulting in a mortal affront to his good friend.

But in the light of morning he was more honest with himself.

"The truth is I cannot bear to part with these things! I won't do it, I can't do it, not if I have to bury them in a trunk and only bring them out in the dark of night, like a miser. . . ."

He wondered if that was how a gambler felt, blood racing and heart hammering, as he staked on a single throw of the dice borrowed money his family needed desperately for food, for shelter. And then a more pleasant thought consoled him. Why, *Hadji* Irza's gifts were treasures that would one day embellish the home he would make for Regina. He must write her at once and tell her about them.

When his landlady knocked with breakfast a few hours later he was, as usual, at his writing table, deep in an account of how he had come by the prized possessions he would be bringing home. And as he tried to convey to her his excitement and delight, it never occurred to him that the young girl to whom his words were addressed would hear in them only what she was capable of hearing: that he was showering her with extravagant gifts from the Orient, rare wondrous gifts to which ordinarily only the very wealthy might aspire.

❧ *Two* ❧

THE COURTYARD of the house where the Segals lived faced a blank stone wall twice a man's height and mossy with age, and beyond it stretched a private park belonging to a convent. The convent buildings themselves were completely hidden from view, for the far end of the gardens, uncultivated, had been allowed to grow into a veritable thicket so that the tops of the aging oaks, honey locusts, and lindens formed a rippling sea of greenery directly below the balcony of the Segals' apartment.

The linden fronds overhanging the yard kept it in cool, deep shade in summer, and in season carpeted the paving stones with fragrant blossoms. Some years earlier the first few branches had started pushing against the walls of the building itself, and by now tendrils of delicate leaves were showing through the balcony grillwork. Once a gardener from the convent had come to offer to prune the trees, but the Segals liked the effect and were content to leave things as they were.

Shortly after Adam Fabian left for the Caucasus, Regina, with time on her hands now that school was out for the summer, made the balcony her own private domain. She would spend whole afternoons with a book of poetry in her hands, open it at random, read a page or two, then lose herself in daydreams. The dreams were mostly sad ones, since so much of romantic poetry is sad, and she happily let her heart break again and again as she wept at the poignancy of some poet's lament.

Toward sundown the trees came alive with the evening song of birds. The chapel bells rang out, calling the nuns to prayer. The fragrance of the blossoming trees carried Regina into another world, where she was no longer just the middle child in an ordinary middle-class family but someone infinitely special, a young aristocrat of the senses, keenly aware of beauty and all things noble, a heroine waiting for her story to be written.

In time, borrowing a phrase from the poet Mickiewicz, whose verse novel *Pan Tadeusz* she knew practically by heart, she began calling the balcony her "temple of meditation" after the wooded retreat of a character in the book, the affected lady of fashion Telimena. Beguiled by the lyricism but missing entirely the sly satire of the poet's pseudo-Byronesque lines, Regina had very simply made the mistake of taking the whole passage at face value: Telimena's ennui, her distaste for country life, her longing for escape to the glittering capitals of Europe, if not Paris then Vienna or at least St. Petersburg.

Then one day, proud of her literary allusion, she made the further mistake of boasting about it to her brother and older sister.

While neither especially close nor really fond of each other, Kuba and Jadwiga were always delighted to join forces against their next-younger sibling, who was at an age to give herself airs and needed to be taken down a peg. After hearing her out poker-faced and without comment, that same night at supper they regaled their parents and a couple of guests with the story. Everyone burst out laughing, with even the younger children joining in, shrieking with joy, not because they understood the joke but because the grown-ups thought something was very, very funny.

Like all persons who take themselves seriously, Regina could not bear being laughed at. She threw down her knife and fork with a clatter and leaving her meal unfinished fled from the table. The rest of them heard the door of her room slam, and for a moment there was uneasy silence. Then Jadwiga said with a satisfied smirk, "Oh, dear me, the princess has had her feathers ruffled." And she reached over for Regina's untouched dessert.

Alone with her humiliation, Regina threw herself on her bed, ready to give in to a storm of weeping. But her ears remained alert for whatever sounds might reach her from the other end of the apartment. Any moment she expected to hear hasty footsteps down the hall as her mother—no, let it be her father—rushed to her to apologize and beg her to come back to her charlotte and her tea.

But no one came. True, the laughter did subside, but only to be followed by the normal hum of conversation. No one was even upset. She chalked it up as yet another score to be settled in the internecine warfare of the home, and vowed that someday, somehow, she would make them all sorry. The tears dried before they really started.

After a time, restless for something to do but determined not to leave the sanctuary of her room, she turned up the light and opened her Mickiewicz. But even he seemed to have betrayed her. And she raged at her own stupidity for having missed the point of his lines, which now came through so clearly. But most of all she raged at her family, whose behavior she considered unforgivable.

Putting Mickiewicz down, she looked around for another book, but nothing tempted her. At loose ends, frustrated and restless, she remembered the packet of letters from her cousin Adam in Erivan. Why she had saved them she wasn't altogether sure, since her true feelings for the writer were anything but clear. But there they were, tucked away between pages of copybooks and, she hoped, safe from prying eyes—the very first love letters anyone had ever written to her, interesting, "different," one might even say exotic.

Why, only last week the postman had given her another envelope from what he termed "that far-off heathen land." And she had blushed, then blushed again as she started reading what Adam had to say. For he spoke not just of his undying love, but of how he was collecting art treasures—imagine, *real art treasures!*—for the home they would some day have. Nothing had really been settled between them, she had promised merely to *think* about being engaged to him, and here he was already laying fairy-tale gifts at her feet!

A little ashamed, she remembered how casually she had skimmed the pages because her mother had called to her that they were due at the dressmaker's and were already late. She had stuffed the envelope into her purse to finish later and forgotten about it. Now she found it again, smoothed out the rumpled pages, and began reading. And the highly charged words became balm to her wounded pride. She found in them nuances of tenderness and appreciation that earlier had escaped her entirely. Why, this wonderful man, so perceptive, so understanding, would never dream of laughing at her, not even if she made the most grievous errors! He would just put it down to her youth and inexperience, and be charmed, and kiss her hands, and tell her how imaginative she was.

One thing led to another. She dug up all his other letters and began rereading them one by one. And they all took on a different dimension. His patient devotion brought tears to her eyes. And he seemed suddenly very near and dear, and she was horrified that for so long she had remained unfeeling, indifferent, often neglecting to answer, or just shrugging him off with a few hastily scribbled words.

Well, that would all soon be rectified.

And she was at her desk, pen in hand. "Dear Adam," she began. No, that would never do. She crossed the words out—which didn't really matter since she always made a rough draft of all her correspondence, then copied everything out carefully on the pale mauve notepaper Aunt Salome had given her on her last birthday. "Dearest Adam. . ." She crossed that out, too. "My dear, dear Adam. . ." There, that was just about the right tone. "I've been thinking a great deal about you lately, thinking how lonely you must be so far away from those who love you. . . . And I began to feel ashamed that I'd done so little to ease that loneliness. . . ."

From there on the words flowed. She told him how she, too, was often lonely, for really she had very few friends, especially now that "practically everybody" was off to the country for the summer. As for her brother and sister, they didn't seem to like her very well and were always picking on her. Then she told him about the old park and her own leafy retreat and what she called it—only this time she was careful to allude to everything with just a hint of implied amusement—and about how sometimes, as she sat on the balcony reading, she would see the postman crossing the courtyard and know, just know in her bones, that he had a letter from Erivan for her.

By the time she had covered eight pages in her large, square, carefully stylish hand, she believed every word she had put down on paper. She relished her own eloquence, her spirits lifted, and she thought how, if not for Adam, she would still be wretched. Instead, she had turned defeat into a kind of victory. Therefore thank heaven for Adam, dear, kind, wonderful Adam. And vowing she would never again underestimate him, she signed herself, "Your very loving Regina."

The next day, returning from piano practice at Aunt Salome's and a stroll in the Saxon Gardens afterwards, she stepped into a veritable hornet's nest the moment she came through the door.

"Ayayay, Miss Regina," the chambermaid, Magda, whispered warningly as she took her hat and light wrap. "Your Papa wants to see you in his study the moment you get here—and he's fit to be tied."

It turned out that another letter from Adam had arrived in her absence, along with a package containing a rather extravagant gift, a heavy silver-and-enamel Kirghiz warrior's belt with dagger buckle, the kind the Caucasus was famous for. To make matters worse, Adam had enclosed a card that read, "Think of me when this clasps your lovely waist!" Both letter and package had been opened, and Karol was livid.

Since he was not in the habit of censoring his daughters' correspondence, Regina was at first at a loss to understand what had prompted him to do so now. Then she noticed the pile of crumpled notebook pages on his desk. She gasped, feeling a little sick. For this was the penciled draft of her own letter of the previous night, the draft she'd tossed so casually in the direction of the wastebasket, that Jadwiga must have come upon before Magda had had a chance to tidy up the room.

"What's the meaning of this?" Karol began to shout as she stood wordless before him. "Love letters? At your age? And from your own cousin? Who gave you two permission to . . . ? The very idea of writing as though you were engaged! I'll break the young rascal's neck when I get hold of him! As for you . . . shaming us like this, acting like a harlot, a streetwalker!" In his rage he was forgetting that a young girl brought up the way his daughter had been wasn't even supposed to know the meaning of such words. "Now don't go thinking you're too old for a good whipping, young lady! I've always spared you the cat-o'-nine-tails, but now I've a good mind to give you what you deserve, right on your bare behind!"

Regina blanched. The cat-o'-nine-tails that hung on a peg in the study was hardly ever used any more, not even on the younger boys. But it could be a terrible weapon in the hands of an irate father, and once she'd been made to watch as Jadwiga was given a taste of it. It left bloody welts that took weeks to disappear. And even worse than the pain was the humiliation.

She must try to talk her way out of her predicament. She thought fast, and one of Aunt Salome's favorite precepts echoed in her mind. "The best way to handle men—I don't care who they are, fathers, husbands, brothers, all men in general—is with a show of meekness. And in case of real trouble, repentance. Tears, if need be. A vow to do better in the future. Keep your fingers crossed and promise them anything they want to hear. You can always get around them later, after they cool off."

Regina had no idea what Adam might have written, but it could hardly be anything that would seriously compromise her. After all, she'd given him so little encouragement in the past! She decided to gamble on that. Assuming an innocent, injured air, she let her lips tremble and the tears gather.

"Why, Papa, how can you say such cruel things to me! Is it my fault Cousin Adam sent me a present? He never asked and I never said he might. Well then, how unfair to put the blame on me!" Now the tears rolled down her cheeks in all earnest. "As for that foolish scribble Jadwiga dug out, like . . . like a scavenger," she searched for the most damaging epithet she could find, "like a Black Hundred informer . . . why, I only wrote those things because I was so hurt and miserable last night. But I never intended to mail any of it, I didn't, I didn't! You can see for yourself I threw it all in the wastebasket. . . ." And she began to sob pitifully, as though the lie were God's own truth.

Like so many men, Karol never could hold out long against tears, and, after all, this was his favorite child and he asked nothing better than to believe her.

"Hm. Well. Yes, I see. I suppose what you tell me does make a difference." He spoke grudgingly, for one must not disrupt discipline altogether by too quick a show of forgiveness. "Do I have your word for it that you've told me the absolute truth?"

She crossed her fingers more firmly and blessed Aunt Salome. "Oh, yes, Papa!" She gave him the full benefit of her moist gaze and repeated still more emphatically, "Yes, yes, a thousand times yes!"

"Well then, in all fairness," Karol relented, "before we go any further I suppose I ought to let you read your mail."

"Yes, please!" Then, realizing she must not appear overeager, she added submissively, "That is, if you really think that's best."

The ghost of a smile crossed Karol's face, though he still tried to sound stern. "Now don't you try to get around me, you little bag of tricks!" But he handed her Adam's letter, which this time, mercifully, was rather impersonal.

Chiefly he was describing the wonders of the marketplace in Samarkand. "I wish you could see the turbaned men, the women carrying pitchers of milk on their heads, the street musicians with their weird wailing instruments and the jugglers and the snake charmers. . . ." And a little further on, "I was tempted to buy a present for you, but the native friend who brought me—his name is *Hadji* Irza, and the *Hadji* is a title, not a first name, it simply means 'one who has made the pilgrimage to Mecca!'—the *Hadji* wouldn't let me. Said the prices were highway robbery, which of course I have no way of judging for myself. Your belt comes from a regular shop in Tiflis, and it's made to fit a grown man, would you believe it? These mountaineers are built like reeds. . . ." Hardly a love letter. Regina breathed easier.

Having gambled and won she now decided like a cautious strategist to hedge her victory. "Papa, if you wish, I can ask Cousin Adam to address all his letters to the family from now on, not just to me. And I can show you the ones I write to him before I send them off."

To her intense relief her father smiled, the sun breaking through the thunderclouds. *"Dzierlatka,* little minx! I hardly think that will be necessary! But you *have* learned your lesson, haven't you?"

"Oh, yes, Papa, indeed I have!"

"Well then, we'll say no more about it."

As she left the room she found Jadwiga prowling in the hallway, and knew her sister had been eavesdropping, possibly in the hope of hearing the sound of blows and shrieks of pain. It was her turn to smile a superior little smile.

That night Regina came to the supper table proudly flaunting her new belt, after lacing her stays at least an inch tighter than usual. It made her feel faint the moment she started to eat, but she hoped she would get used to the discomfort. It would be worth it, especially when she wore the lovely thing to parties next winter for everyone to admire and envy. As for Jadwiga, just let her ask to try it on! Big sister could huff and puff, she could hold her breath till she was blue in the face. Never in a million years would she manage to clasp it around *her* fat middle!

✼ *Three* ✼

THE TOTALLY UNEXPECTED, unhoped-for tone of Regina's letter had the effect on Adam of deliciously unhinging his mind. It seemed to him that a miracle had taken place, the impossible was coming true. He felt the past was now truly over and only the future mattered, a future he was free to paint in glowing colors. He loved and was loved. His life had a goal. He was Tristan after drinking the magic potion, gazing with fresh eyes at Isolde. "You've made me the happiest of men," he wrote back instantly. "What have I done to deserve you, my darling?" Shopworn phrases that to lovers are forever fresh and new.

And now the letters between Warsaw and Erivan flew back and forth. Neither Adam nor even Regina waited any longer for the other to answer before writing again. They filled page after page with observations on every conceivable subject, thinking aloud, as it were, eager to give of themselves, to share every impression and every fantasy. And it became all too easy for each to build an image of the other suited to his own need, an image unflawed, untouched by the drawbacks of reality, unblemished. Thus a separation which normally could have been achingly painful became for them a source of feverish delight.

Regina especially found the situation to her liking. Very early in the newly meaningful correspondence she became aware that now she really must take good care to keep her cousin's ardent love letters secret: let the family get wind of their content, and it would not be easy to talk herself out of trouble a second time! She cast about for solutions, and finally a plan that was practically foolproof evolved in her mind.

She bided her time, then, on an afternoon when both her mother and sister were out of the house, beckoned the chambermaid Magda into her room, and for extra precaution conspiratorially closed the door. "Magda, Magdusia," she began in a whisper, "how would you like to make a lot of extra money? You'd be doing me a great big enormous favor into the bargain—a favor I'd bless you for the rest of my life!"

The girl reflected she could well do without her Jewish young lady's blessing, but money was another matter. "What would I have to do?" she asked with slow caution.

"Oh, little enough—practically nothing!" Regina assured her. "Just whenever the postman has a letter for me, slip it into your pocket and pretend it's for you. Or better still, I could see that the letters were addressed directly to you." Before Magda could say yes or no, she pressed her, "There'll be ten kopeks in it for you every time—and I get a lot of letters. Imagine, you'll be making an extra ruble a month, maybe even more."

It was a tempting offer, considering the wages she got. A body could buy a laying hen for twenty kopeks. If she squirreled away all that silver, her sweetheart in the village wouldn't half mind. They could get married a lot sooner. Still, there were risks.

"I don't know, Miss Regina, I just don't know. Suppose they catch us. You'd only get what-for, but me, they'd ship me back to my father's house and he'd skin me alive and set me to tending the pigs. . . ."

"Silly, why should they catch you?" Regina coaxed. "You've a right to get mail like everyone else! Besides, you're the one that answers the door. Fifteen kopeks?" she added softly, when the other girl still looked dubious.

They settled for twenty. In the end they made a solemn pact, Magda swearing by the Holy Virgin and all the Saints in the calendar that wild horses couldn't drag Regina's secret out of her. The next day she collected her first reward. From then on the hoard of coins inside her straw mattress grew and grew, until she could translate the money into a suckling pig to fatten for market, and a newborn calf, and if everything went smoothly perhaps even a milch cow. Still, just to be on the safe side she was always careful to keep out a few coppers for candles to burn at the altar of the Virgin Mary on Sunday—the surest way to keep from being found out and having to pay the piper.

As for Regina, the secrecy only added an extra fillip to an already piquant arrangement. After a while she forgot the original reason for all the shenanigans and with each letter convinced herself more and more deeply that she was in the throes of a great love. Her imagination did for her what Adam's honest devotion might never have accomplished of itself. She thought about him constantly, carrying on endless imaginary conversations with him, in which he invariably repeated how remarkable, sensitive, talented, and beautiful she was. And when she practiced the piano, she pretended she was playing for him.

Thus a whole year passed. Another cotton crop was ready for market. There was no longer any question about Adam's being one of the most successful buyers in the Near East. The merchants continued to offer him the cream of their crop directly at their plantations, while forcing other "Christian dogs" to do business in town, at the maddeningly slow pace of the region. The benefits to Pozner were spectacular.

Adam never deluded himself into believing that all the cordiality, the cooperation extended to him, was purely the result of the good relationships he had established. The men he dealt with knew perfectly well that he represented a giant in the textile industry, that backing him were the Pozner mills and the Pozner millions, and that this in turn meant a firm foothold in the distant city of Lodz for anyone able to make the right arrangements. Lodz, as everyone knew, was to the Russian Empire what Manchester was to Great Britain. Corner the Lodz market, and, Allah willing, you need never again worry about finances.

The Caucasus needed Lodz quite as much as Lodz needed the Caucasus. For although Lodz, like the rest of Poland, had its strikes and revolutionary unrest, foreign capital continued to flow into its modernized factories. In this it had a great advantage over the textile centers of Great Russia proper, for these, having in the past few years established a kind of monopoly for themselves geared to their own people and ignoring the export market, were now reaping the whirlwind in the general crisis. A populace hungry for bread was not buying their products, neither new clothes nor lace curtains.

But even the economic slump did not tell the whole story. Slowly it was becoming apparent that the Tsarate was no longer having everything its own way in the rest of Asia either. Nicholas' plans for a "yellow Russia" in Manchuria, nurtured by the failure of the Boxer Rebellion and the completion of the Trans-Siberian Railway, were being seriously threatened by the looming strength of the newest upstart in the Far East, Japan. Japan, no longer content with the limited share the world's great powers were willing to allow her in China as a sphere of influence, was also eyeing Manchuria, to say nothing of Korea. A clash between the two rivals seemed imminent.

More and more frequently one heard talk of war. And while it was true that war, with conscription on a mass scale, might mean orders by the million bales for cotton and wool for the army, the merchants of the Caucasus and Transcaucasia were not anxious to do business with the Tsar. Too many bribes had to be slipped into too many pockets, some of them royal and near-royal. And Petersburg had a reputation for not paying its bills, sometimes on the pretext of a national emergency, sometimes with no pretext at all. Indeed, the Polish-Jewish firms of Lodz and its environs made far better customers than Greek Orthodox generals.

Thus the cotton growers wooed Adam Fabian more and more openly, often sending him word by special messenger whenever a particularly fine field was being harvested or a shipment was due by caravan from some distant point. He did even better for his employer than in the past. After he had been in Erivan for a year he got his second substantial raise. A month or two later Pozner wrote to announce that he had decided to pay him an agent's commission in addition to his salary. He also suggested that Adam might consider buying a modest block of stock in the business. This was indeed a lavish gesture, since by and large the Pozner holdings were a closely guarded family affair.

Adam was overwhelmed, exactly as Pozner intended him to be. Long before the term "enlightened self-interest" came into general use, the old man had learned how to cement the loyalty of valued subordinates. Adam wrote back: "You're being wonderfully good to me. But in the matter of stock purchases I'm completely a novice. Please advise me. Just how much is a 'modest block'? The equivalent of my raise? My year's commissions? My savings? I'm ready to follow your advice to the letter, knowing you wouldn't, you couldn't, steer me wrong." He was not trying to be shrewd, but it was the shrewdest move he could have made.

Later that night he wrote two more letters, one to his mother and one to Regina.

The letter to his mother was in answer to one he had received a few days earlier. He carefully brought her up to date on his new financial status, and in light of this was able to be not only definite but generous in regard to several family matters that had been of grave concern to them both. First there was Izidore. Izidore's case, Bluma had recently told him, might finally be coming up for trial. If it did, could they possibly afford a lawyer, she wanted to know.

Now Adam wrote, "Get a lawyer by all means, and a good one. Uncle Leon should be able to help you find the right man. But please, Mama, not a *Gmina* lawyer. Let's be practical and hardheaded for once and not insist on a Jew, not even a *converted* Jew. We want someone well-born, who speaks fluent Russian. . ."

Bluma had mentioned other problems. There was Rosie, head over heels in love and wanting to get married. Her mother had nothing against the idea in principle, in fact she rather liked her younger daughter's intended. But she couldn't help feeling there was a kind of injustice in Rosie being the first to find a husband. By rights, the older sister Idka should be first.

"Of course, I have to be honest and admit our poor Idka doesn't have any such prospects. Even so, perhaps we should make Rosie wait—maybe tell her she'll have to be patient until the money's been saved for both dowries? In the meantime I could talk to a good, discreet marriage broker. Idka's a good girl, *someone* ought to appreciate her!"

But Adam thought only of how waiting could hurt and twist and blight even a great love, until it soured and turned into its opposite. Let his gay, lighthearted little sister be spared! "If you really approve of the man, why not just go ahead with the wedding plans? Give Rosie her full dowry and don't let's worry about short-changing Idka. When her time comes she'll be taken care of, I promise. So don't let's stand in the way of Rosie's happiness. . . ."

This done, he sat for a long time motionless, pen in hand, before starting his second letter. He was thinking of all the things he wanted to say to his own dear love. It seemed to him that he must find words as memorable as the night was memorable. For this was the watershed of his life, an end and a beginning, and it called for some special kind of eloquence.

But though his heart was pounding and he was beginning to feel lightheaded, only the same old phrases suggested themselves. "My dearest dear," he finally began, "At long last I have wonderful news. I am finally in a position to talk to your parents about us." He outlined the details of his new arrangement with Pozner and what this would mean financially. "To sum it all up, my responsibilities to my family are being discharged in full, and soon, very soon, I shall be free to think only of you, live only for you. Nothing more need stand in the way of our happiness. Of course, there will always be my mother to take care of, but that's hardly a burden. And one of these days, when both my sisters are married and even Kazik is on his own, perhaps you'll agree to have her come to live with us. You know she has always loved you as a niece. Now she'll be able to love you as a daughter. As my wife. Oh, the beautiful word—my wife. . . ."

In the flush of his excitement he forgot entirely about going to bed. The room grew chilly in the small hours, and to make matters worse a storm broke, sending the temperature down another ten degrees. Presently Adam became aware of icy toes and fingers. He went to bed and pulled the covers up to his chin but could not get warm. By morning he was feeling feverish but ignored the malaise since he had an appointment to keep. As the day wore on he felt better, but the following morning was worse again.

This went on for the rest of the week. On Saturday morning his landlady found him burning up with fever, and since he was now too weak to protest, summoned a doctor. The doctor diagnosed pneumonia. Forgetting her indignation about the way her young lodger lived his life, and even ignoring her husband's admonitions that this was none of her trouble, the good woman took care of the sick man as best she could, dosing him with herb tea and frequent cuppings, wondering all the while what she should do if he died on her hands.

Then, on Monday, a manservant arrived from *Hadji* Irza's house to invite Adam to dinner. The landlady, only too happy to have someone else take over, led him up to Adam's room. The servant took one look at the semidelirious foreigner and fled, calling upon Allah to protect him from such a plague. But later he did have the wits to report what he had seen to his master. Within the hour the *Hadji* was having Adam moved out of his lodgings and into his own town mansion. Within another hour everything was being done for him that could be done.

Even so, for days he hovered between life and death, out of his head most of the time and difficult to control. But finally the crisis passed, the fever broke, and he began to mend. Maurice Pozner, notified of what was happening, immediately made all necessary arrangements to have his young agent sent to a sanatorium in the Crimea as soon as he was well enough to travel. But it was going to be a long convalescence, and many weeks before Adam could go home.

❧ *Four* ❧

B<small>Y ONE OF THOSE WHIMS</small> of an inefficient postal system, Adam's letter to Regina was misdirected and not delivered until weeks later, leaving her wholly in the dark about his news, both the good and the bad. In the meantime she was allowing mounting anger to build against him for his sudden, apparently inexplicable silence. How dare he ignore her like this when she, because she'd decided to be faithful, wasn't even thinking about a social life even though she had already turned seventeen!

Had she been honest with herself she might have admitted that the indignation and fury were a mask for feelings that had been simmering all summer long. The plain fact was that after a year and a half of waiting—a long time in any circumstances but an eternity at her age—Regina was no longer sure she wanted to remain engaged. There were times when she could hardly remember Adam's face. At other times all she really asked was to enjoy herself, have lots of new, pretty clothes and start going to lots of parties, dance and flirt and be admired and maybe break a heart or two. Marriage, engagement even, could wait.

By summer's end she had already found it hard to continue resisting temptation, had begun flirting with a few of Kuba's friends, and in a couple of cases was dangerously successful. Her appetite whetted, she cast about for a more serious challenge. The next time Henryk Meisels called, she thought she had found it.

But to her intense chagrin Henryk's only response to all her wiles had been a faintly amused, big-brotherly tolerance. *He thinks I'm still a child,* she thought, outraged by his implied condescension and at the same time annoyed at herself for having courted it. *But I'll show him, I'll show him!* With her characteristic penchant for keeping grudges, she chalked up a mental black mark against Henryk.

Her outrage deepened when she found out the real reason for his lack of interest. About this time Henryk became engaged to Missy Pozner. "Well, no wonder he's afraid even to look in my direction!" Regina wrote in her diary. "He's found himself an heiress worth millions and won't risk losing her!" She chose not to remember that once Missy had been fond of Adam but that Adam had preferred her, Regina, who had nothing.

What she had no way of knowing, and wouldn't have been able to understand had she been told, was that a great deal more had led up to the impending Pozner-Meisels match than mere convenience or money. It was an arrangement based on friendship and genuine liking, as well as self-interest, between two extremely complex and realistic people. Both Henryk and Missy would be getting out of the marriage exactly what they needed and wanted. Neither had any romantic illusions about the other, nor about much of anything else for that matter, but this only meant they would be able to accept one another, without demanding more than each was able to give. Henryk was no adventurer; Missy's fortune would merely help him build one of his own while at the same time leaving her independently wealthy. Later, he would stay married to her as long as they both wished the relationship to continue, and in the meantime she would be free of her parents and free to lead her own life, as would her husband. They both wanted to take up residence abroad. Neither wished to be encumbered with children.

A great deal of this Regina was actually able to piece together from conversations overheard between Henryk and Kuba, and also between Salome and Eugenia and some of the ladies who came to tea. But it was still beyond her to believe that such considerations might outweigh a sudden onslaught of the kind of overwhelming emotion—knowing nothing of desire, she called it love—which she herself had hoped to kindle. Therefore, having failed with Henryk was a blow to her pride. But since she really cared nothing about him as a human being, she came out of the experience with her nose out of joint but otherwise unhurt.

Then she forgot all about him as the schools reopened and the Grossglik household, where daily she spent so many hours, filled with young boarders once more. And among the boarders there was one not quite so young as the rest, a graduate student in law at the university, who instantly commanded her attention.

"Allow me to introduce you," Aunt Salome said one afternoon, interrupting her piano practice. "Here's one of my faithful *old* boys, come back to his second home and his second mother!" Playfully, she stood on tiptoe to pat the cheek of a tall, slender, wonderfully handsome man in his early twenties. "Prince Alfred Czartoryski, my niece Regina."

He bowed, clicked his heels, and said he was charmed. She looked up shyly, her eyes widening. "Not one of *the* Czartoryskis!" Instantly she could have bitten her tongue out for having sounded naive and gauche.

But he only laughed, putting her at her ease. "If you mean the would-be Kings of Poland of ignominious memory, thank heaven that's another branch of the family. Me, I'm just the younger son of a younger son, which makes me a minnow among whales."

Now she did not know which to admire most in the young aristocrat with the illustrious name: his patrician bearing, the disarming egalitarian simplicity that softened it, or his profile which was so much like Lord Byron's.

Alfred, it turned out, was an accomplished musician. "In the country, one has no choice but to learn—it's either make our own music or go without." His instrument was the cello, but he was also a fair pianist, thoroughly familiar with all the literature transcribed for four hands, and a far better sight reader than she. In a matter of days he knew exactly when Regina might be found at the Bechstein and began coming in punctually half an hour before the end of her practice period.

Soon they were playing duets, or else he would stand beside her turning pages, gazing meaningfully into her eyes, accidentally brushing against her now and then and softly humming. She, in turn, became acutely aware of how bright his sun-bleached hair was, how blue his eyes. Just to hear him speak her name became a thrill, and the first time he asked if he might see her home she walked on air.

Salome, not unmindful, as she put it, of which way the wind was blowing, did not discourage the budding relationship. "After all," she argued against a somewhat disapproving Leon, "stranger romances than this have come to happy fruition. Let's not stand in the young people's way and maybe something good will come of it."

"Or else something very bad," Leon muttered. But he had to admit that this was only cautious common sense speaking. Certainly he didn't have the heart to oppose his wife, not if nurturing whatever attraction was—or wasn't—there gave her pleasure and put fresh sparkle in her beautiful eyes. The sparkle, he had been noticing with concern, had been missing for many months, ever since she had finally recognized the futility of all her efforts to help Izidore. The failure had sobered her, as though undermining the very mainspring of her being, for she seemed to interpret it not as just another manifestation of the mindless ruthlessness of Tsarist autocracy but as a personal defeat, due, she felt sure, to a waning of her power over men. In this she was not unlike her pretty niece, a resemblance which was hardly surprising considering how long and persistently she had worked to mold Regina to her own image.

"No one will do what I ask any more!" she wailed more than once, and wept real tears in Leon's arms. "That just means I'm getting to be middle-aged, a dowager! No, no, dearest, don't deny it, it's so! Oh, I know that in your eyes I'll always be beautiful, and I bless you for that. But," and the tears kept coming, "the truth is I must be losing my touch. . . ."

She slipped away from him, went to stand before a mirror, and searched for nonexistent wrinkles in her perfect face. "Well, if that's how it is, then *let me be* middle-aged. Tomorrow I'm going to shop for one of those little lace caps like Mama likes to wear. . . ." Having cast herself in this new role, she began to embellish. "Henceforth I'll just do what other matrons do: run my home, see to your comfort, maybe help launch our nieces socially, help the boys make the right connections. . . ."

Leon knew better than to reason with her when she was in this mood. Therefore, when in discussing Regina she switched to spinning fantasies about a romance with Prince Alfred, he put up only token opposition. For now at least her mournfulness vanished, self-denigration was forgotten, and she was once more at the top of her own inimitable form. If it came to choosing between his wife's well-being and his niece's, there was no question in Leon's mind which he would do. He only hoped Regina might be spared any unnecessary hurt and avoidable complications.

In a matter of days Regina and Alfred were taking their walks arm in arm, lingering in the archway of the tree-shaded courtyard of the Segals' house. It was becoming harder and harder to say goodbye. Finally one night they kissed. Alfred's lips were gentle at first, for he was genuinely stirred, and afraid of frightening her.

But as he felt her responding his mouth covered hers, his tongue parted her lips and darted in deep, hungry, exploring. And she shivered and for a moment was submissive and soft against him.

But only for a moment. "Oh, we mustn't," she whispered. "We mustn't! It's wrong!"

"Why? Is love ever wrong? Darling, tell me you love me!"

"I don't know. . . . I don't know. . . ."

He knew better than to press her. "I'll ask you again tomorrow. For I shall see you as usual, shan't I?"

"Yes, oh yes. . . ."

She fled from him, fled inside the house and up the stairs. She was trembling. She who had known only Adam's reverent touch could not believe what was happening to her. Her body felt on fire, her heart pounded, her skin tingled whenever she let herself dwell on the sensation she had just experienced—and she dwelt on it constantly, savoring again and again the strange new taste that lingered in her mouth. In her mind she began composing the letter she must write to Adam, terminating their engagement.

The following day she arrived at the Grossgliks' early, still undecided after a wakeful night whether to tell Alfred that her feeling for him must indeed be love or to let him wonder a little longer. She was forcing herself to keep in mind some of Salome's precepts. "Never let a man think you're overeager, no matter how much you love him and how sure you are of him. After all, you're not an apple, ripe and ready to fall into his lap. Rather, you're a pomegranate in an enchanted garden, which he must scale high walls to reach. In the end he'll only appreciate you more. That's the way men are, dear heart—they have to have their quest. . . ."

Pomegranate or plain apple, she was ready for plucking. The Bechstein took a lot of punishment that afternoon. She couldn't concentrate, couldn't practice properly, making the same mistakes over and over in a relatively easy passage of *Moments Musicales* which on other days she could do in bravura style.

Finally, in exasperation, she brought both hands down hard on the keyboard in hideous dissonance, which was a mistake, for instantly Aunt Salome called from the little sitting room beyond, "Dear heart, whatever is the matter?" She hurried in, then urged in gentle concern, "You're pale, and you do seem distrait. Come have a cup of tea with me. Tea is always good for the nerves."

So much for the day's practice. Regina abandoned it gratefully, sank down into a soft chair, and accepted the proffered tea and biscuits. "Thanks, Auntie. This was a *good* idea!"

"Something bothering you?"

"N-no. . ."

"Well, if there is, you know you can confide in me."

"Thanks, but it's nothing, really." *I must learn to be more careful! She mustn't guess, and she's got eyes in the back of her head!*

Salome thought, *A lovers' quarrel—so soon? But perhaps that's a good sign, perhaps they're really getting serious!"* Aloud she said, as though deliberately changing the topic, "We had a most interesting evening here yesterday, my dear, and such fascinating things developed! Aunt Bluma came over—she's been looking for a lawyer to take your cousin Izidore's case and she wanted to consult Uncle Leon. Because I don't know if you're aware of it or not, but your cousin Adam has had another big promotion and now there's money for that sort of thing, quite a bit of money, his mother tells me. . . ."

Although only yesterday she had decided she no longer cared, Regina, on hearing this, put her cup down with the greatest care lest the sudden shaking of her hands betray her. Inwardly she was seething. Well, now wasn't *that* nice—a big promotion, and Adam hadn't even thought fit to let her know directly! She had to find out this roundabout way! Very well, that settled it. She needn't feel bad any longer about breaking off with him.

"As I was saying," Salome went on, serenely unaware of her niece's state of mind, "there *is* going to be enough money for a change, and Adam very shrewdly suggested that we must at all costs retain a Gentile lawyer. Well, to make a long story short, our dear darling Alfred came in while we were talking, and would you believe it, he actually *asked* to be allowed to handle the whole thing! Not that he's an experienced attorney yet by any means—in fact, he's not even a full-fledged solicitor, and technically only clerking in a relative's firm—he himself was the first to make that point. But," she paused for effect, deliberately nibbling a sweet, "he also assured us that the case would have the benefit of the aura of the Czartoryski firm, and of course the full backing, the behind-the-scenes advice of their whole staff. Oh, he was extremely matter-of-fact, extremely practical about it! And who knows, it might be just the miracle we need! Izidore might even become a *cause célèbre.* With international implications. And it also might be the making of Alfred himself!"

"Why, how perfectly wonderful!"

Regina forgot Adam, forgot about her annoyance. She was seeing Alfred—and herself with him—at the center of a dangerous and exciting crusade. Seeing Izidore, to whom she had hardly given a thought in those interim years while he languished in prison, leaving the Pawiak a national hero. And everything became for her one with the glory of the fight for the White Eagle, for an independent Poland, for freedom.

She quickly thanked Salome for tea and forced herself back to the piano. When Alfred came in a while later, she was just launching into Chopin's *Revolutionary Étude*. She had no chance at all to speak to him alone and had to go home unattended, but when their eyes met she managed to signal to him with a quick nod of her head. Her lips formed a single soundless word: "Yes."

❧ *Five* ❧

Now she would have just as soon forgotten all about Adam and everything connected with him. So it seemed to her particularly unfortunate, when she got home, to find his mother there, big as life and deep in conversation with her parents. And this in itself was odd, since everyone knew that ever since the "illness" following Jacob's death Bluma hardly ever went out alone, especially toward dark. Nor was she in the habit of dropping in without invitation, and Regina was quite sure she hadn't been expected.

Regina was further puzzled to hear her mother say in a voice curiously edged with unspoken concern, "But of course you'll stay and have supper with us. You have to eat, so don't argue. I won't take no. It'll make you feel better, and afterwards we can have Kuba see you home. We wouldn't dream of letting you go back alone, especially feeling the way you do."

"I'm all right now, really I am," Bluma insisted. But she didn't sound like herself at all. "I'm just going to have to learn— I *am* learning—not to fall apart when bad news hits."

Bad news from the Pawiak maybe, Regina wondered. If that's what it was she would find out soon enough. She started to tiptoe down the hall to her own room in order to avoid facing her aunt, at least until suppertime. For although she had by then convinced herself that she was fully justified in feeling aggrieved and wanting nothing more to do with Adam, she also knew that any harsh move on her part would hurt him, and hurt him badly, just as she intended it should. Therefore his mother, a kind of extension of him, somehow became a rebuke to her conscience.

She had almost got past the half-closed living-room doors when her mother called to her, and she had no choice but go in. Dutifully, she leaned down to kiss Bluma's hand and was herself kissed on the forehead. "What news from our fabulously successful Cousin Adam?" she asked a trifle maliciously.

"Only very sad news, child, I'm afraid," her aunt answered, and too late Regina became aware of the pain and fear in her eyes. "For a while everything was going so well—so well maybe it was too good to last. And now my Adash is terribly ill. I just got word." She drew a shuddering breath. "It's pneumonia. *Pan* Pozner sent over to tell me, and that's why I'm here. So your father could explain it to me." And she repeated what sketchy information she had.

Pneumonia, Regina thought. *Why, people sometimes die of pneumonia!* And then a thought came to her of which she was instantly ashamed. *If Adam is so ill, how can I break the news to him that I don't want us to be engaged any more? Common decency wouldn't allow it. Now what'll I do?*

"Is he being sent home? What about his position? And what about all those wonderful plans to help poor Izidore?" Even as she asked this, she was grateful no one could possibly suspect that her concern was less for the fate of the young Pawiak prisoner than for his newly appointed counsel.

But Bluma, taking her interest at face value, actually managed a pale smile. "Bless you, child, I never knew you cared so much! I suppose Salome has been talking to you. But thank heaven at least we can go on with the defense. *Pan* Pozner sent word we needn't worry about finances, that Adam's salary will continue no matter how long he's out. He also said he personally is taking care of all the doctors' bills, I'm not to concern myself. . . ."

She broke off and sighed deeply, but when she spoke again her voice was steady. "Not worry? Of course I worry, how can I help it?"

Regina sighed, too, but wished she could slip away. "I understand, Auntie. And you're being very brave." She excused herself. She had a lot of thinking to do.

Alfred Czartoryski proved as good as his word. Without wasting a day he threw himself heart and soul into planning the defense which, he insisted, must extend beyond Izidore's case alone.

"Not enough, not nearly enough has been done for the victims of the Black Hundred dragnet raids! We're allowing hundreds, no, thousands to rot in jail while we hide our heads under silk eiderdowns. We keep warm, safe, we risk nothing, we hear no evil and see no evil. We've grown deaf to the voice of our national conscience, for isn't that what political prisoners are—our conscience?" Listening to him gave the family a feeling of hope.

Even the cautious Leon was impressed. "He's a born courtroom orator. And young and full of fire into the bargain. And ambitious. Maybe at last our poor Izidore's in luck."

Just as he had anticipated, Alfred also managed to stir up the senior members of his illustrious firm. "Let's say I've made my uncles anxious to help blot out the stain our late relative left on Poland's history. I get considerable pleasure out of picturing my blackguard of a great-great-great-granduncle sizzling on his perch in Hell—and by the way, is it a perch, or are they tied to the stake?" He paused, his mouth quirking humorously. "Be that as it may, it's eternal damnation. I think of him and I tell myself, what Adam Czartoryski sold to the Tsars, Alfred will help win back! Long live national honor!" Listening to him, Regina thought he was being absolutely splendid.

When the next visitors' day rolled around for the Pawiak prisoners, Idka Fabian was able to give her brother a whispered account of this verbal manifesto. It cheered him up for the rest of the week. He began looking forward to an eventual meeting with his defense lawyer, and even his friend Antek Rosol became infected with his enthusiasm.

The only one whose enthusiasm soon began to flag was Regina. For she was torn between pride in Alfred and a creeping uneasiness. It now seemed to her that he had less and less time for her. He still came in early several times a week, early enough to play a duet or two and walk her home in the dusk and whisper ardent phrases, and his hands when she was in his arms had grown bolder, his kisses longer. "But," she confided to her diary, "all this isn't getting us anywhere! All he talks about these days is the defense. Never about his love for me or our future. I suppose I just have to be patient. . . ."

Fall came early that year, with cold rain and sleet and an occasional premature snow flurry. Illness in the damp prisons increased, labor unrest was at a peak, and the newspapers again began to appear with wide white swaths slashing across front pages where the censors had pulled stories at the last minute. Rumor had it that the deletions had to do not just with unrest in Poland but with demonstrations all through the Empire. Something was also brewing in Mongolia and even farther to the east.

Talk about war with Japan became more and more insistent.

Alfred reported that the Czartoryski firm had it on good authority, from highly placed but trustworthy contacts in St. Petersburg, that persons who had the ear of Tsar Nicholas were strongly urging amnesty for political prisoners at Christmas. Such a move, even if it did not include those accused of the gravest crimes, would, they argued, add immensely to the Little Father's dubious popularity. But whether the mulish, self-willed young Autocrat of All the Russias would heed his advisors was a moot question.

"Of course, we can't just take it for granted such a thing will happen," Alfred warned. "We can't begin to act as though it might. But it does indicate one thing: dear Nicholas and his Alexandra are having some sleepless nights!"

Regina's diary entry for that day read, "Right now I wish there had never been an Izidore Fabian! Alfred has become so preoccupied, half the time he pays more attention to the family, yes, even that homely Idka, than he does to me. . . ."

In mid-October the Kronenbergs gave a ball in honor of Missy Pozner and Henryk Meisels, and because so many influential persons of the Jewish community were included in the guest list, Alfred suggested it might be politic for him to be invited as well. In such a warm, festive atmosphere it would be easy for him to approach a dozen men whose support might be specially useful in any future defense campaign. For even considering the risks, many a Jewish financier would find it hard to refuse a Czartoryski.

The night of the ball was unseasonably warm and balmy, which mercifully meant no chilled blue fingers, no red and shiny noses after exposure. Regina, for whom Salome had also wangled an invitation, dressed at the Grossgliks' and she and Alfred drove with them to the Kronenbergs' in the carriage Eugenia sent for them. As she mounted the stairs in the brilliantly illuminated mansion, Alfred whispered, "You're going to be the belle of the ball, my sweet. And I mean to monopolize you when the dancing starts, but I also have work to do. I'm sure you understand."

She punished him by saving him only half the dances on her program. She was very much sought after, and even Henryk asked for a waltz. "You're looking very charming tonight. And, I see, you're much in demand." She thought she detected a mocking note behind the compliment.

The dance ended and Alfred claimed her for the next one, saving her from answering Henryk. Later, as she went in to supper on his arm, he urged, "Let's go hide in the conservatory! I don't need champagne and caviar—only you!"

It took all of her willpower to refuse. Had he simply said, "I love you, come with me," she might not have been such a stickler for convention.

But he's going to say it, he's going to say it, he's going to. . . .

While the footmen glided about, refilling glasses and plates, Alfred remarked, eyebrow cocked, "You know, I do believe I'm the only Christian here, except for the servants."

"And," she pointed out, "those who have converted."

He laughed as at a very funny joke. "And you know what they say about *those,* don't you, my dear?"

"No, tell me."

"Same old Yids only they stink worse."

"Alfred, how can you!" she cried out, shocked. She hadn't known words could hurt so much.

He appeared unconcerned and a little surprised. "Oh, I'm only quoting. You mustn't take it so to heart."

She thought this was her chance to pin him down. "Alfred, seriously, does it matter to you that I'm Jewish?"

"Why should it?" he answered easily. "It only adds to your piquant, exotic beauty."

"You *really and truly* don't mind, then?"

"Don't be a child, my sweet."

But he didn't say what she had hoped he would, that between them nothing could make any difference, that he loved her as she was and for what she was, and that this was all he cared about.

❦ *Six* ❧

O N A CHILL, DRIZZLY Sunday afternoon later that month, Idka Fabian stood shivering in the line that snaked round the courtyard of Pawiak Prison, a shawl around her shoulders and a basket over her arm, waiting as she had done on countless other Sundays for the massive iron doors to open and the guards to start letting visitors in.

She had long ago learned always to include among the gifts she brought her brother extra packets of cigarette tobacco, tea, sugar, sausage, and cheese, alternating the food packages with the books he wanted. This made it easy for the guards, who systematically helped themselves to half the provisions as they searched visitors, to take what they wanted while giving the books only a cursory glance.

After all this time, Idka remained Izidore's most faithful visitor. She hardly ever missed, especially now that she was old enough to come alone. The guards, who by now knew her, had gradually forgotten her exact relationship to the prisoner Fabian and began to assume she was his wife, which led to the standard crude jokes about lusty young grass widows.

"Hey, girl, don't it get lonely for you in bed on cold winter nights? I got something would cheer you up no end, make you feel better real fast! How about it? I'll be coming off duty just when you leave!"

At first she used to be mortified, reduced to rage and helpless tears. Then she learned simply not to listen. She was only glad her mother never suspected what she was being subjected to—she might have forbidden the visits.

The waiting line was just beginning to move when she heard her name called. *"Pani* Idka! *Pani* Idka!"* She turned to see the father of Izidore's bunk-mate, Antek Rosol, waving to her.

She had come to know Jan Rosol from standing on innumerable such waiting lines, from sitting side by side with him on a hard, narrow bench as they faced the prisoners in the enormous barracks-like visitors' room where all semblance of privacy, save the privacy created by confusion and noise, was denied. She was rather in awe of him, for he seemed to her a legend come to life. In his late fifties, he was a pavior by trade. His father had been executed after the rebellion of '63, his brother was even now serving twenty years at hard labor in the Urals, his son was "sitting," and he himself was a veteran of two prison terms. Jan Rosol, or "The Old One" as he was called in the movement to differentiate him from "The Young One," Antek, was a man totally without hesitation or fear, totally dedicated, a tireless organizer. At the same time he was warm and easygoing, with an inborn optimism that never failed to buoy the younger people.

"I belong to the Good-Soup dynasty of the labor movement," he liked to quip, referring to the literal meaning of the family surname, which was "broth." He was fond of telling a story, doubtless apocryphal, about the hanging of his father.

"He stood straight and proud on the slope below the Citadel where the execution was to take place. And he yelled to those who'd come to see the hanging. 'Think this is the end of me? It's not the end, not on your life! For who could put an end to Rosol! I'll live as long as the good soup boils and bubbles on the back of every Polish stove! And some day the pot will boil over, and it's going to scald the Tsar to death!'

"They say he began to sing then—he had a fine bass voice— *Poland is not yet lost so long as the good soup simmers. . . .* He sang till they strung him up and choked the voice out of him." Jan used to tell it all proudly, then add, "I wasn't there to see him off, being under arrest myself for the first time."

Idka let a couple of people get ahead of her and waited for him. When he caught up with her he put a huge horny hand on her arm. "Glad I ran into you," he said heartily. "My wife was saying only last night, 'If you run into Idka, tell her I'd like to see her again. In fact, bring her home to supper. Tell her *I'm cooking up some of my special soup.*' "

Idka had never met Jan's wife nor had she been to their house. She had no trouble translating the invitation: "We're having a meeting with a special speaker. Join us."

She nodded to indicate she would be there. She knew that a great many such meetings were being held around town lately, secret meetings in people's homes, the speakers mainly exiles smuggled in from various parts of Europe where they continued to be active. They came bringing directives and reporting on discussions, on theoretical congresses held by the leaders, Polish and Russian, of the Socialists and the Economists and the Jewish Bund and the PPS, the Polish Socialist Party, which covered not only the Congress Kingdom but also Galicia and German Poland, and the SDKPiL, the Social-Democrats of Poland and Lithuania. The Russian Social-Democrats, Idka had recently heard, had by now split and were calling themselves Bolsheviks and Mensheviks, and the Polish SD was considering joining forces with one of the groupings, she wasn't sure which. She found it all pretty confusing, sometimes wishing someone would explain to her how much the labels really meant so long as they all represented patriots. She was also anxious to learn to distinguish between them now that she had become serious about doing underground work.

"I'd love to come and eat with you," she told Jan, raising her voice above the general din. "I do so enjoy *Pani* Rosol's cooking."

Izidore's gaunt face brightened when he saw his sister.

"I knew you'd come, you always do, but at the last minute when they start calling off names I never can help thinking maybe this time no one will show up." He kissed her, smelling of dampness and unwashed clothing, and voiced his standard warning that was only half-humor: "When you get home be sure to check for lice."

"Yes, I know."

She reached into the basket and brought out a fresh apple, and he sank his teeth in it. But his real hunger was for the books. She had brought a Greek grammar that he had long wanted, and a special gift from Uncle Leon, Shakespeare's tragedies in one volume, leatherbound and printed on India paper.

"Thanks, Idziula," he said, using the old pet name. "And be sure to thank Leon for me. The Shakespeare is supposed to be a magnificent translation. Pretty soon," he grinned wryly, "I'll be the best-read and most cultivated convict in the city."

"Pretty soon we hope to have you out of here." And she began to tell the latest news on his case, how Alfred was pushing to expedite the inquest and secure his release, and how, with the Czartoryski connections and sufficient pressure there was a chance—"Just a chance, mind you, so don't get your hopes up too soon!"—to have his sentence, once it was handed down, confined to the time he'd already spent in jail, which God knows was long enough, especially considering the charges. "Floating garlands on the river . . . what a terrible crime!" she finished bitterly.

He had finished the apple and was now attacking the cheese. "Tell me about everyone at home."

She said Viktor was getting married soon and bringing his bride home to live, and that all Rosie could talk about these days was her own wedding. "All we hear about is linens and featherbeds!" she commented a trifle contemptuously, then added, "It's Adam's last promotion and big raise that are making Rosie's marriage possible. And that goes for your defense, too." She decided to say nothing about Adam's illness. Izidore had enough on his mind as it was.

Her brother's comment was typical. "Well, well, so big brother is turning into a real success. He might even end up a capitalist. You know, when I think how it used to be, him and his old friends, especially that Olek, I have to laugh." But he wasn't laughing. Seriously, he asked, "Any idea what changed him?"

"Who's to know? Maybe it's like Mama always says—no one really knows his own family till something happens. Or maybe it was that girl who went off and left him. Still, give the devil his due—he's always generous with us." And with this bit of lip service to tolerance, she dismissed Adam. "But I didn't come here to discuss him. Tell me about you."

"What's to tell?" Izidore sighed, looking at her with Bluma's clear, tired gray eyes. His domed forehead, too, was Bluma's— especially, his sister realized with a start, now that his hair had begun to recede. He was too young for a receding hairline. But what remained of his bush of hair, badly in need of trimming, gave him, she decided, an interesting resemblance to Socrates. And had Socrates, too, developed this same prison pallor in the days before it came time for him to drink the hemlock?

She told him about the similarity and it seemed to amuse him. "Thanks. Only Socrates had a bigger head—ergo, a bigger brain."

All too soon the visiting hours were over. A bell clanged, guards shouted orders.

"I didn't have a chance to tell you," Idka said as she rose to go. "I'm going home with *Pan* Jan—he said the good soup was bubbling and I must share their meal. It's the first time he's asked me."

"I envy you," Izidore said. "And wait till Antek hears! Well, sister, eat hearty for all three of us." They hugged and kissed. "And," he added, quoting a popular motto of the times, *"Sursum corda!* Be of good cheer." Prison guards did not understand Latin.

The Rosols' flat, in an old wooden building across the river in the Praga district, was already crowded when Idka came in. There were no empty chairs, people sat on tables or cross-legged on the floor. A man was giving a report. He was telling his audience about what he called a militant new labor tactic developed by the Social-Democrats and endorsed at some recent meetings in Brussels and later in London—the tactic of the general strike.

"Consider our situation, brothers and sisters." As she listened, Idka thought there was something familiar about him. "Historically, the moment is ripe to start giving direction to our seething masses. The revolutionary ferment exists, that's undeniable—we can feel it not just here in Poland, but everywhere. The whole Empire is a powder keg, and when the explosion does come, our country with its passion for freedom and its tradition of independence will inevitably—and when I say that, it's not just my own way of thinking—it will inevitably become a key center of struggle. But heaven help us if we allow the holy fervor of our people to turn into a mere nationalist uprising, as always happened in the past—if we let the aristocrats and the big bourgeoisie have things their way. Because if we do, we'd just be exchanging a set of foreign masters for domestic ones. . . ."

"All right, all right," an impatient voice interrupted from the back. "But what's all this got to do with the general strike?"

"Everything." The speaker paused, looking first nettled, then sheepish. "Bear with me, comrade. I know I may sound long-winded, but that's because I like to begin at the beginning, with the nature of things." Thoughtfully, he rubbed the side of his neck with a powerful hand, and in that instant Idka recognized Olek Piotrowski, though she hadn't see him since Adam's university days.

"Now about the general strike," Olek began again. "We're all familiar with the sympathy strike, like the one in Lodz last summer when all the men at Scheibler quit once the women weavers struck. From this to a general shutdown is only a step. Give the signal at the right moment, and everything will shut down—the mills, the retail shops, schools, railroads, streetcars, even the mails, even the newspapers and telephone and telegraph.

"The telephone and telegraph are especially crucial." He was warming to his subject. "Cut off communications, and the whole country comes to a standstill. The local garrisons are paralyzed without orders from the top. The army becomes useless. When orders don't come through, what's the military reduced to? So we take over, the government topples, and all before the Tsar can say boo. And by the time he starts screaming, it'll already be too late. Because by then the people will have discovered their own strength. And that's not a pipedream, either."

"Sounds great in principle," the same heckling voice called out, "*provided* we can do it. Which I submit is questionable. Whoever heard of a hundred Poles agreeing on a tactic, let alone a million!"

"In that case," Olek insisted, "it's up to us to change that. I'm not saying it's going to be easy—only that it's possible. And the secret is organization and more organization. We must organize and we must educate. It's going to take time, sure, but it can be done."

The formal part of the meeting ended and was followed by open discussion, detailed and often personal, about how to handle this factory, that sweatshop. Idka listened attentively but soon lost the thread. Now she understood how little she really knew and wished she had more theory. What she was witnessing here today was a far cry from mere slogan-shouting like "Down with the Tsar, Up the White Eagle!" She had never suspected before that revolution—the fight for true freedom—was such hard, painstaking, systematic work.

When the crowd finally began to thin she made her way to where Olek was standing deep in conversation with Jan and his wife. "You probably don't remember me. I'm Idka Fabian."

Olek looked vague at first, then his face cleared. "Of course! Adam's little sister! But you were just a youngster then. You've changed, you've grown, and if I'm not mistaken," he pumped her hand, "your thinking has developed in a very healthy direction!"

She flushed beet-red. "I suppose that was inevitable."

He laughed. "Well, you know the old saying: 'Drop a pebble in a pool and watch the ripples spread.' "

Jan put in, "Her brother Izidore is a pal of my Antek. Two years now they've been sitting together."

Olek sobered. "That tells me a lot." They talked on for a long time after everyone else left, the Rosols bringing out wine and bread and sausage and urging them to make themselves at home.

She brought him up to date on everything that had happened to her and hers while he was out of the country. She spoke of Izidore's arrest and her father's death and her mother's illness, and about Adam's going to work for Pozner and the Caucasus venture and finally the pneumonia which had nearly cost him his life. "He's better now, he'll be coming home soon. But, of course, it'll take him a long time to mend."

Olek said he was sorry to hear the grim news, but mostly seemed interested in finding a younger Fabian here at the meeting. "You've no idea the pleasure it gives an old war-horse like me to see new faces, feel there's new blood flowing in."

She insisted he was giving her more credit than she deserved. "After all, someone in the family has to keep doing things . . ."

"Girl, if more people felt like you do, we'd be invincible. Too many are summer soldiers, vanishing at the first sign of trouble."

About his own work he remained carefully vague, volunteering only the information that he was living in Lodz, where his wife and her old friend Wanda Borowska had started a children's clinic. "You remember Wanda, don't you? She hid out at your house that time. Well, they both practice under their married names, and so far the police have made no connection between them and those girl students who. . . Lord, what a lot of water has gone under the bridge!"

When it was time to go home, Idka asked eagerly, "Will I see you again?"

But Olek was vague once more. "It all depends. On fate, on luck, on circumstances. Just don't be surprised if one of these days someone—maybe myself, maybe my wife or Wanda or someone we send—comes knocking on your door asking for help. One never knows any more who may turn up where, or when. The main thing is to be sure that when there's the need, we have good friends we can count on."

They said goodbye at the Alexander Bridge. The weather had turned piercing cold, but as Idka waited for her omnibus on a street corner she hardly felt the wind.

❦ *Seven* ❧

The success of the women weavers at Scheibler's that Olek
had mentioned proved to be a morale booster for the whole working population of Lodz. Their anger, long banked and steadily
smoldering since the May Day and May Third repressions of the
past couple of years, was now perilously close to bursting into
open flame, and the preceding summer had done nothing to cool
it.

Actually, the summer of 1903 had been neither better nor
worse than most. It was simply that the hot months were always,
for Lodz, a season of dysentery, diptheria and colitis, since the
city's sanitation system, long a national scandal, was only a trifle
less primitive than in the Middle Ages. Its cisterns and cesspools
a breeding ground for bacteria, its muddy little river hardly better than an open sewer, Lodz breathed fetid menace in the faces of
its inhabitants. Neither water nor milk was fit to drink unboiled,
an unpeeled apple constituted clear and present danger, and garden lettuce bought in the open stalls could kill.

And since, unlike tuberculosis or rickets which could be decently contained within the slums, the summer diseases were no
respecters of class, each spring the rich and the well-to-do fled,
like the British in India, to more salubrious locations. In summer
only the workers and their families remained, along with their
resentful overseers and a few factory owners so dedicated to
money-grubbing that not even threats of an epidemic could drive
them away. And of these it was said among the workers that

nothing could harm them—they were so mean neither God nor the devil himself would want them.

Every spring city officials talked piously about the crying need for a proper, modernized sewage system, but nothing was ever done about it. In the backyards of shacks and fine mansions alike, horse-drawn sanitation carts stopped regularly to siphon off human excrement out of pits where it was allowed to collect. On the days the carts came, the air filled with insufferable stench. And the flies, buzzing their indignation at being disturbed, settled on the faces of sleeping infants, who promptly sickened and died. And the distracted mothers, often already again big with child, prayed to the Virgin Mary, "Holy Mother, you who yourself once bore a son and suffered His loss, intercede for us with our Heavenly Father! This time let it be different. Let my baby live! Or else may all seed dry up in my belly!"

At the peak of the heat the news began to spread through the tenements that a couple of new doctors had opened consultation rooms in a modest house way out on Ogrodowa Street. The place was something the like of which the city had never seen. Bright and cheerful, homey, and the fees so low a body didn't have to be afraid to go in. Most unbelievable of all, the doctors were both women. True, one had a husband working with her who was also called *Pan Doktor* and wore a white smock, but he himself was quick to explain he wasn't the kind of doctor who saw patients. Seems he only worked with microscopes and blood and sputum and urine samples, in a room in the back they called their laboratory.

Another thing, the ladies Piotrowska and Gronowicz—*Pani Doktor* Maryla and *Pani Doktor* Wanda as their patients were soon calling them—always tried to work it so that one or the other was available no matter what time of day or night a person needed help. Never did you hear either of them say, just because you were too poor to pay extra for disturbing them at some ungodly hour, that you could jolly well come back at a regular consultation time or else try the city charity wards. And those two were real angels with the children.

"You should see the toys and coloring books in the waiting room!" women told one another. "Ever hear the like? Kid starts to play, by the time it's his turn to be looked at, he forgets to be scared!" Even mistrust of women doctors quickly vanished in the face of such an approach. Soon people in the factory compounds were calling the new offices *"our* clinic." "Our clinic" was where you brought the children to be vaccinated against smallpox. The priest might try to forbid you, calling vaccination a flouting of God's will. But he didn't have to be told, did he?

"God's will, my ass," one woman with a pockmarked face summed it all up for the two doctors' benefit. "Just tell me how would it add to His glory for my Hanka to go through life with a mug like mine? Naah," she made short shrift of the argument. "Better let her be safe. And if later on she turns out too pretty for her own good, I'll handle that, too. Whale the living daylights out of her if I have to. And that'll be that, I promise you."

Could anyone, Maryla commented later as she told her husband about the conversation, hope for more complete, wholehearted acceptance?

"Just goes to show," Felix Gronowicz enlarged on the subject later that same night, "what can be accomplished when the historical conditions are ripe." He had just finished tidying up his laboratory and now joined Wanda and the Piotrowskis in their communal apartment at the back of the house. "There may be times when clothes make the man, but," he shrugged out of his white smock, white no longer at the end of a long day's work, "it's not our medical garb that's the making of us. No, it's history we have to thank!"

"History and maybe a few other things," his wife contradicted. "For instance, we happen to be good doctors but we don't charge an arm and a leg." She poured Felix a glass of tea, added lemon and sugar, and pushed the concoction across the table to him. "Even the poorest patients know they'll be well treated. They trust us. Don't you think that's what makes the difference?"

Over the years Wanda Borowska-Gronowicz had grown to love her scarecrow husband more and more deeply and never gave a thought any longer to the circumstances that had led to their marriage. She who could be so rigidly intolerant, so unforgiving, was not in the least disturbed by the clowning Felix still often indulged in. She even regarded his tendency to make grandiose, sweeping statements as an endearing foible. But it was not in her nature to let those statements go unchallenged.

"We're earning the reputation we have, Felix, as you very well know. Earning our patients' trust, and their affection, too. Only this morning a woman said to me, 'One reason we all come to you, *Pani Doktor,* is you never act like you're a fine lady and we're dirt. The city hospital doctors, bah, even the *felczer,* the barber-surgeon, they all lord it over us. But you people—you treat us all like we're your equals."

"And what did you tell her?"

"Just that we believe all people are equal."

"And doesn't that prove my point?" her husband crowed. He dropped more sugar into his tea, stirred thoughtfully, and forgot to drink it. "Don't you see, everything you're doing is based on sound revolutionary theory!"

"It's based on my own deepest convictions, and you know it."

"Sound revolutionary theory!" he insisted.

"Felix, for pity's sake!"

"When your husband gets stubborn," Olek put in, reaching for the teapot, "It's like arguing with a mule, Wanda."

Felix defended his position. "But don't you really see, any of you? There's no contradiction. It's elementary, it's what we all have learned. I quote: 'to build up the strength of the masses one must educate them while at the same time appealing to their enlightened self-interest.' I apply this theory to our own practice; and I translate: each youngster whose tonsils you girls swab, each smallpox vaccination, may one day mean another convert to the cause."

"You talking about the child or the parent?" his wife asked.

"What's the difference?" Felix looked elaborately pained. "After all, the revolution wasn't built in a day!"

By now they realized he'd been pulling their leg. "All right, all right," Olek laughed. "So you weaseled out of that one, old son. It's just that when you try to sound cold-blooded you don't ever convince me."

And yet, he reflected, in a very profound sense Felix was right.

For while it was true that setting up a model medical practice in a working-class neighborhood had been both his own wife's and Wanda's goal ever since he could remember, they knew they were also serving the needs of the movement. That, in fact, was one reason they'd left Switzerland when they did. That was why they had settled in Lodz. No, there was no contradiction here at all.

Week by week the work went on. Week by week the stream of patients grew. Women in rusty black, drab kerchiefs over their heads, brought children for treatment, advice, information. And if some of the information had nothing to do with medicine, well then, that only went to show how much the lady doctors knew!

Afterwards, at home, usually late in the evening when the last chores were done and the children safely asleep and out of ear-shot, the women talked to their men about things they had learned. "Tomorrow night there's a protest meeting about this last cut in pay. It's free, everyone's welcome, so why don't you go?" Voices would drop to a whisper. "Want to know what else the *Pani Doktor* told us today? That it isn't enough to hate the Tsar, we also got to stand up to the bosses. . . ."

And if at this point the man urged caution, if he asked how could his wife be so sure the doctors weren't deliberate govern-ment provocateurs, she would just shrug the question off as pure male imbecility. "You wouldn't say that if you met them face to face, you oaf. But me, I got eyes in my head and I got a heart, so I know. Informers, *them?* All you got to do is watch 'em with a sick child. Especially the tall, dark, skinny one that's got a baby of her own."

Since Wanda and Felix had no other choice, they were com-pelled to keep Felka's crib where one or the other could always keep an eye on it, which meant she was generally in sight of ev-eryone who came in. The little girl was technically long past in-fancy and her physical development was normal, but she didn't sit up or talk or laugh or cry, except for an occasional odd little whimper. She seldom even moved. To mothers of normal chil-dren her condition was painfully, glaringly apparent.

They made abundant comment, drew their own conclusions, and their sympathy for Felka's parents swept away any remaining reserve. "Can you imagine, fine educated people like that, and the kid's an idiot. Sweet little mite, pretty, and good as gold, but an idiot. Four years old and has to be spoon-fed. What a cross to bear! And the mother and father are so good to her, so patient, always doing for her. And still hoping, hoping, hoping that one of these days a miracle will help her. Breaks your heart to watch. Plenty of people in the same boat would just have her put away and forget about her. But not them. They're saints, I tell you. So don't talk to me about *them* being informers!"

And neither Felix nor Wanda, yearning over their helpless little cretin daughter, guessed how much their personal tragedy affected the feeling for them in the community.

As summer turned into fall, the doctors' house became a meeting place, a center of secret after-hours activity. A small, crude, hand-operated printing press was installed, hidden securely away in the back of a closet full of medical supplies. Ream upon ream of onionskin paper lay buried under piles of soiled linens. The tea kettle was always at a simmer.

Leaflets run off early in the evening were dry and ready for distribution by midnight. As visitors rose to say goodnight, each would slip a small bundle under his coat. The leaflets were frankly inflammatory these days. They did not mince words.

Workers of Lodz! Do you understand the huge swindle of which you are being made victims? In the name of a business crisis your wages have been cut and cut again. At the same time you're forbidden to form trade unions for your protection.

They sweat you for taxes, and those same taxes go to pay for an army and a police force to keep you enslaved! And in the meantime your city remains one big sewer, and it kills your children as surely as if they were drowning in filth. But dare speak up, and the bosses sic the cossacks on you!

Workers of Lodz, the time has come to revolt! How long will you let your own taxes pay the Tsar's bloody henchmen just waiting to cut you down? How long

will you go on watching your little ones go hungry—
and die?

HOW LONG, BROTHERS AND SISTERS?
HOW LONG?

Workers of Lodz, forget your fears and unite! Together
you can be strong! So close your ranks, stand up for
your rights! The time to act has come! The time is
now!

The leaflets turned up everywhere, and it was the women who
responded to them with the greatest passion. And at about that
same time a song became popular in the city, a long-forgotten
peasant chant singularly fitted to the needs, the mood of the
hour. It had no title that anyone knew, so the women called it
The Hungry Lullaby. And just because it was a lullaby, the censors
took a long time catching on to what it really meant, and the
women sang it openly for weeks. They even sang it at their looms
like a work song, the supreme and satisfying irony being that the
overseers encouraged the singing because it always helped performance.

The lullaby was in a minor key and began softly, plaintively,
like a mother's keening:

> *Oh, we've no bread*
> *Though all our days are spent in labor,*
> *To feed our young ones we've no bread. . .*
> *Milady's dancing*
> *And milord's romancing*
> *And our kids go hungry to bed. . .*
> *That's our fate, the poor man's fate,*
> *Nothing for our babes but death . . . and hate. . .*

The women seldom risked singing the second stanza aloud, for
even a mindless overseer might be able to distinguish between a
plaint and bitter defiance.

> *But dare speak out, my little one,*
> *And you're silenced with a gun!*

And just dare to dream you're free
It's Siberia one-two-three!
That's our fate, the poor man's fate,
Ours a heritage of blood . . . and hate!

Few of the women weavers were aware that it had been
Wanda, their own *Pani Doktor,* who first started them on the
song. She hadn't even known she knew it until it surfaced, unexpectedly, out of some deep-buried storehouse of childhood memory, out of a time when her own peasant nurse had lulled her to
sleep with it in the town of her birth. She had sat crooning it late
one night to her wakeful child, and it had had a magic effect on
Felka. So the following day she tried it on a small, fretful, very
sick patient, and he, too, instantly stopped crying and went to
sleep. She tried it again, and then again, and soon a few of the
mothers picked it up. Now it was sweeping the city.

Oh we've no bread
Though all our days are spent in labor,
To feed our young ones we've no bread. . .

From Lodz *The Hungry Lullaby* traveled along the railroad
spurs to Zgierz and Pabianice, to one after another along the
string of cheerless industrial towns and settlements that led north
to Warsaw, east to Lublin, south to Kielce and Przemysl and
Lwow. It echoed wherever there were women at work. In the capital it became not just a work song but a street song, a prison
song, and even, for a few nights, a cabaret song.

The cabaret was promptly raided, but the swarming gendarmes and Black Hundred agents who questioned management,
entertainers, waiters, and patrons alike came up against a blank
wall of injured innocence. Lullaby? What lullaby? Who in his
right mind would choose a lullaby as a number for singing in a
night spot? A person would have to be crazy. . . .

The police, knowing they were being lied to, made a quick
search in the hope of uncovering, if not a conspiracy, then at least
a stack of forbidden sheet music. But all they managed to unearth
was a score of *The Merry Widow* and another, all dog-eared, of

The Count of Luxembourg. Furious, and swearing to come back and catch them all yet, they finally left, and the story promptly made the rounds, a boost to the city's morale.

Within the next twenty-four hours snatches of the song were heard along the main thoroughfares and in the parks. Handbills with the words turned up in streetcars, in hotel lobbies, in public buildings, and, of course, as broadsides pasted on walls and fences. The police went about tearing them down, but just as fast as they did this, new ones appeared. Schoolchildren brought the handbills home in their book bags and housewives in their marketing baskets.

Alfred Czartoryski brought a handbill triumphantly into the Grossglik household, along with the story of the cabaret raid.

Idka Fabian learned *The Hungry Lullaby* at a secret meeting one night, memorized it, then taught it to everyone at home, including her new sister-in-law, Tynia, Viktor's bride. Tynia was still an unknown quantity, too new to the family for Idka to be able to gauge what went on in her pretty blonde head. But she taught school, and maybe, Idka reasoned, would find someone to pass it on to. You could never tell about those things. You just dropped the seed and watched it germinate.

Izidore Fabian and his cellmates heard the song at dawn one cold morning when a new group of women prisoners were herded into the Pawiak courtyard under heavy military guard. The women, prodded by knouts and rifle butts and the tips of the soldiers' black-tarred boots, sang as they stumbled in. Then there was a sharp command, a blow, a scream, and finally silence. But the next day they heard the song again.

And finally Adam Fabian, too, heard the song.

He heard it during his first hour back on Polish soil.

The Orient Express bringing him home at last after a month of convalescence in the Crimea had been rolling all morning through flat cultivated fields. His meager reserves of strength already taxed to the limit by the long tedious journey, he sat listlessly at the window of his compartment, only half seeing, only half awake.

Barely formed thoughts floated in drowsy patterns through his mind. Well, at least he hadn't died, he was mending, he had strict orders not to worry, and anyway there was nothing left to worry about for he was going home, home to Regina, and as soon as he had his strength back he would talk to Uncle Karol man to man and everything would turn out for the best. *For the best, for the best, for the best,* echoed the wheels. He drowsed off, his head nodding in rhythm.

Around midday he woke as the train ground to a stop. The door of his compartment slid open and the conductor poked his head in. "Forty-five minutes layover, sir. We're taking on water. If you've a mind to, now's your chance to buy a lunch. No need to hurry, eat hearty. . . ."

Adam thanked the man, stretched, and stood up. He wasn't hungry but a turn on the platform would be a welcome break. He reached for his coat. As he did so, he heard steps along the corridor outside his compartment. Someone went by, whistling a haunting tune.

The railroad station was large but primitive, with no real waiting room and no buffet facilities of any sort. But half a dozen peasant women had improvised stalls along the wall of the barracks-like wooden structure. They sat, each surrounded by baskets of food, hawking their wares in the sing-song dialect of the eastern provinces.

"Black bread, white bread, sausage, cheese, fresh sweet milk, clabber, hot tea, what's your pleasure?"

The last one in the line, large, heavy-breasted, with chipped yellow teeth, surveyed him from under her flowered red shawl. "Pot of clabber for you, young mister" she pronounced it "clyabber." She tried to tempt him further. "Nice hunk of chicken, maybe? Still warm, fresh from the oven only an hour ago!"

She lifted the white cloth off one of her baskets and the aroma of home cooking awakened his appetite. "Piece of chicken and some black bread would be fine, Mother."

She reached in with her bare fingers, choosing and picking. As she did so she hummed. "Oh, we've no bread, though all our days are spent in labor. . ." Adam recognized the tune he had just heard, which had so intrigued him.

"What's that you're singing, Mother?"

She looked up, half surprised, half suspicious. "And where've *you* been that you don't know?" Then with elaborate unconcern she offered, "Just a song I learned from my granny. Heard it from the cradle, I have. Now, would you believe it, the whole country's taken to singing it like mad. How could you miss it?"

He explained that he'd been out of Poland for well over a year. "I'm only now on my way home to Warsaw."

The explanation seemed to satisfy her. "That's a horse of a different color." She was mulling something over, coming to a decision. "Say, you can read, can't you, mister? But that's a stupid question! A fine lad like you, well dressed and from the city, of course you can read! Well, I think I have something for you." And from under the mound of dismembered chicken parts she pulled out a sheet of tissue paper, crumbled and stained, the print on it smudged with grease.

"Here, take it along. Enjoy it." She winked at him. "It's your dessert."

He glanced down at indistinct words, but she stopped him with a quick impatient gesture. "Not here. You born yesterday or something? Stick it in your pocket! Wait till the train starts, and make sure you're alone."

Suddenly he felt he had never been away. "So that's how it is, eh?"

"And how did you think it would be? Same as always, only different. Because this time, who knows, this time maybe. . ."

The next instant she was gruff with him. "Now don't stand there like a boob, blocking the way, mister! You want something else, say so, pay for it, and move. I got to find me a couple other customers before the train leaves!" And the chanting began again. "Black bread, white bread, roast chicken, fresh sweet milk, clyabber . . . what's your pleasure?"

He paid her with a silver ruble and waved away the change. "Light a candle in church for freedom, come Sunday."

She crossed herself. "May the sweet Jesus forgive me, there's better things to do with money these days than waste it on wax and wick!"

Then the boarding bell sounded, and Adam sprinted for the

train, forgetting he was forbidden to exert himself. He swung up the steps just as the wheels began slowly to turn. Only then did he realize he was out of breath. The effort had exhausted him, and his heart was pounding. He drew in a shuddering lungful of air.

"Goodbye and God bless you, Mother!" he shouted, waving. And was as pleased as a child when the old woman waved back.

❧ *Eight* ❧

A DAM'S MISDIRECTED, long-delayed letter from Erivan finally reached Regina in the same post as his hastily scribbled note announcing his arrival in Warsaw within a matter of days.

"At last, at long last the doctors are letting me out and I'm coming home, home to you, my dearest dear!" Here, whether due to weakness or excitement, his handwriting became barely legible. "They keep warning me I'm not altogether well yet, that I must remember to be careful. But I suspect everything will cure itself as soon as I'm with you again. . . . ."

She looked at the postmark, compared the date with the one on her calendar, and was thrown into a panic. Time had betrayed her. He was already on the way. She could all but hear the wheels of his train rolling across the eastern plains, closer and closer, louder and louder. A little more, and she must face him. He would cease to be merely an embarrassment that she could conveniently shut out of her mind. He would become—no, he already was—an immediate, living threat. And between her and Alfred nothing was settled.

In fact, she had been seeing less and less of her young prince since the Kronenberg ball, for he had thrown himself wholeheartedly into plans to make of Izidore Fabian's case a true *cause célèbre,* or at any rate something close to one, and seemed to have no time left for anything else. When they did meet, it was only fleetingly. He remained unfailingly charming and occasionally whispered words she chose to interpret as a promise of greater ardor in the future. But that was all. She had to resign herself to being patient, waiting for Izidore's case to come to trial, so that their love could once more take what she felt was its natural course.

Now she couldn't wait any longer.

But how did one prompt a man with other things on his mind to declare his feelings and his intentions? What did other women do under similar circumstances? What would Aunt Salome have done? Regina spent a night tossing and turning and in the morning was none the wiser. Perhaps, she finally decided, she ought to spend all her time these next few days at her aunt and uncle's, waiting, watching her chances for something to suggest itself. Probably all Alfred needed was to be made aware of the awkward position she was being forced into on his account, and as soon as he knew he would make everything right.

But although she sat practicing on the Bechstein long beyond her usual hours, Alfred did not come. Only Bluma, again venturing out alone, which probably meant she was on urgent business, stopped in briefly one afternoon to discuss something with her sister-in-law. Through the closed doors of the adjoining small sitting room Regina could hear the two women in earnest conversation. But inasmuch as Adam's mother was the last person in the city she cared to face right then, she pretended to be engrossed in her Czerny exercises and did not stir from the piano bench.

Shortly afterwards she heard Bluma leave, and presently Aunt Salome called to her. "Regina, Ginia darling, surely you've worked long enough! Come join me in a cup of tea! For I've the most delicious little cakes for you. And the most delightful news!"

She'd had enough of practicing, and tea sounded tempting. She wondered whether she dared—oh, very obliquely, of course—to allude to her problem, hear what Salome might have to suggest.

She never got the chance.

"And now for my news," Salome started as soon as she'd filled their cups. "You'll never guess what Aunt Bluma had to say! Adash is due home even sooner than we expected! There was a cancellation on the Orient Express and he was able to leave two whole days ahead of schedule. He telegraphed, he's on his way now and arriving tomorrow. Imagine, tomorrow by sundown!"

I mustn't drop my cup, mustn't drop my spoon, mustn't spill my tea. And I must say something, she expects it! "Aunt Bluma must be very happy!" she finally managed to choke out.

"Happy is hardly the word! She can't contain herself! And that's not all. She and I just decided that it will be best for our beloved invalid to bring him here rather than to their Nalewki flat. All those steep stairs would be bad for him. And they're so crowded, now that Viktor has brought his little bride home to live. And it's all so shabby—though, of course, I wouldn't dream of letting Bluma think I think so. . . . Well, anyway, I managed to convince her how much better off Adash will be, staying here with us. Don't you agree, Ginia dear? And don't you think if we move the little *récamier* out of here, and set up a bed and a washstand in the alcove, where they won't be eyesores, this will make an ideal convalescent room? So convenient when friends drop in on Adash. . . . As for you, if you want to help pamper the poor darling, as I know you will, you can play for him— you know how he's always enjoyed your playing. So you see. . ." Suddenly she became aware of her niece's silence and staring eyes. "Little soul, don't you feel well? You're white as a sheet. . . ."

"It's nothing, Auntie, nothing at all. I just felt faint for a moment. But now it's passing. Don't pay attention. . . it's probably something I ate. . . ."

Salome, however, was not to be put off. She took the cup from her niece's trembling hands, made her sit back, even offered to loosen her stays. Regina, of course, wouldn't hear of it. Suppose Alfred were to walk in just then! "I'm better already, really I am. Please, please don't fuss!"

She did see him at last, but only on the stair landing as she started to leave, and he was in a great hurry, obviously preoccupied, politely regretful because he couldn't walk her home. "I'm just rushing in to change, then I must be off again. Someone's arranged a dinner at which I'm to meet a man who has the ear of the governor-general. I'm told this personage also has a lot of influence in the courts. Of course, there's no guarantee he'll want to lift a finger to help a Pawiak prisoner. But it's a chance one doesn't dare pass up. . . ."

She said, with what she hoped was plaintive charm, "But Alfred, I haven't really seen you, not to talk to, in ever so long!" Then, urgently, "Please, there's something we . . . I . . . I mean, I've got to discuss something with you, and. . ."

He frowned, then gave her a smile that was like a pat on the head. "Nothing I'd like better, my sweet. But not now."

She swallowed her pride. "Alfred, this is important."

He seemed startled at her insistence and none too pleased. "Dearest child, I thought I just explained. . . ."

"I know what you said. I heard you." Even in her own ears her voice sounded shrill and she forced a velvet quality back into it. "Oh, I didn't mean you're to drop everything this minute. But surely you can find time tomorrow. Please? For me?"

"I'm afraid tomorrow night I have another meeting."

"Oh, not at night, I couldn't get away at night!" *And anyway, by tomorrow night it would be too late.* "But how about around this time tomorrow afternoon? It just happens everyone will be out then—we could talk without being disturbed. Please say you will manage it, please!"

She knew how badly she'd mishandled the situation from the guarded way he answered. "Well, if it's really that important to you. . ."

"Oh, it is, it is!"

"In that case I suppose I shall have to make the time. Four o'clock?"

By four, Salome and Leon would have left for the railroad station to meet Adam's train. And trains were always late. "Yes, that will be fine."

"Very well, four o'clock it is. See you then, pretty child."

Did she imagine it, or was there condescension in his tone? But surely he had no reason. He must just be annoyed with her for having pressed him. Never press a man, Salome always warned, or he'll shy away like a frightened horse. She resolved to be more careful tomorrow.

Twenty-four hours later, having rehearsed all her lines like a scene in a play, she was saying meekly, a penitent in a confessional, "I hardly know where to begin and how to explain. I'm so ashamed. . . . Oh, Alfred, I wish I didn't have to tell you all this, but I must—I simply must get it off my chest, throw myself on your mercy, and then hope you'll find it in your heart to be generous and understanding. . . ."

She had chosen to sit on one of Salome's delicate little brocade sofas where there was just room for two. She had hoped Alfred would join her, but he continued to stand facing her, leaning against the curve of the piano. So far he made no comment, but then she really hadn't given him much to go on. She was forced to struggle on, and as she hunted for the right words she realized that instead of mouthing the phrases she had prepared, she was really doing her best to be honest, both with him and with herself.

"Certainly as I look back on what I've done I can't even understand it myself. How could I have allowed this . . . this mess . . . to happen?"

Alfred continued to say nothing. Only his eyebrows shot up quizzically, giving his handsome face a curiously old, worldly-wise look. She tried again.

"You see, this man, this relative who's coming here to stay . . ." She gestured toward the small sitting room, metamorphosed overnight just as Salome had said it would be. And the freshly made bed with its covers turned down reminded her that no matter how late Adam's train, time had run out for her. "This man," she went on desperately, "my cousin Adam, Izidore's brother . . . he, well, he's in love with me. He's been in love with me a long time, almost two years. . . ."

Alfred spoke for the first time. "He shows good taste."

She brushed aside the comment. "Just before he went away he proposed. Quite unexpectedly. I wasn't sixteen yet, a baby really, childish, foolish. And it was my first proposal. Naturally I was terribly flattered. . . ."

"Oh, naturally," he echoed, and she couldn't tell whether he was serious or not. "Tell me, my dear, why are girls always so flattered when they're proposed to? I've noticed it often has little to do with how they feel about the man himself. Could you explain the phenomenon to me, perhaps?"

"Now you're making fun of me! Please don't! Don't make it any harder. . . ."

"Sorry, pet."

"Well, as I said, I was flattered but wouldn't give him an answer—how could I when I didn't even know how I really felt? Then, later on, other things happened. I wasn't very happy at home. And he kept writing. And I answered. And one thing led to another. And we became kind of engaged. . . ."

"*Kind of* engaged? That's interesting. Wouldn't some people call that playing both ends for the middle?"

"No, Alfred, no, it wasn't like that, I swear! I honestly thought I was being sincere! But that was before *you* came along. And now everything's changed. And I haven't had a chance to tell him about you . . . about us. And he's coming home ill and . . . oh, don't you see . . . ?"

"No, I don't see. Especially not what all this has got to do with me." His voice was the voice of a stranger. "Obviously you've some reason for telling me your unsavory little saga?" Before she could pull an answer together he asked a second question. "But just what is it that's really bothering you? Are you afraid I'll talk out of turn, tell your—er—fiancé what you've been up to behind his back?" She gasped, tried to protest, but he ignored her. "Because if that's what's bothering you, you can set your mind at rest. Remember, I'm a gentleman, and gentlemen don't kiss and tell, they only kiss."

"Darling," she begged, abject, "don't talk like a cynic! It isn't like you."

"Isn't it? Perhaps you just don't know me as well as you think."

Now finally she was beginning to understand that this was true, even though she still refused to accept it. "But, Alfred. . ." Not "darling" this time. "Alfred, I thought you loved me the way I love you! I thought . . . You said. . ."

"A man says many things, my dear—he even means them—

while he holds a pretty girl in his arms. If you don't know that, you're still as much of a baby as when what's-his-name proposed. . . ."

"Adam," she said mechanically.

"Adam, Alfred . . . you're going through the A's."

"You're cruel!"

He started to laugh. "Just what did you expect as the climax to this little scene? That I'd fall on my knees and ask you to marry me?"

Because that had been precisely what she had expected, she sat silent. But the pain in her face gave her away. And he said, half smiling, "Yes, I can see now that's exactly it. But seriously now, can you picture a union between us? My parents, and the bishop who married them in the chapel of our estate, waiting to greet your parents. The Czartoryskis and the Segals. Oh, really!"

"You snob," she whispered. "You insufferable snob."

This time he laughed out loud. "That's right, call me names." Then, "Of course I'm a snob. Also a realist. And now be honest—did I ever say I'd marry you? Did I make any promises?"

She shook her head, more in shock than in denial, and suddenly he took pity on her. "Face it," he said more gently, as if doing his best to teach a child its ABCs. "Marriage is a serious business. It'll be years before I'm ready to take a wife. And when I do, well, the plain, ugly truth is the Czartoryskis seldom marry for love, though that, too, has been known to happen. Mostly we marry to perpetuate an illustrious bloodline. We choose our brides like highly pedigreed brood mares. We also choose great fortunes—we have to, for it's the only way to keep our estates intact even while some of us, like my own father, gamble away their patrimony. . . ."

She was crying, not for effect this time but in heartbreak and humiliation and shame. But he had still more to say. "Of course, if you were an heiress with a dowry of many millions I'm sure the Vatican would cooperate and even my sainted mother could be persuaded to be gracious. But after all what are you? A little middle-class Jewess with a pretty face and, I'll wager, an even prettier body. And I admit I'd love to take you to bed. But not the marriage bed."

She put her hands over her ears to shut out the insulting words, forgetting, among other things, to act out the accepted fiction that a well-bred young girl didn't even understand such allusions. "Oh, you're unspeakable," she whispered. And her anger was so thorough that her tears stopped. And to bolster her reviving pride she permitted herself one final pretense. "I'm glad I found out *in time* what a cad you are! I wouldn't want you now if you came begging!"

He bowed gravely, imperturbable, scornful, and so handsome she wondered bleakly how she could go on living without seeing him, touching him, feeling the caress of his lips. He said, "Well spoken, my dear."

She was beginning to feel hysteria mounting in her. "Get out of here! You're not fit to black Adam Fabian's boots! If you had any decency, any decency at all, you'd pack your bags and move out of this house today, right now!"

"Not a bad idea," he agreed smoothly. "As a matter of fact I've been thinking for some time I should do just that. And now I've been given the impetus. We Czartoryskis," he added, "may be without morals, but never without tact."

"All I ask is that you not be here when my people come home."

"I won't be, you may be sure. There are always hotels. And friends with cozy little flats their wives know nothing about. Anyway, I promise I won't remain underfoot." As he turned to go, he stopped for a final word. "Just be glad, in case you've given any thought to that other cousin of yours, that poor chap Izidore in the Pawiak, that I am not a petty man. Otherwise what happened here between us might have affected him badly. But of course it won't, because handling his case is a matter of principle with me. In fact," he pulled out his watch, "I'm just in time to get to another meeting. Well, goodbye, Regina. I expect we won't be seeing much of each other from now on."

I ought to go home, she thought. *I ought to get out of here while the road is clear. I can't face anyone now or talk to anyone!* But she couldn't get herself to move. She just went on sitting very straight in a straight little gilt parlor chair where she'd dropped, her knees buckling, once Alfred had left the room.

She felt numb—not in pain yet, but numb, unreal. Her first serious defeat, her first great loss, and it didn't even hurt. *I'm like those men you read about in books,* she told herself, *who have accidents in the wilderness. They'll wander on for miles with a broken leg looking for help, and not even feel anything until afterwards.* Only for her, Regina Segal, the little bourgeois Jewess with a pretty face, there would be no help. No matter where she went she would always be exactly what she was. . . .

Dusk changed to night, the long row of street lanterns outside flicked on one by one as a lamplighter went whistling down the block. She listened fearfully for the sound of approaching carriage wheels. *If I don't go now they'll find me here.* Retreat would be cut off. And still she could not move.

Miss Julia padded in, a fresh black dress on, her lace apron stiffly starched and her frilled cap in place. She went from window to window, drawing the draperies. Then she, too, like the lamplighter, busied herself with the lights. Only then did she become aware of someone in the room with her.

"My word, Miss Regina, what a start you gave me! What're you doing all alone in the dark and quiet as a mouse? I thought surely you'd be down to the station with the others, welcoming our *Pan* Adam home!"

I must look a fright, Regina thought, and stayed in the shadows so that the housekeeper might not notice her swollen eyes. "I had a little migraine," she murmured vaguely, "I was resting. . . ."

"Resting on *that?*" Miss Julia sniffed, pointing to the little chair. "It's hard as a rock! Even if your aunt says it's real Louis-something-or-other and very valuable. . . ."

"Sixteenth," Regina supplied mechanically, wondering why she bothered. "Louis Sixteenth."

"Whatever it is, it's not for sitting, if you'll forgive my saying so. Anyway, ducky, if you're poorly, go lie down and I'll make you some chamomile tea. Chamomile tea is good for most anything that ails you."

"Thanks, but I really should be on my way."

"What, and not wait for *Pan* Adash, and him gone so long and coming back so sick! And all on account of a little pain in the head!"

You're wong, it's a pain in the heart. But talking to the old retainer was forcing her mind off herself. There was odd comfort in picking up the routine of familiar living.

"You know, Miss Julia, you're right, I shouldn't give in so easily." Besides, maybe it would be best to face Adam right now, while she was still too numb to care about anything. She made her voice sound bright. "You've changed my mind for me, I do think I shall stay. They should be along any minute. But in the meantime I need something to do. Isn't there something I can help you with?"

The old servant, who had found from experience that whenever her ladies helped it was likely to end with more work for herself, mumbled ungraciously that whatever needed doing had been done already. Then she thought better of it. "Matter of fact, Miss Ginia, there is something. The flowers. Generally *Pani* Salome arranges them herself, but today they were late getting delivered. And I'm a poor hand with them. Maybe you could do that."

Fifteen minutes later, when the hacks carrying Adam and the welcome party rolled into the *porte cochère*, Regina was standing with her arms full of white snapdragons and pink carnations and red roses, trying to decide whether to separate them or arrange everything in great colorful masses.

So determined was she to shut everything out but the problem of the flowers that when steps sounded on the landing she paid no attention. A door opened and closed, the house filled with voices, and still she continued with her task. Slowly the steps came closer, then Adam was in the room.

He was pale, and older, and walked slowly, leaning heavily on Uncle Leon, who carried his greatcoat. His tiny mother trotted beside him carrying his hat and his travel rug. And Salome and Miss Julia and Idka made up the rear.

"Here he is! Home at last and he's going to stay!"

Regina turned and looked at him and hardly saw him. What she did see was safety, a haven from hurt, her passport to a carefully ordered, sheltered existence with a man who would cherish and pamper her and forgive her all her peccadilloes. This was the second time she was turning to him, like a child with a bruised knee, who whimpers please, make it stop hurting. And she knew he would always do everything in his power to make her happy. And she would never let him suspect his real role. As for her, the pain would continue, the sense of loss remain as acute as ever for a long, long time. But she would learn to live with it. And then one day—though she wasn't ready yet to believe this even while she told herself it would be so—the suffering would be over, until finally it would be just a memory. Oh, yes, Adam Fabian would make her a good husband, an ideal husband.

Over the armful of flowers she raised her eyes to his and smiled, and instantly saw color flow into the tired, pale, invalid face, saw the admiration and the worshipful love. Her lips formed the single soundless word, "Later." Later on today, or maybe to-morrow, they would manage a few moments alone and they could talk. She went on smiling.

PART SIX
Early Winter 1903–
February 1905

❧ *One* ❧

FROM THE MOMENT of his encounter with the old peasant woman a healing change had begun to come over Adam. The lethargy that had protected him like a cocoon all through his illness seemed to burn off as the night mists burn off at the start of a new day. He was stirred at last by the knowledge that he was going home, home to the land he loved and the woman he loved. And he found himself starting to think like a well man again, living in the present.

Already his time in the Caucasus was receding into unreality. Who was it had said that man was a political animal? He couldn't remember, but the observation seemed to him wonderfully apt. He thought about the old crone with her pots of clabber and her roast chicken and the tissue-thin leaflet stained with chicken fat. A political animal. Wouldn't she be surprised if he tried to tell her that was what she was?

He spent the rest of his journey trying to picture his homecoming. Would Regina be meeting his train together with his mother? No, how could she possibly explain wanting to do that? Since at her own insistence secrecy had continued to surround their relationship, he had even resisted the impulse to telegraph her directly. She was probably reduced to pretending only the most casual interest in his return, when in reality she was counting the hours, scheming her innocent little schemes to maneuver a meeting.

As the train rolled into the long station platform he spotted his mother and Salome and Leon.

Bluma could barely hold back her tears at sight of him. "It's for happiness," she lied, dabbing impatiently at the corners of her eyes. "Because it's so good to have you back." But in truth the tears were for his waxy pallor, for the way his shoulders drooped, as though somewhere along the course of his relatively brief time on earth life had already defeated him.

She knew illness sometimes does that to a person, and that, given time and the will, the harm can be undone. She remembered her own terrifying collapse following Jacob's death and the long, slow journey back until the pieces had been put together. Everyone said she was whole again, yet deep down she never did feel completely whole. Sometimes she thought of herself as a vessel that had been shattered, then skillfully repaired by a master craftsman: the cracks don't even show—just don't try to put it to daily use. It has been permanently flawed.

Now, looking anxiously at her firstborn, she could only hope that no such permanent damage was threatening him. Well, she tried to console herself, his had been only a physical illness, not the devastation of loss. And he had youth on his side. Or did he? As she searched his face it struck her that he was no longer really young—and where had his youth gone so soon?

Taking his arm, she steered him slowly toward the street exit while Leon took charge of the luggage. "We'll have to fatten you up," she chatted with forced cheerfulness. "Nothing like good home cooking to thicken tired blood. . . ."

"Oh, I'm really a lot better than I seem," he quickly reassured her. "The doctors in the Crimea all agree I've the constitution of a horse. But, of course, if you want to pamper me, I won't fight you!"

"We all want to pamper you," Salome chimed in. "And you mayn't know it yet, but we're kidnapping you, Uncle Leon and I. I mean, you're coming to stay with us instead of going home. It's on account of the easy stairs," she hastened to explain as though to ward off hurt feelings. "All we're thinking about is your comfort."

"I do hope you won't take it the wrong way," his mother

added in that diffident manner of hers. "You mustn't think I'm afraid of the little bit of extra work. . . ."

The idea of his mother shirking a responsibility amused him. "You, Mama! That would be the day!" Actually, it was the best news they could have given him. He would be seeing Regina whenever she came to practice on the Bechstein. Maybe he would see her tomorrow.

By the time they reached the street the exertion of the long walk caught up with him. Leaning on Uncle Leon for support he allowed himself to be helped into the waiting cab. The rumble of the wheels on the paving blocks seemed to take on the rhythm of the moving train, his head began to nod, and he no longer cared where they made his bed so long as he could lie in it. It was not an unpleasant sensation: like being wrapped in swaddling clothes and put into a cradle. He was only vaguely aware of being helped down again, then stumbling half dazed up the stairs.

The short climb ended, doors opened, they were inside the familiar apartment. The house, he noticed with some surprise, was ablaze with lights as though for a gala occasion. When he mentioned this, Salome laughed. "Well I should think so! Isn't it an occasion that you've come home? And now," she went on in a flurry of solicitude he felt wasn't really warranted, "suppose we take you straight to your room. You'll want to have a nice rest before supper." He followed her. And there, smiling up at him, her arms full of carnations and roses, stood Regina.

They moved toward each other and he was finally able to speak her name. He took her hands in his and kissed them, spilling the flowers. "Regina . . . oh, my dearest dear," he said, low enough so that only she could hear. "I was beginning to think I had imagined you."

She kept on smiling and there seemed to him to be no break, no break at all between his long dream and reality.

Some time in the course of the night he woke, and was surprised that the bed was so soft and the darkness and silence so deep. Then it came to him where he was, and instantly his mind cleared. Tomorrow Regina would come again, and perhaps then they could talk. And make plans. It was high time. He'd had enough of secrecy, and she was no longer a child. As soon as he was back at work he would go to Karol and formally ask for her hand in marriage. Thinking it all through, he had a moment of pure exhilaration. Desire swept through him like a hurricane, clearing way the last cobwebs of lethargy and shattering the capsule of isolation. He slept again, deeply.

Great as had been her initial relief at having someone immediate to turn to, Regina was finding it hard to bring much enthusiasm to her newly revived relationship with Adam. The disenchantment, the blow to her pride, and indeed the genuine pain of losing Alfred Czartoryski would have made any other reaction impossible. Maybe, she thought, if she could just keep Adam at arms' length until she recovered a little, allowing him to adore her from a distance, as it were, she might slowly recapture her old feeling for him, the excitement of the best days of their courtship by mail. Or maybe—and though she instantly rejected this idea as unworthy she was never quite able to rid herself of it altogether—their romance would last, sustaining them both, only so long as both were convalescing, he physically, she spiritually; and later on something else—something unforeseen and exciting—would take its place.

She therefore continued to beckon him on, then elude him. "We must be twice as careful as ever before," she pleaded, whenever they were alone for even a few minutes and he tried to make the most of it. "Besides, you aren't at all well yet." If he took her in his arms she would slip away, or turn her head if he wanted to kiss her. "Please, someone might come in. If there was a fuss, I'm sure it wouldn't be good for you. . . ."

He felt it was useless to explain to this virginal child that a man's body dictated in no uncertain terms what was best for it. He also remembered that she had a lifelong distaste for illness and wondered whether it was this that made her involuntarily stand-offish, even though she was too kind to say so. Well, if that was the answer, time would soon take care of the whole problem. In the meantime, since his flesh, for all that it clamored for her, was still far weaker than his spirit, he did not press her.

Otherwise his convalescence was rapid, for he did have youth on his side. He was getting restless. "I've lazed about long enough," he was soon complaining over the late breakfast that was served on a tray in his room and that Salome, generally still in lacy peignoir, liked to share with him. "I should be thinking about getting back to my desk!" But he said it without any real urgency, savoring the unaccustomed luxury of his surroundings and the still greater luxury of leisure, time which he was free to fill as he chose—with reading, with meditation, with what he called putting his thoughts in order.

Occasionally he reflected, a shade guiltily, that he might indeed get used to being a rich man with no trouble at all, though the possibility of accumulating a fortune had not yet become plausible to him and he merely toyed with it as a theory, wishing he might argue out the pros and cons of such an end with Olek. But Olek seemed to have vanished like a stone in a millpond. Whether he had returned to Switzerland or some other haven of exile, or was perhaps in hiding and active somewhere close by, or even, like Izidore, rotting in a Tsarist prison, Adam had no way of knowing.

He continued to grapple alone with questions the daily newspapers kept thrusting at his conscience. Once he had the physical energy, would he search out Olek and maybe move closer to the movement again? Or would he, like his other old friend Henryk Meisels, simply turn his back on what went on in the land? He cast about for some third, less sharply defined road to follow, but could find none. Here at home the war clouds looked far more ominous than they had against the fairy-tale tapestry of the Near East, and revolutionary ferment was everywhere. Arrests kept mounting. The Tsarate was moving with special ferocity against the Jewish masses, particularly the Jewish labor groups. Cool detachment, a purely philosophical interest, would be progressively harder to maintain.

Once or twice he tried to talk some of this over with Regina but she warded him off, preferring topics like her music or the people they knew. He told himself he really had no right to feel disappointed or to expect more from her, and finally decided that for the time being he must find something to do that wouldn't commit him too deeply, like helping in Izidore's defense. This, he knew, was as far as he dared venture, now that to his other responsibilities would soon be added the responsibility of marriage. As a married man it would be his duty to protect and cherish his young bride, not expose her to dangers and possible hardships. Later on he hoped he might help her develop some interest in politics and the liberation battle. But he would have to be patient.

Two incidents, one coming directly after the other, forced Adam to this conclusion.

Not long after his homecoming, on a night when Regina stayed to supper, conversation at table, which Salome generally tried to keep light and inconsequential, had taken an unexpectedly serious turn. One of the young boarders had come home with the shattering news that half a dozen youth leaders were to die on the gallows at Citadel Prison at dawn the following morning. Someone mentioned fresh rumors of a contemplated prison break. But Uncle Leon said no, he had it on good authority that the action would center on freeing the condemned men. Instantly an argument arose, sharp and passionate, between supporters of such dramatic tactics and those who claimed that the movement was better served by a less flamboyant approach.

At first Salome tried, with all the skill at her command, to guide the talk away from what she termed "these grim masculine topics." But when the boys ignored her and even her compliant husband for once pretended not to hear, she pouted and finally announced, "Tomorrow I shall hang a little calligraphed card from the chandelier. It's going to read: POLITICS AS TABLE CONVERSATION STRICTLY FORBIDDEN. What you gentlemen discuss over your brandy and cigars is up to you. But must we ladies be exposed to all this unpleasantness?"

Stony silence greeted her words. Then Regina giggled. "It certainly would make for pleasanter meals, wouldn't it?" When no one seconded her, she added defensively, "No, but seriously, what sense is there in making ourselves miserable when we aren't really helping those poor wretches at all!" In spite of himself, Adam wished their aunt had had less influence in shaping the outlook of her favorite niece.

He was equally distressed by Regina's seemingly unexplained

dislike of his brother's lawyer, whom he had met immediately upon his arrival and with whose dedicated approach he was becoming more and more impressed. By now Alfred Czartoryski, having long since decided to handle Izidore's case as something that went far beyond the injustice done one young student, was embarked on organizing a campaign that would reach beyond the borders of the Empire and stir international protest. Adam especially admired the tact and gentleness with which Prince Alfred handled timid little Bluma and his way of treating Idka as a comrade-in-arms, so that she unbent and was able to forget, maybe even forgive, his aristocratic lineage and his near-royal manner and thought only of getting more backing for his plans.

But Regina refused to see any good in him at all. On one occasion when Alfred came in while she was playing for Adam she had been ungracious to the point of rudeness, so much so that later on he'd felt impelled to question her. At first she merely hedged, trying to shrug the incident off. "Do I *have* to like all of Aunt Salome's boys?"

"He's rather more than that," Adam argued. "He's—but don't you really appreciate the wonderful, courageous thing he's doing?" He elaborated: "To take on the defense of a political prisoner, and not just any prisoner, but a Jew—why, it may cost him his career before he ever gets started!" And when she continued to look unimpressed he added, "I just wish, dearest, that you could find it in your heart to feel more friendly toward him."

She said mysteriously, "And suppose he's defending a Jew for reasons of his own?"

"Now what do you mean by that?"

"That's up to you to find out. I just happen to know he's a filthy anti-Semite."

"Alfred Czartoryski? I can't believe it!"

"He is. And you don't know everything."

"But, my darling, that simply doesn't make sense! In the first place he'd lived here at the Grossgliks' all through his school days. He came back as a graduate student. He has the warmest personal relationship with Uncle Leon as well as with Aunt Salome."

"He probably kept coming back because he was smitten with

her. All the boys are. It's a phase for them, like growing pains or measles, and quite as harmless."

"That's true enough," he conceded, "but now I believe he's really a friend. And just look at the way he is with my mother. The only word I can think of to describe it is, well, tender. Alfred an anti-Semite? Whatever put the idea into your head?"

She was on treacherous ground now and must give guarded answers. "If I told you, you wouldn't believe me."

"Try."

She knew she'd gone too far now to back out, and thought fast, and found a way to bend the truth just a bit and twist it to her purpose. "Well, about a month before you came home we all went to a ball at the Kronenbergs'. It was when Missy Pozner and Henryk got engaged, and the place swarmed with rich girls, very pretty girls, and Alfred danced a lot and flirted outrageously. But then he told me that no Czartoryski would be caught dead marrying a Jewess. Unless, of course, she was an heiress and worth millions, in which case a papal dispensation could be obtained easily enough. Now if that isn't filthy! And cynical!"

But to her horror Adam only shook his head. "Cynical it may be. But that doesn't really make him an anti-Semite. Why darling, don't you know our own families would take just about the same attitude? It's the same the whole world over, when it comes to marriage. Just let me give you an example. Remember that man I wrote you about so many times, my good friend from the Caucasus, *Hadji* Irza? Remember how good he was to me when I first got ill? And before that, how he opened his house to me, and gave me all those wonderful gifts? Well, he has a daughter just about your age. And do you know what he told me? That he loved me like a son, but if he'd ever found me looking at her as a man looks at a woman, I'd have ended up with a dagger in my back. And I didn't for a moment doubt he meant what he said."

This gave her a chance to change the subject and she seized on it. "And it would have served you right!" she cried in mock anger. "The very idea of your trailing after some veiled Persian enchantress!"

He laughed indulgently. "It wasn't even an idea, sweet. Just an improbable example. There was never anyone in my thoughts but you."

To make sure Czartoryski was forgotten, she made use of that, too. "Prove it."

This was the first time since he was home that she invited his caresses, and he took her in his arms and kissed her, long and lingeringly. And she wondered if enough kissing would make her forget the touch and taste of Alfred's lips. Almost at once, involuntarily, she turned her head away. "Oh, do be careful. Someone might come in!"

He stopped kissing her but continued to hold her, stroking her silken hair. "Which brings me to the next point. Our engagement. Our marriage. Don't you think as soon as I stop looking like a scarecrow I ought to go talk to your father? Isn't it time we got things settled and started making plans?" When she didn't answer he urged, "I know girls like long engagements, and I don't grudge you that special time. But tell me, how long does an engagement have to be? How much time does it take to get a trousseau ready, and all that?"

"I don't really know," she said vaguely, "I haven't given it enough thought. And anyway, there really isn't any hurry. My people would never let us get married before I'm eighteen. That's next summer. And then we'll have a whole lifetime ahead of us, won't we? So first let's just concentrate on getting you well. . . ."

She knew that no miracle was going to give Alfred back to her. But she needed a little more time to accept the cold fact.

❧ *Two* ❧

IN MID-DECEMBER a heavy snowfall blanketed the city, to the noisy delight of vacationing schoolchildren whose days were made perfect with sledding and skating and making snowmen and pelting one another with hard, well-aimed bullets of near-ice. But among Warsaw's adult population there was little joy. Thousands were out of work. Rumors of war were growing ever more insistent and alarming. Arrests on the slimmest pretext, or for no reason at all, became a daily occurrence.

In other years the Tsar had sometimes celebrated Christ's birthday with a political amnesty, and as the holidays neared even the worst pessimists among the Pawiak prisoners allowed themselves to be infected with the virus of hope. On Christmas morning, as the sun came up and church bells tolled, involuntarily they began waiting—for the Magi, the miracle. But the day wore on and there was no word from the governor-general's palace. By the time the visiting hour approached they knew they had deluded themselves.

In Pawia Street, among the men and women waiting on the long line that had formed early in front of the prison gates, Adam and Idka Fabian stood stamping their feet and flexing numbed fingers that even heavy-lined gloves could not keep warm.

"Maybe you shouldn't have come," sister said to brother as she saw his face turn an alarming grayish-blue. She knew he'd had to argue down his doctor, who felt that even an hour in the clammy, fetid atmosphere of the old dungeon might have dangerous aftereffects. But the doctor hadn't considered the more obvious hazard of exposure to weather. "You haven't seen Izzy in so long, another couple of weeks wouldn't have made much difference."

"I'm not all that cold," Adam insisted, refusing the scarf she had taken off and was trying to wrap around his neck and shoulders. "Besides, the line is finally beginning to move."

It was, but at a snail's pace. While they inched through the courtyard he had time to observe, with increasing interest, his sister's relationship with other "regulars" among the visitors. He was startled to see how much at ease she was among them though they came from all classes, all walks of life. Shabby, often ragged, but just as often luxuriously dressed in furs, knowledgeable and filled with anger or cowed and frightened, they were all united by the single bond of love and loyalty to someone behind bars. But between many there was also another bond, that of knowing exactly why the prison was full.

Used to Idka's rather sullen silences at home, Adam now saw another side of her. He watched her wave a smiling greeting to a broad-shouldered, middle-aged man in work clothes, whose high cheekbones and handlebar moustache made him look like Matejko's Polish peasant grown old. He saw her put a protective arm around the thin shoulders of a young girl in the final stages of pregnancy.

"My dear, remember what you promised," he heard her say. "You're to send for me the moment the pains start coming. Word of honor? You must, you know. For your man's sake, if not your own. So that when he finally does come home, he'll find a healthy wife and a fine son waiting. . . ."

"You've changed, Idka," he said, when he had her attention again. "I never realized how much. It's as though Izzy's being in there had made *you* stronger."

She seemed pleased but also embarrassed. "Well, things do have to get done and someone has to take over," she said, half truculent, half apologetic. But when he tried to question her about her new friends she quickly put him off. "Later maybe. Not now." And he understood how much he had forgotten, during his time away from home, about the never-ending need for caution. He felt lonely and vaguely ashamed.

He found Izidore even more changed than his sister. Young-rooster arrogance had given way to controlled, quiet purposeful-ness. Never again would Izidore waste his time in futile grand-stand gestures. "What babes-in-the-wood we were that May Sunday!" he remarked at one point. "Babies trying to start our own Childrens Crusade! But here in jail," he added, purposely loud so the guards might overhear and misinterpret, "here we've no choice but to learn discipline!"

"And if you had it to do over again?" Adam wanted to know.

The bony, pale, bearded man who was his younger brother considered briefly. "Oh, I'd probably do exactly the same thing. That's the *price* of learning—the only way you ever start is by making mistakes. But the *point* of learning is not to make the same mistakes twice in a row. For if you do, you're a fool—which I flatter myself I'm not, any longer."

"And otherwise—no regrets, Izzy?"

"None. Just plans for doing better later on."

"You know," Adam said, the hum of a hundred conversations around them making him feel they were an island, private and alone, "this may be a hell of a thing to tell a man who's sitting, but jail has improved you."

"Well, thanks, big brother! Care to join me sometime?" They laughed companionably, feeling really close for the first time in their lives.

Idka, of course, was scandalized. "Iz, you shouldn't say things like that, not even in jest!"

"Why ever not? Do you think the stoolies will report us? Philosophical discussion bores them. What they're after are names, places, dates. But if it'll make you happy I'll change the subject. What books did you bring me? What's new at home? How's Mama, how's everybody, including the new sister-in-law I've never even met? And what about that swell of a lawyer you got for me? Anything to report? Or is no news bad news?"

The hour was soon over, guards hustled them out like so much troublesome cattle, prodding them with curses if not with whips down the long corridors, past rows of heavily barred doors, and down the worn stone stairs. Then once more they passed through the courtyard and the outer gates, which quickly and noisily clanged shut behind them.

Not until they were in the street was Adam able to breathe again. Filling his lungs with clean, sparkling winter air made him a trifle light-headed. "Out here it smells of freedom," he startled even himself by saying, and added, "That sounds pretentious, but how else put into words what I'm trying to say?"

That same week the doctors at last agreed to let him return to work. "But don't overdo. The lungs are still delicate. These things take time." To ease the strain, it was agreed he would stay on at the Grossgliks', since Count Berg Street was, in Salome's words, "just far enough from Pozner's for a brisk walk in fine weather and near enough so you can afford to take hacks."

The arrangement suited him, and slowly it began to suit Regina. Bit by bit she reminded herself of all the things her aunt had ever said about the advantages of marrying an older man. *You'll be his precious darling till death do you part. . . .* Never again was she going to let herself be hurt as Alfred had hurt her. Let Adam be blessed for giving, then. She would be content to receive.

Again she set about creating the atmosphere of secrecy that was so to her liking. She came every afternoon to play for him or to read aloud, mostly poetry, which she read extremely well, and now she no longer turned away when he touched her. To his more and more insistent questions about how soon she thought he might speak to her father she still answered vaguely, "Soon. Don't be impatient. Soon." But one day she finally added, "Maybe when you're back at work full time. That'll mean you're completely well, and then we can start planning our wedding. . . ."

In the meantime Missy Pozner and Henryk Meisels were planning theirs. They set the date for April, and Regina found herself involuntarily caught up in the excitement.

"We've picked April because that's the most beautiful month in Paris," Missy explained one evening while she and Henryk were visiting, "and that'll be our first stop on our grand tour of Europe." *Europe* was then the fashionable word for all lands west of the Oder, while Russian Poland, along with the rest of the Empire, was *Asia*. "We're going to take a long, *long* honeymoon, maybe months."

"What about your trousseau?" Regina asked, curious and thinking enviously that with the Pozner money such mundane matters would be merely a mass of troublesome detail. "I suppose you're very busy with that?"

"Oh, I'm mostly letting Mama worry about it," Missy said carelessly. "Monogrammed linens and silver and eiderdowns bore me. But my own personal trousseau is another matter—for my clothes I plan to shop in Paris. With my bridegroom! Which is giving Mama fits because it just isn't done!" she added, looking pleased with herself. "It's all Henryk's idea really. Henryk tells me no really chic European woman would dream of going to a couture house without a man in tow. If she can't bring her husband or her lover"—she used the word deliberately, and Regina did her best not to look shocked—"she'll at least drag her brother along. How else is she to know what really appeals to the masculine taste?"

"How else indeed?" echoed Regina, whose own experience was limited to her mother's seamstress and Salome's little dressmaker. She hoped she had manged to sound properly worldly. But she chalked up the interchange as something to hold against Missy. She was beginning to think the Pozner heiress was putting on too many airs.

What she really resented, though she would have been incapable of putting this into words, was not so much Missy's fortune and social position as the fact that, securely engaged and more than half in love with Henryk for making freedom possible after all, the young heiress was completely at ease both with him and with Adam, her former tutor. This made it possible for the friendship between the two men to reach out and include Missy, creating a kind of comradeship in which Regina felt no part and which made her suspect she was tolerated like a child that is loved but for whose sake conversation is kept on an elementary level.

In an odd sense this fancied grievance had a salutary effect. Regina became so intent on proving to Adam, and especially to herself, how important she was to him that in the doing her last regrets over the fiasco with Alfred Czartoryski gradually began to fade. She no longer wished to keep Adam at arms' length and even invited his caresses. After a while she started to enjoy them. Unfortunately this did not lessen her almost peasant suspicion of the fine lady that was Missy and the very polished Henryk. Nor could she quite forgive Adam for being so thoroughly at ease in their company. She was constantly torn between a desire to avoid them as much as possible and an equally strong determination not to let Adam, if it could possibly be helped, see much of them without her being present.

Generally she was successful. But one night after she'd already gone home Henryk dropped by unexpectedly without his fiancée. The Grossgliks were entertaining a group of older friends and Adam had gone to his room. Henryk was told not to stand on ceremony but to go right in, and for the first time in several years the two old friends had a chance for a long talk alone.

"So you've finally been snared," Henryk remarked at one point in the conversation. "Is it official yet? Are congratulations in order? If so, I wish you both happiness. And I hope Regina appreciates what a prize she's getting. Missy isn't half so lucky. You're one of the few men alive who won't chafe at the confines of marriage. Given half a chance, you'll never even look at another woman. . ."

To his vast amusement Adam began to look uncomfortable.

"I wonder why it always embarrasses a man to be told he's the type to stay faithful?" Henryk went on. "And yet I mean this as the sincerest compliment. In fact, I envy you."

"Rubbish. Any man can stay faithful if he wants to," Adam snorted.

"I rather doubt that." Henryk shook his head and smiled. "Somehow good intentions alone aren't always enough. One just has to be built a certain way. Otherwise, why haven't a thousand years of Christianity been long enough to make Europe a model of monogamous society? By now adultery should be unheard of, crimes of passion nonexistent. And just think how much less trouble we humans would make for ourselves if we mated for life, like the wolf or the wild duck."

"Considering our lifespan," Adam said, his mind suddenly on the past, "perhaps it's just as well that we don't. After all. . ." He hesitated, then forced himself into an oblique confession. "What about all those who think they're mated for life and then lose out? What a grim future, never to be given a second chance!"

Henryk caught the allusion. "That, my friend, is one reason I'm happy for you. You'll thrive on domestic happiness. Unlike me. For myself, I doubt that I'll ever really settle down until lovely women themselves stop finding me attractive. And by then I'll be too old, and reduced to paying for youth and beauty. Fortunately Missy and I understand each other."

"You work hard at being a cynic," Adam said.

"Not really. It's become a habit. But it's also a dreary subject so let's drop it. Let's talk about you. What are your plans for the future? Or would you rather hear about mine first? I'm not being a pig—they may have a bearing on yours. In fact, that's the real reason I wanted to see you alone."

Aware that he had succeeded in intriguing Adam and enjoying the effect, Henryk settled back in his armchair, took a fresh cigarette from the thin gold cigarette case he always carried, snapped the case shut, pocketed it, and lighted up. "First," he resumed, "let me refresh you on a few things you already know. I needn't remind you that neither my brother nor I have ever felt we really belong here once we'd had a taste of life abroad. I think I mentioned that Juzek married a Belgian girl and is living in Brussels—his wife wouldn't dream of moving elsewhere. Which is fine with him, especially since it was her family's connections in banking in the Low Countries that started him off in the first place. Add to this how much he enjoys life in a part of the world where anti-Semitism is not virulent. Well, Juzek has long been after me to go into partnership with him."

"And?"

"While our parents were living I kept putting him off. But now there's nothing left to hold me here, and Missy is as anxious as I to make the change. Mainly she wants to put distance between herself and her people. They don't much like it but they aren't stopping us either. And the Pozner money won't be exactly a hindrance—I'll be joining Juzek on more than equal terms."

He shifted in his chair and recrossed his long legs. "But it isn't as though I were entirely beholden to my father-in-law either," he hastened to add. "Once I sold the family business we were left a tidy little fortune. Then, too, my brother—he calls himself Joseph now, by the way—is a high-ranking Mason. There are Rothschild connections. As for me, I've been talking to our mutual good friend Kronenberg. Just between you and me the poor old Baron is so disappointed in his own son, he feels privileged to lend a hand when someone of the younger generation, someone with imagination and initiative, approaches him. . . ."

"But international banking? Isn't the field crowded by now, the competition brutal?"

"We've considered all the angles," Henryk said calmly. "We propose to make our big push where everything is still wide open and development is mainly in the future. Italy first. Then the Balkans, Greece. Maybe Asia Minor."

Adam remembered hearing talk in the Caucasus about how smart European capital was being channeled into all these areas. French and British money developing the oil fields around Baku. American money flowing in. German. And the Tsarate, hungry for immediate profits, giving all comers development concessions on the most advantageous terms. Uncharted territories, *Hadji* Irza had said.

"Uncharted territory," Henryk said now. "In some ways not unlike America, or I should say the America of fifty years ago, for the trend is reversing by now. We're expecting high yields, yet paradoxically it's not much of a gamble. To misquote the old song, 'Today is uncertain but tomorrow is ours.' Well, I've been wondering. How would you like to come in with us, Adam?"

"You'd like me to be your representative here after you leave?"

"We shan't be needing a Warsaw representative. We're cutting all ties with the motherland."

"Then I don't see where I'd fit in." For a moment Adam was mildly puzzled. Then the full implications of what Henryk had been saying hit him. *"All* ties?" he repeated. "But why?"

"Because," Henryk answered carefully, making it clear he'd

given this a great deal of thought, "I don't like half-measures. We'll simply be turning our backs on the past. For poor people that's called emigrating. For us there are more elegant words. We'll be expatriates, cosmopolites, citizens of the world. I find the prospect rather attractive."

"But . . . to tear up all one's roots . . ."

"What roots?" Henryk scoffed. Some inner honesty compelled him to add, "I'm lying. It's far more complicated than that. True enough, like my brother I'm anxious to go where being a Jew, no matter how remotely a Jew, doesn't stand in a man's way. But that isn't the whole story."

He got up and began restlessly pacing the floor. "We all know war with Japan is in the cards. Supposing the Tsarate topples and the Empire starts falling apart—what next? A Polish national uprising? A revolution? If anything like that happens, I want both my carcass and my money to be well out of harm's way."

It came to Adam then that Henryk was afraid. *He's dead earnest about all this and he's afraid! He's running.* "Don't you think," he finally asked, "you may be exaggerating?"

"If I am, I'm not waiting to find out. Really, how much chance is there of either of us remaining on the sidelines once things start boiling up? And I for one don't care to sacrifice my life on the barricades. Or risk jail if the other side wins, for that matter. So I'm moving out of the way of temptation while there's still time."

"*Et tu, Brute?* I always thought you were above the battle."

Henryk laughed, but without mirth. "That's the impression I try to convey. But since I'm not altogether a scoundrel, I do want to avoid having to deny my old friends, let alone playing the martyr. How about you, Adash? How do you look at it?"

Adam thought of Izidore, of Idka, of his old friends whose very whereabouts were a mystery. "I hardly know how to answer."

Henryk changed his method of attack. "What about Regina? Don't you think she'd enjoy living someplace like Paris?"

"I can't answer that either. Perhaps, like your brother's wife, she mightn't want to be torn from everything familiar, her family. . ."

"I should think," Henryk pressed, "she'd find it exciting. So much so, it might outweigh her filial devotion. And besides," his eyebrow quirked, "you'd end up making a lot of money, which she would hardly find unpleasant. As for yourself, you'd be within a stone's throw of the Sorbonne—and doesn't that open up possibilities?"

Mention of the Sorbonne made Adam jump. "Don't tempt me. I'll have to think, long and hard. When must you have an answer?"

"Oh, not for months," Henryk said. "And just remember, the day may come when you'll be grateful for having had this chance to turn your back on patriotism while there was still time." He rose to go. "And now goodnight, I've kept you up long enough." It was a rather dramatic exit.

❧ *Three* ❧

HENRYK'S WORDS kept Adam awake half the night. But it was
not the flattering offer of a whole new way of life that disturbed
his sleep. What he couldn't get out of his mind was something
else Henryk had said. *After all, I'm not altogether a scoundrel.*
Henryk, always so cool and detached, had put into words what he
himself was still trying not to face—that it would be a great
comfort to find an honorable path away from the recurring pull of
the political movement.

And he was tempted. He had long come to understand and
even accept the fact that the quiet heroism of those he most admired, heroism as a way of life, would never again be for him—
he'd lost his one chance to embrace it. And heroism as an avocation he saw as a fraud. He remembered Olek's contempt for those
indulging in the sometime struggle, in talk and plans that led
nowhere. Besides, he had none of the capacity for self-delusion
one needs for playing such games. Yet to remain wholly on the
sidelines when the hour of decision came, as it must, would be
unthinkable. Henryk had put his finger on the sore spot.

He continued to toss and turn in his comfortable bed until the
silk eiderdown slipped to the floor. He retrieved it, wrapped
himself in it as in a cocoon, and felt oddly secure. The tightly
drawn draperies shut out every vestige of light and muffled
sound, and there were only the occasional footfall of a lone passerby, the distant beat of horses' hooves, and the whirr of rubber-

tired wheels on wood paving blocks to keep him aware of the city outside.

How different from the house where he'd grown up. In the Nalewki district the streets and courtyards never slept. Men left their beds in the dark of night to go to work, the homeless huddled in doorways, drunkards brawled, while the very pavements of rough cobblestone magnified rather than hushed the sounds. Thus, even in sleep the poor were different from the rich.

A man must choose, Olek had liked to remind him in the old days, he must run either with the hares or the hounds. He must become either one of the hunters or the hunted. "And that's the whole gist of the social struggle, even including the independence movement. There can be no fence-straddling. Anyone who tries finds himself impaled. . . ."

The hell with you, Olek, old friend. Perhaps you didn't have all the answers at that. Perhaps there is a third way after all—a way out for people like Henryk and me. And can we really help it if we're born fence-sitters?

The real question was, were he and Henryk really all that much alike? But how was he to find out, so he could know beyond doubt and be sure in the core of his being? The old question again—*quo vadis,* where are you going? He must think it through in broad daylight, when his mind was clearer. And he must talk it over with Regina. He must let her have a say in his final decision, and hoped she would understand when he told her why he needed to turn his back on the old pain, the old waverings— why it would help him to start anew in a world where a man is not necessarily a political animal. . . .

And so at last he slept, bone-weary and in a sense defeated, a soldier conquered without battle, the casualty of a war yet to be fought. And as he slept escape beckoned to him all the more invitingly. He dreamed the old recurring dream about his father. The heavy curtains at his window parted and Jacob stepped in from the balcony and sat on the edge of his bed.

He looked younger than Adam remembered, and rested, his face no longer wrinkled. "You still haven't found the right answers," Jacob said in his old normal voice, free of the terrible rasp of his last illness. "How many times must I warn you business is not for you? You aren't ruthless enough. Find work you're fitted for."

"I'm trying," Adam pleaded, like a child anxious to justify himself. "You must help me—tell me which way lies escape? Is it science? The academic world?"

But his father only shook his head. "That I may not do. In the end you'll have to help yourself." He rose and, silent now, backed toward the balcony.

"Don't go! There's so much to talk about!" his son begged. Jacob smiled then, and beckoned to him to follow. But Adam in his haste could find neither slippers nor robe, and when at last he dashed out after the retreating figure, it had vanished. Instead, Regina was there, waiting to comfort him.

They embraced and remained standing tightly pressed against each other, watching the night. The air was clear, the sky luminous, star-studded as one never really sees it in cities. They were able to trace all the familiar constellations, the Big Dipper, the Little Dipper, Orion, Gemini. And the stars danced and dipped, forming and reforming into symmetrical patterns. First the six-pointed Star of David. Then snowflake designs. And finally, as once in the past, the great brilliant letters—R.F.

Even in the dream he had the distinct feeling of *déja vu*. Only now the sky seemed to be telling him what his father had refused to divulge. "Look, look, Regina! It's an omen—République Française and your own future initials too! Now I know exactly what I must do. Accept Henryk's offer and . . ."

But she shook her head and stamped her foot impatiently. "What has the French Republic to do with us?" Then quickly her mood changed and she asked sweetly, "Does the place where we settle really matter? Wouldn't you be happy anywhere, just so long as we could be together?"

In the morning he told himself his dream had indeed been prophetic, if not a literal answer. He must go at once to Regina's father and formally declare his intentions. Then some old-fashioned scruple, or perhaps it was simple consideration, prompted him to discuss his plans with his own mother first.

He found Bluma in the dining room of the Nalewki apartment, in her special chair by a window where the light was best, a large basket of mending beside her. As always at sight of him her worn face lit up with pleasure. But when he started to talk he found her, to his distress, strangely thin-lipped and disapproving. She who never pressed advice on anyone and was generally so diffident about voicing an opinion now said bleakly, "I've nothing against Regina personally, you understand. She's a lovely child. But a child just the same—and it's your happiness I'm thinking about." She bit her lip in an effort not to say more. "Sure you aren't just charmed by what's on the surface?"

He held back a sharp answer. "I've loved her for a long time. We corresponded all the while I was in the Caucasus. Yes, Mama, I'm very sure. This is no sudden infatuation, if that's what you're hinting."

She saw that she had wounded him and tried to make amends. "Of course, plain women like me are never really fair to the beauties. We just don't quite trust them, I suppose. Now you take your Aunt Salome. She's made Uncle Leon a fine wife, they're devoted to each other, but the first time he brought her to meet us—well, I can't begin to tell you how I felt about her. Oh, I kept quiet, I never let on, not even to your father. But my back was up. I was sure she couldn't possibly be good for Leon. See how wrong I was?"

He heard only what he wanted to hear. "Well, then, you yourself admit. . ."

"If you're sure in your heart, if you are both sure," she said, patting his hand, "why then all I can say is, be happy together." Again she hesitated, undecided whether she had the right to say more. "Adash, I hope you'll forgive me for bringing this up. But somehow I always hoped it was going to be that first one . . . the *shikse* you brought here that time you all had to leave the city. What was her name?"

"Wanda. Wanda Borowska."

"Yes, Wanda. She was—how shall I put it?—not just a girl but a woman. Not even Jewish, but you two were right for each other. What happened? I've never asked. Maybe I shouldn't ask even now. . ."

"It's over," he said, his voice rougher than he had intended. "It's been over a long time—never mind the reasons. She's married and has a child. She . . . I don't want to talk about it."

"In that case," his mother said gently, "I'm glad you've put it behind you. Spilled milk is spilled milk. And it's time you were taking a wife." She kissed him. "You must bring Regina here— how shall I say? Officially. As your future bride."

Salome took the news much less philosophically. In fact, she wept copious tears in Leon's arms, for this was far from the brilliant match she had intended for either her nephew or her niece. And she blamed herself for allowing it to come about, for not having been perceptive enough and vigilant enough to intervene while there was still time.

"It's all my fault. . . I let them be together too much. . . . And after planning such wonderful things for them both. . . ."

Her husband soothed her, pointing out that after all love was what made the world go round. And since there was very little else she could do, she allowed herself to be comforted.

The real explosion faced Adam when he called on Regina's father.

Karol Segal would doubtless have been dead set against any man asking to marry his favorite daughter. And here was her cousin, her own first cousin acting as though the proposal were a mere formality, a polite afterthought, as though the young people had already settled everything to their own satisfaction. Too late, he remembered their correspondence of the previous year and his original objections, and wished he had had sufficient foresight to forbid it as instinct had dictated that he should. He felt outwitted, outmaneuvered. So he raged at his daughter, who was not present, and at her suitor, who was very much there.

"I forbid it, I absolutely forbid such a union! Have you no decency, to go behind my back this way? Have you no shame? You, a grown man, to take advantage of a young girl, innocent, impressionable. . ."

"What do you mean, take advantage?" Adam shot back, matching Karol's anger. He had been prepared for opposition, but not for the violence, the unfairness of the reaction. "Just what are you trying to suggest, Uncle Karol? I respect Regina. I think of her as my future wife. . . ."

As suddenly as it had flared, Karol's fury died down. Even in his own ears his outburst, his choice of language, had sounded false.

"All right, so maybe you've been the soul of discretion. Maybe I had no business to yell at you." And using the very words Bluma had used, he went on, "I've nothing against you personally, Adam, don't misunderstand me. I even like you. But it's my child's future, her happiness I'm thinking about. She's too young for you. And it's not as if we were anxious to marry her off. With her looks and her charm and her talent, she can afford to pick and choose."

"Who knows that better than I?" Adam said, now feeling truly humble. "I'm reaching high, and Regina deserves the best. But one thing I can promise you. No one could ever love her as I do. I want to devote the rest of my life to making her happy." The words were hackneyed and he wished he knew a more eloquent way to plead his case.

But Karol was touched. "I don't doubt your sincerity, Adash, nor your love either. But when you've reached my age you know that love alone isn't enough. There are other considerations that can't be ignored. You two are first cousins, and there are bound to be children. I speak now not as Regina's father but as a doctor. In addition to the blood relationship there's the difference in ages. And your recent illness. Frankly all this worries me."

Adam tried a new, desperate tactic. "If you forbid this marriage, we'll be wed without your blessing!" Then, on impulse, "And don't think I'm making an empty threat. Regina feels the same way. Moreover, I've just been offered a position—an excellent position—abroad. I could simply accept and take her with me. . ."

Karol's answer was a counterthreat. "You do that, and I'll cut her off without a penny." It was his trump card. But the effect was not at all what he'd anticipated.

"I never counted on a dowry," Adam said coldly. "I wouldn't

accept one if it were offered. Do you think I'd want Regina to feel she had been bartered off? All I want is the privilege of taking care of her."

Unexpectedly, Karol no longer felt like the proverbial irate father. "You really do love her, don't you? Well, you've just proved it. There aren't many men who'd take this attitude."

"You mean," Adam said, hardly believing he was hearing right, "that you aren't going to try to stop us?"

"Not so fast. Let's just say I'm willing to listen to reason. Mind you, I'm not giving you a categorical no, but neither am I saying yes. You and Regina may become officially engaged. But only on certain conditions."

"Anything, Uncle," Adam stammered. "I'll go along with anything you say."

"Hm. We shall see. Here is what I propose. There's to be no talk of a wedding for a full year. Frankly, I'm counting on time to do its dirty work. With everyone treating her as your fiancée, Regina will soon get a taste of how it feels to have other young men keep their distance. She's always been used to a lot of attention, a lot of adulation, and she may not like what happens. She may get bored, or simply change her mind. I wouldn't be too surprised if she did."

"If that's what you think, you don't know your own daughter!" Adam began indignantly. Then gratitude overwhelmed him. "But thank you, Uncle, thank you just the same!" At a loss what else to do, he shook Karol's hand, then kissed it. "If I believed in God I would call down his blessing on you."

Karol awkwardly patted the younger man's shoulder. "Don't thank me yet. I want it clearly understood that what I'm doing is done with malice aforethought." And to indicate he considered the interview over, he rang for the maid to bring in tea and ask Miss Regina and her mother to join them.

Karol's gambit may or may not have been a shrewd one. It was never tested. Time turned out to be not his ally but his enemy. The following week he suffered a near-fatal heart attack. As soon afterwards as he was able, of his own accord he sent for Adam.

"It looks as though I'm the one on whom the dirty trick's been played." He was whispering, for it was a great effort for him to talk. "I won't be around long enough to watch over you children and your long engagement. . . ."

With tears in his eyes Adam did his best to reassure him, saying all the things a well man says when he visits the ill and the dying. But his uncle stopped him with an impatient grimace.

"Save that for the women, they're going to need comforting a lot more than I. One advantage of being a physician," he smiled feebly, "is that you only lie to patients, not to yourself. I happen to know my days are numbered." This time Adam did not even argue. He merely listened while the sick man unburdened himself.

"I'm leaving my family not too badly off," Karol began. "There's a nest egg for each of the children, enough to see even the youngest through until they're educated and on their feet. And Aunt Balbina will be comfortable. But she's going to need someone to lean on, advise her on finances, that sort of thing." His breath was coming hard. He signaled for water. Adam helped him to raise himself on the pillows and held a glass to his lips.

After a while Karol began again. "So you see, everything is changed. I was going to outfox you, remember? But now I'll die more peacefully if I can see Regina safely married to you. For regardless of anything I may have said, I know I'll be leaving her in good hands. Just remember, Adash, she's such a child still. I, especially, have petted and spoiled her. She'll need a husband who in many ways is a father to her. . . ."

Beyond the tightly closed and sealed windows of the sickroom the convent park stood stark and lifeless, the trees naked except where snow clung to their branches. The golden cupola of the chapel, clearly visible through the stripped branches, shone blindingly with reflected winter sunset. As Karol paused to draw breath, the chimes began to ring for vespers.

He made a futile attempt to reach the bell-pull. "Get Regina and her mother here, will you? We have to make plans. By the way, Ginia already knows, I've told her." Adam couldn't be sure whether Karol meant his daughter knew he was dying or that there was to be a wedding. "And before they come in there's something more I have to say to you, son. There's no need for pride any longer, so don't turn down her dowry. If you don't want to use it, invest it for her. That way she'll always have something completely her own. Just in case anything happens to you—though, of course, you're too young still to believe such a thing is possible. Just the same, no one is immortal. . . ."

And so, with Regina sobbing and Adam holding her, aware as never before that he was making himself completely responsible for her at last, they planned a quick, simple family ceremony. Now there would be no time for all the customary rounds of shopping, the trips to dressmakers and lingerie shops and linen shops and conferences with the needlewomen who monogrammed what had been bought. Just barely time to whip up a wedding gown. And Adam thought what a pity that his little bride should be cheated of that innocent bit of excitement. But Regina, in the midst of the bittersweet preparations, thought fleetingly, *May God forgive me for such sinful thoughts at such a sad time, but I'm going to be just like the chic Missy Pozner! I'll have to buy my trousseau after I'm married, with my own husband helping me choose!"*

She found the prospect rather intriguing.

Had it been up to Adam, he would have chosen to be married in the City Registry, with only Regina's parents and his mother present. He hated the fuss, even such as it was. He resented the prospect of having to submit to the elaborate religious ceremony, the wedding canopy, the broken wine glass. But since that seemed to be what everyone else expected, he didn't even attempt to fight it.

As the wedding day approached, Karol improved visibly.

"Well, at least I shall be up and about to give my daughter away," he announced cheerfully, "and drink a toast to your future. And if the drinking kills me, why, what pleasanter way is there to die!"

He continued to feel better, although neither he nor anyone else was fooled as to the ultimate outcome. He wore his frock coat to the wedding, the same one he'd worn to his own, and looked less pale and nervous than the bridegroom. When his wife tried to get him to sit down halfway through the service, he waved her impatiently away.

As for Regina, she made a storybook bride. The dressmaker had done wonders on such short notice. Making a virtue of necessity, she'd advised the simplest of styles: a tight bodice above a draped skirt with a short train, leg-o'-mutton sleeves, the whole thing done in rich, creamy brocade satin but with no frills and no lace—"No need to gild the lily. With that marvelous rose-point veil and the string of pearls twisted to hold it, and all those orange blossoms. . ." The veil was Salome's gift and had once been her mother's. The pearls, real ones, small but perfect, came from the Kronenbergs—"Mademoiselle will look like a pure, floating angel. . . ."

And an angel was what she seemed to Adam as she came to him on her father's arm. They exchanged rings. The rabbi blessed them. They drank the sweet red sacramental wine and Adam crushed the glass under his heel as he'd been coached to do. By then there wasn't a dry eye in the room. It was as though Karol's illness, in addition to melting parental opposition, had made even Salome forget her objections to the match. Toast after toast was drunk to the bridal pair.

When at last everything was over, when everyone had kissed the bride and Regina had changed to her traveling suit and she and Adam were able to get away, they left with every blessing their families could think to heap upon them. Never had a marriage begun in an aura of greater confidence. And no one, Adam least of all, was aware that between the man and the woman just joined in holy matrimony not a single serious word had been spoken that had a bearing on their future.

❦ *Four* ❧

Aʟʟ ᴛʜʀᴏᴜɢʜ ᴛʜᴇ ʏᴇᴀʀs she had devoted to shaping her favorite niece's personality, Salome Grossglik had promised herself to have a long talk with the girl on the eve of her wedding. That would be the moment to share with Regina her own most cherished nuggets of woman wisdom for keeping romance alive in marriage. It would also be the time to warn her—oh, ever so tactfully, of course!—about certain physical things that went on between a man and a woman in the bridal chamber. Strictly speaking this should be a mother's responsibility, but Salome didn't put it past her sister-in-law Balbina to shirk such unpleasantness. Yet obviously it had to be done, if only to save the bride from being terrified on her wedding night!

Salome planned the conversation with the greatest care. Having managed a half-hour of total privacy, she began by reminding Regina about the remark Leon had first made on their seventh wedding anniversary, the remark she so loved to repeat that by now the whole family knew it by heart. "What he said to me—and I give you his exact words, I remember them just as if it were yesterday—what he said was, 'My darling, you're so pure and lovely sometimes I still think of you as my betrothed. . . . I even wonder if you couldn't happily remain an engaged girl all your life. . . .' "

To make things clearer to her niece, she added, "And he still says that every time he takes me in his arms he feels as if he had to win me over again. Now I expect that doesn't have much meaning for you yet, Regina darling—how could it when you're still all innocence?—so let me explain. . . ." Hastily, then, she launched into confidences on what to her was the genesis of the matter.

"You see, my dear, no matter how wonderful you think a man is, he still has certain baser instincts that can't be denied. And as a good wife you'll have to let him . . .well . . . ah . . . have his way with you. But that doesn't mean you have to allow your husband every liberty every time! If you do, he'll only begin taking you for granted. And grow bored. Maybe even, God forbid, for that's how men are, start straying. So you see, dear heart, the wisest thing is to keep him guessing. Be kind sometimes, and at other times distant. . . ."

Fortunately for Regina, Salome's veiled hints about the beast in man went in one ear and out the other. Like Missy Pozner before her, she, too, had recently read *Memoires de Deux Jeunes Mariées* and she was so entranced by Balzac that she related all of Salome's well-intentioned advice to what the novel's two protagonists had said to one another about their relationships with their husbands: *To keep the bloom on marriage, to make your husband your slave, always make sure he looks at you in wonder and delight. Take infinite pains with your looks, keep your skin glowing, your hair a halo of glory and your perfume subtle.* It was harmless advice, and it kept her from having the usual fears dinned into her. So that when at last she faced the marriage bed, she brought to it not only the smooth, flawless body of a plump bisque shepherdess but the undistorted instincts of a healthy young pagan.

Adam's surrender to his bride was complete. His body on fire after its long ascetic fast, he had nonetheless been ready to be endlessly patient, to initiate her slowly, step by step, into the mysteries of physical intimacy. Instead, here she was, matching him caress for caress, as innocently sensual as a kitten yet with just enough innate shyness to make it necessary for him to woo her, just enough reticence to keep him aroused and give the game meaning.

The little gasps of pain and then of pleasure, the clinging to him for reassurance, and finally, as ecstasy mounted, the look of wonderment in her eyes—all of it doubled his own pleasure and his own delight, filling him with tenderness and a kind of pride known only to the victorious male.

For Regina, dazzling as was the discovery of her own body and the pleasures it could bring her, even more heady was the knowledge of how she could affect a man by the mere fact of being herself. And while still too new to lovemaking to see it as a sharp and cruel instrument of power, she was not unaware of the possibilities. She merely tucked the secret away in a recess of her mind, to use later if need be.

They were spending their honeymoon at the Pozner estate in Milanowek, where Marek had once said she might care to watch him play polo. Old Maurice, who enjoyed such gestures of largesse, had put the place at their disposal for the month. The villa, a miniature baroque palace surrounded by formal gardens in the center of a vast park, snow-covered now, might have been the Ice Maiden's castle as one approached it in midwinter. Inside it was furnished grandly if in execrable taste, and while Regina was well aware of the vulgarity, she did enjoy the opulence. Here she had servants to wait on her hand and foot. The lady's maid who unpacked for her also served her breakfast in bed in the morning, drew her bath, helped with her clothes and hair. Lunch might be served among the palm and orange trees of the conservatory, afternoon tea in an upstairs sitting room. And dinner was a feast of baronial splendor, with gleaming silver and crystal and gold-and-cobalt china, and white-gloved footmen stiffly in attendance behind her chair and Adam's.

On crisp, clear days they would go for drives through the sparkling countryside, skimming the ground in a great sleigh drawn by a pair of fine black Arabs. Snug under fur lap robes, they kissed behind the coachman's broad, impassive back. In gloomy weather they stayed indoors, sipping hot mulled wine before a roaring fire. Or she would go to the grand piano and play all of Adam's favorite pieces. Or they would read aloud or play dominoes. And once or twice they made love in broad daylight, the awareness of servants gliding about the corridors almost within earshot making them feel deliciously guilty. Afterwards, dressed again and again decorous, they couldn't help wondering if their drowsiness, their heavy-lidded languor, didn't give them away.

Regina liked to pretend that the luxury and the grandeur were not borrowed, that she was mistress here, free to give orders. She began to see herself in the role of young chatelaine, and it seemed to her a perfect piece of casting. From there it was only a quick step to other conjectures. She was prettier than Missy, wasn't she? And who were Missy's parents that their life style should remain unattainable? She had met them both; fat, coarse-grained, they made their own children shudder. Gossip had it that *Pani* Konstancja could barely read. . . .

"Wouldn't it be delightful," she murmured one evening as she and Adam sat gazing into the fire, "if all this really truly belonged to us? Would you have to work terribly hard to become really rich?"

He had been lost in a dream of his own, and it took him a moment to return to the here and now. "What? What did you say, sweet?"

"Only that it might be fun to be rich-rich-rich. Like the Pozners and the Kronenbergs. Like your friend Henryk is going to be. Don't you think it would suit us, too? Can't you just see us. . . ."

A plan, only half articulate still, was forming in her mind. What was that motto engraved inside her school graduation ring? *Per aspera ad astra?* No, that was the wrong sentiment—she had no desire to make her way to the stars through any cruel thorns. Then she remembered what she was after. *Too low they aim who aim below the stars.* She had no idea where the quotation came from, and it didn't really matter. She was thinking of that dream of Adam's he had told her about in such detail.

Well, dreams like that could be interpreted in more ways than one! After all, if it took only one generation to establish an industrial dynasty like Pozner's, then why not a Fabian empire? All Adam really needed was a little skillful prodding. "You haven't answered me, dear," she pouted.

He stroked her hair. "I didn't think you were serious. How could being millionaires make us any happier than we are now?"

She almost said, "Must I spell it out for you?" Some instinct stopped her. She was forewarned by an inflection in his voice, a withdrawal so slight there was no defining it. One of Aunt Salome's favorite dictums echoed in her memory. *One catches more flies with honey than with vinegar. Never be crass, dear heart, when it comes to letting your wishes be known. Men hate to be led by the nose. Let them think they make the decisions and you're just falling in with their plans. It's so easy, and so much more pleasant, to be the quiet power behind the throne. . . .*

She heeded the warning and shifted her tactics. She smiled—a trifle mysteriously, she hoped. "Ah, well, if I please you just as I am, without jewels or furs or wonderful clothes, I suppose that's all that matters." She snuggled against him. "I know it's childish of me to dwell on *material* things, even if they *are* lovely . . . lovely but not in the least important. . . . So be patient with me, and I promise to grow up."

Instantly Adam's arm tightened around her and he kissed her, assuring her he didn't want her to change, that she was his own precious darling and he adored her and all he asked was a chance to make her happy. And she rubbed her cheek against the rough stuff of his coat, pleased with what she had managed to accomplish and thinking how smoothly the future would take care of itself.

Their month in the country was cut short by a telegram from Warsaw.

FATHER HAD ANOTHER HEART ATTACK. COME AT ONCE. It was signed by Kuba.

Without stopping to pack, they were on their way as soon as the horses could be harnessed, catching up with an express train at the nearest junction. Even so, they were already too late. Karol's heart was still beating when they reached Regina's old home, but he was in a coma. He died in the night without regaining consciousness.

Regina sobbed brokenheartedly in her husband's arms, all the little artifices swept away by grief. But her mother, who for weeks had waited for this final blow, remained controlled and dry-eyed. Bluma was with her, and the sisters knew a kinship they hadn't known in years, the kinship of loss and bleakness. It was the kinship that comes of donning widow's weeds and slipping a second, too large wedding band onto one's ring finger.

Yet even as she tried to comfort her younger sister and wept with her, Bluma knew that Balbina would very soon find her balance again. For Balbina's center of gravity had always been within herself. She needed no one—not husband, not children—to maintain her equilibrium. And in a sense Bluma envied her, yet at the same time she felt pity for her. Balbina might be spared the price in pain of giving fully of herself, but Bluma would not have traded places with her. *For I have known real happiness with my Jacob,* she thought, *while my sister, I suspect, has known merely a well-ordered life.* That was when she understood that the tears she was shedding were less for Balbina's than for her own ever-fresh bereavement.

The funeral procession was large and most of it was shabby, so shabby Regina was secretly relieved that the hired coaches, closed and with curtains drawn, in which family and friends followed the hearse were clearly unrelated to those mourners who came on foot. It irked her (in death as it had in life) to have to acknowledge the slightest connection with her father's numerous neighborhood patients. Now here they were pouring out of their flats like ants out of a tumbled antheap, the women with black shawls over their wigs, the men in long kaftans and skullcaps, all of them anxious to pay their last respects to their trusted *Pan Doktor.* He'd been a generous man, they whispered, in the Yiddish jargon Regina despised and didn't even understand so that Adam had to translate for her. He'd been a good man and a learned one and would be much missed. Lucky for his widow she already had grown children to care for her. Though who knows, she might be in need for all that, and perhaps now was the time to search one's soul and make a real effort and pay up those long-overdue bills. The only question was, where was a person to find the cash? You can't squeeze blood out of a turnip, and who understood that better than the dear departed himself?

The uncollected bills remained uncollected. And it was not on her grown children—actually, only Kuba was of age and what would a candidate for a doctorate in philosophy, and a musician

« 533 »

and poet by avocation at that, know about managing finances?—
it was not on her own grown children but on her new son-in-law
that Balbina Segal thrust the responsibility of handling her business affairs.

Karol's estate turned out to be more substantial than anyone,
including his own wife, had suspected. Each of the children was
left a tidy ten thousand rubles while their mother received as
much as all five of them together. In his will, read at a family
conference at which Adam quite naturally was present, Karol's
last request to them all was to consider very carefully what to do
with their inheritance.

"Each of you is free," he'd written on some long-ago occasion,
"to take what belongs to you and either put it by as a nest egg for
a rainy day or spend it recklessly. I can't dictate to you—besides,
whatever you decide, your mother will still have a competence all
the rest of her life. She'll be a burden on no one, beholden to no
one. So you see, I'm not trying to put pressure on you. Just the
same, I should like to suggest a better way to handle your money.
If none of you were to touch your capital for a while, if you agreed
amongst yourselves to pool your shares for careful investment,
the total would add up to the kind of money that can talk. I am
not now thinking of immediate income, which would merely
permit your mother, and those of you who continue to live at
home, to exist in modest comfort. My concern is for how all
this could be made to pay off in the future. . . ." There was
more in the same vein, shrewd advice, measured, sensible.

The reading over, all eyes turned to Adam. Finally Balbina
said, speaking for the lot of them, "Well, Papa died in peace
knowing we now had a man in the family who understood about
such things. I know, because he said as much toward the end.
What he was hoping for, Adam, was that with your experience
and your connections you might want to use the inheritance to
start a business of your own, in which all of us, your wife's people, would be your silent partners. I might even say this was
Karol's ardent wish. . . ."

It was the last thing in the world Adam wanted. He thought
of his own father's warning in another time of crisis, and of his recurring dream that served as a periodic reminder. And he felt

trapped. After the long years of caring for his own family—at what cost to himself no one would ever know and only his mother suspected—after making a new beginning, straightening shoulders that had been bent too early and for too long, he was aghast at the idea. A business of his own, financed out of funds he must husband more zealously than anything belonging to himself, would mean a kind of intolerable slavery to balance sheets and profits and dog-eat-dog competition. He did not want that as a way of life.

"I just don't know, Aunt Balbina," he began defending himself. "I doubt if I have this special kind of talent. Perhaps I could just ask Pozner about investing in his company, and let it go at that?"

It was then that Regina, tragic and pale and lovely in her heavy mourning, looked up at him, her beautiful eyes swimming with unshed tears. Her soft, cool hand slipped trustingly into his. "But, my dearest, wouldn't it be better for all of us if you did it yourself, if you built up something that could be truly ours? I know you'd have to work harder at first, but just the same . . . for my sake, for the sake of those I love best in the world . . . wouldn't you be willing to . . . sacrifice?"

"Is that what you really want?" he asked, and wondered why she had never before made it plain how deeply she cared about her people, and thought it must be a lack in himself that he hadn't guessed without being told. "Because if it is, then yes, of course I'll do it. Only I want to make one thing clear to all of you. I'm no business genius, I can't promise you mountains of gold. But I'll do my best—I'm sure all of you know I will."

That night in their bed in the guest room of the Grossgliks' apartment, where they would be staying until they could make other plans, Regina clung to him, whispering her gratitude and her love and her belief in him. "You'll do wonders, I know it, I can feel it! And oh, Adash, how good and generous you're being to my poor family. . . ."

Her lips were soft, her body fragrant and responsive and capricious and eager. When finally she slept, it seemed to Adam there was nothing in the whole wide world he wouldn't be able to accomplish for her sake.

❧ *Five* ❧

BUT IN THE GRAY LIGHT of morning doubts began to assail him again. He felt as though he were being forced from one treadmill onto another. For this was exactly the effect of Karol Segal's last will and testament. Intending only what was best for everyone, reaching from beyond the grave, his father-in-law had forged for him a harness of iron.

Nor did it really matter very much whether he ended up taking the money and starting some independent venture of his own, as Regina wanted, or else, staying on as an employee at Pozner's, invested and then watched over the combined family inheritance. It was the prospect of the responsibility that overwhelmed him. And while he hesitated to admit it even to himself, he resented being saddled with it.

Troubled, he had the impulse to wake Regina, tell her she mustn't press him. But she was sleeping so soundly he didn't have the heart to disturb her. She slept on her back, one plump white arm thrown above her head, her hair spilling over from her pillow to his, her breasts only half-covered so that the pink nipples showed above the lace-edged sheet. *If I do wake her,* he thought, *it won't be so that we can talk.* He sighed, edged himself out of bed, got into his clothes, and tiptoed out. The next best thing was a long walk to clear his head.

The house was quiet, and only the aroma of fresh-ground coffee told him there was already activity in the kitchen. On the hall table the morning papers waited. He glanced at them idly. Half the columns had again been pulled by the censors so that the front pages, as usual these days, were slashed with great gaping swaths of white. He was startled to notice the date. Only the 10th of February, yet so much had happened since the Christmas holidays it was as though months had already gone by.

He was reaching for his hat and coat when Miss Julia padded out in her carpet slippers. "Going out without breakfast, *Pan* Adam, and you so recently sick! Can't let you do that!" She sounded properly outraged. "At least have some coffee and rolls, everything's ready for *Pan* Leon anyway, it's not as if you'd have to wait. . . ."

Rather than argue he drank the coffee in big gulps. It burned his mouth, but he was anxious to be off before anyone else came out. If it wasn't possible to talk things over with Regina he wanted to be left completely to himself, and perhaps his thoughts would begin to sort themselves out and he could start rationally to consider the decisions he was being forced to make.

He walked fast if aimlessly, gradually becoming aware of the city waking up around him. The men and women out in the street at this early hour were, like himself not too many years ago, hurrying to poorly paid jobs. They were the ones who opened the shops, lit the first lights, pushed back shutters. The ones who swept floors and sidewalks and wiped off counters. The ones who got everything ready for the more privileged employees.

It was a long time since he'd been out among them, and suddenly the clock was turned back for him and he was reliving the past. He was a schoolboy again, hearing the tower trumpeter while rushing to this place or that to tutor some dunce incapable of getting admitted to the *Gymnasium* on his own. He was in the upper grades, beginning, for good pay now, to tutor Marek and Missy Pozner and Lucio Kronenberg. He was a student at the university and his father was dying and Wanda and Maryla were dodging the police and he was learning from Olek Piotrowski the rudiments of conspiracy and survival.

Unexpectedly a great wave of nostalgia swept over him for the vanished days and the old friendships that had slipped from his life but had never been rooted out of his heart. There had been a purity of purpose about it all which he now missed, a clean selflessness that he yearned to retrieve and that he knew would elude him altogether if he became embroiled in the building of a possible fortune with his in-laws' capital. It was a startling insight and one which only added to his distress. For how was he ever going to explain his thoughts to Regina? How convince her that to become her family's banker and broker was all wrong for him? And even if he did manage that much, how persuade her that the past, in which she had no share and which right then he saw as a great raveling tear in the fabric of his being, must remain forever part of him without including her, even though it in no way threatened or diminished his love for her?

He had been walking along familiar streets and unexpectedly found himself passing the building where the Meisels had lived for as long as he had known them. Henryk still kept the old apartment while winding up his father's affairs in preparation for his coming marriage and move abroad. Adam thought of their talk of a month ago and Henryk's flattering offer. In a sense going into partnership with the Meisels might be no more to his taste than any other business venture, but, as Henryk had pointed out while trying to tempt him, if he went to Paris he'd be within a stone's throw—and not just physically but intellectually—of one of the world's great science centers. If he were to throw himself body and soul into the making of money for a period of, say, ten years, with any kind of luck he might yet be able to change careers before he was forty.

The city was now fully awake. Adam pulled out the heavy silver watch his father had given him on his birthday nearly fourteen years ago. Over an hour had passed since he'd left Count Berg Street. It was still early, only a little after eight, but not too early to ring the bell of an old friend.

He found Henryk at breakfast, handsome and splendid in a Jaeger robe with satin revers and slippers of dark morocco, but looking curiously rumpled in the morning light. Adam noticed that the maid who let him in was much too young and pretty to be housekeeper to a bachelor. After she'd served them fresh coffee she continued to stand about, her spaniel eyes gazing at her master with such mournful adoration there could be no doubt as to her true function in the household. Adam guessed she was being discarded along with whatever furnishings Henryk decided to leave behind.

"I'm moving into a hotel in a few more days," Henryk spoke as though the girl in the room weren't there. "This place is becoming depressing." With a wave of his hand he indicated the packing cases spewing straw and filled with what must be personal treasures, the crates containing a few choice pieces of furniture, the bare unfaded rectangles of wallpaper where until recently paintings had hung. "Missy and I have gone over everything with a fine-tooth comb and there isn't much we really want."

Adam heard the young housekeeper suck in her breath, but she only asked if there would be anything else.

"Nothing. You can go now and clear later," Henryk said curtly. When the door had closed behind her he added, "Sniff-sniff-sniff, cry-cry-cry. I've told her a dozen times she was welcome to anything we leave behind, that she's free to sell or set up a place for herself and do business—a rooming house, or better still a house of assignation. And do you know what? She didn't appreciate the humor. Women! Always wanting what they can't have!"

Not until then did he become aware of Adam's horrified expression. "Oh, sorry. I forgot I was speaking to an idealist, and a man in love besides. Let's change the subject. What brings you out at this ungodly hour?"

The morning had soured for Adam. He was thinking of Olek discussing the corruption of a social system in which women were chattels and money was tainted, Olek insisting that no one who did not consciously and consistently work against the status quo could avoid being tainted by it. "A man can't wallow in shit without some of it sticking to him," was how he'd once put it. Nevertheless he, Adam, didn't feel corrupted, only trapped. Could one perhaps subdivide oneself into cells like a beehive, some pure, some impure? That remained to be seen. In the meantime he was just as glad to have had this glimpse of the shoddy side of his old school friend and possible future partner. It had the odd effect of completely depersonalizing the interview.

"I'm here on a matter of business," he finally said. "Things have moved faster for me than I expected and I'm faced with some major decisions. About that offer you made me just before I got married—does it still hold? And another question, which by the way I want you to consider separately. Quite aside from whether or not I decide to come in with you, would you be interested in cash for capitalization? If so, what do you figure as a return on such an investment?"

"How much cash?"

"A hundred thousand."

Henryk whistled. "Not that it's any of my business, but how do you come by such a sum?"

"It's what my wife's father left. Now the whole family look to me as their miracle man. Regina's share is only one-tenth of it."

"With you as part of the deal her share'd be worth a hell of a lot more. Come to think of it, we'd make quite a triumvirate, Juzek, you and I. For a start, Paris, Brussels, Milan. Later on, the sky's the limit. We'd all get rich together."

"Aren't you indulging in pipe dreams?" Adam asked soberly.

To his astonishment Henryk answered just as soberly. "My future father-in-law doesn't think so. Seriously, can you see him backing Missy's husband in anything less than a spectacularly promising venture? Not that I also haven't full confidence in my own ability. Arrogant? Of course I'm arrogant. How else are fortunes made?"

"You haven't answered my main question," Adam persisted. "Forgetting about me—what kind of returns could the Segals expect on their investment?"

Henryk sipped cold coffee. "During the first few years not more than good current bank rates. Six, maybe seven per cent. The real cream will be for skimming later. Because in the early stages we plan to concentrate on growth. Think they'll be satisfied with that kind of arrangement?"

"I'll let you know when I talk it over with Regina's mother."

"And you," Henryk prodded. "What about you?"

Adam thought fleetingly he wasn't really sure he wanted a close association with a man who, even though formally engaged, was already taking infidelity for granted. He said vaguely, "I haven't got your drive, your ambition. I've been drawn into the business world willy-nilly, as you know. What I'm actually looking for is an arrangement with an eventual way out. That's what attracts me most about your scheme—a possibility to make my way to the Sorbonne. If I slaved away at—forgive me—at moneygrubbing for X number of years, in the end I might buy my freedom." The old impossible dream beckoned, shimmering, no longer altogether unattainable, and he allowed himself to toy with it. "Someday I could teach, or else go into research. That would make the whole thing worthwhile."

"You and Maria Curie-Sklodowska."

"No need to poke fun at me."

"You know me better than that," Henryk protested. "Anyway, *chacun son goût*. Eventually, I suppose, we could work out some sort of royalty arrangement. I presume Regina agrees?" he added pointedly.

Adam thought of the sleeping girl he'd held all night in his arms. "We've barely had time to discuss details. But she always says she wants whatever is going to make me happy. On the other hand," he felt impelled to concede, "she's also immensely concerned about the well-being of her family. So naturally she'd also want me to be practical."

"Oh, naturally." Henryk suppressed a sardonic smile. From what he knew of her, he found it hard to imagine Regina welcoming the role of dedicated scientist's wife, whether now or ten years hence. But he made no further comment. "Well, whatever you decide, let me know. The wedding isn't until late April, so you've plenty of time. And afterwards there are always the mails and the telegraph."

Adam asked to be remembered to Missy, and left.

A little later in the day he called on his employer.

The old man had not expected to see him so soon after the funeral, said as much, expressed his condolences, and remarked what a pity it was to have one's honeymoon thus interrupted. He also inquired after the bride. Then, assuming this was no social call, he asked Adam what was on his mind and whether he could be of help.

Adam had decided in advance to be completely frank. He mentioned the reading of the will and the position vis-à-vis his wife's family in which he now reluctantly found himself. Then, omitting only his own future hopes, since intuition warned him Pozner would have scant sympathy with any leanings toward the academic life, he went on to the Meisels' new venture and Henryk's proposal to himself.

"At the risk of sounding like an ingrate, I want you to know I haven't turned him down."

He said it with considerable apprehension, expecting fireworks, but to his intense relief Pozner chuckled. "Well, I've lived long enough to expect these things. The fledgling itching to try his wings, one's children growing up and going off. The best you can hope for is that at some future date the younger generation won't kick you in the teeth. Beyond that. . ."

Adam, sincere and earnest, started to protest but the old man imperiously silenced him.

"I know what you're about to tell me. It isn't in you to bite the hand that fed you. You're probably right. But the fact is we'll never really know, for to put it bluntly I'm too big and you're too puny to present a threat. On the other hand, your going in with my girl's husband appeals to me. You're a loyal cuss, and no matter what the future holds you'd continue to watch out for Missy's best interests, not just your own. Not that I don't trust Henryk, you understand, especially since well he knows which side his bread is buttered. But I go by the old saying—forewarned is forearmed."

Apparently, like his daughter, the old man had very few illusions, Adam reflected. He offered no comment, none being called for. Pozner had launched on one of his long discourses, which could be not merely interesting but illuminating.

"Those two young squirts have a sound idea," he was saying. "Might even turn out profitable for all of us, seeing how shaky the Empire is these days. An international banking operation specializing in undeveloped countries—it's an inspiration. Wait ten years." The magic number again, Adam noticed. "Wait ten years and there's no telling how it will spread. And now let's get down to cases. How seriously are you considering the offer and what's your timetable?"

Adam said he was still of two minds about everything.

"Well," his employer said, "I should hate to lose you, but if I were thirty years younger that's exactly what I'd do myself. Leave the country. Join the mainstream of civilization. I'm all for it." Apparently he had given the subject a great deal of thought and saw far beyond the immediate goals.

After a while he continued through a haze of cigar smoke. "Another few years, and Western capital will be invading the field in earnest. It's already fighting for spheres of influence in the Balkans, the Caucasus, the whole Mediterranean—you've had a glimpse of some of this at first hand. The Tsarate is hungry for hard cash and giving away all kinds of concessions in return, and who do you think will develop all this natural wealth? The French, the British, the Germans, the Americans." It was more and more obvious he had considered the subject from every conceivable angle. "The only thing is, they're also busy with China, all of Asia, in fact. Much too busy to worry over a country like Italy, for instance, which by the way is still as backward as Russia in some ways, and that's saying a good deal. So you see, there's a big juicy melon waiting to be cut, and that's a good way out if one has the misfortune of having been born a subject of His Most Gracious Majesty, the Autocrat of All the Russias, and a second-class subject to boot for having been born a Pole, third-class for having been born a Jew. . . ."

Henryk had spoken of all of this, but never so concretely. Adam listened spellbound as Pozner, his imagination inflamed, continued the analysis. "Go abroad while you're young, go by all means. Acquire French or English or Dutch or even Italian citizenship. Then you'll really hold freedom in your hand. Plus a key to a fortune. At any rate, shake the dust of Poland from your feet. So long as you have *Pole* and *Jew* stamped in Cyrillic letters on your Russian passport, you're crippled. I'm happy so many of you younger men are finally able to see this, that you're no longer waiting around for the millennium of independence. Because for us Poles patriotism is worse than an illusion, it's a sickness.

« 543 »

I'm especially happy to find *you* thinking this way—it's the last thing I would have really expected."

Adam was beginning to feel that words were being put in his mouth. *"Pan* Pozner, I never said. . ."

The old man waved away the protest. "You needn't be ashamed. I promise I won't hold any of this against you."

"But really, I. . ."

"I *said* no disclaimers were necessary. It's simply going to give me considerable pleasure to see you get out of this stinking, decaying land, where in order to make headway a man has to kiss every official ass that presents itself. Oh, I know all about the sentiments that have been dinned into you ever since you were old enough to listen. *Pro patria. Gloria victis.* But honestly, Adam, when one comes right down to it, what is this hallowed love of country? And do we Jews really have a country here? Does Poland want us? Even in the patriotic underground aren't we barely tolerated?"

In spite of himself, in spite of recognizing the partial truth of what the old man was saying—in spite even of the sometime temptation to turn his back once and for all on the long, hard struggle—Adam was experiencing the same kind of revulsion he'd felt earlier, with Henryk. Only this time it was more than a matter of personal morals. He was astonished to find that when he heard love of country attacked, his response was totally visceral, involuntary.

For the second time that day he was finding at least partial application for something Olek had been fond of dinning into him: that money and big business cut clean across class lines and also national loyalties, that capital and capitalists have their own special kind of International. And also out of the past he brought out a symbolic answer. "Sometimes," he told Pozner, not sure it was going to do any good, "a bad mother is better than no mother at all. Children seem to sense this. You watch them being cuffed around, then clinging to the hand that has just been cruel. I suppose deep down they always hope love will some day break through the denial. Besides, aren't bad mothers mostly the fault of the society we live in? What makes anti-Semitism? If you're born into a brutal, bigoted world you grow up a brute."

"You sound like a socialist," Pozner shrugged. "But that's always been your weakness."

The conversation was interrupted by a footman coming in with the afternoon papers. Again half the front pages were blank. But the remaining headlines screamed about the treacherous attack by Japan on the Imperial navy at Port Arthur. General mobilization orders were being issued. This was war.

For several minutes both men read in silence. The censored dispatches were neither informative nor accurate, and they both knew the war had been brought on by the stubbornness of an ill-advised autocrat who cared nothing about the welfare of his people or how many of them he sent to their death. It was, in fact, a war that should have been avoided at all costs, for it must end in unavoidable, ignominious defeat. Neither the Russian army nor the Russian navy could sustain the onslaught of a well-prepared adversary, especially when the battleground was thousands of miles away from the country's bases of supply.

After a time Pozner quoted a favorite *bon mot* of the moment. "No wonder they call him the great autocrat from neck to toe! A head on his shoulders he hasn't got!" Then, unbelievably, he winked and began to laugh. "All this may prove fatal for the Empire, but not for the textile business! Want me to give you the soundest advice of all under these new circumstances? Stick with me till after the peace. Take the money the Segals give you and do as I tell you, and by the time the army's demobilized you'll have tripled their capital. Afterwards you can always invest in other things or think about emigrating. And by then, who knows, you may already be rich."

It was a reaction so spontaneous and so frankly callous that Adam recoiled. His head bursting with advice that he knew was sound but that sickened him, he finally took his leave and started for home. His route took him past the statue of Copernicus on Nowy Swiat, that monument to Poland's past glory below which once Izidore had met his young comrades for the national demonstration that had cost them so dearly. Adam hadn't the slightest doubt that soon there would be fresh popular outbreaks, fresh repressions, fresh arrests and killings and torture.

"And is it really all for nothing?" he kept asking himself. He refused to believe it. For the moment his personal decisions diminished in importance. He was thinking how ever since he'd been conscious of political ideas people had been saying that war, any war the Tsarate began, might turn out to be Poland's salvation. Perhaps this time the theoreticians and prophets were right.

❧ *Six* ❧

Ｎ EWS OF THE WAR stunned the city. For once the defiant gaiety of its streets was stilled, the cafes were gloomy, the boulevards deserted. Things got so bad, one wit was quoted as saying, that a whole week went by when no one cracked a single political joke. All Poland seemed to go into premature mourning for the future victims of Tsar Nicholas' colossal ineptitude.

When a free nation goes to war the people are caught up, for better or worse, in patriotic fervor. But the Poles knew—and no amount of propaganda could make them lose sight of the fact— that this was an alien battle in which they had nothing to gain, and much to lose. Hating their masters and wishing them ill, yet with no stake in the victory of the adversary, they saw war with Japan only as a senseless bloodletting, a tightening of already murderous police regulations, new waves of house searches, arrests for cause and without cause.

That the war might have been avoided through diplomacy was an open secret long before whispered reports and, later, illegal writings trickling in from abroad began to prove the point. The daily papers now seemed to carry twice as much white space as print, and one needed no special political acumen to interpret this, too. Very simply, the Russians were losing. In the meantime the tyrant of St. Petersburg continued to show his customary capricious disregard for the advice of either statesmen or competent military men.

Russia had a raggle-taggle, ill-trained, ill-equipped army, huge, but, except for its officer corps, composed largely of conscripts from non-Russian areas. It had a badly functioning system of communications and supply and a hierarchy so riddled with corruption that even the supreme command was not above taking bribes, provided, of course, the sums were large enough to tempt princes and grand dukes. And facing it was the deadly Japanese war machine, honed to perfection, disciplined and in preparation for a decade. Japan's army was much the smaller but it was composed of soldiers who'd received long and superb training. Its navy, under the command of the brilliant Togo, was modern. Having been designed specifically for the narrow waters of the Yellow Sea, it was formidably maneuverable.

There was also the matter of strategic advantage. Japan was fighting in its own back-yard puddle, so to speak, while the Russian giant suffered from the unwieldiness of overextended bulk. Some of the obstacles Russia had to cope with were climate and terrain and distance—four thousand miles of steppe and taiga stretching between the capital and Port Arthur. And east of the Urals, along the whole length of the single-track Trans-Siberian Railroad, the local population consisted of what official reports euphemistically described as unreliable elements. They were Tartar, they were Mongol, with slit eyes and yellow skins, and they had a long memory for insults.

In building their Empire Tsar Nicholas II, and his father before him, had cared little whether or not they had the loyalty of the populace so long as they had its taxes. The unruly could always, after all, be brought to heel. Now Nicholas cared equally little that the war was not a popular one, nor that the general mobilization ordered with the outbreak of hostilities should spell calamity for the cities and total disaster for the countryside, where not enough men were left to plough the fields and do the spring sowing. The situation, alarming enough in Great Russia proper, threatened the non-Russian peoples on the Empire's periphery with starvation pure and simple. In Poland and Lithuania, in the Baltic provinces and the Ukraine and the Caucasus, there was consternation and weeping. Petitions for easement only brought the answer, delivered largely from the pulpit on Sundays and sometimes in secular public announcements, that it was an honor for humble subjects to suffer and die for the Little Father. The "natives" were learning in the most direct terms what it meant to be considered ideal cannon fodder. Briefly, they became paralyzed with shock.

But the paralysis soon wore off and a healthy anger took over. So the resistance began, sometimes subtle, sometimes open and erupting into violence. To evade conscription became a way of life. Young men everywhere seemed ready for anything rather than to go into the hated Russian army.

In the villages, cases of self-mutilation were frequent. Peasants getting their tools ready for work reported a sudden rash of accidents. Recruiting officers were often found badly beaten, or even with their throats cut, by the roadside.

In the city, doctors and surgeons and barber-surgeons and plain quacks worked around the clock, performing hernia operations and appendectomies on sound young bodies, slicing off a toe here, a finger there. Countless healthy eyes were infected, sometimes causing blindness. "No one," men said to each other, "has ever accused us Poles of being cowards. Our fathers died for the motherland and so would we, tomorrow. But the Tsar's war—we spit on it!" Then the voices would fall to a whisper. "Where can I find someone to bribe, someone with enough influence so I'll be let off? How much should I offer? And how know he won't just take my money and do nothing?"

Even older men did not feel safe from the draft. For who was to say when the age limit for army service might be raised? There might be a new edict tomorrow! Those with relatives abroad wrote frantic letters, seeking emigration as a way out. "Answer at once—we can't afford to wait!" Anxious to make their point clear, they quoted the old, old joke of the Underground: *You know how it is—a man can't be too careful. First they'll have your balls, and then go prove you're not a camel!*

In Warsaw, the Governor-General and the Chief of Police Noltke put their heads together and decided something had to be done to bolster the city's morale. During Easter Week, a command performance was given at the Grand Opera House of Glinka's *A Life for the Tsar*. It was a glittering social event supported by the military in full dress uniform and those among the Polish nobility who found it expedient to make a show of loyalty. But the gallery seats were empty, and the following morning the city had a new slogan: "Better lose an eye for your own sweet sake than your life for the Tsar!" Warsaw was able to laugh again. It laughed in relief, laughed as it made ready for the long hard haul, for the old battle waged in new form.

At the Grossgliks' uncertainty hung heavy over everyone, since several of Salome's young boarders, in the last year of the *Gymnasium,* felt threatened in spite of family connections and plentiful means. As if to illustrate the point, one evening directly after supper Alfred Czartoryski stopped by unannounced. He was in officer's uniform and had come to say goodbye. "I was inducted earlier today and tomorrow they're sending me to the front. I suppose," he added acidly, "they figure it's a way to render me harmless. Or at least they mean to try."

"But . . . an officer's commission just like that, one-two-three . . . ," someone objected.

Alfred shrugged. "I once had the misfortune to spend a year in military school—and take first prize in horsemanship. That makes me a cavalryman. And it's a neat way to separate me from the Fabian case. Which reminds me." He turned directly to Adam. "Would you convey my regrets to your brother? And if you can think of a way to do so, tell him for me also that I don't intend to twiddle my thumbs in the army. Plenty to do at the front, I hear."

He considered a moment, then added, "Rumor has it that a delegation from the Polish Socialists, the PPS, headed by Josef Pilsudski, has set out for Tokyo with a memorandum for the Japanese War Office. They're offering to blow up bridges in Siberia and sabotage various routes of supply. In exchange they want a Polish Legion to be formed, consisting first of all of Polish prisoners of war in Japan, to be augmented in time by other volunteers. The legion would fight alongside the Japanese now, and later on, when the Tsar has been defeated, would return home as a liberating army, sweeping the Tsarist government out of the Congress Kingdom. Who knows," Alfred mused, "if it works I may find myself marching back as a liberator. . . ."

Leon was quick to ask, "Do you seriously think there's any hope in something like this?"

But the young aristocrat, perhaps feeling he had already spoken too freely, became carefully noncommittal. "One hears all kinds of rumors. About violence in unexpected places. About mutiny. In some regiments officers are joining forces with mutinous recruits. Who can tell where all this may lead? But one can hope."

How handsome he looks, Regina thought, as the men went on talking. *How handsome and splendid and brave. And how lucky I am to be married to Adam, not to him!* In that moment she forgave Czartoryski all the old slights. And when he was taking his leave she even spontaneously held out her hand and wished him luck. "Come back to us safe and sound, Prince Alfred. And do take care of yourself." To her own surprise she realized she had spoken from the heart.

Soon afterwards Salome's rule about avoiding politics at table became a thing of the past, she herself having rescinded it. She seemed to change overnight, her flirtatiousness dropping away without warning, as she went stoutly into action on behalf of those she knew and loved who needed army exemption.

"Even if my 'boys' don't need me," she explained to her husband, "our own real relatives have no one to depend on but me!"

There was Lucio Kronenberg to worry about, even though his father had already taken certain steps. There was Regina's brother Kuba, even if as a university student he was likely to be given preferential treatment. Among the young Fabians, Adam was already too old and still considered sickly, and Viktor was disqualified because of a recently discovered congenital heart murmur. But there was still Kazik, and also Rosie's fiancé, both of them exactly the right age and both healthy as bulls.

Indefatigable as in the early days following Izidore's arrest, Salome again took to sweeping into the sanctums of the great, even those who once had received her with frigid courtesy. She sailed in defiant, prepared for fresh rebuffs. But this time the rebuffs did not materialize. Instead, men were cordial to her and occasionally quite helpful, as though even in high places resistance was now considered a possibility.

In May, Lucio's crossed, shortsighted eyes turned out to be his passport to safety.

In June, Rosie and her young man were married in a hasty ceremony, packed up the linens and laces Rosie had been collecting so lovingly and so long, and left for Hamburg where steerage passage to New York had been booked for them. They were planning to live with distant cousins of the bridegroom's on a street named Hester Street, obviously after the Biblical queen. And he was going to learn to tailor pants, and she would help out, at least until the children started coming, by making artificial flowers right in their home. They were going to be established in no time.

"So you see," Bluma Fabian pretended to look on the bright side, as she kissed her younger daughter one last time, "it really is an ill wind that blows no good. In a country where they even name streets after Jews how can you help but be happy!"

Her new son-in-law, carefully coached by Rosie to keep things cheerful during the final leavetaking, promised, "One of these days we'll send you a paving brick of pure gold, see if we don't!"

She had the impression he half believed it and went along with the game. "When it comes, I'll pawn it and use the money to visit you." She had never seen an ocean liner and was convinced she would die of sea-sickness if ever she had to set foot on one. But promises like that were not expected to be kept, and never hurt anyone.

And now there was only Kazik left, the child of Bluma's middle years, the petted, pampered, handsome baby of the family. Nineteen, tall and straight and bursting with good health, it seemed to his mother inconceivable that he, too, could have the good fortune to avoid the uniform without having to endure some sort of maiming. But late one afternoon Kazik came home from work to announce that as far as he was concerned Aunt Salome could stop running. He had solved all his problems on his own, without any help from her.

"And just wait till you hear *how* I solved them! Seven at one blow!" he boasted gleefully. "Not only is the army off my neck, but I'll never again have to worry about money. Never so long as I live!"

It was all really very simple, he went on to explain. The gold-smith to whom he'd apprenticed himself instead of going on to the university, like his brothers, had angina and shortness of breath. He also had a daughter, an only child. She was three years older than Kazik and no beauty, but she was going to inherit. And she doted on him, as did her mother, something of which he had been aware for some time.

"So now I'm going to marry her and I'll be made full partner in the business. Then, very suddenly, on the advice of his doctor the father decides to retire. And that leaves me in full charge of the family enterprise, which, by the way, pays Class A taxes. An automatic exemption from military service, see, Mama! Pretty smart, huh? Could I have done better with a university degree?"

This time Bluma didn't ask, as she had asked Adam, "Are you sure, my son?" This time she only sighed. But later on, alone with Idka, she made what her daughter was long to remember as a significant remark. "When I think of our poor Adash," she said, "and the way he sacrificed all those years. Giving up his own youth, his own life, really, coming back from Berlin that time when Papa was so sick." She sighed. "And we never even stopped to ask ourselves if that's how it had to be, we just took it for granted that the family must come first. Well, now sometimes I wonder. What would have happened to us if he hadn't come? Probably nothing so different from what did happen. The rest of you would have managed. People have a way of landing on their own two feet, I'm beginning to notice. And Adash . . . I've always regretted that. . ." She stopped herself. "Ah, well, what's done is done, I daresay."

It was a long and harsh speech for Bluma to make, and Idka understood she was bitterly disappointed in Kazik. She also suspected her mother was not wholly reconciled to Adam's marriage, even though for the time being he seemed happy enough, and in love. Idka herself had reservations about her beautiful cousin, now her sister-in-law, for she considered her an empty-headed flirt. Whereas that other girl, of whom she had only the vaguest memory, had assumed legendary stature in her mind.

But to continue delving into the might-have-beens would only add to her unhappiness. "Speaking of landing on one's own feet,

Mama," she said in an awkward attempt to change the subject, "there's something I want to talk to you about. You know how I feel about dowries—it's like bribing a man to marry you . . . so. . ."

Not knowing where this was leading, Bluma made no comment and waited.

"So I've decided," her daughter went on, "that I'd rather learn to support myself. And I've been wondering—do you think Adash would mind if I used my dowry money to learn something useful, like nursing? Then, if ever I did marry, it wouldn't be for demeaning reasons. . . ."

"Nursing!" her mother exclaimed, not sure whether to be alarmed or look on her daughter with admiration. "You know what they say about nursing—that it's for old maids! You want to be tagged an old maid before you're twenty-five?"

"Weren't you tagged an old maid by the time Papa came courting?" the girl said gently. "Besides, times have changed."

She did not add that her real hope was someday to put her future skills at the service of her comrades in the movement.

❧ *Seven* ☙

IN JULY word came that Alfred Czartoryski had been killed at
the front. When she heard the news Regina fainted, and later
went into a paroxysm of uncontrollable weeping. Fortunately for
her, only Salome and Miss Julia were at home at the time, and
both were much too upset themselves, and much too busy un-
dressing her and putting her to bed, to pay attention to the
strange things she was babbling.

"Never to see him again. . . . Gone, gone. . . . I can't
stand it. . . ."

"Dearest child," Salome said, doing her best to calm her
down, "you really mustn't let yourself go like that. And over a
mere acquaintance! I know how soft-hearted you are, but *really!*
What would happen to you if it were, God fobid, someone of our
own!"

When she saw that her words made no impression whatever on
the hysterical girl, she sent for the doctor. He came quickly,
prescribed valerian drops and rest, and was just packing his bag
when Adam came home. Immediately he requested a word with
the husband in private and the two men stood talking together in
the foyer, Adam in a state bordering on anguish, the medical
man professionally calm, benign, even fatherly.

"Your wife seems to be in shock. Was the young man whose
loss she's mourning very dear to her?"

Adam shook his head. "That's what I simply can't understand.
She didn't even like him very well."

"Ah! In that case I think I have the true answer to the riddle. You're recently married, aren't you? Practically newlyweds?"

"Four months," Adam said. "Nearly five."

"And hasn't it occurred to you that *Pani* Fabian might be in a—er—delicate condition? What could be more natural!"

"You mean—there's going to be a baby?"

"There *was* going to be a baby. Not any more." The doctor, looking solemn, put a sympathetic hand on Adam's arm. "These things happen constantly, no one knows why. They're especially likely to happen in the early days of marriage when passions run high. A very early miscarriage, the kind that often goes unnoticed, is nothing to worry about. As for the shock and hysteria, I'd say the bad news only brought them on because she was already aborting. Coincidence. Anyway, young man, don't take it too hard. She's young and healthy and there'll be other babies. . . ."

Adam said he didn't care about other babies so long as his wife was all right, and the doctor smiled. "You young husbands! After a while you'll change your mind!" But he agreed that a little pampering and a change of scene would be beneficial, and suggested Regina might join her mother for the rest of the summer at the cottage the Segals still rented every year in Otwock. The arrangement suited her perfectly. Looking wan and frail and saying very little she let herself be bundled off, and when Adam assured her he would take every opportunity to come out and visit, if only overnight, she begged him not to worry about her but watch his own health instead. It made her sound appropriately brave.

Since, just as the doctor had known, there really was nothing wrong with her, she improved rapidly, got color back in her cheeks and sparkle in her eyes, and in no time at all was playing croquet and even badminton. It was like all the vacations of her girlhood except that her brothers' friends seemed to find her more attractive than ever now she was a married woman. With Alfred dead and her own extravagant outburst a kind of last rite for him, she really seemed to get him out of her system and firmly out of her mind. At the same time she decided, just as firmly, to keep her husband at arms' length for a while. It couldn't possibly hurt and might on the other hand pay handsome dividends.

Whenever Adam did manage to catch a late suburban train and dashed out, weary and dusty, for an overnight visit that must be cut short at sunrise, she was affectionate as a kitten, but refused to share his bed. "Not yet. You know what the doctor said. . . ." Actually the doctor hadn't been very explicit. But she enjoyed punishing her husband—for her bad experience, for having become pregnant so soon, but mostly, even though she no longer yearned for Alfred, because she had so very nearly given herself away.

For Adam, it was a cheerless, singularly rootless summer. With Henryk and Missy married and out of the country permanently, he had no real friends left in the city. He continued to stay at the Grossgliks' but came and went like a stranger, for the first time in his life acutely lonely instead of just solitary. Having once learned to share his waking and sleeping hours with a woman who mattered intensely to him, he hardly knew what to do with himself in her absence.

He resumed his old habit of taking long walks through the city at odd hours, and to his mother's intense pleasure tried to make it a point to visit her a couple of times a week. He became reacquainted with his family, playing occasional chess again with Viktor, even though Viktor's bride, Tynia—not unlike Regina, although he never thought to make the comparison—did not encourage any activity of her husband's that did not include her and chattered incessantly as the men tried to concentrate on their game. Finally, he began to feel a new closeness with his sister Idka.

One night as he was about to start the long climb up to the old apartment he met her in the courtyard. She said she was on her way to a meeting at the Rosols' and invited him to come along. "Mama doesn't expect you, so she won't be disappointed. And this will interest you. Rosa Luxemburg has just arrived from Berlin, and she's hiding out, on her way to Lodz. She's going to talk to us about the work her group is doing abroad. And about what they think is going to happen if the war drags on." He agreed readily and was surprised at the sudden surge of excitement the prospect aroused in him.

On the streetcar Idka talked about the nursing course she was attending, and in his present mood he was inordinately proud that she was showing such independence of spirit. He started to tell her how he felt, but she shrugged it off and spoke instead about Izidore and the need to find a new lawyer now that Czartoryski was dead.

"Such a pity. When we first knew him he seemed just another young aristocrat looking to make a name for himself. But then he began to change, you could feel it. Jan Rosol and the others said he had the makings of a great patriot. Not many like him among the nobility."

Adam reminded her of his own long-ago experience with the Korszas, father and son, and she admitted her statement was too sweeping. "It's just that among the high-born, the Tsar-lovers are the ones mostly in evidence. If you've been reading the papers this past week you know what I mean." She was referring to a petition that representatives of some of Poland's most illustrious families, including dignitaries of the Church, had just addressed to the Tsar. In it they pledged loyalty to the crown, at the same time suggesting that "in these difficult times" strong measures be enacted against "the unruly mob" threatening His Imperial Majesty's empire from within while a foreign foe threatened from without.

"It's revolting! I know no other word for it—revolting!" Her voice started to rise to a shrill crescendo. "They call themselves National Democrats, but those *Endeks* are really the most reactionary. . ."

"Hush, you're in a public place," her brother warned. He was relieved when at last they reached their stop that no one else got off the streetcar with them. It was all too easy to attract the attention of some two-bit informer.

The meeting was about to start when they reached the Rosols' flat. As usual, the place could hardly hold all the guests. Adam and Idka threaded their way from the hall to listening posts in the kitchen doorway just as Jan introduced the speaker.

"You all know who she is," he was saying. "We've managed to smuggle her in, and when the time comes we'll smuggle her out. She's been a German citizen for years, and as such is entitled to political immunity. But would a detail like that stop our gendarmes if they picked her up? Why, they'd just forget to read her passport!"

It was the calculated light touch and brought a murmur of amusement. "And now let me stress," he went on on a serious note, "that you're all pledged to secrecy. Not a word about tonight to anyone. Most particularly, there's to be no mention, no hint of Rosa's presence here, in our own secret press. The news will have to wait until she's safe again across the border. Do I make myself clear?"

"What d'you take us for, Rosol, a bunch of children?" a burly man in work clothes grunted. "Come on, let's get on with the business!"

"Just an ounce of protection," Jan answered. "Better forewarned than . . . but let that pass. Now then, in Rosa's person you're greeting our exiled brothers and sisters far and wide, those in Paris, London, Zurich, even New York. Even—and don't ask me how they keep in touch, but they do!—even those in the jails, in the penal colonies of Siberia. In short, the cream of our patriotic, revolutionary cadres. Our best theoreticians, our most courageous activists. . ."

There was applause, muffled lest neighbors overhear. Rosa stood up. For all that he'd heard so much about her, Adam had never seen her and wasn't sure what he had expected, but certainly not this tiny, crippled woman with the long nose and the flashing eyes, who after the long years abroad spoke her native tongue like a foreigner, stumbling now and then over a simple word. Rosa Luxemburg, known as the mother of the general-strike tactic, had the reputation of a firebrand. But here in the smoke-filled room where there was no need for oratory, she sounded rather like an earnest schoolteacher.

"My friends," she began, raising a hand for silence, "my dear friends, I'm honored to have been chosen for this liaison task. Times being what they are, mine may be an important mission. In a little while I'll come back to this point, but first let me bring you up to date on Europe's overall labor movement. This is something you will not find mentioned in our controlled press—yet it's germane and vital to our cause."

She then began telling them how the highly class-conscious, literate, articulate, and organized workers of every country in the industrialized West were holding protest meetings to condemn Tsarist oppression, how Russia was spoken of everywhere as "the prison of nations." Trade unions abroad were passing resolutions to express solidarity with Russia's unwilling army conscripts and with the millions in the rear now forced to labor longer-than-ever hours, making uniforms for the Tsar's army, supplying arms, building roads for the soldiers to travel toward almost certain death.

"And that isn't all," she went on. "More and more, one hears special mention in the resolutions—and I quote directly from a leaflet I brought to show you—of 'our Polish brethren who suffer under the double yoke of capitalist as well as foreign enslavement.' Now and then the question is even raised of Polish reunification and independence. And that, of course, means not just our own Russian Poland but the lands annexed by Germany and by the Austro-Hungarian Empire. Just think, an aroused world opinion may finally help us regain what's rightfully ours!"

"Words!" cried the same man who earlier had interrupted Jan. "Sounds to me like our European comrades have an uneasy conscience so they're shedding a few crocodile tears. What good will that do us?"

"Words have their uses," Rosa answered evenly. "Let our people hear how the whole world cares about them, and they'll take heart. Let the message spread through the factories, the peasant huts, the slums, the schools, the prisons." Her voice grew eloquent, the awkwardness of speech forgotten. "It's going to take courage, it's going to take daring to prepare for what lies ahead. . . ."

The room grew still again and she knew she had all their attention. "Shall I tell you how we outside analyze the situation? Only please don't think," she interrupted herself, "that we're trying to foist our views on you. It's just that abroad we have the advantage of a clearer perspective. Which is natural, with an uncensored press. Also, we're free to travel, we can consult each other, the various groupings keep in constant touch. And that, by the way, includes close contact with our comrades in the Russian underground."

At her mention of Russians a hostile murmur began, which she did her best to stop. "Hear me out. And try to remember that very soon great, sweeping changes may be coming. Once this senseless war ends in disaster, as it must, the Tsarate itself may topple. What's at stake is not a handful of minor reforms thrown to us like a sop. Oh, no! What we envisage is revolution, then independence, and our own Polish Republic. But, brothers and sisters, *we cannot accomplish this alone!*"

Now the room was so quiet Adam could hear his own pocket watch ticking. *Dare I believe her?* he wondered. *During all those years when Olek and I talked of independence, nationhood was always a dream for the future. Something you spent your life working for but never really expected to live to see—something for the time of your children's children. And here this woman talks as if it might come tomorrow!*

Experienced speaker that she was, Rosa waited for her words to sink in. Then, before an argument could start, she again took the floor. "Everything I have told you, friends, we're convinced is possible. That is the heart of our theoretical evaluation of the forces at work. It is also, I might add, our evaluation of the Social Democratic Party of Russia. We do not always see eye to eye with them, but in this area we have no disagreements."

Having made this point, she quickly picked up another thread. "So you see, an independent Poland need no longer be a pipe dream. It can be reality. But a reality only we ourselves can make happen. And then *only* if we work carefully, in the most disciplined fashion, without letup. And *only* if we have agreement amongst ourselves. Yes, there has to be a master plan for the whole Empire. We have to have united action—no one single party can be victorious alone. Nor can we Poles break out of our chains alone—we need the help of Russia's revolutionary masses!"

Again the murmuring, and again her skillful brush past it. "I know, this sticks in the craw. Yet it shouldn't. Russians or Poles, Christians or Jews, what matter? Proletarian solidarity must rise above nationalism, above sectarianism, above religious prejudice. . . ."

Her audience would not quiet down and she plowed on with a kind of desperation, "Just ask yourselves, who is the real enemy: the Russian worker, or the Polish factory owner who'll see you shot at dawn if his profits are threatened? In the final struggle, where will you find the rich? On our side, helping a revolution that would destroy them, or hand in hand with the Tsar's men, ready to crush us for the sake of their own profits? If you don't believe me, think what happened in Lodz two years ago!"

"Still and all, to work with *Moskals,* any *Moskals*—tfui!"

"Not *Moskals,* brother Proletarians like ourselves."

"But *Moskal* proletarians." The heckler in the back was on his feet to make his point more emphatically. "Give me one good reason why we should pull their chestnuts out of the fire!"

"The revolution is international. There's no such thing as their wrongs and our wrongs."

"I say let them make their revolution, and we'll make ours."

There were cries of "Sit down!" but also a scattering of applause. The meeting broke up, factions shouted at each other. Adam whispered to Idka, "Traditional Polish behavior. One small roomful of people, and they manage to reduce everything to chaos."

"They'll learn," she whispered back. "We shall all learn."

"I wish I had the strength of your convictions," her brother said. He was feeling the old familiar urge to withdraw to the sidelines.

Jan Rosol finally succeeded in separating the sides before a fight started. One group ostentatiously pulled on their caps and stalked out. Others stayed behind for more discussion. A circle formed around Rosa, bombarding her with questions. They were eager for more details of what was going on abroad. Were the exiled leaders really drawing up a timetable for an uprising? Were they truly sanguine? And if she, a woman, wasn't afraid of entering the country illegally, wasn't it time some of the men were doing as much?

Adam wondered whether she knew anything specific about his own old friends in Zurich. She probably did, but she was answering guardedly, generalizing, naming no names. He knew why. While there was no reason to suspect anyone the Rosols vouched for, there was always the chance that a police spy had wormed his way in. That was how the whole organizing committee of the Social Democratic Party had been arrested a year earlier.

Rosa, of course, had no intention of publicizing the plans of her comrades either abroad or in the Congress Kingdom, nor was she letting it be known that the following day she would be meeting first with the Warsaw leaders, then with a cell in Lodz. She had, in fact, exactly a month in which to visit all of Poland's major industrial centers, after which she would carry all the messages, recommendations, and conclusions she had gathered back to Zurich to be coordinated. In the meantime she and those working with her must at all costs avoid arrest.

Jan and his wife brought out beer and wine, bread and cheese for their remaining guests. The conviviality helped smooth down any feathers that were still ruffled, but a few mumbled comments could still be heard about Rosa Luxemburg being an extreme Leftist and a troublemaker. On the other hand, her aims seemed the aims of any patriotic Pole—she had spoken of an uprising for independence.

"What did you think of the evening?" Jan Rosol asked Idka and Adam as they were leaving.

"I'm glad I came, but there's a lot that troubles me," Adam said. He was even more troubled when his sister excused herself, and linking her arm in Jan's took him off into the kitchen.

Don't let her get too deeply mixed up in all this! he was praying. But already he knew that no amount of wishing could keep her away from the movement. Unlike himself, she had no hesitations. She was ready to take a clear-cut, determined stand and would never be content with halfway gestures.

And he saw it beginning all over again. One person lays a burden down, and two others pick it up. Thus it had been for a century and more, thus it was going to continue—for how long? There could be no sitting out a crisis, not if one were a Pole with a glimmer of a conscience.

❧ *Eight* ❧

IT WAS FALL AGAIN. Adam was on a slow train, returning to Warsaw from Lodz. The countryside stretched ahead and around him flat and bare, the fruit trees already stripped, the harvested fields dark gold with stubble. Here and there women in stooping rows dug potatoes. Flaxen-haired children tended skinny cows.

> *Hushed our quiet Polish village*
> *Hushed our joyous Polish farmland. . .*

The lines echoed and reechoed in his head.

The train stopped, moved on, stopped, and was shunted to a siding to make way for cattle trains filled with army recruits in gray-green uniforms. At stations along the way more young soldiers waited for other trains. Pushing up from their over-stuffed packs were loaves of bread, strings of sausages like over-size worry beads, white heart-shaped cheeses dried in the sun— whatever their womenfolk had been able to spare them for the journey to the front. To Adam it seemed they handled their bayoneted rifles like so many scythes and rakes.

He had spent the past week inspecting one Pozner mill after another, talking to plant managers. Old Maurice had sent him on a kind of reconnoitering mission. "I need to get a feeling of what's really going on. Can't trust written reports—half the time those flunkeys only tell you what they think you want to hear. 'Indeed, sir, things are just fine, couldn't be better, sir.'

When all the time they're falling apart. It's a way to protect their jobs."

There was trouble, Adam soon discovered, even in the factories working on foreign orders, where logically the crisis was not an issue. For they, too, were being plagued by shortages that disrupted schedules. Deliveries of cotton from the East were at best slow, jammed by the war traffic. Sometimes whole shipments were intercepted, requisitioned—always without warning—by the army apparatus.

The situation got so bad that for a while before Adam's tour of inspection Pozner talked of sending him to the Caucasus instead. "That new agent of mine is no replacement for you, he's a glorified clerk! Does everything by the book! What I need is for you to go back for as long as it takes to renew old contacts, warm up personal friendships. Go mend my fences for me and I'll ride out the war." But then strikes and rioting broke out in Baku, fierce and bloody, and travel in that part of the Empire became out of the question.

Strikes were also constantly breaking out the whole length and breadth of Poland. They were mostly spontaneous, ill-prepared, ill-organized. Yet Adam couldn't help wondering if there was a connection between them and Rosa Luxemburg's flying visit to her homeland. Not too likely, he finally decided. The Social-Democrats, with their strict discipline and, above all, their leanings toward cooperation with the Russian Left, were not really popular among the passionately nationalistic masses of Polish workers, who accused them of a lack of patriotism. The reception Rosa herself had received at the Rosols' on the night Adam had met her was a fair sample of the general mood, with which in spite of himself he tended to be in sympathy. Often he wished he knew where Olek was and what he was thinking.

Once or twice he even tried to question Idka, but not unexpectedly his sister had turned stubbornly silent. Still, he could see for himself what really prompted the general unrest. It was not ideological agitation but hunger, want, unemployment and fear of unemployment, falling wages, and a workweek that, with the war serving as an excuse, had again been lengthened from a hard-won fifty-four hours back to sixty-five. Men and women alike labored eleven hours a day and ten on Saturday. And still their children didn't have enough to eat.

Oh we've no bread though all our days are spent in labor. . .

"Go find out what's happening and give me an honest account," Pozner had ordered, taking Adam away from desk work that would simply have to pile up and wait. "And about the Caucasus. Write those friends of yours, promise them bonuses, promise them *anything* to keep the cotton flowing. But first I've got to know what's going on in my own compounds. Just whom do the workers hate?"

Mostly, like everyone, they hated the Tsar and the unpopular war, and this led them into a dozen different political camps. The least realistic advocated armed rebellion now, to culminate in war with Russia, for hadn't a righteous David once slain Goliath? Others, particularly those who followed the old guard of the Polish Socialists, still believed Japan might be induced to champion Polish independence. True, the call for volunteers to form a Polish Legion to fight side by side with the Japanese hadn't produced any results to speak of. But it had been a chivalrous gesture, and perhaps, they said, when Russia was brought to her knees a grateful Mikado would remember it and include freedom for Poland as a condition for peace.

But all this did not keep the weavers from hating the big industrialists as well, and it was even whispered in Lodz that the city was no longer safe for the bosses. One rich family after another closed its home, moving to the capital for the duration. Others, Baron Kronenberg and Pozner himself among them, siphoned off large cash reserves into West European banks. "One hardly knows what to fear most these days—the Tsar, or our own Polish mob," they commiserated with one another.

A drizzle started. The train was stalled again. Chilled, Adam wished that next time it would stall in some railroad station where at least he could buy a glass of hot tea. He was feeling profoundly depressed. His trip hadn't been exactly productive and he wondered what he was going to tell the Old Man.

Pozner's general manager in Lodz, *Pan* Cybulski, resented

being checked on and made no bones about it. "Tell the old bastard for me to call off his dogs. What does he want from me—miracles? Personally I think he's real lucky to have an honest-to-God Pole, a *genuine* Catholic, to stand between him and the men. I understand them, they understand me, and no shit." It was arrogant and intentionally vague and obliquely anti-Semitic, and he seemed to be defying Adam to carry the message back, word for word, to their employer.

Stubbornly, Adam had tried to talk to some of the workmen in the Cegielniana Street compound. But to them he represented management and they became as uncommunicative as Cybulski himself. Well, they'd say, things weren't as bad here as at Scheibler's or Heinzel & Kunitzer's or Grohman's—at least they didn't time and dock you when you went to the privy. But pay was so low it hardly bought bread, and they piled you up with work and rushed you and then charged you for spoilage, and if you squawked the answer was always, you don't like it—you know what you can do. "Well, and what can a man do, with so many mouths to feed?"

One day he even tried to track down the weaver at whose place he and Wanda had stayed over during her flight. But at mention of the man's name the gatekeeper froze up. "Mister, what would a fine gentleman like you be wanting with that . . . ? Besides, he ain't here. Been gone a long time. You want my advice, you get gone, too." Whether it was a threat or a friendly warning Adam couldn't be sure.

He felt so useless he began to suspect Pozner was inventing work for him. It even occurred to him that his livelihood might be threatened. Without really believing it, he speculated on how he could ever face Regina with such news. True, they wouldn't be left instantly penniless like factory workers, and, of course, there was always Henryk's offer, which in fact Henryk had renewed before leaving. But by now Adam was fairly certain how his wife felt about the whole proposition. As for his own dream of leaving the business world once he had an assured modest income, she didn't encourage it at all.

In fact, the last time he had tried to talk to her about it, she seemed to have very little patience with it. "Oh, Adash, isn't that rather selfish of you? I mean, well, it isn't as though you had only yourself to think of. Or even only the two of us. Because, of course, if that were the case I'd tell you to do whatever makes you happiest. But there's my family now, and your mother, and . . . well . . . the children we hope to have some day. Would you like to condemn *them* to growing up in . . . shall we say shabby gentility?"

Adam had never thought that a life of dedicated research might be considered selfish. And yet, weighed against the comfort real money could buy, perhaps it was. Regina made him feel as though it were indeed a kind of self-indulgence. All right then, so be it, he would have to learn not to indulge in fantasies. Only that being the case, to continue working for Pozner and earning advancement became doubly important. He took out a memo pad and began making notes for his report.

Presently the rains brought Regina and her mother back to the city. The Grossglik household filled once more with its customary quota of boarders. Schools reopened despite widespread rumors about an impending nationwide student strike which might soon shut down all institutions of learning in protest against the continued use of Russian as the teaching language. Sporadic demonstrations increased, and news from the front went from bad to worse.

In December Henryk and Missy came home for a brief holiday visit. But no one was celebrating Christmas that year and they might have been visitors from Mars. They did, however, give one small dinner party to which the Fabians were invited.

Missy looked stunning and was so cool and self-possessed in her new role of hostess that Regina hated her, hated the outrageously becoming Paris gown and the pompadour hair style held up by jeweled combs and the emerald and diamond necklace that Missy wore so unselfconsciously. Later it also turned out she had taken up smoking. And when someone commented on it, she replied airily that all chic European women were doing it. Regina at once decided this could be turned to her own advantage.

She waited until she and Adam were driving home from the

party. "That's an awfully unfeminine habit she's developed, don't you think?" she asked, stroking her husband's hand.

"What? What habit?" He had spent the evening discussing the military situation with Henryk and Henryk's father-in-law— five thousand of the Tsar's soldiers, mostly non-Russians, frozen in the Manchurian snows; the rout following General Kondratenko's death in mid-December; Port Arthur ready to fall like a sugar plum into the Mikado's lap. "Sorry, I wasn't following," Adam said, his mind still thousands of miles away.

"I was talking about Missy and her smoking. Don't you think it's unfeminine?"

"Come to think of it, I suppose it is. But Missy is Missy. A law unto herself," he said, not really caring one way or another.

"Yes, but what would you say if I tried it?"

"That's different. I hope you're never tempted, darling."

"You wouldn't like it, then?"

"Frankly no. It wouldn't become you."

"In that case," she said, smiling up at him in the semidarkness. "I promise you I never shall. You know, dear, I'm relieved you've decided to keep your distance from the Meisels in the future. Missy is so . . . *sophisticated.* I can't help feeling she'd be a very *bad* influence on me. She's such a strong personality that . . . well . . . I'd be bound to change. . . ."

"Don't ever change," he said instantly, pulling her close.

She put her head on his shoulder. "I'll try not to." There, she had put her oar in, and the threat of Adam going in with the Meisels brothers receded even further.

Immediately after the New Year news came of the fall of Port Arthur. This was followed by the call-up of reservists, including many who until then had considered themselves safely exempt. At the same time factories were swamped with army orders and began to work double shift. The Lodz industrialists quickly seized on this as an excuse to add yet another hour to the already brutally long workday. The rationale was elementary. Let a man protest, and he was threatened not just with dismissal but conscription. It was exactly as Pozner had prophesied: the war might be a calamity for the rest of the land but it was a fine thing for the textile business.

That same week the price of bread and potatoes doubled.

Then without warning the weavers' midday dinner break was cut by fifteen minutes. This meant they barely had time to get from their looms to the courtyard gates, grab their lunch pails from waiting wives and children, wolf down the meal and relieve themselves. Not even time for a smoke afterwards. That small pleasure too must wait until after work—and by then a man was too done in to eat, let alone relish his pipe.

The shortened lunch break was the last straw. The following morning Lodz woke to a general strike, something no one had quite believed was possible. As each night shift went off the job, the day shift did not take over. Like clockwork, in the cold, gray dawn, first one compound and then its neighbor stopped humming.

Power was shut off. Chimneys stopped smoking. By the time the rest of the city stirred, no streetcars were running, so people couldn't go to work. Children and their teachers had no way to get to school. Offices didn't even attempt to open, shopkeepers kept their shutters closed, the city library and the museum and even the telephone exchange remained locked. The strike, the first general strike in the city's history, seemed a total success.

With the city thus paralyzed and even the violet uniforms of the police nowhere to be seen, crowds poured into the streets in a holiday mood. Those who remembered it said afterwards the day had been remarkable for many things, not the least of which was a total absence of looting, thefts, hooliganism, arson. Men and women paraded down the main avenues through the dirty snow, six abreast and arms linked, singing patriotic songs. The flower vendors gave away sprigs of mimosa to all comers.

By mid-afternoon the factory owners sent word to the city organizing committee that they were willing to negotiate. They proposed that three of their number meet with a delegation of workers to iron out grievances. The three men chosen were princely young Miecio Silberstein who headed the industrial complex belonging to himself, his mother and four of his five brothers; one of the German-born Scheiblers; and finally Pozner's

Catholic manager, Jan Cybulski. The time was set for the following morning and already the strikers congratulated themselves on an easy, bloodless victory.

They were wildly optimistic, all caution forgotten. But in a carefully shuttered room behind the doctors' offices in the Piotrowski-Gronowicz household a handful of old revolutionaries sitting down to a strategy meeting were not half so sanguine. They were preparing for a larger, city-wide conference of all strike leaders to be held later in the evening, a conference of the kind that in future years would come to be known as a united-front gathering. Unfortunately, this whole approach was still so new, so largely theoretical, that no one—either in Poland or anywhere else for that matter—had any very clear idea about applying it.

One of the participants in the conspiratorial session was Dr. Julius Silberstein, Miecio's eldest brother, black sheep of his wealthy tribe, and just then head of the strikers' medical committee, on which Wanda and Maryla were also serving. Another was Rosa Luxemburg. Rosa, who ever since her arrival in Lodz a week earlier had been a secret guest in the household, had somehow managed without once venturing into the streets to initiate and help direct the planning of the general strike that erupted following the weavers' spontaneous walkout. Now, her work done, she was getting ready to leave town.

"The important thing to remember," began Julius, who by virtue of his age and white hair was acting as chairman, "is that there must be no unilateral agreements. Nothing without collective approval. Otherwise we may win a battle and lose the war." Since no one was disposed to argue the point, he turned to Rosa. "I think you should take over now. Tell us everything you can think of—especially since after tonight we won't be able to rely on your experience," he concluded.

Rosa sighed. "I only wish I could stay. But you all know the situation. It won't be long now before the authorities start putting two and two together, recognizing certain strike patterns that parallel certain events in Galicia, in German Poland. Once that happens they'll be combing the city for me." Rosa did not propose to be taken.

Her plans made, she was only waiting for darkness to be on her way. Then a stooped little woman wrapped in a black shawl, a market basket full of cabbages over one arm, would clip-clop down the street. At an appointed corner a peasant cart would hail her. And she'd climb in and roll past the city gates to vanish in some village with a heavily Jewish population. Rosa anticipated no trouble; her forged papers had a look of total authenticity.

"What can I say, comrades," she spoke quietly, "except to wish you well? By now you know as much as I. Everything Brother Julius has said is right—it's borne out by our experience in the West. When you negotiate with the bosses, never forget to demand guarantees. Not just promises. Gains have to be spelled out, consolidated, before you call off a strike. Right now your biggest bargaining advantage is that the city is shut down tight. See that it stays that way. Keep checking and double-checking, and above all don't relax round-the-clock discipline and vigilance." She rose to go. "Factory owners will do anything they can to outsmart you."

"What you're really telling us," Olek Piotrowski said as they embraced in parting, "is—above all, no gentlemen's agreements. But that's easier said than done, considering the Polish tendency toward panache. Unfortunately it's a trait that cuts across class lines."

"Well, be on guard," she repeated, picking up her shawl and her basket of cabbages. "I may see you all again, or I may not."

After she had gone Dr. Julius took the floor again. He proposed himself, and the others agreed, as the logical spokesman for their group at the night's meeting. "Knowing my own relatives as I do, knowing some of their cronies personally, I might be able to caution the delegates against some obvious trap."

He did his best at the general conference, but his best had no weight against an appeal from the owners, which, when read, produced cheers and *vivats*.

"The Polish factory worker," the statement read, "is the key to the country's well-being. We employers have long recognized this. Now let us prove to you how well we know it! Let us all come together in a spirit of good will!" And not a word about wages or hours.

Dr. Julius tried to point out how little substance there was in the deliberately flattering phrases, but no one listened. "We have them on the run!" people laughed at him. "Stop worrying! Go home like the rest of us and have a good night's sleep!"

"Not yet," Julius pleaded. "Please, stop and think! Beware the Greeks bearing gifts! What will your families live on? Love and kisses?"

But things had gone too smoothly, and only the other two doctors on the committee, and they women, sided with him. Eventually the representative of the Lodz PPS organization, which advocated moderation in everything and especially the class struggle, demanded the floor. He spoke with heavy sarcasm about "certain people" who refused to recognize the difference between "our own" industrialists and the Tsarist stooles, treating all employers with equal, ill-advised mistrust. Ergo, while one might conceivably condone Brother Silberstein's inability to maintain a fair and objective attitude—"We all understand about family antagonisms"—that shouldn't prejudice the rest of the delegates. Why assume the other side was acting in bad faith?

"Above all don't let us forget, brothers and sisters," the PPS delegate concluded, "that there's a great deal more at stake here than just your wages or even the general strike itself. As this war progresses we may be moving toward an upheaval that will result in the independence of our beloved motherland. And when that glorious day dawns, we shall have need of our own non-Tsarist Polish industry—an industry that flourishes, not one that's bankrupt and ruined by our own hand. Indeed, we shall need everyone—everyone ready to line up with us for the great job of reconstruction. *And that must include the Polish factory owners!*"

He had a golden orator's voice and used it to the hilt, and whatever Julius Silberstein might have said in rebuttal was drowned out by applause. The meeting broke up in celebration and singing. No one was interested in reviewing the work of the safety committee or checking arrangements for the night, much less in listening to suggestions about various precautionary measures.

It was a fatal oversight. With traffic moving freely, the owners, having recovered from their initial state of shock, dispatched messengers posthaste to a couple of the nearest garrison towns. At dawn a detachment of government troops marched in and put the city under martial law. The leaders of the strike, the PPS man along with all the others, were arrested in their beds. By the time the sun rose the streets swarmed with Russian uniforms and anyone who put up resistance paid for it in blood. The jails filled up and the factories reopened under armed guard.

Now that the strike was broken the rest of the country shouted its indignation. Even the cautious, the conservative, those who ordinarily gave such problems little thought, were suddenly voicing sympathy for the downtrodden. Everyone agreed that the ferment in Lodz was really an expression of protest against the war, against the Tsarate in all its naked brutality. *Polish* ferment, that's what it was, people said, and therefore, proletarian or not, deserving of respect. On the other hand the factory owners had deliberately—deliberately, mind you, for hadn't they called in the Russian military and the secret police?—aligned themselves with the archenemy. The average Pole felt he could forgive anything except that. To the Polish mind, seeking the help of Moscow in a purely internal dispute was the worst of all crimes. Many went so far as to call it treason.

As always, the people turned to their national poet for an appropriate quotation. Mickiewicz did not disappoint them.

> *. . . for Poles to deal a mortal blow so slyly*
> *To other Poles, with Muscovite connivance. . .*

Thereupon the line of demarcation between the national liberation struggle and the economic, possibly revolutionary, struggle of the proletariat seemed to obliterate itself while exact labels ceased to matter. From Austrian Poland, Joseph Pilsudski himself sent a sorrowful message to the Lodz workers, deploring his colleague's tragic lack of judgment. The Silbersteins were divided by fratricidal war. And Maurice Pozner, never before distinguished for either liberalism or patriotic fervor, summarily fired his Lodz manager.

Since no one required him to say what he himself might have

done had he been in Cybulski's shoes, the gesture cost the old man nothing and made him appear a benevolent employer deserving of his workers' loyalty. That much accomplished, he sent for Adam.

When the summons came, Adam was at his desk in the ground-floor wing of the mansion, where the offices were situated. He was waiting for a clerk to bring in the afternoon papers. As the day wore on he was finding it harder and harder to concentrate. A clock somewhere in the hall chimed the quarter-hours, marking the passage of time, but it seemed to be moving at such a snail's pace he was constantly pulling out his old silver watch to make sure it hadn't come to a standstill.

He was hoping for more explicit news from Lodz.

At breakfast the papers had been full of the strike and its aftermath, and for once the censors were glad to allow all the details to be published. There was an account of how the strike was broken, a statement from the chief of police, another from the governor-general. Then followed triumphant lists of the men and women already arrested and lists of others still being hunted. In some cases real names were used, others were referred to by their *noms de guerre,* their underground aliases.

Idly at first, Adam had scanned the long columns. Then his eye caught the name of the weaver he had tried to locate at the Pozner compound only a few weeks earlier, the man who was Olek's uncle's friend. He felt old emotions stirring and was overwhelmed first by a sense of helplessness, then by the profound conviction that there was something urgent he ought to be doing in order to help those who no longer came to him for help. In fearful fascination he continued reading, like those after a mine disaster who try to find out whether beloved names are on lists of the living or the dead.

He was unable to shake the wholly irrational feeling that something important and unpredictable was about to happen, and this gradually changed into a belief that someone out of his past was close by and trying to get in touch with him. By midday the conviction had such a grip on him that instead of going home for lunch he drove across town to his mother's house hoping to find Idka, who might know more than he did.

His sister wasn't even at home.

"She rushed out early, without breakfast," his mother explained. "Read the paper and mumbled something about having to see a friend right away. Maybe it has something to do with a new lawyer for Izidore. She never says." Bluma sighed. "I'm not complaining, you understand, I know that's how it has to be. Just the same, it isn't easy. . . ."

Adam kissed her, managed a few soothing words, then, restless, said he must be off.

"But you just got here! At least have a glass of tea!"

"Mama, please!"

She made no attempt to urge him further. "I know, I know. All my children. . . ."

Only then did he remember guiltily that he had promised to go with Idka to visit Izidore the previous Sunday and then, at the last minute and without letting them know, had gone back on his word. On Sundays no one ever got up for breakfast at the Grossgliks' and when he'd stirred Regina wound her arms around his neck and they stayed in bed until past noon. By the time he was dressed and shaved, visiting hours had come and gone.

The feeling that he must reestablish contact with his old friends kept growing stronger, and he had just made up his mind to stop off on his way home to see Olek's Uncle Jacek when Pozner's summons came. Adam's first reaction was pure annoyance. *Not now. Not now when I have other things on my mind.* But, of course, Pozner could not be ignored.

Hastily he telephoned Regina, warning her he might be late coming home, and started up the great curved stairway toward the study. The doors stood wide open. For once the old man did not try to force a cigar on him.

"Well," he began without preamble, "a lot of history has been made since you and I had our last chat. In fact, the picture's changing so fast it makes a man dizzy. Sit down, listen to what I have to say. And if your head isn't already spinning, it soon will be. A glass of port? Don't say no, you might need it!"

Adam, not usually put off by the old man's verbal flourishes, was tempted to growl. *Oh, come to the point, you old windbag!* And

Pozner, misreading his expression, smiled. "Hah. I've succeeded in making you nervous. And yet I didn't ask you here to play cat-and-mouse with you. I'm going to put my cards right on the table. Here's my proposition: Instead of all that talk about leaving the country one day to make your fortune, how about hitching your star to my wagon? What would you think of being put in charge of all my operations in Lodz, young man?"

Whatever Adam had expected, it was not this. "What did you say?"

Maurice laughed uproariously. "I knew that would bowl you over! In plain words, what I'm offering you is Cybulski's job. I just got rid of him—after that shameful sellout he was party to, did I have any choice?"

He let the news sink in. "So now, as you can see, I need someone to take his place. Someone I can trust and the workers can trust. Considering your whole past, the friends you once had and your brother in jail all these years, I can't think of a more fortunate choice."

By now Adam had caught his breath. "But," he said slowly, "I don't know the first thing about administration. All I know is cotton in the boll. Not machines. Not conversion. Certainly not how to deal with the men who run the machines."

"And how much did you know about cotton when I first hired you?" Pozner shot back. "But you learned. You can learn this, too. In fact, it's easier. And this time you have me and my whole organization close at hand." Now he leaned back, and with the calm of one for whom the issue is already settled refilled both Adam's glass and his own. "One thing I can promise you. No one either here on my Warsaw staff or in Lodz will be digging holes for you to break your neck in. Cybulski was never popular, not even with his overseers. So you won't be resented, which means if you make a few mistakes it won't be fatal. And I've a hunch that having a Jew in the job isn't a bad idea either. You know how many of the weavers are Jewish. It might make a difference."

In spite of himself Adam admired the old industrialist's cool, analytical handling of the situation, even though the timing appalled him. "You've thought everything through very carefully."

Pozner shrugged. "In times like these one can't afford to over-look a thing. As I was saying, you'd be starting off with everyone for you, not against you. Not many managers are that lucky."

"You're assuming I'm accepting your offer?"

Pozner chose to ignore that. "About your salary. I'll pay you whatever it's worth to you to pull up stakes and settle in Lodz."

He knew, and Adam knew he knew, that there were no stakes worth mentioning to pull up. But it suited him to put it that way. "Oh, Lodz is a dreadful hole and your wife won't like it, don't I know! Missy and Marek haven't set foot in our house on Cegielniana in years. Wouldn't be caught dead there. So you must point out to *Pani* Regina that there will be compensations. Money. Quite plainly, lots of money. Am I making myself clear?"

"And may I also point out to her that it won't be forever?"

"By all means. I don't expect you to sell yourself into bondage. In fact, when the war is over you and I can rediscuss everything, and if you still want to go in with my son-in-law, I promise not to hold that against you. But on the other hand you may well decide to stay on. After all, with my own son turning up his nose at the family business, you'll be pretty high up in the hierarchy, a grand duke if not exactly the crown prince. You might very well mention that to *Pani* Regina as well. And about those family in-vestments. Now more than ever I would consider it a pleasure to help and guide you, and between us we can turn that little nest egg into a big, fat ostrich egg. . . ."

It was slyly put, an offer Adam could not possibly afford to turn down. Nevertheless something impelled him to say he must think about it, discuss it with his wife as well as with her family, since it concerned all of them.

"By all means, by all means," Maurice agreed grandly. "I'm not asking you for an answer this minute. Take your time. Tele-phone me during the evening. Or else let me know when you come in in the morning. Well, then, *prosit!*" He raised his glass, and the wine sparkled through the crystal.

❧ *Nine* ❧

THAT SAME DAY a noontime emergency conference at the *Gmina* delayed Leon Grossglik so long that finally Miss Julia, insisting everything would spoil if they waited another minute, persuaded her mistress and Regina to go ahead and have their midday meal alone. They were just finishing their dessert and coffee when he came in. His face was grave. The conference, he informed them, had been called because of persistent rumors of pogroms in the little towns of the Pale in the east—a sure sign that the Black Hundred were on the march. The afternoon papers, after running detailed accounts of the Lodz arrests in an earlier edition, were again full of white space, a bad sign.

"And even that isn't the whole story," he said, toying with the cutlet Miss Julia set before him. "One of our directors got word privately from St. Petersburg. Things are bad there, too. Seems on Sunday there was a huge demonstration before the Winter Palace—workers coming to petition the Tsar about their starvation wages. Everything was peaceful and orderly, they were led by an Orthodox priest, the *Pop* Gapon, and people even brought their children. But the Tsar figured this was a mob ready to riot and he personally gave orders for soldiers to fire on them. The whole thing turned into a bloodletting, and there's a story making the rounds that Gapon, for all he's a man of the cloth, is a provocateur in the pay of the secret police. Already people are calling it Bloody Sunday."

Leon pushed back his plate, sipped coffee that he'd forgotten to sweeten. "The upshot of it all is that the Putilov Works are on strike to protest the mass killings. Imagine, a country's largest iron-and-steel works shut down tight in the middle of a war! And they say the protest strikes are spreading. To Moscow, Tula, Kiev, everywhere! It's a real revolutionary upsurge. The Empire is ready to explode."

"My dear," Salome exclaimed, "that's exactly what the baker was telling me only this morning!" Having once rescinded her own ban on politics as table conversation, she now seemed eager to encourage it, as if to show the world what a serious person she had become. " 'Pani Grossglik,' he said when I started to pay him, 'sorry, but the price of kaiser rolls has gone up another grosh since yesterday. We're going to have a revolution,' he said, 'you mark my words!' "

She waited for this bit of information to produce its effect, and continued, "Well, when he said that, he looked so frightened, the poor man, I thought I'd cheer him up. So I said, 'Why, Pan Kowalski, but surely you're not afraid! Anyway, if it does come, it'll be a real Polish revolution—some of the best people will be for it!' And he said, 'God bless you, Ma'am, spoken like a true patriot!' He perked right up. 'You're right, and it's not as though we had a king of our own to send to the guillotine!' And everyone laughed and we all felt better. It wasn't until later I realized we might all have got ourselves arrested, talking like that!"

"And so you might have," Leon said, smiling gently, distracted for the moment from his own news. "Darling, you must promise me to be more careful from now on. Oh, it's all very well to be brave and I'm proud of you for it—just don't go around making a noise about it."

"That's what Eugenia said, too," Salome admitted, "when I told her."

Listening to the two of them, Regina couldn't help a twinge of impatience. Everything was beginning to seem out of kilter to her. Salome was really ill-cast in this new role she affected. And life generally was too complicated, not at all the way one's first year of marriage ought to be.

Here it was nearly a twelvemonth since her wedding, and Adam had yet to make a single important decision. Granted the war made a difference. Nevertheless she felt she had been patient with him long enough. The honeymoon, her father's death—all that was in the past now and it was the future that concerned her. Mainly she was anxious to start savoring the new sense of importance which being a married lady, *Pani* Adamova, should give her. And this, she knew, just wasn't going to happen so long as she remained a guest, no matter how welcome, in a household where everyone still thought of her as a girl.

Oh, it was all well and good for her husband to treat her like a baby—it had its own advantages. Besides, he only did it during the daytime hours. In the privacy of their big double bed there was no doubt at all he considered her a woman grown. And that, too, as Salome had hinted, was as it should be. But by now she felt she'd absorbed enough of her aunt's unending good advice on how to handle a man. There was a point at which the advice might be called meddling.

To add to her irritation, her mother stopped by unexpectedly later in the afternoon, demanding to know why nothing had yet been done about investing their common inheritance. Fortunately, Adam telephoned before Balbina had a chance to say very much.

"He's going in to see Pozner right now, Mama," Regina was able to announce triumphantly, her tone implying vast secret possibilities. "Yes, I know there's been a lot of shilly-shallying. But what can you expect, times being what they are?" Once someone else ventured to criticize Adam she was fiercely defensive of him. "Would you have him jump at the first thing that offers itself? Really, Mama! A good businessman can't be too careful. Look before you leap—isn't that what you yourself always say?"

"What about that foreign venture?" Balbina asked, a trifle less sure of her ground.

"Mama, please. . ." Carefully casual, she threw in, "Of course, if you'd rather someone else handled your money, all you have to do is say so."

It was a well-calculated risk and she had the satisfaction of seeing her mother back down hastily. "No, oh no. That isn't what

I meant at all!" *Of course not,* she thought maliciously, *Who else but a son-in-law would manage your investments without charging you a commission!* Aloud she said, "Well then, don't push! Just let me handle this my own way, and I promise you won't be sorry!"

They parted amicably enough, but both were relieved when the visit was over.

After her mother left, time really began to drag for Regina. As she waited anxiously to learn what had occurred during her husband's interview with his employer, she came to the conclusion that there must be no more putting off the serious talk she meant to initiate. Whatever news he came home with would give her the opening she needed. She hoped he would be back long before the evening meal, for this was no conversation to embark upon while waiting for the roast to be served. Unless the timing was right, it would be an opportunity lost.

She began to plan her approach. First she would draw him out with a few subtly phrased questions. Then, depending on his responses, she would make everything she had to say sound as though it stemmed spontaneously from his answers. After that she anticipated little difficulty. *I can make him agree to anything I want, lead him anywhere I want him to go,* she crooned inwardly in unashamed satisfaction.

She had already proved this to herself at least once: the threat of going to Paris, first to play second fiddle to Missy Pozner Meisels, and later to end up as the shabby wife of a penurious professor, had safely receded. Now he must be persuaded to stick close to Pozner, invest their money as the old wizard suggested, and start getting rich. Already she could see herself in her own elegant drawing room, entertaining her own elegant guests, the center of an admiring coterie. Not only that, but once Adam did start making a lot of money for her family, her position in relation to her brother Kuba and her older sister would be a deliciously superior one. As a sort of Lady Bountiful, she could lord it over them—oh, quite subtly, of course!—and thus have an opportunity to settle old scores, especially with that viper Jadwiga. What a pleasure to get even with her sister for the thousand youthful humiliations she had neither forgotten nor forgiven. What a joy to see her eat crow!

To make doubly sure her husband would see things her way, she decided to make herself lovely and desirable for him. She went to freshen up, brushed and repinned her hair, rubbed a piece of her new, delightfully scented rice-paper over her already flawless skin—to make it glow, as Adam put it, like mother-of-pearl. Then she sat down to the piano to practice his favorite Bach toccata and fugue. She was going to pretend not to hear him come in, give him plenty of time to watch and listen. Then he would walk up behind her and put his arms around her while her hands were still on the keyboard, and only then would her fingers slow down, and she would lean back against him and turn her head so that he could kiss her. . . .

But it got to be five o'clock, and still he did not come. Then Miss Julia broke in on her, asking, as she sometimes did, would Miss Regina please go buy some fresh flowers for the table. With all the day's bad news and everyone so upset, *Pani* Salome had neglected to do it herself and the dining room looked like a funeral chapel the morning after, and really it was a shame. The request, perfectly natural and reasonable, somehow seemed to her the last straw. *Miss* Regina indeed! Even the servants in her aunt's house treated her like a schoolgirl. Enough was enough. High time for Adam to take her out of this.

Once out in the street, she actually rather enjoyed the short walk. The air, unusually mild for midwinter, smelled of rain. There was an aura of mystery about the buildings shrouded in fog, the softly glowing street lights. Soon now the days would be growing imperceptibly longer. The thaw was like an optimistic reminder that eventually it would be spring again.

She was in no hurry, but she walked briskly in order to avoid giving passersby the wrong impression; a young woman alone couldn't be too careful these days even in broad daylight, and here it was already dark. As a minimal precaution against purse snatchers, she hugged her reticule to her instead of letting it hang from her arm.

She turned into Nowy Swiat, toward the corner where Salome always bought flowers. Along the main thoroughfare the traffic seemed unusually heavy, but Regina didn't stop to ponder the significance of this. In a doorway a street urchin was peddling the latest papers, chanting in the dialect of the riverbank slums, "Latest news from the front! Japs give the *Moskals* hell! Read all about it!" Luckily no police uniforms were in sight, for the young-old voice went on, exulting, "Read all about it, people, read all about it! Mikado's got the Tsar by the balls and he ain't letting go!"

Regina quickened her pace, pretending not to hear. She even crossed the street. There, at a regular newspaper kiosk, a dozen persons were queued up, waiting for the final editions. This time she decided to stop. Knowing how passionately Adam cared about everything political, she thought it would please him if she came home with a paper.

Someone tried to push past her and she had to stand up for herself or lose her place in line.

"Good heavens, my good woman!" she spoke coldly to the middle-aged biddy behind her, noting with distaste her shapeless body, the musty-smelling shawl she wore in lieu of a coat. "Can't you wait your turn like the rest of the people?"

She knew she was risking a string of abuse and rather expected it. Instead, she got a civil answer.

"Indeed you're right, missy, it's just I'm not myself these days. It's my son. He's at the front and every day I expect bad news. But that's no reason for pushing and shoving, maybe you got somebody out there, too. . . ."

Already Regina was feeling contrite. "No, no, and I'm sorry I was so sharp. Here, you may get ahead of me."

Now the woman gave her a tearful smile. "May God bless you, missy! At first, to look at you, I thought, she's all dressed up, a lady, a swell. But anyone can see you've a good heart. You're one of our own. . . ."

"Well, I should hope so," Regina answered, involuntarily stung. "Just because a person wears good clothes needn't mean she doesn't care! Why, anyone with an ounce of decency in his bones can't help feeling today that. . ."

But the woman, looking fearfully about, wouldn't let her finish. "Hush, missy, hush, lovey. I understand. And the less said aloud the better."

"But . . . but. . . ." Fortunately, the line began to move. "I hope you hear from your son soon," Regina said, anxious now to cut the conversation short.

Just then a woman a few places ahead of them turned. "Regina!" It was Adam's sister Idka, of whom she was not especially fond. "I thought I recognized your voice. Suppose I buy us two papers, that way the whole line can move faster."

Thinking only what an unattractive, loud, really *plebeian* sister her husband had, Regina thanked her. Then, because something else seemed to be expected of her, she asked as they walked away together, "What are you doing in our part of town at this hour?"

With an intimacy she really felt was unwarranted, the other girl took her arm. "As a matter of fact I have business with Adam. I . . . I was killing time to make sure he'd be home, before ringing your bell. But then I heard you and that woman talking, and the way you sounded, well, I decided I could risk being frank with you. . . ."

They were at a safe distance from the crowd by then. Even so Idka's voice dropped to a whisper. Regina was honestly puzzled. "Whatever do you mean? I don't understand."

"Don't you, dear?" And Idka smiled warmly. "Ginia, you don't have to pretend! When she said, 'One of our own,' and you said, 'Well, I should hope so,' that told me everything. Everything fell in place, though of course I had no right to assume anything else about you to begin with! I guess what used to put me off was that you're always such a lady, always so . . . kind of stand-offish. . . ." She smiled again and patted the other girl's arm. "Now I've learned better."

"Honestly, Idka," Regina tried again. "I still don't follow."

"Think, my dear. Nowadays, when everyone knows how careful we all must be, when there's likely to be a snooper in every crowd, it takes real courage to. . . I mean, I didn't hear the *whole* conversation, but I did hear the end. *You're one of our own!* And here all the time I thought you were just another little flibbertygibbet like Salome! Oh, I've done you a terrible injustice!"

She's hysterical, Regina thought. Then she remembered Salome and the baker who called her a patriot and Uncle Leon telling her not to be brave in such a loud voice, and she had to make an effort not to giggle. Everyone's hysterical these days, she thought. They walked another block in silence. Then finally Idka ducked into a *porte cochère,* drawing Regina in after her.

"There's something I want to show you, but not in the street."

She opened her copy of the newspaper. And there lying inside was a smaller sheet, the illegal paper *Red Banner.* In it was an account of the St. Petersburg massacre Leon had mentioned. The priest Gapon was flatly called a paid Tsarist agent, an accusation for which later there would be incontrovertible proof. There were also details of the protest strikes already under way in Great Russia and a call for a general strike throughout Poland. "In solidarity with our Russian brothers let us lay down our tools!" Finally, there was a brief account of how troops which could ill be spared from the Far Eastern front were being used against the strikers and demonstrators. Then came a fresh list of victims, the dead and the jailed.

"And that's not all," Idka whispered when Regina finished reading. "I have some personal news Adam would want to know. His oldest friend has been arrested in Lodz. He and his wife and the husband of another old friend. . . ." Her voice shook. She gulped, drew a painful breath, and went on, "But we've been standing here too long already, we're only attracting attention. Were you on your way somewhere? I'll walk along with you."

"Only to the next corner, to buy flowers for the table."

"Flowers, at a time like this?" Idka moaned. "But, of course, that isn't your fault, I know Salome!" Then urgently, "Look, Regina, Ginia darling, do you have any money—real money, I mean—that you can spare? Like fifty rubles maybe? Does Adam?"

"Fifty rubles?" Regina was instantly wary. "That's a lot. Why would you need fifty rubles suddenly like that?"

"It's not for me. It's. . ." Idka hesitated, then quickly seemed to come to a decision. "All right, I'll just have to trust you all the way. I'll tell you the whole story, and then you can tell Adam. Like that I won't have to wait for him, I can use the time to visit other people. . . ."

Again she looked about, making doubly sure they were not being spied on. "Let's start walking." And again she took Regina's arm in that uncalled-for, intimate way.

Idka, too, was acutely uncomfortable, but for altogether different reasons. She was trying to find some tactful way to speak to her brother's wife about the woman in his past. In her new-found warmth for Regina she hated to think of hurting her. Yet this was no time for letting niceties of feeling get in the way of what had to be done. "Did Adam ever mention Olek Piotrowski to you?" she began tentatively. "Or his wife Maryla? Or a girl named Wanda?"

Vague memories, from the first year she'd stayed, off and on, at the Grossgliks', came floating back to Regina. She remembered a day early that summer when Adam had dashed in to see their aunt. Later he brought a large, ill-dressed, uncouth young man and a young woman, thin and dark and forbidding, a Gentile and a student, and afterwards it had been impressed upon her she must never, under any circumstances, mention their having come. Still later she heard they were all hiding out in the country, then had to flee abroad. And Adam was so in love with the dark girl that when she went away his heart was broken. And all of it was mixed up with underground politics.

Once, during their honeymoon, the whole episode had somehow surfaced in her mind and she tried to question her husband about it, but he absolutely refused to speak of that year of his life. In fact, he'd practically growled at her, like an ordinarily gentle dog if you touch him where he has been hurt. It had made her both curious and suspicious. Now she had a chance to find out more about it. "What about these people?" she asked cautiously.

"Well, you see," Idka began, "Wanda showed up at our house this afternoon, looking for a place to stay. Naturally, Mama put her up."

"Was she. . . ?" Regina's voice shook a little. "Was she looking for Adam?"

"Oh, no. Just she had her little girl with her, and had to have someone reliable to leave her with during the day. The poor little thing's an idiot, you see, a cretin or something. Such a shame. No more trouble than a vegetable, is the way Mama puts it. It's terribly sad."

Yes, but what has all this to do with us? Regina wanted to ask. But she knew that if she were going to find out anything, she must let Idka ramble on in her own way. She bit her lips even though it made them rough, and said nothing.

"The long and the short of it," the other girl went on, "is that Olek and his wife and Wanda and Wanda's husband are all up to the hilt in the events in Lodz. And now the two men and Maryla have been arrested—all the strike leaders were, that's in the morning papers. But what the papers didn't say is that now they're all here at the Pawiak. In fact, they're in the same wing as Izidore. . . ."

"Go on," Regina murmured, horrified and fascinated in spite of herself.

"Wanda told us it's the first leg of a trek into northern Russia, no one knows yet exactly where. The convoys will be starting in a day or two by *kibitka*—imagine travel by open cart in midwinter! How many will survive? Naturally Wanda is frantic. She's running here and running there, trying to raise some money so she and the little girl can follow Felix, that's the husband, to Moscow or Tula or maybe even Siberia. . . ."

Suddenly the accumulated anger for which Regina badly needed a target found one. "What!" she cried. "You mean to tell me that at a time like this, this woman had the gall to come to your house? Why, she could stir up all kinds of trouble for all of us!"

"But, my dear, where else would she go?" Idka answered simply. "Where if not to old trusted friends?"

Regina realized she had almost betrayed herself. "You're right, of course. I simply wasn't thinking. . . ." But in her mind's eye she had a vivid picture of the woman who once had meant everything to Adam and who now might try to contact him, a bereaved woman with a helpless child, whose plight was enough to wring a heart much tougher than her husband's. Then she also remembered this was to have been her night, a night when no intrusion was to be countenanced.

"Idka," she said with a new urgency, playing for time, "just first let me take care of those silly flowers. Then you can walk back with me and we'll talk some more." She let the flower vendor press a great bunch of mimosa on her, paid whatever was asked, and was free once more to give all her attention to the problem at hand. "Now then, exactly how much money does your *Pani* Wanda need?"

"A lot. No matter how cheaply one travels, it costs."

Regina dug into her reticule and emptied her change purse. "Not much here, is there? Not nearly enough."

"Possibly," Idka offered, "Adam keeps money in the house."

"No, I don't think so," Regina said, too quickly. Then she knew what she must do. "But wait." She made a good show of suddenly remembering something. "Let me see now." She stopped under a street lamp, rummaged through her bag, pretending to explore. "Yes, just as I thought. . . ." From an inner compartment she extracted a roll of large-denomination bills, money she had been saving over many months.

It was to have bought her a round seal muff, the latest fashion, which would have gone beautifully with her new sealskin coat. But first things first. Instead, it would buy her this evening alone with Adam, and maybe even ward off all contact between him and Wanda. And if the two did see each other in spite of everything, after tonight she was confident she could handle that, too.

"My savings," she said with a great show of innocence. "How lucky I didn't get around to putting it in the bank! Here. . . ." She began to count the bills. "Twenty, thirty, fifty, seventy-three rubles. Take it, Idka, take it all. It's in a noble cause. . . ."

"You're giving all of it?" Idka stared at the crisp new banknotes, then as usual when she was moved her nose turned a strawberry red and her eyes watered. "Oh, thank you, thank you!"

Regina had the grace to be embarrassed. "It's little enough for me to do."

But her sister-in-law had to have her say. "You're too modest.

Darling, darling Ginia! Oh, will you ever forgive me for the way I've misjudged you! And now I must run. You'll tell Adam everything for me, won't you, darling? Tell him to come over or not, whatever he thinks best. She's going to be with us until tomorrow at least."

"Leave everything to me. I know what to tell him."

Idka thanked her again, then finally left her. Breathing deeply of the mimosa, Regina turned toward home. Her plans for a scene at the piano might be ruined, and she would not be the picture of fashion until another winter. But providentially a crisis had been averted, of that she was certain.

❧ *Ten* ❦

AFTER ADAM LEFT POZNER he turned in the direction of
Marszalkowska, intending to catch an omnibus and head straight
home. But on every corner hoarse child voices hawked the news,
and he bought several papers to scan anxiously while waiting at
the bus stop.

There were fresh details of the Lodz arrests, and as he began to
read he was rooted to the spot. An omnibus halted directly in
front of him, disgorging passengers while those trying to get on
jostled past him, but he paid no attention. Olek's party name
leaped at him from the printed page. There were others he recognized, at least one the *nom de guerre* of a nationally known underground leader.

"And this is the hell hole my benevolent employer wants me to
work in! Among the butchers of my old friends!" He wadded the
paper and flung it into the gutter like something live and slimy
and evil. He hadn't realized he had spoken aloud until next to
him someone snickered.

"What's the matter, my friend? Can't take it?"

Adam looked up, not really focusing on his neighbor. "Maybe
you don't understand."

"What's to understand?" a mocking voice answered. "Another
roundup. We let them do it to us every time. We rebel just so
long, then we fight among ourselves and they pick us off like clay
pigeons. Oh, we're great with the words, the national songs."

The man spat noisily, accurately, at a crack in the pavement. "But organization! Tfui!" Behind the graying mustache, the beetling eyebrows bristling under the blue worker's cap pulled low, Adam recognized the printer Jacek Piotrowski.

Olek's uncle seemed to have aged ten years since they had last met. All except in spirit. "Uncle Jacek!"

"In person. And if I weren't so goddam mad I'd say I was glad to see you!" They shook hands. "Anyhow, let's go somewhere and have a beer." They turned into a side street.

Like Idka, Jacek had a copy of the *Red Banner*. "You hear about Bloody Sunday? Not yet? Well, take it from me, this is the beginning of something tremendous." Briefly, he brought Adam up to date on the events in Russia's capital. "After the massacre, barricades started going up in the streets of Russian cities. By next week we shall have them here, too. The Tsarate is rotten from top to bottom. It can be toppled. If only we don't bungle things again. . . ."

Then, essentially repeating the information Idka had given Regina, he told Adam about the Lodz prisoners being moved into the Pawiak prison. "Olek is there, and his wife, and Felix Gronowicz—that's your friend Wanda's husband. We don't know about Wanda, so maybe she's slipped through the dragnet. The ones who've been caught are to go by convoy into Russia. There's a housecleaning at the Pawiak and the Citadel, to make room for new prisoners, no doubt. On the morning the convoy starts there's to be a big demonstration. First one in Warsaw. I only hope it's decently organized this time. We want to jam all the streets leading to both prisons."

They came to a tavern, the kind where workingmen stopped off on their way home from factory or shop, the kind Adam hadn't set foot in since he'd lost track of Olek. The place was dark, smelling of hops and sweat and clothing that didn't often see a cake of soap. But it reminded Adam of a past he cherished and he felt suddenly good just to be there.

Jacek was hailed by several of the patrons. "Hey, you're late! There's work to be done, or have you forgotten?" Adam with his good clothes and clean hands they eyed with suspicion. "Who the hell is that with you?"

"A friend. I'll vouch for him," Jacek said. "Moreover," as if presenting an honorary pass, "he's got a brother in the Pawiak. A political sitting out his fourth year."

"In that case let him have a drink on the house!" the barkeep cried.

Jacek nodded agreement. "And now, like someone just said, there's work to be done, brothers."

It was long after dark when Adam finally started on his way home. His pockets were empty, for he had given away all his money, even the change. And he had helped write a handbill that by now Jacek would be running off on his secret press. The first copies would then go to other printers, and by dawn, as Warsaw woke and made ready for work, thousands of leaflets would blanket the city, calling the people to action. Adam was staggering with fatigue but it was a good kind of weariness, and he felt more at peace with himself than he had in a long time.

He had no sooner let himself in with his passkey than Regina burst into the hallway, already in her night clothes, hair flying, face white, eyes sending out sparks and nostrils quavering with controlled fury. "Where have you been? Don't you know what time it is? I've been nearly out of my mind with worry!"

At sight of her, and because he had time for it now, he at once felt contrite. "Dearest, forgive me, I should have sent word but there just wasn't any way. Let me explain." And he tried to draw her into his arms.

But she would have none of it. "Doesn't it matter to you that your wife sits home worrying herself sick while you're out gallivanting till all hours? And with the secret police swarming everywhere? Don't you even care what you put me through?"

"Don't say such things! Don't be angry with me! Regina, beloved child, please, please listen. . . ."

"I'm not a child."

"Please, my darling." He took her hands and kissed them, and slowly she allowed herself to be mollified. "You're quite right," he went on. "In times like these anything can happen. And it did. Oh, nothing bad, now don't start worrying again. Just I met an old friend who had news of other old friends, and one thing led to another." He told her then exactly where he had been and what he'd been doing. "When I knew I could be useful I had to stay. And now I'm so exhausted all I want is to fall into bed and sleep and sleep."

Her rage spent, she herself was nearing exhaustion. She was ready to call a truce, but on her own terms. Still feigning reluctance, she allowed him to kiss her neck and press her close. "I forgive you. Maybe I, too, have been a little foolish. Here I was, imagining all sorts of things. I was sure you were with *her*. . . ."

"Her? You mean you thought I was with another woman? Whatever gave you the idea? Dearest love, don't you know no one exists for me but you?"

By then she could have bitten her tongue out. Had she been less overwrought, less weary, she would never have let this slip out like an accusation. And now it was too late. The only way to undo the harm, she decided, was to be meticulously frank about her meeting with his sister. "Adam, I ran into Idka earlier on, and, well, it seems an . . . an old friend of yours has come to stay at your mother's. In fact, she'll be spending the next couple of nights there. . . ."

Adam seemed to come wide awake, and watching his face she had the oddest, most terrifying feeling that he was slipping away into a world where she could not follow. "Adam," she whispered, "oh, Adam, I was so afraid! You see, long ago, when I wasn't supposed to understand what went on around me, I used to hear the family talk about . . . about you and her. So naturally I know. . ." She let the words trail off eloquently.

"Wanda," Adam repeated, and she had the impression he hadn't heard any of the other things she'd said. "Wanda at my mother's! But Jacek was so sure no one had even heard from her." Suddenly his arms around his young wife tightened protectively. "Oh my poor darling, what you've been through! But you are never, never to worry about such things again so long as you live. Because, don't you see, you are all that matters, all that ever will matter to me."

She sighed then, like a child well consoled after too much crying, and nestled against him. "Then you won't even try to see her?"

"Sweetheart, be reasonable. Of course I must see her. She's a wonderful person and from what I learned today she's in deep trouble." He felt Regina stiffen in his arms, but she did not protest. "In fact, I would never forgive myself if I did nothing to try and help her. But not tonight any more, it's much too late. Besides, if I started to wake the concièrge in my mother's building it would only attract attention. Last thing Wanda needs. But in the morning I must go there."

"In that case," Regina said with finality, "I shall go with you. No, don't try to spare me. I'm your wife and my place is at your side."

"I might have known," Adam said, profoundly moved as she had intended him to be. "Oh, I might have known you would take it this way."

And pressed close together, they moved toward their room, and bed. In the excitement both had forgotten about Adam's interview with Pozner, but that could wait. Within ten minutes, arms tight around one another, they were asleep.

There was no sleep at all around the Pawiak that night.

For days the grapevine had been busy, the rumors flying, spreading like wildfire. No one knew exactly what was truth and what wishful invention. A revolution would be erupting tomorrow, a revolution compared with which the French one would seem to have been child's play. Already, from the Urals to the Baltic, from the Arctic to the Caspian Sea, enslaved nations were rising against the despot, breaking out of their chains, standing free. The *Internationale* was being sung in all four corners of the Empire. Rumor said the Tsar was shaking in his boots. . . .

In Poland, the song of the day was *Warszawianka,* the Song of Warsaw, *Whirlwinds of Danger.* Proscribed, it echoed through the streets. It found its way into the corridors of dungeons where silently, soundlessly, prisoners beat out its rhythms so that the guards were constantly conscious of it without ever hearing its tune or its words.

Whirlwinds of danger are raging around us
Forces of deepest darkness assail us
Many must die as we march into battle
Many must die—yet one day we'll prevail!

Brothers and sisters, shed your blood freely
Raise high the red flag, raise the red banner
Forward to justice, liberty, freedom
Death to the tyrant, the future is ours!

Every child and every crone in the city knew the words. Every prisoner knew them. And no one, not even those in the dankest solitary cells, felt alone these days, abandoned, forgotten.

The communal cell which Izidore and Antek Rosol and a dozen other men had shared for so long they no longer remembered what it was like to eat, sleep, or even perform one's natural functions in private, faced the huge cobblestoned prison courtyard. There the prisoners from Lodz, too numerous to house inside the buildings, had been bivouacked since the previous day. Considered a prize catch and dangerous, they were under heavy guard around the clock. And the old inmates, watching through the bars and even occasionally managing to communicate with them, felt themselves honored merely to share jailing with these national heroes.

"It's like sharing a moment in history," Antek Rosol said to Izidore. "Someday, when scholars write about January 1905, we'll be included." The idea buoyed and awed him. Antek needed buoying. He had been spitting blood for the past month.

Hard-bitten veteran of the struggle that he now was, and not easily roused to emotion, Izidore, unable to tear himself away from the narrow window, spent his waking hours observing the new arrivals. Long after roll call he rose from his pallet and barefoot, shivering in the dark, crept back to his vantage point. The grapevine, as always surprisingly accurate, had furnished all the important details of the Lodz events as well as the names of many of those who huddled freezing in the yard below. The realization that among the sleepers bedded down on the cold paving stones was a boyhood friend of his brother's, someone who in another time had had the run of his parents' house, seemed to bring the Lodz action oddly and personally close. It somehow made his own empty prison years singularly worthwhile.

In spite of himself he felt a mounting excitement and a stirring of new hope. He tried to imagine the demonstration forecast for the morning. It could, after all, be the beginning of a new era. He began to dream of the storming of another Bastille. Already he was half-convinced that out there just beyond reach lay freedom, and if only his arm were long enough he could reach out and touch it. Perhaps tomorrow he would. Tomorrow. . .

Among the captured strike leaders down in the courtyard there was no such optimism. Talking in whispers after the guards had dozed off, they kept punishing themselves by reviewing the events of the past week. They tried to draw lessons for the future. "We let ourselves be led into a trap. We acted too hastily, we should have waited, preparing and protecting ourselves better. Mostly, we should have built a second and a third line of defense so that if we failed, others might carry on without us. Dr. Julius was right—we won a battle and lost a war. Now maybe we'll have to pay with our necks. And just at a time when everything is really starting to move in good earnest—just at a time when not a man can be spared. . . ."

They had heard, as Izidore had, about Bloody Sunday and the demonstrations sweeping Great Russia from border to border. But they had also heard the ever-recurring rumors about a prison break to free the "politicals" here and at the Citadel prison when the convoys started to roll in the morning. And they knew such an action would be premature. The city had not yet risen in armed rebellion. The break couldn't possibly be carried out successfully. In the narrow streets leading to the Pawiak the people would only be cut off and massacred. *Lord, you who've watched o'er Poland through the ages / Once made her mighty, covered her with glory, do not permit this senseless bloodshed! The battle for freedom needs living heroes, not dead martyrs! Oh, Lord God, protect our brothers!*

Was it God himself, or Satan, or the Tsar's deputies who heard their prayer? Long before the winter sky turned gray with reluctant light the guards started to rout the prisoners out of their improvised bunks. "Up! Up! Up with you bastards!" Throughout the prison buildings, too, lights flickered on a full hour earlier than usual. "Up! Up! Everybody up!"

Morning roll call was rushed, curt orders barked out over and over to hurry, hurry, make it snappy, you fucking mothers' sons, if you know what's good for you and don't want a hobnailed boot in your ass! We want the last goddam one of you ready and out and standing at attention in the yard by the time the Citadel trumpeter plays reveille!

"Ready for what?" some unfortunate had the temerity to ask.

It got him a clout on the side of his head that sent him reeling against the wall. "Do as you're told and keep your stinkin' trap shut!"

They kept quiet after that, wondering whether it was fresh punishment or death that lay ahead.

Except for the wing where common criminals and murderers were held, all inmates were ordered to pack their belongings, as much as they could carry in a single bundle. This meant they were all being moved. But where? A still more secure jail—the Butyrki in Moscow after all? Siberia, without even a trial? Perfectly possible. But not the gallows. You weren't told to pack your gear if you were being sent to the gallows.

They descended the rotting, crumbling stairs silently, in two long lines. On each landing the lines were swelled by other groups, each man with his bundle, and finally by several dozen women. "Maybe they're letting us go home," someone whispered out of the side of his mouth. "Maybe they got tired of feeding us."

"I could use a change of menu," Antek Rosol whispered back. "How about the rest of you?" He doubled over in a fit of coughing.

Izidore put his free arm around his shoulder to help keep him walking. As the prison doors clanged open and they stepped into the icy air he became aware that his friend was finding it increasingly difficult to breathe.

In the yard the Lodz prisoners were already through with roll call. The place teemed with soldiers, Cossack and Kalmyk. Bayonets bristled. Orders were given in Russian. "Atten-*shun!*"

They obeyed, row upon row of weary, unarmed men and two rows of women, groggy with want of sleep, most of them beyond fear now but worn down by an uncertainty that is worse than fear.

A subaltern detached himself from the rest of the armed group and solemnly, if haltingly—since he had difficulty with words of more than two syllables—began reading the Tsar's newest *ukaze*. This stated that, as dangerous elements, they would no longer be permitted to remain, even confined in prison, in an area so close to their former sphere of activity; though how these men who had spent years in total isolation were now suddenly endangering the Crown was not explained. "Moreover, since drastic steps must be taken to ensure subordination throughout the Polish provinces—subordination as well as domestic peace—and wishing to safeguard Our subjects in all Our domains against insurrection, We graciously decree that the prisoners here assembled be transported under guard to a destination inside Great Russia to await trial, said destination to remain secret so as to avoid further crimes against Holy Mother Russia. . . ."

So it sounded like Butyrki after all, Izidore thought. Well, at least the waiting was over. Now there would only be the farce of a trial, the outcome of which would never for a moment be in doubt. They would all be found guilty and sent to Siberia. The only unknown quantity was the length of each individual sentence, and whether that sentence would be hard labor or merely exile in a penal colony. How many would live long enough to return to the homeland was another matter.

The reading over, the bustle of preparations began again, this time more purposeful. It became clear there was to be no waiting for daylight to move the prisoners out. Whether the prison authorities had gotten wind of plans for the demonstration or merely wished to forestall any kind of goodbyes, like families coming to weep and wail on the sidewalks outside the gates, was never quite clear. A curt order, and the rattle of wheels, the rhythmic beat of horses' hooves, began to be heard. From around the corner of Pawia Street the first of the empty *kibitkas,* the convoy carts, appeared.

A collective sigh, partly sorrow but largely relief, went up in the crowded courtyard. At least there was going to be no slaughter in the streets. And then, as they were being herded and pushed and booted by their jailers, somewhere in the ranks the singing started. In defiance of the guards with their knouts and their bayonets it rose and swelled, cheering the dejected, restoring hope to those who were losing hope. It was a mocking song they had all known by heart ever since they could remember, as their fathers and their fathers' fathers had known it, a song future generations might someday be allowed to forget.

> *Damn* kibitka's *got the shakes*
> *Got the shakes, got the shakes,*
> *Wracks our carcass till it quakes*
> *Till it breaks, ouch!*

The guards, enraged, were shouting, "Silence! Silence, you bastards! Shut up and get going!" No one listened. And the song, life-saving because it still made laughter possible, was picked up by a hundred voices and would not be stilled.

> *Damn* kibitka's *got the shakes, the shakes-o*
> *Got the shakes, the shakes-o*
> *Got the shakes, the shakes-o*
> *Wracks our carcass till it breaks, it breaks-o*
> *Till it breaks our goddam necks!*

As the first of the convoy rolled through the open prison gates, all the windows in the houses along Pawia Street swung open. Unmindful of the soldiers' shouted threats and obscenities, people still in their night clothes leaned out to wave. "Go with God! And come back with the Tsar's head on a platter!"

The same subaltern who had read the ukase now asked an officer, "Want I should give orders to fire, Excellency?"

"No, you idiot. That's what they're after—confusion, so some of them can get away."

The prisoners' spirits were lifting.

As cart after cart filled up and found its way into line, Izidore heard his name shouted. "Hey, Fabian! Izzy Fabian! Hey!" He turned. Olek Piotrowski waved at him from a moving vehicle. He was standing between a distinguished white-haired man of medium height and a tall, cadaverous stranger, a Don Quixote, an El Greco Christ come to life. "A pleasant journey, Izzy! We'll meet in Siberia!"

Gripped by a strange kind of exaltation, carried on the wave of their collective strength, Izidore waved back almost gaily. "And a pleasant journey to you all!"

Then the song with its gallows humor drowned out everything else. The earliest crowds of demonstrators converging on the Pawiak from the four corners of the city were just in time to see the last of the convoy disappear.

"She isn't here," Bluma said an hour later, as she opened her door to her son and daughter-in-law. "Left at the crack of dawn without a bite of breakfast. Idka, too. She'll be back, though, for she's left this poor little mindless mite of hers with me. This is no day to be dragging a child around the streets, not even if it's no more trouble than a cabbage head. . . ."

She led the way to the back of the house, where, propped by pillows so she would not roll off her improvised crib, Wanda's cretin daughter was placidly sucking milk out of a bottle. Her face was large, vacant, yet singularly good-natured, like a contented infant's. *She's my daughter, too,* Adam thought in total disbelief, shocked to find that this meant nothing to him and merely grateful that Regina remained ignorant of this part of his story.

Yet he continued staring at little Felka in morbid fascination. Would she perhaps have been born normal had he been there to take care of her mother right through her pregnancy? Olek had said cretinism had something to do with prenatal deficiencies, that it was common in Switzerland. Still, if things had been different. . . . How much of it was his fault? But this was a riddle to which there would never be any answers, and suddenly he was impatient to turn his back on it. "Did Wanda say where she was going, Mama?"

"Just . . . out." Then, after a moment's hesitation, she drew her son aside and whispered, so that Regina need not hear, "I don't want you to think I'm criticizing, but do you think it's right, bringing your wife with you? I mean," she looked pain-fully embarrassed, "what if she finds out something she shouldn't? You could hurt her badly." It was as much as she dared say.

Adam hastened to reassure her. "Don't worry, Mama. Regina knows. She understands. She's been wonderful. Of course, she also knows Wanda means nothing to me any more. Just an old friend in trouble."

"Still, it might be best if she weren't around when you and *Pani* Wanda meet."

He said emphatically, *"Especially* if we meet I'd want Regina there with me."

"I just hope you know what you're doing," his mother said.

Just then the child dropped her bottle and began to whimper. Bluma turned, retrieved the milk, then took Felka into her lap to cuddle and soothe until she finally succeeded in getting her to start sucking again.

It seemed a good moment for them to leave.

"Tell Wanda I was here, Mama," Adam said.

And Regina added, "No, tell her we were *both* here to wish her well." Bluma, watching from the window, saw them cross the courtyard a few minutes later, and they were holding hands.

❧ *Eleven* ❧

Prevented from demonstrating at the Pawiak gates, where they were met by a forest of bayonets and a wall of mounted cossacks, the citizens of Warsaw seemed to lose all sense of personal danger. They did not go home, nor did they go to work. Many were holding in their hands the call Adam had helped write, the call for a general strike in protest against Bloody Sunday in St. Petersburg. Factory after factory was shutting down. By the time Adam and Regina left Bluma's house, half the population was pouring into the streets.

Men and women who never before had raised a finger in the interests of independence were now spontaneously joining the crowds, shouting patriotic slogans. People weren't questioning one another's politics. They were all Poles together, banded against a single oppressor. A common hatred made them all brothers. It would be some time before the Pope in Rome issued his encyclical enjoining the faithful to remain loyal and obedient to "that great Monarch, Nicholas II," whose "wisdom and tempered leniency" Pius X extolled. The priests had not yet started to enjoin their flocks that they must at all costs defend the faith and the fatherland against godless agitators. In that last week of January there were no radicals and no conservatives, no proletarians or rich men or nobles, no Gentiles or Jews, even. There were only those who shouted "Down with the Tsar!"

Thus, for the authorities, the spiriting away of the prisoners turned out to have been a colossal blunder after all. All over the city policemen were being disarmed by the populace and locked up. Russian petty civil servants grabbed up what gold and valuables they could and, prevented from leaving the city, hid in attics and cellars. The Tsar could punish them later on if he wished; right now all they asked was to keep safely out of the way of danger. His Majesty's loyal, obedient servants were taking no unnecessary risks.

January 26, the day that ushered in Poland's own Revolution of 1905, doomed but glorious, was a day of judgment, a day of reckoning, a day for action. The people did not stop to think they were making history, only that the time had come to stop counting costs. Even the elements seemed to be on their side. The morning that had loomed gray and bleak after a bleak and bitter night suddenly seemed to shake off its shroud. The sky cleared, the sun broke through to cheer the demonstrators on.

By midday no one remained indoors. In the public squares, in parks, on street corners, improvised rostrums went up, from which speakers representing every shade of public opinion openly addressed the crowds. "We demand independence, freedom, a Polish Republic! Down with the Tsar!" Workers already on strike were going from one still-operating factory to the next, urging the crews to join them. Even the PPS and the Social-Democrats acted together. A parade of fifteen thousand, carrying red banners and placards that read "Down with the bosses!" marched into Sigismund Square. It was a political uprising and a social revolution rolled into one.

Adam and Regina spent hours walking the streets, losing themselves in the crowd, whose spirit, as the day wore on, was becoming more and more self-assured and festive. Everywhere they kept running into people they knew, close friends and casual acquaintances who greeted them like friends.

"They've thrown up barricades in Lodz, did you hear?"

"Zaglembie Dombrowskie is shut down tight."

"The university has called its own strike. The schools, too."

At a gate to the Lazienki Gardens they met Viktor and Tynia, who regaled them with the latest joke. "Have you heard about the telegram the Tsar sent the Mikado? 'Give me half your army to fight my own subjects and I'll give you half of Asia.' And the

Mikado wired back, 'Do you take me for a fool? I already have half of Asia. Soon I shall have the other half. So why should I give you anything?' "

Afterwards they all wandered together through the gardens. The fountain, drained at this time of year, made an excellent podium. A speaker, perched on the raised pediment from which in summer water spouted, was just winding up an appeal for funds. "We're asking you, ladies and gentlemen, brothers and sisters, patriots, comrades, friends, to give whatever you can spare for the relief of the first victims of this week's brutalities. Dig deep into your pockets, you who still have your freedom! The wife of one of the jailed leaders is right over there," he said, pointing to a park bench beneath a naked maple, "ready to take your money and see that it's turned over to the relief committee. . . ."

Adam, his hand already reaching for his wallet, turned, then stood stock still. The woman the speaker had pointed out was Wanda.

As he stared, rooted to the spot, she turned in his direction and their eyes met. He came alive then, moved swiftly. "Wanda! It's really you!"

"Adash!"

The years rolled back and they were seeing the fountain shaded by flowering trees in summer twilight and on its marble rim two youthful conspirators whispering together.

The moment of illusion passed. Wanda was the first to return to the present. "It's good to see you, Adash. I was hoping I would." She held out her hand rather formally.

Just as formally he took it, automatically bending to kiss it. "I tried to catch up with you at my mother's, but you'd already left." He was thinking that she was not as he remembered her, yet exactly as he had always imagined she must someday become. Thinner, more austere, every line of her face more sharply and finely etched. The hair, he noticed, was already showing gray. The mouth was tired, the skin that had once been drawn so smoothly over the beautiful cheekbones was crisscrossed with tiny premature lines. She was wearing something dark, a little shabby, and she was totally without artifice of any kind.

Yet in spite of it all there was no longer anything forbidding about her, as though time had softened and love warmed her. And she seemed not to hold any grudge against him at all.

"Wanda, my dear, can't we take a little time to talk?"

But a dozen people were claiming her attention, handing her paper money, dropping copper and silver coins into the box she held, asking where they might send donations of food and clothing.

Between answering their questions she said, "Look, Adam, I can't stop now. But I haven't eaten all day. Can you pick me up in twenty minutes?"

He searched out Regina and the others in the milling crowd, explained he had just met a very old friend and arranged to find them again, in a cafe they all knew, in half an hour. Then he went back for Wanda, who was beginning to collect her things. On the way out of the park he took her arm to help her over some piled-up snow. It was like touching an electric wire after the current has been shut off. No spark passed between them. Nothing. Earlier, he'd said of her: just an old, old friend in trouble. And that's what she was. That's all she was.

And yet it was important to him to know more about her. "Tell me about yourself. About what happened."

Briefly and with a minimum of personal detail she sketched in the years between. Her marriage, her work, the political activity that had never stopped. And finally, hesitantly, she spoke of her little daughter. "You've seen her, haven't you?"

Adam nodded.

"Then you know. It hasn't been easy for us." She fell silent. And then, as if making up her mind, "Adash, there's something I've wanted to say to you for Lord knows how long! For years I've wanted to say it. I know now, maybe I've always known, that I had no right to be so high-handed with you. Call it pride, plain stupid pride. I hurt you. And yet, believe me, it has all turned out for the best all around. For you. For me. For . . . everybody."

He was able to read between the lines. She was admitting the child's paternity, yet at the same time absolving him of guilt. He felt touched and deeply grateful. "What a remarkable woman you are!"

She smiled a little. "Ah, well, the important thing is to learn to let go of the past. It's really a terrible waste of time to agonize over yesterday's mistakes!" That much brought out into the open, she began talking quietly, without the least self-consciousness, about Felka. "She's really such a good child. But these last few days she's cried a lot—misses her father." *Her father!* Here was final forgiveness. "Felix always knows how to handle her, he's wonderful with her, much better than I really, though I must say I'm getting better. . . . And she, the little mite, she's a lot smarter than people realize. And she's improving all the time, we can see it. . . ." She was a physician, yet like other parents similarly afflicted, was trying to convince herself, by convincing him, that one day her child would be like other children, that it was all merely a matter of time and patience and extra love.

Vaguely Adam remembered reading somewhere that cretins seldom lived long. For Wanda's sake he hoped this was true. He also hoped her husband would come back to her before they were too old to have another, normal child. "I, too, have wanted for so long to tell you how sorry I've been for my share in . . . the stupidity. . . ."

They reached the cafe, which was overcrowded, and far in the back he saw Regina waiting at a table with some people he barely knew. "Viktor and Tynia couldn't wait," she said by way of a greeting. "You're very late!" He started to apologize, and she put her hand on his arm possessively. "And Adash, you haven't introduced me to your . . . *friend.*"

He was taken aback by the sharp edge of his wife's voice. Fortunately it softened almost at once. One look at Adam and Wanda together, and Regina realized she could afford to be gracious. This woman was no threat to her.

Since Wanda was planning to take a train into Russia the following day so as to overtake the convoy, then travel with it, she had dozens of errands still to do and had to leave almost immediately. But they arranged to meet again in the evening, in Philharmonic Hall, where a symphony concert had been canceled in favor of a great public rally. Rosa Luxemburg would be one of the speakers, Joseph Pilsudski was expected to arrive from Galicia or at least send a representative, and there would also be someone who had escaped arrest in Lodz.

As the afternoon wore on and their energy ebbed, Adam and Regina finally turned back toward Count Berg Street. At home they found Salome alone except for Miss Julia, for not only Leon and all the young boarders but even the second maid had been out roaming the street since morning. Salome was having a *crise de nerfs,* convinced that her loved ones would all end up in jail before the night was out.

"Oh, I know you all rely on me to get you out of trouble every time. But please, my darlings, please stay home tonight! When your Uncle Leon gets back I mean to go on my knees to him, beg him to stay in, too. . . ."

They calmed her down as best they could and went to their room. There Adam found a note from Maurice Pozner, delivered some hours earlier by messenger. "I hope you've come to a decision by now. Please let me know at once. This is urgent."

Adam crumpled the paper, feeling his gorge rise. "He has no right to push me like this! Not today of all days!" Without other comment he passed the note to his wife.

As she read, Regina's heart began to beat faster. In the general excitement she hadn't questioned Adam about what had happened between him and the old textile magnate, but she had a general idea of what might have. A secure future seemed to her so close, so easily within reach. But she also realized this was ground she must tread on with the greatest care.

"Darling," she handed the note back, eyes open wide and looking very innocent indeed. "You never said—did he make you an offer by any chance?"

"Oh," Adam said, "in all the excitement, with so much else happening, I forgot to tell you." Quickly, then, he outlined for her his conversation with Pozner of the day before. "But right now it's hard for me even to think about it. How can I possibly make up my mind? A manager's job, in that . . . slaughter-house? Regina, Regina, what am I to do?"

She said demurely, "I'm a woman, it isn't my place to decide. Naturally I want what's best for you, for my family, and for the children we're going to have. Still, I would never urge you to go against your conscience."

"Thank you, my darling. I knew you would understand."

"Tell you what," she suggested, again playing for time, "it's much too late to do anything about it now anyway. Let's sleep on it. Give him your answer tomorrow, when your head is clear."

"You're right, that's exactly what I will do." As happens so often when a person is torn, and hoping against hope to avoid a painful decision, he was feeling desperately tired.

She felt suddenly sorry for him, and tender. "Try taking a nap, you look all in. I'll wake you when dinner is served." He nodded, fell across the bed, and instantly escaped into heavy, fatigue-drugged sleep. An hour later Regina hardly had the heart to shake him awake.

"Come, you really must get up or we'll be late to the meeting. You do want to go, don't you?"

He was wishing he could avoid even that. He sat on the edge of their bed, his head in his hands. "Right now what I think I would most like is to get out of the country. You and I will have to talk some more about that before I get back to the Old Man. Can't you see the trap I've set for myself! If I do take this job in Lodz—and it's a big job—I'll feel like Judas. And yet this much I also know. I was never really cut out for being part of the underground. I finally understood that once and for all today, when I saw my—when I saw Wanda. It was always mainly a matter of personal loyalties. And now my loyalty is to you. Why couldn't I have been born the kind of man who's content to live for himself and his family and let the rest of the world take care of itself! Then everything would be simple."

She was beginning to feel a mounting impatience and did her best to control it. When will he learn to stop tilting at windmills? she thought. She sighed to indicate sympathy, but she really felt like shrugging her shoulders. She heard Salome's voice whisper in her ear, *Don't push, little heart! Never push a man or he'll do exactly what you don't want him to do!*

She finally urged him to throw some cold water on his face and come to dinner. "It'll make you feel better, darling, I promise you."

Philharmonic Hall was already filled to near-capacity when they arrived, but Wanda and Idka had come early and were saving them seats far down front, in the orchestra. It was a strange experience to walk down the carpeted aisle and see men in work jackets and women in kerchiefs instead of hats occupying the red plush chairs. Gone for the moment were the accustomed elegance, the rustle of silks, the scent of costly perfumes. The very lights in the great chandeliers flickered uncertainly, as if themselves surprised to be shining on such a spectacle. To Adam, the really strange thing was the absence of musicians, their chairs strung out in a couple of long rows to accomodate speakers and strikers' delegates. There was nothing to remind one that this was Warsaw's great music center except the philharmonic organ, the city's pride, the columns of its pipes dominating the whole back wall.

It was a rough crowd, noisy, uncouth, shouting and waving at each other, and restless in their seats. When at last the meeting was ready to begin the chairman was forced to rap his gavel again and again before there was relative silence. "Friends, comrades," he finally began, "I needn't tell you what a momentous occasion this is. The time of freedom has come at last. Therefore, we propose to open our meeting with the singing of our forbidden national anthem. Not since this hall was built have its sacred strains been heard under its roof."

Now they all stood, hushed as in church. And for the first time in the memory of the oldest of them they let their voices swell, full-throated, in the open:

> Lord God who've watched o'er Poland through the ages,
> Who made her mighty, showered her with glory. . .

The anthem rang from the rafters, not a lament any longer but a song of thanksgiving. Then, joyously and without pausing, they went into *Poland Is Not Yet Lost*. And men and women wept unashamed. And strangers pressed each other's hands.

Now the first speaker was introduced.

"Brothers and sisters," he shouted from the huge stage, "we who have been born into slavery never thought we should be the first Poles in a hundred years to see freedom! We shall be the first since Kosciuszko's day to die free men!" The crowd roared its approval. "We have the cossacks on the run. . . ."

Some of the speeches were pure emotion, others clear and sane, a sober call to action. Some aimed at the heart, others at the head. A young dandy jumped up to demand restoration of the ancient monarchy. He was hooted down. A textile worker bringing fraternal greetings from the embattled mill complexes of Lodz province cried out that it was not enough to overthrow the foreign masters. "What shall it avail us to rid the country of Moscow's yoke if we exchange it for the yoke of domestic capitalism?"

Adam began to shift uncomfortably in his seat. He was wishing the speakers would stay with more lofty concepts. His hours of work with Jacek Piotrowski the night before, weighed against the note from Pozner which seemed to him to be burning a hole in his pocket, refused to cancel each other out. The mention of Lodz was particularly disquieting.

As if to taunt him, Rosa Luxemburg was the next to take the floor. The diminutive gnome of a woman still spoke with an occasional foreign intonation, but Adam noted with impersonal interest that her rusty Polish had improved since he'd heard her at the Rosols'. The rest of the audience did not seem to have his critical ear. Her thoughts were so lucid, so well organized, that she commanded both instant respect and total silence. The audience became completely still, letting her strong, resonant voice easily fill the hall.

"Brothers and sisters, I represent the comrades abroad and as I've been telling our people again and again this past month, I'm here with the message that all Europe is aware of what's happening here today. The working class of industrialized Western Europe is with you. I bring you greetings, expressions of solidarity, words of encouragement from the organized labor movement of the world. . . ."

In spite of himself Adam found he was caught up in what she was saying. Now, he thought, the meeting has dignity. All through the audience people began to applaud. Rosa signaled for quiet.

"But let me also warn you: you will need the strictest discipline, unity, order, organization. There can be no other way to sustain what today you've only begun. Without organization and discipline all you would have is daydreams, and dreams have a habit of vanishing in the merciless light of day. Comrades, friends, listen carefully! Be guided by the experience of the international working class. All of us joining together, and uniting with our equally oppressed, equally exploited proletarian brothers in Russia—there lies the only road to revolutionary success. . . ."

Again there was applause, but also shouts of "Goddam Social-Democrat! Bolshevik! Damn Jew!" Without warning rotten eggs pelted the platform. "Shut her up! We don't need her kind of advice! The hell with her and her party and the Russians!"

"Shut up yourselves!" A dozen fist fights erupted in the aisles like flash fires. "We want to hear what else she's got to say! Let her speak! Come on, Rosa! Rosa!"

In an effort to control the near-riot the inexperienced chairman, sweating, hoarse from trying to outshout the others, called for the singing of the *Warszawianka,* hoping that the universally popular song would help unify the crowd and bring at least temporary order. But even that was a mistake. For it was not the customary opening stanza people chose to sing, but the final one, with its clear if unsubtle revolutionary call:

> *Shame on the rich when thousands are starving!*
> *Shame on the toads who wallow in comfort!*
> *Shame on all those who lacking in courage*
> *Dare not speak out or stand to be counted!*

"Bravo! Bravo!" someone yelled to thunderous applause. "Stand up and be counted, brothers, like the song says!" From the gallery a chorus answered, "We need a real revolution, a revolution that will give the people power!" Men were clambering onto the stage dragging a great red banner to plant next to the Polish white eagle on its field of amaranth.

"Brothers, who can lead us in the singing of the *Interna-*

tionale?" a nameless man cried. "Born of the Paris Commune, may it also inaugurate the Commune of Warsaw!"

There was more applause as a hundred voices from all parts of the hall responded: *Arise, ye prisoners of starvation. . . .*

Now others from the audience crowded onto the stage. Seemingly from nowhere, huge blown-up photographs of Marx and Engels appeared. Those who brought them were looking frantically about for a way to hang them in full view of everyone. A youth wearing the leather apron of a cobbler produced a hammer and nails, then realized there was no wall to hammer them into. He stood uncertainly looking about until someone yelled to him, "There, up there!" pointing to the great organ. The boy moved, and in headlong unthinking passion began pounding the nails in. As they penetrated the metal a strange moaning sounded from the pipes that always in the past had played Bach and Handel and Mozart.

Unbelieving, sickened at the wanton destruction, Adam watched from his seat.

The portraits finally hung to his satisfaction, the youth with the hammer stood back and faced the hall, as if inviting approval. A girl cried out shrilly, "Well done! That'll show them nothing can stop us!" She jumped up on her seat, waving her arms. "Now then, let's start over again, all of us together! *Arise, ye prisoners of starvation. . . .' "*

Abruptly, Adam had had enough. "Stop it! Stop it! You're nothing but an uncivilized mob!"

There were jeers. "Ho-ho! A second fine gentleman heard from! A great *Pan* with delicate nerves! Hey you, *Pan,* you another one of those who want to set up a Polish kingdom with a real Polish king on the throne!?"

Shaken with helpless rage, on his feet now, Adam was shouting, "Just stop this senseless vandalism!"

A couple of large men rushed him and before he knew what was happening or could defend himself, he felt a glancing blow to the side of his head. He stumbled. Between them, Wanda and his sister managed to pull him outside.

A moment later Regina made her way out. She had lost her hat and her hair was awry. "Are you hurt?" Her eyes were wild with terror, her face white. When he shook his head to reassure her, she turned on him. "Whatever came over you? You fool, you might have got all of us in trouble!"

In the cold night air his breath came with difficulty. For a while he found himself unable to make a sound. And when at last he did speak, it was to Wanda and Wanda alone.

"Well, now I've seen them, your proletarians in action. I've had a taste of what it's like when they get the upper hand. I know what comes of it. Mob rule." He was making it a personal accusation against her. "Mob rule, and I want no part of it." And it seemed to him in that moment that his sight had cleared after years of not seeing, and that he was suddenly free of the past.

"Now at last I understand why people say radicalism is merely *jugendkrankheit!*" he said contemptuously, in that one statement about starry-eyed immaturity denying the long, agonized years during which he had tried so futilely to live by the ideals of brotherhood and humanism she represented. The ideals themselves now seemed to him to have turned to mockery. Humanism—after what he'd witnessed in there, in the great hall? The moaning of the organ as the nails sank in had seemed to him the death knell of his own illusions. And he felt betrayed, without for a moment suspecting that one day he would discover he had, instead, evolved a rationale for betraying himself.

All this time Regina stood watching him, saying nothing at all. It was wholly beyond her to understand her husband or even follow his thought, but unerringly she sensed that whatever was happening was to her advantage. Wanda, on the other hand, having known an Adam who to his wife was a stranger, could guess exactly the tortured workings of his mind.

For years—and this was the root of his ultimate defeat—he had wanted just what the song described: to cling to his comforts, lacking the courage to speak up and be counted. Yet he was also a man of conscience, and so for a long time had burned with unavowed shame, until in the end, unable to bear being constantly torn, he'd had to search for a scapegoat. He had just found it. He called it "the mob."

Standing there beside him on the public sidewalk, preparing

to leave for the frozen North, she remembered another leave-taking, on a railway platform in a foreign city. Remembered the lover who was letting her face her great trouble alone because he was without the kind of courage that can disregard convention. Because he hadn't yet put a wedding ring on her finger. Even though he already called her wife, he hadn't found the strength to follow her. And she had pitied him, for all that in loving him she had been cruelly wounded. Now she no longer loved him but she pitied him more than ever.

"I'm going away tonight and we may never see each other again," she said. "So perhaps you'll forgive me if I speak my mind. You're wrong about so many things! Oh, I don't deny that what we saw tonight was indeed vandalism. I don't condone it any more than you do. But try to remember the circumstances. Think, Adam. Ask yourself, who are these people? Our dark, unlettered masses. All their lives they've been brutalized, and believe me, poverty and hunger do make brutes of men. I can remember a time when you were able to understand such things."

"In that case," he said bitterly, "I'm glad I have forgotten. Now all I ask is, let them stay in their place!"

"No," she said. "Let them crawl out of their holes and into the light. Let them make mistakes. They'll learn. And even if they don't, their children will! Their children will know that an organ is for making music. More than that, their children will make the music."

"You were always good with words," he said bitterly, "only this time you can't win me over. I'm sorry, Wanda. Go sacrifice yourself for the masses, if that's what you want. For myself, I no longer think it's worthwhile. I've better things to do."

A cab clattered slowly by and he hailed it, helping Regina in, not even asking to take Wanda and Idka wherever they were going. Then, as he himself climbed in, he turned for one final word. "Well, goodbye, old friend. I wish we might have parted on a happier note." He gave the driver directions and the man flicked his whip, urging his tired nag to a trot. Adam sank back in his seat, his breath coming in hard sobs. Suddenly he reached for Regina's hand and began kissing it above the glove.

He did not speak again until they were home and in their own room.

"Tomorrow," he announced, "I'll see Pozner and tell him I'm accepting his offer. You have been very wise, my dearest, very patient with me, and I'm beginning to think you know me better than I know myself." He stood watching her as she removed the pins from her disheveled hair. "I'm so lucky to have you! So very, very lucky. . ."

While she sat brushing her hair the traditional hundred strokes, he went to draw the curtains. The streets had grown quiet; the city was making ready for the night and for a new day. But somewhere in the distance there was still singing. The strains of the *Warszawianka* could be clearly heard.

Shame to all those who lacking in courage. . .

Adam slammed the window shut with such violence that the panes rattled. He jerked the heavy drapes together. Then he turned his face back into the room. He took Regina in his arms, and the brush slipped to the floor, and she smiled, and he buried his face in the warm, thick, heavy, fragrant hair.

❧ *Epilogue* ❧

ON A COLD, penetrating evening in the late winter of 1907 a pair of unexpected visitors were ushered into the Adam Fabians' elegant new apartment, situated in the same building as Baron Kronenberg's Lodz *pied-à-terre.* The woman wore a white nurse's coif above her bulky, fur-lined coat. The man, prematurely gray and prison-pale, coughed a great deal, at least in public. They were given warm welcome, and since supper was about to be served Regina ordered a rather startled servant to take the guests' things and set two more places at table.

The unprepossessing newcomers were Adam's sister Idka and Michal Winawer, secretly her husband. Officially he was a very sick patient she was accompanying to Davos, where the pure air of the Swiss Alps was to effect a cure of his nonexistent tuberculosis. But in truth, as she remarked after first whispering to her brother and his wife that their papers were as kosher as Friday-night carp, the Swiss air was just then indicated for both of them.

Idka and Michal had met at the Rosols' shortly after the death in Butyrki prison of Antek Rosol, whom Michal had known there. He had known Izidore, too, and had a great deal to say about him. The two young people felt an instant kinship, one thing led to another, and soon Idka, who like her mother a generation earlier was already resigned to spinsterhood, was feeling about this man who fell in love with her as Bluma had felt about her Jacob. Added to everything else they shared their political passions, which made her happiness complete. For the first time she was consoled over the loss of her beloved Izzy, by now serving out a five-year sentence in a Siberian penal colony.

The Fabians' apartment was even more luxurious than Idka had expected, and her sister-in-law, in the last stages of pregnancy, was very much the queen of her domain. Idka's practiced nurse's eye noted that her belly was huge, out of all proportion to her tiny size; yet she indulged at supper in second helpings of rich foods, remarking gaily that now she must eat for two. Obviously, like the healthy young animal she was, she bloomed with the experience, not in the least concerned over her ungainly bulk, wearing it like a badge of success, letting Adam hover over her and the household staff wait on her hand and foot.

But to Idka these were details and she gave them no more than the fleeting attention she felt they deserved. There was so much else to talk about, most of it important: her mother had finally been convinced that it was best to give up the Nalewki apartment and come to live in Adam's house; the arrangements were already being made; there was, heaven knows, room enough and to spare, and once the baby came, even if there would be a nurse for it, Bluma could give Regina a hand now and then and thus feel useful.

Other family news was then disposed of. Viktor and Tynia were doing well enough, but no baby in sight yet. Kazik, as might have been expected, was having a love affair with the jewelry business. And Rosie wrote from her crowded flat in Hester Street, New York, that she was yet to see a single gold paving-block anywhere in the new country, but soon, God willing, things were bound to improve.

As for herself and Michal, once safely out of the country and settled in Switzerland, they hoped, as Idka put it, to be able to start being useful again to the underground. Right now things were bad, very bad, and a far cry from the glorious days of 1905. This past year, in fact, had brought everything to a standstill.

"No leadership left," Michal put in. He had a deep voice and spoke out of the side of his mouth, doubtless a prison habit. "They're all either dead, or in jail, or abroad. The Tsar couldn't win the war but he certainly did us in." He was referring to the succession of events since the Revolution had first broken out, exactly two years earlier.

For a while its tide had continued on the rise, growing to formidable proportions by the time the Russians met defeat at the hands of the Japanese. Inside Great Russia, the soldiers returning from the front joined the people at home to form *soviets,* or councils, of Workers' and Peasants' Deputies. In the provinces the nationalist forces were demanding independence. But the Tsar, in mortal terror of his embattled subjects, was at last free to give full attention to crushing them. On the advice of his new favorite, Piotr Stolypin, who had succeeded the more liberal Count De Witte as prime minister, in October 1905 Tsar Nicholas II issued the infamous manifesto designed to undermine unity and disarm all but the most militant and most far-seeing among the rebels. It was a manifesto that promised everybody everything, including civil rights and civil freedoms and even a legislative Duma patterned after the parliaments of the West.

To the vast body of men and women of good will, the middle-of-the-roaders, the new proposals seemed attractive, indeed, civilized. Not until the whole country's guard was down did they realize that the Duma was without any real law-making powers. Yet even this pale gesture in the direction of democracy was not to the Tsar's liking. Before an effective protest could be organized, the first Duma was dissolved in favor of another, still less liberal one. In the meantime, parliamentary immunity notwithstanding, many former left-wing and even mildly progressive deputies were summarily arrested and sent to prison. And finally a third Duma, this one completely the mouthpieces of the government and the great landowners, was set up. It was the beginning of what came to be known as the period of the Stolypin reaction.

Soon a revitalized Black Hundred assumed full sway in both town and countryside, spying, informing, denouncing, indulging in provocations. In the villages it encouraged the richer, land-owning peasants, the *kulaks,* to grind their landless neighbors into the dirt. And, of course, wherever possible it instigated pogroms, spreading tales about ritual blood murders, teaching the hungry masses to blame their misery on the Jews.

"And the worst of it is," Idka summed up the situation, "just as Michal said—no leadership. With five thousand death sentences this past year and God knows how many arrests, we've hardly anyone left except those who've managed to escape abroad." Her figures were for the whole Empire, but the Congress Kingdom had had more than its share of casualties. "We're going to have to regroup on foreign soil."

As she spoke she looked once more about her brother's well-appointed home. Ironically, Polish industry had richly profited by the rout of labor and the inevitable demoralization that follows such defeats. Wages had recently again been cut and hours lengthened. And though the economic predictions were for another crisis in the near future, right then in Lodz the mills were humming.

Adam Fabian sat listening to his sister with rather academic interest. He had long since convinced himself that the disaffection of the working class was purely its own fault and the revolution a lost cause—*Jugendkrankheit* after all. He thought of the past with nostalgia and sadness, remembering his old friends as so many tilters at windmills. It was a comfortable viewpoint and suited his new life perfectly, his and Regina's, and while he was glad enough of this chance to see Idka, to know that in her personal life she was at last happy, he also knew he would be glad to see her and Michal leave town the next day.

The talk went on and on. They continued to sit around the dining table consuming innumerable glasses of tea. Though her other luggage was sparse, Idka had brought a whole satchelful of illegal literature, and somewhat to his own annoyance Adam found himself eager to glance through the various pamphlets, eager to know what was really going on. It was as though a spark that had never quite died down was fighting to be rekindled. Regina sensed this and was troubled. As midnight struck she suddenly pushed her chair back. "To bed, to bed! I for one can hardly keep my eyes open. We can continue at breakfast tomorrow."

She led her guests to the room that had been prepared for them, quickly said goodnight, as quickly went to the big master bedroom where the big double bed waited, snowy sheets turned down, shed her unbecoming pregnancy clothes, and lay waiting for Adam with the satin eiderdown pulled up to her chin. When he turned the lights out she rolled over on her side and after making herself as comfortable as her condition allowed, let him hold her close. The baby kicked. "Another few weeks," she murmured, "and all the bother will be over! What a relief!" Then, unexpectedly, "You know, Adash, sometimes I wonder. Are you really happy with the decision you made—I mean, working for Pozner?"

"Whatever makes you ask? You know I'm happy with anything that makes you happy, my dearest."

"You're so good to me," she answered, drowsy and content. "Well, goodnight."

Twenty minutes later they were roused from a first deep sleep by the raucous sound of the doorbell. Since the maids all slept at the other end of the house, it was Adam who jumped up to answer it. Regina, hastily throwing on a robe, then a large shawl for added warmth, padded out after him.

"Telegram," a gruff voice said through the crack of the door on its chain. "Open up."

It was the standard ploy of the secret police intent on a surprise search. What had prompted them? Had someone routinely checked old files and brought to light the fact that Adam had once been connected with a group now in prison? Or the fact that Izidore was his brother? Or did they have a new lead, connected with Idka and her man?

This was no time to make guesses. Instantly alert, Adam and Regina could think of only one thing. The dining room table was just as they had left it, strewn with illegal leaflets. When the police started their search of the house they would find them. And that would be the end of everything.

Regina was the first to move, to act. While Adam fumbled with the door chain and stood talking to the intruders she silently glided into the dark room beyond. She swept the papers on the table into a small pile. After making doubly sure nothing was left behind, she slipped everything under her heavy shawl. Then she wrapped the shawl more securely around her swollen body. Her fleeting thought was, *I'm so big already, who'll even notice?* And she went to stand beside her husband, pretending a great sleepiness. "What is it, dear? What's wrong?"

He said it was a house search and that they must wake all the servants and their guests, too. His eyes showed fear and she dared not warn him. In the meantime the gendarmes were already heading for the dining room. But when the lights were lit, he saw that by some miracle the table had been cleared.

They ransacked everything, pulled books out of bookcases, clothes out of closets. As in the past, they poked inside the tile stoves, spilling ashes onto Persian rugs and parquet floors. They found nothing. Next, each person was questioned in turn. And finally they began the frisking—first the men, then Idka, then the cook and the maids.

Was it pure luck, or because she was so very pretty and so very young and so very pregnant that they left Regina alone? She would never know, and it hardly mattered, and eventually, after the usual threats to come back another time and catch them Jew-bastard Polaks dead to rights, they were gone. Only then did she feel her legs giving way. Her arms loosened and a shower of pamphlets tumbled to the floor. Everyone stared at the pile at her feet.

"My literature!" Idka cried. "Michal, how could we. . . ."

Regina was looking from one to the other, triumph in her face. For a while, in their intense relief, none of them could speak. Finally Adam said, "Well, my dear, we've got our unborn child to thank for this! Still in the womb, and already the future generation is making its contribution to the fight that will go on and on. . . ."

Regina frowned, and Adam saw the frown and was puzzled. She was looking straight at him, ignoring the others. "On the contrary," she said in a thin, clear voice, "it is we who are being forced to defend the future generation—against, I may say, incredible, unforgiveable carelessness. . . ."

Only then did Adam understand that she was angry. And now that the crisis had passed, he, too, felt a stir of anger taking the place of exhilaration. She was right, of course. It had been unpardonably careless of Idka to expose them thus.

Still, one mustn't insult guests in one's own house. Gently, he put an arm around his wife's shoulders. "Darling," he soothed, "you're all in. You've had a shock. Come and lie down."

"Not yet," she said, throwing off the protective arm. "First I want to say something, and say it while everyone is still here. There must be no more risks of this kind taken in our house. Not after tonight. Please. Never again. I couldn't stand it. I . . ." Her voice broke dramatically.

He said, "After tonight you've a right to ask. But we can talk about it later, tomorrow. Right now you must let me put you to bed. And tomorrow we're going to make a few decisions. Even . . . even if it should mean cutting ourselves off from. . ." He did not finish.

Only then did she permit herself to be appeased. But afterwards, as she slept in his arms and he continued to lie awake reliving the scene, his mind began to see again the startled glance his sister and her husband had exchanged. And the way Idka had stared at him, pain clear in her eyes, before she finally turned away.